Jan

THE SHORE OF WOMEN

Pamela Sargent was studying philosophy, ancient history and
Greek at the State University of New York at Binghamton
when she wrote her first published story. Her novels include
Cloned Lives, *The White Death*, *Earthseed* and *Venus of Dreams*.
She is also the editor of *Women of Wonder*, a popular collection
of science fiction written by women. She lives in New York
state.

Pamela Sargent

THE SHORE of WOMEN

Pan Books
in association with
Chatto & Windus

First published in Great Britain 1987 by
Chatto & Windus Ltd
This edition published 1988 by
Pan Books Ltd, Cavaye Place, London SW10 9PG
in association with Chatto & Windus
9 8 7 6 5 4 3 2 1
© Pamela Sargent 1986
ISBN 0 330 30116 0

Photoset by Parker Typesetting Service, Leicester
Printed and bound in Great Britain by
Richard Clay Ltd, Bungay, Suffolk

For Shirley Sargent

The glory about us clinging
Of the glorious futures we see,
Our souls with high music ringing,
O men! it must ever be
That we dwell, in our dreaming and our singing,
A little apart from ye.

Arthur O'Shaughnessy,
'The Music Makers'

The
ENCLAVE

LAISSA

I had expected Birana to weep. I had thought that when she was finally led to the wall, she would plead with the city, even though her plea would have been futile. Instead, she gazed steadily at the women who had pronounced her sentence, as if condemning those who had condemned her.

It was Yvara, Birana's mother, who had committed the first crime, and who had thus led her daughter into committing the second. Yvara had fought with a woman named Ciella; in a moment of rage, Yvara had picked up a knife and had stabbed the other woman.

At that moment, Yvara must have realized that her punishment would be severe. She would be punished not just because of this deed, but because of who and what she was.

Yvara might have won a little sympathy, or at least some understanding, if she had summoned a physician to Ciella's side. She might have avoided our worst punishment. Instead, she had stood over the bleeding woman and had waited for her to die. Birana might have saved herself had she gone for help, but she had waited with her mother and had done nothing.

Only with Ciella dead could Yvara have found a way to conceal her crime, or to argue that she had acted in her own defence. It was no secret among Yvara's neighbours that the two women had often had violent disagreements, that both had been warned before. With Ciella dead, perhaps Yvara could have made a convincing case for herself; so our city's Council had argued before passing sentence. Birana would then be the only witness and might have lied to protect her mother; even under questioning, the two might have found a way to conceal the truth or to cast doubt on events.

This was what our Council claimed, but I saw matters quite differently. I imagined Yvara, frozen with fear, suddenly unable to act. I saw Birana, out of loyalty to her mother, refusing to leave her side and reveal her deed to others.

But the two were discovered. Ciella did not die, though she would carry the scars of her wounds for the rest of her life. She told her story calmly before the Council in a gentle, subdued voice, condemning Yvara and Birana with each soft word. Yvara was still when she heard her own sentence; she screamed out her rage only when her daughter's was pronounced, though she had shown few signs of concern for Birana before. They would both be expelled from our city and would never enter another. It was a death sentence, for all knew that they could not survive outside.

A few, even then, claimed that the two had not merited our most severe punishment; Ciella, after all, had lived. The Council called such thinking misguided. Ciella had survived, but Yvara had clearly been prepared to watch her die; she was a murderer at heart, and her daughter had connived with her to hide the deed. Threatening the life of another woman could not be tolerated; any woman's life was too precious. Had such deeds gone unpunished in our past, we would never have been able to build our world on the ruins of the old; we could not have survived that struggle.

Yvara had tried to kill another; she had made her daughter an accomplice. Our city could not allow two such women to live in our midst. An example had to be made, or the life our ancestors had so painfully created for us over the centuries would be endangered. Had Yvara been only another woman, one without her particular responsibilities, she might have paid for her deed in another way. But she was one of the Mothers of the City, and one of those who were, or would be, the mothers of men. More was asked of her than of others.

I watched Birana as she stood inside the wall next to the door of the chamber through which she was to pass to her death. Her blue eyes seemed to accuse us all of cruelty; she might have been passing sentence on us. She and her mother had been given some food and water, but no tools that might help them survive; the provisions would only prolong their punishment for a little while and allow them to reflect on their deed. They would die in the world outside our city's wall, but we would not strike the fatal blow ourselves; we would let the world render that judgement.

At that moment, I found myself thinking that, if anyone could survive outside, Birana might have more of a chance than most. She had always been strong. During the time I had spent with her, she had thrown herself into physical efforts almost recklessly. She could outrun most girls; she had galloped through our parks on horseback while the rest of us kept to the paths at a trot. There had been times when I had wondered if our city could hold her wilder spirit.

Then Yvara spoke. 'I have something to say.' The women standing with her in the long corridor inside the wall were silent, perhaps expecting some show of repentance. 'I won't let death take me,' Yvara continued. 'I'll find a way to live. I might have wounded Ciella's body, but she was killing my soul. I acted in self-defence, whether you see that or not. We'll live, and we'll come to haunt this city and all our cities. I think that others who were condemned still live outside, and I'll find them. There is much hidden from us, lands over which our ships never pass. These will be a refuge for us, a place where other exiles have learned to live apart from the cities. You'll have no victory over me.'

As strong and resourceful as the two were, I could not believe that. I was certain that Yvara did not believe it, that she was only striking a useless blow at her judges, refusing to show the fear she must have been feeling.

Birana did not speak. Once, I had called her my friend. She was eighteen at the time of her sentence, less than a year older than I. We had been close as young girls, but as we grew older, her forceful ways and her constant questioning of our teachers began to disturb me. Birana questioned everything and argued with the answers she was given. Soon, I no longer sought her out, for I was afraid to admit that I had many of the same questions. I had been wise to avoid her; her questions and her carelessness had condemned her. If she had asked fewer questions, if she had accepted the world as it had to be, she might have understood her duty and might not have been expelled.

I might have wept for my former friend as the door of the chamber closed behind her and Yvara. I might have felt more than a momentary pang as I pondered what awaited them on the other side of the wall amid the snow-covered hills. I sorrowed, but part of me was grateful that I had grown apart from Birana and that therefore her act could not tarnish me. I did not go to see her and had watched her expulsion over my screen, telling myself that she would not have been comforted by my presence, although I also knew that it would have done me no good to seek her out then. I could do nothing for her. I felt no shame, no sense of having failed her.

Instead, Birana's fate only made me dwell more on my own situation. At that time, my mother was moving dangerously close to a different kind of disobedience, and I feared what might happen to me if she persisted in her ways. I would be taking on the responsibilities of a woman soon; I had waited a long time for

13

that, and my mind was on my approaching celebration.

Birana had once been close to me. We had shared secrets while playing our childish games; then we had drifted apart. She was gone, and I had to forget the blue-eyed girl who would touch my life no more.

Eilaan came to speak to Mother two days later. At first I thought she had come to wish me well; now that I was a woman at last, I was to celebrate with my friends that evening. But Eilaan's old face was solemn. She barely glanced in my direction.

I was sitting on the floor with Button, trying to teach him a card game. As Eilaan walked across our white carpet, Mother stood up, but did not smile.

'Dorlei,' the older woman said quickly, 'I must speak to you. I have left messages, and you refuse to respond to them.'

My mother sat down again. 'I know what you're going to tell me.' She waved a hand in my direction. 'Laissa, take Button to your room.'

'Let her stay.' Eilaan sat down on the couch near me. 'She might as well hear what I have to say. She's old enough. Womanhood came later to her than it does to others.'

This was so. I was seventeen, older than my friends had been when they had celebrated menarche. Women of our clan often matured late, according to Mother; she had refused to hasten my growth, though she might have done so. Our trait was a useful one, she believed; it had perhaps kept our ancestors from wearing out their bodies with birthing children too soon. A long childhood, so she thought, was a fitting prelude to the long life I would have as a woman.

Eilaan tugged at her white pants nervously and smoothed her green tunic, then frowned. 'Button.' Her mouth twisted as she said the name of Mother's son.

'It's just what I call him,' Mother said. 'It's his nose. It looks like a button, don't you think?' Her voice was high and strained.

'He's only a boy. He doesn't need a name. How old is he now?'

'You know how old he is, Eilaan.'

'Over five. Nearly six years old, I think. You should have sent him outside before now.'

Mother leaned back on her couch. 'He was so small. And then there was his illness – you know that. I couldn't have sent him out then. I was trying to build up his strength.'

'The boy looks healthy enough to me.'

'Yes, he's well now, and strong.' Then Mother told a lie. 'But

I've tried to contact his father, and I can't reach him. He hasn't been to a shrine in a while.'

I kept silent, even though I knew that Mother had not sent out such a call. Button picked up a card and peered at it.

'Then send him out with someone else,' Eilaan said.

'I would rather not,' Mother responded, and this time her voice had an edge. 'I think a biological father is more likely to care for his own child.'

'Don't be ridiculous, Dorlei. It may be customary to send them out with their fathers, but those creatures can't tell who carries their genes and who doesn't. One boy is like another.'

'I think they can tell.' Mother lifted her chin. 'I think somehow they sense it.'

'The boy's father might be dead, in which case you'll have to give the lad to someone else.' Eilaan leaned forward. 'And you're not helping the boy by keeping him here. He must be sent out soon so that he can learn how to survive. The longer he stays here, the harder it will be for him to adapt.'

'I know that. But it's still winter outside. Wouldn't he have a better chance if I waited until spring?'

I looked at Button, wondering how much he understood. He glanced at Eilaan warily, shook his blond head, and went back to his cards, turning them face up on the white carpet.

Eilaan sighed. 'I don't want to say this, but it's best that you hear it from me. You are getting very close to outright rebellion, to setting yourself against our city and our customs. If you persist, the Council may have to speak to you. You are one of the mothers of men. You have a place of honour because you're one of those entrusted with that duty. Perhaps you should not be one of us. Perhaps you should take your place among those we serve, if you cannot manage your obligations, and let another woman take your position.'

I froze, unable to look at either woman.

'I am not rebelling,' Mother said very slowly. 'I have every intention of doing what I must. I only want to be sure that Button – that the boy has a chance.'

'Your disgrace isn't the worst than can befall you, Dorlei. There is also expulsion.'

'You have no reason to threaten me, and certainly not to expel me.'

Eilaan shook her head. 'I'd like to trust you, but I can't. The Council will be watching you. If you don't call a man to take him, someone else will hand him over to the next man who is called to the wall. If you persist in your disobedience, you'll pay the penalty. If you don't care about yourself, think of Laissa and the shame you'll bring to her.'

'I understand,' Mother said.

I glared at her. How could this be happening, on the day of my party? It was all I could think of – that the party celebrating my menarche would be ruined.

Eilaan held out her hands. 'I know I sound harsh,' she said in a gentler tone, 'but much is troubling us now. I spoke to a friend in Devva today. That city is divided, even though the women there know that they must act soon. There are men within sight of Devva who have built a town and have united several tribes. They must be destroyed, as an example to others and for our own protection, and yet there are women in Devva who believe that those men should be allowed to live. It seems that there are others as sentimental as you.'

'Those men cannot threaten Devva.'

'They don't threaten it now, but their arrogance will grow. We must strike at the root. We've been complacent for much too long. If Devva doesn't act, another city will. The man leading that pack has not even troubled to conceal his thoughts and hopes when praying to us. He dreams of challenging the Goddess.'

'The Goddess.' Mother laughed. 'You speak as if She were real.'

'The men believe in Her. We had better see that they keep doing so, that they both worship and fear Her – it's the only way we can control them. But the way in which we present the Deity to those outside doesn't affect my belief. We have to give men a belief they can understand – they aren't capable of anything more. My belief is more complex.'

Mother shrugged. 'You know that I'm not a believer, yet you keep trying to make me one.'

'It might be better for you if you were.'

My mother and Eilaan gazed at each other in silence as Button slapped down his last card and then climbed to his feet. He took a step toward Mother, holding out his arms. I grabbed his hand as Mother warned him away with her eyes.

Eilaan had seen the boy's gesture. 'You give that lad too much affection, Dorlei.'

'I don't.'

'Oh, yes, you do. It's not good for him.' Eilaan plucked at her long silver hair as she watched Button; I pulled him to the floor, picked up his cards, and handed them to him. 'You have to let him go.' The old woman said the words softly. 'I know what it's like. I had to send out two boys when I was younger. I know how one can come to feel that they're more than they actually are. But they aren't like us. Their feelings are shallower and more violent; they cannot give life and so must deal in death; their minds are narrow and incapable of higher intellectual functions. They seem most like us when they're children, but their true nature is revealed when they grow older. If your boy lived among us for long, he would sense his limitations, however dimly, and would only grow more unhappy. This isn't new for you. You've sent out a boy before.'

'I understand,' Mother said.

'I'm sure you do.' Eilaan rose. 'I trust that you'll do the right thing.'

When Eilaan had gone, Mother sent Button to his room while she reviewed my lessons with me. She had always believed that a mother should take an intense interest in her daughter's studies, but I also sensed that she wanted to take my mind off her conversation with Eilaan.

'Have you decided what you'd like to do?' she asked me when we had finished.

'I'm not sure.'

'Well, you've had a long enough time to think of it. You celebrate your womanhood tonight, and your tests are coming up. Are you still thinking of mathematics?'

I stretched out on the couch and rested my head in her lap, wishing that I were already old and at the same time wishing that I hadn't grown up quite so soon. 'I don't know if I have the skill for mathematics – I have more trouble with it now.' Birana, I recalled, had shown a talent for mathematics. I pushed the thought of her aside quickly; thinking of her only reminded me of threats, of possible punishments.

I considered my choices. Mother had studied medicine, but I wasn't interested in that. I was beginning to see that I didn't know what I wanted to do.

My body had betrayed me. I had waited impatiently for this day, with my maturing and sometimes troubled mind trapped inside my narrow-hipped, flat-chested body. I had thought that the onset of womanhood would change everything for me, would be the outward sign of all that I was becoming inside. Then the bleeding had come, and the pain; my body was not yet a woman's, but only an awkward, gawky shell that refused to obey the mind it still imprisoned.

'Maybe I'll try engineering,' I said at last, without much enthusiasm, although the thought of pursuing a study with few ambiguities held some appeal.

'You need maths for that, Laissa.'

'I know, but not the same sort of maths, just practical problems. You know, Button's good at arithmetic – he's been playing with the calculator. He seems to figure it out all by himself.'

Mother was silent.

'But he's limited.'

'Of course.' She had not said a word about her discussion with Eilaan, and that was making me uneasy.

'It seems hard to believe that when I see him with the calculator,' I said.

'His limitations don't show at his age.' Her voice was toneless, but her hand trembled as she rested it on my head. 'Oh, Laissa – I've grown to have feelings for Button I shouldn't have. Sometimes I even believe that if he could grow up here, he would become like us. It wasn't this way with your twin. When I sent him out, I still had you. I think that was why I didn't feel the same way about him. It's why I chose to have you both, so that it would be easier.'

I had not thought about my twin in a long time. He was only a dim memory, a little boy with my blond hair and grey eyes. I had rarely played with him, perhaps because Mother had not wanted us to grow too close. I could not even recall his departure. Mother had sent me to one of the dormitories for girls my age, and the boy had been gone when I returned.

I thought of Eilaan's threat, and my throat tightened. 'Did Eilaan mean it when she said you might be expelled?'

'No, dear. She only said that to show the seriousness of the matter. You know that expulsions rarely take place.' Mother's words did not console me; I was thinking again of Birana and her mother.

But Mother's case was different from Yvara's; Eilaan had only been trying to frighten her. Others had said for years that Yvara was bound to commit some dreadful deed, while Mother had always respected custom. Yet I thought of Birana, and it occurred to me that, if I aided Mother in her disobedience, or ignored it, I might also share her punishment.

We were among those who were the Mothers of the City. We looked out for our city, and watched over its people, and gave birth to the boys who would be given to the men outside; in return, we had honour and respect. There were times when I envied the more carefree ways of those who could live their lives, do their work, and raise their daughters without our responsibilities, but I did not want to become one of them. Eilaan might send Mother to live among them if she failed in her duty, and I might have to go with her if I were not careful.

Others would take our place, and we would be disgraced. I did not care that we might then be relieved of painful or difficult decisions, but thought only of the shame.

'I've been wrong in putting this off,' Mother said. 'I knew all along that Button couldn't stay. You'd better get up, Laissa. I must summon his father to take him away.'

She got up and went into her study. I trailed after her and stood in the doorway as she went to her mindspeaker, put the circlet on her head, stared into the lenses on the wall, and spoke her message aloud, as if afraid that the mindspeaker might otherwise transmit her unspoken thoughts.

I had learned how to use a mindspeaker in the dormitories. We had begun by sending images and messages to one another, learning how to focus our minds and how to keep our surface thoughts unmuddied. I had found it hard at first to keep stray, conscious thoughts from intruding. Then we had been shown, those of us who were to be the mothers of both men and women, how to send recorded tapes to the shrines outside. The innocuous ones, those of women who would soothe men and ease their fears, did not disturb us, but the erotic ones were more embarrassing to contemplate.

I knew that these tapes were centuries old, the women who had made them long dead, and that they had created them only out of a strong sense of duty. Images of women, naked and seductive, would appear to men in shrines when the men were wearing mindspeaker circlets, and the men would experience the sensation of lying with these women. My teachers at the time had told me little more than that, but I shuddered to think of how the men dealt with those images.

The tapes had been both a source of amusement and disgust to us all; some of my friends shrieked or laughed nervously as we prepared such transmissions. I often refused to view the tapes; although I knew that they were needed in order to condition men, I had always found them distasteful. It was said that, very rarely, a woman might feel perverted longings if she thought too much about such tapes; I was never able to believe that, to think that a woman might imagine a man with her. Once, women had lived with men; the thought was appalling.

Mother removed her circlet when she was finished. 'What did he say?' I asked.

'I didn't speak to him. The message is there for him, though – if he goes to a shrine, he'll receive it. It hardly matters if I speak to him directly since his responses are so ritualized. He goes to a shrine quite often.' She waved a hand at the console in which past transmissions were stored. 'There are his prayers. An erotic tape is sent once in a while, just to keep him happy.'

'What's he like?' He was my progenitor, too, and I was curious.

'Big, strong, hale and hearty. His hair is like yours, and his eyes. He's a man – that's all you have to know. He's a man, and Button will be a man, too. I must keep thinking of that. It'll make it easier to let him go.'

ARVIL

Tal had been called to the enclave before. I had never been called but prayed for it. I had grown tall, and my voice had changed, was like that of a man. I would rub my face and long for the down to become the bristles of a beard. Soon, I hoped, I would be called.

Tal had brought me out of the enclave, so I had been there before, but I could not remember anything about it. Sometimes, I would have a dream: I was in a room with a soft covering under my feet, a covering softer than grass, but white instead of green. Someone was with me, and I would feel arms around me and smell flowers and rest my cheek against a shirt as soft as fur while a high voice sang to me. Sometimes, I was in a different place, and other times I was surrounded by darkness, but the voice was always singing. The voice was high and light, like a boy's. The Lady had never sung to me when I was blessed in a shrine, so I might have been dreaming about my time inside the enclave. But I could not be sure, so I always told Tal I did not remember anything about that time.

Tal thought that was good. 'You should not remember,' he would say. 'Young ones who remember too much don't last. They don't learn fast enough. They keep hoping to get called back, but they never are called because they don't live long enough to become men. You cried when you came out, and I had to beat your tears out of you, but you learned. Be glad you forgot.'

I accepted that during the first eleven winters I was with Tal, but in my twelfth winter, I began to question him more.

'Did you ever see a young one who remembered?' I asked him while we sheltered under an outcropping of rock, waiting for the snow to stop so that we could follow fresh animal tracks to game. We were alone, so I could ask him. The rest of our band was back at our winter camp.

'I did see one,' Tal answered. His eyes were as grey as the winter sky, and others had told me I had the same eyes. 'It was before I brought you out, boy. This young one came out with Hasin. He had to carry the child back to our camp trussed and gagged because the lad wouldn't stop crying. Hasin spoke gently, and when that didn't work, he beat the boy. The child would cry at night when he thought we were asleep, but Hasin was sure that would pass.'

'What happened?' I asked.

'One night, the boy slipped away. We did not want to go after him, but Hasin said we must. I knew we would find him dead, if we found him at all, and I was right.'

I said, 'An animal got him.'

Tal laughed. 'An animal – yes. Somehow, the boy made his way toward the enclave. He should have known he could not go inside without being called – we had told him that often enough.' He paused. 'Another band found him and killed him. We came upon them while they were stripping the body. We struck down two men, but before we drove them off, they had taken Arvil's life as well.'

He had named me after Arvil, the man who had taken Tal out of the enclave when Tal was a boy. He had never told me before how Arvil had died. 'So you were even. Two lives for two.'

'Yes, we were even. I wish we had killed their whole band. I saw the signs on those creatures – the shreds of cloth, the bits of metal they scavenged from the grounds near the enclave. Those signs showed that the band never ventured far from the wall. They lived on what they could find and on what they could steal from those coming out or those being called back. They were animals, not men.' Tal rubbed his hide-covered hands together, then folded his arms. 'Such bands do not last long, and catch little game. Those who stay near the enclave are never called, and so no new young ones come out with them. But there are always other bands to take their place.'

I had heard about such scavengers often; Tal was one who said the same things many times. 'Why do they stay there, then?'

Tal shrugged. 'Because they are cowards. Because they grow weak, perhaps, and cannot leave.'

'When will I be called?'

Tal glanced at me, scowling under his blond beard. 'I cannot say. When you are older. I had been with old Arvil for nearly sixteen summers before I was called.'

'I might be called sooner.'

Tal cuffed me on the side of my head. My eyes stung and my head throbbed a bit, but it was a gentle blow, meant to teach me my place and not to punish me. 'Sooner! You think too much of yourself, Arvil. Do you think you'll go before I did? Sixteen summers before I was called – you won't be called before that. You will be lucky to be called then.'

Tal had been called three times – once before I knew him, again when he brought me out, and another time after that. Only Geab, our Headman, had been called as many times, and he was an old man with grey in his black beard.

Geab had not gone to an enclave in a long time. One day, I was sure, Tal would be called again, and then, when he returned, he would be the Headman and Geab would become an Elder. Geab would hunt his last meal, take his last hide, and make his last cloak, the one in which he would die and which the next Headman would take from his body. I believed that Tal would be called again, and hoped for it. If he were not, he would have to wait for Geab to die.

The snow had stopped. We picked up our spears and left the outcropping, searching for fresh tracks.

We found only two rabbits on our way toward our camp. The sky was already darkening when Tal stopped, took my shoulder, and steered me east.

'Where are we going?' I asked.

'To the shrine.'

'But then we won't get back before . . .'

Tal hit me, knocking me into the snow. 'You listen. When you are near a shrine, you pay your respects, even if it means going out of your way.' He dragged me up and brushed the snow from my back.

I knew that he was right, but I wanted to get back to camp, to a fire and a meal. The shrine would be warm. That thought startled me. I should not have been thinking of a holy place as a spot for my comfort.

'You wonder why I have been called three times,' Tal went on as we stumbled through the snow. 'It's because I never miss a chance to pray, and the Lady knows it. Don't ever forget to pray.'

'I pray every night.' Almost every night, I told myself silently, promising Her I would try to do better.

We came to the top of a hill. The shrine was below us. On top of its curved, metallic walls sat a golden dome with a white cap. The snow around the entrance to the shrine was unmarked. No one else was near; and although no man would attack another on holy ground, I preferred to pray alone.

We waded toward the shrine as I tried to banish unholy thoughts. I had prayed at shrines many times. When I was a young boy, my soul was sometimes called to the Lady, and an aspect wearing Her form would come to me and hold me gently. When I grew older, other aspects had shown me Her true blessings. At the thought of those blessings, I felt a powerful longing for Her. Suddenly I wondered if She would ever hear my prayers again, if She would withhold Her blessing from me, if She would turn from me, and trembled.

Tal's big hand clutched my shoulder. 'Easy, boy.'

I swallowed. I was thinking unholy thoughts on the shrine's threshold and prayed that I would not be punished. The door in front of us slid open, and we entered.

The shrine was warm and the air bore a musky scent; the dome overhead glowed as the small room grew lighter. We knelt, cupped our groins, and pressed our foreheads to the floor, then rose.

Twenty couches, covered with red cloth, stood in a row near one wall. Circlets of gold rested on each couch, and, above each, a round piece of glass set in the wall caught the light, winking. We walked past the couches and knelt again in front of the altar.

An image of the Lady smiled down at us. I lifted my eyes to the statue and was at peace. This shrine was to Mary, the aspect of the Lady I had always loved the most. I had seen Her in other guises, in other shrines – as the Warrior, with black hair, slanted eyes, and a spear, or as the Wise One, with slender glass tubes and strange tools, or as Venus the Lover of Men, with bright red hair and bare breasts – and I had heard that there were other aspects in more distant shrines. But it was Mary, the Mother, the most familiar aspect to me, to Whom I prayed most often.

We prayed for a few moments in the holy speech, the tongue I had known before I learned the words of men. Then Tal got up, went to a couch, and stretched out upon it. I took the couch next to his, put the circlet on my head, and waited. Tal, eyes closed, was still, his blond beard and hair as golden as the circlet on his brow. His lips moved, and I wondered if the Lady was speaking to him.

He twitched and began to moan. His arms slapped the couch as his body arched. He kicked with his long legs and moaned again and shook so much that I thought he would fall to the floor. At first, I believed only that the Lady had decided to bless him, and then he smiled. I had seen Tal smile like that only once before, in another shrine, when he had last been called.

I closed my eyes. Perhaps the Lady would call me, too. No joy I had known had been greater than Her blessing, and I burned with longing, but She did not speak, did not appear to me.

Tal would leave me once again for the enclave. I tried to give thanks for him, but could think only of myself; I had not been called. I pushed that thought from my mind. Tal would be our Headman when he returned. I knew I should not be thinking of that, either, but only of the Lady.

Tal was removing his circlet. I took mine off and said, 'You were called.'

He sat up slowly and rubbed his arms. 'Yes.'

'Your fourth time.'

'I must go to the enclave.'

'Take me with you.' The words were out before I could hold them back. I glanced toward the altar, afraid.

'Arvil, were you called?'

I shook my head.

'I thought not. You cannot deceive the Lady. If you haven't been called, you cannot enter the wall. I shall have to leave you behind.'

'You're going to make the Stalker my guardian again.'

'He did well enough last time.'

'He'll try to beat me.'

'If he does, then you will deserve it, although I think he would find it harder to beat you now.'

'And Cor will beat me when the Stalker is out of sight.'

Tal sighed. 'Stop whining. If you cannot get along with that boy, then fight him. You ought to be able to beat him by now – you have grown taller than Cor.'

'He'll summon the Stalker then, and I cannot raise my hand to my guardian. Leave me with someone else.'

'If you don't stop this talk, Arvil, I'll beat you myself. You are in a shrine. You are the height of a man, but you're still a boy, and the Lady doesn't take kindly to boys who disobey their guardians.' Tal stretched out again. 'Now, I want you to take the rabbits outside, skin them, and cook our supper. We'll eat what is left tomorrow.'

'Aren't we going back to the camp?'

'We'll go in the morning. The Lady has favoured me. The Mother will not mind if we sleep here. Now go outside and gather some wood before it grows darker.'

As we neared our camp, I worried again about what Geab might do when he learned about Tal's fourth call. He might go to the shrine in the hope that the Lady would call him, too, but men his age were rarely called. He would have to hope that Tal did not return safely from the enclave. Perhaps Geab would even move our camp to make it harder for Tal to find us again.

I had seen a Headman become an Elder once before, two winters after Tal had become my guardian. The Wolf had led us then. He had broken his leg badly in a fall and knew that it would not heal. He had declared himself an Elder, knowing it was for the good of the band; caring for an old and crippled man would have made life harder for all of us.

The Wolf had gone on his last hunt, although others had to help him take his last hide. He had sewn his cloak and eaten his final meal, then given away his things. Geab, the new leader, had been given the Wolf's precious knife, made with a sharp metal blade taken from a scavenger.

Geab struck the first blow with that knife, cutting the Wolf's throat. By the time the rest of us pricked the Wolf with our spears, he was already dead.

The Wolf had met death willingly. Geab would not.

I had dreamed of the white room during our night in the shrine, but the Lady did not speak to me. Tal, however, had communicated with Her again, mumbling as he slept. Like all men, I had a stain on my soul, yet prayed for purification and the Lady's blessing. Tal was a good man and had been called, but it was the fate of all men for ever to fall away from grace and be forced from the enclaves. Again, I wondered: Could a man become so holy that he could dwell within an enclave's wall and never come out?

As we came toward the hill leading to our camp, Tal suddenly grabbed me, startling me out of my daydreaming, and pointed at the ground. He had already loosed his spear from his back. The tracks of horses marked the snow and led up the hill toward our camp. I pulled at Tal's arm, wanting to flee.

At that moment, a horse carrying two riders came around the hill and trotted toward us. Tal lifted his spear.

'Hold!' a familiar voice shouted. I recognized Cor's furs and hides. He was sitting behind a stranger on the horse's back; his legs dangled, and his arms were tight around the other man's waist. I was too startled by the sight of Cor on a horse to be afraid then.

Cor released the other rider, slid awkwardly off the horse, sprawled in the snow, then stumbled to his feet. Tal saluted him with his spear. 'Who is this man?' he asked as he waved his weapon at the stranger.

The horse whinnied, but the stranger was silent. Cor smiled, showing white teeth under his thin red mustache. 'Another band is in our camp. We're having a parley.'

Tal frowned as he glanced at me.

'You should have been back last night,' Cor went on. 'This stranger here is helping me guard the hill. The rest are above.'

Tal adjusted his hood. 'I shall go up.'

'Geab is busy with the parley.'

'So you told me.' Tal's voice was angry.

We climbed the hill. Our winter camp was near the top, so that we could watch the land around it; but when the winds blew strong, we often had to take shelter in the hollow space we had dug below ground, where we stored the dried meat and plant food we had gathered for the cold season. In winter, we did not wander far from the land we knew. We knew about winter, and what we had to do to live through it. We did not know what dangers we might face if we left for lands where strange bands roamed.

Outside one lean-to, Geab sat in the cleared space around our fire. The stranger nearest to him was a large man in a bearskin. He looked well fed, as had the man with Cor. Ten other men were with him, all large, some dressed as he was. They did not sit but stood stiffly, their spears at their feet. Each held the reins of a horse, while one man held two horses.

I had seen such men only once before, at a distance, and they and their tamed horses had struck fear into me. Seeing such men in our camp frightened me even more.

Our band had always been small. There were Geab, Tal and me, Cor and the Stalker, Eagle Eyes and the boy Hawk, and Arrow. Arrow had brought our newest member, Stel, out of the enclave to the north the winter before. Hasin was dead, struck down in a battle with another band. We could not have fought these strangers and their horses, so I well understood why Geab had agreed to talk instead. But what could such men want with us? Why hadn't they attacked us, when they could have so easily?

Tal squatted near a small snowbank as he watched the parley. I turned and went to a lean-to under the trees, a shelter I had built myself of wood and branches covered with hides. Hawk was sitting under it with Stel.

'Who are they?' I asked Hawk as I sat down.

'A band from the south.'

'And they came north in winter? What are they doing here?'

Stel giggled. His chubby, dark brown face reminded me of his guardian's; Arrow was the only dark man I had ever seen. I poked Stel with my elbow and told him not to giggle. He rolled his dark eyes. I poked him again, and he blinked back tears. He was small and afraid to hit back.

Hawk rubbed his pointed chin. 'They are treating with Geab. They came here at dawn when I was on watch, put down their spears, and asked for truce. It was hard for me to understand them at first, for they use strange words, but their leader and another man know our speech, and we all know holy words, so we were able to talk. Did Tal bring us some fresh meat?'

'We found nothing except two rabbits, and we ate those.' I took off my empty pack.

Hawk pouted. 'Those horses would make good meat. The dried meat is . . .'

'What about the strangers?' I said.

'They want us to join them.'

'*Join* them!'

'That's what their leader said. They have a large band, Arvil. That is only part of it there. The leader held up ten fingers, and then ten more, until he had held out his fingers nine times. They number ninety, and they have built a wall, and have huts, and plenty of food, too – that is why they're so fat. The leader told us that their men have been called to two different enclaves and that they control the paths to four shrines.'

'I don't believe it.'

Hawk drew up his hood, hiding his brown braids. 'He says they do. They fed us dried meat of their own before, and leaves with grain. He says they grow some of their own grain and don't often have to forage for it. He says they keep herds of animals with them and have fresh food in the winter without having to hunt for it.'

'If he has such a large band, then what does he want with ours?'

Hawk leaned forward. 'Unity. He spoke of unity – strength in numbers, he called it. He says bands do not have to fight other bands or avoid them. He says that one day, they will be so strong that they'll destroy any band that isn't part of theirs, and that all the weaker bands will die out, and that some day, they will be as strong as an enclave. And then . . .'

Stel's eyes were wide as he listened. Hawk shoved the boy. 'Go away, Stel.'

'Why?'

'Just go. Practise with your spear or gather wood.'

Stel wandered away from the lean-to as Hawk drew closer to me. 'And then,' he whispered, 'they will go to an enclave when they want to, and not just when they're called.'

I hid my face with my hand for a moment. 'Do not say it. The Lady will hear.'

'Their leader says he serves the Lady. He says he can hear Her even when he is not in a shrine wearing the Lady's crown. He's touched with holiness, and, when he is entranced, the Lady speaks through him. He says that She has told him that a new day is dawning for all men.'

It sounded unholy to me. I sent up a silent prayer to ward off the Lady's anger. 'What happens if we don't join them?'

'We shall have a truce for now, but in the spring they will declare us their enemies and be free to hunt us down. They can do it, too. We cannot fight men on horseback.'

'We can run from them.'

'We would have to run far.'

'Tal will never agree,' I said.

'He'll have to go along with what the others decide.'

I wrapped my arms around my legs. Tal was watching the strangers, but I could not read his face.

When the parley was over, the strangers rode down the hillside to make camp below and sent Cor up to us. They moved in a line, one horse following another, each man holding his reins in the same fashion, as if the thoughts of one ruled all.

We gathered around the fire while Geab talked of what the strangers had said.

'What do you think, Headman?' the Stalker asked.

'I say we join,' Geab answered. 'We need no new enemies, and their band has been blessed. We must join them.'

'I agree,' the Stalker said.

Arrow was nodding, and so was Eagle Eyes. Hawk, Cor, and I had no right to vote since we had not yet been called, and Stel was only a child.

Tal shook his head. 'We cannot do this. We live well enough.'

Geab said, 'We can live better.'

'We'll have to do what they tell us and live among strangers. We don't know their speech. We may not have our own Headman.'

'We all know holy speech, and I'll still be our Headman,' Geab replied. 'They have something they call a council, and I will speak for our band there, but we must obey their Headman.'

'You will speak for us?' Tal scowled. 'Do we not speak for ourselves?'

'You will speak to me, and then I'll speak to them.'

'But you will not be our Headman then, Geab.' Tal showed his teeth. 'I spent the night in Mary's shrine. I've been called again. When I return, I shall be the Headman, and you will be an Elder.' Tal had saved that news.

Geab narrowed his brown eyes and grinned; he did not seem disturbed. 'There are no Elders in their camp. Their leader told me that. He says that they keep their old men and listen to their tales and make use of their wisdom. I'll still be our Headman until I die – and, in a place like that, I may grow very old.'

'We haven't joined them yet.'

'But we will.'

'You must wait until I return from the enclave.'

'We cannot. They leave tomorrow and have asked us to ride with them. They can tell you how to follow us to their home ground. We will join them, Tal.'

Geab was right. I could see it in the eyes of the others as they dreamed of food and huts. Geab was afraid of death; he would give up being a true Headman in order to live. And if Tal never reached the land of the strangers, that too would serve Geab's aims, for he would then have no rival.

'It is unholy,' I cried out.

'Silence!' Geab shouted at me. 'Your body may be much like a man's, Arvil, but you're a boy until you are called.'

'It's unholy. Hawk told me that they dream of becoming as strong as an enclave and of going to enclaves without being called.'

'Is that true?' Tal asked.

Geab nodded.

'Then it is unholy. I serve the Lady, and She has favoured me again. I won't join them.'

Arrow pulled at his kinky black beard; Eagle Eyes was frowning. The Stalker waved an arm. 'I'm with Geab,' the Stalker said. 'The Lady has favoured the strangers, has She not? They say they have brought many young ones out of the enclaves. They shared food with us willingly, for they have much more. I say we go.' I knew then that Eagle Eyes and Arrow would follow Geab as well.

Tal rose. 'I must go to the enclave. I must pray, and purify myself in a shrine, and travel to the Lady. But I won't return to you if you go with them.'

Geab laughed. 'Then you will die. You'll be alone, with no band.'

'I am at the mercy of the Lady. We shall see what She wills for me. I may find a new band. The Lady will know I wasn't tempted by evil.' Then Tal spoke these words, chilling me. 'I withdraw my allegiance from you, Geab. You are no longer my Headman, and I am no longer of this band.'

'And I expel you,' Geab answered as he jumped up. 'If the Lady hadn't called you, you would die now. But I believe death will come for you soon enough.'

Tal gazed down at me. The other men were watching him. I was frightened; I was still Tal's charge, and what became of me now was in his hands. I could not go with him to the enclave and wondered if he would leave me here alone to survive however I could while I waited.

Tal pulled me to my feet and led me to the Stalker. 'Will you be Arvil's guardian?' he asked. The Stalker nodded. 'Very well, then – it is done. Farewell, Arvil.'

I wanted to cry out, but that would have been unseemly. Tal stood near me while I struggled with myself, wanting to cling to him. 'You were not called,' he said, 'and I cannot take you along.' He drew me to one side, away from the men and the warmth of the fire. 'You must go with them to that unholy place, for you would die here alone, but the Lady will guide you. Pray often, and follow Her way – reject unholiness. We may meet again when I can take you from that place.'

'Do not lie to me, Tal. We'll never be together.'

His fingers dug into my arm. 'Resist evil. Whatever they tell you, don't fall into evil ways.'

I said, 'I must live as they do while I am among them.'

'Think of the Lady. Your only chance at life is to go with them now, and that is why you must, but if they punish you for

keeping to holiness, then you will have to bear that punishment.'
He released me. 'Farewell, Arvil.'

Tal picked up his spear and bow, shouldered his quiver, and walked down the hill alone.

LAISSA

My friends began to arrive for my party. I greeted them while trying to forget my worries. After they had sung the traditional song of approaching womanhood, and I had accepted their gifts, we sat down on the carpet and began to nibble at candies and fruit.

All of my friends had already passed menarche, and they had advice to offer. 'Find a room in the north quadrant, Laissa, but not in one of the outside towers.'

'If you decide to follow your mother and study medicine, stick to research. Doctors and nurses have to go to the wall sometimes and deal with men.'

'I'm thinking of joining the patrol for a while when I'm through with my studies. The work isn't much, but it's chance to meet a lot of women and help them.'

'I'm concentrating on astronomy and astrophysics. It's exciting to look at all those plates and records, to understand what was discovered in the past.'

'Get some pilot training if you're suited for it. The cyberpilot does most of the piloting anyway, and you'll get to see other cities. We went as far as the Ridge on a training flight once.'

'Cybernetics is interesting, and it's a good way to win a place on the Council someday.'

'Cybernetics.' Zoreen, in her low voice, almost spat out the word. 'Isn't everything cybernetics, in a way? How much real work do we have? The doctors stare at a lot of screens and scanners, the pilot stares at a screen, and the cybernetic intelligences tell us what to do. The cyberminds do most of the work, and we don't do anything new. We don't know anything that wasn't known two centuries or more ago. We probably know less. We hold ourselves back.'

The other young women looked away from Zoreen; a few made faces, while others pretended they hadn't heard. I hadn't wanted to invite Zoreen, but we had been close once, and she had invited me to her celebration.

'We have to understand what the cyberminds do,' Shayl responded. 'They just save us the trouble of doing a lot of tedious tasks they can manage more quickly.'

Zoreen's mouth curved into a half smile. 'And it makes things easier for us, too. Do what was done, follow past procedures. Once there were satellites scanning the heavens, and now we're content to stare at astronomical plates made centuries ago. Once our ships flew over the oceans, and now we're content if they fly as far as the Ridge. We build no new cities. Even on our own continent, there are lands almost unknown to us now.'

Shayl sat up straight and pointed her chin at Zoreen. 'Would you want us to be like the ancients?' she asked. 'They nearly destroyed the world with their overreaching. You, of all people, ought to know that.'

'We might do more,' Zoreen said.

'We have obligations,' Shayl replied. 'We'll be the Mothers of the City. We have to serve all those women here who depend on us, we have a duty to them to keep their lives as peaceful and untroubled as they are. I wouldn't wish to change that.'

Shayl, my best friend, had been studying physics. Her life was already planned; she would master her work, perhaps elaborate a little on what was already known, have her children, and then divide her time between her work and tutoring in a girls' dormitory. Thinking of the dormitories, I became solemn; my life there, and in Mother's rooms, was over. Soon, I would move to my own rooms. Shayl and I had already planned to live together until it was time to have children and perhaps even after that; but I hadn't seen much of her since her party and wondered if she had changed her mind. Jenna and Carlea, still inseparable, sat together holding hands, and I felt a pang.

'What are you going to do, Laissa?' Carlea asked.

I said, 'I don't really know.'

'An adviser'll talk to you after the tests,' Jenna said in her lilting voice. 'You should follow her suggestions.'

'Do the general science course,' Carlea said as she shook back her dark curls. 'It's a good choice for anyone who's uncertain. You really can't go wrong, and it's useful as a base.'

'There's always history and human culture,' Zoreen offered. Another girl giggled; I felt myself blushing. 'It would certainly enliven your days of study.' She leaned forward; her green eyes glittered. 'Men and wars. Boys and girls together, without any protection. No insemination – they actually had to touch the men.' Zoreen, it appeared, was deliberately being offensive; she must have known that the others hadn't wanted her there.

'It sounds disgusting,' Shayl said loftily. With her large brown eyes and dark brown skin, she had always been the most beautiful girl I had known. 'I think a lot of perverts and disturbed women do history.'

Zoreen looked down. My cheeks burned. I had read some history, finding myself oddly drawn to a few of the old stories, but had never intended to study it.

Shayl glanced at me. 'You should do physics,' she went on. 'That way, we could study together.' I gazed uncertainly at her. 'Well, we are going to share rooms, aren't we? I thought we'd decided that a while ago.'

She spoke casually. I wanted to leap up and throw my arms around her but only smiled instead. 'Of course.'

'Look!' Miri shouted.

Button had wandered out of his room. He rubbed his eyes sleepily as he watched us and pulled at his brown nightshirt with his other hand.

'Come here,' Jenna said as she held out her arms.

Button toddled to her. As he reached out to touch her long brown hair, Jenna pushed him away with both hands. He sat down hard on the carpet. 'What a little beast he is. He looks even uglier than my brother.'

'Do you know what's going to happen to you?' Carlea murmured as she crawled over to him. 'Do you know?'

Button's eyes widened; he did not speak.

'You're going to get sent outside,' Carlea shouted triumphantly. 'You're going to live with big, hairy, wild men, and, if you don't do what they say, they'll kick you and beat you.'

'Look at him,' Shayl said as she leaned over and lifted Button's shirt. 'Isn't it wretched? It just hangs there like a little sausage.'

Everyone giggled. Button turned toward me; his grey eyes glistened. I wanted to get up and lead him back to his room, where I could have comforted him a little, but couldn't bring myself to move.

Carlea got to her feet and lifted Button, swinging him in a circle before throwing him to Shayl. Zoreen watched silently; unlike the others, she was not laughing. Shayl swung Button in an arc, and he screamed. As she set him down, he kicked her leg hard with his bare foot and then slapped her hands away.

'Button!' I cried out.

'He's already getting nasty,' Miri said. 'He should have been sent out a long time ago.'

Button glared at me. I did not speak. He ran back to his room and shot an angry glance at me before the door slid shut.

'Of all the things we'll have to do,' I heard myself say, 'bearing boys is by far the worst.'

Everyone began to murmur in agreement, but I hated myself for saying it.

I began to worry again after my friends had left. I should have been happy, but I was thinking of Button and was suddenly angry with Mother for not sending him away sooner. Because she had grown to care about Button too much, she had brought me to care about him, too, and had endangered us both in the process.

I found Mother in her study. She was slumped in a chair by the mindspeaker console; her long auburn hair hid her face.

'I came to say good night.'

She looked up at me. Her eyes were red; her face seemed swollen. 'Did you have a nice party?' she asked.

'Oh, yes. Shayl still wants us to live together. Her rooms are in the south quadrant, too, so we'll be close by.'

She stared at the floor. 'Button's father has already received my message. He should reach the wall in a few days, and then Button . . .' Her voice shook a little. 'He's looked after your twin. Button will have two men to look out for him.' She stared past me. 'I did what I had to do. There won't be any more warnings from Eilaan. We needn't concern ourselves with that any more. I did it for you, Laissa. I wanted you to have your celebration without worrying about this.'

I kissed her and went to my room, then remembered that I had left a jade bracelet, Shayl's present, in the outer chamber.

My door slid open. Mother stood in front of Button's room, weeping.

Both Shayl and my tests dominated the next few days.

When I got up, I walked through the botanical gardens near my tower to a training centre and sat before screens and scanners while cyberminds tested my brain chemistry, reactions, and reflexes, then displayed questions for me to answer. The lenses and lights of the artificial intelligences winked at me as their questions and diagrams danced across the screen, and their soft but stilted voices chattered. I had been tested often enough before and could not imagine what else they would learn about me, but these tests were longer and more extensive than those I had undergone earlier.

During the afternoon, I would put on a circlet and find myself in a ship about to crash, then in a garden tending flowers, then with a small infant, then with a patrolwoman aiding a lost child. I moved through so many scenarios that I soon lost track of the number.

At the end of each day, several old women, all psychologists, questioned me; their inquiries seemed either obvious or silly.

'What is a boy?'

'Which would you rather be, an architect or a veterinarian, and why?'

'If a close friend lied to you about a trivial matter, and you discovered the lie, what would you do about it?'

'If you were in love with someone, and she didn't love you, what would you do about it?'

'Why must men live outside?'

In the evening, I came home to dinner and then a visit from Shayl. One night, she took me over to her rooms, which were near the top of her tower, and we stood on her balcony and looked up at the stars. On another night, we went through my possessions as she advised me on what I should leave behind.

I had no time to think of Mother. She was a silent presence at dinner, and withdrawn at other times. I assumed that she was trying to reconcile herself to the loss of Button whenever I thought about her at all.

On the last day of my tests, I was sent through the curving corridors of the centre to a small room.

An old woman I hadn't met before was sitting behind a desk. Her face was wrinkled, her chin sagged, and her hair was grey. She, like Eilaan, had reached that time in her life when rejuvenation begins to fail and a woman starts to prepare for death. This woman, I was sure, had seen almost two centuries of life, and I wondered if she would be sorry to leave it. Then I asked myself why, if we could live this long, we could not find a way to live as long as we chose. Before I could ruminate on an answer to that question, I was thinking of the men outside and of how short their lives were in comparison to ours.

'My name is Bren,' the old woman said as she stood up and led me to the couch. A console with a small screen sat on the table before us; Bren pressed a few keys, gazed at the lettering, then turned toward me. 'I am to be your adviser, Laissa. I'm here to deal with any problems you might have during this time of transition, when you're preparing for the future course of your life.'

I said, 'I've already decided to do physics.'

'Let me ask you something, then. Are you planning to do physics because you really want to, because something in you cries out for a deep understanding of the physical universe, or because your friend Shayl is studying that subject?'

I hesitated. At last I said, 'I would have considered it anyway, but I'll do better at it with a friend to help me.'

Bren's smile seemed stiff; her small black eyes were glassy. 'I recommend that you consider the general science course instead. You'll get some physics there, and you can always explore the subject in more depth later. But I would also suggest that you supplement your studies with some work in history and human culture.'

I was stunned. Swallowing hard, I tried to compose myself. 'I'm not interested in that, Bren.'

'That isn't what your tests show.'

'Anyway, you know how everyone feels about that. They think it's odd to study those things, that a normal woman wouldn't be interested in them.'

'I once expected to hear such talk only from those we serve, but it seems more and more of the Mothers of the City feel the same way.' She leaned back. 'I did some work in human culture myself, and you might be surprised at some of the others who have dabbled in it. Oh, I know that many young ones find it strange and disturbing – they can't imagine what it has to do with their lives now, and they want to fit in. When one gets older, though, one sometimes wants to understand the past, and what made us as we are.'

I brushed at my sleeve nervously. 'Well, I'm not old. Besides, what would I use it for? I don't want to be a recordkeeper or a historian, and I'd have to learn at least a couple of the old languages to read the records anyway.'

'There are translations, but your tests indicate that you have an aptitude for languages. And a knowledge of history and human culture can be useful.'

'But what would *I* use it for?' I repeated.

Bren put her hand on my shoulder. The gesture seemed rehearsed. I imagined her thinking: Now I should pat her on the shoulder, now I should smile and look reassuring. She smiled and tilted her head to one side. 'Everything on your tests shows that you might make a fine chronicler. By looking at the past, you will come to understand why we are as we are. By writing about your feelings, your perspective on our life, you might illuminate . . .'

'But I don't want to be a chronicler. I never thought of doing that, ever.'

Bren drew back. 'Some seem to be born with the desire, while others come to it later. I can only tell you what your tests show. Chroniclers are rare, and their stories now are often repetitions of what has often been told.' She paused. 'Be honest, Laissa. Do you passionately long to understand the principles of matter, the underlying structure of the universe, or are your questions about us and our ways?'

I leaned away from her.

'Don't you sometimes feel as though you're an observer, some-one apart?'

'I don't know,' I replied.

'Don't you have your doubts about the way we live?'

'No,' I said forcefully. 'Not really. Not any more than anyone else.'

'You can't lie to me, Laissa. I know that you doubt. Your responses to many questions show that.'

I wondered how that could be. I had answered carefully, going out of my way to seem conventional.

'Listen,' Bren continued, 'you're not alone. There are others who doubt. They ask why we cannot live outside our cities, why men cannot live as we do, why some women rebel, why we have grown complacent and unadventurous. Some of those who doubt chronicle their feelings or embody them in stories, and others read them and are enlightened. They come to see our world as an outsider might see it and thus gain a perspective on our lives. They come to see what we have kept of the past and what we have rejected. They question and, by questioning, may come up with a way to make things better. Sometimes, one has to doubt, go through a painful questioning of everything one holds dear, in order to come to acceptance of our way. You see, we can make use of doubt – expose it to the light, so to speak – so that it doesn't fester below the surface and poison us. Chroniclers – good chroniclers – are usually doubters. They show others who have questions that they are not alone, and aid them in reaching an acceptance of our way in the end.'

The conversation was making me uneasy. If a chronicler's doubts were supposed to lead to acceptance, then what would happen to a chronicler who could not overcome her doubts? I pushed that question aside.

Bren was making me doubt. It was another test; it had to be. I had read some of the tales of chroniclers; their stories were little more than recollections of individual lives, mingled with dubious ideas, or recountings of experiences they had never had or had made up altogether. There could be nothing in my tests to show that I was such a person; Bren was only trying to see if I knew my own mind.

'I know your mother, Dorlei, has had her own questions,' Bren was saying. 'Perhaps that has influenced you. Or maybe it's a quality you carry in your genes. Diversity is important for survival – we must have doubters, as well as followers and leaders. Doubt can show us how we might make things better.'

'Mother doesn't doubt, not really.' I felt that I had to say it. 'She does what she must. And I don't want to be a chronicler.'

'I cannot force you to be one. Force would be useless for such work in any case. I simply advise. We give our tests so that we can save young women from painfully attempting work for which they aren't suited. You may not believe this now, but in time you are likely to find yourself growing more interested in our history, and wanting to record your thoughts, and then you'll regret the time you lost. Study physics, if you must, but you may find that it's not where your true talents lie.' She waved a hand, dismissing me.

My life was beginning, and I was suddenly afraid of what it might hold.

ARVIL

The home of the strangers was six days' journey on horseback to the south. We took what remained of our provisions and left our camp with them. The strangers shared some of their food with us as we travelled and sheltered us in their tents during the night; we shared our food with them in return.

The Stalker and Cor cuffed me often. I accepted the blows, knowing that Tal had given me to the Stalker rather than to Eagle Eyes or Arrow because the Stalker was stronger. Tal had done only what he thought was best, but I felt anger toward him. He spoke of keeping to the Lady's path, yet he had abandoned me.

The leader of our new band was called by the name Truthspeaker. On the first night we camped together, he went into a trance and spoke in the holy tongue. 'Our sin is to be washed from us,' he chanted. 'The day approaches when we will live with the Lady and all Her aspects, and men will fight other men no more.' That was all I could understand, for Truthspeaker then fell to the ground and uttered a stream of gibberish while two of his men held his arms and legs. I made a sign and prayed silently, but my mind was not only on guarding myself from unholiness. My thighs burned from riding on a horse behind a stranger all day, and I ached as I thought of the journey still ahead.

The stranger with whom I had ridden came to my side while Truthspeaker was still babbling. 'It is said that Truthspeaker was felled by a powerful blow to the head by an enemy long ago,' the stranger murmured to me. 'He lay as one dead and then arose, and it was as if he had come back from the realm of the dead with visions of the truth.'

This man, named Bint, took a liking to me. I was shy of him at first. Geab and the Stalker had sometimes taken their pleasure roughly with those in my band who were younger, but Bint did not force himself on me. He treated me as if he were my guardian and thus forbidden from using me in that way.

By the third day of our journey, I was at ease riding with Bint and had overcome my fear of his beast. He pointed out landmarks as we rode and even prayed with me before we slept. The Stalker was content to leave me with Bint much of the time, although he would strike me once in a while just to remind me that he was still my guardian.

Bint spoke our speech but called on me for words he did not know. He told me much about life in his camp. 'See this?' he said once, pulling his coat open. 'Sheepskin. We keep sheep. We keep them with us and always have food and coats.'

'Did you always live with this band?' I asked.

'Ever since I was a boy. I, too, am from the north, but I cannot remember much of that life. This band was smaller then, but two bands have joined since – yours is the third. You will like it in our camp. You'll learn how to grow some plants and grain, which is hard work, but, when the ones below us are shivering through winter, you'll be in a warm hut with plenty of food. But you will have to do as you're told.'

'Will Geab tell us what to do?'

'The council will, and he will follow them. Work is given to you. If you disobey, there are punishments according to what you have done wrong. But you won't be punished without a hearing – that means you get to tell your side of the story and can call witnesses. Of course, if you've done an evil deed, you might die for it, but you will have a hearing first. We practise justice.'

It all sounded strange and wondrous. It came to me that, with a band as large as theirs, things were not so simple.

'Don't other bands try to take what you have?' I asked.

Bint laughed. 'Oh, they can try. They don't if they are wise. We train to defend ourselves. Some are archers, others fight with spears, and some fight on horseback.'

'We can each fight with spears, and knives, and arrows, as well as with slings.' I spoke with pride. 'We do not fight in only one way.'

'Our way is better,' Bint said. 'We train each in what he is best at, and, when we fight, we work together, but with a plan. It is not just every man fighting for himself or his young charge. Maybe, if the other bands got together, they could give us a battle, but they never do. They fight each other while we grow stronger.'

I thought of Tal often during the first days of our journey, squeezing my eyes shut at night before sleeping so that I would not cry. Soon, I no longer thought of him, and even came to think that he had been wrong not to promise to join us when he left the enclave. Bint was a good man. He prayed every night and told me he had been called to an enclave three times. I began to believe that Tal would come to see that he had made a mistake and would seek us out after all.

We left wooded hills by the fourth day of our travels and then rode across a snowy plain. On the last day, we prayed at a shrine to the Witch before going on.

Here, in this shrine, I was again uneasy. Hecate glowered at us as my band knelt before Her, and then I saw that Truthspeaker's men did not kneel but gazed directly at Her image as they prayed. We lay on the Lady's couches, wearing Her circlets, but She favoured no one, and no one was called.

The shrine was on the plain. Above it, to the south, was a high plateau. Bint gestured with one arm. 'Up there,' he said. 'Our settlement, Arvil. Our town.' I could dimly make out a barrier near the plateau's edge.

We rode to a path leading up to the camp. This passage wound among the rocks along the steep incline, as if a large hand had carved it out with a giant stone. We passed snow-covered boulders as the horses climbed with sure feet. I did not dare to look to my side or toward the land so far below. We came to a cave guarded by two men; one of them mounted his horse and rode ahead of us. We passed another cave where others guarded the way, and they shouted a welcome in the holy speech.

As we climbed higher, I saw a long, low barrier made of wood and stones piled upon dirt. This was the wall my new band had built. Then huts seemed to rise from the ground above us, and I heard the sound of many voices. The band was singing, and their song was filled with a joy I had rarely heard.

Boys ran toward us. They climbed over the wall and held out arms to the smaller ones. They were smiling, and their faces were round and full. As we dismounted, one boy ran to Bint, and he hugged the child with his big arms. At that moment, I longed for Tal.

I could see this band's wealth. Meat, enough for days, turned on spits in the centre of the settlement. Logs of wood, enough for many fires, sat outside each of the huts. Bint chattered in that band's tongue to the boy who clung to his hands, while Geab danced lightly on his feet and then shouted, 'The Lady is good.'

I said, 'We are blessed.'

'And your old guardian,' Geab answered, 'is a fool.'

I stared at my new home. These men had built on high ground that could be defended. Each hut seemed large enough for five men or more, and an enclosure inside the wall held a herd of sheep. There would be much work for me in the settlement, for I saw that such a camp needed the labour of many. But the smiles of the young boys told me I would also find contentment.

I had been taught to fear strangers; I had thought my own band knew as much as men could know. Now I felt how small and weak we were.

The boy with Bint handed him a skin. Bint drank from it and handed it to me. 'Mare's milk, Arvil.' I tasted the unfamiliar drink and made a face. The boy laughed. I had grown more used to the horses during our travels, had taken to riding more easily than I had expected; I supposed I would get used to the milk.

'Look there!' Eagle Eyes cried out. He was gazing toward the horizon, where I could barely make out the shimmering spires and the vast wall of a distant enclave. Five tiny globes suddenly rose from the wall, hovered, above it, and then flew in our direction. We gaped at them, marvelling at the enclave's magic.

The globes grew larger as they approached until I could see

that each was even larger than a hut. They glittered in the sunlight. They swept toward the plateau and circled us while several men sang loudly, threatening to drown out the hum of the silver balls.

'The Lady favours us,' Bint shouted. 'She is welcoming you to our home.' The boys near the barrier cheered.

I could not speak. 'Does this always happen when a band joins you?' Geab asked.

Bint shook his head. 'It has never happened before. This must have a special meaning. What a glorious day!' We stood there and smiled at the globes as their glassy eyes winked at us.

Then the Lady rendered Her judgement.

Rays brighter than the sun shot out from the globes. I heard a boy scream and saw three huts catch fire. A man near me fell. His head was gone, and his blood spurted over the snow.

Truthspeaker held out his arms. His face was twisted, and he seemed to be entranced. 'Lady!' he called out in the holy speech. 'I have stood before You! I turn from You now! I would embrace evil rather than join You in Your realm!' His words were horrible to hear, and, as he spoke, two boys fell at his feet.

Cor was struck as he ran toward me. One man lifted his spear and launched it at one globe before he fell under another ray. Beams struck along the wall as flames leaped from the roofs of the huts.

I was stiff with terror, unable to move. The boy near me dropped his skin of milk and screamed as a ray caught him. Bint knocked me to the ground. I rolled down a slope and was caught under a boulder, then threw my hands over my head. I could still hear the screams of both horses and men.

Tal was right, I thought, then tried to silence my mind, afraid that the Lady would hear my thoughts and find me. Feet ran past me as men fled down the path. Peering through my fingers, I saw the runners fall under the rays of a globe. I heard other voices full of rage, some cursing in the holy speech. Even now, while the Lady was showing Her power, some were refusing to plead for mercy; they would only condemn themselves in the next world.

Truthspeaker had doomed my band as well as his own. The cries of rage and pain became a single cry, the cry of a maddened beast. Rays flashed as the globes hummed. Their hum reminded me of a swarm of bees, those creatures so loved of the Lady, those creatures that sometimes gave us their honey yet stung those who did not approach their hives with care. I pressed my face to the ground, praying for a quick death, as I listened to the agony of others.

I lay there for a long time until I could hear no more screams, only the hum of the globes and the crackling of the fire. The humming grew faint and then died away.

Slowly, I got to my feet. The globes were gone. Bodies were strewn about on the reddened snow. I staggered toward Bint. He was on his back, his chest burned open, his face stiff with terror. Geab lay next to him. Truthspeaker's face was frozen in a snarl.

The huts continued to burn. Each blackened structure caved in with a creak until there were only charred mounds.

I felt that I must do something for the wounded and stumbled from body to body until I understood that all were dead and that I was alone on cursed ground. The settlement's sheep milled about and bleated in the distance, having escaped through a breach in their enclosure. Two wild-eyed horses near me whinnied and then galloped away.

I looked down toward the plain. A few men were riding southeast, and I guessed that they had escaped from the caves we had passed earlier. I could not have caught up with them, and perhaps they would not have accepted me, thinking that my band had somehow brought this punishment upon them. Perhaps we had. I could not know the Lady's mind.

I moved as if under a spell. I took charred meat from one of the spits and packed it in my pouch. Near one hut lay a pack. I put more meat inside it and tied it to my back, then picked up my bow and spear.

I prayed for the dead, hoping that the Lady, having punished them in this world, might show them mercy in the next, but the words seemed useless. I wondered if the few who had escaped, instead of repenting, would only harden their hearts against Her.

Eagle Eyes had taught me the lore of mushrooms and how to forage for wild plants. Arrow had shown me how to shape my weapons and which stones were best for them. Hawk had gazed at the stars with me. Stel would never grow large enough to challenge me when I chided him. I had hunted with the men of my band, and they had shown me how to make fires with my flints and how to make clothes out of hides. Now they were gone, and I had no band. After praying, I took Geab's metal knife, for there was no one else to claim it, and thrust it into my belt with my own.

I could not remain on unholy ground. I left the plateau, crept down along the path, and wandered aimlessly until dusk, when the bitter wind of evening bit into my face and brought me back to myself. I could not remain out there alone. If I could make my way north, I might find Tal when he returned from the enclave there, but I would have to avoid the scavengers near the wall. Then it came to me that Tal might leave the wall before I could reach him, and that I might never find him.

I was near Hecate's shrine. Tal had told me always to stop and pay my respects, and no man could harm me there. But the Lady had judged my new companions and had destroyed their camp; She might strike me down as I prayed.

At that thought my numbness vanished, and I knew terror. I clung to a tree and moaned, trying to hold back my tears. In that state, I somehow cleared my mind. If the Lady knew I was alive, She could take me at any time. I could not hide from Her, so She had to know where I was, and that meant She had decided to spare me. If I did not stop at Her shrine and thank Her for my life, She might be angered.

I went into the shrine.

I knelt before the Witch and prayed until my knees were sore and my forehead hurt from striking the floor before the altar. The image glared at me but did not speak, and I began to hope.

I got up, went to a couch, and put on the Lady's crown, knowing what I had to say.

I prayed silently, below a whisper, shaping the words of the holy tongue as I had been taught to do by Tal. 'Lady, please speak to me. Our Headman led us to the plateau where You struck down the sinners who sought to challenge Your way. I was given to another man by my guardian, Tal, and had to follow that man, for I am only a boy. But I am still Your servant and did not sin against You. Guide me – tell me what to do.'

She was silent.

'Tell me what to do. I am alone, without a band. You have called my old guardian, Tal, to You, but I cannot follow him to Your side. What shall I do? Speak to me, please.'

I kept praying in that way until I grew so weary I could not rise from the couch. Curling up on my side, I clung to the soft red cloth, still pleading.

An invisible hand reached out and touched my face. A form took shape, and I saw that an aspect would appear to me. I was on the couch, but no longer in the shrine. The Lady had taken my soul, through Her magic, to a smaller, darker room.

She moved closer to me and touched my face once more, then drew back. 'What is it you want?' Her hair was blond and Her tunic white; Her eyes were the wintry grey of Tal's eyes. 'Why do you call Me?'

I told my story again, and She was silent. Then She said, 'Wait,' and stepped back. I could see Her more clearly; the body under Her clothing was slight and unformed. She lifted Her hands to the circlet on Her head and faded from sight.

I stared into blackness until another voice spoke, a lower voice, but still soft and musical. Somehow, I felt that I had heard this voice before.

'You seek My guidance,' this voice said. Another manifestation of the Lady appeared; Her hair was auburn, Her voice kind. 'You say that you are alone. I can help you. Your guardian, Tal, is with Us, and I have decided to call you to Me as well. Go to the southernmost side of our enclave's wall, to where Tal entered, and wait there before the door you will see. You will be allowed to enter and will find your guardian again. Spend the day before you approach My city purifying yourself in a shrine. You are a strong boy, and I believe you will overcome the dangers of your journey. If I do not behold you within fourteen nights, I shall send your guardian from Me.'

My joy unbalanced me. I should have abased myself and offered thanks. Instead, my mind cried out, 'Why did You punish those on the plateau? They were not all evil – the man called Bint prayed often and was Your true servant. The boys could not have been evil – they were only children. Could You not have punished the evil ones while sparing the good?'

She drew back and Her eyes narrowed; She seemed almost to be sorrowing for the condemned men. Then She said, 'Men are tainted. When their sin grows larger than their virtue, and they must be punished, there can be no mercy. The Lady, Who gives life to men, may take it. Those who live with evil will be struck down as surely as the evildoers themselves. It is ordained that you shall wander the world in bands, but those men sought to unite themselves against the Lady's aspects. That cannot be allowed. Remember that.'

She turned Her face from me and covered Her eyes, then looked up. 'I send you a visitation,' She said, 'so that you will know you are blessed. The Goddess be with you.'

She disappeared and another took Her place. This aspect was naked, Her hair was black, and Her brown eyes were rimmed with gold. Her hands drew away my clothing as Her fingers caressed me.

45

'Come to Me,' She said, and I held Her. She guided my hands to Her body, and this was part of the magic of Her blessing – that She seemed to take pleasure from my touch as well as giving pleasure to me. My member swelled, and I felt Her breath on my ear as I entered Her, and was one with Her as I felt release.

She disappeared, and slowly I came to myself. My muscles ached, and my groin felt sticky and wet. I had been called, and the Lady had blessed me. I opened my eyes; I was in the shrine again.

A man and a boy were kneeling at the altar. As they stood up, they turned to look at me. I struggled to sit up. Their furry hoods were thrown back, showing their black, frizzy hair. Their broad faces were much alike and their skin was as dark as Arrow's. I felt sorrow again as I remembered that Arrow and Stel were dead.

These worshippers could not harm me there. I said, 'I have been called.'

The boy snickered; the man shot him a look. 'I saw,' the man said. 'You were thrashing about possessed, as your soul travelled to Her realm. I thought you had only Her blessing until I saw the joyous smile on your face. Are you older than you look?'

'This is my twelfth winter outside the enclave.'

'I do not know why the Goddess would call one so young, but Her purposes are unknown to us.'

He led the boy toward the couches near me, and both lay down, closing their eyes and donning the circlets. It was soon clear that the Lady would not speak to them. At last, the man sat up.

'Where is your band?' He spoke each word slowly, as if unused to my language. I, in turn, was surprised that he knew it; we had spoken in the holy speech before. 'Are these not your words?' he continued. 'You have the look of men who speak in this way.'

'It is my tongue,' I admitted.

'Where is your band?' he asked again.

I was suddenly cautious. I could not lie to him in a shrine, where the Lady would take offense at false words. 'They are elsewhere,' I replied; the Lady could not consider that a falsehood.

He looked at the sack beside my couch, then raised his eyes to me. 'And you have been called. Your band will be pleased when you run to them with the news.' He rose. 'Peace be with you.' He led the boy from the shrine.

I slept in that holy place, hoping that the Lady would again visit me. I had been given Her blessing before, and yet I had never felt such pleasure at other times. I had been near death, and She had restored me to life. She had called me to Her enclave, and that meant that She had forgiven me for falling under the spell of Truthspeaker's band. I had learned why men obeyed Her call, why some even forsook taking such pleasure with other men when they were blessed often enough in shrines. But She did not return to me that night.

I ate some of my meat and left the shrine at dawn. The weather had grown warmer. The snow was beginning to melt and the ground was muddier. I warmed snow in my hands and drank of it.

I had been called. I would be a man when I came out of the enclave. I said it to myself again and again, exulting in the words. Even Tal had not been called so young. For the first time in my life, I wished that Cor were with me so that I could glory in the triumph, and that thought gave me pain. I wanted to tell everyone of that summons, and there was no one to tell.

As I walked north, I recalled the landmarks Bint had shown me. I wondered if I could have controlled a horse by myself and was sorry I had not tried to bring one with me from the plateau. I would have to move quickly, and my body was still stiff and sore from the days of riding. Soon, I came to a small hill, topped by a few thin trees, where we had stopped during our journey. As I climbed, I began to feel that I was not alone.

Eyes were watching me. Tal had taught me to trust such feelings. When I reached the top of the hill, I knelt as if to examine the ground, then peered quickly through my legs.

Below, someone disappeared behind a rock. I caught only a glimpse of my tracker's furry brown cloak, but I knew who he was. The dark man I had seen at Hecate's shrine was trailing me, and if he discovered I was alone, I would be in danger.

LAISSA

Inside my tower, a few small girls were playing near the entrance. I crossed the lobby and entered the lift; the platform carried me up through its transparent cylinder and stopped at my floor. Women leaned over the railings on other floors and called to the girls below; I hurried along the walkway to my door.

Button was sitting on the couch playing with a pocket puzzle. I felt a twinge as I compared his lot to that of the girls in the lobby. 'Where's Mother?' I asked. 'It's nearly suppertime.'

'She had to go to the wall.' He lifted his head and glared at me. I went to the screen in the corner; Shayl had left a message saying that she had to study that evening but would visit next day to hear all about my tests.

Button said, 'You're sending me away, you and Mother.'

'You should be in your exercizer, not sitting here with a puzzle. You have to get strong.'

'You're sending me away. You hate me.'

'I don't hate you, Button.'

'You do, and so does Mother. You're sending me away.'

I went over to him and sat at one end of the couch; he recoiled from me. 'I'm going away, too. I'm going to live with my friend Shayl, and I'll have to work hard at my studies. All of us have to go and live somewhere else someday.'

'I don't want to go.'

'You have to, Button. You're a big boy now. A man will come for you, and he'll take care of you. You'll go outside, and meet other boys, and learn lots of new things from them. You'll be with your own kind. You'll like it a lot more than here.'

'No, I won't. I want to stay here.'

'Well, you can't.'

'Why?'

'Because you're a boy, and boys have to go outside.'

'Why don't girls have to go?'

'Because this is our home.' I tapped my knee impatiently. 'And sometimes girls have to go, too, if they're very bad.'

'I have to go away because I'm bad.'

'No,' I said. 'You go because you're a boy, and you wouldn't like it here later on – really, you wouldn't. You see, girls who are very bad go outside, but boys who are good go outside so they can be with other boys, you know that. And girls have to stay here and look after the city. That's hard work. You can go outside and see new places, and you don't have to worry about the problems we have.'

'You're lying, Laissa.'

I wanted to hit him. What good would his questions do? 'I'm not lying. And you'll forget all about us anyway, wait and see. They put a mindwasher on your head before you go, and you forget us, so there.'

Button screamed. I had said the wrong thing.

'It doesn't hurt,' I shouted. He dived at me and pounded me with his fists; I slapped him. 'If you're going to act like that, go to your room.'

'No!'

'Yes!' I got to my feet and pushed him toward his door. He walked away stiffly, his head up.

I picked up his puzzle and peered at the maze. I could not have solved that puzzle at his age, and yet Button had. I threw the puzzle on to the couch, then went to the study; I didn't want to sit in my disorderly room, where I was still sorting out what I would take to Shayl's.

The door slid open. A light on the wall had lit up; someone was calling from outside the city. Our mindspeaker could pick up transmissions from any of the shrines outside, but Mother had long ago set it so that it would signal to her only when the brain pattern registered was that of my progenitor or my twin. My father had, according to Mother, already entered the wall, so my twin had to be calling.

I had practised on a mindspeaker often enough and knew some of the ritual for men, but had never spoken to one directly. I thought of the boy I barely remembered, wondering if he had been like Button. I went to the table, picked up the circlet, and put it on my head.

A voice screamed at me; I felt an overwhelming fear. Somehow I found the modulator and pressed it. The voice softened.

I closed my eyes and saw a tall young man stretched out on a couch. I tried to concentrate on what the mindspeaker was showing me, on the lifelike image it had created with the aid of the lenses and sensors in the shrine. Only the couch was visible to me. The young man's shoulder-length, blond hair was matted and his even-featured face was dirty; his hands were covered by filthy leather gloves. He wore brown leather leggings and a coat of hide; the opened coat revealed a worn leather shirt.

I reached out with one hand and felt his face, then drew back, telling myself that I was not actually touching this creature, that this was only an illusion. A memory came to me of a little boy who had sat at Mother's feet with me, who had shoved me when Mother wasn't looking, but who had also repaired one of my broken toys. I touched his cheek again, imagining how rough his skin must be, then pulled away.

'What is it you want?' I asked, forgetting the ritual. 'Why do you call Me?'

'You must help me, Lady,' the young man said. His lips moved only a little as I picked up his subvocalized surface thoughts. He was saying that he was alone, that his guardian had left him to travel to a city, that his band had then travelled south with other men only to die under the beams of a city's ships. 'I am alone,' he finished. 'Please help me, please tell me how I can find my guardian, Tal, again.'

'Wait,' I said, then removed the circlet as I recalled what Eilaan had said about Devva. That city, it seemed, had acted, and this young man had been with the men Devva had attacked. I clasped my hands together. Mother had been accused of disobedience; I had been told by Bren that I doubted, and now my twin was telling me that he had narrowly escaped Devva's action.

The door behind me slid open. I spun around, startled. Mother waved at the light on the wall. 'Laissa, what are you doing?'

'My twin is calling you,' I said. 'Devva's destroyed that settlement of men they were so worried about.'

'What does that have to do with him?'

'He was there. He escaped.'

Mother covered her mouth. 'But his band roams the lands beyond our southern wall. He shouldn't be so far south.'

'He says that they travelled to that other place. He's alone now. He says he wants to find his guardian.'

'He means his father. The boy can't live out there for long if he's alone – men live in groups.' She went to the console and played back what the boy had told me, then scowled. 'This isn't good. I must think of what to do.'

'I know I probably shouldn't have talked to him, but I was careful. I . . .'

'It's all right, Laissa. Leave me alone now. I'll speak to him.'

I paced the outer chamber as I worried about what Mother might do now. At last she joined me, but she did not speak until she had taken a bottle of wine from the dispenser in our wall. Her hands shook as she poured wine into a glass.

'I've called the boy here,' she said in a low voice. 'If he's strong enough to make the trip, he'll be with his father again, and Button will have two males to look after him. They might find another tribe.'

I folded my arms. 'But he's only seventeen. He's young to be called, and he was with those men Devva attacked as well. You shouldn't have done that.'

'I had no choice!' she said harshly. 'The boy is alone. His father has no tribe now. Even with two males, Button's chances won't be good. With only his father, they'll be much worse.' She gulped her wine and poured more. 'I just hope the boy can get here. I'll have to wait for him. It means I'll have to keep Button a little longer.'

'But Eilaan told you . . .'

'I had to do it!' she shouted. 'As it is, I may only be sending Button out to die. If only he could stay even a year or so longer. I know it's wrong to think it, but I do.' She downed the wine and set the glass on a table.

'You didn't have to do this,' I said as calmly as I could. 'You might have given Button to a man who has a group to return to.' I paused. 'We'll be disgraced.'

She came to me and grabbed my shoulder; her fingers dug into me painfully. 'This isn't disobedience. This will test their strength. I haven't violated my duty.' She seemed to be saying the words more to herself than to me. 'If your twin can make such a journey alone, it will only show that he and those with his traits are strong and should survive to pass on those traits to future generations of women.'

'That isn't why you're doing this, Mother. You could still send Button out with someone else.'

'I've already promised his father a young one.' Her mouth twisted. 'The Lady cannot break Her promise.'

'You just want to hang on to him. You've gone mad. You're still hoping some miracle will save him.'

She turned away. Once again, she had endangered us both.

ARVIL

I kept to rocky or frozen ground, not wanting to leave many tracks. I spent part of the night in a tree and built no fire for warmth. The man and the boy were still following me the next morning, and they no longer troubled to conceal themselves. They were keeping well behind me, near the horizon to the south, but always in sight.

I had some meat left in my pouch. Hunting near the home ground of other bands would be risky, and I could not look for food while being tracked. Why were they following me? They had to believe that I was heading back to my band, that they might be attacked if they followed me. Then I remembered

Geab's knife. The man might have seen it while my soul was with the Lady. A man would kill for such a weapon. The two might be waiting to fall upon me before I could join others.

As I made my way through territory where I knew nothing of the nearby bands, I understood how alone I was. We had seen no bands while travelling south, but other men would have hidden themselves from a large band passing on horseback. A lone boy was an easy target. I held to my faith in the Lady, yet I had seen good men die before. I could not know Her will.

A flock of sparrows had alighted on the snow in front of me. They hopped away, took to the air, and flew toward the sky. I thought of my band, lying dead on the plateau, and of their souls now flying toward the heavens. Would the Lady forgive them and accept them? Would She grant them the blessings in the next world that She allowed other living things in this one? Only death would bring us the happiness the sparrows and other creatures enjoyed in this life, for they dwelled with females and their young, while we had only the boys given us by the Lady to raise. We were of the world, yet apart from it, and the sight of animals doing what we could not was one of our punishments for ancient sins.

Once, we had been with the Lady, living in Her realm, and then we had been cast out. My loneliness was unbalancing me, for I was pondering this truth as I walked, hearing a voice inside me questioning it. Had we truly been of the spirit and then forced into our earthly bodies, as I had been told? Or had Earth borne us and given birth to us as She had to all other creatures? Where did the boys who left the enclaves come from?

I tried to silence my questions, knowing that they would only lead to unholiness, but my mind's voice persisted. Why did the Lady, knowing men were sinful, allow us to live? Why did She give us boys? There was a holy mystery here, and all the words I had heard from older men about the Lady granting us boys so that men would move closer to redemption did not answer my doubts.

We needed the Lady, and She somehow needed us, too. That notion made me draw in my breath. 'Silence,' I said aloud to my mind. I looked around hastily, afraid another might have heard, but saw only the patches of melting snow on the brown land that stretched to the horizon.

I had picked up my pace. I strode quickly, then ran, then slowed to a rapid walk again. In the afternoon, I came to the edge of a wood. Bint had told me that there was a shrine to the east, just beyond this patch of forest, but we had not gone to it because it would have meant a half day's travel out of our way. If I could get to that shrine, I would be safe for at least one night.

I moved through the woods stealthily, wondering if I was still being followed. The man trailing me might not know about this shrine. I soon came to a pathway, seemingly well-travelled and with the recent marks of feet, that wound among the trees, and I guessed that it led to the shrine. My own trail would not be so obvious on this path, but I would also have to be careful to avoid other travellers. At one point, I heard distant voices and hid in a tree until I could hear them no more. It grew dark and harder for me to see; I was forced to move more slowly.

It was night when I reached the edge of this wood. I was about to step from the trees and walk toward the shrine ahead when its door opened and I saw a group of shadows against the light. I rolled under a bush as the men walked toward me; twigs cracked as they passed by. I held my breath and was not discovered.

Climbing to my feet, I sprinted toward the shrine and was panting by the time I reached it. The door opened, and I stumbled inside, shaking mud and snow from my boots. My stomach ached. I tried not to think of food. My meat would have to last for some time.

I went to the altar. The Warrior dwelled in this shrine. She watched me from behind Her shield as I prayed, and then I went to a couch and donned the Lady's crown. I called to Her, telling Her of my journey and asking for Her help in finding more food, but She did not speak.

I was tired and drifted into drowsiness. I do not know how long I lay there. The whisper of the door made me start, and I sat up quickly, knowing that I had slept while wearing the circlet. As I took off the crown, the dark man and the boy glanced at me, then went to the altar.

They had followed me here; I trembled with fear and rage. They finished their prayers, went to the couches, and put on circlets. I wanted to run from the shrine, but would be no safer outside. I waited until the man sat up and gazed at me.

'We saw the signs of two bands along the way,' he said. 'You didn't join either.'

I said nothing.

'Maybe·yours is farther away than you thought. Or maybe they are hiding from enemies. Or they're dead, or they broke their bond with you for some reason, or they were forced to move their camp.' As he spoke, I was wondering where his own band was and why he and the boy were still alone.

The man held up his hand, palm out. 'Don't look so angry. We are in a shrine – we cannot hurt each other here. There is always peace in Her presence. Truce.'

The truce would be over once I stepped off holy ground. The man watched me for a while, then gestured to the boy, who opened his small pack and threw me a burnt bird's wing.

I gnawed at the wing, sucking on the bones after devouring the meat. The man gave me another wing, and I finished that one, too.

'Truce?' he said again.

'Truce,' I answered. 'Where is your band?'

The boy narrowed his eyes. The man plucked at his thick, curly beard, scratched his head, and then said, 'You are alone, are you not? You must speak the truth here.'

'You must promise me that there will be peace between us when we leave.' I turned toward the statue of the Warrior. 'Swear it, by Her.'

Both raised their hands and promised peace, and I swore peace as well. We were now bound by our vow, for we had made it before the Lady.

'I am alone,' I admitted, telling myself that they would not have offered food and then sworn an oath if they meant harm. 'The rest of my band is dead.' I sent up a silent prayer to the Lady. I could not lie in a shrine, yet could not admit to these two that I had narrowly escaped Her wrath. 'But my guardian, Tal, was not with my band when they died, because he was called to an enclave. I'm going to him now. I prayed to the Lady at the shrine where you first met me, and She called me to Her, and now I am travelling north to find Tal.'

'What is your name?' the man asked.

'Arvil.'

'What does that mean?'

'It is an old name – the meaning is lost.'

'I am Wanderer. I had another name once, but that is how I am known now. The boy is Shadow, because he follows me. I guessed that you had no band near here, for the men in these parts have a different tongue.'

'Where is your band?'

'You see it here.' He waved a hand at Shadow. 'We travel by ourselves.'

'But that cannot be.'

'We are here, are we not?' Wanderer reclined on one elbow. 'I lost my band as a boy. Since then, I've been alone, but I have made peace with many groups. They find me useful because I know the speech and ways and lore of others and can be a messenger or go-between when there is ill feeling between bands. I have dwelled with and hunted with many groups of men, and I have travelled far and can entertain them with tales of my adventures. I have even aided some bands in treating with others so that they do not fight over a herd or a territory. But I have no band of my own.'

'The Lady cannot approve.'

'I am here, saying it before Her. I have been called three times to an enclave, and Shadow was given to me. The Goddess has not condemned me.'

I shook my head, trying to accept this tale. 'What do you want with me? Why did you follow me?'

'Because I suspected that you were alone when I first saw you in the Witch's shrine. I spoke to you in the northern tongue, and you understood and answered me in it. You had been called, and that means you must be especially loved of the Goddess, for one so young is rarely called. Then I wondered how you had come south, for I was certain you could not have made the journey by yourself. What could it be that brought your band south in winter? It could not be a hunt, for you would stay on familiar ground during this season with stored food to save your strength, and move on in the spring.' He leaned forward. 'I have guessed. Your band sought to join those behind the wall on the plateau.' He watched me calmly. 'Am I right?'

I refused to answer.

'I saw the judgement from below. The fire blazed brightly. But you escaped somehow and then were called, so the Goddess has pardoned you. You should have nothing to fear from Her, and Shadow and I will do you no harm.'

'But why did you follow me?'

'I grow older,' Wanderer said. 'I now need a band, for an old traveller will be of little use to strangers. And you are alone, so you need me. I think we should travel together.'

'I must go to the enclave first and find Tal.' As I spoke his name, I felt again how much I missed him.

'We can travel with you for part of the way. When you find your guardian and come outside, we can become a band if he wishes. If not, we still have our truce. But I think he will agree. After all, he has no band now.'

'I must sleep,' I said, 'and consider this.'

'Very well.' He murmured a few words to Shadow, then stretched out, his back to me.

I did not know what to think of his offer. A stranger was saying he would help me, yet my band had always distrusted strangers, and those strangers we had followed had led my band only to death. The Lady had decreed since the beginning of time that only the strong would live and the weak would die, yet here was a man ready to help someone weaker – for I was weaker, whatever blessings the Lady had bestowed on me.

I would have to travel with Wanderer and Shadow. Tal could decide whether we would be a band later. I knew that without Wanderer's help, I was unlikely to reach my guardian.

The next morning, I accepted Wanderer's offer, and we shared most of what was left of my meat. We said our prayers together and put on the circlets once more. The Lady said nothing to me or to Shadow, but Wanderer was given a visitation. As he thrashed about, I recalled my own visitation and longed for another. When Wanderer rose from the couch, he glanced at Shadow and shook his head. I knew by that gesture that he had not been called.

We left the shrine and went north, then turned west, skirting the wood, until we were again following the route I had travelled with Bint. We turned north again and soon came upon a snare in which a rabbit was struggling.

As I took out my metal knife, Wanderer grabbed my hand. 'No. I know this kind of snare – a band I have treated with near here set it. We must leave it for them.'

'They won't know who took it,' I said.

'The Goddess will know, and we may soon meet this band along the way. My truce would be at an end if they saw me with their game, and the snare has marked that rabbit on its limb. Leave it.'

We walked on, satisfying our thirst with handfuls of melted snow, and soon came upon two red-haired young men. I readied my spear, then lowered it as the men greeted Wanderer and Shadow. As Wanderer spoke to them in their own speech, they glared suspiciously at me. I longed to run from the strangers but controlled my fear. I could make out only a few words of their talk; some were northern words, while others resembled the holy speech of the shrine. Most of the words were unfamiliar.

'What is he saying?' I asked Shadow.

'Wanderer says you are his charge and that the Goddess guided you to him.' One of the young men uttered a stream of words. 'He says that his camp will give us meat for one of Wanderer's stories.'

I was astonished. 'They will feed us in return for words? You have an easy life.'

'Do not think that, Arvil,' he answered as we followed the young men. 'Last season, we were offered food for a story, but that band did not like the tale and drove us away with beatings from their spears. Only our truce with them saved us from death. Usually, it is better to do our own hunting, or to aid a band with theirs in return for a share.'

The men lead us to tents on a hillside, where the haunch of a deer was cooking over a fire. Five older men with reddish-brown beards sat with four tow-headed boys. As with another band I had once seen, they had grown to resemble one another.

We squatted near the fire to warm ourselves, and Wanderer began his story. He sang the words and, at times, leaped to his feet, waving his arms while his deep voice swelled.

'What is he saying?' I murmured to Shadow.

'This is a new one. He told it to another band a moon ago, and they liked it so much that we got extra portions.'

'What is it about?' Wanderer was kneeling now, bowing toward the ground as he spoke.

'He is telling them of a band far to the south, where it never snows and the water never grows stiff. Once, there was a boy who was the best hunter and the best tracker and the best forager who ever lived. The Goddess loved him so much that he was called to an enclave six times, for his looks were fair and pleasing to all and his spirit was brave. But when he grew older, he became unhappy and went to live in a shrine so that he could always be near the Goddess. Men for many paces around brought him food and pleasured him and prayed with him because they believed he was holy – otherwise, the Goddess would have ordered him from the shrine, as She will if someone tarries there too long.'

The red-haired men were staring at Wanderer, their mouths open. 'One day,' Shadow continued in a low voice, 'when the man's own band came to him, they saw that, under his shirt, he had grown breasts. he disrobed before them, and they saw that his member was gone and that he bore the pouch instead.'

Wanderer, still chanting, was holding his arms to the sky.

'Then,' Shadow went on, 'the Goddess spoke, and said, "This is My Child, in Whom I am well pleased." And the man, who had become one of Her aspects, was lifted up and taken to the moon, where he lives with Her in bliss. You can see him there when the moon is full.'

I gaped at him. 'Is that true?'

'There is more to it than that,' Shadow said. 'Wanderer puts in more details.' He lowered his voice to a whisper. 'It isn't really true, but Wanderer found out long ago that most bands like a story with bits of truth and a lot of invention more than one that is all true.' He paused. 'We did hear a tale from a band long ago about a man who tried to live in a shrine, but the Goddess ordered him away. And some legends say that men once lived on the moon with the Goddess before the Judgement. So part of the story might be true.'

We all knew of the Judgement. Men had sought to rule over the Lady and all Her aspects; that had been our ancient crime. Fire and ice had been sent to punish us, and we had been cast out, condemned to our present lives in bodies of flesh and bone. But I had never heard of men treading the holy orb of the moon.

'Isn't it wrong to tell such falsehoods?' I asked. 'Some of these men might want to live in a shrine, thinking that the Lady will raise them up as well.'

Shadow shook his head. 'Only a foolish man would do that. It is a story. They will believe it happened long ago, in another place, but that it has nothing to do with them. Still, it might give them hope, and some may try to serve the Goddess better because of it. I don't think She would mind a story that honours Her.'

Wanderer finished his story, uttering the last words in the holy speech. The red-haired men smiled and clapped and gave us generous portions of their meat along with dried plants.

We slept in their tents that night and left in the morning.

We travelled on together for four days. My mind held the images of streams where I had stopped for water on my way to the plateau, and Wanderer had travelled in these lands before. The snow had melted, and we did not have to crack ice to get our water. We lived on the fish we caught at these streams.

I was beginning to feel a bond of friendship with Shadow. I had been called, as he had not, and he respected me for that, but he had travelled to many places with his guardian, and I could honour him for his courage. Shadow said little about his life, but I felt easy with him, as if he had always been part of my band. Perhaps Shadow, having spent so much of his life among strangers, knew how to ease the suspicions and fears of another.

We shared no pleasures together, for it was now the Lady I longed for most, though we did sometimes speak of the Lady's blessings; he had received Her blessings before in faraway shrines. I was sure that the Lady would call such a good soul to Her before long.

On the fifth day, we met men of another band, and one of their number recognized Wanderer. They renewed their truce, and we were taken to the hollowed-out cave that was this band's camp. I could understand most of their speech and was able to hear another story of Wanderer's without Shadow's aid.

This story was of a man who had killed a doe. The doe's orphaned fawn cried out to the Lady as the doe lay dying, and the Lady, clothed as the Warrior, hunted the man down for his crime and killed him with rays of fire. The fawn, under Her protection, grew into a doe and lived with that man's band, which no longer hunted does with young.

This band did not seem to like the story. Their Headman scowled as he threw a small piece of meat to us. Wanderer quickly told another story of other men in the south who lived by a great, salty body of water and caught fish with nets given to them by the Lady, Who had blessed them with an easy life but had also cursed them by calling few to Her side. This tale earned us one more piece of meat.

We had not gone far from that camp when Wanderer stopped and made us kneel. 'We must pray,' he said. 'we must give thanks that those men liked the second tale I told, and we must ask for guidance.' He put his his hands on our shoulders and began to chant. 'As the doe rules the buck, as the cow gives life to the calf, as the stallion must fight for the mare, as the spider weaves her web of beauty and death, so do You rule us, and so do we serve You. Guide this boy Arvil to Your side and bless us all.'

We stood up. 'I have not been this far north in many seasons,' Wanderer went on, 'and we will be in more danger. Some of those who knew me may be dead, and their truces with me would then be at an end. Arvil, you will have to help in guiding us.'

His words frightened me. 'I don't know if I can.'

'I think we should travel to a shrine for safety, but we will have to avoid other bands.'

I thought for a moment. 'There is another shrine to the Warrior in the west. My band was there two springs ago, and the men near it will stay by their river in this season.' I paused. 'But we'll be farther from the enclave, and I must get there soon, or . . .'

'I know.' Wanderer might have abandoned me then; we had a truce, but he owed me nothing more. 'How far to this shrine?'

'From here, it should be a day's walk, but we can't reach it before night.'

'Then we must be quick.'

I looked at Wanderer gratefully as we set off at a trot towards the trees to the west.

The Lady's moonlight guided us through the thickening trees, but soon clouds and the evergreen branches overhead hid our path. We were forced to move more slowly, afraid of losing our way.

Suddenly, a twig cracked. Men leaped upon us.

I knocked one attacker aside and heard a grunt, then blocked a blow with my spear. Another man was near me; I grasped my knife and thrust it at him. He shrieked; my metal blade had drawn blood. Pine needles whispered as feet pounded away; there was a shout in the distance.

'Come,' I muttered to Wanderer. I was surprised that we had driven off our attackers so quickly but knew that we had to reach the shrine before they came at us again.

I heard a moan. Wanderer bent over a dark, huddled shape. 'Shadow is hurt,' Wanderer said.

'We must go.'

He picked up the boy and threw him over his shoulder. Shadow groaned. I led the way, trying to keep to the path. Wanderer was soon panting under his burden, for Shadow, though young, was already quite tall.

'Leave me,' I heard Shadow say.

'No,' I said before Wanderer could reply; I would not abandon my new friend so quickly. Just as I was beginning to think we would never find the shrine, I saw it ahead in a clearing. The golden dome glowed faintly.

We hurried toward the shrine and were soon inside. Wanderer put Shadow down on the floor and opened his jacket, feeling for wounds. I saw much blood. Shadow pressed his lips together, trying not to cry out.

'Will he be all right?' I asked.

'Be quiet, lad.'

'We must pray. Perhaps the Lady . . .'

'It is a time to act, not to pray,' Wanderer replied. 'The Goddess will understand.' It came to me that Wanderer often seemed willing to state what the Lady might think.

After pulling up Shadow's torn and bloodied leather shirt, Wanderer found the wound, an ugly gash under one rib. Blood oozed from this gash as Wanderer examined it. 'Arvil, you must go out and gather kindling and wood.'

'But the strangers . . . they might . . .'

'Get the wood, boy. If you're quick, they won't catch you.'

I went out and gathered the wood, wondering what the man wanted with it. Shadow's wound had looked deep; it might not heal at all. When I returned, Wanderer took out his flints and soon had a small fire going just outside the doorway of the shrine. The door remained open, and I sat with him, watching as he reached inside his pack, removed a small pot with a handle, and filled it with water from his skin.

We were safe for now. Even if the fire in the open doorway attracted other men, we were on holy ground. 'Where did you get that?' I said as I gestured at the pot.

'From a man I had to kill. I expect he took it from a scavenger.' He stripped off his leather hand-coverings and washed his hands. When the water in the pot bubbled, Wanderer handed the pot to me and took out a small leather pouch. He sprinkled a few herbs into the water.

'Hold that pot.' He scrubbed at his hands again. 'Now watch me, boy, and learn. A band south of that cursed plateau gave me this substance – it cleans wounds and keep the blood from becoming poisoned. It can be gathered, if you know where to look for it.'

He rummaged in one pocket and took out something else. 'Cloth,' he said, waving it at me before dropping it into the water. Stel had worn garments of such a material when he had been brought to my band. 'Another man gave this to me.' Taking the wet cloth out, he leaned over Shadow and bathed his wound. The boy smiled a little, as if trying to reassure us. Then Wanderer took out a bone needle, the thinnest one I had ever seen, threaded it with a long, thin piece of gut, and dipped that into the pot of hot water.

'Now,' he said, 'I am going to sew up the gash.'

'Sew it?'

'Wounds, like rips in leather, can be sewn. In a few days, I'll cut the stitches out with the edge of my knife, but the knife must be clean, and the wound will have to be bathed again.' He gazed at Shadow. 'It's going to hurt you.'

The boy gritted his teeth. I watched as Wanderer sewed.

61

Shadow reached for my sleeve and held it tightly. He moaned a little but did not cry out.

'There. It is done.' Wanderer bathed the wound with the cloth once more, then poured out the few drops of water left and put away his tools. I put out the fire and covered the burned wood with dirt.

The door slid shut behind me as I came back inside; we carried Shadow to the nearest couch. Wanderer and I said our prayers at the Warrior's altar, then donned the circlets, but heard no words from the Lady.

Wanderer glared at me as he took off his circlet. 'You told me that the men near here would stay by their river.'

I felt ashamed. 'I thought they would. They never attacked my old band, even though we had no truce, as long as we didn't approach their camp and took only what game we needed.'

'You have given poor advice, Arvil.' I thought that he might strike me, but he did not. 'Did you draw blood?'

'Yes.'

'That's bad. It means, if that man dies, they might return and wait for us to leave holy ground. If they find that we are alone, and we cannot reach a truce, they'll kill us.'

'Then we must leave now.' We would be safer away from the shrine, where the strangers might expect us to stay.

'We cannot leave. Shadow must rest until he is healed. He's lost much blood already. If he is moved now, he'll bleed again.'

'How long?'

'Two days, maybe three. He is strong and should be able to travel at a slow pace by then.'

'But you said those men might come here.'

'Then we must pray that they don't. I cannot leave my charge.' I had to get to the enclave; I could not wait three days. I sat on the edge of my couch and stared at the floor, afraid to look at Wanderer.

He said, 'You know what you must do.'

I looked up. 'I can stay. I will hunt for your food.'

'You cannot stay. Your first duty is to the Lady. You have to leave us.'

I knew he was right. 'I'll come back for you,' I said, unable to believe my own words, sure that they would both be dead by then. Tal would never travel here for the sake of men he did not know.

I stood up. 'Goodbye, Wanderer. Shadow, farewell.' I

swallowed hard. 'May the Lady protect you.'

'And may you reach Her enclave safely,' Wanderer said.

As I turned from them, our enemies entered the shrine.

There were seven men in this group. As the door closed behind them, they knelt quickly and made signs in the direction of the altar. One of the strangers was injured; a bloodied arm in a torn sleeve hung at his side. Another man caught him as he fell toward the floor.

'A truce while we speak,' Wanderer said in the holy speech, and then repeated the words in my language.

'There is always peace in Her presence,' a man with a grey beard answered in my tongue.

'You have injured the boy there.' Wanderer pointed at Shadow. 'But I've hastened his healing, and I can tend to your companion's wound. I must speak truth here – I know some healing arts.' The greybeard frowned. 'I must tend to him before he loses more blood. Give me a truce, and I'll heal him.'

The greybeard nodded. 'Truce. Until you heal him. We swear a truce by the Lady. But if Firemaker dies, we must take a life from you outside.'

I would be the one to die, for I had led my companions here; Wanderer would never let them take Shadow.

The strangers helped their wounded companion to a couch while Wanderer rummaged in his pack, then told me to gather more wood.

I built another fire outside the door. Wanderer stripped off the man's shirt, and I saw the gash my knife had made; the wound was ugly, but not as deep as it might have been. I began to hope. Wanderer took out a piece of cloth and tied the man's arm above his wound.

'What is that?' the greybeard asked.

'He mustn't lose more blood,' Wanderer said. 'I'll loosen this in a little while and see if the bleeding has stopped. Heat more water, Arvil.'

When the water bubbled, Wanderer bathed the arm. Firemaker's jaw tightened above his short brown beard; his large blue eyes showed fear rather than pain. I had seen wounds washed before, but never as Wanderer cleaned them, with water heated over a fire. The men I had lived with had washed with what water they had, and if a wound festered, that was the Lady's will.

Wanderer loosened the cloth, then peered at the arm. 'You are fortunate,' he said. 'Your muscles aren't cut so badly that you cannot use your arm again, and the blood isn't pulsing from your wound, but I'll have to sew it closed if you're to heal.' He took out his bone needle again and dipped it into the water I had carried to him.

'What unholiness is this?' the greybeard asked.

'Do you think I would practise unholiness in a shrine?' Wanderer bent over Firemaker. 'You've pledged to take one of our lives if I cannot heal him. You must let me do what I can.'

I looked down, praying silently for Firemaker's life and my own.

LAISSA

Eilaan came to see us again. This time, Mother sent me out of the room while they spoke.

I went to bed, but was unable to sleep. Mother might be disgraced, deprived of her position as one of the Mothers of the City; and, if I aided her or did not separate myself from her deeds, I would share her punishment. We might be expelled. I could not rid myself of worry over that extremely remote possibility, could not forget the look in Birana's eyes when she had been forced to leave us for ever.

When I went into the outer chamber, Mother was lying on a couch, one arm thrown over her eyes; her auburn hair was loose and tangled. She lifted her arm and gazed at me with weary eyes.

I said, 'We're going to be punished.'

Her head rolled from side to side. 'No. We'll be watched, and our mindspeaker will be monitored for a time. After Button is gone, an adviser may have to decide if I need counselling – the Council is still discussing that. Eilaan persuaded them not to remove me from my work, since she thinks it's better that I keep busy and not brood, but I imagine some of my patients may request another physician.' She paused. 'Have I done anything so wrong?' She did not wait for me to reply. 'Of course, they must be firm even with minor infractions, and especially with women like me, or everything would unravel, wouldn't it?' She sounded bitter as she spoke. 'I must set a good example for others.'

'What about me?'

'Nothing's going to happen to you, Laissa. I told Eilaan you'd been quite critical of me. You'll be living with Shayl soon anyway, and once you've moved in with her and taken up your studies, nothing I do can affect you. At worst, I'll be an embarrassment.'

I had been delaying the move, was still anxious about leaving. Now I saw that my own safety lay in leaving as soon as I could.

Mother sat up. 'You should be asleep. I thought Shayl was coming over early tomorrow.'

'I can't sleep.' I sat down across from her. 'You know that Eilaan's right. If you start stretching the rules for Button, other women might do the same, and then . . .'

'I know. I haven't been fair to you, either. I haven't even asked you about your tests, or what you're going to study.'

In her worry over Button, I doubted that she had thought about me at all. 'I'm going to study physics.'

'But the maths . . .'

'I'll get through it somehow. Shayl can help me.'

'Then the tests didn't make you change your mind.'

'No.' I didn't want to talk about that. Bren had intimidated me to the point where I was thinking of changing to general science, but I didn't want to do that until I talked to Shayl. I suppose that I was hoping she would talk me out of the change.

'I remember when I took my tests,' Mother said. 'I was advised to become a historian.'

I stiffened. 'Why didn't you?'

'It isn't just that it seemed so sordid. The more I learned about the past, the more hopeless the present seemed, the more imprisoned I felt we had become. I wanted to lose myself, forget the questions I had, be like everybody else. I wanted to stay busy so that there wouldn't be time to think, and in obstetrics and midwifery, I would be doing something useful.' She sighed. 'It's odd. When they're born, it doesn't seem to matter whether they're male or female. All I worry about is their well-being.'

'Mother, send Button out now. If you do that, you'll be left alone. Don't wait.

'It's too late. I've already summoned Button's brother. I have to hope he finds his way here and that Button will get the best chance I can give him.'

Shayl did not come to our rooms the next morning. I waited and then called her. She was out, but had left a message saying that she would call me later. She never did.

I called her again the next day. This time, her message was apologetic. She was busy, she was behind in her studies, I might want to put off moving until she had caught up with her work. She had been impatient for me to move before.

I went to Shayl's tower. When her door opened, I saw that she was sitting with a group of young women; none of them seemed to be studying. Shayl bit her lip as she looked at me, then quietly ushered her friends out.

We were alone. I went to the window and stared out between the surrounding towers at the distant wall of our city. She came to my side. She didn't kiss me as I had expected her to do; she didn't even reach for my hand. 'Laissa, I . . .'

'Why did you leave those messages?'

'Because I didn't want you to worry. I've had so much to do.'

I turned to face her. 'That isn't true. If you're behind in your work, why were you sitting here talking to your friends?'

Shayl tilted her head. 'I was going to study. I was just about to ask them to leave when you came.'

I was ready to apologize until I recalled the rest of her message. 'Why did you say that I might want to put off moving?'

Her brown eyes widened. She took a step backward. 'Because I thought . . . well, I thought you needed more time to get ready. And I can help you more when I've caught up. You're still going to do physics, aren't you?'

'I don't know. I wanted to talk to you about that.'

She sighed. 'Let's talk, then.' She didn't seem to care whether she talked to me or not; I had never seen her so distant. I followed her across the room; we sat in chairs, facing each other. 'Well?'

'I was advised against physics. I was told to consider general science instead.' I paused. Shayl was my best friend, the first girl who had made love to me, the one I loved most deeply; I had always been able to tell her almost anything before. But I had hidden a few things from her – my questions, my doubts – and they now seemed more important than the thoughts I had revealed to her. 'The adviser told me I might want to study history and early human culture, too, but I told her that was out of the question.'

Shayl pursed her lips. 'Why would you study that? What would you do with it?'

'Well, I asked the same thing, of course. Bren – the adviser – said I could be a chronicler, but I certainly don't want to be, so I'm thinking of taking general science and concentrating on physics later on. I could use more preparation anyway.' I was shielding myself from her disapproval, as I always had.

Shayl leaned back and drummed her fingers on the arms of her chair. 'Maybe you should live with someone else, then. It always helps to live with someone who's studying the same thing.'

I was numb. She stared past me, refusing to look directly into my eyes.

'It's just a suggestion,' Shayl went on. 'It might be better for you.'

'That's why you left the messages. You don't want me to live with you.'

'I didn't say that, Laissa.'

I leaned toward her. 'Tell me the truth. You don't want me here. You can at least tell me why.'

'It isn't what I want. It's my mother. She told me I should reconsider.' Shayl still refused to look at me. 'She told me the Council was watching your mother because she'd kept her boy too long. She told me your mother might be . . .'

'Who told her that?'

'I don't know.' Shayl's voice had risen; I had never heard her whine before. 'Maybe someone on the Council told her. Word gets around. I always knew your mother pampered that boy too much. With all the Council has to do, they wouldn't be bothering with her if they didn't think it was important.'

'What do my mother's actions have to do with me anyway?'

'You might be disgraced along with her. I haven't noticed that you've gone out of your way to bring her around, or to criticize her. And then there's that business with Yvara's daughter – everyone knows you and Birana used to be friends.'

I couldn't imagine why she would bring that up now. 'That was a long time ago.'

'Maybe it was, but it's just one more thing against you. You're heading for trouble. You're still living with your mother, and, if you don't watch out, you'll both be disgraced. Now I know why Dorlei's lovers never stayed with her. Anyway, Mother said it might hurt my own reputation to live with you.' Shayl was no longer whining; her voice had become harsh. 'And now you say that you were told to study history. Everyone knows how filthy that is. I know someone has to do it, but Mother wouldn't want me living with a historian. She doesn't like me to see Zoreen because of that.'

'But, I'm not going to do that. And Bren told me I might be a chronicler later, not a historian.'

'A chronicler. In some ways, that's worse – writing lies, making everything seem worse than it is.'

'But I'm not going to be . . .'

'It doesn't matter.' She twisted a curl of her black hair as she fidgeted. 'Mother doesn't think I should live with you now. Try to understand. She can really make things hard for me with all her nagging.'

I wanted to rage at Shayl, lash out at her. Yvara, I thought, must have felt this way when she raised her knife against her lover; perhaps Ciella had wounded her with crueler words. I remembered the times Shayl had touched me and I had returned her love; I felt betrayed.

I stood up slowly. 'Shayl, stop telling me about your mother. You're not living with her now, and you don't have to listen to her. At least be honest with me.'

She shook her head, close to tears.

'You're the one who doesn't want to live with me, and you couldn't even come to my rooms to say so. You probably thought I'd get the message after a while. You say I'm in trouble, and you won't even stand by me or try to help me.' At this point, I nearly faltered, recalling how I had begun to avoid Birana, with no explanation. But this wasn't the same; I had never been as close to Birana as to Shayl.

'Well, that's fine with me.' I went on. 'I don't want to live where I'm not welcome. I have more pride than that. I wouldn't live with you now if you begged me.'

I turned and walked slowly toward the door. I was in front of it before I realized that I was waiting for Shayl to come after me, to ask forgiveness, to tell me that she hadn't meant what she said.

I stepped through the doorway, still waiting. Shayl did not speak. The door slid shut behind me.

As a child, I had often gone to play in the shadow of the wall, but later I began to avoid the barrier that bounded our city.

Now I was speeding toward it with Button, clutching his hand as I nursed my anger at my mother and at Shayl. I had lost Shayl; I was ashamed that I had loved her, that I had believed she loved me. I couldn't mend the breach with her, but I had thought of a way I might protect myself against the worse consequences of Mother's actions.

The city outside the transparent tunnel whipped by us; the towers and then the smaller buildings surrounding the spires became a series of blurred vertical images as the current carried us forward. Button was gaping at the sight; he had never travelled so far from our tower before. The last building flashed past; the flat parkland around the city was a sea of green. Button leaned forward in his seat.

The car in which we were riding floated to the left and slowed as it approached our destination. I stood up as it stopped behind a few empty cars, then opened the door, took Button's hand, and led him outside.

Five young girls were playing in the area between the tunnel exit and the entrance to the wall; as they caught sight of Button, they waved. 'What's your name?' one brown-haired girl shouted as she ran up to us.

'Button.'

'Button!' The little girl giggled.

'Leave him alone,' I said.

The girl stepped back. 'It's a boy!' She motioned to her friends. 'They're sending him out!'

Her companions squealed. 'So long,' one cried; it was soon a chorus. 'So long, so long.'

From where we stood, the grey, flat wall seemed to reach nearly to the sky. Button looked up, then began to pull at my arm as we came to the entrance. 'Laissa,' he said.

'Hush.'

'Are you sending me away?'

'Be quiet.'

'You are. Laissa!' He dug in his heels; I had to drag him to the entrance. 'Where's Mother? I want Mother!'

The door slid open. The wide hall, its white walls and silvery floor gleaming, stretched to my right and to my left, seeming to reach into infinity. Three women rode by in a cart and frowned at me as Button wailed.

Two patrolwomen were approaching us on foot. Button tugged at my hand as he whimpered; one of the women pulled him away from me, shook her finger at him, and told him to be quiet.

'What's this all about?' the other said.

'He's my brother. He has to be sent outside.'

'With which male?'

I gave her the particulars, which I had learned after searching Mother's records at home – his number, the room in the wall that held him. 'He calls himself by the name of Tal,' I added, although that hardly mattered. 'I'm supposed to give the boy to him.'

'You, and not your mother? What's your name?'

'Laissa, daughter of Dorlei, Alta's Clan.'

Button suddenly threw himself at me; his screams echoed down the long hallway. I pried him from my legs. 'Be quiet,' I said.

'I hate you! I don't want to go!' He screamed more loudly and began to cry. The taller patrolwoman gave him a piece of candy; he dashed it against the floor's silver tiles.

The short, stocky patrolwoman muttered a few words into her wrist-link, then looked up at me. 'I don't find any authorization for this. Your mother is the one who should be here with him. Why isn't she?'

'She couldn't come. She sent me instead.' I had to shout to be heard over Button's loud weeping; I had expected the patrolwoman's response. The two exchanged glances, and then the shorter one motioned to me.

She led us down the hall to a door. The tall woman picked Button up and thrust him inside the small room. 'Wait here,' the short one said to me.

'Why?'

'Just do what we say.'

'He has to go outside,' I said. 'He should have been sent out before.'

The shorter woman shoved me into the room; the door slid shut. I touched a panel on the wall, then realized that we had been locked inside.

Button lunged at me; I knocked him aside. He slid across the shiny floor and hit a wall. As he stumbled to his feet, I raised a hand. 'You'd better behave.'

'I hate you. I wish you were dead.'

'You have to go outside. You're going, whether you like it or not.'

Button ran to the door and screamed as he beat it with his fists. I sank to the floor. When his voice grew hoarse, he went to a corner and curled up, whimpering. I tried to pity him but could not. It was his fault that Mother was being watched, his fault that Shayl had rejected me.

The room was bare, without even a screen; I was sure we would not be kept there long. The patrolwomen would have to summon Mother, and maybe my action would convince her that she should let Button go now.

He stopped crying. 'I'm sorry,' I said. He glared at me. 'I don't know why you have to make such a fuss. You'll have to go out sometime, and nothing's going to change that.' He didn't reply.

We waited in silence. At last the door opened again. Mother

was outside; the patrolwomen were with her. I forced myself to look up.

Button ran to her; she patted his head as she gazed at me. 'What were you trying to do?' she said sadly. I had expected a harsher tone.

'I was taking him to his father.' I stood up. My legs were shaky, my hands cold. 'You wouldn't bring him, so I did.'

'But you know they wouldn't let him go without my authorization.'

'I don't care. I thought you'd finally see things my way. Eilaan would be on my side. You've ruined everything for me. Shayl doesn't want to live with me now.' Mother lifted a hand to her lips. 'Let him go now, Mother. Don't wait.'

'I have to wait. You know that. I have to wait for . . .' Her voice trailed off.

'He looks old enough to go, older than many,' the tall patrolwoman said. 'Maybe you should listen to your daughter.' In spite of her words, she seemed to sympathize with Mother, and her tone was gentle; perhaps the patrolwoman had once grown too attached to a son.

'He'll be going soon enough,' Mother replied. 'I'll take him home now.'

I followed Mother back down the hall; the patrolwomen saw us to the door. It was already dark outside; the tunnel was a long snake of light over black ground. Button kept near Mother as we walked toward the tunnel and shrank away from me whenever I came too close to him.

'You should have let him go,' I said. 'It's just going to be worse for him later.'

She stopped next to the tunnel entrance and turned toward me. 'Do you hate him so much that you can't let him have the bit of time that's left?'

Button would not look up. I knew that I had frightened him badly, that he would be fearful during the days he had remaining to him. 'I don't hate him,' I said. 'I hate what he's done to you. I don't want to see you in trouble.'

'You don't want to see yourself in trouble. People will know that my own daughter turned against me. That was what you wanted, of course, to protect yourself, but it won't make things easier for me, and you've made the whole business harder for Button as well.'

'I want people to know I brought him here,' I burst out. 'At least they'll see I know my duty. I don't want anyone to think I'm like you.'

'Of course.' Her voice was flat. She led Button to the tunnel, not seeming to care whether or not I followed.

I did not ride with Mother and Button but took another car. I forgot to punch in my route, and my car came to a stop at an exit near the southern edge of the city. As I was about to direct the car along a route that would take me nearer my own tower, my hand froze above the panels. I couldn't go home now, couldn't bear the thought of facing Mother again. I could stay in a dormitory for a little while, but the counsellors there would urge me to find my own rooms soon, if I didn't plan to go home.

Then I saw where the car had stopped. I got out and left the tunnel. I was standing on a brightly lit street just south of the towers. A few young women had gathered across the way to talk; through a window behind them, I could see several women of various ages around a table, sharing an evening meal. Along the street, on tables outside the small, square buildings, a few wares were still being displayed. I passed tables filled with pieces of embroidery, jewellery made of metal, enamel, or bright gems, glazed pottery shaped by hand, and woven cloth. A girl behind a table laden with candies and other sweets called out to me, but I walked on, having nothing to trade for her wares.

I was among those we served, those over whom the Mothers of the City watched. Here a girl could grow to maturity in a household of women, could pursue what art or craft she liked. When it was time to have her children, she would go to the wall and, with the advice of a geneticist, choose a man's seed based on his characteristics and traits. She would never have to call a man to the wall or communicate with him over a mindspeaker. She would never have to think of the outside or concern herself with what lay out there. Whatever children she had would be daughters; she would never have to bear a son and take him to the wall. She would grow old among a community of women, a house filled with others like herself.

Theirs was a carefree, placid life, and yet it was possible only because of what my kind did. My friends and I had lived among such girls in the dormitories; we had learned how to cooperate and to share, while they had learned how to live outside their close, affectionate households for a time. I had made friends with a few such girls, had encouraged those who seemed curious or quick to work at the lessons through which, if a girl shows promise, she can win a place among the Mothers of the City. Now, as I glanced at their smiling faces and heard their cheerful babble, I wondered why any of them would want to be like us.

For a moment, it seemed that the punishment of being sent here to live as one of these women might in fact be a blessing. But even they would scorn a disgraced woman. I could not become one of them; I was condemned to be what I was.

I came to a playground below the towers overlooking this part of the city. I was near Zoreen's rooms. I hurried along the playground's winding path and came to her tower's entrance. Zoreen had chosen to live here, as far from the city's centre as she could move.

Her rooms were at the top of this tower. She lived alone, and no one was with her that evening. She seemed surprised to see me as I entered and watched me without expression as I crossed the room, then said, 'Whatever brings you here?'

'I had a fight with my mother.'

She cleared a space among the papers and books on her couch so that I could sit down. 'Can't say I'm surprised,' she said. 'I know she's had problems lately.'

I told her a little of what had happened as she gazed at me impassively. 'I can't live with Shayl now,' I finished, 'and I really don't feel like going home.'

'Shayl always was stodgy.'

'I don't know what to do, Zoreen.'

'There's always a dorm.'

'They won't let me stay long, not at my age. I don't want to go through all this with an adviser.'

'They'll find a set of rooms for you. You can always live alone, as I do.' Her mouth twisted. I had never known whether Zoreen had chosen to live by herself, or if she had been unable to find anyone to share her rooms.

'I thought maybe I could stay here with you, at least for a while, if you don't mind.'

'You can't ask your other friends?' Her green eyes narrowed. She must have known that my other friends might want to keep a discreet distance until my mother's position was clear; it was a useless question.

'I thought you were my friend,' I said at last.

'I see,' she murmured. 'We haven't exactly been very close lately.'

'I know that. I did ask you to my celebration, though.'

'Yes, you did. How very kind. I really enjoyed being with people who didn't want me there.'

'I wanted you there, Zoreen.'

'No, you didn't. You just felt obliged to an old childhood friend.'

'Then I suppose you don't want me to stay.' I was about to rise.

'Oh, Laissa. You can stay.' She pulled at a few loose strands of her dark brown hair. 'That is, if you don't mind living with someone who's doing history and early human culture.'

'I don't mind.'

'Then I guess I don't care about having someone here whose mother's in trouble. I can't really be choosy.'

I was about to reply but swallowed my words. Zoreen had the right to say what she had; she knew that I would rather be with Shayl.

'Zoreen, I know how you feel,' I said finally. 'I don't ask you to be anything more than a friend. I know I haven't been a very good friend to you for a while. If you don't want me here, I'll go.'

She gazed at me; I could not read the expression in her eyes. 'You can stay as long as you like. I've been lonely. I could use a friend.' I understood what I was seeing in her face as she spoke; she had the look of one used to solitude, to standing apart from the world. I had feared loneliness, had suppressed anything that might separate me from others. Zoreen had been an outsider for some time, ever since taking up her studies; now, I would be one as well.

'Thank you,' I said and saw her smile a little. 'I'd better leave a message for Mother.'

I went to the screen and recorded my message so that I would not have to speak to Mother directly. I said that I would be staying with Zoreen, that her rooms were now my home, that I would pick up my things soon. In that way, I cut my ties. I was safe; whatever punishment Mother brought upon herself would not touch me.

ARVIL

The colour had returned to Firemaker's face by morning. The members of his band examined his arm and saw that it was healing. The strangers said nothing to us then, but later that morning, while they were eating, they gave us a little of their small supply of dried meat. This meat was hardly enough for one mouth, but they had little for themselves.

I said a prayer of thanks, knowing that men did not feed those they planned to kill, and then drew Wanderer to one side. 'How soon will Shadow heal?'

'I told you before. I don't want him to move from this shrine for another two days.'

'But I must leave.'

'I know that, but we had better have a truce with these men before you go.' Wanderer frowned. 'They did not stay by the river, as you said they would. I wonder why. They carry only pouches and waterskins, but no packs, and two of the men have no spears.' I had seen this as well. It was as if they had travelled to the shrine quickly, without forethought.

We turned toward the strangers, who had said their prayers and were now reclining on the couches, awaiting the Lady's blessing. Firemaker was soon sitting up and gazing at his arm while Shadow rested.

We went to Shadow's side. 'It hurts a little,' the boy said, although he looked ashamed to admit it. 'It burns.'

'I'll give you a potion for the pain,' Wanderer replied. 'Then I'll walk outside with you for a little ... otherwise, you will grow weak.'

Shadow nodded. Firemaker was grooming his curly hair with the fingers of his good arm. 'What about you?' Wanderer said to him.

'I feel well.'

'Your arm may be stiff for a while. Don't pick at the wound.'

The other men removed their circlets. The grey-bearded Headman sat on the edge of his couch and gestured to Wanderer. 'We must talk.'

The two walked to the altar and seated themselves under the statue of the Warrior. I trailed after them and sat behind Wanderer while the other men grouped themselves around their leader.

'Before we talk,' Wanderer said, 'we must have a truce.'

The leader leaned forward. 'What have you done – used magic on Firemaker? Will you remove your spell if no truce is granted?'

Wanderer was silent.

'Grant him the truce, Wise Soul.' Firemaker had followed us and was now sitting on the nearest couch. 'I'm healing. I need his spell.'

The greybeard scratched his head. 'Very well. I grant you a

truce. But we must have your promise that the rest of your band will not harm us, either. I hope you have the power to grant that.'

'I do,' Wanderer said. 'For how long?'

'For as long as any of us lives. We grant you the same.'

This was a surprise. Wise Soul would not need such a long truce unless he felt his band was in some danger. Their enemies would become ours if we had a truce with them.

Wanderer was agreeing, as I knew he would have to do. He and Wise Soul murmured oaths to each other and sealed the truce. Then Wise Soul asked, 'Where is the rest of your band?'

Wanderer held up a hand. 'Answer me this. Why are you not at the river where I was told you dwell?'

The strangers stirred. 'I asked my question first.'

Wanderer waved a hand. 'You see my band, Wise Soul. It is these two boys. I have no other.' Firemaker was shaking his head. 'Shadow was given to me in an enclave. This boy, Arvil, joined me south of here because the rest of his band are dead.'

'Then we have been deceived,' Wise Soul muttered. 'We have no truce with a band, but only with three, and two are boys.'

'The Goddess saved Arvil from the fate of his band and has blessed him. He has been called.'

'He looks young to be called.'

'The Goddess has called him. He'll be a man when he comes out of the enclave. Would I lie in front of the Goddess, in a shrine?'

Wise Soul lowered his head and glanced at me for a moment; I thought I saw respect in his eyes.

'I am called Wanderer,' my companion continued, 'because I travel from place to place without a band. I have learned much. I have learned some healing arts and can teach them to you.' He paused. 'Now answer my question. Why did you leave the river? Was it to come here to worship? Or was it to set upon travellers seeking out this shrine?'

'My men have endured much. The lust for blood was in them. They couldn't strike at our enemies, so they struck at you.' Wise Soul looked up at the image of the Warrior. 'We were driven from the river. These men are all that remain of our band. Our boys are dead, our camp is gone. We barely escaped.'

'Who did this to you?'

'A band we have never seen before. A band of horsemen.'

'I have seen horsemen,' Wanderer said. 'I didn't know they had come so far north.'

'These men spoke our speech,' another man said. 'I was at the edge of the camp when they attacked. I fell and struck my head on a rock. When I came to my senses, I heard a boy pleading for his life, begging for mercy in the Lady's name. A horseman answered in our speech, saying that his band had, not long before, come upon a traveller who had also pleaded for mercy, who spoke of seeing with his own eyes two aspects of the Lady outside a shrine, who swore powerful oaths that this was true, and yet the horsemen slayed him. The horseman said this and then took the boy's life. I knew there would be no mercy for us then and that I would have to flee.'

I pondered this strange story. How could a man see aspects of the Lady outside of a shrine? Would a man be so desperate for life that he would risk punishment in the next world by swearing falsely to such a tale? I had uttered my share of falsehoods, but never with holy oaths, and never when I believed I might not live long enough to win the Lady's forgiveness for speaking a lie. The man must have been maddened by his fear of death.

Wanderer seemed deep in thought. He was no stranger to falsehood, yet even he did not claim too much truth for his tales; they were only stories that might have happened in another time or in a faraway place. He would not have sworn to their truth, and most men had tales that grew in the telling. A man might lose sight of the truth, when an event lay far in his past, and thus not be truly guilty of a lie.

I thought of legends I had always believed were true. They also spoke of times no living man had seen. Could untruth have been mingled with them? I stilled my thoughts quickly; this was not something to ponder in a holy place.

Wanderer spoke. 'I didn't know horsemen had come so far north. If they speak the northern tongue, they must have dwelled in this region for a time. There are more bands of such men now in other places, and they may one day overpower those on foot. When they hunt, they don't need to track a lone animal, or chase a straggler into a trap – they can ride after a herd and kill more than they need. They can travel farther from their home ground, and they can fight those on foot, even if the ones on foot outnumber them.'

'They do not fight,' Wise Soul said. 'They slaughter. They do not fight man to man.'

'I have talked to such men and have lived among a few. I have learned something of their arts and can teach them to you. With horses, we can have the strength of ten bands.'

'But it is unholy,' one young man said.

'It is not unholy,' Wanderer replied. 'The Goddess has said that we must hunt, must live as we can. She has not said that we cannot use horses to aid us. I know how to ride, as does Shadow, and how to train a horse.' He paused. 'I have travelled far. I have even heard of unknown lands where men have mastered the art of tilling the soil, or of shaping hard objects from soft clay. I know that what one band despises, another band may practise.'

Wise Soul's eyes widened; he seemed drawn by Wanderer's talk. 'You can teach us some of these things?'

'Yes, and tell you many stories of far places.'

'Could you pledge yourself to our band and become our brother?'

Wanderer nodded. 'I have thought of having a bond with one band, for wandering grows wearisome. But first you must do something for me.'

'And what is that?'

'The boy Arvil has been called to the enclave north of here. He must go there, and soon. His former guardian is there now, and I believe he will also join your band, for he has no other now. I cannot travel with Arvil because I must tend Shadow, but Arvil must reach the enclave soon, for the Goddess has commanded it. I ask that your men travel with him.'

'We don't know that region well. When we have wandered, we have moved west, and the Lady has always summoned us to the enclave south of here.

'The boy can guide you,' Wanderer said, 'and you can offer him protection.'

Wise Soul stroked his beard. 'We must move along the river and find a place for a new camp.'

'Do you think you are safe here, so near the horsemen who have driven you away from the river? They will range far on horseback. I know the ways of such men. They will claim all the land along the river for their own.'

Wise Soul said, 'I must talk to my band.'

We left them by the altar and went back to Shadow. 'Do you think they'll come with me?' I asked.

'They are in danger here, and your band no longer dwells on your home ground. They could claim its territory before another band does.'

'But you and Shadow must stay here until he can travel.'

'That cannot be helped. If I pledge myself to them, we can follow when Shadow is better.'

I gazed at our new band, for such they would be. 'Is that the kind of band you wanted to join?'

Wanderer shrugged. 'They are men, no better or worse than others. Maybe I can teach them to be better than they are. Wise Soul has the look of a thoughtful man, and the others are young, and that means some of them may be called by the Goddess and given boys. I did not choose these men, but perhaps the bargain will be a good one.'

Wise Soul spoke to his men for a long time before he beckoned to us. We went back to the altar, and Wanderer was soon pledging himself to this band. His pledge would bind his charge, Shadow, as well.

'Wanderer has been like a guardian to me,' I said when he had finished, 'but I'll be a man when I leave the enclave, and I can become your brother then. I am not a man yet, so you do not have to heed my words, but Wanderer thinks you should take your band to the land where mine once lived. I don't think another will have claimed it yet.'

Wise Soul nodded. 'It may be best to move on. The horsemen have cursed this land for us. You should lead us to your old camp.'

I looked back at Shadow. He was my friend now, and I did not like the thought of leaving him and Wanderer here alone. 'I can tell you how to reach the camp,' I said, 'but I cannot lead you there myself. I must get to the enclave soon. I must go north, while you will have to go north-east to reach our camp. I must think of Wanderer and Shadow as well, for they are my friends. You should all leave this place, yet Shadow cannot walk far. You could make a conveyance of wood and hide, and carry Shadow upon it. You will have to travel slowly then, while I must move as swiftly as I can, but you'll still be safer than if you remain here.'

Wanderer did not speak, but his hand rested on mine for a moment.

'Wanderer won't leave without Shadow,' I went on, 'and you may have need of his arts.'

'You speak wisely, boy,' Wise Soul said, 'but can you travel alone through the land to the north?'

'I shall try.'

'If you are to have a bond with us, we should aid you. I should send companions with you while the rest of us travel to your camp.' I guessed at what else he was thinking. He wanted me to have a chance to reach the enclave safely and to bring Tal out to join his band, but he also wanted most of his men to survive. If I met danger along the way, the rest of his band, travelling east, might escape it.

Wise Soul then agreed to send two of his men with me, a skinny man named Hare and a burly one called Ulred. I told them how to reach my camp, describing the landmarks and the distance to each, then led the men outside, where I drew pictures in the dirt until I was sure they could find the way. When I left the enclave with Tal, I said I would go to Mary's shrine, the place where my guardian had been called. It had come to me that Tal had always distrusted strangers, and that he should speak to them first in a holy place.

Wise Soul assured me that at least one member of his band would go to the shrine from time to time for two moons before I was given up for dead. I did not think of what might happen if my new band failed to reach the camp.

Just beyond the clearing around the shrine, Ulred and another of Wise Soul's men were able to bring down a small deer. After thanking the Lady for providing us with meat, we butchered the deer, and I quickly cooked the pieces my companions and I would take on our journey, searing the meat in the flames of a fire, for there was no time to do more. The others would carry what meat they could and leave what they could not, for they wanted to leave soon, and there was still the conveyance for Shadow to make.

I bid farewell to Wanderer outside the shrine and prayed that he and the others would be safe. I feared for them, for they would have to travel with an injured boy and a wounded man. I was filled with foreboding, in spite of my luck so far, and beginning to think that my fortune would change again.

My companion Ulred, who had a bristly black beard and heavy eyebrows, turned out to be a friendly fellow, while Hare, whose thin face bore only a downy moustache, spoke little. Hare, I discovered, was close to my age and had not yet been called.

We loped through the forest, speaking only when we stopped to rest. 'I lost a boy in that damned raid,' Ulred told me. Though the wind was warmer, Earth was hiding from the sun behind Her thick grey veil, as if not wishing to reveal Her thin layer of dirty, encrusted snow. 'A little fellow, he was – just out of an enclave last spring.'

'You have been called, then,' I said.

'I have once, but the Lady did not give me a child then. The boy's guardian, before he joined the Lady in the next life, gave him to me as my charge, for he was my true friend and knew I would care for the boy as he had. I had been looking after little Sunchild since autumn.' Ulred wiped his eyes with the edge of his coat. 'A wretched horseman dashed his brains out with a strange weapon, a long piece of shiny metal shaped like the shaft of a spear. At least the lad died quickly.' He sighed. 'Sunchild was a good boy, golden-haired like you, always smiling, always with a song . . . it was a joy to have him in the band. I tell myself now that perhaps the Lady loved him too much to let him suffer in this world.'

If the Lady had truly loved him, I thought, She would never have sent him out in the first place but would have kept him at Her side. My mind was leading me astray once more. It was man's nature to sin and to be a prisoner of this world for a time.

Ulred sighed again, and I uttered a few words of comfort. Tal had often said that it was useless to love a boy until he had grown tall and his guardian knew that he would live to manhood. Observing Ulred's sorrow, I saw the truth of those words.

We left the woods, and I guided them north. Once we came upon horse tracks, and I grew fearful before seeing that they led west, away from us. At night, we sheltered ourselves in a wind-break of sticks and Hare's hides, and I fell asleep to the moans and sighs of the men as they sought to reproduce the blessings of the Lady with their own hands. Hare offered to aid me in such pleasures, but I refused, knowing that he could not give me the joy I had known in the shrine.

As we travelled, Ulred often spoke of those in his band who had died at the hands of the horsemen, while Hare nodded sorrowfully, interrupting his friend from time to time to murmur, 'The Lady's will be done.' I said little, sensing that Ulred gained some comfort from his memories, which were all he had left of his friends, and which also served to remind him that he still lived. I too had felt the odd, triumphant joy that follows sorrow, that comes from knowing one lives while others lie in the ground.

We came to wooded lands again, although the trees were not thick and there were spaces of empty land to cross. We met no other bands and saw few signs of their presence. Within four days, we were near the shrine where I was planning to pray and purify myself before approaching the enclave. I was not thinking of the scavengers I would have to evade on my way to the Lady, for dangerous as they were, I could not believe that She would let me fail. Once again, my spirits were high, I had a new band, I would see my guardian again, the Lady would visit me.

I did not know how soon my faith was to be tested.

My destination, a shrine to the Wise One, was near the shore of a small lake where I had often hunted geese and ducks. The birds had flown south, but the ice in the lake had melted, and they would return before long. Forays to the lake in warmer weather were risky, for other bands sometimes hunted birds there and fished as well, and although we had been able to make truces with some for a season, others would try to kill or drive off weaker bands. We had once been forced to take shelter in the shrine, chased there by two bands, and had escaped only when the two bands began to fight each other.

During winter, this part of the lake was usually abandoned by men as well as by birds. We crept through the wooded land bordering the shrine cautiously, but I expected to see no one by the lake. I was thinking of the times I had waited there with Tal, and also with Geab, Cor, Eagle Eyes, Hawk and Arrow – all dead now.

Ulred grabbed my arm suddenly. 'Look.'

I had already seen where he was pointing. We had a closer look as we emerged from the trees. A body lay on its side near a leafless shrub, its back to us. The feet were covered with a kind of boot I had seen only on boys newly out of enclaves, dark leather boots with heavy soles. The garments were more cause for wonderment, for the pants were of a green cloth, as was the hooded coat.

'A dead man,' Ulred whispered.

Hare looked around uneasily, in case the attackers were still nearby. 'Why didn't they strip the body?'

'Maybe he is only hurt,' Ulred said.

'Look at those boots and the clothes,' Hare muttered. 'I have seen such garb only on small boys. Do men wear such things here, Arvil?'

'No.' I approached the body. There was no sign of life. Footprints marked the ground around the body, and the ground had hardened a bit, I saw what had happened. Three men had set upon this lone traveller, and the struggle had been brief. But the attackers had fled without taking the clothes, and that puzzled me; I would not have let such garments out of my hands.

I leaned over and lifted one gloved hand. The wrist was small, the skin cold, the arm stiff, and I felt no pulse.

Ulred and Hare came up to me as I heaved the body on to its back. It had been lying on top of a metal receptacle. I picked that object up, shook it, and heard the sound of liquid. I dropped it and studied the body. The throat was bloody where a knife had slashed it, and the blood had dried.

'We can take the garments,' Ulred said. 'That coat is too small for you or for me, but Hare might find a use for it.'

The victim's beardless face stared up at me with unseeing blue eyes. The curly dark hair was matted with blood. That face frightened me, for there was something strange about it. The shirt, also stained with blood, had been pierced by a knife. I ripped it open and saw round breasts and a body no man could have.

My thoughts tumbled inside me. I remembered the story of the man who had sworn aspects of the Lady had appeared to him.

Hare let out a shriek. Ulred caught me as I staggered, for terror had made me faint. 'Unholiness!' Ulred said, and we both shook so violently that we collapsed to the ground.

Hare sprinted toward the shrine. He tripped, fell and rolled in the dirt, as if possessed. We stumbled up and ran to him, then dragged him to his feet.

Ulred slapped him. 'The Lady!' Hare cried. 'The Lady!' Ulred slapped him again.

'Stop gibbering!' I shouted, though I was as frightened as Hare. 'We didn't harm Her. That was another's doing.'

Hare began to grow calmer. 'What world is this,' Ulred said, 'where one of the Lady's aspects lies dead so close to a shrine? How is this possible?' I now knew why those who had killed Her had left the body, and wondered how they had been judged, for I was sure they had been punished. They might even have taken their own lives.

'Listen,' I said, trying to control my own fear, 'we cannot leave Her there. We must take Her inside the shrine and pray. The Lady is powerful. The Lady may restore this part of Herself and bless us for bringing Her there.'

'The Lady,' Hare responded, 'may think us guilty and condemn us.'

I shook my head. 'The Lady knows everything. She will know we aren't guilty.' I wished that Wanderer were with us; he had travelled so far, and knew so many strange tales that I was sure he would know what to do.

We went back to the body and lifted it, holding it as gently as possible as we carried it toward the shrine. I almost expected Her to come to life in our arms. Bowed forward under the weight, I saw another set of tracks leading to the door. Someone in the same kind of boot had fled into the shrine. I shuddered and nearly dropped my share of our burden.

Hare moaned. 'Oh, Lady, have mercy.' The door slid open and we stumbled inside, then set the body on the floor.

Someone else was in the shrine, lying on a couch. This stranger wore boots and pants of grey cloth; a grey coat lay on the floor. The stranger moved and sat up. I had only to see the face, the long, flowing, dark brown hair, the shape of breasts under the grey shirt, and the rounded hips, and I knew.

Ulred and Hare threw themselves on the floor and grovelled; I stood gaping until Ulred pulled at my leg. 'Bow, you fool,' he whispered. I knelt and hit my forehead against the floor several times.

She walked toward us. I was afraid to look up and heard the sound of weeping, as though She were crying for all the sins of men. At last I lifted my head.

She was near the body; She gave a cry and turned away. 'What have you done?' She spoke in the holy speech. 'Why did you bring her here? You didn't have to kill her.' She was not using the words a man would use to speak of an aspect, but only those we would use to talk of Earth's female creatures. 'She's dead. I might as well be dead, too. Why don't you kill me and be done with it?'

I gasped as I straightened and sat back on my heels. 'We cannot commit such a deed,' I said in the holy tongue. 'We did not kill Her. We were passing and saw Her outside. She was already dead ... that crime was the deed of other men. Have mercy.'

Her mouth twitched. 'Yes, I see that now.' Her voice was faint. 'You don't look like the ones who ...' She covered Her eyes.

'We could not leave Her out there,' I said, 'and brought Her here, so that the Lady can restore this aspect of Herself to life.'

She let Her hands drop. She seemed tired and weak. It was odd to see an aspect of the Lady that way, for in my imaginings and in the visions the Lady had granted to me, She had always been strong. Her blue eyes were large and Her lashes thick and long, but there were shadows under Her eyes and hollows in Her cheeks. She swayed. I leaped to my feet and caught Her as She fell.

'Forgive me for putting hands upon You,' I murmured.

'Help me to the couch.'

I led Her there, struck by how frail She seemed, how small She was – Her head reached no higher than my shoulder. I could see no sign of Her magic, of Her power. As She reclined, Hare and Ulred crept up to the couch and settled themselves on the floor. I knelt at Her side and covered Her with the grey coat.

She sobbed, choking as She wept, while we waited, unable to offer comfort and afraid to speak. I felt that I was in another place, outside the familiar world I knew.

She sat up and pulled a receptacle from the coat, then dropped it. 'I need more water,' She said, 'and some food.'

'You may have ours,' Ulred said as he pulled out his waterskin. Hare offered Her our remaining cold meat. She drank some water and gnawed at a small piece of meat, making a face as She did so, then rested on Her elbow as She gazed at us. Her blue eyes were cold.

'Please tell us what to do,' I said. 'Tell us if we can help You restore Your fellow aspect.'

'She's dead. She can't be restored.' She was silent for a while. 'Her soul is somewhere else now . . . that body is only where it lived for a time. She has shed that body to return to the Lady's realm. She should be buried.'

I wondered then why the aspect seemed so unhappy. If her fellow aspect were with the Lady again, if a body, to the Lady, were no more than a garment to be cast aside, why did this aspect not show joy? Men could not see beyond death, could only hope that the next world would bring them blessings and not punishment. Death could hold no sorrow for the Lady, Who was eternal. Perhaps it was the sins of men that caused Her to weep, the evil of those who had raised their hands against an aspect.

'Her body will lie outside this shrine, Holy One,' I said.

'Bury her, then.'

We hastened outside to do Her bidding. We dug on our knees with flat rocks until the hole was large enough. The sun was setting by then. We carried the body to the grave and laid it in the ground.

She came to the grave as we began to fill it in, and watched us at our work. When we were done, we set stones around the grave, and Ulred rolled a large rock on to it.

'Farewell,' She said softly as tears trickled down Her face.

When we went back inside the shrine, we lingered near Her as She sat down on Her couch. Her face was filled with grief, and I cursed my kind silently for our wickedness.

I had no ritual to guide me; the old one would have to do. 'We must pray,' I said at last, 'and then put on the circlets.'

Her eyes widened. I thought I saw fear on Her face. But what would an aspect have to fear from us? 'Listen to Me.' Her voice was low, but commanding. 'Pray if you wish, but don't put on the circlets. I am with you now, so you need not put them on.'

'No circlets?' Ulred said. He had clearly been hoping that the Lady would give him Her joyous blessing.

She shot an angry glance at Ulred, and he cowered a little. 'No circlets,' She replied. 'The Lady sorrows now. There will be only a curse for you if you put them on.'

I nodded, not wondering at Her remark, thinking only of obedience.

We went to the altar, where the Wise One stood in a long white robe amid Her beakers and tubes. I fought to keep my mind on my prayers, although it seemed strange to be kneeling before a representation of the Lady when a living aspect was with us.

I tried to sort out my thoughts, certain that Hare and Ulred were doing the same. The aspect was holy, more powerful than we, yet She was weak and had needed our food and water. She was fair, but Her face did not have the blinding beauty of the aspects Who had blessed me before. Her form was the Lady's, but if it had not been for Her belt, which made the swell of Her hips and breasts more evident, I might have taken Her body for a boy's. I had touched Her body briefly, and had seen the lifeless one of another aspect, and was sure that both were only flesh and bone and blood. It had to be a test of some kind. The Lady had come among us to see how we would act. If we aided Her, we would be blessed.

I said more prayers and asked the Lady to guide me safely to Her enclave. As I stood up and turned toward the couches, I noticed that the aspect was watching me. 'You have blessed me, Lady,' I said. 'May You protect me as I journey to Your enclave.'

She started. 'What do you mean?'

I was surprised at Her question; surely She knew. But perhaps not. She had needed food; she still seemed weak. She had not prevented the death of Her fellow aspect. She walked among us in a frail body and might have forgotten what She once had known. Long ago, Tal had heard an old story about the Lady appearing in flesh in order to die and be reborn, taking upon Herself the sins of men, and although Tal had considered the story blasphemous, I saw now that it might have been true. 'I have been called,' I said.

'Called!' She raised Her hands to her mouth. 'But you seem young.'

'I have been called. It is no stranger than finding You among men, Lady. I came here to purify myself, but I do not have much time to do so. The Lady wants me with Her soon.' I bowed my head, remembering to show respect. 'I thought . . . forgive me for thinking so highly of myself . . . that You might have come to guide me to Her enclave.'

'No, I did not come to guide you.'

'You must advise me. Now that You are here, does that mean I do not have to go?'

She stood up and came to the altar, then turned to look at us. Hare flinched as She glanced at him. 'Holy One, we are Your servants,' Ulred said. 'We shall do what You ask.'

'Listen carefully, then. I have come among you for a purpose, to see if you follow the right way. You must protect Me from others and feed Me and, in return, you will have the favour of the Lady and a place in Her heart. If ill befalls Me, you will be cursed. There is no need for you to don the Lady's crown in shrines while I am with you. If you do not honour Me, the Lady will take Me from you, and you will die condemned.' Anger flashed in Her eyes. 'In return, there are things I can tell you, stories of the Lady's magic.'

Ulred and Hare were on their knees again as they nodded their heads vigorously. I knew that I should kneel, but instead, I repeated my question. 'Does this mean I do not have to go to the enclave?'

She did not reply. 'I have been called, my guardian is there, and the Lady has promised that we will be together again, but only if I reach the enclave soon.'

She stared at me a long time before answering. 'No, you must go. If you do not, the Lady may discover that you've disobeyed, and then . . .' She paused. 'You will have to go, but I give you a warning. Do not speak of Me, or think of Me. Your mind will be filled with Her blessings, so you will not have time to think of Me, and I can teach you how to keep thoughts of Me from your mind.'

'But why must I . . .'

'Do you dare to question the Holy One?' Hare burst out.

'The Lady is testing your will,' She said. 'She wants to see if you will obey My commands. If you do, holiness will be yours, and you will be blessed above other men. If you do not, you will die in this world and be denied the next.'

I knelt and swore to obey.

She turned away. 'I must sleep.' She lay down on the nearest

87

couch and closed Her eyes. I went to Her side and stood there, worshipping, until She opened Her eyes again.

'I beg Your pardon, Holy One,' I said. 'Is there a name by which this aspect is known?'

Her eyes seemed fogged with sleepiness. 'What?'

'The aspects in Your shrines have names by which They are called. Is there a name of You?'

She curled up on the couch. 'Birana,' She whispered. She lowered Her lids. Tears rolled out from under Her dark lashes.

I slept only a little while and awoke early to begin my purification. I longed for more time to clear my mind and prepare myself, then recalled the events of the day before. The aspect called Birana was with me; Her presence would aid my purification.

The others were still sleeping. I went to the altar, knelt, recited every prayer I knew, then stood up. Slowly, I removed my clothing, until I was naked, and began to dance in front of the Wise One. I opened my arms and swayed, then bounced on my feet, whirling as I began to hum. The Lady, I thought, will bless me. She will make me sing, She will come to me with Her blessing. I danced and leaped, and my soul flew out from me, crying out to Her. I was strong, I was pure.

A longing for the Lady took possession of me. I was aflame and filled with holiness. I danced and swooped and then found myself over the still body of Birana. Suddenly, I was sure of Her purpose. She had come to the shrine to grant me Her favour, to purify me further for my journey to the enclave. I thought of the aspects in shrines Who had captured my soul with Their magic, how They had held me, how They had guided my hands to the cleft they had instead of a man's parts.

I fell on the couch and embraced Her; I pulled at Her shirt and felt Her warm flesh.

She moved under me, screamed, and pushed me away. I fell on the floor, cowering as She struck me with Her fist. 'What are you doing?'

I was terrified, certain that I had failed a test of some kind. 'I am purifying myself,' I cried as I covered my member and pressed my forehead to the floor. 'I longed for Your blessing, that is all. Forgive me, I meant no offence.'

'You fool,' I heard Ulred say in our speech.

'I longed only for . . .'

'I know,' he said. 'It is hard not to feel it. But we must do Her bidding. We cannot take Her blessing, She must give it.'

I looked up. Ulred was standing near Birana's couch, bowing his head. 'Forgive him,' he said in the holy tongue. 'His purification made him long for a visitation. His mind was filled with holiness, and Your spell was upon him. It will not happen again.'

'It had better not.' Her face was pale. 'He will be punished if it does.'

I danced before the Wise One some more, but my fear of losing control again made me unable to purge my mind. I was afraid of the enclave now, afraid that the Lady would be disappointed in me when I finally reached Her realm.

Birana covered Her eyes. She seemed to hate the sight of my body. I stopped dancing and put on my clothes awkwardly.

She said, 'Remember what I have told you.'

I bowed.

'I must instruct you now in how to meet the Lady. Your companions will find us food.' She gestured at Ulred and Hare as they scrambled to their feet. 'You'd best be careful outside,' She said to the two men.

'We have You to protect us,' Hare replied.

'All the same, the Lady doesn't protect those who are careless.'

They hastened from the shrine. I followed Birana to the altar, and we sat on the floor, facing each other. I was uneasy with Her so close to me in Her earthly body. I kept expecting Her to vanish, to fade from sight as other aspects did after They had given Their blessing. She drew back from me, as if wanting to disappear.

'I'll teach you how to keep your mind still,' She said. 'You must do this when you enter the enclave and don a circlet there. When you wear one, the Lady hears only what is on the surface of your mind.'

'But She knows all.'

'That is why She does not have to hear your deeper thoughts then. Remember, you're being tested – that's why you must keep all thoughts of Me from your mind when you are before Her. You will break a powerful spell if you say My name to Her, and you'll suffer for it, and I will be taken from you.'

'I understand.' It seemed a strange test. If I would break a spell by saying Her name, then why had She given the name to me? But I could not question Her will.

'What are you called?'

'Arvil.' I wondered why She did not know that. 'My friends are Ulred and Hare – Ulred is the bearded one. But do You not know all the names of men?'

'I wanted only to hear your name from your lips,' She said hastily. 'Well, Arvil. We must begin now.' The sound of my name from Her lips made me shiver.

She lifted a golden chain from Her neck over Her head and held it in front of my eyes. From this chain hung a strange object with markings and what looked like a metal needle. She instructed me to watch this object as She spoke. We sat together for a long time while She taught me how to keep my mind still, how to keep all thoughts of Her from me with one holy word, and as She spoke, Her voice seemed to fill my soul.

Ulred brought back a rabbit, while Hare had caught three fish. We cooked our food over a fire outside the shrine. After Birana had taken Her share, I ate as much as I could, knowing that I would need strength. When we had eaten, we filled Birana's bottle and our waterskins at the lake.

We walked for most of the morning. When Birana began to fall behind, Ulred waited for Her and then gently took Her arm. She pulled away and flailed at him, then relented and allowed him to support her.

She was slowing our pace. When Ulred guided Her, he had to walk more slowly. She hobbled, as if Her boots were blistering Her feet. She did not speak, but I could see the weariness in Her face. The Lady's spirit, held by this body to our world, seemed to be weakening.

At last we stopped for a time to rest. 'I can go on alone,' I said to Hare and Ulred in my speech.

'You don't want us to come farther with you?' Hare asked.

I shook my head. 'I can travel faster alone, and I have little time. We'll soon be near scavenger territory. It would be safer for you to go to where you are to meet the rest of our band. It would be safer for Her, since we promised Her our protection.'

Birana did not seem to understand our speech, although I had thought that the Lady knew all languages. That was yet another of Her limitations in Her present form. Again, I wondered. An aspect of the all-powerful Goddess had to be honoured, yet also treated as one who had our flaws.

'Wish me well, and I shall pray for your safe journey,' I said. Hare and Ulred bowed their heads and murmured some holy phrases. 'I ask that You bless me,' I said to Birana in the holy speech. 'I must leave You now and travel to the enclave, but Ulred and Hare will lead You to safety and to the rest of our band. They will all protect You, as we have.'

'I bless you.' She glowered at me. 'Those creatures around the wall might kill you, though.' I recoiled, as if She had cursed me. At that moment, it almost seemed as if She wanted me to die before I entered the wall. I looked down at Her upturned face, searching for some sign of mercy.

She lowered her eyes and sighed. 'May you return safely.' She said the words as if She did not mean them, and then Her face softened a bit. 'Those men usually rummage near the western side, where . . .' She paused for a moment. 'If you approach from the south, you may not see anyone. If you do, and they're near the entrance, wait until they leave before you enter. They'll grow tired of waiting.'

'I shall remember Your words,' I said gratefully. I gave directions to Hare and Ulred, drew pictures on the ground to show them their route, then watched them depart.

I went on my way, my mind filled with both anticipation and fear; they seemed almost the same feeling. I saw dimly, although I could not admit it openly to myself, that my faith had been altered. Somehow, the presence of the Lady in Birana's body had changed me, and I was moving toward the enclave with unholiness within me.

I could not put my thoughts into words. I could not admit that my reverence for the Lady had been poisoned by doubt, and – worst of all – by a buried rage at the life I had always accepted.

I was thinking: We are the Lady's fools. She has made us mindless creatures, no better than the animals we hunt. She toys with us, then casts us aside. My thoughts were not words then, but only a weight on my heart.

LAISSA

I had acted to establish my independence from Mother, but still had the chore of moving my personal possessions to my room in Zoreen's quarters. After checking to make sure that my mother wasn't home, I went to my old room.

I had left only a few of my belongings at Shayl's and sent her a message, telling her that she could send them to Zoreen's tower. I was sure that she wouldn't want to keep them, and I didn't particularly care whether she sent them on or threw them out. I only wanted her to know that I had found another companion, that she had not been the only one I could have chosen. I wanted her to be jealous, and perhaps to regret what she had lost.

I went into my old room and stared at the boxes, surprised at how little I wanted to take. I had packed old toys, pillows, message spools marking special occasions, gifts from Mother and my aunt and my grandmother, and had planned to take it all, along with my clothing, to Shayl's rooms. Now my belongings seemed only a reminder of times I preferred to forget. As I looked down at my wrist, I realized that I was still wearing Shayl's bracelet, the gift she had given me at my party. I tore it off and left the room.

Button had wandered into the outer chamber. He retreated to the window and watched me warily. As I moved toward him, he lifted a hand, warding me off.

'Button, I'm sorry for what I did to you.'

He turned from me and gazed out the window.

'I shouldn't have done what I did. I didn't mean to frighten you.'

He was silent.

'But, I also thought I was doing the best thing for you.'

'No,' he said. For a moment, I thought he understood what I was trying to explain, but he probably would have said 'no' to anything I had to say. 'Mother says you don't live here now. Go away.'

I walked toward the door, thinking of how lonely his life had been. He had never gone out of the tower except with Mother or with me; his toys were his only companions. He had met other boys infrequently, for we had been told often enough that boys were unruly and hard to manage in groups. Visitors usually ignored him, and often he had been sent to his own room before they arrived. His only obligation was to stay as physically strong as possible, doing his exercises under Mother's guidance, working out on his machines. Learning anything else was useless, for the mindwasher would erase it before he was sent out, leaving only his ability to speak, a sense of something lost, and perhaps a residue of memory to fuel his dreams.

The contrast with my own life was striking. I tried to imagine myself growing up that way and being forced to live outside. Would I become like a man? Would men, living here, become more like us? Everything I had been taught denied it; men had a propensity for violence that was both genetic and hormonal. The biological well-being of humankind as a whole required some of their qualities, but the survival of civilization demanded that women, who were less driven and able to channel their agressiveness constructively, remain in control. Over these harsh facts, many of us had erected a structure of suppositions to soothe ourselves, believing that men were happier as they were, that they were capable of little more, that they would destroy everything we had built.

I considered what history I knew at that point. Once men and women had lived together and had formed bonds. The old records showed that a woman might love a man as I had loved Shayl. Such love had been, of course, a trap. I could not imagine a woman willingly putting herself in the power of a man; women had given power to men, and men had nearly destroyed everything. It could not be allowed to happen again.

I glanced at Button before leaving the room. History, I was beginning to see, might be instructive. I had read a few tales of women bought and sold, of depending on men for food and shelter, of being forced to endure contact with male bodies, of being murdered by men. Our ways were surely better.

Zoreen was sprawled on the floor among her papers and books, reading. I tiptoed over the floor, careful not to step on anything, and sat on the couch.

'Are those real?' I asked, waving a hand at the piles of paper.

'Real documents? Of course not. These are copies – they'd hardly let a student handle the originals.' She picked up one book, a thick pile of paper, and waved it at me. 'The real books don't look like this at all. The pages are bound together, or decorated.'

'Then why have all this paper? Why don't you just use a screen, or a reader and microcopies?'

Zoreen sat up. 'I do, for most reading, but sometimes I want to make a note on a page, or underline a passage, and it's easier to have the paper in my hands. Eventually I'll just put my notes into the system, and then I can get rid of some of this. Why, does this mess bother you?'

'Not really, but it would still be easier to make your notes another way.'

She shrugged. 'I know it seems odd, but you'd be surprised at how many historians keep piles of paper in their rooms. One of them told me it's because they start thinking of how much from the past has been lost, how easily things can disappear, so they make microcopies and keep papers, or give them to other historians, as well as recording it all on spools. The more copies there are in different forms, the more likely the past is to survive.'

'You sound as though some might want to lose it deliberately.'

Zoreen nodded. 'Let's put it this way. There are those who think much of it's best forgotten.'

'Anyway, it seems to me that, with all these copies around, it might just become harder to find the one you're looking for,' I said. 'And if so much was lost, then how can you be sure that what you learn about the past is true? How do you know that your own assumptions aren't shaping the way you interpret and understand these documents?'

She smiled. 'Why, Laissa, you surprise me. You sound as though you're interested in the subject. I didn't think you cared.'

I waved a hand dismissively. 'Oh, I don't, not really.'

'Are you still going to do physics?'

'I don't know.'

'I suppose you wanted to do what Shayl was doing when you thought you'd be living with her, and now . . .'

I shook my head. 'That isn't it. It's just that I was advised against it. I was thinking of doing something else even before I decided not to live with Shayl.' I had altered the details of my confrontation with Shayl when telling Zoreen about the incident, making it seem that I had decided not to live with my old friend because of her doubts about me. 'I'll probably do general science. I can go on to physics later, maybe.'

'How utterly useless.'

I leaned forward. 'Why do you say that?'

'I don't mean the subject itself is useless, but the way we go at it is. All we do is study what's known, what was discovered ages ago. After all, we wouldn't want to push too far, considering the violent applications of science in the past. It's stultifying – perfect for someone like Shayl.'

'You're hardly one to criticize someone else for keeping to what's known,' I said. 'Besides, we should be cautious. Using scientific knowledge to build weapons perverts the whole enterprise.'

Zoreen's eyes widened. 'What a proper statement that is, and yet our past achievements in the sciences, the most important ones, took place during times when people were building their most powerful weapons. One might almost say that building the weapons brought about other, more constructive discoveries that otherwise wouldn't have taken place.' She tilted her head; her long, brown hair swayed. 'You know, most of the physicists in ancient times, before the Re-birth, were men.'

'It's hard to believe.'

She chuckled. 'Oh, Laissa. You sound like so many others. Even the Mothers of the City often sound like those we serve, those who don't know any better.'

I seized on one point. 'If what you say is true, then it's because men worked in the sciences that their efforts were directed toward such enterprises.'

Zoreen laughed even more at that. 'And we made most of our advances when we had to find ways to enclose our cities, to secure our walls, to build weapons our ships could use to strike at men. Since then, we've done very little. Unpleasant facts, Laissa. I'm not saying that the need to push against the boundaries of knowledge has to be linked to such aggressive impulses, but, for whatever reason, we haven't managed to replace it with another motivation. And in the past, there were men who questioned how science and technology were used, who saw the dangers. Iree of Teesa's Clan is the expert on the period just before the Destruction. She's written about it; she knows more about it than anyone else. Iree deals with primary sources, records of the period, not post-Rebirth documents. There were many men who saw what was coming and tried to work against it.'

'Men wouldn't have had the ethical sense.'

Zoreen pushed a few papers aside. 'Let me ask you this. Why do you think so many women don't want much to do with history or historians?'

I smiled. 'Oh, come now, Zoreen. You know why.'

'Because it's sordid? That's what girls think, and a lot of the Mothers of the City as well, even though they once knew better. It isn't the real reason. Most women just don't want to admit that men had the capacity to think and act in certain ways. They'd rather believe that men always had certain innate limitations, because to believe otherwise raises a lot of questions about the way things are.'

I could not think of a reply.

'Look,' Zoreen said as she held out her hands, 'it doesn't really change things. Whether or not men could behave ethically or peacefully isn't the point. The point is that they used their power, the power women gave them, to destroy the world, and can't ever be allowed to do that again. Nothing changes that. Most historians simply think it would be better for more of us to admit that ancient men weren't quite what a lot of women prefer to think they were.'

The Destruction and the Rebirth are two periods of history we are all taught to some degree, since those events are part of religious doctrine as well. Mother, like many, was not a believer, and I had always been a sceptic, believing that religion was of use only to those women the Mothers of the City served, but I had been taught my share of doctrine.

Once, women had given men the power over life that women had held since the beginning of human history; so we have all been taught. Men had used their power for evil, and the world had been devastated and poisoned in ancient times by the weapons men had controlled. The great fire came and, after it, the long winter. Only scattered communities in isolated places had survived, living for ages in underground shelters, for life on the surface was not possible. Earth refused to yield crops, animals sickened and died, and humankind's damaged genes whelped monsters.

Below ground, life had gone on, in a fashion. Even in the shelters, many did not live, and tunnels holding the dead were sealed off from the living. These shelters, we are told, were our purgatory, places in which to pay for our sins. Gradually, Earth began to heal itself, and in time, it became necessary for some to venture above ground.

At first, only men who had fathered all their children were sent out, for the communities had to be preserved from genetic damage, but these men, weakened by age and inexperienced in the wild, often could not fend for themselves. Younger men were sent outside, along with women who could not bear children – and there were many of those in ancient days, for the Earth had punished us by robbing many women of their ability to give life.

Those women who remained behind had to teach their children while doing much of the work of the community. As they gained more control of the biological sciences, they learned how to find out which men had sustained the least damage to their genes, and how to sort them out from others. To love one man, and to bear only his children because of that love, was a luxury these societies could not afford; it was soon clear that such love had always been an evil, had brought women to forgive men instead of protesting their foolish ways. One judged a mate on his health and strength – nothing else mattered. Defective children died out; other children grew stronger. Women regained their ability to bear healthy young, and those who did so ruled.

Perhaps those early men, living outside and returning to the shelters only infrequently to donate their sperm, their game, and their news of the healing Earth, still believed that they would regain their power, that in time, their lives would be as they were before. Perhaps, guilt-ridden over what their kind had wrought, they were content to let women take over more responsibility. Or maybe they welcomed their life of hunting and roaming and adapted to it readily because it was the life to which they were best suited. But the pattern had been fixed.

Our scriptures tell us that the spirit of Earth, in the form of the Goddess, soon began to speak through the mouths of women. 'You continue to sin,' She said. 'You readily allow men to come among you, even though they have scarred Me. You gave men power over Me, and they ravaged Me. You gave them power over yourselves, and they made you slaves. They sought to wrest My secrets from Me instead of living in harmony with Me. You have sinned and have not yet turned away from wrongdoing.'

So the Goddess spoke, and many women abased themselves and wept over their foolishness and promised to keep to the right way. Those who were wisest became the Mothers of their communities, contributed sons to the world outside, and guided other women, who bore their daughters and lived their lives apart from men. But history also shows that some women turned away from the Goddess and often had to be expelled, and that a long time passed before women reclaimed their true place.

The Rebirth came. Here, and on other continents as well, we left our shelters and retreated inland, away from the greatest devastation, and built our cities and the shrines that would guide men to us. Much of the land beyond was surrendered to the Goddess, left to renew itself untouched by humankind. The ten thousand years of man's rule, an aberration in human history, were past.

That is our story, but in the light of Zoreen's speculations, the story seemed to take on a new meaning. If men, even some men, had once been capable of the compassion and intellect that were the proper province of women, then our way of life was not merciful and just, but only a cruel necessity, a way to survive and no more. Civilization had been preserved at the cost of depriving all men of it. We also paid a price for we were bound by these patterns, unable to alter them, for our survival still depended on them. Those who had become the Mothers of our cities were not only the wisest, but also the most merciless. Those sciences that might lead to new and more powerful weapons were controlled, and innovation discouraged; and because of this most of us still learned only what women hundreds of years ago had known, for to know more might risk the death of all. Even the surrendering of much of the Earth's lands to the Goddess in atonement for our sins might have been only an act of fear and cowardice. We had made our world a small one. Our cities stand on only part of our continent, and rarely do our ships travel through the skies over the oceans to far cities; the women there remain images and voices on our screens. We send few ships to map the lands we have abandoned.

What Zoreen had said at my party was true; we did little that was new.

How could thinking of this ease my mind? It would replace my doubts with a cold practicality. For all to live, some would have to suffer, and all would have to hold to the ways that had made survival possible.

Zoreen shuffled a few papers. 'At any rate,' she murmured, 'ancient men might have done some good deeds, but they also committed most of the evil ones. They had armies with weapons, not just unarmed patrols. They beat and killed women, beat and killed each other, raped, terrorized whole cities – you should read some of the old literature. It was quite commonplace. In a city like this, we wouldn't have been able to walk down a street without fearing for our lives in the time before the Destruction. We do have different natures, I fear. Men destroy; women build and nurture. It's because we carry our children inside us, and men can't. Even the most exceptional men probably had to fight their own impulses constantly.'

I was thinking of Button, the only male I had known. What if the boy were capable of more than I had imagined? What if he could have been trained for much more and instilled with an understanding of our ways? Maybe we could have been helping men adapt to our cities in some manner. I tried to push that thought aside. We could not change the natures of men, could not allow them any power again.

Zoreen grinned suddenly. 'You actually seem interested in all of this.'

'Oh, I don't know.' I looked away. 'I guess I should tell you. Shayl, needless to say, wasn't too happy when I told her. I was told I could take general science, but I was advised to concentrate on history and human culture, too.'

'Really?'

'I didn't want to,' I said. 'I'm still not sure I will.'

'You ought to consider it. Not because I'm doing it, but because there's a lot going on in the subject now, which is more than you can say for other things. We're revising a few old assumptions, sorting out more of the pre-Rebirth documents from post-Rebirth ones, seeing which ones were altered the most. It's exciting, Laissa. It might change the way we look at the past.'

I was thinking to myself that historians would alter only the way historians themselves viewed the past; no one else would care, especially if it raised disturbing ideas. 'But I wasn't told to be a historian, or a recordkeeper. I was told I might make a chronicler, although I can't imagine why.'

'A chronicler.' Zoreen let out her breath. 'I was going to say I'm surprised, but for some reason I'm not. It seems to fit you somehow. The tests and advisers are usually right. Maybe you should listen to them.'

'But . . .'

'Oh, I know. Don't think I didn't notice how my old friends started avoiding me as soon as I started my studies. Even my mother isn't happy about it. I was surprised you asked me to your party at all, in fact.'

'And then you came and joked about what you were doing. You really made it sound . . .'

'Well, what else could I do? They were going to think badly of me no matter what I said.' Zoreen stood up and stretched. 'I've done enough for today – I feel restless. Let's go out.'

We left the towers behind and wandered in the streets among the houses nearby. Zoreen examined several tables of handicrafts before trading a small music box for a silver necklace. Some of the women behind the tables of wares greeted Zoreen by name, and she seemed to know others as well.

'At least here,' Zoreen murmured to me, 'no one's going to care much about what I do. I'm just one of the city's Mothers, and history's just a lot of stories that have nothing to do with them. Some of them like hearing stories about the cities when they were new.'

We came to a hydroponic garden, where tables were arranged around the glassed-in complex. Below, women in green smocks were tending to the vats while others served meals at the tables. Here, we could eat for nothing in trade except praise for the food or advice on what new seasonings might be tried. We selected salads and then sat down at one small table.

As we were finishing our food, a group of young women crossed the grass and giggled as they sat down at a long table near the grape vines. Shayl was with them. I looked directly at her. She did not greet me.

I set down my fork, imagining that Shayl was mocking me in front of her friends. 'Let's go,' I murmured. Zoreen nodded. As we stood up, I encircled her waist with one arm.

When we reached the path bordering the lawn, Zoreen pushed my arm away. 'Don't.'

'I didn't mean . . .'

'I know what you meant,' Zoreen said in a low voice; I had to bend my head forward a little to hear her. 'You wanted Shayl to think we're more than just roommates and friends. You want to get back at her, make her think you have someone else now. Fine. Just don't use me to do it.'

'I'm sorry, Zoreen.'

The anger in her green eyes faded. 'It isn't that I couldn't care more about you, Laissa, but even I have some pride. I don't want to be just a replacement for someone you loved, who doesn't love you. Shayl was the one who rejected you, wasn't she? It wasn't the other way around.'

I nodded.

'I guessed it before. You didn't have to make it seem otherwise. It wouldn't have changed my feelings.' She took my arm as we walked toward the street. 'Come on. I'll take you to one of my favourite spots. It isn't a place I'd go with many others.'

'Where's that?'

'The wall.'

I tightened my grip on her arm. 'I don't want to go there.'

'I don't mean inside the wall. The patrol wouldn't want us wandering around in there anyway without a reason. I mean on top of the wall. You must have been there at least once.'

'Only when some of us were taken to Devva. I didn't like it. I went straight from the lift to the ship.'

'Then you have to come, just this once.'

I sighed and gave in.

We rode through the tunnel and entered the wall, where one of the lifts carried us to the top. I thought of what was behind the doors of the wall and wished that I hadn't agreed to come. Men were in some of the rooms on the first floor, lost in an imaginary world of erotic images provided by their mindspeakers as sperm was taken from their bodies to be analysed in the wall's laboratories and used for impregnation if it was found suitable.

Although I looked forward to becoming a mother, I did not look forward to the day when I would go to the wall to receive sperm, but consoled myself with the knowledge that, unlike women of ancient times, I would have no physical contact with the child's father. I intended to be very careful about which progenitor I picked, unlike some of the Mothers of the City, who settled for anyone who was strong and without defects. I would answer many prayers, and call many men, and ask for analyses of all of them before I chose. Strength and health would not be enough; I would pick one with the rudiments of intelligence and sensitivity. I would probe their thoughts with the mindspeaker before I decided.

The lift came to a stop. The door opened, and we walked outside. A wind struck me in the face, a wind from outside cold and biting. We were beyond the force field that protected our city.

The field was behind us, arcing up from a low railing. Zoreen turned toward the invisible shield. 'There's our tower.' She pointed toward one of the distant spires.

'How can you tell?' I asked. The towers, some pointed, others with flat roofs, looked similar to me from this perspective; in fact, I was struck by their uniformity. The small variations in materials or design were not as apparent from the wall, and I suddenly felt that the women inside them were themselves only variations on a theme, that individuality was an illusion, only life's way of endlessly reproducing itself until it found the perfect form.

'But that isn't what I wanted to show you.' She steered me away from that railing and we ambled toward the opposite side of the wall. Far to my right, a few women were boarding a ship. The round golden globe of the ship soon lifted and fled from the wall. I pulled up my thin collar against the cold and thrust my hands into the pockets of my tunic.

'Look,' Zoreen said as we came to the railing.

The hills near the horizon were brown and covered with leafless trees. Patches of snow dotted the flatter ground beneath us. A thick forest of pines, not far from the wall, and evergreen spears on the hills were the only bits of bright colour visible. It was untamed land, and I wondered how anyone could live there.

'Isn't it a sight?' Zoreen asked.

'It's terrifying.' The images of the outside I had seen, even the quick glimpses I had caught from a ship the one time I had left the city, had not prepared me for this. I had expected to see a place more like an untended park rather than this wild landscape.

'It's not like this all the time,' Zoreen said. 'In the summer, it's all green, and you can see flowers. In the fall, when the leaves start to turn, the hills are different colours, green and red and orange and yellow. You should see it then.'

I tried to imagine it, having spent all my life protected from seasonal changes. 'It didn't look this way from the ship.'

Zoreen laughed. 'You probably took one peek and hid in your seat with your hands over your eyes.' She was silent for a bit. 'Sometimes I think of going out there.'

I was shocked. 'You can't mean that.'

'I meant in a ship, of course, with a destination. There are things out there no woman has ever seen. Sometimes, I hate being closed in. The city doesn't seem so big when you look outside. Sometimes it seems that men have more freedom.'

'I suppose they do, in a way,' I said. 'They're free to freeze to death, or starve, or pick up some disease, or be killed by some animal or by another man.' I put my hands on the railing for a moment, then slipped them back inside my pockets. 'They must have stories to tell. That would be real work for a chronicler, setting down some of their tales.' I paused. That was the first time, since speaking to Bren, that I had, however dimly, seen some work I might do. 'Not many women would want to read them, of course.'

'I've sometimes thought of an expedition,' Zoreen said. 'A lot was taken out of the ancient shelters, but I wonder what we might have left behind, what documents and artefacts might still exist in the places we've abandoned. But we'll never do it. No one's brave enough to go. I might be afraid to go even if I could.' She pulled her collar close around her neck. 'All we'll ever see is another city, and the inside of a ship while we're travelling there.' She turned toward me. 'Birana's out there now. She was, anyway. She couldn't still be alive. Even someone with her strength couldn't survive.'

'I didn't know you knew her.'

'I wasn't a friend, but I used to see her sometimes out here on the wall, and we'd talk a little. She told me about some of the things she'd seen. She said some of the men scavenged for whatever they could find near the eastern and western sides of the wall, near the recyclers. Sometimes a few men will dig for whatever old stuff might be buried, even though there's little they can find. Birana said that some tribes seem to stay near the wall most of the time, that sometimes they attack others travelling here. She could recognize a few of them by what they wore.

The patrol usually checks to make sure those tribes aren't nearby before they send men back out.' Zoreen gazed out at the hills. 'Poor Birana. I don't suppose she ever thought she'd have to go out there.'

I shivered. If Birana had kept away from her mother or if she had summoned help for Ciella immediately, she would have been safe; she might even have been standing on the wall with us now. 'I wonder,' I said aloud. 'Yvara said at the end that she believed other women might be alive out there, other exiles – that they might have found a way to live. I wonder if it's true.'

Zoreen shook her head. 'Look at what's there, Laissa. An expelled woman couldn't survive alone – she wouldn't know how. The men are used to it, and even they have to struggle. Yvara would have said any wild thing by then.'

I was not so sure. There were many areas of Earth over which ships passed only rarely, that were abandoned. I was deluding myself, trying to believe that some sort of safe place might exist for the young woman I had forgotten and neglected. It would be better for Birana if she had died quickly instead of having her suffering prolonged.

'I tried to see her,' Zoreen said, 'before they sent her out.'

This revelation surprised me. 'But you said you weren't her friend.'

'I was feeling guilty, I suppose. No one spoke for Birana. I certainly didn't. Maybe it wouldn't have made any difference if I had – at least that's what I tell myself. There are those on the Council who think we must be firmer than ever with transgressors, especially those who are Mothers of the City, as Yvara was. A lot of women will remember what happened to her. They'll think of what happened to her daughter. If someone doesn't care about her own fate, she'll still have to consider what might happen to her child.'

'What did Birana say to you?' I asked.

'She didn't say anything. I wasn't allowed to see her. I asked again if I could, and a woman told me it wouldn't do any good to ask any more. I got the message. They wanted Birana and her mother to believe at the end that no one in the city cared, that there would be no mercy for them. They wanted them to go out from the wall believing that. That's why they're probably dead now. They'd have no reason to cling to life, no hope that they would ever be forgiven. Imagine believing that every woman in the city cared nothing for you, had accepted your sentence.'

I tried to imagine it, could almost feel the despair of an exile. It would have been useless for me to try to see Birana, but knowing that didn't ease my guilt at not having made the attempt.

'Some might say,' I murmured, 'that your ideas could lead you astray.'

'I'm cautious enough. I know how far I can go. I just don't deceive myself about how things really are.' Zoreen peered through the rungs of the railing again, then grabbed my arm and pointed. Far below, a group of men emerged from the evergreens, ran toward the wall, then stopped. They were tiny figures, clothed in what looked like the furs and hides of animals. I was sure that they could not see us, so far above them. They swayed and then began to dance, lifting their arms as they pranced before the wall.

'What are they doing?' I asked.

'I think they want to be called.'

'Then why aren't they in a shrine?'

'I don't know. Maybe they think we'll let them in anyway. We won't, of course. If one came inside, and it was found he hadn't been called, they'd punish him and send him out as a warning to the others.'

The men danced some more. They strutted like birds, threw open their coats, and lifted their hairy faces toward the sky. One man leaped into the air, extending his legs, then dropped into a squat; another opened his shirt and showed his chest.

They stopped dancing and held out their arms toward the wall. Poor creatures, I thought then, oddly touched by their yearning.

When they saw that the wall would not open, they retreated, wandering back toward the trees with bowed heads and slumped shoulders. We watched them go. The wind tore at my face and shrieked past the wall.

ARVIL

As I drew closer to the enclave, my fearfulness grew. Much as I longed for the Lady's grace, part of me still wanted to hide from Her, afraid She might hear my unspoken and unformed questions and doubts.

From a hill, I gazed out over the tops of the trees below me on its northern slope. The enclave was visible even from this distance. A great wall surrounded it on all sides, but I could see only the southern side clearly. The eastern and western sides stretched on toward the horizon, beyond which the northern part of the wall was hidden. The tops of towers far from me caught the light of the sun.

As I looked at the wall's flat, shiny surface, I seemed to remember being nearer to it, crying out as I was dragged away. I found it strange that I could not recall my life inside the wall, even though it was best not to have such memories. Holiness lay inside the enclave, and it was part of our punishment not to recall the time when we had dwelled near the Lady. Even Birana, Her aspect, was weaker in our world. The Lady and all Her aspects represented a unity, a whole, while we were those who had fallen away from that unity, to be reunited with it only when we were called and, if we led proper lives, at our deaths. I pondered these holy matters, and the place in them of Birana, Who had appeared among us.

Tal was inside. My wish to see my guardian again was so strong that I almost ran down the hill toward the wall. Tal would be pleased with me; he might even offer some of the praise I had so rarely heard from his lips. I would be bringing him not only myself, but also a new band. Now I needed to be even more cautious. I was in scavenger territory and had already sighted one band in the distance.

I thought of what Birana had told me. I could barely see the indentations in the wall that marked the entrance. I would get as close to the south end of the wall as I dared, wait until nightfall, and then sprint toward the entrance. As I made my way down the hill and moved through the trees, the enclave seemed to get no closer. Its wall was so vast and so unlike the usual landmarks that I could not gauge its true distance.

As I stepped over dead twigs and trod lightly on old leaves and pine needles, I heard a hum, and knew the sound. I fell to the ground, and rolled toward a log, then flattened myself against it as a large globe flew over the treetops toward the wall. I trembled as it passed, thinking for a moment that the Lady would deal with me as She had dealt with those on the plateau. But the globe continued on its way and finally disappeared over the top of the wall.

As I came nearer to the edge of the wood, I saw that I would have to cross an open area to reach the enclave. I could now make out the entrance clearly. It was at least twenty paces wide and perhaps thirty paces in height. My memory jostled me again; I seemed to recall the door closing behind me. I also saw that my way was blocked. Near the entrance, a group of seven men squatted, as if waiting to fall upon whoever came out.

Scavengers, I thought, and all the stories I had heard about them came back to me. They hunted men as others hunted beasts. Tal had declared that they dined on the flesh of men. Other bands would not wait so near an enclave for one of their members, for most men made such a journey alone or only in the company of another who had been called. No truce was possible with scavengers. I remembered Birana's advice. I would have to wait until they grew tired and left.

It came to me then that I need not enter, that I might wait until Tal left the wall. My fear of the Lady was growing as great as my desire for Her. I could meet my guardian outside, would not have to pass through the test Birana had set for me, would not have to risk betraying Her. This was a thought I cast away at once. I could not refuse the Lady's summons and knew She would find a way to punish me if I did. I had Birana's spell to protect me. I was angry with myself for having such unholy thoughts so near Her enclave and quickly said a prayer.

I retreated, careful to make no sound, then climbed up into a tree and concealed myself among the boughs. Needles tickled my nose and pricked my face. I took a sip of water. I was almost out of time and had to enter the enclave soon.

The wall, although still tens of paces away, dominated all I could see. It seemed to reach the sky and was so long that I could see only a small part of it. The scavengers got to their feet, stretched their legs, and began to dance, swaying in front of the wall as they held out their arms.

Tal had told me of such sights. Scavengers sought to appeal to the Lady directly, rather than going to a shrine, but were never called, for the Lady scorned those whose cowardice kept them near Her enclave. I watched them as they leaped and pranced, despising them for their foolishness and villainy. One man spun, arms out. He stopped suddenly and pointed to the west. The others froze, some with a leg extended or an arm raised.

I heard thunder.

Clinging to the tree, I looked up at the cloudless sky. The thunder grew louder and rolled toward me from the west. The scavengers milled around and then started to run toward me. I readied my spear.

The thunder was not an approaching storm, but the sound of horses' hooves. Twenty horsemen rode swiftly toward the scavengers. I heard a cry above the thunder, and then a shriek.

When the men on foot were still several paces from the forest of evergreens, the horsemen bore down upon them and, as they encircled the band, struck at them with their spears. The scavengers tried to fight back and stabbed at the horses with spears and knives. Hooves struck one man's head as a horse reared. One horseman, his legs tight against his horse's flanks, shot arrows into two men, hitting one in the back and another in the chest. He leaped from his horse, went to the twitching bodies, and drew out his knife. Others dismounted and quickly cut the throats of wounded scavengers. The slaughter was over in the time it had taken me to draw only a few breaths.

The horsemen stripped the bodies and divided the spoils. One man waved a pot like the one Wanderer carried. Another held up a shiny piece of metal and grimaced at it as he drew it closer to his face. For the first time in my life, I felt pity for the scavengers; the haste of the slaughter horrified me. I did not stop to think that the horsemen had done me a service, clearing the obstacle that had barred me from the wall, while ridding the region of one evil band.

When they had finished loading the dead men's possessions on their horses, they mounted and trotted off toward the west while I gave thanks that they had not ridden through the trees.

I now saw the wisdom of what Wanderer had told Wise Soul's men back at the Warrior's shrine. We would also have to master the horse to have a chance against such bands. Yet it seemed a way that would lead us to greater cruelty. When killing was easy, men embraced it and rejected truce. The horsemen would kill not only scavengers but also other bands; Wise Soul and his men had barely escaped them. In time, one band of horsemen would fight another, and that would lead men to find yet other ways of killing – sharper spears, stronger bows. It might not end until every man was dead, and the Lady was doing nothing to stop it, for the butchery had happened in front of Her wall. My thoughts were leading me along a dangerous path. Men who had reached out to other bands, trying to unite them, had died on the plateau, while those who killed without mercy lived on. I saw no good in that.

I was judging the Lady, Whose ways I should not have questioned. She had killed Truthspeaker and Bint and their companions because they had sought to challenge Her. I had to clear my mind of heresy before I entered the wall. She had shown me this killing for a reason. If my band were to live, we would have to become like these horsemen. She had appeared to us as Birana in order to show us our destiny and to test us. I had to hold to my faith and reject my doubts.

After taking another look at the land around me, I climbed down from the tree and stretched, preparing myself for my sprint. It was growing dark, and I hoped that any men lurking amid the trees had been scared off by the appearance of the horsemen. I flexed my muscles, took several deep breaths, and ran.

I looked away from the bodies as I passed them. Someone shouted. My foot hit a stone, my ankle twisted, and I fell. As I scrambled up, two men emerged from the shadows of the trees to my right.

My terror spurred me on. An arrow struck the ground near me. As I came to the wall, I lunged toward it and pressed my hands against the door. Another arrow flew past me and bounced from the wall.

The entrance did not open. The two men were drawing nearer. I beat on the door with my fists, then turned, readying my spear. Suddenly the door whispered past me and I fell inside. One man launched his spear toward me, but the door closed as the spear was still in midair.

I was alone, safe, in a darkness blacker than a moonless night. I clung to my spear, imagining first that the Lady might impose new tests upon me before I entered the enclave, then that She would find me lacking and expel me.

Gradually, the room grew lighter. Ten couches, each with a circlet, were against one wall, reminding me of a shrine, but there was no image of the Lady here. Uncertain about what to do. I knelt and prayed silently.

As I prayed, a low voice filled the room. 'Go to a couch,' it said in the holy speech, 'and don a circlet.' I looked up, but the Lady had cloaked Herself in invisibility. 'Go to a couch and don a circlet,' the voice repeated.

I had to use my spell. As I went to a couch, I quieted my mind and said the holy word Birana had taught me. She sank to the bottom of my thoughts, hidden by a dark barrier. I had forgotten Her; I was entranced. I would keep my promise and follow the Lady's will.

As I put on the circlet, I was swallowed by darkness again but felt no fear. This darkness soothed me, warming my body and calming my mind. 'Wait,' the voice said inside me. 'The Lady will speak to you soon.'

I do not know how long I lay there, drifting through the

darkness, but I would have been content to stay for ever in that state, freed both from fear and longing for Her.

At last She spoke. 'I am with you now.'

The darkness parted. She stood before me in a guise I remembered, as the auburn-haired One Who had spoken to me after I had fled from the plateau.

'You have come at last.' She smiled. 'Your guardian, Tal, is with us. I have touched his thoughts and know of you, Arvil, and have waited for you. I am glad you are here. You must be brave and strong for coming so far alone.'

I basked in Her praise but could not accept it without admitting the truth about my journey. She, I thought, might grow angry if I did not speak up for my comrades, for I was sure She was aware of them and was testing me.

'I could not have made the journey alone,' I replied. 'I was aided by two of Your servants, Wanderer and Shadow, and was later helped by a band with whom we have made a truce. They are willing now to accept both Tal and me as members of their band.' I told Her a little of my adventures, but as my mind drifted toward my meeting with Birana, a wall rose in my mind and hid the thought of Birana from me. Birana's spell had power, and I did not think or speak of Her.

'I was alone, without a band,' I finished. 'Now, I have friends and a new band. You have blessed me, Lady, and I shall always serve You.'

She smiled again as She clasped Her hands together. 'Thank you for telling Me this – it is more than I hoped for.' Before I could wonder at those words, She said, 'You must rest now, and then you will be blessed and reunited with Tal.' As She spoke, the darkness came upon me again.

I had slept. Another aspect of the Lady, naked, black-haired, and golden-skinned, came to me. She bent over me, speaking soft words in the holy speech as She embraced me. Her skin was smooth and warm, and She smelled of flowers. As She drew me toward Her, I was suspended in the holy state, held there by the touch of Her hands.

Another aspect appeared, younger and red-haired. Her breasts were high and round. Her nipples the pink of wild roses. As She came toward me, I reached for Her, unwilling to wait, but She guided me in touching Her body before opening Herself to me. Cursed we might be and condemned to live apart from the Goddess, and yet the sighs of the aspect told me that Her pleasure was as great as my own. This was part of Her blessing – the knowledge that She welcomed me to Her side. I felt Her nails on my back as She moved under me.

Another aspect was lying at my side, caressing me as the red-haired One put Her lips to mine. This aspect had long, brown hair glittering with threads of gold, and a shiver ran through me as I looked at Her. Something in Her youthful face reminded me of Birana and the longing I had felt for Her.

'Birana.' The name flew through me, flitting from darkness into the light. It shattered the barrier and escaped in a sigh before I could call it back. 'Birana.'

The spell was broken. I recalled Her holy word, too late; I could not force Her from my mind. As the brown-haired aspect stroked my belly, I reached for Her and was suddenly holding air. She faded and I was alone, surrounded by mist.

I knew the greatest terror I had ever felt at that moment. Birana had given me a powerful spell to test me, and I had broken it.

'Arvil.'

This voice was harsh. The mist parted, showing me the auburn-haired aspect I had seen before. I cursed my weakness, knowing I would be punished.

'Arvil. You said "Birana." Where did you hear that name?'

I did not answer.

'Where did you hear it?'

'It is only a name.'

'It is not only a name.'

My head was beginning to ache. My throat tightened. 'I heard it spoken, Lady – that is all.'

'How, and where? Tell Me.'

My head throbbed. A sickness was in my stomach. 'You do not need to ask,' I said. 'Do You not know everything that comes to pass?'

'Do not be disrespectful. You cannot lie to Me. You sought to keep something from Me and were taught how to do so. Foolish boy – you're too weak to do such a thing. You haven't the power – your mental blocks cannot deceive Me. You must wait.'

The mist enclosed me again. I sank into it, supported by pillows of fog. My pain disappeared. She was angry; I had seen Her rage. In my holy state, I had betrayed Birana, yet the Lady had seemed angriest when I refused to betray Her further. I had failed. I wondered if Birana had already been taken from my new band.

Perhaps I was not yet lost. I would be examined to see if I

would betray Birana further, and perhaps this was part of the test. If I spoke of Birana again, I would lose my soul. If I did not, I might avoid the worst punishment. This hope was all I had left.

I drifted up through the fog. I was on a couch in a pale, empty room. The auburn-haired One reappeared and next to Her stood another, a silver-haired aspect with the fierce eyes of the Witch.

'You said the name of Birana,' the auburn-haired aspect murmured. 'I am going to ask you again – where did you hear that name?'

'From another band.'

'You are lying,' the witch-aspect replied. My head began to ache once more. My torment was beginning. I tried to rise from the couch, but my limbs refused to obey me. 'Do you not know that you cannot deceive Me? Where did you hear the name?'

I was silent.

'Where did you hear it?'

My skull seemed to be shattering, and every nerve in my body was on fire. I twisted, and the torment worsened. My teeth sang with the pain as knives cut through my skin. I was bleeding, I would die, but still I refused to speak.

'Where did you hear the name?'

I screamed as my bones cracked and somehow managed to clutch at my head with one broken hand, feeling the circlet under my palm. The Lady's crown was biting into my scalp. I tore off the circlet.

At once, the aspects vanished. The pain was gone. I was inside my body, which was still whole. I looked down at myself, bewildered.

I was naked. A clear, slender tube attached to my member curled under the couch on which I lay. A ceiling of light was above me, and my body glittered with metal threads that bound me to the couch as well as to several metallic objects near me. Lights on the surfaces of these strange, square objects winked and flashed. Where was I?

Two metal arms suddenly appeared at my side and reached for me. I tore at the shiny threads, ripping a few away, and then saw that another man was in the room with me.

'Tal!' I cried as I recognized him. He did not respond. He was also clothed in metal threads, a circlet on his head, a tube enclosing his organ. His mouth twitched, and saliva trickled into his blond beard. His penis stiffened, flexing the tube. 'Tal!'

What could this mean? Was the Lady showing me that She would also punish Tal for my misdeed? Was this room a place where both body and soul would be tormented? The metal arms seized me and forced me onto my back. I struggled helplessly as one arm pressed against my chest, pinning me with its shiny claw as the other lifted the circlet. I tried to pull my head away, but the claw pressed the crown down upon me.

My pain returned. This time, I struggled against it, aware that my soul, not my body, had suffered the tortures inflicted on me. But my struggle was useless. The pain was greater than any I had ever known, and I was unable to ward it off.

'Where did you hear the name of Birana?' the witch-aspect cried. The other aspect's face was pale as She held a hand to Her lips.

Punishment and the loss of my soul could not be worse than my present torment. 'I shall tell you,' I cried, ready to condemn myself in order to escape the pain. I was weak; Birana had imposed too great a test on me. I had failed Her, and my band would lose Her. I would lose Her, and that thought was nearly as painful as my torment. The pain faded, leaving only dull aches in my limbs and head.

I told them of my meeting with Birana. Once I began to speak, there was no purpose in hiding anything, and so I spoke of all that had passed. When I was finished, the witch-aspect nodded while Her companion turned away.

'You have done the right thing by telling Us this,' the silver-haired aspect said, 'and you will break the evil spell that bound you.' The mist returned, concealing the aspects, and I waited, wondering what my fate would be.

After a time, the auburn-haired aspect returned to me. Her eyes gazed at me gently, but I could no longer think of Her as truly kind.

'Arvil, I must tell you something now about the one you call Birana. She claims to be of the Lady, but she is not. She is an evil one who has taken on the guise of an aspect in order to lead men into wickedness. She seeks to deceive you. If you worship her, or honour her, she will lead you away from good while trying to convince you that she represents holiness and truth. She is not of us but is one who has fallen away. Do you understand?'

'Yes,' I said, as I tried to absorb this new knowledge.

'Men can easily be led astray, and you should not berate yourself for falling into Birana's trap. I know you are strong and can resist evil. You have done a good thing by revealing this to Me and will be rewarded for it. I did not want you to suffer, but we had to purge the evil from your soul. You will soon hear how

We plan to deal with the one called Birana, but now, receive Our blessing.'

She faded, and three aspects appeared, one golden-skinned, one dark, a third fair. They touched me, leading me back into the holy state, yet part of me seemed distant from their ministrations, was an onlooker apart from the pleasure the three were giving me with Their hands and lips. I thought of what I had seen after removing my circlet, and it was enough to tell me one thing: The Lady was not what She seemed. I kept that thought deep inside me, refusing even to form it into words. The Lady was not what She seemed, and I was lost in an illusion, unsure of the truth.

LAISSA

The sight of the world beyond the wall had altered the way I looked at the city. Glimpses of a landscape on a screen, even the simulated sensations produced by a mindcaster, had not prepared me for what I saw with Zoreen.

With the mindcaster, I had experienced what it might have been like to walk across a plain, to huddle in a tent near a fire, to journey on foot through a wood, but, however vivid such sensations were at the time, I had known that I was safe inside the city's walls. I had studied maps but had paid more attention to the locations of cities and shrines than to the land around them.

The city seemed smaller as I walked along its lanes and streets. I had lived my entire life among three million women. I had solitude when I sought it – in my room, during a night-time stroll through a park or garden – but I was always within sight or range of others.

As is true of all of us, my upbringing had strengthened the bonds between me and other women. Even the historians and chroniclers, perhaps the loneliest and most solitary of women, sought to share their insights with one another and with those who were interested. This, I knew, was right and necessary, yet I thought of the outside and wondered what it was like to wander there apart from others, what it was like to hear only the voice of one's own mind. We hid from the world instead of exploring it; I began to think we hid from ourselves as well.

I did not seek such absolute solitude. My training and the fear instilled in me of wild, untamed regions had made such a goal seem impossible. Even so, I found myself thinking: If I dwelled apart from others, how then would I see the world? What would I continue to accept, and what would fall away?

On the day after Zoreen and I returned from the wall, I spoke to Bren, intending to tell her that I was going to pursue general science, but after mentioning that, I heard myself say, 'I'd also like to do some reading in history.'

I saw her frown before I looked down from the screen. 'Is this only because you're now living with someone who's studying that field?'

'No. I see things differently now. It's hard to explain.'

'Well, then. I hope this isn't just a temporary change of heart. We'll see.' Bren stared at the console in front of her, tapped on the keys with her fingers, then assigned me two mentors, Lorell for science and Fari for history. 'You'll be given a list of readings,' Bren went on. 'After that, you'll speak to each mentor, and begin to attend classes and discussions. You'll have a lot of freedom during this first year – use it wisely.'

In spite of Bren's promise, I had very little freedom after contacting my two mentors. The lists of readings were so long that I had no time for anything else, and I spent the next few days poring over my reader while Zoreen did her own work.

I did not, however, mind the reading. My worries about what my old friends would think about my choice had vanished, at least temporarily. I fed the hunger for knowledge that I had denied in myself for so long, but I was also feeding my doubts. Each document about past events revealed a layer in our society of which I had been unaware earlier, and disturbing questions would rise unbidden to the surface of my thoughts.

I was in my room, lost in a hypnotic trance as I sought to reinforce what I had studied with the aid of a mindcaster, when Zoreen touched my arm to rouse me, then waited as I removed my circlet.

'Your mother wants to talk to you,' she said.

I glanced at my room screen, wondering why I had heard no signal. 'Tell her I'll call her back.'

'I can't. She's here. She says she has to see you.'

I went to the outer chamber. Mother was sitting on a cushion, legs folded, her fingers drumming against the floor. The sight of her face shocked me. Dark shadows were under her eyes and she had the pallor of a woman recovering from an illness. She had grown thinner; her inner struggle seemed to be consuming her. I was suddenly ashamed of how I had acted toward her.

Zoreen murmured a farewell and retreated from our rooms, leaving us alone. Mother frowned, as if disapproving of the piles of documents and the lack of furniture; Zoreen's papers were on our only couch, and a jacket was draped over one of our two chairs.

'I suppose you came to see how I was doing,' I said. 'Zoreen and I are getting along, and I've decided to do general science and some history. I guess that surprises you.'

She said, 'I didn't come here about that.'

'Why did you come, then?'

'It's time.'

At first, I didn't know what she meant; then I guessed. 'Time to send Button away, you mean.'

'Yes.'

'Mother, I . . .' I paused, not knowing what to say. 'You didn't have to come here to tell me that.'

'Button's brother is here – he has been inside the wall for a few days. He accomplished more than I hoped for – he not only made the journey, he also found a new group of men to live with, so Button has more of a chance to survive.' Her voice was flat. 'It's good that he'll be with one so resourceful. I was right to wait, wasn't I?'

'You didn't know that ahead of time,' I said. 'Well, it doesn't matter now. Everything will turn out for the best.'

Her mouth twisted at those silly, useless words. 'There's more, Laissa. I'm going to tell you something you'll have to keep to yourself. Sit down.'

I seated myself on the floor in front of her, apprehensive at the expressionless tone of her voice.

'Your twin, the boy called Arvil – he and his new friends found Birana alive in a shrine.'

I looked up, startled, unable to believe it.

'Yvara is dead, but Birana still lives. He said her name just as I was about to disconnect from my mindspeaker. I contacted Eilaan, and we soon got the story out of him. It seems that Birana was able to plant a suggestion in Arvil's mind and set up a block so that he wouldn't give her away. It might have worked, too, given his fear of her and his belief that it was part of a test, but something in the tape he was receiving unlocked it – a word, perhaps, or an image that reminded him of her.'

I felt numb as I tried to imagine Birana alive outside, among men.

'I may have prevented great harm by finding this out, and that works in my favour. Eilaan isn't chiding me now.'

'Birana's still alive,' I said, marvelling at that fact.

'They worship her. They think she's an aspect of the Goddess. I had to tell him that she isn't, that she's evil.'

'But why?'

'Don't be stupid, Laissa. From her, they can learn more than they should know, and that could lead to dangerous notions.'

'Oh, Mother. What can men possibly do against us?'

'We can't take the chance. The longer she stays with them, the more likely it is that they'll see things aren't as they believe them to be. They'll see that we're beings like them, that we're not all-powerful. They may learn how to cloak their thoughts successfully. Don't you realize that if they learned enough, they might find a way to enter the wall and attack us? Our true protection doesn't lie just in our wall and our weapons, but in what they believe about us.' I knew then that I was hearing Eilaan's words, even though my mother was speaking them. 'Birana has to die.'

'No,' I said.

'Do you care so much about her? You didn't seem so concerned when she was expelled. You've been reading history. You ought to know what can happen, how even an isolated event can change much. Eilaan says that Birana presents a problem. She was sent out there to die, and she must. I shall see to it.'

I had not spoken for Birana before; guilt over that was forcing me to argue for her. 'She's one of us,' I said. 'She was punished for her mother's deed. The council could have shown some mercy. You can't just kill her.'

'She's not one of us now. An example has to be set. She was supposed to die. She should never have been able to live out there, and yet she's alive. We can't leave her outside, and she can't come back here. What's the difference between sending her out, knowing she'll die, and acting against her more directly?'

It seemed to me that there was a difference, but I could not express it. If Birana had somehow survived outside, then hadn't she earned the right to live? Her life was likely to be short enough as it was, with all the dangers she would face.

'There's another way,' I said slowly. 'Birana could live in a shrine, and men could visit her with food and other offerings. She could reinforce their beliefs.'

Mother laughed harshly. 'You speak as though we could control her, and we can't. She has no reason to do anything for us. Having men see her age or get ill, as she inevitably would, is hardly going to reinforce their beliefs. Anyway, it's too late. The young man has been told that she's an evil being in the guise of a woman and has to die before she can lead men astray. I'm doing Eilaan and all of our cities a service. That band of men will probably spread their story afterward, and that helps, too. If anyone's expelled in the future, men will be more likely to think that she might also be an evil one sent to tempt them.'

I recalled what Yvara had said about a refuge for exiles. Our city had found Birana out, but perhaps other exiles had survived and had not been discovered. Images of women concealed in hideaways in unknown lands filled my mind before I realized how impossible that was. There would be no insemination for such women, and therefore no daughters to preserve such a refuge; the alternative was too repugnant to consider. I had seen the outside; that Birana had lived at all was a miracle. She could never have escaped discovery; a careless word from any man who had seen her, uttered during prayers in a shrine, would have been enough to give her away.

'How are you going to kill her, then?' I asked.

'Arvil will do that for us. He'll be afraid not to. We'll embed the suggestion in him. By the time he leaves the wall, he'll be itching to do away with her and save his band.'

'I see,' I said bitterly. 'You want to make sure that no one acts against Arvil's band, as we could. You want to make certain that the city doesn't send a ship against them, because then your precious Button wouldn't have a band to protect him.'

Her face grew even paler.

'I'll bet this was your idea and not Eilaan's.'

'Eilaan has her own reasons not to bring this before the Council.'

'You didn't want the Council to handle it, either,' I said. 'You'd rather send my twin out to kill Birana so that Button still has a chance to live.' I could see by the pained look in Mother's eyes that I had hit close to the truth. My arguments were pointless and futile; I was only trying to ease my shame at having done nothing for Birana before. 'It doesn't seem right. Birana didn't deserve to be exiled. She doesn't deserve such a death. You want her to die and Button to live.'

Mother's face contorted. She clutched at her belly, as though I had delivered a blow. I should have understood the struggle going on inside her, how torn she was by everything that had happened; instead, I was thinking that if she had sent Button out earlier and had not summoned Arvil to the wall, she would not be facing this dilemma now.

'I thought you would understand,' she said hoarsely. 'I've seen my duty, as you hoped I would. I was thinking of you, too. I didn't want to see more shame come to you because of my actions. I said I was going to talk to you. Even Eilaan thinks it's time that you learned about difficult and unpleasant decisions.' She was silent, and then continued in a calmer voice. 'I'm taking Button to the wall today. I want you to come with me.'

'Why?'

'So that you'll see what it's like. So you'll be prepared when the time comes for you to send a boy of your own out. You were anxious enough to take him there before.'

I wanted to refuse. Those were not her reasons; she needed me with her for obscure motives of her own. She wanted to share her deeds and perhaps to punish me in some way. But her cold gaze cowed me, and I was unable to stand against her.

I said, 'I'll go with you.'

Button was silent as we entered the tunnel and boarded a car, but when he saw that we were speeding toward the wall, he began to scream.

Mother raised her hand. The slap reddened his cheek. Mother had never struck him before; she covered her face as if ashamed. Button shrank from us and hunkered down on the floor; he glanced at me and then turned away.

As we left the tunnel and walked outside, he freed himself from Mother and sprinted away. I dashed after him and grabbed him by one arm, not caring how hard I gripped him. Mother caught up with me and took his other arm; we dragged him to the wall. He shrieked.

'It'll be all right,' Mother said as the door opened. 'You're going to have a wonderful time. You'll meet other boys and learn all sorts of things.'

Two patrolwomen hurried toward us and took Button's hands as Mother told them who we were and why we had come. Button, screamed and kicked one patrolwoman in the leg. 'You didn't prepare him very well,' she said accusingly to Mother. 'Others don't scream this much.'

'Let him scream,' Mother said.

'It's unpleasant enough without all this fuss,' the other

patrolwoman said. We followed them down the hall; I wondered how many others the two had sent out. Button was between them being dragged backward by his arms; his face was red. 'Mother, Mother! I won't do anything bad. I promise! Take me home! Mother!' He twisted but was unable to free himself.

'Take a last look,' Mother said to me as we stopped in front of one numbered door. 'That's the last you'll see of the Button you know.' The patrolwomen dragged him away as the long hallway echoed with his sobs.

The door near us opened. I entered quickly, unable to bear the sight of Button any longer. Mother and I were in a large room; the walls were covered with screens. Two women sat in one corner, while another sat near the centre of one wall; all three wore circlets. One woman removed hers, stared at the screen while she rubbed her temples, then put on her circlet again.

I followed Mother to a screen; we sat down in front of it. 'Do we have to stay here?' I asked. 'Couldn't we go back to your rooms?'

She reached over and punched out a few numbers. 'There they are.'

The screen showed me a blond, bearded man and a younger unbearded one lying unconscious on beds. When I was able to gaze at them without flinching, I recognized the younger one as my twin. They wore circlets, and their naked bodies were covered by the thin wires of the webbing that would stimulate their muscles and keep them from growing weaker. Their mouths sucked at the tubes that fed them nourishment. I studied the younger one's even features. His cheekbones were a little higher and broader than mine, his chin more prominent, his straight nose larger, but he resembled me; the similarity made me uneasy.

'The man is Tal, your father. We've taken sperm samples from Arvil as well. They're both strong and seem resistant to disease – we had to tend to only minor infections when they entered, so we were able to convey them to that room right away. Some will probably choose Arvil as a progenitor, in spite of his youth.'

The feeding tubes retracted from their mouths and slid into the wall behind them. I felt only repulsion as I gazed at these images. 'Are they all so hairy?' I asked, noting the feathery hairs on my twin's arms and legs and the chest curls and thick beard of the man.

'A lot of them are. A few aren't. They're tall, even taller than you or I. They tend to be taller than most women.'

They had once ruled by brute strength, and by force; they had needed no other tools. I tried to imagine Birana among them and shuddered. Living among them would be worse than death; maybe Birana would not mind dying. The men before me, with their flat chests and larger, more sharply defined muscles, seemed deformed.

Mother pressed a key; the images vanished. I said, 'Why did you bring me here?'

She picked up a circlet. 'I must speak to them now.'

'Mother . . .'

She put on the circlet. I got up and began to pace, longing to be away from the wall. There was no reason for me to stay, but I was afraid to leave my mother alone. Why had she brought me here? Did she want to harden me to what I would have to do some day, or did she want me to share her pain at losing Button?

I thought of the women the Mothers of the City served. They would never have to sit in this room or see the image of a man. They would give birth to no boys; men to them were no more than fabled, distant creatures, beasts of the earth. They were shielded from the difficult, painful decisions the city's Mothers had to make.

Now I was beginning to see those we served as our means to keep our own power. By shielding them, so that they would accept our decisions, we had kept them from the doubts that might have led them to question our ways. By protecting them, we had made them weaker. It seemed uncomfortably close to what men had done to women in the past.

Two of the other women had left the room; one still sat alone. She took off her circlet and looked up at me; I was surprised to see the brown eyes of Fari, my mentor in history.

She beckoned to me; I took a seat next to her. 'Fari,' I said.

She raised a brow. 'You look familiar.' She tapped a finger against one cheek. 'Of course – you're Laissa. How is your reading coming along?'

'Fine. I'm already learning quite a bit.'

'You're young to be here, Laissa.'

'My mother's sending her boy out today. I think she wanted me to come along, so I'd know what it's like.'

'I see. I suppose she knows what she's doing, but I think it's easier to handle when you're older. It's hard to look at them so directly, even if it is only a screen image. I don't much care to come here myself, but I'll be preparing to have another daughter before long and have to select a progenitor.'

'Have you had a boy yet?' I blushed, wondering if I should have asked the question.

'Oh, yes.' Fari's reddish-gold curls bobbled as she nodded her head. 'A few years ago. I cried when I sent him out.'

'You did?'

'It's not so uncommon. It's not something one talks about readily, but it happens. One grows attached. That's why the penalties for disobedience are often so severe – if we behaved as we should easily, without hesitation, there would be no need for harsh punishment, or punishment at all.'

'I wonder . . .' I said, then paused.

'Go on.'

'Oh, it's nothing.'

'You're supposed to wonder, Laissa, and share your questions with your mentors – that's what we're for. What did you want to say?'

'It seems to me,' I said, 'that we could take all the sperm we needed for ages to come and never call in men again. One man can father thousands.'

'It's been considered from time to time, but then we'd lack diversity, which is essential. Biological organisms must be adaptable, and diversity aids that adaptability.'

I had, of course, expected that response, but now found it unsatisfactory. 'We could take enough samples to ensure diversity,' I replied. 'Anyway, we've been as we are for ages. We don't need to adapt to anything else.'

'Conditions could change. Also, men need the reinforcement of being allowed inside the wall occasionally – they hope for it as a reward and might begin to doubt the faith we've given them without it. And women enjoy having some say in who the father of their child is to be. It's an old instinct with us even now. Do you know what I think?'

I shook my head.

'No society can live without change for ever,' Fari continued. 'At least that's what I believe, even though we've been as we are for so long. Eventually we may choose another way, and men may vanish from the world. There are already fewer than once existed, and perhaps it would be better if we went on without them – less cruel to them as well. We cannot possibly live with them, not as we are and they are – we couldn't share our lives. So it might be better if they died out completely.'

'I don't know what to think,' I said cautiously.

'We're becoming more rigid, more bound by custom. The

essentials of our lives haven't changed for centuries. And we can't change too much, or too rapidly, without affecting how we deal with those outside. Therefore, we don't progress, and don't become what we might be. We're still bound by our biology to the men outside and don't develop the tools we could to change that fact. We only elaborate on what's already been done.'

I shrank back in my chair. This conversation was taking a dangerous turn. She was saying out loud what I had been thinking as I read.

'We may be in decline,' my mentor went on. 'We have fewer children. We build no new cities, for some of us would have to go outside to do so. Doesn't it follow that we must either free ourselves by developing ways to reproduce without men, or change the way in which we deal with them, or even alter our natures and theirs as well?'

'No,' I said forcefully, but I was unable to counter her with an argument. My mentor, it seemed, was unorthodox.

'Once,' Fari said, 'we dreamed of leaving the Earth, of travelling to the stars, yet now we no longer probe the space nearest our world. Do you know why we abandoned that dream?'

I said nothing.

'Because to go on such voyages, we would have to become something other than we are now. We might have to live much longer than we do, perhaps, but that is possible. Or we would have to bring up new generations aboard ship, and that too is possible. We might even be able to train a few men to make the journey with us if that was thought to be necessary. But we don't, for such a project would alter too much. Those who returned to Earth might be changed also, might make us question how we are. We would be reaching out, instead of conserving and protecting what we have, and that might result in our repeating the sins that almost destroyed us long ago.'

'We could never make such a journey,' I said. 'To think of never seeing Earth again, of possibly never returning – no one could do that.' But I was also thinking that one might not be content with Earth once one had gone so far from it.

'Men sinned in the past by denying us a full life, by ruling over us. They justified this by saying that we were incapable of such rule ourselves. Now we rule over them and call it right.'

'It was to save what was left to us,' I said. 'Had we done otherwise, men might be ruling over us now. They might be threatening our world once again.'

Fari frowned. 'Are you saying that we're so feeble that this would have been inevitable? Do all our accomplishments show, not our strength, but a need to cloak our weakness? There were those who once thought another way was possible, that true love and friendship could exist between a man and a woman. I'm not talking about an enslaving love, or its sordid physical expression, but a love in which each could draw on the strengths of the other and become more than each might have been alone.'

'Men made that impossible,' I said. 'Only women are capable of such a love.'

'And yet men are born of our bodies and share certain traits. Are they as they must be, or have the lives they must lead made them that way? We might have kept a few inside our wall and seen what emerged.'

'Never,' I said, shocked by her words.

'Never. Of course. Because I discuss a possibility doesn't mean I seek it. But one should face such ideas instead of shying away from them. I consider possible changes, even while hoping they don't happen too soon.'

I was suddenly sure that meeting Fari here was no accident. She might have called my room, or learned where I was going; she might have decided to observe me or draw me out. Perhaps she wanted to see what sorts of thoughts I harboured; she would have seen my records. She might be aware of my mother's unusually strong attachment to Button and be wondering how that was affecting me.

I said, 'I wouldn't want our lives to change. Things are better as they are.'

'Why?'

'We've survived. We've preserved the knowledge and accomplishments of our kind. You know what we have, Fari. To gamble on change would be reckless – we could lose everything we've built.'

'Perhaps.' She rose, looking oddly disappointed. 'I must go, Laissa. I'll look forward to our future discussions.' She walked away, leaving me to puzzle over her words.

A cart was waiting for us in the hall. Mother motioned to me; I glanced at her uncertainly as we climbed into the cart. 'Where are we going?' I asked.

She keyed in her destination and leaned back. 'To the south exit, to see Button off.'

'But why?'

She did not reply. She was clenching her teeth, and her hands trembled. She was tormenting herself needlessly; I was afraid of what she might do. We rode through the hall, passing other carts as well as women on foot. The exit was on our left; several patrolwomen were standing by a cart. As we came nearer, I saw that three bodies lay in the cart – my progenitor, my twin, and Button.

I wanted to run from them. I had never been so close to grown men before and understood why members of the patrol spent only short periods on duty inside the wall. The three males were unconscious, yet I felt that they might awaken at any moment, might leap from the cart and strike at us before they saw who we were. The two men stretched out on the cart's seats were clothed in their hides and leather garments, which had been cleaned and mended; Button was wearing woollen pants, a sweater, and a brown coat. All three wore circlets.

Our cart rolled to a stop; Mother and I climbed out. One patrolwoman was holding two spears, another had bows, quivers of arrows, and slings; still another wore knives in her belt and carried a few small pouches. Men had made these weapons, used them against one another without a qualm. Birana had been expelled here, at this same place; now a man would be sent out to kill her. I gripped Mother's hand; her fingers were cold.

The door slid open, revealing a large chamber. The cart wheeled the males inside, lifted them with its arms, and laid each on a couch. While the metal arms were still lifting Button, the patrolwomen hurried inside and put the weapons and pouches on the floor.

The three seemed at peace as they slept; Button wore a smile. The mindwasher had done its work; he had forgotten us already.

Suddenly Mother pushed past me and ran to the boy, laying a hand on his head. A patrolwoman tugged at her sleeve. 'You must come away. It isn't wise to get too close to them.'

Mother shook her head and sat down on the floor.

'Come away,' the patrolwoman continued. 'We have to run a scanner check, make sure they have a clear path to the trees before they leave. We have to go – they'll awaken soon.'

'No,' Mother said. 'No, no, no, no.'

'What's wrong with you, woman?'

'I've done what I'm supposed to do,' Mother said. 'You can't say I haven't. I wanted him safe. I want him to live, and he'll live, but she'll die. I haven't failed you. I've done my duty to the city, but you asked too much of me.'

'What are you talking about?'

'Mother.' I went to her quickly, held out a hand, and then drew back, afraid to touch her. Her eyes were glazed, her jaw tense; a muscle twitched near her mouth. 'Come to your senses.' My voice was harsher than I had intended. 'You have to leave.'

One patrolwoman waved an arm. 'Take her out.' Two women dragged Mother up by the arms and led her from the room. As we entered the hall, Mother twisted away and struck one woman, nearly knocking her down.

'Hold her!' A tall woman gripped Mother's arms, pinning them behind her back. Not now, I thought: Please, Mother, not now. One woman pulled out a pocket speaker and muttered into it while the others led my mother into another room.

I said, 'She'll be all right. She's been under strain. This isn't like her. She'll be all right.'

'I've seen a few cry,' the patrolwoman said. 'I've never seen a display like this. This woman's ill.'

'You don't understand. It isn't just ...' I choked back my words. 'I have to go to her.'

The patrolwoman held up a hand. 'That wouldn't be wise. We've got to calm her down. You wouldn't be much help.'

'She's my mother!'

'All the more reason for you to stay out of it. A daughter shouldn't see such scenes. You can visit her when she's better.'

I backed away helplessly, then fled down the hall.

The sky was red in the west, casting a pink glow over the brown land. A few green shoots had poked their way out of the earth, and a flock of black birds had alighted on the ground far below. I peered down at them and then saw that they had landed near the remains of a few corpses. I shuddered as I turned away.

Ever since coming to the wall with Zoreen, I had begun to have nightmares about the outside, imagining that I was out there, alone, trapped far away from the city and unable to get back. My dream would be real for Birana. Her nightmare would end not with awakening, but with her death at Arvil's hands.

The wind bit at my face. I would freeze if I stayed up on the wall. Zoreen would be wondering where I was. My mother might need me at her side soon.

I walked back to the inner railing and stopped near the entrance to the lift. I knew why Mother had brought me to the wall. She had wanted me to help her cling to her reason, and I had failed her. She had tried to convince herself that she was right in doing her duty, and she had not persuaded herself in the end. Her mind had broken under the strain. She might have endured the inevitable loss of Button, but having to send her other son out to murder a young woman had been more than she could bear.

I might have sympathized with Mother, might have been a kindred spirit to whom she could have turned. Instead, with my cruel words, I had only added to her sorrow and isolation.

The lift door opened; the silhouette of a woman appeared in the rectangle of light. I did not speak until she stood before me. She was wearing a cape; a hood framed her old face.

'What do you want, Eilaan?' I asked.

'You were seen entering this lift. You didn't stop at any of the floors. I knew I would find you here.'

'What do you want?'

'We must speak. We should go inside, away from the cold.'

'You may speak to me here,' I said, wanting the wind to chill her old bones. 'What is going to happen to Mother?'

'Dorlei needs to rest. She'll be taken back to her rooms, and we'll find women to tend to her. She'll be better in time.'

'You're going to punish her.'

'Eilaan shook her head. 'There's no need for punishment. Dorlei has done nothing wrong – quite the contrary. To do what one must in spite of one's feelings, in spite of one's inner struggle, is always praiseworthy, is it not?'

'What do you want with me?'

She pulled her cloak more tightly around herself. 'We have a slight problem now. Your mother will be unable to see to certain matters for us. I'm sure you know what I'm talking about. She said she was going to speak to you about it, and I agreed to allow her to do so. I thought it might ease her a little.'

You wanted to test us both, I thought. You wanted to see if I might be unreliable. 'She spoke to me,' I said.

'I can't tend to this matter alone. I may need your help, Laissa.'

I drew back. 'You've got the Council to help you. Mother did all she had to do when she told you Birana was alive. You didn't have to involve her in what you decided. You didn't need my mother, and you don't need me now.'

'But I do. Why should others on the Council hear of this until it's necessary? It would be better for me to present them with an accomplished fact – otherwise, there might be unpleasant consequences.' Eilaan paused. 'The one called Arvil has been told to go to a shrine and report to us when he has taken care of our problem. It would be best if you were the only one to pick up that message.'

I clenched my fists. 'Why don't you say what you mean? You want me to find out when he's killed Birana, and if he doesn't, you'll want to know that, too.'

'Oh, he will, never fear.' Eilaan did not sound so sure. 'Or another in his band will take care of her when those creatures find out what he's been told. Anyway, the girl may already be dead – life is hard out there. Perhaps the pack she's with has been attacked. If so, the matter is out of our hands.'

'You expelled Yvara because she tried to kill another woman, the greatest crime there is. Now you want me to be a party to the same crime.'

'Birana is guilty. She was expelled.'

'Then let the world outside decide her fate.'

'Things have gone too far for that.' She lowered her voice. 'I have to work through that young man quietly and pray that I don't have to take other action. This puts me in an awkward position. I can be forgiven for not being more severe with Dorlei to begin with, when she first showed signs of her instability, because her subsequent actions brought this problem to my attention. But others on the Council will remember that I convinced them to expel Birana with her mother when others were pleading for mercy.'

'Then bring Birana back. Show her mercy now.' I had said nothing in Birana's defence; that fact tore at me again. I had not known that some on the Council were willing to spare her.

'It's too late, Laissa.'

'Why should I help you? You're only thinking of your own position. I know why you need me. If anything goes wrong, you can blame the whole business on me and my mother and claim that you had nothing to do with it.'

'You fool.' She grabbed me by the shoulders and shook me. 'You'd better think of your own position. I can make things easier for you in the future – you might need me later.'

She released me. 'You're like your mother,' she went on. 'You set yourself apart and doubt. If the preservation of our way, or my problems, means nothing to you, consider this. What happens to Dorlei is in your hands now. She can recover and return to a peaceful life, but if Birana doesn't die, we'll have no choice but to strike out at the whole band she's with in order to kill her. That would mean the end of any chance at life for that little boy Dorlei's so concerned about, and you can imagine how that would affect her, given the precarious state she's in. You don't have to do a thing except to receive that young man's message, when he goes to a shrine to tell us of his deed, and convey the news to me.'

She was threatening me with my mother, and Birana would die in any case. I couldn't help her, but I might help my mother. Zoreen had told me that she knew how things were, how far she could go, what the limits were. I wondered if even Zoreen could imagine my dilemma.

'You will be a Mother of the City, Laissa,' Eilaan said. 'Did you think you could pass through life as thoughtlessly as those we serve? It is we who must preserve the happiness of the majority of women by taking upon ourselves the burden of any sins the city must commit. It is the Goddess Who acts through us, and She is no stranger to what may seem heartless. She will forgive us if we act to preserve Her way.'

I had no such belief. I would carry my sins and there would be no Goddess to forgive me for them. It was futile for me to resist. Arvil would act no matter what I did, and I could not help Birana. I could not fail my mother again.

'I'll do what you want, Eilaan.'

She began to talk to me of how to question Arvil, of how the mindspeakers in the shrines outside would channel his messages, and any from his band, to my mindspeaker alone. I listened carefully, hardening myself; I seemed to be watching events from afar. Though I did not realize it at the time, I was thinking: I will set this down, I shall open our darkest ways to the light. I can change nothing, but my words can illuminate the truth.

Perhaps if Eilaan had known how her request would affect me, she would not have drawn me into her web and might have chosen another course, but she was too old to question her wisdom: I was too young to realize that I was only beginning to travel a dangerous path.

ARVIL

I had longed to enter the enclave, and yet there I knew little true happiness. My desire for the aspects Who appeared before me made me powerless to resist Them, yet a part of me could not be soothed by Their pleasures. The mission that had been given to me was not an honour but a frightening task, for I feared Birana almost as much as I feared the Lady.

As I departed from the Lady's misty realm, my soul returned to me. I opened my eyes. I was in the room I had first entered, lying on a couch near the door that led outside. I took off my circlet and sat up.

Tal lay on the couch next to me. Next to him was a fair-haired child. We had been given a boy and our new band would be pleased at that, but I could summon little joy. I was remembering the disturbing vision of Tal covered with metal threads, of shiny claws pressing my body down, and wondered if I had dreamed it all.

Our weapons lay on the floor, along with our sacks and pouches. I picked up one pouch and peered inside, then plucked out one of the orange balls it contained. I bit into it and tasted a tart, fruity sweetness; the Lady had given us food for our journey.

Tal stirred. I swung my feet over the couch and leaned toward him. 'Tal.'

He opened his eyes, removed his circlet, and sat up. 'Arvil! She told me you would be with me.' He held me by the shoulders. 'We are blessed. I had to give you up, and now you're restored to me, safe from those unholy horsemen. The Lady has rewarded me for keeping to Her way. She told me that you had been given a task – to strike down an evil one.' He lowered his voice. 'You must tell me more of that, but not inside this holy place.'

I shivered as I thought of the Lady's demand. Before I could speak, Tal caught sight of the boy. He went to the lad and took the circlet off his head. The child threw up an arm, then shook his head as he sat up. His blue eyes stared blankly at us.

'I am your guardian,' Tal said. The boy shook his head. Tal pointed to his chest. 'Tal.'

I said, 'He doesn't understand.'

'He will learn. You knew only words in the holy speech when you were given to me.' Tal turned back to the boy. 'I am your guardian,' he said in the holy tongue and then repeated the words in our speech.

'Guardian,' the boy said.

'Arvil.' I pointed to myself.

'Arvil.'

Tal swatted him gently on the arm. The boy whimpered a little. I handed Tal his belongings and he held each item up, giving its name both in the holy speech and our own. I plucked at my garments, noting that they were clean and that I no longer itched.

'He needs a name,' Tal said, gesturing at the boy, who blinked as if holding back tears.

'Call him Bint,' I said quickly.

Tal frowned. 'Whose name was that?'

'He was with the horsemen our band joined. He was a good man and would have cared for me if the Lady had not struck down his band.'

'Struck down?'

I told him what had happened on the plateau, and the terror I had felt then returned to me. The Lady had shown Her power to me then and would strike at me if I failed Her now. Tal's eyes narrowed as I spoke. 'You see,' I finished, 'you were right to say we should not join them. But Bint was kind to me and saved my life and tried to serve the Lady.'

'If he had been a good man, She would not have punished him. You say that all died, and only you were spared – She would have spared him if he had been worthy.'

'He was a good man, I tell you. I came to know him while we travelled, he prayed with me before we slept.'

Tal's lip curled. 'And perhaps he took his pleasure with you as well, and that is why you want him honoured.'

I shook my head. 'He treated me as his charge.'

'I can't name this boy after such a man. The name would leave a curse. He shall have Hasin's name, for Hasin was one who avoided wickedness.'

I shrugged, trying not to think of Bint. Tal was quiet for a time before speaking again. 'It is a blessing to be given a young one, Arvil, but without a band to help us, he may not live long. Our own days may be few.'

'I have much to tell you, Tal. I have found new friends, a band willing to let us join them. I could not have made my way here without their help. Let me . . .'

'What band? What sort of band welcomes strangers into it so quickly, or helps a lone boy? Is this another like the horsemen's band?'

'They are from the river to the southwest where we have hunted. They are good men, Tal, and we need a new band.'

He slapped me. I jumped up and strode to the other side of the room. 'I am your guardian,' he shouted. 'I'll decide what sort of men they are. Better for us to find a band near our lands that shares some of our ways, instead of strangers we do not know.'

'The bands near us would be more likely to kill us if they

believed we were alone with no band to avenge us.'

'I can deal with them. I am your guardian, and you'll listen to me!'

'I don't need a guardian now,' I shouted back. 'I have been called. I am a man now. I'll have as much to say in meetings of the band as you and will join them even if you don't.'

'Do not speak that way to me.'

'You may do as you like,' I answered. 'You can come with me to Mary's shrine, where these men are to meet us, or you can wander alone – that is your choice.' I pointed at Hasin. 'The Lady has entrusted him to you, and he'll be safer with a band.'

The boy began to cry. Tal shook him, then slapped his face. 'No crying!' He released the boy. 'Do not cry,' he said in the holy speech. 'If you cry, I shall beat you.'

The joy I had felt at being with Tal again was fading. I had believed him to be strong, and now I began to see him as obstinate. All that had befallen me had changed me, and I was seeing Tal with new eyes. 'We should not be fighting about this,' I said at last. 'We're in a holy place and have not even thanked the Lady.'

I knelt in prayer, but my mind was not on holy words; I was struggling against my anger with Tal. I had risked much to find him again, and now he scorned the tidings I had brought him. I tried to summon up a prayer, but the words seemed empty and useless.

I do not know You, Lady. At last I had come to that. My visitations, the pains and pleasures the Lady had given me, were not what they seemed. I had sensed that, somehow, when I had glimpsed myself on a couch and saw my body covered with metal threads. I thought of the hands and mouths of aspects upon me. I had touched Their bodies and known the smooth wetness of Their women's parts, and yet in my memory They seemed spirits and not creatures of flesh. *I do not know if I believe, I do not know if You are real or an illusion.* I said this to myself silently as I knelt inside the wall, and yet the Lady did not strike at me.

I stood up. Tal had forced Hasin to his knees and was instructing him in prayer.

'You must leave Me now,' a voice said. Tal scrambled to his feet and pulled the boy by his hand toward the door. 'My blessings are with you. Farewell.'

The door slid open and we sprinted into the night.

We did not stop running until we were hidden among the trees. I carried Tal's pack, along with my own and my weapons, while Tal carried the boy. Hasin's cries grew louder until he was wailing.

Tal dropped him, then struck him on the side of the head. 'Be quiet!'

The wails became whimpers. I leaned over the lad. 'Be quiet, Hasin,' I whispered in the holy speech. 'Others will find us and kill us if they hear you.'

That silenced him. He climbed on to Tal's back without a sound.

We spent the night in a tree, where Tal and I took turns on watch. In the morning, we travelled swiftly through scavenger territory and nibbled at food from our pouches as we walked. Tal murmured prayers of thanks to the Lady for Her food as we ate, for She had given us small fruits, flat cakes that crumbled as we bit into them, and salty brown squares that tasted of meat and mushrooms. I seemed to remember tasting this food before but had no time to savour it. My mind was on the scavengers who might kill us for our food.

When we were safely away from scavenger land, we set Hasin down and turned east toward Mary's shrine. Tal had said little during our journey, for we had to be alert to the sounds and signs of danger, but I sensed that he was also pondering what I had told him inside the wall.

We camped that night under a rocky ledge that bordered a creek. 'Now we shall talk,' Tal said as we ate more of the Lady's food. 'Tell me about these men I am to meet at the shrine.'

This eased me, for Tal was now agreeing to meet them. I told him of everything that had passed after I fled from the plateau. He scowled when I told him of Birana, but did not interrupt me.

Hasin was already asleep when I finished, curled up inside his coat. Tal was silent for a while, then said, 'You have kept company with two who willingly wander without a band and who tell foolish tales to strangers. Now you want to join others, who have been guided to our old camp by your words and given what is ours. And you have consorted with an evil one who claims to be of the Lady and allowed her to cast a spell over you inside a holy shrine. You have done badly, Arvil.'

'I have done well enough. I would like to know if you could have done better.'

'I would not have treated with one who chose to wander alone.'

'Then you would have died. You would have been such a man yourself if I hadn't found friends.'

'I would not have been blinded by an evil spirit.'

'She wears the form of the Lady. You would have bowed before her yourself and longed for her blessing. But the Lady has ordered me to destroy her, and I shall do so.' In spite of my doubts, I was holding to that purpose. The Lady was more powerful than I and found ways to punish those who disobeyed, and the memory of my own suffering at Her hands was fresh. I felt the power of Her command as I remembered. Had Birana been before me at that moment, I would have taken her life then.

'I'll see that you obey,' Tal said.

I rested my back against the rock. 'But you mustn't speak of Birana and what I have told you when you meet the band. They believe she is an aspect, and I don't want her to use her powers to turn them against us. She may have cast a spell on them.' It had come to me that the others might try to protect her from me. Wise Soul's men did not yet know me well and might not take my word against hers.

'At last you're using your sense,' Tal said grudgingly. 'But if she is so powerful, then how do you plan to destroy her?'

'I'll find a way. The Lady would not have given me such a task if it couldn't be done. She would have used Her own magic against Birana instead. I saw the magic She can summon on the plateau.' Even as I spoke, I remembered that Birana had cast her spell on me in a shrine, and that the Lady had not prevented it. Birana had some power, then. I pushed such thoughts aside, since they would lead me only to more doubts.

'We must be cautious, Tal,' I continued. 'I must try to keep the rest of the band from harm.'

'You show great concern toward men you hardly know.'

'It is Wanderer and Shadow I think of most, but I have also pledged a truce to the others.'

He grunted. 'Tell me more of this band. Who will be its Headman?'

'I think Wise Soul will remain so. The others are all younger men. Wanderer might be next if he wins their trust.'

'Who would be next?'

'I do not know. If you join, you might be next, but I cannot say. I don't know their customs.' I glanced toward him, unable to see his face in the dark. 'Is that what you want? A promise you will be Headman someday? You'll have to earn their trust first.'

'If those cursed horsemen had not come, I would have been Headman after Geab.'

I let out a breath. 'That's why you were so angry then. That's why you wouldn't join the horsemen, and why you left me with them even while saying they were evil. It wasn't because they were unholy, but because you were not to be our Headman.'

He slapped me. Hasin awoke and gave a cry as I jumped to my feet. 'Don't ever do that again, Tal.' I spoke softly. 'I am a man now, and the time when I'll be able to fight you is not far away.'

He said no more that night.

It took us four days to reach the shrine, for Hasin slowed our pace. We soon finished the Lady's food, and I sighed as I ate the last of the sweet fruits. During this time, Hasin learned a few more words of our speech as well as how to clean the fish we caught at a stream. He seemed quick of thought, and I hoped that he would grow strong as well.

Tal had stopped confronting me, and soon I saw that he had decided to throw in his lot with the new band, although he would not say so outright. He asked me about the men, and I told him what little I could, unwilling to admit that I could not tell him much.

I spoke mostly of Wanderer and Shadow. 'Wanderer knows much lore,' I said one night as we made a shelter of tree branches against the early spring rain. 'He says we may have to master the horse if we are to survive.'

'Horses,' Tal muttered. 'Potions for wounds. The man is a fool.'

'Changes are coming. We must learn new ways and change as well.'

'Changes are not coming. The Lady will forbid it.'

'The Lady will not forbid it. If we are to serve Her, we must be able to stand against those who would kill us, and that means we must learn their ways.'

'Listen to me, Arvil. You say that two of those men were under that evil one's spell when you left them. She may have bewitched them all by now. I would not heed the words of men who can be so easily misled.'

I had told my new friends that I would bring them a good man; now I wondered.

The shrine was empty when we reached it. We would have to wait there until someone came for us. I wanted to search our old campsite for the band but knew it would be wiser for Tal to meet them on holy ground, where a truce would be in effect and he would not be moved to a rash act.

It came to me then that the band, or some members of it, might not have survived their journey to this region. They might have tarried too long near the shrine where I had met Wise Soul and been found by their enemies, or they might have met danger elsewhere. If they did not send a man to this shrine soon, I would have to search for them and might find that we had no band after all. Part of me hoped for that, so I would not have to face Birana again, yet I also wanted the band to be safe.

We went through our rituals as Tal showed Hasin how to pray. I put on a circlet and told the Lady that I would soon join my band and rid it of Birana, then took the crown off, not caring if the Lady blessed me with a visitation or not. Although I still longed for that pleasure, a part of me recoiled from it.

I gazed at Tal and Hasin. They lay on their couches, their eyes closed. I was lost, alone, apart from the Lady and the community of men. I thought: The Lady needs me to defeat an evil one instead of using Her own powers against that evil. I thought: A soul can wear the form of the Lady, yet not be one of Her aspects. I thought: If men, who are thrown by the Lady into this world, can win their way back to Her realm with their prayers and be reunited with Her at their deaths, then why can Birana not do the same, and renounce evil? Why must she die now?

My doubts had grown. I did not know if I could find my way back to the shelter of faith. I went to the altar but did not kneel before Mary. I would do as the Lady had bid me in the hope that Birana's death would restore my peace of mind.

We dwelled in the shrine for two days. We made journeys outside to a stream for water and feasted on a small pig Tal and I speared. I showed Hasin how to gather watercress at the stream and pointed out the small reddish clumps of new dandelions. I told him of the berries we would find on bushes later in the season and of trees that bore fruit. I held him back when he reached out for a mushroom. 'Those you must not gather,' I said. 'The lore of mushrooms takes time to master. Some can be eaten, while others will poison you. Pick nothing until you are sure of what it is.'

The boy had learned more words in our tongue. 'Fish. Mud. Water Pig.' He grinned as he spoke each word. He no longer cried, though I sometimes saw a sorrowful look cross his face. He seemed unhappiest when we were with Tal, who was often impatient with him. I tried to recall if Tal had treated me the same way when I was first given to him, but my memories of those early days were few. Perhaps he had been kinder to me, but he had been part of a familiar band then, had not faced the prospect of joining strangers.

On the third day, I said to Tal, 'Perhaps I should go to our old camp.'

Tal scowled and shook his head.

'You could wait here,' I went on, 'and I could see . . .'

'No,' he answered. 'You shouldn't go to them. They may have turned against you and, away from holy ground, they could strike at you.'

'We have pledged . . .'

'Don't talk to me of pledges, Arvil. Who knows what lies in the hearts of strangers? I shall see them here, where they must speak the truth.'

I was about to speak angrily to him of his stubbornness when Shadow and Ulred entered the shrine.

I ran to Shadow and pounded him on the back. 'You are well!' I shouted, and my joy at seeing him safe and strong made me forget my fears. Shadow opened his coat and pulled up his shirt, showing me his scar. Ulred gripped me around the neck with one arm and jabbed me in the belly with the other; I caught him around his leg with mine and sent him sprawling on the floor. We laughed together until I saw that Tal was watching us with narrowed eyes.

'A boy,' Shadow said as he pointed to Hasin.

'We were blessed.' My joy was fading, for I was again thinking of Birana. I could speak of her true nature in this shrine. Surely Shadow and Ulred would believe me then, for a man could not lie there.

'We have been fortunate also,' Shadow replied. 'Birana has brought us luck.' I started as I heard her name, and the warmth and awe in Shadow's eyes kept me from telling what I knew. He would not listen to me. He would have more faith in a false aspect than in me and would think I was the one under an evil spell. He would say that Birana had been found in a holy place and would wonder why the Lady had not struck her down then instead of allowing her to live.

I should have spoken then, but I did not, and then I remembered Birana's face and form and how I had longed for her. I could not let her die yet.

I led my friends to Tal and Hasin. They said their names to Tal, but my guardian hesitated before telling them his own. As we squatted by the altar, Tal said, 'Say your prayers now and put on the Lady's crown. We can talk after you have given Her what She asks of those in Her shrines.'

'We don't have to pray here, or wear Her crown,' Ulred said, 'for as long as Her aspect dwells with us. That is what Birana has commanded, for is She not with us to hear our prayers? Only if She leaves us must we return to a shrine.'

Tal made an angry gesture and was about to jump to his feet. I motioned at him to be still. 'That seems unholy,' I said carefully.

'How can it be unholy,' Shadow said, 'if it is Her will?'

I could not reveal what I knew. Shadow went on to speak to Tal of how he would be welcomed, while Ulred told him a little about the band. Tal frowned and plucked at his beard.

'Will you join us?' Ulred asked outright.

'I shall,' I said, knowing that if I did not join the band, they might wonder why and grow suspicious of me. 'Tal must speak for himself and for Hasin.'

'I shall pledge a truce for a time,' Tal said stiffly, as if granting a great favour. 'I'll decide what to do when I meet the others.'

We travelled back to the camp along a familiar route. I remembered the last time I had travelled that way, when I had been returning with Tal to tell our band that he had been called again. I had not known then how soon the world I knew would change. Now the land was growing green, promising a new season, yet I felt the chill of winter inside me.

'Much has happened,' Ulred said to me.

'Tell me of it.'

'You will see for yourself. You'll be surprised. Birana gives us courage.' He cast a sly glance at me. 'We have been lucky.' He would say no more.

As we came to the hill leading up to the camp, I heard the sound of horses' hooves. I was back in that other time, when the horsemen had come to treat with us and had led my old band to its death. I was about to pull my spear from my back when Wanderer, riding a white horse, rounded the hill.

'Hold!' I cried to Tal, as he prepared to loose an arrow. Hasin screamed and clung to Tal's leg. 'He is a friend.' Tal lowered his bow.

Another rider on a second horse was behind Wanderer. Birana was the rider, and for a moment I could not gaze up at her.

Ulred howled with merriment as his elbow dug into my side. 'How amazed you look, Arvil. I wanted to see your face when you saw this.'

I was angry with him for this joke; in another moment, Tal's arrow might have found Wanderer's chest. 'You were foolish not to warn us,' I muttered. 'She won't protect you from your own carelessness.' I was about to say more, but Birana was staring at me coldly. I shrank from her gaze. Tal's hand tightened around his bow.

Birana and Wanderer rode up the hill ahead of us. Tal wore a grim look on his face, and his lips moved as if he were whispering a prayer. As we neared the camp, Wise Soul emerged from a lean-to and greeted us. He laughed as he swept up Hasin, who wriggled out of his arms. 'A boy! That's a good sign.'

Wanderer dismounted and tied his horse to a tree. Birana remained on hers and gazed steadily at me. She is with them, I thought. She has not been taken from them as she said she would be if I betrayed her in the enclave. That proves she is not what she said she was. I wondered if she knew, or could guess, what I had been sent to do.

'What is all this?' I asked as Wanderer strode over to me. 'Where have you found horses?'

'We captured them a few days after we reached this camp. Two horsemen, alone, had stopped to rest not far from here, and we attacked. They were careless. It is a lesson to us. We must not let greater strength overcome our caution.'

'Aren't you afraid that the rest of their band will seek you out?' I asked.

Wanderer shook his head. 'It was my wish to see if we could gain a truce with them, but their band is far from here, and the men with us still remember how horsemen dealt with the rest of their old band. Wise Soul is not ready for a truce with such men yet. His men made certain that other horsemen would not seek out those two and then took their lives.' He did not tell me how the two dead horsemen had been brought to reveal that.

Birana's horse whinnied. Tal shook his head as he retreated toward a lean-to. 'That is Tal, my guardian,' I said as the other men greeted me. 'He's afraid of horses.'

'So am I,' Hare said, laughing. 'But I grow braver.'

I looked up at Birana but did not meet her eyes. 'You know how to ride?' I said in the holy speech.

'I learned long ago. It's harder without a saddle, but I can ride.'

'A saddle?'

'I know many things. Do you doubt Me?'

'No,' I said quickly.

'She fell off once,' Wanderer said. 'We feared She was hurt. She mounted again. Now She rides like the wind.' Birana slid off and led the horse away as Wanderer leaned closer to me. 'This aspect has forgotten some of what the Lady knows,' he murmured, 'but She regains a few powers as the days pass. She can ride, and She speaks some words in our speech now. Our band is learning of these horses and we shall capture others in time.'

The shadows of the trees had grown long. We settled around the fire for our evening meal. Tal crouched apart from the group with Hasin and gnawed at his meat as he looked from one face to another. The boy seemed about to crawl closer to me until Tal pulled him back.

'There is a story I told on the first night we were all together again in this place,' Wanderer said. 'The three with us today have not yet heard this tale.' He turned toward me. 'I heard it in a place far from here, from a band whose oldest man had heard it long before that.'

Wanderer began his story, saying the words in the holy speech. He told of an aspect of the Lady Who had come to dwell for a time among men. As She walked by a stream, an arrow struck Her in the heart, for a man had not clearly seen the form She wore and had shot Her from afar. The man soon sickened and died, and the rest of his band lay under an evil spell. They brought down no game, and no rain came to their lands. The stream where the aspect's body had fallen dried up, and no plants grew there. The band's members were no longer called to the Lady's enclaves. No boys were given to them. All the men in that cursed band died until only one was left, and as he lay dying, the Lady appeared to him. But no one knew what She had said or whether She had finally forgiven that band.

'That cannot be true,' Tal muttered when Wanderer had finished his tale.

'How can you say that, now that you have beheld the One called Birana?' Wanderer responded. 'Another aspect died near the shrine where Arvil found Her. Those who raised their hands against Her will for ever be cursed, while we shall be blessed. I tell you this also. The man who told me this tale had spoken to one who had seen that lifeless form of the Lady, and saw the arrow in Her heart, and the sight turned his hair white in a day.'

This was not a tale I wanted to hear. I remembered the body I had found outside the shrine by the lake. Had that form been worn by another evil one? Birana had mourned for the other as if sorrowing for a companion. Or had the other been a true aspect Whom Birana had led into danger? Perhaps her grief had been false. Birana might have powers unknown to me. I longed to question Wanderer, who had seen and heard of many things; but he, like the others, was under Birana's spell.

'When I first heard this tale,' Wanderer went on, 'I did not understand its meaning fully, but it has come to me during the days we have passed here. I think I know what the Lady said to that man when he was dying. She was telling him that not every stranger is an enemy and that a lone traveller may be a Holy One in disguise. She was telling him that one should not be so quick to strike out at what one does not know.'

Tal grimaced. 'That cannot be the meaning,' he said. 'Strangers are enemies. A man makes truces when he is weak. When he and his band are strong, there is no need for truce.'

'I have travelled among strangers,' Wanderer said. 'I wasn't their enemy. We must know who our true enemies are, but also who may be a friend.'

'Unholiness,' Tal grunted.

A few of the men were near Birana, waiting to offer her food. Firemaker, stretched out at her feet, held out a piece of meat. She ignored him but accepted a drink of water from Hare. He gaped at her as she took his waterskin, gazing at her with adoration. I would never convince them of her evil; I saw that clearly. She handed the skin back to Hare, who clutched it to his chest.

She looked across the fire at me, as if something in my soul drew her, as if I might be one she knew well, and yet her look did not frighten me.

At that moment, when the light of the fire made her skin like gold, and her blue eyes shone, and her dark hair seemed redder in the light of the flames, even I could not accept her evil. I thought of disobeying the Lady and allowing Birana to live among us, but knew that the Lady would find out if I disobeyed. All of the band might then be punished, while I would suffer most of all. Before being sent from the enclave, I had been given another taste of the torment that would be mine if I did not act; I would not willingly visit that torment on my new band. Whatever my doubts and questions, I would have to act alone to protect them as well as myself.

'Birana has blessed us,' Shadow said to me as we ate. 'We have drawn together to serve Her. I think we would not have had the courage to attack the two horsemen if we had not known we were doing that to be better able to guard Her. She is our soul.'

I forced myself to swallow. 'Has She spoken to you of the Lady?'

'She had told us that She will speak to us of some of the

Goddess's magic. She has told us that we are greater than we know and that we will be granted many blessings. We are pledged to Her for as long as She chooses to remain with us.'

I knew then that the others would kill me if I told them of the Lady's command.

I did not act. I also did not tend to Birana as did the others, for I feared her spell and saw that she noticed how I shied from her. She gazed at me piercingly whenever I passed, as if seeing what was in my mind. I stared back boldly, unwilling to let her see my fear. Often, she seemed about to speak to me before she drew away. I told myself that she could not know of my purpose, or she would have ordered my death at the hands of the other men.

At last Tal took me aside. 'The Lady has commanded you,' he muttered as we gathered wood on the hillside. 'Yet you still wait.'

'I must choose my time.'

'She will ensnare you as she has the others. Hasin goes to her side when I'm not there to prevent it.'

'Let the boy be. She's gentle enough with him.'

'She is evil. How can you question the Lady's will?'

'I have grown to question much,' I said rashly.

He threw down his wood and lashed at me with a twig. I darted out of the way. He hurled me to the ground, dug a knee into my back, and lashed me as I struggled to throw him off. Swinging with my free arm, I struck him in the face. His twig whistled, then broke against my brow, narrowly missing my eyes. I jumped up and punched him, knocking him flat.

'Don't ever beat me again, Tal. Next time, I shall beat you.'

He panted as he stumbled to his feet. 'You wait too long. If you do not act soon, I will, and the Lady will bless me and curse you.'

'If you act, the others will kill you.' I knew also that, if Tal failed, Birana would be more closely guarded. The others might even punish me for having brought Tal to them. 'Listen to me, Tal. I must be careful. I must be sure that, when I strike, I do not fail.'

Tal turned away and picked up his wood. I left him there and descended the hill. Below me, Wanderer was leading the white horse by the reins as Hare rode, his body slouched over the horse. The reins had been made with strips of leather, and we had examined them so that we would know how to make our own. Birana sat on the bay horse, watching. I summoned up my courage and went to her.

'You did not betray Me,' she said, but her voice rose a little on the last word as if she were asking a question.

'You were with us,' I answered. 'The Lady has not taken You from us, and I have returned safely, while my guardian was blessed with a boy. Does that not show that I obeyed You?' Her mouth twitched a little. 'Teach me to ride,' I went on.

She raised her eyebrows. 'Wanderer will teach you.'

'But You have greater knowledge than Wanderer. You are an aspect, after all.' She looked at me sharply as I spoke, and I lowered my eyes; I was being too bold and might betray myself. 'I ask You humbly to teach me. I have ridden a horse before and know a little. I would be grateful for Your help.'

'Very well, but if you don't learn quickly, I won't teach you any more.'

'I shall learn, if it is Your will.'

She dismounted. 'Let me see you get on.'

Bint had taught me how to mount. I vaulted on to the beast's back. It danced a bit, reared, and dumped me to the ground. Hare laughed as Birana steadied the horse.

'I see you know something,' Birana said, 'but you did not stay on for long.'

'I should have said,' I answered, 'that I did not ride alone before.'

'Go on, try again.'

I was able to stay on this time, gripping the horse with my legs and clinging to the mane as Birana led it around the hill.

I spent the rest of the morning on the horse while Birana taught me how to sit, how to hold the reins, and how to guide the creature, while Hare watched. His eyes were narrow with envy, for Birana had not taught him. She did not ride with me but walked at the horse's side as she told me what to do. I did not think of my task then, but only of what stirred in me when I was near her.

I was sore when I dismounted, and the insides of my thighs burned. 'Thank You,' I said to Birana.

'You need practise.'

'I would be grateful if You taught me more tomorrow.'

She shrugged. 'You're quicker than I thought. You might learn.'

'Tomorrow?'

She shook her head as she glanced at Hare and Wanderer. 'I can't spend all my time with you.' She mounted. 'The day after, maybe. We'll see.'

Ulred and I went to catch fish the next day. His talk when we filled our skins at the stream was of Birana. Hare had spoken to him of how Birana was teaching me to ride. Now Cloudgazer, another of our band, was begging her to instruct him as well instead of leaving it to Wanderer.

'How happy Hare and I were,' he said, 'as we travelled with Her. One night, as we slept, I heard Birana whisper in Her sleep and saw Her tremble in the cold. I longed to press nearer to Her, to give Her warmth, but saw during the journey that She shied away from our touch. I took off my coat then and laid it over Her.'

'You must have been cold, I said.

'The air chilled my bones that night, but I was happy knowing that She was warm.'

'It would not have helped Her,' I responded, 'if you had grown ill and couldn't protect Her.'

When we had caught our fish, we washed as well as we could with the cold water, and Ulred told me of how he had carried water to Birana so that she could bathe inside a lean-to, hidden from the men by a curtain of hides. Ulred and the others, I had seen, now spent more time grooming their beards and hair. He glanced at me as I cut at my hair with my own knife. 'You are fair enough,' he said, 'but you wish to be even fairer now, do you not?'

I shook my head, although he had guessed at my thoughts. I would have to act against her, and yet I wanted her to think of me as fair.

'Your guardian Tal does not speak to Her,' Ulred continued.

'He doesn't wish to offend Her.'

'It does not seem so to me. I see no respect in his eyes when he gazes upon Her.'

'Tal is afraid,' I said hastily. 'All of this is strange to him. He has beheld an aspect and must live among strangers as well. He was told that all strangers are enemies.'

'Most strangers are.'

'But our old band perhaps feared them more than others. He must grow used to you, and he respects Birana more than he shows.' I was beginning to fear then that Tal might betray what he knew to the others.

Birana spent more time teaching me how to ride. As the days passed, my stiffness and soreness lessened, and I came to regard the horse almost as a companion.

The horse was a mare, Birana told me. She had named it Flame for its reddish colour. I refused to ride the white stallion, which Wanderer called Storm, but the mare was gentle, and I grew to like its quiet temperament.

I had wanted to lead Birana into trusting me by passing this time with her, but instead my own will grew weaker. I would burn with the desire to strike out at her and bring an end to her spell, and then she would gaze at me kindly for a short moment, or say a few words, and a longing for something I could not name would fill me. It came to me that our battle had already begun, and that Birana, in some hidden way, was bending me from my purpose.

She had begun to help the others with their riding, but it seemed that she was favouring me, and this was creating hard feelings. Hare glared at me more often, Ulred grew sullen, and Cloudgazer often wore a frown on his dreamy pale face. Even Shadow was beginning to resent me. Birana, I thought, might be making these men weapons against me.

Tal was growing impatient, yet I could not strike, for Birana was never alone. I told myself that I was only waiting for my chance, but I was already hoping that chance would not come.

I needed to leave the camp for a time and went hunting with Tal. A flock of returning ducks had altered their course, bringing them near the place where our stream widened into a small river, and we were able to bring a few down with our arrows. The early return of these birds was, I hoped, a sign of a long spring.

A darker spirit had entered Tal's soul. He cursed me whenever my arrow missed its mark, although his missed almost as often as mine. He did not talk of our new band, while we camped by the river, but only told tales of our old one – tales I had heard often. It was not until we were returning to our camp that he spoke of what I was compelled to do.

'How long will you wait?' he asked.

'Wait for what?' I said foolishly.

He struck me such a blow to my head that I dropped my ducks, too stunned to fight back. I winced as I picked up my game. 'You know what I am asking, Arvil. How long will you wait?'

'Until I have learned what I can about her. I must be sure that she doesn't use her powers against me.'

'She has no powers. She is as we are, even if those other fools can't see it. She must eat and sleep and hide herself behind a bush to piss. She has no magic, only unholiness. Only an unholy one would tell us to keep away from shrines. How does she expect us to be called? She has no powers and deceives us.'

'She may be hiding her powers.'

'You spend too much time with her. She'll lure you from your purpose.' Tal had hit close to the truth, for I was finding it hard to see evil in her. I had lost my fear of Birana, yet part of me still revered her; I had honoured the Lady for so long that part of me still continued to worship anything that wore Her form. I was fighting myself, imagining her death, yet unable to harm her.

'I must get her to trust me,' I said. 'I don't think she does. I can strike at her when we are away from the others.'

Tal grunted. I felt sorry for him then. He had pledged himself and Hasin to Wise Soul's band, as I had, but he was unhappy. Wise Soul made decisions with his men or consulted with Wanderer, while Tal did as he was told, rarely speaking up. Hasin was his charge, and yet the boy sought out the other men more often. They, rather than Tal, were teaching Hasin what he had to know.

Tal was growing older. It was not likely that he would be called to an enclave again, and he had once looked forward to being a Headman. Now he had only the tasks of any band member. He could have learned much from Wanderer, but he scorned Wanderer's tales and refused to learn how to ride or how to bandage wounds. Had he not been a good hunter, the others might have grown impatient with his stubborn ways.

I wanted to ease Tal somehow. 'The bears are awakening from their winter sleep,' I said. 'Our band should hunt one soon for we grow leaner without their fat. You might lead us on the hunt and show some of your skill to the others.'

He cuffed me again, hard. I was dizzy from the blow and longed to strike back. 'Now you listen to me, Arvil. Strike at her in the camp if you must. What does it matter if you die as long as the Lady's will is done? Let the others fall upon you – your soul will be welcomed by the Lady to her realm.'

'I shall do Her will,' I managed to say, 'but I'm not yet ready to die.'

'That doesn't matter. The Lady should have given the task to me, but She did not, and I must leave it to you until I am certain that your will has failed you. If I see that it has, then I'll strike at her myself and kill you afterward for failing the Lady. It is I you had better fear now.'

Firemaker was on guard by the hillside and Cloudgazer had come down to relieve him. As they spied us, Cloudgazer leaned toward Firemaker and whispered to him.

'Here he comes,' Firemaker shouted as we approached. 'The Lady's favourite.'

'Do not let him hear you,' Cloudgazer said as he arched his pale brows. 'He's favoured, and he may grow angry.'

'Maybe She has missed your presence,' Firemaker said. 'Are you going to Her now?'

I was silent.

'Do you think She will bless you?' he continued. 'Do you think She will raise you up and set you over us? Do you believe the Lady is entranced by you?'

I walked past them, gripping my bow.

'He dreams of blessings,' Cloudgazer cried. 'He thinks that She will come to him and lead him into the holy state.'

I spun around at that. 'Be quiet,' I said. 'You don't know what you're saying.'

Firemaker threw down his spear and pulled a stone knife from his belt. 'You struck at me once. I bear your scar on my arm.'

'I was not of your band then. We've pledged ourselves now and must put that behind us.'

'Maybe your face needs markings, Arvil. Perhaps then She won't find it so fair.'

I dropped my ducks and lunged at Firemaker, wrestling him to the ground. He tried to jab at me with his knife. I pinned his arm. Tal stood aside, refusing to help me as a smile played around his lips.

My head swam, still aching from the blows Tal had given me earlier. Cloudgazer pulled me up by the hair, then held my arms while Firemaker punched me in the belly. A sour taste filled my mouth. I kicked Firemaker in the leg. Cloudgazer held me more tightly as Firemaker thrust his knife toward my face.

'Stop!'

Firemaker stumbled back. Cloudgazer released me. Birana had ridden down the hill on Flame; her face was pale.

'You mustn't fight each other.' Her voice shook as she spoke the words. 'Save your fighting for your enemies.'

Firemaker and Cloudgazer backed away. Tal began to climb the hill, ignoring me. I picked up my weapons and my game. As I passed Birana, I muttered, 'We fought over You.'

Her eyes widened. 'There is no need for that.'

'Perhaps it would be better if You were not with us, Birana. I don't think we can survive Your blessing.'

She dug her heels into Flame's flanks and rode away from me.

Leaves were appearing on the trees, and the weather had grown warmer. Wanderer rode away on Storm to scout out the land, while Tal went off on yet another expedition alone. I suspected that he would go to Mary's shrine to pray. The Lady might inflame him, bring him to act against Birana when he returned.

The other men were with Hasin, teaching him how to use the bow Tal had made for him. I had to act soon. Birana had been avoiding me since my fight with Firemaker and Cloudgazer. This had gained me an uneasy peace with the rest of the band, but I did not know how long it would endure.

I cleaned my metal knife, then sharpened my spear, chipping away at its stone point as I watched Hasin struggle with his bow. I told myself that only an evil one would divide a band against itself, but I knew too much about our nature to believe that.

I looked past Hasin toward the trees around our clearing. Birana stood next to Flame; her arms were around the horse's neck as she whispered to it. My feelings warred inside me again. I thought of the pain the Lady had inflicted on me; I thought of how my murderous desire faded when I was near Birana.

Suddenly a vision of such power came to me that I nearly cut my hand. I imagined Birana's hands on my body, as she whispered to me, and almost cried out before seeing that Shadow was at my side. 'Arvil,' he said, 'we must gather wood.' The vision faded, but not my longing.

Shadow motioned with his head, and I saw that he wanted to speak to me alone. We rose and walked down the hill until we were out of sight of the others. 'Wanderer has spied the tracks of horses not far from here,' Shadow said. 'He saw them the other day.'

I tensed. 'Horsemen.'

Shadow shook his head. 'These weren't the tracks of horses ridden by men. Those ridden by men make deeper tracks. These are horses without men, and Wanderer thinks of capturing another horse or two, but he also believes that the presence of that small herd might lure horsemen to this region.'

'Then we may have to fight,' I said.

'That isn't what Wanderer wants. He believes that we might be able to make a truce with such a band.'

'I have seen such men,' I said. 'I saw them strike, just outside the Lady's enclave. You heard what Wise Soul said when we met him. No truce is possible with them – they kill without mercy. We can only be stronger than they are.'

'I've lived among such men. They may not be so willing to strike at us when they know we have horses, too. We would not be so easy to kill as a band without horses. And we have an aspect of the Lady with us. They may want a truce with us so that She will protect them as well. Life would be much easier for us if we had no enemies nearby.'

'I was with a band of horsemen who sought truce with others. The Lady punished them.'

'I know of that, but Birana is with us now.' There was an odd tone in Shadow's voice as he spoke of her. 'This is what I want to say to you, Arvil. Birana begins to divide us. When She smiles at Cloudgazer, Firemaker glowers. When She speaks kindly to me, Ulred frowns. And you are the one whom She favours most.'

'I am not. She avoids me now.'

'Do not deny what I say. I see how She looks at you even when She doesn't speak. It is as if She has known your soul before somehow.'

'I can do nothing about that.'

'I speak to you as your true friend,' Shadow said as he put an arm around my shoulders. 'We cannot live with such feelings building inside ourselves. If we make truce with others, they may come to our camp. They too will seek Birana's goodwill, and such feelings may build inside them. We cannot have that.'

I wondered if I could now speak to Shadow of what I knew. 'I must ask you something,' I said. 'What if – what if Birana is not what She seems?'

'But I have seen that already.'

I pulled away from him, startled.

'Do you think I'm a fool?' he said. 'I see the truth. Wise Soul has come to it also, and Wanderer as well, for Wanderer has seen many things and heard many tales. We say nothing in front of the others, but they will come to see it.'

'What have you seen?' I asked.

Shadow did not say what I had expected to hear. 'Birana lives among us in a body of flesh and bone,' he murmured. 'She is an aspect, and yet in some ways She is weaker than we. She has asked us not to pray in shrines or wear the Goddess's crown, and that means we are deprived of the Goddess's special blessing in the holy state. Yet that desire is still with us, I know what this means, and the others will soon see it as well.' He paused. 'We must seek such blessings with Birana Herself. It is why She wears this body. We must each enter the holy state with Her in turn, and then we'll ease the feelings inside ourselves and be truly bound to Her. Those who become bound to us by truce can also receive Birana's blessing, and we will see that no one is favoured above another.'

I gaped at him. 'You're wrong. She may smile upon us from time to time, but She resists even a touch.'

'It is a test, Arvil. The Goddess is testing us. She is waiting for us to see what we must do. Birana has said we cannot go to shrines while She is with us, so we must go to Her. How do you think we can be called and given boys otherwise? Birana will bless us, and through Her, the Lady will summon us to Her enclave. She wants us to see this holy way for ourselves. She's setting the barriers in our path to see if we are brave enough to overcome them.'

How could I tell Shadow about my mission now? He plucked at my coat. 'This is why I'm speaking to you,' he went on. 'She favours you, and I have seen that you have courage. It is you who should seek Her blessing first, and then the rest of us can follow.'

'She will strike me down for it.'

'She won't strike you down. I would go to Her myself, but I am still a boy, and it is a man who should receive Her blessing first.'

If I did this, if I went to Birana, I might never break her spell. 'I must think,' I said.

We climbed back to our camp. Birana was upon Flame, watching as Hasin drew his small bow and aimed his arrow at a tree. He let it fly and it struck near the root. Birana smiled. 'Try again,' she said in our tongue, then repeated the words in the holy speech.

I shouldered my quiver and picked up my spear and bow. My knife and sling were in my belt, and a waterskin as well. It was time and I did not know how soon I could return after finishing my deed.

I took a breath and walked toward her. 'I must speak to You, Lady.'

'Speak, then.'

'Not here,' I said in a low voice. 'There are things to say that You might not wish the others to hear.'

I was taking a chance. She gazed at me for a long time, then said, 'I'll ride down the hill. Follow Me.'

Flame carried her down the hill slowly. Firemaker glanced at me angrily as I followed. When we were out of sight of the camp, Birana stopped. 'Get on behind Me.'

I slipped my spear under the straps across my back and then mounted. I sat with my back straight and my arms tense, conscious of Birana's waist under my hands as Flame trotted down the slope. I had not been this close to her before. I felt only the cloth of her coat, but my mind dwelled on what lay under the garment. She needed no weapons against me, for my longing had already weakened me.

Ulred was on guard at the bottom of the hill. He saluted as we passed, but seemed surprised to see me riding with her.

We rode east. I felt a chill in the air, winter's farewell and a reminder that the cold would one day return. I could pull her from the horse, finish her before she knew I had struck.

'I suppose,' she said, 'that you think I'm not pleased that you went to the enclave and returned safely. I couldn't tell you before, but I am.'

I said, 'You don't often speak to me now.'

'I must be careful. I don't want the others to think I like you more, especially after that fight.'

'Do You?'

'No.' She reined in Flame. 'Get off, you can walk. I'll ride.'

I slid off and walked at her side. She was silent until Flame stopped to graze on a few green shoots. 'I thought I would never be able to let one of you touch Me without getting sick. I suppose I'm getting used to you.'

'Surely the Lady can prevent an aspect's illness.'

She tossed her head and her hood fell away. She had tied her brown hair back with a leather thong, but a few strands curled around her face. 'You're smarter than the others, Arvil. Wanderer and Wise Soul probably know more, and Shadow's no fool, but I think you're quicker. Maybe you're too clever.'

'Not too clever, just clever enough.'

'What did you want to tell Me?'

'That I know you are not what you seem.'

'Be careful, Arvil.'

I stepped back. 'Let there be truth between us. I do not say this in front of the men, but to you alone.'

'You didn't say it in front of them because they would have torn you apart for speaking that way to me.'

'Can you be so certain of that?'

She lashed me in the face with the reins. I threw up an arm. 'Don't get Me angry.'

'My only wish is to serve the Lady.'

She seemed bewildered as she gazed down at me, as if she were wondering what I knew. 'I thought . . .' she began. 'I thought you might be someone I could talk to more freely.'

She did not sound like an enemy, like one who sought to ensnare me in evil. I narrowed my eyes. I had my weapons, and our camp was safely distant, yet I hesitated.

Ulred had seen me ride off with Birana. The others had seen me follow her down the hill. If I returned without her, I would have to explain that. I practised a few stories silently. Another band attacked us. I rejected that, for there would be no signs of such a band, and I would have to explain how I had escaped. The others might not forgive me for my carelessness.

She was thrown by the horse. But she rode too well, and Flame was gentle. The men would be suspicious if I did not come back with her body.

She was called by the Lady and ascended with Her to the heavens. That was more promising, but I wondered if I could tell such a story convincingly. I thought of what Shadow had said to me and did not think he would believe such a tale.

'What are you thinking about?' Birana asked when we stopped again.

'Nothing.'

'Wanderer and Shadow told me about you. You were with a settlement that was destroyed. I imagine those men must have thought they were wiser than they were. You'd better remember that.'

'I know only what I need to know.'

'And what is that?'

I readied my spear. I would bring this into the open and see what weapons she had; I was now sure that she had none. 'If you will stand before me,' I said, 'I shall tell you what I know.' She did not move. 'Are you so frightened of me that you cannot do that?'

I was ready to pull her from the horse before she could ride away. Instead, she dismounted. 'I don't fear you. What can you know?'

'That you are not of the Lady,' I answered. 'That you are not a true aspect and not part of the Unity.'

'You learned something in the city!'

I forced myself to look directly into her eyes and saw her fear. 'Do you think I can't reason?'

'You betrayed me! I should have known you would! You weren't strong enough, you . . . I should have . . .' Her throat moved as she swallowed. 'I can ride back and tell the others to kill you.'

'They may not listen. They begin to question the meaning of your presence among us. Shadow spoke to me of that today. Can you be certain that they won't listen to what I have to say?'

'Why are you telling me this? Do you think you can win some power over me?' Her face was pale; her hand trembled as she held on to Flame's reins. 'I don't want to be here. I shouldn't be here – I should be dead. I don't know how long I can bear it. Sometimes I wish I would never wake up, and other times, I wish I would, so I could find out it's all a dream.'

I shivered. She was speaking as though she knew what the Lady had ordained. She was telling me she knew my purpose. She wanted to die, she had accepted that. I gripped my spear.

She backed away, then mounted Flame. I did not move, could not move to stop her. She kicked the horse with her heels and galloped south. I dropped my spear and readied my bow, but could not shoot. Birana disappeared below a rise in the land.

I picked up my spear and ran after her. Lady, I prayed, do not make me do this. Tell me it is only a test, and that Birana cannot die. I suddenly knew that to see Birana lying dead would cause a pain that might burst my heart, and then it came to me that this feeling was one of Birana's weapons. She had unmanned me.

I tracked her to the stream. She had tied Flame to a sapling and was sitting on the bank. She might have ridden far, and yet she sat there, waiting.

I went to her side. 'I can't run,' she said. 'Where would I go?' She turned toward me. Her eyes were rimmed with red, and tears streaked her face. The sight of those tears made me tremble – made me despise myself for causing them.

At that moment, I understood at last that she was one like me. I could have slain her then, but did not, for I was gazing into another imprisoned soul reaching to me for help. If the Lady had heard the thoughts racing through my mind at that time, She would have detroyed me, yet I stood there and lived.

'Arvil,' Birana said, 'tell me what you think I am.'

'The Lady broke your spell,' I said. 'Your name was torn from my lips. I was told that you are an evil one sent to deceive us, to lure men from the right way.'

'Is that what you believe?'

I would speak the unholy thoughts inside me. 'I think that if the Lady is all-powerful, She wouldn't suffer you to come among us for such a reason, for there is wickedness enough in the world to test us and many ways for us to fall into evil. When I was in Her realm, I had a vision of a room with strange objects where my guardian lay bound in a silver web. It wasn't a place where souls reside, but another place, and it showed me that the Lady is not what She seems. I see you among us and although you wear Her form, your body has the weaknesses of ours. Birana, I was sent out here to kill you.'

Her eyes widened; she covered her throat with one hand. 'And will you?'

'How can I kill you? You are one like me; I see it now. You live in our world, and something in you calls to me.' I looked toward the sky. 'What has the Lady done to us? Is it She who has cast a wicked spell on the world? Has She led us to falseness and made us believe it is truth?'

I was not struck down. The Lady did not appear with Her weapons of fire to destroy me. The murderous impulse She had planted inside me was gone, but speaking those dread words tore at my soul. The world I knew had vanished. There was nothing left to guide me.

I fell at Birana's side and wept. The cries of a beast came from my throat. I wept for my lost faith and my wretchedness, then felt a hand on my brow.

'Arvil,' she said, 'you glimpse the truth.'

I sat up. 'The Lady may not be what She seems,' Birana went on, 'but the Lady is powerful nonetheless. She can still destroy.' She closed her eyes for a moment. 'She'll want to destroy me, to be certain I'm dead. I wish I didn't want to live so much. Even out here, I want to live.'

'You aren't safe here,' I said. I was thinking of what I had witnessed on the plateau and what the Lady might send here against us, but I was also thinking of what Shadow had told me. 'Others in the band are coming to question your nature. Shadow believes that you came among us to give us the blessings the Lady sends those who wear Her crown in shrines.'

Birana started at that and drew away from me. 'What can I do?' she whispered. 'I might escape you. I might ride away on Flame and never set eyes on you again, but how will I live out here? Another hand might kill me. Even if they don't, they'll come to see what I am, as your band is beginning to see. If the city knows I live . . .' She gazed out over the stream. 'It might be better for you if you killed me now and found a story your band could believe.'

'I cannot do it. You are all I have now. I have nothing to guide me and have lost what I took to be the truth. If you die, I may never come to know what the truth of the world is. I cannot kill you, Birana.'

'I don't think you can prevent my death.'

'Then I'll do what I can for you and learn what I can before I die also. Your soul has called to me, and I . . .'

The horse lifted its head and whinnied, then pawed at the

ground. I heard a rustling on the slope behind us and was on my feet in an instant, raging at myself for my lack of caution as I whirled to face what was there.

Tal walked toward us. 'You grow careless, Arvil,' he said in our tongue. 'I can still sneak up on you, I see.' Birana pulled her coat closer about her as I lowered my spear a little. 'You will not have a better chance,' he muttered as he came near.

'This is not the time,' I said.

'It is.'

He was next to Birana in one bound. He yanked her up by her hair. Her eyes were wide with terror. 'Strike!' he shouted as he raised his spear.

'Arvil!' Birana cried.

'You must die,' Tal said in the holy speech. 'The Lady has commanded it, and Arvil must strike the blow. You won't trap me in your evil ways. Strike!'

Tal thrust her toward me. She fell at my feet. My hand moved. My spear found Tal's heart.

His grey eyes looked at me not with rage, but with shock and bewilderment. He was my guardian, and I knew his spirit would haunt me during the time I had left, but I could not take back that deadly thrust. I slashed at his throat, then pulled my spear from him as he fell to the ground.

Birana's shoulders shook. A hoarse, rasping sound was coming from her throat. It came to me that she had led me into evil after all. Then a black sea flooded into my soul, and I knew no more.

The
REFUGE

BIRANA

I thought he was dead.

He lay on the ground without moving. His spear was stained with the blood of the man he had killed to save me. I could not look at him. My hands were cold; my body icy with shock.

I had wept over my mother's body but had no tears for this man. I had been sent outside to die; it seemed that the harder I tried to escape my fate, the more death would surround me.

Then I glanced at Arvil and saw that he still breathed.

I could not go back to his tribe. I might have ridden away from that place and left Arvil, but I also knew that I wouldn't live long alone.

I began to shake until my body was shivering violently. Flame pawed at the ground as though scenting the death around her. I was surrounded by beasts. I had forgotten that fact during my short time among men, when the light of reason flickered dimly in their eyes, and their mouths uttered familiar words in my own language.

Arvil's knife lay next to his hand, I could take that knife, cut my throat, and end my struggle, but my will to live was still too strong. Even then, I clung to the hope my mother had aroused in me.

There was a refuge, she had said. Against all of the evidence, she had believed that.

We will be spared, I thought. The Council will only frighten us and then forgive. I held to this hope until the wall closed behind us.

I hardly saw where we walked. No one in the city had spoken for me; no one had visited me. I thought of one former friend, the grey-eyed girl who had once been close to me, but who had grown more distant as my feeling for her grew. I had waited for the time when she might notice me again, would no longer care what her friends thought of me, when she might return my love. She would forget me as completely as though I had never lived; that thought was the most tormenting of all.

We were in a forest; the trees were so thick around us that we could not see what lay ahead. 'My mistake,' mother said suddenly, 'was in not making sure that wretched Ciella was dead.'

'You would have been found out anyway,' I replied.

'True enough, but I would have had that satisfaction.'

I did not want to hear more; her deed had condemned me. I had gone to her rooms that day only out of concern for her. I should have left before she and Ciella began to lash out at each other, but I had not, and Yvara had struck before I could stop her. My mother's love for Ciella had somehow fed on the pain, the cruel remarks, and belittlement that Ciella had inflicted on her. Ciella had bent my mother to her will before striking the one blow Yvara could not stand – the announcement that Ciella was leaving her. I had waited while Ciella's life was seeping away, and had done nothing although part of me rejoiced that Yvara had finally struck at her tormentor.

'I'll tell you why I was punished,' she continued. 'Ciella lived, so they might have shown some mercy, but the Council fears it's losing its grip, and Ciella was so convincing when she spoke against me. I have only one regret – that I brought you to this.'

'It's too late, Mother. You don't have to pretend you feel something for me now.' Yvara had given birth to me only reluctantly; that was one of the truths Ciella had revealed to me in her insidious way. My mother had not thought of me while striking at Ciella, but then she rarely had.

She groped at her neck and pulled out a necklace; a compass hung from the gold chain. 'Where did you get that?' I asked.

'Someone gave it to me long ago,' she answered. 'It was useless in the city, of course, so I wore it only as an ornament once in a while. I happened to be wearing it when they came for us, and no one thought to take it away.' She stopped and pulled the chain over her head, then pushed back my hood. 'You wear it, Birana.'

'Why are you giving it to me?'

'Take it and speak more softly.' She hung it around my neck and covered it with my coat. 'If we're separated, you may need it. You're younger and stronger than I am, with more of a chance to survive.'

'We mustn't be separated,' I said. I was not thinking of survival, but only that I did not want to die alone. I touched the necklace, thinking of other small gifts my mother had given me, gifts that were substitutes for the feelings she lacked.

We walked through the wood for most of the day without seeing signs of men. The forest was thick and often the sky was hidden from us, but the compass guided our steps. At last the trees grew more sparse, and we were able to look back at our wall from a hillside.

I gazed one last time at the city that had condemned us. We had been given warm garments, some water, a little food. This, I saw now, was not an act of mercy, or a way to be certain that we died at some distance from the wall and any witnesses there who might pity us; it was part of our punishment. It would have been kinder and quicker to strip us of everything and thrust us from the wall.

The sun was setting; the lights of the distant towers winked on. I thought of the world I had lost and wept.

We took shelter at the bottom of a hill. The air had grown colder; the ground was blanketed with snow.

'We can't rest long,' Yvara murmured as we huddled together. 'We'll freeze to death if we do.' She swallowed a handful of snow. 'Eat only a little food – it has to last as long as possible.'

'Why?' I said. 'So that we can postpone our deaths?'

'We're not going to die. I won't let us die, do you hear? Other women have been expelled. Some of them must have survived.'

'The cities would know if they had.'

'They could be hidden. There are many places to hide: lands we haven't mapped for ages, places our ships rarely see. There are lands to the east and west we surrendered to the Goddess, where no man can dwell. We might find a refuge there, where women wait to welcome other exiles.'

'You're not defying the city now,' I answered. 'You don't have to say such things to me.'

'Do you think I didn't believe it when I spoke? We've been fortunate so far. And you forget one thing, Birana. These men have been taught to worship us; we can use that to survive.'

She was mad. A tribe of men spying two lone travellers would not see what we were before taking our lives. She was deluding herself with her talk of refuges and survivors. I shivered, afraid to look up at the sky, remembering that a force field no longer protected us.

'There are places to hide,' Yvara continued, 'wildernesses we haven't mapped, shores near the oceans where women might hide. The cities have grown lazy and complacent and are no longer as vigilant as they once were. Earth could hide many things from their eyes.'

'And what good will staying alive do?'

'Living, when all the cities believe one is dead? It would be my triumph over them. When I'm older and ready to give up my life, I'll return to the wall of our city and show those who condemned me that it was I who defeated them.'

Her exile had unbalanced her; whatever shreds of rationality she had possessed were gone. Her talk of growing old only reminded me that, even if we avoided starvation, a violent death, or a thousand other perils, disease could still claim us. Unlike the men who were called, we could not enter the wall to be cleansed of infectious diseases. Our immune systems, untended, would start to weaken. Without rejuvenation, we would age more rapidly.

I despaired, and yet a bit of hope had been planted in me. I was just beginning to nurture the seed of my own delusion – that if I could survive, my city might choose to forgive me and take me back, believing I had been punished enough.

'Exactly how do you plan to live?' I asked.

'We must get to a shrine. We'd have warmth there and a place to sleep.'

'Men would come there.'

'They can't attack others in shrines, you know that. Keep this in mind, distasteful as it is – we'll need the protection of men.'

'If they put on the mindspeaker bands,' I objected, 'they might reveal we were there, and then . . .'

'Think, Birana. We might show them how to cloak certain thoughts. We could even tell them that they don't have to use a mindspeaker in our presence.'

Yvara went on to tell me that, once we gained the protection of a tribe, we would have a chance to stay alive. Eventually, we might hear of where other survivors could be found. I tried to listen but could think only of the cold and my weariness.

Arvil stirred, then opened his eyes, but moments passed before he seemed to see me. He groaned and hid his face as he whispered words in his own language.

'Arvil,' I said.

'My guardian,' he replied in words I could understand. 'He brought me out of the enclave, he cared for me, he taught me what I know. Now he lies dead because of you.'

'I can't fight you, Arvil. You can take my life as well.'

'Then his death would be for nothing, and your death won't cleanse my soul now.' He stood up and went to Tal's body. The dead man, I was sure, was Arvil's father; I had noted the resemblance. The man had seemed to have little affection for Arvil, but perhaps he had not always treated him that way. Arvil let out a cry, then fell at Tal's side; his shoulders shook.

I thought of what he had told me earlier about his tribe and their changing feelings toward me. They would use me as they used the images presented to them by mindspeakers, as they used one another; I had heard the groans in the night. I couldn't go back; I would come to welcome death if I did.

I waited for Arvil to purge himself of his grief as I wondered what he would do.

Through the mindcaster, I had experienced something of life outside our wall. I had built a simulated fire and had gazed out over the re-creation of a plain. For most of the girls I knew, one such experience had been enough, for their fear ran deep, but I had experienced such imaginary journeys several times.

Those mental tours had not prepared me for the aching of my body, the fear of injury, the pangs of hunger, the dirt I could not wash away, the need to squat over the ground to relieve myself. For the first time in my life, I saw myself as physically weak.

We did not rest long by the hillside. The wind picked up and we pulled our hoods around our faces. Before morning, snow began to fall; it was soon so thick around us that we could hardly see each other.

We stood under a tree, clinging together as the storm swirled around us. My body grew numb; we stamped our feet in an effort to keep them warm. 'I won't let you die,' I heard my mother whisper; the wind swallowed the rest of her words. I do not know how long we stood there, but at last the snowstorm began to abate, although flakes still sifted down from the sky.

We stumbled on. A shelf of rock suddenly loomed before us; a creature crouched against the stone.

I nearly screamed as the creature's hand gripped a spear. My mother cried, 'The Goddess is with you!' She quickly threw back her hood and opened her coat. 'Look at My form,' she shouted, 'and know that I am of the Lady.'

She stood there before the man as the flakes fell on her hair and on to the shirt outlining her full breasts. The man was clothed in hides and fur, and hair concealed the lower part of his face; I shuddered at his ugliness. His small dark eyes glanced from my mother to me; he called out strange words and then threw himself to the ground.

'Why have You come before me?' he called out. His hands,

covered in leather, clawed at the snow. 'Am I to be blessed or punished? Oh, Lady, forgive me my sins.'

I was surprised to understand his words, but remembered that the men knew our language, for they used it in their prayers. His fear of us astonished me. Then I thought of how easily he might have struck at us, before seeing what we were, and nearly collapsed myself.

'I come among you to test you, to see that you are truly My servants,' Yvara answered. 'Rise, and answer the Lady's questions. Where are you bound, and where is your tribe?'

The man climbed to his feet. 'Oh, Lady,' he whimpered. I opened my own coat quickly and his eyes widened. 'Two aspects! Never could I have dreamed – I am Your true servant, I swear it. I am now travelling back from Your holy enclave to rejoin my band.' He knelt. 'They roam in the west, some five days' travel from this place.'

'I shall test your devotion to the Goddess,' my mother said. 'She knows of your worthiness and will have a special place in Her heart for you if you serve Me. First, you must lead us to a holy place, to a shrine where My spirit resides.'

He stood up again. 'I was to stop at a shrine not far from here to pray,' he said. 'I shall take You there.'

'Are there other tribes near that shrine?'

'Not in this season. But surely you know that, Lady, for we can hide nothing from Your eyes.'

'I am only testing your honesty. Remember, you cannot lie to Me.' Yvara took a breath; her voice showed none of the fear I was certain she felt. 'You will travel with Us to that shrine. If you show Us what a worthy servant you are, you and your band will for ever be blessed.'

'I will take You to the lake shrine,' the man responded, 'where the aspect known as the Wise One dwells. I'll be a worthy servant to You, Holy Ones.'

That man was the first I had ever seen in the flesh, for I did not count those I had watched at a safe distance from the wall. He was called the Bear, and in his hides with his thick brown beard, he had seemed much like that beast, but a beast that spoke words.

Our weakness seemed to puzzle him. He believed in the Lady's strength, yet during our journey, we often stopped to take shelter under the tree limbs and hide he would set over us. Yvara directed him to turn his eyes from us whenever we knelt to relieve ourselves. He guarded us while we rested, then rested while we watched, ready to awaken him if we saw any distant movement. Our feet grew blistered and sore, and it was soon hard to walk at more than a slow pace.

Yvara explained to the Bear that, in our bodies, we shared some of the weaknesses of men, that this was necessary if we were to live among men without harming them with our greater powers – yet I wondered if, in time, the Bear might see what we really were. He could read signs in his environment invisible to us; he seemed capable of some reason and thought. Brutal as he was, he remained patient as he guided us to the shrine.

The Bear dwelled with us in the shrine for three days. He fetched water for us to bathe our blistered feet and caught fish for us through the ice of the lake; we had none of our own food left by then. He sat on the floor before the altar and gazed at us with awe; pathetic as he seemed, I was touched by his devotion. Yet he was a man and used to violence; I could not forget that.

He left us with some dried fish and enough water for a few days, promising to return soon with his band. When he was gone, my mother spoke of her plans. The Bear's tribe would know of others; we might find one who could guide us to a refuge.

'He told us nothing of any refuge,' I said.

'We'll find one, and then, someday, I'll go back to the wall and show everyone that I prevailed.'

'You dream of women who don't exist,' I shouted. 'You think of nothing but revenge, revenge against Ciella, against the city. You would destroy it if you could.'

She leaped up and struck me across the face. 'Yes, I would, and you should feel the same way. Hold to your hatred – it'll keep you alive. No one spoke for us, remember that. You're all I have left, and you're going to live.'

'You brought this on me. You don't care about me. You only want to ease your guilt by thinking you can bring me to a safe place.'

'Believe that if you like.' She turned away.

As I waited for the Bear to return, my despair deepened. My life would never be more than a struggle, and a short one in all likelihood. I could accomplish nothing by staying alive.

We left the shrine only to relieve ourselves near the door and still saw no sign of the Bear. We brooded in silence, afraid to eat what little food remained. At last, there was only one piece of dried fish left; Mother handed it to me.

'You eat it,' I said. 'My life is over.'

'Take it.'

'I don't want to live,' I said.

'You must.'

'Why must I?'

'Does anyone know the answer to that?' she said. 'All we can say is because our lives are all we have. I thought I wanted to die before, back in the city. I struck out at Ciella instead of at myself, but it was all part of the same impulse. It wasn't until I was awaiting my sentence that I decided to live, whatever happened.'

'I don't want to stay alive.'

She took my hand and stroked it gently. It was an uncharacteristic gesture; she had rarely shown me much affection. 'You're not being honest, Birana. Dying is simple enough. I can't restrain you if you're determined to die. You could find death outside in any number of ways, but you don't. You don't really want to die, but you haven't made up your mind to live. You'd better decide what you want.'

I was silent.

'We've survived this long,' she said. 'We've found a man to help us. It means others could have done so. You must hold on to that hope. Women in ancient times found ways to live when the Earth was in ruins. Surely some could do so again. If they have, then in times to come the cities may learn of it, and it may be that by then they'll have need of those outside and of what they have learned.'

She was, without knowing it, renewing the hope I harboured – that there might be forgiveness of exiles, forgiveness for me.

'Decide, Birana,' she said as she let go of my hand. 'Decide to live or to die, and at least that torment will be over.'

We ran out of water and still the Bear did not return with his men. 'He will come,' my mother said, 'or another will. This is a shrine – men have to come here.' But even her spirit seemed to be failing her. She began to pace the shrine restlessly, wasting her strength, then paused for long moments to stare at the door.

I don't know how many days we passed this way – perhaps only a few. I was soon too weak to stir from my couch. I was lying there when Mother rose and walked toward the door.

I struggled up. 'Where are you going?'

'Down to the lake.'

I didn't want her to go even that far from the shrine. 'Don't go.'

'We have to have water. I must go before I'm too weak to fetch it.'

'I'll get the water,' I said, but she was already gone. Fearing for her, I managed to cross the room; the door opened as I went outside.

The darkening sky and the dusky light made it difficult to see. I squinted; she was near the edge of the lake. She bent over, then stood up as she began to walk toward me.

She was near a small shrub, only a shadowy form, when I saw other shadows move. I tried to cry out as they raced toward her, but my voice was locked inside my throat. The men were upon her in an instant; their long fur cloaks swirled around their legs. I saw her fall, saw a blade move toward her throat. She was given no chance to speak, no chance to call out, to reveal what she was.

One of the men bent over her. I nearly ran to her murderers myself, and then the man let out a howl of such pain and terror that I staggered back. The door closed; the floor rushed up to meet me.

I was lying on a couch, with no memory of how I came there. My mouth was dry, my strength gone.

The door opened. Three men entered, carrying my mother's body.

I do not know how I found the strength to rise. My body shook with sobs and I walked toward them; my voice screamed accusations as the men threw themselves down, and then one of them looked at me.

He was a blond beast with a hairless face, but he was gazing at me with Laissa's eyes, with the grey eyes of the girl who had once been my friend. The shock of seeing those eyes brought me to myself. I noticed then that these men were not wearing fur cloaks; they could not be my mother's killers.

The blond one caught me and guided me back to the couch. Even in the ugliness of his face – the skin browned and roughened by wind, the high cheekbones and angular jaw, the straight, hard mouth with none of a woman's gentleness – I saw a resemblance to Laissa. He was only a man, and yet in him there was something of one I had known and loved.

I did not realize it then, but at that moment, I decided to live.

Arvil stumbled to my side and sat down, his features distorted by his grief. I had to speak, had to find out what he would do now.

'Arvil,' I began.

His head jerked up. I did not look away. Occasionally, when he spoke to me or asked a question, a gesture or expression would recall Laissa to me; at those moments, I could feel some kindness toward him.

'Arvil,' I continued, 'I must explain something to you. The Lady is not what you have believed She is, but She is powerful and can still harm you. The Lady will guess that I'm still with your band if we return to your camp, and we would not be safe for long. My city, the place you call the enclave, can easily find your band's camp and might destroy all its members to be certain I was dead.'

'I have seen the Lady's weapons of fire and have witnessed Her wrath.' His grey eyes gazed past me. 'I know what She can do. Are you so evil, then? Perhaps They were right when They told me you were.'

'I'm not evil. I did nothing. I was punished for the crime of my – of another – because I stood by and did nothing to prevent it. My city did not have to punish me, but cruel ones refused to show me mercy. Weak and foolish I might be, but I'm not evil.'

'That other – the one we found by the shrine – was it she who committed this crime?'

I nodded. 'And she has paid for it, as you saw. The enclave doesn't want me dead because I'm evil. I am to die so that you and your kind will never know the truth.'

His eyes narrowed. 'What truth could the Lady teach if She has deceived us all this time?'

'You've already seen part of the truth. You told me what I was – a weak creature, like you.'

'There are many questions I would ask.'

'Arvil, you can save yourself and your band. You can do what the Lady ordered you to do and return to your camp. You can tell them that I chose to return to the Lady. Or you can take the horse and leave me here. I would die soon enough. I can't survive alone.'

He lowered his eyes. I was reminded of Laissa once again and of all I had lost. I thought of my mother; her struggle to live had been useless. I gazed toward the body of Tal, who had died because of me.

Arvil lifted his head. 'After I had taken your life, I was to go to a shrine and tell the Lady of my deed. The Lady was to reward me for that and spare my band. If I do not go . . .'

He did not have to finish that statement. Terror nearly overwhelmed me, but somehow I held it back and was able to think.

The city might have stuck at Arvil's band immediately, yet they had not. They could not be concerned with the lives of the band; they were only another tribe of men. Why hadn't they acted? Some might have scruples about taking a woman's life so overtly instead of leaving her to die, but the Council could not let an exile live.

There was one possibility. Some in the city might not want others to know that I lived, as they would if ships were sent out to strike at the band's camp. Someone was fearful of what might happen if the city learned I was still alive.

This possibility, however mistaken, was enough to renew my determination. Perhaps Yvara had been right about the existence of refuges, and others feared I might find one. If someone in the city wanted to keep my existence a secret, it meant I might have a chance to escape, that the city would not turn all its resources against me. I had some power over the city's actions even now.

'I must be honest with you,' I said. 'The Lady is powerful, and we may not escape Her, but there is still a chance. Her power does not extend over all of the Earth.' A look of doubt crossed his face, yet he seemed to accept this, for he already knew what I was. 'We might find a place of safety.'

'Even if we could not, I cannot kill you. I would never know the truth then, but it isn't only my curiosity that holds me back. I do not know how, but something in your spirit calls to my own.' The intensity of his gaze as he spoke made me turn away. 'We cannot return to our camp.'

'I wouldn't be safe there,' I said.

'It is not only that. They dream of the blessings of your body. It angers me to think of their hands upon you.'

I got to my feet, sick at the thought. 'I must bury Tal,' he continued, 'but he cannot lie here. The others will find the grave, when they come for water, and wonder whom it holds.' He stared down at the dead man for a long time. 'He brought me out; he raised me. He deserved a better death.'

He reached down and pulled the coat from Tal's body. 'Take off your coat and put on this one,' he said.

'But I . . .'

'Take it off. A man seeing that coat will wonder why you wear such a garment, where you found it, who you are. You might be taken for a scavenger, and they are despised by all.'

I shuddered as I handed my coat to him and put on Tal's. The sleeves hung down to my fingertips; the hem fell past my knees. A dead man had made this coat, had worked at the hide to make

167

it supple, had cut its pieces with sharp stones, and sewn them with bone needles. His blood was on the coat; I nearly cast it off.

'Steady yourself,' he said fiercely. 'His spirit will haunt me, not you. Bring Flame to me. We must carry him to another place.'

He strained as he lifted Tal and slung him across the horse's back. I saw no tears, only cold and angry eyes. Arvil knelt and dug at the ground, pushing dirt over the signs of blood, then threw my coat down on the bank.

'Here is what my band will find,' he said. 'A man will come for water, or they will search for us and follow our tracks to this place. They will see your coat, and believe that you have departed from them, and if they do not know it then, they will see it as the days pass and you do not return. Wanderer knows many stories, and he will see one in these signs. He'll know that I am gone as well, although he will not know if I was blessed or punished. He will think you have ascended to the heavens at last.'

'How do you know they won't follow us, instead?'

'We will leave them no tracks to find.' He took Flame's reins and led her down toward the stream.

We walked over the rocks at the edge of the stream, the sun at our backs. Finding our footing on the rocks while being certain we left no signs of our passing slowed us, yet by mid-afternoon, we had reached a place where the stream widened. My feet were sore by then, but I trudged on behind Arvil, unable to bring myself to mount the horse that carried Tal's body.

We pressed on until the stream was narrow enough for us to cross to the southern side. We were able to walk over a few half-submerged rocks while leading Flame through the water. We did not stop then but moved on along that bank. Arvil was silent throughout our journey, and I worried about what he might be thinking. Was he remembering Tal, was he regretting what he had done? He knew what I was, knew my weakness, knew I was powerless against him. I had much to fear from him still.

When the sun was low in the sky, we stopped and Arvil began to dig at the ground with his stone knife. It was long, hard work; by the time he finished, the sun was setting, and he had hollowed out a shallow grave where Tal could lie. Remembering how he had buried my mother, I began to gather flat stones from along the bank and set them by the grave.

He lifted Tal from the horse and laid him in the ground gently, then set his quiver and bow next to the body. 'I shall keep his spear, for no enemy can threaten him now, but he must have his other weapons so that he can hunt in the next world.' He closed his eyes and I heard him moan softly. 'What foolishness I speak. The Lady tells us of another world and yet She has lied. What world can there be for him now? Where will his spirit find rest?'

'There may be a Goddess,' I said without conviction. 'Many of my kind believe there is. We may not be what you thought we were, but there can be a Goddess Who hears prayers and watches over us.'

'She will not hear mine. Perhaps She hears no one's if She allows those who wear Her form to deceive us. But Tal tried to do what he thought was Her will. He was hard and stubborn in his ways but tried to keep to what he thought was right. Perhaps he will find some peace.'

He covered the grave with dirt and then set the stones on the mound. The evening light was fading quickly, but I could see the guilt and anger in his face as he stood. I wondered if he would strike out at me after all.

'Arvil, I am sorry,' I said. 'I've also lost one who was close to me. I didn't want Tal to die.'

'If I had done nothing, Tal would have taken your life and then mine. He told me that himself. He was willing to kill you and to strike at me. If the Lady cares more for those aspects in the enclave than She does for you, then She will bless Tal's soul.'

His words chilled me. I took a step back. He bent to pick up Tal's spear, took a strap of leather from his shoulder, then tugged at me roughly as he tied the spear to my back.

He mounted Flame and pulled me up behind him, refusing to look back at me as we rode away from the grave.

ARVIL

Birana had trapped me in her spell. My guardian was dead because of her, because of the spell she had cast over me. The world I had known was gone. The Lady Who watched over the world had been taken from me, and I had a vision of others like Birana whose spirits were housed in the Lady's form, but who had none of the Lady's strength. With their magic, they had hidden the truth from us, and the Lady had not punished them for their deed. I had refused to do Her bidding and still lived.

All that I had thought of as good had become something else, and the Lady Herself seemed part of the evil. My spirit, with its questions and doubts, was a curse. It had set me against the world, and I wondered where it would lead me.

Birana's arms were around my waist. Again the longing I could not name rose up inside me. Her soul had called to me, and whatever misery she brought, I still ached to learn from her what I could. More pain lay ahead of us, I was sure. Alone, I had little chance of surviving. With Birana to protect, my chances were even less. Silently, I cursed the spell she had cast on me, while resolving to learn from her what I could before death claimed me. Turning back now would not bring back what I had lost.

I had chosen my path; yet, as I rode, I hoped a vision would come to me, that the Lady would appear and with Her words restore my world to me, even if that meant that She would condemn me for my deeds.

The night was growing cold, and we had to find shelter. As we rode south, I thought of Mary's shrine, but knew we could not go there. I wanted to be away from the lands near my camp.

I thought of my band, of the friends I would see no more. They might already be searching for us. One might have found Birana's coat. The men would wonder at that, and their fears would give rise to many imaginings. I was certain that their bewilderment would lead them to Mary's shrine to pray. It came to me that the Lady could not hear their prayers unless they wore Her circlets, for I was learning Her limits. When the men understood that Birana would not return, they would have no reason not to don the Lady's crowns.

'Arvil,' Birana whispered behind me, 'I fear what I've brought you to. You've lost Tal and now your band. It might have been better for you to have taken my life.'

'It is useless to speak of that now.' Her words made me burn with rage at her for entrancing me. 'You will have to repay me for your life by telling me tales of what you call the truth. If I don't like what I hear perhaps I will find that I am able to carry out the order the Lady gave to me.' Her arms tensed around me as I spoke, and I was sorry for what I had said. It was part of her spell – that she could transform my anger into longing for her.

We soon came to a small hill. The few trees at the top would hide us, and we could see any movement below. I heard no sound, saw no sign of men. We rode up the hill and dismounted, then sat down after tying Flame's reins to a limb.

'I have questions for you,' I said. 'Answer them well, for our lives will depend on those answers. My band will see soon that you are gone, and I believe that they will go to Mary's shrine to seek counsel from the Lady. You are no longer with them, and at least one will find courage to don a circlet. The Lady will then learn that you are no longer with them. Will that keep Her from searching for you?'

She was silent for a moment. 'The city would learn that I'm not with them. They might believe you killed me, and were afraid to return to those men, but they wouldn't be sure.'

'Will the enclave search for you? Will the Lady believe you are dead?'

'I don't know. Your band would be safe from the city if they reveal I'm not with them, but how can you be sure they'll go to that shrine?'

'They will go,' I said. 'When they find your coat and see that you have vanished from the earth, their terror will take them to the shrine.'

'They may not go right away. Until they do, they're not safe, either.'

I pondered her words and felt concern for my band. I had not thought of the danger to them while we fled; I had not thought of protecting them against the consequences of my deed. They had befriended me when I had no one, and I felt shame at having abandoned them to their fate.

'If the city sends a ship against them,' Birana continued, 'then the city may believe that I died with them, but perhaps not. The ship might take images of the bodies back for study, to be . . .'

'Do you care so little for those who cared for you?' I burst out. 'Are we only creatures to be cast aside?'

She shrank back in the darkness. 'I did not mean that I wish them dead.' She paused. 'I don't know how much I can tell you. As far as I know, the cities have never had this problem before. A woman is sent out, and nothing more is heard of her. Many things can kill one out here, and we don't know how to live outside the wall. We cannot take another's life ourselves – it is our greatest crime to do so. That's why women are sent out instead.'

'The Lady takes the lives of men.'

'Yes, but not the lives of our own kind. That must be why you were sent, you see – even though I was condemned, they would rather send a man against me, so that they wouldn't have to act themselves. But they will act if there's no alternative.'

I sighed. 'I was told that, when you were dead, I must go to a shrine and speak to the Lady once more.'

'I know. The city will begin to wonder why you haven't done so.'

'Tell me this, Birana. If I go to a shrine and do as I was asked to do, will we be safe from the Lady's wrath then?'

She caught her breath. 'If they believe you, yes – but they have ways of getting the truth from you. You'll find it hard to hide the facts from them.'

'You put a spell on me before, at the shrine by the lake.'

'And you see how easily it was broken. It wasn't strong enough to keep you from betraying me.'

'The Lady put a spell on me,' I said. 'It was a powerful spell, enough to make me feel some joy when I thought of striking at you. Yet, when I saw what you are, that spell was broken, for your spell on me is stronger. I know a little more about the Lady's true nature now. She no longer has as much power over me. You must teach me what to do to hide my thoughts, and then I shall go to a shrine.'

She jumped to her feet. 'You might as well take my life now! They would send a ship with weapons to that shrine – they'd destroy everything around it to be sure . . .'

'Sit down,' I muttered, 'and keep still, or you may call death here.' She settled herself on the ground. 'We have little chance at life by ourselves, even with Flame to carry us. We'll have none at all if I must fear the Lady's magic, for I'll be watching the sky and fearing Her weapons instead of seeing what dangers lie around us. I must go to a shrine. If the Lady breaks your spell and learns the truth, we'll only meet our death sooner. If She does not, and believes me we have a small chance at life.'

'You cannot do this, Arvil.'

'I must. There is my band to protect as well. They will not be safe until the Lady knows you are not with them. I won't have them suffer because of me.'

'You cannot . . .'

'You treated little Hasin with kindness. Would you see him struck down by the Lady's rays?'

'No!' My talk of Hasin had moved her. 'I suppose I must do what you ask.'

I let her sleep for a time, then roused her when the Hunter's Belt was higher in the sky. I pointed out the stars to her and told her to wake me when they were lower in the west. 'Most men will sleep at night,' I said, 'but you must wake me if you see anything move.'

She nodded as I stretched out on the ground. I supposed that she was hungry, but we had no food. I closed my eyes. No dreams came to me as I slept. When I awoke, I imagined that I was back at my camp and then remembered.

It was still night. The dark shape of Birana was black against the starry sky. She stood a few paces from my feet, keeping watch.

She was the danger closest to me, more threatening than anything below. I could take her life quickly and see that she did not suffer. I could go to a shrine then without fear of her enclave. I could bury her and return to my old band, or find another band I might join.

I had worshipped the Lady and those aspects who wore Her form. Although I knew that Birana was not what I had believed her to be, awe of her was still inside me, mingled with that longing that burned in my soul. I wanted to know the truths she could tell me but wanted something more as well. I thought of what Shadow had said about the blessings Birana might grant us in her body. There was no one to stop me from receiving them – from taking them.

She had kept apart from my band. She had granted a smile, or a kind word, but had not called any of us to her side. I remembered how frightened she had looked when I told her of the men's wishes.

I forced myself to ignore my longings as I sat up. 'The sky will grow lighter soon,' I said as I rose. 'We must go. We can travel far by dawn.' I helped her mount Flame, then got on the horse behind her.

I had decided to ride south, along the route I had travelled with Bint. If we kept in the open we could flee from any men on foot, and I would watch for signs of horsemen while avoiding regions where men lived.

'There is a shrine to Hecate in the south,' I said. 'It isn't likely that other men will travel to it now, for any near to it will have seen the Lady's ships strike at the plateau. They will fear the Lady's wrath and believe that land is cursed.'

'Is that where you saw men die?'

I told her then of how my band had joined Truthspeaker's men and how we had travelled to that plateau only to meet death at the Lady's hands. As I spoke, I thought of everything I had lost – my old band, the friendship of Wanderer and Shadow, my new band, my guardian Tal. I wondered if Birana, and what she might reveal to me, could ever replace what I had lost.

'I am sorry,' she said when I had finished my tale. 'You have suffered much.' I wanted to learn more from her, but we needed food, and there was little time for questions.

Throughout this journey, we stopped when I could see a place of safety for Birana, a grove or a hollow in a hillside where she could hide herself while I hunted. I dared not go far from her or leave her alone for too long, but at one small stream, I caught fish, and another day, I brought down a duck with an arrow. Plants were beginning to sprout, and I was able to gather green onions, mushrooms, and spears of young asparagus. Birana, I saw, would be useless in helping me find food. She did not know what plants to gather, and it was easier for me to hunt alone.

Whenever I returned to her side, she would wipe tears from her face before greeting me. Often, she would smile a little, and warmth would fill me at the sight. I felt joy when I could bring her food, shame when I found little. She did not weep in my presence. She did not complain, although I saw the weariness and despair in her blue eyes. I learned not to relieve myself in front of her and to turn away while she tended to herself.

In the evening, and in the morning before we rode, she dangled her golden chain before me and spoke to me of the spell I would need in the shrine. With her soft words, she would entrance me and then call me back from her spell. I had no memory of what happened under her trance, but my longing for her seemed greatest when my soul returned to me and I saw her once more.

'You are doing well,' she told me on the fourth day of our travels as we rode. 'You fall into the trance more easily. You're more suggestible than I thought.'

'I must not let your spell be broken.'

'I'll do my best to see that it isn't. You will not know that I live when you speak to the Lady, you won't be aware of me. You won't even know me until I speak the words that will call you back. Then you'll remember everything that happened, and I'll know from what you tell me whether we're safe. You must trust me, Arvil.'

'I want to ask you another question now,' I said. 'Once men dwelled in the Lady's realm – so we have always believed, and yet I wonder at the truth of it now. Then we committed a great evil and were cast out. Is this so?'

'It's true. It happened long ago, long before anyone now alive

174

lived. Men nearly destroyed our world. You need not doubt that.'

'How could men do such a thing!'

'They knew much of what you call magic. They used it to fight among themselves, and millions died – many, in numbers you cannot count. Those who lived saw that it couldn't be allowed to happen again, so women, the aspects of the Lady, sent men from their midst and kept the magic for themselves. This brought peace to the world, for women swore that there would be no more battles.'

'There is little peace in my world,' I said.

'At least you have a world.'

I struggled with my thoughts. 'You say that those who committed this sin are no longer alive, and yet we are punished for what they did.'

'Your natures are violent ones. You must be kept from bringing destruction to the world again.'

This was in keeping with what I had believed, that our souls were stained with the evil of the past. Yet questions still came to me. 'Boys are given to us. I was given to Tal in an enclave, although I have no memory of it. We found Hasin inside the wall. Do you allow men to live so that they will be forgiven someday?'

'I do not know,' she said, 'if you can ever be forgiven.'

'But can a boy be so evil that the enclave must send him away? If we are truly so evil, why do you allow us to live at all?'

'You are needed,' she said but did not explain what she meant. 'Some of us believe that the Goddess appeared to us long ago and directed us to live apart from men. Others say that this is only a story, that the Goddess does not work in such ways, or that there may be no Goddess at all, but that our way is right nonetheless because it has preserved Earth.'

If there were no Goddess, then Who watched over us? What was there to hold back evil? The thought that She had turned away from the world was not as fearful as the notion that She might not exist at all. 'What do you believe?' I asked.

She kept her face turned away from me. My hands tightened on her waist. She said, 'I think we've lived as we have for so long that we can't change, regardless of what may be right, or what the truth might be.'

My head throbbed. I slid from Flame's back and landed on my feet.

'Arvil . . .'

'I must walk,' I said. I had wanted to know what Birana called the truth. I was hearing it, and my soul recoiled.

I had learned that Birana, outside her enclave, had little of the Lady's magic, that other aspects were not as powerful as I thought. Doubts had troubled my spirit even before I entered the enclave, and the strange vision I had seen there of Tal bound by thin metal threads had fed my doubts. I had felt the pain the Lady could inflict. Yet I had somehow hoped that Birana's truth would reveal a purpose, a reason for our lives being as they were.

Now she was saying that we lived as we did only because her kind would not change it. I thought of Bint and his band, who had wanted a better way and had died for that. I thought of the Lady I had worshipped. Only my faith had made me able to bear hardship in the hope that I might at last be forgiven.

Flame halted, then lowered her head to graze. I put my hand on her flank as I looked up at Birana. 'I must ask you this,' I said, 'although I think I already know the answer. Are all those in the enclave only other creatures as weak as you? Would they be without their power outside the wall? Do they just cloak their true nature with their magic?'

She nodded her head.

'And is the Lady only one of your lies? Have we been taught to worship Her so that we can never know the truth?

'I cannot say if the Goddess is only a lie. Many in the cities believe in Her reality, though they don't see Her as one who acts as we have taught you She does. She is seen as the spirit of Earth, or as the intelligence that brought our world into being. Others are doubters. We are free to believe as we like, as long as we follow custom. For many it's easier to believe in Her, for then they do not question. It's true that a belief in Her serves our purpose and maintains our power.'

I wanted to pull her from the horse then, to release my rage with my fists. Her eyes widened as if she had seen my angry thoughts.

'Arvil, it's better that you know all of this now. If you are to speak to someone in the shrine, you'll be stronger if you understand that those who hear you are more limited than you thought.'

'That is so,' I said bitterly.

'Please try to understand. Long ago, we had to rebuild a world. We did it in the only way we could, however cruel it might seem to you now. Many fear that if we chose another way, that if we kept your kind in our cities, we might risk destroying what we have built.'

'Be silent,' I said as I mounted again. 'I don't think I can endure more of your truth now.'

*

I travelled more slowly with her than I had with Bint's band, but we were soon on the plains north of the plateau and Hecate's shrine. The last time I had entered that shrine, I thought that the world had punished me as much as it could.

Birana's truth was harder to bear than my earlier suffering, but it was all I had left. If I lived, I would force more truth from her and learn what I could of her enclave's magic. If I could find a way to turn that magic against the enclaves, I would do so. If I could not, I would seek a way to let other men know of the truth. Birana could remain alive until I had learned what I could from her. I told myself that I no longer cared what became of her after that.

There was now fear in Birana's eyes whenever she glanced at me, as though she sensed my musings. I left her side one evening not only to hunt, but also because I might have lashed out at her in my anger. I needed her spell.

I returned with a rabbit. She offered to skin it for me, but I refused.

'Please,' she said. 'I feel useless. I've watched you and the others with game. I can do that much. You have to teach me what to do.'

I raised my eyes to her face. My anger left me. Her brown hair was looser around her face, and her smooth skin had grown darker from the wind and sun. The night was warmer, and she had opened her coat; I saw how thin she had become. Her grey clothes were loose on her body; her form now seemed more like a boy's than an aspect's. She had little of the beauty of the aspects who had blessed me in the past, yet my soul stirred again as I looked at her.

She looked away quickly. 'You're angry with me,' she said, 'and I know why. You feel rage at all of my kind who have deceived you, but you can't strike out at them, only at me. You must be wishing you had never found me.'

'You are with me. I cannot undo that.'

'You can still take my life.'

'That thought has come to me,' I admitted, 'but your spell stays my hand.'

'Then if I am to live,' she said fiercely, 'you have to show me what I must know. You must teach me how to hunt, even how to fight if it comes to that. I have no power here except what you give me.' Her eyes were hard, and I saw strength in her gaze.

Those in the enclaves had destroyed the refuge I had hoped to find with Bint's band. They had called me to the enclave not to bless me, or to reward me for my courage, or to restore Tal to me, but for some unknown purpose. They did not seek only to follow the will of the Goddess, but to preserve their power from men. Yet they had also sent Birana from their midst. Their cruelty to one of their own kind was as great as their cruelty to men.

I thought of how I had ached when Tal had abandoned me to the Stalker. Tal, however, had believed that I would live. Birana's kind had sent her out to die. I felt pity for her then, and more than pity.

I reached for her hand and gripped it in my own. I had touched her at other times, but only for a purpose – to help her mount, to guide her, to steady myself as I rode behind her. This was the first time I touched her for no reason but my longing for her soul.

Her hand was cold. I saw from the tenseness of her body that she wanted to pull away, but she kept her palm against mine. Joy filled my spirit, a joy I had felt only when in the holy state.

I let go of her quickly, afraid that her spell would overwhelm me if I held her hand too long, then stood up. 'I shall show you what I can,' I said. 'I'll teach you how to build a fire.'

The sun hid in the east, although the sky was growing lighter as we came to Hecate's shrine. I gazed south, toward the distant plateau, and saw a bit of light flickering in the darkness.

Birana sat behind me. I pulled at the reins and Flame slowed to a walk. The light seemed to be that of a fire, burning just below the top of the plateau.

'Something burns near the plateau,' I said.

'What could it be?'

'Perhaps men have found shelter in one of the caves below that camp, although I don't know why they would remain on such ground.'

Her hands gripped at my coat. 'Then they may come to the shrine.'

'We can be gone before they can reach it, and perhaps they won't come, but we cannot be harmed in a shrine. I have reached a truce with strangers before, and I can tell them that the rest of my band will seek revenge if we are harmed outside. There is nothing now to keep me from speaking false words in a shrine, and they will believe them to be true.'

I urged Flame on, and we rode quickly toward the shrine. When we had tied her reins to a tree outside the door, we entered. I took out my skin, swallowed some water, then moved toward the altar out of habit until I remembered that I no longer had to pray.

I sat down and set my weapons by the couch. 'It is time,' I said. 'I must do this thing, and, if I do not betray you, we must leave this place and think of where we might go.'

'You will not betray me. I have had time to prepare you, and the Lady won't know you are under my spell.'

'Then cast your spell on me.'

Her face grew pale as I stretched out. 'Listen to me,' she whispered. 'There may be pain for you while you're in your trance, because you'll remember things that haven't happened and will believe they are true. You will not recall coming here with me, but will think you travelled alone. When you are in the trance, I will tell you what to say, and you will not return to yourself until you take off the circlet and see me again, at which time I'll say some words to you. Then you will recall everything that passed while you wore the circlet, and we'll know if we're safe.'

She had explained all of this to me before, but I saw that she wanted to prolong what might be our last moments of life if I failed. 'I understand,' I replied.

'I'll sit by the door and wait. Arvil, you mustn't fear. Remember that anyone who speaks to you, stripped of her magic, is only another like me.'

She held her chain before my eyes; her words filled my soul. The shrine disappeared, and my spirit floated in darkness as she spoke. Then silence swallowed me. My hand reached for the circlet and put it around my head.

'Lady, hear me,' I prayed, and fear and despair filled me. Again I stood by the stream. Birana was near me, holding out her hands as she pleaded for her life, I tore her coat from her as she struggled, but she could not stop me with her feeble blows. I pulled her head back as my knife found her throat.

The vision passed. I had carried out the Lady's command, and yet I sorrowed.

An aspect appeared before me, and I saw that she was the golden-haired one I had seen in this shrine before, when I had fled from the pleateau. 'Arvil,' she said, 'you have called to Me. Have you carried out the task the Lady set for you?'

'I have.'

She was silent for a time. She bowed her head and I thought I heard a cry escape her lips. 'You must tell Me of your deed,' she said as she raised her head.

I could hardly bear to think of it. I heard Birana's voice again as she begged for her life. 'Lady, the one You call Birana put a spell on me and it was hard for me to see her as evil, even when I struck. I nearly wept when I saw her blood on my knife. I shall never forget her eyes as she sank before me, when she saw that I had brought her death.'

I went on to tell of what I had done. I could not return to face the men who had worshipped her and could not leave her body there for them to find, for they would know I had killed her and would not rest until they found me. I left only her coat, so that they would find it and believe she was truly gone from them, and I left no tracks as I carried Birana's body east on my horse.

From time to time, the aspect would ask a question, and although I could answer easily, certain memories eluded me. I recalled lifting Birana's body from the horse but not laying her on the ground. I saw myself digging a grave for her but did not remember covering her with dirt. The horror I had felt at killing one who wore the Lady's form had robbed me of the memory of my lonely journey south, yet somehow I had survived to reach Hecate's shrine.

'My fear of You,' I said to the aspect, 'and my desire to be Your true servant overcame Birana's spell, and yet I tell You now that I mourn. I have saved my band from evil, but I shall see them no more.'

'Your band has prayed to Me already,' she said. 'I was sure – I knew then what you would tell Me. Be at peace about those men, for they are safe from Me.' I could almost believe that she felt no joy in my victory, that she sorrowed with me and wanted to comfort me. I imagined then that I heard her weep.

'If the Lady wills it,' I said, 'I shall survive alone, as a wanderer. When She calls me to Her at last, I will die knowing I did Her will. I leave my fate in Your hands.'

'I am sorry you must bear this burden. It is My burden as well.' I could hear the grief in her words. 'But you will be blessed, Arvil, and the Lady will summon you to Her side in the next world.'

She vanished, and another aspect appeared to me. I accepted her blessing, but as she lay with me, I was thinking of Birana, of how, for a time my spirit had communed with hers and seen her as another imprisoned soul. I would have my life, and yet wanted to lose it.

My soul was alone in the dark. My arms felt heavy as I lifted the circlet from my head. I forced myself to rise and then knew terror as I looked toward the entrance. Birana's ghost stood before me, waiting to haunt me, I cried out.

'Arvil, I live – awaken, and know I am with you.'

I remembered. She was alive; she had entranced me. My soul sang within me. I had not taken her life; I was bound more closely to her now. I had believed her dead, and my joy at seeing her unbalanced me.

I began to stumble toward her. 'You are safe,' I said. 'The aspect believes you lie in the grave I dug for Tal.' I came to her side and flung my arms around her, pressing her body to mine. The world she had lived in and the world I had believed in were no more – there was only the world we would share. We would teach each other what we could, and she would soothe the ache in me.

She pushed against me. 'Arvil!' I had forgotten her fear of my touch and released her.

'I did not mean . . . it is only . . .' I stepped back. 'I didn't betray you this time. The golden-haired aspect to whom I spoke believed me and blessed me.'

Her eyes widened. 'A young one?'

'I don't know, but her hair was gold and her form more like a boy's than an aspect's.'

'You didn't see one with silver hair, one with . . .' She shook her head. 'I can't believe that the Council . . .'

'Are you saying that we aren't safe?'

'No, Arvil. We must be safe, or she would have kept you on that couch until the city could send a ship here. I'm grateful to you. There is now one thing less to fear.'

'We should leave this shrine,' I said. 'If there are men near the plateau, I would not have them find us here.'

I fetched my weapons, then followed her outside. The sun was higher in the sky, and I saw that it was nearly noon, although in my trance it had seemed little time had passed. As I moved toward Flame, I heard both Birana's cry and the low sound of thunder.

I turned. Two horsemen were galloping toward us from the south, and they were already too near for us to outrace them. I seized Birana and pulled her into the shrine.

'What can we do? she asked.

I pushed her toward the altar. 'They cannot harm us here.'

'But they'll see . . .'

'Keep your coat around you. They will think only that you are a boy. I'll speak for both of us and try to reach a truce that will protect us when we leave. Say nothing to them.'

'They wouldn't hurt us if they saw what I am.'

'It is better that they don't see that until we learn more about them.'

We sat by the altar with my weapons in front of us. 'Remember, you must not speak for you won't know what to say to them.' I said. 'They will not wonder at that. A man would speak for a boy here.'

'I'm frightened.'

'Steady yourself, Birana. There are only two.'

The door opened, and the two men entered the shrine. As they came toward us, I expected them to bow to Hecate and go through the motions of worship, but instead they strode up to the image and gazed at her face. They did not act as men should in shrines, and I feared the arrogant look in their eyes.

'Greetings,' I said in the holy tongue. One of the men had a black beard flecked with grey; as he lowered his hood, I saw that he was growing bald. The other was younger, with a brown beard. His eyes were cold as he looked down at me. 'A truce while we speak.'

'There is always peace in Her presence,' the balding stranger said, but his lip curled as he spoke and something in the way he said the words chilled me. 'I see you ride the horse, as do we.'

'I do.'

'Yet your band must be far from here, for you are alone, and we have seen no other horsemen in this region.'

'I am alone with this boy now, but others of our band will come.'

The two were wearing sheepskin garments of the kind Bint had worn. It came to me that these men might have been among the few guards below the plateau who had escaped the Lady's weapons. I wondered why they had returned. I was about to tell them that I had been granted a truce by their band, but the hard look in their eyes held me back.

'I have heard tales of the plateau to the south,' I said carefully. 'It is said that rays of fire destroyed a camp there.'

The balding man nodded. 'The Lady sent Her weapons, it is true, and yet we dwell below the land She marked.' He showed no fear as he spoke these words. 'What is your name, boy?'

'I am called Arvil, and I am a man, for I was called to an enclave not long ago. The boy with me is called Spellweaver, for he knows some of the magic of the mind.' This name seemed to suit Birana. I also hoped that they might fear what magic she knew.

The brown-haired one suddenly pulled at Birana's sleeve. She recoiled. I held up a hand. 'Leave him be.'

'He has a fair face for a boy,' the brown-haired stranger said. 'No doubt he warms you at night.'

I was surprised by the power of the rage I felt as he looked at Birana. 'I have taken the place of his guardian. I do not seek such pleasures with him.'

'But I am not his guardian. There is nothing to hold me back.'

'You should not be talking of this to strangers in place where one should be seeking the blessings of the Lady.'

'The Lady will grant me no more pleasures, and I might have those of this boy.'

Even in this place, I no longer felt safe. 'We are in a shrine,' I said. 'It's time to speak of other things.'

The black-bearded man stared down at me. 'All men speak the truth in shrines,' he said. 'I shall tell you our truth. The Lady cursed us. She sent weapons of fire against us, but some of us escaped Her wrath. A vision came to me then, and I saw that my soul was already dead, that the Lady had turned from those few of my band who still lived, and that there was no hope in following Her way. But I tell you that there is a freedom in that. It no longer matters what way I follow, for the Lady binds us no more.'

My hand moved toward the knife under my coat. In an instant, the black-bearded man was upon me, pinning me to the floor. Birana jumped up; the other man seized her by the arm.

'What evil is this?' I cried. 'We are in a holy place. You must be mad.'

'I am not mad!' He dug his knee into my chest while restraining my arms with his hands. 'I know why the Lady struck at us – it was because She feared us, because we grew fat and strong and dreamed of challenging Her. If the Lady Herself were to appear to me now, I would remember what She did to my band and turn from Her. I will tell you what else I saw in my vision – that a man can be free of Her grasp. I say this in Her shrine, and you see that She doesn't act.'

Birana struggled as the other man dragged her toward a couch. She bit his hand, and he howled as she broke away; he struck her, and she crumpled to the floor, senseless. There was no hope for us even if they discovered Birana's true nature, for they felt only hatred toward the Lady. I remembered how some in

Truthspeaker's band had cursed the Lady before dying.

I fought for breath. 'If you don't fear the Lady, fear my band. They will come here and . . .'

'They cannot save you. After we have taken what we want from you, we shall wait until we see signs of them. They will not expect us to attack them in a shrine, and we'll take what they have as well. Let the Lady save you if She can.'

Birana was still, and I feared she was badly hurt. Her body was limp as the other man pushed her aside with one foot. 'Kill him!' the brown-haired man shouted as he stepped in front of her. 'Then we will share the boy before he dies.' I saw her hands tighten into fists, although the stranger did not, and knew that she had heard him.

The man holding me released my arm as he reached for the stone knife at his belt. In that small moment, I saw my chance. My fingers jabbed at his eyes. He cried out and dropped his knife. I grabbed my own knife and struck as another knife streaked past my head. The brown-haired man was coming toward me, and then he fell, knocking his head against the floor. Birana's small hand was around his ankle.

My knife found the throat of the balding man. There was a look of surprise on his face as I struck. I do not know how many times I stabbed him, for it can take a man long moments to die.

I had nearly forgotten his companion. Birana crawled toward me. She picked up Tal's spear, stumbled to her feet, and began to pound at the back of the man on the floor. It was a foolish way to fight. I saw him roll over and pluck the spear from her as easily as he might have taken it from a child.

I grabbed my spear then and hurled it at him as he found his footing. He staggered back, his fingers around the spear embedded in his chest.

BIRANA

Arvil was covered with blood when he came to me. I could not watch when he pulled his spear from the dead man; I had covered my ears to stop the sound of the man's moans while Arvil waited for him to die.

I screamed as his hand reached for me. I screamed again,

unable to stop, and he slapped me, then dragged me to my feet. My legs shook; he caught me and bore me to a couch.

'It is over,' Arvil said. 'You're safe. I did not mean to strike you, but you must not scream.'

I began to shake violently. 'Don't,' I cried as he held out his arms. 'Don't.'

'You are safe now. Please. You helped to save my life.'

A sob escaped me.

'Cry if you must,' he said.

I coughed, but no tears came, and then I began to shiver violently. 'You did well when you tripped that man,' he went on. 'You have a brave spirit. But beating him with the spear was not wise, for you gave him a chance to take it from you. You should have thrust it through his back before he could get up.'

'If this is what we must do to live, I can't bear it.'

'You must learn to bear it. If a man means to take your life, you must take his, or be prepared to run from him for ever.'

I glanced at him, then looked away from his bloodstained clothes. 'You said we would be safe here.'

'No man would expect an attack inside a shrine. These were evil men, and they must have believed, when they saw us, that we would be easy to overcome. It is better that these two will prey on travellers no more.'

He got up and began to gather his weapons and theirs, putting them on a couch, and then went to the bodies. 'These are good coats,' he said in an oddly steady voice. 'We can use them.'

'Leave them!' I cried.

'We must take what we can. Our journey will be hard enough.' He began to pull the coats and trousers from the bodies; I hid my face.

He put these garments on the couch with the weapons, before covering me with one of the coats. I lay down, unable to stop shivering.

Arvil leaned over me. 'Birana, you must steady yourself. We cannot stay in this shrine. There may be other men who dwelled with these two. They may search for them when they do not return.'

'Others!' I clutched at the coat.

'I do not think there can be many – five or six, perhaps, no more. I was on the plateau when their band was destroyed, I saw how few escaped. But they could be as dangerous as many men if they're like those who attacked us.' He strode to the entrance and looked outside, then came back to me. 'I see no signs of other men yet, but if they are up there, they may be watching this shrine.'

I forced myself to sit up. 'Where can we go now?'

'It is I who must ask you. An enclave lies to the west, and we would have to circle scavenger territory. We cannot go north, and it is said many bands roam in the south. I know little of the east – even Wanderer heard few tales of those lands. Can you tell me what lies there?'

I knew even less than he. 'We know little of those lands,' I replied. 'When we built our cities inland, we abandoned much of the land in the east and west to the Goddess. That means we have no shrines there and no cities – even our ships rarely fly over those regions. We left those lands to heal to allow life to return to them. Once, some of my kind dreamed of returning to them and building new cities there, but we build no new cities. We hold on to the ones we have and hide inside them.'

'If the enclaves do not know of those lands, you would be safe there.'

A refuge for me might exist in the east. Such a place would have to be there, or far to the west, safe from men who might betray their knowledge of it in shrines. But I did not know what kinds of dangers might await us along the way, and Arvil knew as little.

'I think we must go east,' I said at last.

He helped me to my feet. 'Take off Tal's coat and put on this one. Make certain that the hood is about your head.'

'But why?'

'If friends of these men are watching, they will see only two small figures far below. It would be best if they took us for their companions.' He picked up the other coat.

I was not sorry the strangers were dead, although I felt horror when I thought of how they had died. They had been vicious creatures preying on others, willing to inflict pain on those who were weaker, ready to violate the code others of their kind followed. Yet it was the destruction of their settlement that had made them that way, and women had done that to them. The cities had clearly wanted to implant fear in them, but instead had only freed their hatred and the violent impulses all men possessed.

The strangers had tied their horses to the trees under which Flame stood. One was a pinto mare; the other was black with a white mark on her head. We approached them cautiously; the pinto whinnied and pawed the ground as Arvil came up to her.

'We should take these horses with us,' he said. 'I hope they will allow us to ride them.'

I went to the black horse and held out my hand; she bent her neck to lick it. 'This one seems gentle enough.'

Two packs had been tied to the horses. Arvil opened each and peered inside. 'There's water and dried meat,' he said. 'We'll have a little food.' He put all the food and water in one pack before thrusting the strangers' pants and boots in the other.

'Take this.' He handed me a stone knife; I secured it under my belt. 'Take these also – they're good flints.' I slipped them into my pocket as he handed me Tal's spear. 'I'll keep the other weapons. Luck is with us, Birana. These strangers have increased our wealth.'

To the west, on the horizon, I could barely see what might have been a wall and remembered that the city of Devva lay in this region. I had travelled to that city once, never thinking to look at what lay outside it. Tears sprang to my eyes; I wiped them away quickly.

Arvil secured our old coats under the pack on the black horse. As I reached for Flame's reins, he motioned to me, then turned toward the plateau. He pointed to a spot near the top of the cliff face, and I was able to make out a thin, dark stream of smoke.

'We must get away.'

'Birana, I fear for us. Madness poisoned the two who lie inside, and I cannot know what their companions might do. Other men would fear to follow two travellers and risk facing the rest of their band in a battle, but that may not restrain men who would defile a shrine with blood. When we leave, they may follow us.'

'What can we do?'

'Do you have the courage to wait? If their companions look down now, they may believe that their friends are only tarrying here, but if they see us ride away to the east, they may grow curious. I would have us wait and ride when night comes, when the darkness can hide us from their eyes. They won't know where we have gone, and we could be far from here before they find our trail.'

He had been wrong about finding safety in a shrine; we might be in greater peril if we waited. I wanted to flee and wondered if I could trust his judgement. He gazed down at me, seemingly waiting for my response.

I had to trust him; he had brought me this far. 'We'll wait,' I replied.

We sat down just outside the shrine's entrance. 'At least the enclave will not search for you now,' he said.

In the aftermath of the attack on us, I had nearly forgotten that more distant peril. 'You're sure of that?'

He told me then of how he had been questioned and how he had responded. There was pain in his eyes when he spoke of his false memory of my death, the one I had implanted in him. 'You did well,' I said when he had finished. 'I can see by what you've said that your story won't be doubted.'

'It was hard to say it, hard to believe you were gone.' I heard the intensity of his voice. His feelings toward me were strong, and I was frightened by them; I had seen how quickly they could turn into rage.

'I am puzzled by one thing,' I said. 'It seems that only a young one questioned you. I would think an older woman, someone of importance in our city, would have done so.' I frowned as I wondered what it could mean.

'Perhaps it is because I had spoken to this young one before.'

I lifted my head. 'Before? Are you sure?'

'I remember, because she has the grey eyes of my guardian. She spoke to me when I first came to this shrine, after I fled from the plateau. She spoke to me and she vanished, and then another aspect appeared and called me to the enclave to be with Tal.' He sighed. 'It would have been better for Tal if I had never found him again.'

I closed my eyes, feeling that my heart would burst through the bones of my chest. There must have been several young women in the city with the blond hair and grey eyes Arvil had mentioned, but I believed I knew who his interrogator was. Laissa had spoken to him. I had imagined that she was indifferent to me, and that had been painful enough. Now she had become one of those actively seeking my death. I felt more grief now than I had when I learned the city would show me no mercy.

A memory returned to me then, one I had long forgotten. I was in Laissa's rooms. I could not have been more than four or five; someone must have taken me there, since my mother usually left such tasks to others. Laissa had gone into her own room to fetch a toy, and then I heard a movement behind me and looked up.

A child was standing there, with Laissa's grey eyes and her wavy golden hair. I knew he was a boy and, although I had never been so near one of his kind before, I was not afraid. He did not speak but gazed at me for a long time before touching my face lightly with his hand. I remembered that I had smiled, knowing he would not hurt me, and then someone – maybe Laissa, maybe her mother or some other woman – had pulled the boy away and had ordered him back to his room.

Laissa had a twin. It had been a fact of no importance, easily forgotten when the boy vanished from her life. Now she had tried to use her twin against me. I did not know what her motive could be, or how she had found herself entrusted with such a task. She had, when she began to avoid me, started choosing friends among those whose mothers were prominent in our city's life, but I had never thought of her as ambitious in the usual sense; she only wanted to be accepted, or so I told myself. She would change when she grew older; she would remember her old friend and turn to me again; she would know that I was one who truly cared for her.

She wanted to be sure that I was dead. She could not be acting alone without someone on the Council to guide her, but she was willing to carry out the city's wishes. She would see me dead in order to get whatever favour or reward she might have been promised.

I thought of Hasin. I had pitied the little boy, had not minded when he thrust his small hand in mine as we walked about the camp. I had felt a bit of warmth for him. Perhaps he had evoked the memory of the boy in Laissa's rooms.

For a moment, I no longer cared if the men Arvil feared found us, and then I raised my eyes to Arvil's face. He was staring toward the plateau, on guard against any sign of activity there. I had seen the same worried look on Laissa's face. The resemblance pained me; yet, at the same time, I was moved by it.

His eyes met mine; he suddenly reached for my hand. 'Your soul calls to me,' he said. 'Can you reach out to mine?'

He had misinterpreted my gaze. I withdrew my hand from his. 'It's only that you look much like someone I knew.'

'A man? But you have seen few, and only Tal was like me – so my old band told me.'

'Not a man . . . someone in the city.'

'Did you know the one who spoke to me?'

I looked down, then swallowed hard. 'I'm not sure,' I said at last.

'It is strange that her eyes were so like Tal's. Tell me, Birana – what was it like for you inside the wall?'

I shook my head. 'I don't know what you mean.'

'I had a vision there of a room where I lay on a couch, with Tal beside me on another, and we were bound in silver threads. Then

189

shining claws put a circlet on my head and I saw no more of that place. This was after I had betrayed you and had spoken your name, when the Lady inflicted Her tortures on me. It was then that I began to know the Lady was not what She seemed.'

I knew the place he spoke of; my cheeks burned.

'I saw only that place and the room where I entered, and then I left the wall. What is it like inside the enclave?'

'The wall surrounds our city, as you know, but we don't dwell inside it. We live in the towers and dwellings at its centre, but there is much land around them. It isn't like the land out here – the grass is tended, and we have gardens of flowers and trees in our parks. A shield you cannot see protects us from the weather, so it is always spring or summer inside. We live in rooms inside our towers or houses and can speak to women in other rooms, or even other cities, with our screens, which are like openings that can show you someone far away and through which you can hear her voice.' My own voice caught on those words; all of that was lost to me.

'Sometimes,' Arvil said, 'I dream of a room with a soft white floor, where someone holds me and sings to me. Tal told me it was a dream of my time in the Lady's realm, before I was given to him. Once, I wondered if I would see that room again when I died and was restored to the Lady's realm, but now ...' He adjusted his hood. 'I don't know what to believe. I see others like you who have strong magic and who seek to keep us from knowing of it. I see boys like Hasin crying for what they have lost and not knowing what it is. I don't know why boys are given to us. Surely, if your kind is so angry with us, you could rid the world of men with your magic.'

'We can't destroy all of you. The cities need you.'

'What could you need us for? Why are we called?' He was silent for a moment, and then his eyes narrowed as he grabbed my wrist and thrust his face toward me. 'It has come to me. Is it only that you seek your pleasure with us?'

'No!' I tried to pull away, but his grip was too tight.

'Is it that we bring blessings to you as you bring them to us? I touched the bodies of aspects inside the wall, and they have the power to come to us in shrines, although I do not know how they can call our souls to them, but inside the wall, it would be easy to come to us.'

'Arvil, I don't want to speak of this.'

'Did you ever go to the wall to take your pleasure with a man? If you did, why do you shrink from me?'

He was angry with me again. I huddled against the shrine's wall. 'I never did such a thing. We couldn't . . .'

'Yet there are those who do. Somehow they come to us and give their blessings and vanish.'

I did not know how to explain this to him; my cheeks were hot with shame at the thought of what he called a blessing. 'Those are not women like me who come to you,' I managed to say. 'They are the spirits of women who no longer live.' This seemed easier to say than that they were images that had never really existed. 'Our magic can call up their spirits and show them to you. No woman could ever seek such pleasures with a man.'

'You call us to the wall and make us long for ghosts? Do we live only so spirits may enjoy us?' He thrust my arm away. 'No, that cannot be the only reason we're given blessings. You send spirit-women to us so that we will love you as well as fear you, so that our longing for you will make us helpless against you.'

From what little I told him, he was quick to grasp a deeper truth. I wondered what else he might see, and how it might change his feelings toward me; the more he knew, the more his anger at what we had done to the world would grow.

'The Headman of my old band was called Geab;' he went on. 'He did not think only of his duty to us, but of the pleasure it gave him to have that place. That must be the pleasure your kind seeks – of knowing that others live who must obey you. You let us live to feed that hunger and destroyed Truthspeaker's band on that plateau because they no longer fed it. Even you would wish such power over me.'

'I didn't make this world,' I said. 'I entered it as you did without the power to change it. My people have been as cruel to me as to you. It wasn't only a longing for power that led my kind to our deeds. We live at peace in our cities, and the other creatures of the world are undisturbed by us and allowed to flourish. This wasn't so in ancient times, when men lived in what you call the Lady's realm and used our magic. We wouldn't harm any men without reason, and we abhor murder above all, because we could not have survived that Destruction without valuing life.'

'Your kind did not value the lives of Truthspeaker's band. They no longer value yours.'

'Even that is nothing compared to the violence you inflict on yourselves. You could make truces with all men, friend and stranger alike, and live at peace. If you had done so in the past, women might have come to think that you could be given some of our magic and that you could change. As you are, you show only that the ancient ones were right. Ask yourself this, Arvil – if men like those who lie dead inside the shrine had our magic, what sort of world would they have made?'

'Would it be crueler to us than yours?'

I could not answer him. He had the traits of a man, and yet he had tempered them. I had seen him kill, but only in self-defence. In my short time with his band, I had seen that he did not often grow angry unless provoked; I had glimpsed some intelligence and even gentleness in his eyes. Hard as his world was, he struggled against the worst of its cruelties. Ignorant as he might be, he thought and questioned and reasoned his way to a truth, however painful that truth might be. He had reached out to me, knowing he might die for it.

'You wanted to know the truth,' I said. 'I'm telling you what I have been taught, and why my kind have acted as they did. Hate them if you must – I have no wish to defend all the ways of those who want me dead. But don't turn your anger against me.'

'It seems I cannot be angry with you for long.'

'I can tell you that there are women who feel imprisoned by the way we live, and who think it may be time to somehow change our way, that if we don't, we'll grow weaker. We create little that is new and only cling to what we have.'

He leaned back. 'I could bear knowing this,' he said, 'if there were some other purpose to your way and a reason for our lives.'

I knew I might eventually have to tell him why men were called, how boys were given to them, yet everything in me shrank from that possibility.

The sun was low in the west. We gazed toward the distant plateau in silence. Arvil got to his feet and cupped his hand over his eyes. Something was moving on the cliff side. I squinted, barely making out what might have been a man on horseback descending the cliff. Someone else was following him.

'We must go,' Arvil said. 'We cannot wait for night now.'

I ran toward Flame and mounted, slipping my spear under the pack. Arvil leaped on to the black mare's back, untied her reins, and seized the reins of the pinto. The black horse did not throw him, but the pinto whinnied a protest as he led her away.

'We must ride swiftly,' he said. 'By the time they have descended the slope, we must be far from here. I think they will go to the shrine to see to their companions first, and it will be hard for them to track us when it's dark.'

He rode away from the shrine, the pinto at his side, and then turned east, I dug my heels into Flame's sides and followed him.

A grassy plain stretched before us, and I was thankful that the flat land offered few places for others to hide. The moon was only a sliver in the sky. We galloped on through the high grass, until the horses were panting with their efforts, then slowed to a trot.

Arvil kept glancing behind us, but there was no sign of horsemen. We came to a grove of trees, circled it, and continued to ride east. A cold night breeze bathed my hot, flushed face; my fear made me alert. I was thinking of how the man in the shrine had pawed at me, of how his breath stank, of his maddened, red eyes. My gorge rose, nearly choking me.

It was still night when we reined in the horses and slowed them to a walk. Arvil lifted his head as he surveyed the land, then turned south toward a dip in the ground.

A small stream wound its way between gently sloping banks. We slid off the horses and rubbed them down with Arvil's old coat before allowing them to drink. Arvil gulped from a waterskin, then filled the other skins with fresh water. I knelt on the rocky bank, drank from cupped hands, and washed my face, wishing that I had a piece of soap.

'We shall not eat tonight,' he said, 'but will save what we have until we need it.' My stomach ached; I tried to ignore its rumblings. 'At least our horses will have their fill.'

We led the mares across the stream and let them graze. The pinto often seemed about to bolt and neighed when we came too near. I doubted she would let either of us ride her, but she seemed willing enough to be led.

We mounted after the horses had eaten; Arvil took the pinto's reins. 'Those horsemen will have to rest, too,' he said. 'Let us hope they lose our trail here and do not know if we have gone north or south.'

I followed him along the bank, seeing that Flame's hooves trod only on the rocks or in water instead of on ground where a trail could be left. From time to time, we stopped to conceal any droppings the horses made. I told myself that any horsemen who might follow us could not pursue us indefinitely, and that they might fear coming after us when they found their dead companions.

Soon the stream, which had grown a bit wider, was bending

east. Arvil turned. 'Watch carefully,' he said. 'Where there is water, there may be men, although, on this land, we will see them from afar.'

In spite of his warnings, by dawn we had seen no men. The stream twisted north; we left it and rode swiftly toward the east. Occasionally, I looked back, but there was no sign of our pursuers.

The plain was a sea of grass under a wide sky; I had never seen land so flat. The plain seemed endless. Although any dangers this land held could be seen at a distance, it frightened me even more than the forest and hills I had travelled through with my mother. No shield protected me from the sky, and a bitter wind nipped at my face. There was no place where I could hide from the openness, and my fear of the outside nearly overwhelmed me. I reined Flame in and pressed my cheek against her mane.

Arvil turned back and came to my side. 'What is it?' he asked. I shook my head, unable to explain. 'Have courage, Birana.'

I nodded mutely.

'When we are able to stop for a time, I will show you some ways to defend yourself. You won't be so fearful then.'

'I'll never be able to fight.'

'I have seen weaker men able to fell those who are stronger, for it isn't only strength that matters in a fight. And you have shown some courage already.'

Somehow his words heartened me, and I was able to ride on.

I had always been more active than many girls. My mother had admired physical strength more than most. She had enjoyed riding the horses and ponies in the stables by our parks, and I learned to ride so that she would spend some of those moments with me. I was trained to run and almost always won my races with other girls. I learned ways of strengthening my upper body and was stronger than many of those I knew. I hoped to win Yvara's affection by being a vigorous girl she could admire; later, I pursued physical activity for its own sake, as a respite from my studies. Yet in Arvil's world, I was little stronger than a boy not long out of a city.

Arvil's back straightened. To the north, barely visible against the horizon, I could see what looked like a few tents. 'A camp,' Arvil said, 'but I see no horses. Those men will not follow us.'

In a while, the camp was hidden from us. By noon, I caught the gleam of a shrine's dome in the south; Arvil saw me look toward it. 'We cannot stop there,' he said.

'I know.' I had no desire to enter a shrine again.

'The evil men following us could surprise us there.'

'We've seen no sign of them yet.'

'I have a feeling about them,' he said. 'They will lose our trail at the stream, but, if they're determined, they can find it again. I do not think they have turned away yet. If they follow us long enough, they will see that we've joined no band and will know that we have none. That is likely to fire their anger against us.' He leaned forward as we began to gallop.

'We cannot run from them for ever,' I shouted above the sound of our horses' hooves.

'There is no way we can stand against them out here. We must wait for such a chance.'

I pressed my lips together. What chance could we possibly have? I looked up then at a gleam in the southern sky and forgot my fear of our pursuers.

A golden globe was flying toward us from the south. I nearly screamed, then lashed at Flame with my reins.

'Stop!' Arvil cried to me.

'A ship!'

'You must stop! We cannot hide from it now.'

I pulled on Flame's reins. The pinto neighed as the hum of the ship grew audible. It was moving in our direction; though it was high overhead, its humming sound seemed to pound against my ears.

'Get off your horse,' Arvil said. I slid off, still holding the reins, and pulled my hood more closely about my face. My legs were shaking. Arvil covered his head. 'Kneel, and honour the Lady. If it is coming for you, there is nothing we can do, but if they still believe you dead, they will see only two men.'

I knelt and bowed my head, expecting the ship's weapons to strike us at any moment. I did not look at the ship closely and could not tell whether it carried passengers or was only a ship sent out to gather images.

When I travelled with others in such a ship to Devva, I had been fearful that the ship might have to make an emergency landing, although we knew men were not likely to attack us and the ship could protect us. We had laughed with relief when we reached Devva; we had dreaded the trip back. I thought of the passengers that might be overhead and wondered what they were thinking as they looked down at us.

The hum of the ship was fading. I looked up and saw it moving north-west, perhaps on its way to my own city.

'We can ride on now,' Arvil said.

I covered my eyes and wept. 'Birana, we are safe.' He touched my shoulder, I pulled away violently. 'What's wrong?'

'I am remembering,' I managed to say. I wiped my face and stood up. 'I can't go on. You'll have a better chance without me, and I won't live long out here.'

'We have lived this long. It would not have been better for me to be without you in Hecate's shrine.'

'I can't . . .'

'You must steady yourself.' He touched the back of my hand lightly. 'I cannot let you die.'

'Of course you can't,' I said bitterly. 'There are too many questions you want me to answer.'

'It is not only because of the questions.'

I drew away from him and mounted Flame, telling myself that I must not give up hope of finding a refuge. But my hopes were fading.

In the afternoon, we spied a herd of shaggy beasts in the north-east. Arvil gazed toward them longingly as we circled around the herd; I knew he was thinking of meat.

Our horses had slowed to a walk. 'Could you hunt one of those?' I asked.

'On this horse, with my spear – perhaps, but I have not hunted in such a way before. I would have to separate one from the herd, butcher and skin the animal, and by then the men following us would be closer.'

'But we haven't seen a sign of them. They might have given up already.'

'We cannot be sure of that.'

Except for the one band we had glimpsed from a distance, we had seen no other men. The farther we rode from regions where cities stood, the fewer men we were likely to find. Men would have no boys to bring into their bands if they dwelled too far from shrines and the cities that might summon the men. I would be safer from men the farther east we went, but there would also be fewer who could tell me of any refuge that might exist.

'It seems few men live here,' Arvil said, apparently pondering similar thoughts. 'I wonder if more may seek these lands out. Long ago, I was told, past members of my first band did not live in the north but elsewhere. Other bands grew numerous in those lands, and so my band sought new territory. Wanderer said that in the south, where the weather makes life easier, there are more bands than Earth can support, and more fighting.'

'Wanderer has travelled,' I said.

'Yes, and farther than any man I have met.'

'Did he ever hear a story of a place, a place outside the cities, far from them, where others of my kind might have been seen, a place where they might live?'

Arvil frowned as he turned toward me. 'Could there be such a place?'

'There have been others who were expelled from the cities. I can't believe they all died. Some might have found a way to survive.'

'Wanderer never told a tale about such a place,' he said. 'He did tell one, when I first met him and Shadow, about a man who lived in a shrine and whose body was changed to a woman's form.' His mouth twisted. 'Wanderer's tales were not always filled with truth.'

I tried not to feel disappointed. Wanderer, after all, would have roamed in lands where men lived.

'I do not recall that Wanderer spoke of the east,' Arvil continued. 'He didn't know what may lie here. Is that what you seek, Birana – a place where others of your kind live?'

'If there is such a place.'

'If that's what you seek, I would have you find it. But you would be with your own kind then. You'd have no need of me.'

'There may be men among them,' I said. 'They may have found a way to live together.' Such women might have mastered the means to inseminate themselves, as they would have to do to keep their refuge alive, to have daughters to care for them when they grew old and sons to learn from any men who had aided them. I refused to dwell on how, without mindspeakers and the images used to rouse men, these women might gather the men's seed.

'If they live together,' Arvil said, 'then they would make the men their worshippers, as those in the enclaves do. It would give me joy to know you are safe, but, among your own kind, I would be nothing to you.'

'It isn't so,' I replied. 'You are my friend now. You're probably the only true friend I have.'

I spoke these words only out of pity for him, and because I feared his darker moods, but his eyes glowed as he looked at me. 'Is that so, Birana? Do you call me your friend?'

I thought of Laissa, no longer my friend. 'Yes, Arvil. You are my friend.'

His chest swelled under his coat; his hood fell back, exposing his blond hair, as he gazed up at the sky. 'I am your friend,' he said, as if those words were filled with a greater significance.

By evening, we came to a small rise in the land, where a few slender trees grew, and stopped there. The horses grazed, and we gave them water from our skins, holding the liquid in our cupped hands as they lapped. 'Star,' Arvil said as the black horse drank from his palms.

'What did you say?'

'Star. She should have a name, and her white marking makes me think of a star.'

'And what shall we call the pinto?'

'Perhaps you can name her.'

The pinto gazed at me balefully as she drank. She was learning to tolerate us, but neither of us had ridden her. Her hide was marked by thin scars. I supposed the man who had once ridden her had lashed her often, but he had not been able to quell her spirit. 'Wild Spirit,' I said. 'That's what I'd call her.'

'It suits her.'

When the horses had grazed, we secured their reins to the trees. I was about to take some food from our packs when Arvil shook his head. We had heard the twittering of birds in the bough above; Arvil climbed up one tree, disappeared in the branches, then dropped down, holding out five small birds' eggs. I forced myself to choke down two raw eggs, while he ate his with relish; the dried meat could be saved for another day.

Arvil kept watch as I rested, then woke me. I sat up, surprised at how soundly I had slept; I was used to sleeping on the ground by then but ached from our long ride. A howl suddenly broke the silence, and I started.

'Wolves,' he said. 'If they come too near, the horses will warn us.' He led me out from under the trees, then pointed up at a group of stars in the east. 'When those stars are above the trees, you must wake me. Wake me also if you see anything move on the land.'

'What if . . .'

He knew what I was going to ask. 'They would still be far behind us, and they will have to stop as well. I shall not rest long.' He gazed at the stars. 'I have been told that the stars are fires so far from us that, if we could walk to them, it would take the lifetimes of many men to reach them.'

'It's true. Long ago, we once dreamed of travelling to them.'

'But how could they be reached if they are so far away?'

'We could have built ships able to travel the distance. Such a ship would have to travel at a speed approaching the speed at which light moves, and then time for those on the ship would not pass as it would for those on Earth. A season might pass here while only a day passed on the ship – a lifetime could go by here while those travellers remained young.'

'The ship would have to be under a powerful spell.'

'You might put it that way. Such a spell is possible.' I did not know how I could ever explain what we understood of the physics of interstellar travel to him.

'It is said that the stars are camp fires set by the Lady for the spirits of men in the next world. If the souls of those in the ship entered that world, they could not return to this one.'

'They are not fires, Arvil. They are suns, like the one you see in the sky.

'They are suns?' he asked.

'Yes. They seem so small because they are far away. Some are much larger than our sun, and our sun itself is so large that you could fit many Earths inside it, hundreds upon hundreds of Earths.'

He turned toward me, rubbing at his chin as he considered this. 'I see. A thing far away seems small and then becomes larger as a man moves closer to it. If this is true about the stars, that each is a sun, they must be even more distant than I can grasp.' He clutched at my sleeve. 'And if they are suns, do they shine upon other Earths?'

His imaginative leap startled me. 'There are other worlds – that we know. But we know little about what they are like. We might have tried to reach them, or to communicate with them, for just as it is possible for my kind to speak with others in distant parts of Earth, it's possible to find a way to speak to the stars. Yet we have not done so. In ancient times, it was because we had to save what had survived and rebuild. Now, we lack the will, perhaps because we're afraid of what might be there, and of how it might change us.'

'Other suns.' He lifted his head again. 'Other Earths. I don't know how this can be, but it gives me joy to think of them. Perhaps men live at peace there. If I had the magic of such a ship as you spoke of, I would wish to see those other Earths.'

'Arvil, you must rest now.'

'This is a wondrous truth you have told me.' He reluctantly settled down under the trees as I paced along the rise, trying to stay awake, but still tired even after my rest.

Arvil's thoughts had surprised me. I had seen that men

possessed more reason than I had once believed. Wanderer and Shadow had shown signs of intelligence, and Wise Soul had been a reflective man, but Arvil could listen to me and then reason to what I had not told him. I wondered how many other men might be as he was. I was wrestling with my thoughts, beginning to see the enormity of the evil we had committed in order to bring about the Rebirth.

I had worried over how much to tell Arvil in answer to his questions. Now I feared that he might deduce the answers with only a few hints from me, and I had seen how angry he became with me before. Whatever qualities he might possess, he was still a man and had grown up in a violent world. If I angered him enough, he could, without intending to, hurt me badly.

The wolves howled again; they seemed to be farther away. I felt how alone I was. I had thought of myself as lonely during the past years in the city, when it seemed that one old friend after another found excuses not to spend time with me. I had been living alone before my expulsion, been kept in a room by myself while the Council decided my fate, but that loneliness could not match what I felt as I stood under the stars that night.

I stopped pacing and looked down at Arvil, my only friend. His face was hidden in the darkness. He sighed once, and I wondered what he was seeing in his dreams.

ARVIL

The lady was drifting toward me, but I could not see her face. My arms encircled Her waist as I sought to join myself to Her. Birana's face looked up at me. I was suddenly aware of some purpose to the Lady's blessing, something more than the need to bind men more closely to Her, and yet I could not grasp it.

'Arvil,' She said. I gripped Her, but Her body became as elusive as smoke. 'Arvil.' She was melting away before I could satisfy my longing.

I opened my eyes. 'Arvil,' the dark form above me said, 'you must wake now.'

I sat up, rubbed my eyes, then got to my feet. The spell of my dream still held me. Without thinking, I pulled Birana to me and rested my cheek against her head.

She did not pull away, but her body was stiff, and I could feel her resisting my touch. Dismayed, I released her. 'I wanted only to hold you,' I said, 'as I might hold a loved friend. If you don't want my touch, then tell me rather than suffering it.'

'I'm afraid to anger you.'

'You anger me more in this way.'

'I anger you eventually whatever I say or do.'

'In my dream,' I said, 'a spirit-woman was with me, but she wore your face. She welcomed my touch, but then . . .'

'You mustn't think of that. I can't endure your embrace. You don't know what it might lead to, what the consequences could be.' She covered her mouth as if afraid to say more.

'Then I shall try not to touch you again,' I said angrily, 'but the spell you have cast on me is a strong one.'

I went among the trees then to relieve myself but still ached even after my water had flowed. My embrace, if she welcomed it, could lead only to blessings, and her kind had made men want them.

'I have no spell on you,' she said as I came toward her. Her head was bowed, and she had folded her arms across her chest as though protecting herself. 'I understand your feelings. I know that men of your band sometimes joined together at night. You wouldn't feel the same way if you had a man to join with – it's only that you lack other companions.'

She was wrong. Her spell was stronger than a man's would have been, for she evoked thoughts of blessings.

'I am not a man who cannot control his needs,' I said firmly. 'There are those who go to boys and prefer them to other men, even when the boy is unwilling, and there are boys who will offer themselves for an extra piece of meat or a gift of some kind.' I thought of Cor, who had given himself to the Wolf when the Wolf was Headman, and then to Geab. I had despised him for it, for I had known he did not go to those men out of love or respect.

'However great my need was,' I continued, 'I preferred to satisfy it alone rather than go to a boy I might overcome or a man I didn't like, for there is no pleasure in that for me. I was happy to grow strong enough to resist those I did not want, and when the Lady began to bless me, it was that I longed for most. I will not touch you again.' In spite of my words, I knew how hard it would be to keep that promise.

'Was Tal . . .' She cleared her throat, and I sensed how hard it was for her to speak his name. 'Was he one you loved in that way?'

I was shocked. 'No guardian would seek pleasures with his charge. I don't think even the men who attacked us would stoop to that, unless in their madness they embrace all evil.'

'Was there anyone you loved before?'

'There were some I did not refuse, but love`...' I paused. 'I think that love might have grown between me and Shadow, but I didn't wish to seek him out until he became a man.' It was hard for me to speak of my feelings for Shadow, now that he was lost to me, and yet his soul had not drawn me as much as Birana's. 'Were there any you loved?'

'Few sought me out. There was no one who loved me.'

I found that hard to believe. How could others not have longed for her? 'What about the one who was with you, the one we buried? Did she care for you?'

'She was my mother,' she replied, 'my guardian. A mother to me is like a guardian to you.'

'I know that is what a mother is. Our legends call Mary the Mother, for She is the aspect that is guardian to us all. Earth is our mother, for we're created from Earth's dust.' Something in my words reminded me of my dream, where my thoughts had seemed slippery and out of reach. 'The Mother brings life into the world.'

'Arvil, we must go before it grows light.'

Suddenly, I saw a great truth. Men were called to enclaves, and sometimes they were given boys. The creatures of the Earth, male and female, joined, and young ones came into being. I had always known this, but had never thought of the Lady's aspects as creatures like them. From Birana, I had learned that her kind had bodies of flesh and bone, as we did. Now I saw that the spirit-women might join with men to create boys. I did not know how it was possible, but their magic was powerful.

Then another thought came to me. It was not only boys they created, but those of their own kind, for animals brought both female and male into the world. Did Birana's kind need us for that as well? Was that what she had meant when she said that men were needed?

All of this came to me in an instant. I groaned and nearly fell to the ground. 'What is wrong?' Birana cried as she stepped toward me.

'I see a truth you didn't tell me. I know why men are called. It is from our joining with the spirit-women that boys come, and perhaps young ones of your own kind as well, unless you have other magic for that. Is this so?'

She sank toward the ground. 'It is.'

I clenched my fists as I glared down at her. 'So that is the purpose for which men live.' I had thought that knowing there was some purpose to our lives would ease my mind, but this knowledge chilled me.

'I didn't know how I would tell that truth to you,' she said. 'From your seed, that which we take from you, others, male and female, are created. You don't have the power by yourselves to bring more of your kind into existence.'

'You need us and make us long for you. What fools men are. If we did not go to the enclaves, we would have no more boys, but perhaps there would be no more of your kind. If men wanted to punish you for what you have done, we could travel to your enclaves no more.'

'You would only bring about the end of your own kind. We have enough of your seed to survive, or could find other ways.' She spoke words then that I did not understand, but somehow I saw that seed from many men was more desired than seed from only a few. 'We might become less adaptable, less varied,' she said, 'but we would live.'

I wanted to strike her and through her strike out at all of her kind. We were not called to be blessed, but to have part of ourselves stolen from us.

'You have come to see the truth,' Birana went on. 'I dreaded knowing I might have to tell it to you, but you were able to see it for yourself. Other men might see it as well, perhaps not so quickly, but in time, if we didn't take so much trouble to hide it.'

I pulled her up roughly by her coat. She put up her hands, and I could not bring myself to strike. 'The smallest creatures of Earth are treated more kindly than we,' I said, 'for although their females rule the males, they allow the males to dwell among them.'

'Arvil, I . . .'

'Do not speak to me now.'

The sky was beginning to grow grey in the east. I went to Star, freed her reins, and mounted.

My mind cleared at last while we rode, although my world was becoming more merciless with every truth I learned.

The plain was giving way to rolling land, and as our horses carried us over a small rise, I saw the dome of a shrine to the south-east. Sunlight danced on a stream flowing past the shrine, and a man was standing near the water.

'We must go to that shrine,' I said as I reined in my horse. 'We may be able to learn something of this land from that man.' I looked back toward the west. I did not expect to spy our pursuers and did not see them. But a man knows when he is being hunted, and I seemed to sense them following our trail.

'I'm afraid to enter that place,' she said.

'We need not fear attack there. What happened to us never happened before and is unlikely to happen again. If this man is with others, we'll ride away and be far away before they can follow on foot, but I think he is alone.'

We rode quickly toward the shrine. Although I would not admit it to Birana, I could no longer look upon a shrine as a safe refuge. The attack upon us had marked me and given me new fears.

The man looked up, saw us, and ran inside. As we rode up to the entrance, I looked down at the ground but read no signs of other men.

We dismounted and rubbed down the horses quickly, then tethered them to a willow near the stream. 'Do not speak,' I said before we entered. 'I shall question this man, and then we'll ride on.'

We walked inside. The man was sitting near the altar, alone, under the image of Mary. He was clothed in a leather shirt and a vest of fur. His leggings were also of leather, and feathers hung from a cord of leather around his neck. His hair was black and fell past his shoulders, but he had no beard.

He looked up. 'A truce while we speak,' the young man said in the holy speech.

'There is always peace in Her presence,' I replied. We went to the altar and sat down in front of him. 'And I pray that there will be peace between us when we leave this place, as we must soon, for we will not stay in this land.'

His brown eyes narrowed. 'Do you pledge, before Her, that you will not harm me when I depart?'

'I promise that.'

'Then I shall promise the same, since I would not wish to battle against two who ride the beasts you left outside. I cannot speak for my band, for I am a boy, but we have always roamed this land freely without the need to fight others.'

'We wish no battle,' I said.

'Yet your presence here could mean that others might follow. I have not seen horsemen in this land, although a traveller has told us of how some men live with the horse.'

'We are alone,' I said. 'Our band has met misfortune, and we must now travel to another place.'

'The camp of my band lies to the south,' he said. 'I am called Ilf, but when I have been called, I'll return to my band and take a man's name. I had hoped the Lady would call me now, but although She sent me Her blessing, She did not call me to Her side.'

'I am Arvil, and I was called not long ago. The boy is called Spellweaver.' That name came to me easily now, for it was what Birana had become to me.

Ilf glanced at her, and she lowered her eyes. He turned back to me. 'Do you wish to pray and don the Lady's crown before we speak further?'

'We will pray, as we should,' I said quickly; I had forgotten to bow and kneel before Mary. My beliefs had been shaken, but I would have to observe their forms before other men. 'But the Lady has already blessed us at another shrine we passed. I think She will forgive us if we are grateful for that blessing and do not call to Her again.'

He peered sharply at me then. Clearly my words had aroused some suspicion in Ilf, but we had pledged a truce, and he said nothing. Birana and I knelt and went through the motions of silent prayer as it came to me how much I had lost my faith. My prayers had become empty words. The image of the Lady was only a lifeless form, placed there to deceive us.

'I must ask some questions of you,' I said as we sat down once more, 'and in return, I'll tell you something it would be well for you to know.'

He nodded. 'I will answer what I can.'

'We are travelling east. Can you tell me what is ahead, and what dangers may lie in wait for us?'

Ilf was silent for a moment. 'I can tell you only what I have heard from others, from the few who have travelled through our land. In three days, perhaps four, you will come to hills, and above these hills to the east you will see what we call the Barrier.'

Birana leaned forward, and seemed about to speak. I put my hand on her sleeve for a moment, then said, 'And what is this Barrier?'

'It is not a range of mountains, but neither is it a wall like that around the Lady's enclave. Some say that the Lady set it there long ago to keep us from straying too far from Her side. I have seen this Barrier once from afar, and the sight filled me with terror. Yet there are men who were brave enough to cross over it, and some men dwell on the other side, so it seems that the Lady will allow some to live there.'

'And what lies beyond?' I asked.

'It is said that there is a vast lake to the east of the hills and that many bands make their camps there.'

I frowned at that.

'There is little to fear from those bands, I am told,' Ilf continued. 'It is said that each band is at peace with those nearby, and that a traveller wishing them no harm will not be harmed by them. I was told that, long ago, a band went to that lake and struck at one camp, but men came from other camps to drive them off. By the lake, it seems, an attack on one camp is seen as an attack on all.'

'That is a remarkable thing,' I said.

'It isn't all that is strange by that lake. It is also said that, in times not long past, one of those bands was especially honoured by the Lady, and that She appeared to them in a vision.'

Birana started at those words. The young man's dark eyes met hers, and in Ilf's glance I saw lust for the one he thought of as a boy. It was natural for him to feel such an urge, and he would not seek to satisfy it in a shrine, yet his look enraged me. I felt as if he had already laid hands upon her.

I swallowed my rage. 'Can you tell me more of this vision?'

'I can tell you little. Of the few who cross the Barrier, even fewer return. I heard this tale of the Lady from one of who did return, but he had not seen the lake for himself. He heard the tale from another man.'

'And these lake bands do not harm travellers?'

'Not if they come in peace. It is even said that strangers can find a place with them.'

'And how far from here is this lake?' I said.

'I cannot say.'

'I don't know,' I said, 'if we'll seek out those bands, but I thank you for telling us of them.' Ilf would speak the truth in a shrine, but what he had said had been told to him by others and was not something he had seen for himself.

'What lies beyond the lake?' I asked.

'That land is unknown.' He glanced fearfully at the image of Mary. 'I don't know how this can be, but it is said that the Lady Herself is unknown there. It would not be wise to travel east of the lake. A man would be lost, without even the Lady to guide him. There may be demons there to rob him of his soul.'

'I thank you again for what you have told me,' I said. 'Now I must tell you something you should know. No more than three days ago, we stopped in a shrine to worship. Two men came there and violated it with unholiness – we were attacked before the altar.'

Ilf's mouth dropped open. 'Inside a shrine?'

'I am telling you the truth, as I must in this holy place. Those men had turned from the Lady and tried to do evil in Her shrine, but the Lady couldn't abide such unholiness. She lent us strength and we were able to take their lives. Those men have paid for their blasphemy, but others of their band may be pursuing us to seek revenge. They may come to this shrine and prey upon anyone who is here.'

Ilf reached for his spear and gripped it tightly. 'I had hoped to be called. I was to spend this day here in prayer and wearing the Lady's circlet.'

'It would be better for you to return to your band. I do not think they will turn aside, but if they come to your camp, you must not trust them. Any oath they might swear to your band will be a false one.'

'I didn't know such evil could exist, but you cannot be lying before Her.' Ilf picked up his pack and weapons and followed us outside.

'This is their garb.' I pointed at my sheepskin coat. 'Those men ride a horse, as do we. There will be no more than four or five of them. If you see them, you must prepare to fight. Do not treat with them; they will only be waiting for a chance to attack you. Do not let them get close – strike from a distance with arrows and wound the horses if you can. I can tell you no more and pray that those men do not seek out your band, but if they do, you must be prepared.'

He stepped back, wary of our horses, then took a piece of dried meat from his pack. 'Take this in return for your warning, Arvil. I have food enough, and you cannot stop to hunt if you are to escape.'

I gave him one of the dead men's knives in return. 'Farewell,' he said as he slipped it under his belt. 'I hope you find safety.'

'Farewell, Ilf.'

The young man ran off through the high grass as we refilled our skins and then led the horses to the stream to drink. Ilf, I thought, was one who might have become a friend. Had I been alone, I might have found a place with his band. I gazed at Birana as she knelt by the stream and drank from cupped hands.

'What can you tell me of this Barrier?' I asked.

She stood up. 'We call it the Ridge. Long ago, even before most of our cities were built, it was to be a great wall around the lands we left to the Goddess, but it was never completed. It may have been that some decided there was no need for it, or maybe the effort simply became too great. Two cities lie far to the south of the Ridge, and any men living this far north would have to travel some distance to reach them. My city's ships rarely fly beyond the Ridge.'

'Then we would be safer on the other side.'

'If we can cross the Ridge,' she said.

'If others have crossed it, we can find a way.' Ilf had spoken of bands by a lake, but I did not see how we could live among those men for long without revealing Birana's true nature. Yet he had also said that one band among them had seen the Lady appear. Could this be only a dream, or the sort of vision that had been visited upon Truthspeaker when he fell into a frenzy? Or could it mean that one like Birana had come among them?

'The refuge I seek may be at that lake, or not far from it,' she said.

'Don't raise your hopes too high,' I replied. 'Ilf told us only what others told him.'

'There's a chance.'

I did not object. It would be better for us to travel with some hope, however mistaken.

We stopped that night but did not rest for long. We ate some of our dried meat and rode on while it was still night. In the morning, we stopped once more near a few trees. I dismounted and secured Star.

'We mustn't stop now,' Birana said.

'We can spend some moments here,' I answered. 'I'll teach you how to use a sling.' It had come to me that it might be easier for her to master this weapon rather than the spear or the bow. 'Our enemies, if they follow, will still be far behind us.' The flatlands stretched far to the west, and yet I still saw no sign of pursuit. For a moment, I hoped that they had given up the chase, then turned to Birana. I did not want her helpless if those men found us, but did not speak that thought aloud.

We searched for stones as I told her which ones were best for hurling; then I showed her how to fit a stone inside the sling. 'You must hold the ends together,' I said, 'and whirl the sling this way so that the stone is held until you release it.' I whirled the sling and sent the stone against a tree trunk. 'Now you must try.'

At first, her stones fell from the sling before she could whirl it.

'You must whirl it with more force.' I demonstrated the sling again, then handed it to her. She bit her lip and tried once more. This time, she was able to send the stone a few paces from her feet.

I stepped back and watched as she hurled more stones. They did not strike at where she aimed, and a few still fell from the sling before she could release them, but she was gaining some control.

'Enough,' I said.

'I still can't hit anything.'

'That will come. You can practise later. You have done well enough for now.'

My praise brought a smile to her lips. We gathered up a few of the stones and continued on our way.

Ilf had said we would come to hills, and already the land to the east was not as flat. On the plain, we could see danger from a distance, while among hills, we could be surprised. We rode more slowly as I searched the ground for men's tracks.

In the evening, we stopped again so that Birana could try the sling. Her stones flew farther now although they still found no target. I sat on her sheepskin coat as she practised, watching her body move. Her small breasts lifted under her shirt as she swung her arm, and I imagined my hands upon them.

A half-moon lighted the sky that night. We rode on until I saw that Birana was growing weary. We came to a small slope where a few shrubs grew, and from where I could see much of the land below. 'You may rest for a little while,' I told her, 'but then we must go.'

She fell asleep quickly, pillowing her head on my old coat. I listened, as her breathing grew steady, then touched her hair lightly, so as not to awaken her. I wanted to lie at her side and feel her warmth against me. Instead, I stood up and paced until the tightness in my groin eased.

There was a torment in being with her, and I worried about how long I could endure it. I could overcome my longing during the day, but at night, when she slept, I had visions of her arms embracing me and of her lips touching mine as those of the spirit-woman had. I might have satisfied my need alone, but I feared that this would only fuel my desire for her. All that she had told me had not robbed me of my longing for her.

'Birana,' I whispered. She stirred in her sleep, as if hearing me, but her eyes remained closed.

We were soon among hills, and our journey was a slow one, for I needed to be alert to danger. As the sky grew lighter, I led us up one high hill so that I could see what lay around us.

These hills were green, and wild flowers had begun to bloom. A flock of birds below us suddenly rose toward the sky in a black cloud. I lifted my eyes toward them and then saw, on the horizon, that which Birana had called the Ridge, and my courage nearly failed me. It was a wall so vast that it dwarfed the one around Birana's enclave. I wondered how we could ever pass over it.

Birana lifted a hand to her lips as she gazed out at the Ridge. 'It doesn't seem to end,' I said.

'It was never completed. To get around it, we would have to go far to the north or south, but I know . . .' Her voice trailed off.

'It is another sign of the power of your kind.'

She shook her head. 'It's only a sign of how much we feared when we retreated from your world.'

I slept uneasily that night, and for only a short time. Birana practised with her sling before we mounted. I had cut away part of the ends to make the sling easier for her to use, and she dropped no stones this time before hurling them, but they did not travel as far. The sight of the Ridge seemed to have robbed her of her spirit.

As we rode east, the Ridge grew higher, and by morning, I could make out some of its features. What had seemed a wall from a distance now looked more like the side of a vast cliff. The Ridge, I saw, had been built of rock, and its surface was uneven, unlike the walls of enclaves. My hopes rose a little. On such a cliff, we might find footing.

Although we had allowed our horses to rest from time to time, I saw their weariness and feared to drive them too hard. They carried us slowly toward the Ridge while I searched for a way over it.

The cliff rose before us. I scanned the expanse quickly, then pointed south. 'Do you see?' I asked. Birana shook her head. 'There, in that place. It seems a traveller has marked the way.'

We rode toward where I had pointed. An arrow was lodged in the ground; I grabbed it and pulled it out. Perhaps a man some time ago had scouted this land and left a mark for his band. A few worn bones, those of a small creature, perhaps a hare, also lay there. I could imagine a man kneeling to pray before crossing the Ridge, offering the hare to the Lady, hoping She would allow him to pass. I scattered the bones with my foot.

I now saw a possible way up the Ridge, but we would have to lead the horses. I dismounted from Star and tied Wild Spirit's reins more securely to my pack.

I led the horses on to the rocks while Birana followed. I had to pause often to test my footing. Ground that seemed solid could be loosened as we trod upon it. I murmured to the horses as we climbed, trying to soothe them, urging them on gently. Once we were forced to creep north, unable to move higher for long moments until I saw a way up. I might have turned back, but there was no room for us to turn around, and we were forced to press on. A stone, loosened by Star's foot, fell, bringing down a shower of pebbles with it; I flattened myself against a wall of rock, then took several breaths before moving on again.

In this way we climbed, and as we moved higher on the Ridge, we found a wider passage among the rocks and firmer footing. I wondered how many feet had worn away this trail, how many men had come here, gazed at the Ridge, and then found the courage to cross.

I did not look up and refused to look down; I did not know that we were near the top until I saw that the passage ended between two sheets of rock. The way was narrow and steep, and I had to pull on Star's reins to urge her through the passage.

I was standing on a flat surface that ran to the north and south and far enough to the east that I could not see what lay on the other side. I bent down and ran my hand along this surface, which seemed like the substance of the enclave's wall. Birana's kind had set this barrier here, must have used some of the mightiest of their magic to build it, and then had abandoned it.

Birana led Flame on to the top of the Ridge. I stepped back to let her pass, then looked out at the land to the west. At first, I saw only the hills, and then movement caught my eye. I squinted. The tiny forms of horses and riders appeared for an instant, then disappeared into a hollow betweeen two hills.

I knew then what I would have to do.

I motioned to Birana and took her arm as she came up to me. 'Steady yourself,' I muttered.

'What is it?'

'Gather your courage and look below.'

I heard her cry out as the riders reappeared. 'Arvil!'

'They will be sure now that we have no band. They must have ridden their horses hard these past days to have come so far.' Their rage and their madness must have been great to have kept them on our trail.

Birana crouched down and hid her face. It had taken us much of the day to climb up, and our enemies would not reach the Ridge before evening. I wondered if they would chance climbing at night. They would see that we had found a way up. They had come this far; they would surely follow.

'Come with me,' I said. We led the horses toward the eastern side. Below lay more hills and the sparkling ribbon of a distant stream. Along this side of the Ridge, the way down seemed wider and less precarious, for the cliff was not as steep. 'Do you think you can lead the horses down alone?'

Her eyes widened. 'Won't you be with me?'

'You must listen. I can run, or I can make my stand here. I count only three of them, and I'll have high ground. We could end this pursuit here.'

'But, then why . . .'

'If you lead the horses down, you'll be safe below. I'll watch to see what they do. They may turn back, they may fear this Ridge, and then I can follow you. If they do not, they may still believe us gone, and I will have a chance to strike at them as they climb.'

'You might be hurt, Arvil. You might . . .' She looked away.

'If I fall, you will still have a chance to escape them. You can find another band to protect you when you reveal what you are.'

'No.' She lifted her eyes to me. 'I'd rather stay with you. I may not be able to fight, but I can't leave you to face them alone.' Perhaps she was thinking only that she would have little chance to find safety without me, but her words heartened me nonetheless.

I pointed to the south. 'Lead the horses away, then, and secure them farther from here on this Ridge. I don't want one of them to give us away.'

As she went off with the horses, I walked to the western side. The rocks at the top of the Ridge would conceal us from the men. I peered through the space between the rocks and saw a small boulder just below, along the passage.

I crept down, put my shoulder to this stone, and pushed it up until it blocked part of the space, then climbed over it. I hunkered down and began to test my bow, welcoming the feel of it in my hands. Birana came back to me, and I motioned her down.

She held out a hand as she seated herself. 'I brought you food.' I chewed at my meat while she nibbled at hers, then drank some of my water. 'What now?'

'We wait, and pray that they turn back.'

*

This waiting was hard for her. She said nothing, but her hands fluttered from time to time, and her lips were raw and bleeding as she bit at them. Once, I reached for her hand and rubbed my fingers against the calluses on her palm. Her hand was cold.

I leaned my back against the rock, and the knowledge that I would need to be alert later was enough to allow me to sleep. I awoke when the sun was setting. Birana was gazing over the boulder, keeping her head low.

The men were below; they had come to the place where we had begun our ascent. As they dismounted, I saw the legs of one horse give way. Its rider lashed at the beast until it got to its feet. They had driven their horses too hard. Perhaps they would have to rest.

One man gestured with his arms, then pointed at the Ridge. I could guess what he was saying. He would be telling his companions that they must press on, that they had gained on us, that from the top of the Ridge they could see where we had gone, that the moon would help to light their way. I did not move. One man raised his head. I was too far from him, and the light of the sun was too faint for him to see me, but he might suspect that we were lying in wait for his band. The men sat down as their horses grazed. They might wait us out, wait until we showed ourselves or gave some sign of our presence.

The sun had nearly set. One man stood up again. The others rose and began to lead the horses to the Ridge. They would not be starting their climb if they believed we were here.

Birana caught her breath. 'Stay low,' I whispered. 'I can do nothing until they are close. You must be still.'

A wind was blowing along the top of the Ridge. I hoped that the wind would not carry my arrows far from their mark. The moon would rise before they reached us. I would have to strike before they could see me clearly.

My mind grew calmer as we waited. I had the advantage of both high ground and surprise. 'When I have loosed an arrow,' I whispered, 'we shall both push this boulder down the side. Can you do that?'

She nodded. I wanted her safe, and yet I was happy she was with me.

The sun was gone and the half-moon beginning its climb before I heard the voices of the men, although I could not make out their words. I shrugged out of my coat and tested my bow again, then readied an arrow. Holding my bow at my side, I peered around the boulder, waiting to catch my first glimpse of them on the passage below.

At last, when it seemed that the entire night might pass before they reached us, I saw the first of the men. His hands were on the reins of his horse, his spear still tied to his back. He climbed until he was no more than a few paces below us. In one movement, I stood, aimed my bow, and loosed my arrow.

The arrow found the base of his neck. I saw him fall against the legs of his horse. I dropped down as we pushed against the boulder. As it rolled, it loosened other rocks, and I heard a scream as a man and a horse fell from the Ridge, bringing a shower of rocks and pebbles after them. The horse struck an outcropping and lay there senseless. The man disappeared. The horse nearest me scrambled for footing, then reared. Its legs flailed as I sent another arrow into its chest. The horse arched as it fell into the darkness.

One man remained. I heard him bellow his rage but could not see him. As I aimed in his direction, a cloud hid the moon. I released the arrow and heard the cracking of crumbling rock as a horse shrieked. Something had fallen, but I could not tell if it was the man or the horse I had struck.

Birana was on her feet, her back flat against the sheet of rock. She reached under her coat. I held my breath, afraid to move, unable to see.

He was suddenly before me, a shadow just below the gap in the rock. Before I could aim, he had hurled his spear. I leaped to one side to dodge his weapon and felt my head strike rock.

I have failed you, I thought. Darkness swallowed me as the surface rushed up to meet me.

BIRANA

Arvil had fallen. I could not tell if he still breathed. My terror nearly paralysed me. Somehow I pulled a stone from my pocket and placed it in my sling as the moon reappeared.

The man was already pulling an object from his belt as I whirled the sling and released the stone. For the first time, I found my target. The stone hit him in the chest, and I heard him grunt as he staggered back.

My stone did not have enough force to injure him badly; I had done little more than startle him for a moment. I saw him teeter as I groped helplessly for another stone, and then he lost his footing. He disappeared over the edge.

My legs gave way. I clawed at my sling, imagining that he would suddenly rise before me, come at me again. I tried to stand, but my legs would not hold me. At last I managed to crawl through the opening and peer over the edge.

He had fallen on to a ledge far below. His body was twisted sharply at the waist. I looked away and caught sight of another body; a horse lay near it. I retched, sick at the sight, heaving until my stomach was empty, shaken by the thought of how close death had been.

I remembered Arvil; I crawled to his side. Please don't be dead, I thought, please, not now. As I leaned over him, I saw his chest move, then felt his head. His skull was not fractured, but a bloody gash marked the spot where he had struck the rock.

I tore a strip of cloth from the edge of my shirt, then pulled out my waterskin. Arvil gave a moan and opened his eyes; he seemed stunned.

'You're safe now,' I said. 'It's all right, the men are gone. I must clean your wound.'

He moaned again as I bathed him, but said nothing. I wiped away the blood, then rinsed out the cloth and bound it around his head.

The wind had died a little, but the night was still cold. I reached for his coat and put it over him. When he closed his eyes, I ran toward the horses, took off a pack, and carried it back to him, kneeling as I slipped it gently under his head.

His eyes fluttered. 'Dizzy,' he murmured.

'You mustn't move. You have to rest.' I checked his wound again; the bleeding had stopped. 'I think you'll be all right.'

'That man . . . he . . .'

'He's dead.' Arvil tried to raise his head. 'Lie still,' I said.

'What happened?'

'I used my sling. Somehow, I hit him. He lost his balance and fell.' My hands began to shake. 'I was lucky. I might have missed. My stone didn't hit him hard. If he hadn't been standing where he was, I . . .'

'You did well.'

A new feeling was rising in me – a wild joy that I was alive and that our enemies were dead. This, I thought, is what a man would feel.

I lay down next to him, pillowing my head on my arm. I did not think then of what lay behind us, or what might lie ahead. Arvil was alive, and he would heal; he would be able to lead me to a refuge. I touched his arm gently as he slept, telling myself that it was only relief at having a protector still with me that gave me joy.

Arvil was able to move in the morning, although he seemed unsteady on his feet as we paced the top of the Ridge. 'Will you be able to walk down the other side?' I asked.

'I must. Our horses will need food, and there is none here for them.' Arvil raised a hand to his head.

'How do you feel?' I asked.

'My head throbs, and the ground seems to sway under me, but it will pass.'

'I can take the horses down alone, let them forage, tether them, and then come back for you.'

'No.'

'You were going to let me take them down alone before,' I said.

'We'll go together.' He turned and walked back to the western side of the Ridge, then leaned against me as he gazed at the bodies below. 'There may be food in those packs,' he said, 'and one horse could feed us for a long time.'

I shuddered. 'No.'

'It's foolish to leave so much, but it may also be foolish to climb down. We might bring more loose rock down on ourselves, and my wound has weakened me.'

Much as I wanted to get away from the Ridge, I was concerned. 'You should rest.'

'I'll rest for a few moments, and then we will descend.'

He sat down while I fetched the horses, then followed me to the eastern side. There was firmer footing here, and a wider way over and down the rock, but we had to stop often so that Arvil could rest. It took us until midday to travel down the Ridge; only then did I see the strain on Arvil's face, and the effort his descent had cost.

He stretched out on the ground, while I gave the horses some of our water and then stood with them as they nibbled at stalks of wild grain. I tethered them at a shrub before checking Arvil's wound. He caught my hand, as I was about to stand up, and pressed it against his cheek; I tensed.

'You have saved my life a second time,' he said.

I drew my hand from his. 'I had luck, that's all. I could have easily been killed. I may not be so fortunate again.' I had only led him into dangers he would otherwise not have faced.

'You have learned one way of fighting. You will learn more.'

I never wanted to fight again. I stood up. 'Can you ride?'

He got to his feet. 'I can ride. We have no one to outrun now and can go slowly.'

We mounted and began to ride east. When the Ridge was far behind us, I glanced back for a moment and nearly dropped my reins. A ship was flying high over the Ridge, moving from south to north. I told myself it could not be searching for me. Any passengers it carried might look at the bodies we had left there and see only another example of the cruelty and barbarism of men. I watched the ship pass and felt dread and regret as I thought of my city.

We came to a stream by dusk. Arvil, who had seen no sign of men in the region around us, felt safe in building a fire. I collected the dead wood, but Arvil refused to light the fire for me; he wanted to see what I had learned. I struck sparks from my flints on to tinder and tried to fan the flames into a blaze. By the time I was able to start the fire, it was nearly night.

Arvil felt well enough to gather cress and berries, which we ate with a little dried meat. After our meal, we stretched out on the ground, the banked fire between us. 'It is said,' he murmured, 'that the Earth is round, like the moon.'

'That's true.'

'If we rode for many, many days, then we would come in time to the place where we began our journey.'

'If we could ride so far,' I said, 'but we couldn't. If we kept going east, eventually we'd reach the ocean, a body of water so wide that you cannot see what lies beyond it.'

'What is on the other side, Birana?'

'More land. Some is wooded; some is desert. On one body of land live animals you've never seen here – giants with tusks and long trunks, and creatures with necks so long they can nibble at the tops of trees. And in the centres of those lands, there are other cities, and men who are called to them.'

'And are those men like us?'

'They live much as you do.'

'I wonder what stories they would tell.'

I propped myself up on one elbow and gazed across the fire at him. 'You wouldn't understand their stories. Their languages are different from yours.'

'We could talk in the holy speech.'

'Even what you call the holy speech is different there,' I said.

'But those women's ways are the same as ours. Their speech may be different, and the Lady has other names, but we follow the same customs. The Lady rules there, as She does here. Long after the Destruction, we found ways to communicate with those in other regions of Earth, and eventually all women came to see what we had to do to bring about the Re-birth. It was women who swore then that there would be peace. There were men even then, when much of the world was in ruins, who would have continued their battles with other men. It was best that they have only spears and arrows for their wars.'

He got to his feet. 'My head is clearer now,' he said. 'I shall keep watch while you sleep.'

I closed my eyes as he stood guard, but even in my dreams, I seemed to sense his eyes on me as I slept.

The next days of our journey passed with no sight of men. Arvil captured two rabbits; from their skins, he fashioned foot-coverings for me to wear inside my boots. My socks were worn and full of holes by then; I was about to dispose of them, but washed them and put them inside my pack instead. I might have need of the cloth.

He asked me few questions about the city as we rode, and that eased me; perhaps his curiosity had already been satisfied. The peacefulness of this part of our journey, the knowledge that our enemies could no longer harm us, and Arvil's calm should have reassured me, and yet I worried. I had believed myself safe once before, with Arvil's band; their camp had not been a haven for long.

The cool but sunny weather did not last. One morning, the sky was red in the east as the sun rose; the light was soon hidden by heavy clouds. By afternoon, it began to rain. I huddled against Flame, miserable in my wet clothes.

There were more trees on the land, and forest ahead, and we were able to escape much of the rain as we rode on under tall pines. Arvil, however, seemed more fearful as he looked restlessly around at the trees. Without the sun's light, the forest seemed nearly as dark as night; we could not know what the trees hid. Arvil stared at the ground as our horses walked on slowly.

Finally he reined in Star. 'We are lost,' he said. 'I see no trail and do not know this land. I cannot even tell if we are still going east.' He pointed. 'Look there. It seems we have met our own trail once more.'

I had forgotten my compass. I reached toward my neck and

pulled out the chain, angry at my carelessness. I was growing too dependent on Arvil, had too easily allowed him to lead. I peered at the needle. 'We've been going south,' I said, then pointed east. 'We must go this way.'

He leaned toward me. 'What is that?'

'A compass. It can show you which way you're going.'

'It is not used only to cast spells?'

'No. You see, this needle always points north. These markings are the different directions.'

He gazed at the compass's face. 'So you have brought some magic with you. Will that magic stay with you out here?'

I tried to explain how the compass worked but was not sure how much he understood. Magnetism, to Arvil, was magic or a spirit that directed the needle. I continued to guide us with the compass until it became too dark to see its face.

We spent that night under a tree, with our horses tied nearby. I could not sleep easily; the mournful whistling of the wind in the pines kept entering my dreams.

The rain stopped by morning. The dark forest was filled with green light, and the weather had grown so warm that I longed to take off my coat. Arvil was alert, refusing to speak, starting at the slightest sound. Once, we heard a shriek in the distance, and Flame's nostrils flared at the sound.

'A cat,' Arvil said; I tensed. 'It will avoid us, unless it has young and feels its cubs threatened.' His words only increased my fear.

It was easy to lose track of time in the forest. Only the increased darkness told me that it was night. We had eaten the last of the food in our packs and had no food before we slept. In the morning, Arvil gathered a few green sprouts and mushrooms before we moved on.

I was still hungry, and tired as well; my clothes were dirty and the heavy coat made me sweat. I itched and needed to wash, but complained of none of these things. I imagined that here, in this strange land, Arvil was thinking of his old band and the lands he knew, of the life he had given up for me. What did he have in return? Only the loss of the beliefs that had made his life easier to bear.

We came to the bank of a stream. I was about to dismount and get water when a golden gleam caught my attention. A shrine, almost hidden by the trees, stood on the other side of the stream. I lifted a hand to my mouth.

'It's all right,' Arvil said. 'Those who did evil in shrines are dead. We'll be safe.'

We let the horses drink before crossing to the shrine. Arvil surveyed the ground carefully. 'It seems no men have come here for some time,' he said, 'but some may travel here in this season.'

This shrine was smaller than those I had seen earlier, its surface more worn, its dome more tarnished. I wondered if anyone still came here. We were far from any city, nearer land we had abandoned long ago.

We tied the horses to trees and sat down in the small clearing around the shrine, letting the sun warm us. 'We need food,' Arvil said. 'I must hunt.'

'But if men come while you are gone . . .'

'They will not harm you here. You have heard me speak and know what you should say. Birana, we don't know how far we will have to ride, or what meat will be there for us. We can rest here for a time and take meat with us. We must use the chance. If I cannot hunt, we should kill one of these horses.' He looked at Wild Spirit.

'Not the horses,' I said quickly.

His lips formed a half-smile. 'Would you starve before you would eat of a horse?' He shrugged. 'It is true that we might have need of that horse later. I'll let it live – for now.'

He explained to me that much of what meat he found would have to be smoked and dried, then set me to work gathering long pieces of wood that could form poles. While I set the poles in the ground, Arvil picked up his weapons and walked away along the stream; he was soon hidden by the trees. With a wide, flat stone, I dug out a pit for our fire, then set stones and rocks around it. It was arduous work, but I welcomed the effort. It was something to do, work that made me of some use to him.

I strolled away from the shrine, looking for firewood. I had my compass but kept the stream in sight. I broke pieces of dead wood with my foot, made bundles, and carried the wood back to the shrine, moving a bit further into the forest each time. The song of a bird delighted me; the scampering of a squirrel across my path made me smile. There was some beauty in Arvil's world, a beauty lost to the city, a beauty its tended parks could not match.

Suddenly I heard a snarl and saw a patch of yellowish fur. I dropped the wood I was holding as my eyes met those of a large cat. I hadn't seen it before, had not heard it approach. The cat was no more than ten or twelve paces from me; it crouched and snarled at me. I froze, afraid to move, fearing that, if I reached for my sling, the cat would leap. It glared at me, seeming to sense my fear.

I stared at it a long time as my heart pounded, then chanced a step back. The cat crouched lower, about to leap. I could not run, would find no safety in a tree. Twigs crackled behind the cat. It turned its head away from me. At that moment, a spear flew and embedded itself in the cat's side.

I heard the animal screech, and then Arvil was upon it, stabbing with his knife. He released the cat as he stood up. 'Why are you here?' he said angrily.

'I was gathering wood . . . I only . . .'

'You didn't have to come this far. If you cannot be alert to danger, it's better for you to keep to a safer place.' He knelt by the dead cat. 'We cannot eat its meat, but I will take the hide.' He gestured with his head. 'The game I have found lies there. You must get it back to the shrine.'

A few paces from the cat, I found the carcass of a small deer. I could not lift it; at last I began to drag it forward by the legs. The effort soon made me pant. I wanted to fetch one of the horses but could not lift the deer to a horse's back alone.

My back ached by the time I reached our campsite. I dragged the carcass toward the poles, then collapsed beside it, exhausted.

Arvil finally emerged from the trees and threw the cat's fur down at my side. 'When you walk in a wood,' he said, 'you must not be careless. You should have been listening and had your sling ready when you first glimpsed it.'

I refused to speak. The beauty of the wood had entranced me; I had forgotten the dangers.

'It is good that I found you,' he said more gently. 'It would have grieved me greatly if you had been harmed.' I sat up. 'You must light the fire and gather more wood, but do not roam far this time.'

He began to skin the deer while I struggled with my flints. I nursed a spark into a flame and fanned it with my hands until a large fire blazed; then I collected more wood while Arvil butchered his game. 'We need more wood,' he muttered as he worked. 'This fire must burn for a time.'

He cut thin strips of leather, bound them to the poles near the fire, then draped thin pieces of meat over them. It was night by the time he had finished his labours. He had cut off two large pieces of meat for us, which were roasting on skewers of green wood. I had thought I would be too tired to eat, but the smell of the meat revived me. Once, I would have turned from it in disgust; now my mouth watered.

We ate until we were full. When I yawned, Arvil said, 'You must go to sleep now. I'll feed the fire. We must keep it going – that meat will draw other creatures.'

I might have gone into the shrine but stretched out on the ground, not wanting to leave his side. I did not dwell long on that thought before falling asleep.

I kept the fire going through the last part of the night; Arvil awoke at dawn. He went to collect more wood, then gathered cress from the bank of the stream. As we ate, he lifted his hand to his head for a moment.

'Are you well?' I asked.

'My head still pains me a little.'

Concerned, I peered at his wound. He had healed, but the injury must have been greater than he would admit. 'How much does it hurt?'

'It lessens. It grows no worse.'

I sighed. 'You have to conserve your strength while we're here. You'll need it when we go on.'

'We have food. I'll be able to rest.' He gave me a sidelong glance. 'Is it my well-being that concerns you, or is it only that you need my help to get to the safe place you are hoping to find?'

My eyes met his. 'I need your help, but even if I didn't, I would be sad if I lost your companionship.' I had intended to say that only to ease his feelings but, to my surprise, found that my words were sincere. 'On the Ridge, when I thought you might be dead, I grieved, and not just because I thought I had lost a protector.'

He reached for my hand. I let him hold it, fearing that I had said too much. 'My soul longs for you,' he said. 'Does yours begin to long for mine?'

I slipped my hand from his. 'I long for a friend, that's all.'

'Two friends can share love.'

I stood up quickly and went to the shrine's entrance. The door opened and I retreated inside. The shrine seemed crowded and cramped; only five couches stood near the wall, and the fabric covering them was worn and shiny. An image of Hecate stood near the altar; I sat down on the couch in front of it. For the first time since I had met Arvil, I had accepted his touch without wanting to pull away; I had wanted my hand in his, and that frightened me.

His footsteps sounded behind me as he came up to the altar.

He gazed up at the image for a while, then turned to face me. 'I have a question, Birana. Why did the spirit-women choose Tal as my guardian?'

'It wasn't the spirit-women who chose him. A woman now living would have chosen him. Those who spoke to you must have chosen him.'

'Why was Tal chosen, and not another?'

'It was thought that he could best care for you.' His eyes narrowed; I would have to say more and dreaded saying it. 'I must explain something to you.' I looked past him at the altar. 'It isn't the spirit-women themselves who bring boys into the world. Those living in the city do that.'

'I thought it must be so, now that I know you have bodies of flesh, but you must tell me how.'

My cheeks burned. 'Men are summoned to the wall, and their seed is taken from them while spirit-women . . .' I bowed my head, wanting to hide my face. 'A woman then takes the seed of a man and combines it with her own, and carries the child that results inside her until it's ready to be born – to come out of her body. When children are born, they're small and unable to care for themselves, so all of them, boys and girls alike, those of your kind and mine, stay with their mothers in a city. When a boy is old enough, he is sent outside with a man as a guardian. All his memories of the city are taken from him so that he'll be able to adapt more easily to his new life.'

Arvil said, 'Memories are taken from him so that he won't know the truth.'

'That is part of it as well.' I stared at my folded hands. 'The girls stay, and the boys are sent out.'

'And both the girls and the boys enter life in the same way?'

I nodded.

'Then a boy and a girl can come from the same woman's body and grow up together, but the female remains in your world while the male is sent from it.' His voice was low, but I sensed his rage.

'Animals must push their young from them when their offspring are old enough to survive. Even a girl must leave her mother's side eventually.'

'But she can live in her mother's world.' He paused. 'There is a man then who gave seed so that I could live, if what you say is so.'

'There is. I think . . .' I forced myself to lift my head. His lips were pressed tightly together; a muscle along his jaw tightened.

'You have a father, a man who gave his seed to the one who was your mother, and the seed of both gave you life. It is our custom, whenever possible, to give a boy to the man who was his father. You and Tal resembled each other strongly. I think he was your father. I think that Hasin, the boy you both brought out, also had Tal as a father.'

He took a step toward me. 'So Tal gave me life, and I brought him death. His seed is in me, his spirit, and this was hidden from me. What kind of sin have I done? He will haunt me even more!'

I held out my hand. He moved toward me, as if about to strike it away, then lowered his fist. 'Once,' he said, 'female and male lived together, our legends say. I believed you were holy, but there is no holiness in what you do. Your magic is only a shield to hide what you are. Except for my member and your female parts, we are the same, as the stallion and mare are, or the buck and the doe. You could allow us to remain among you if you willed it. You could dwell among us.' He stared at me for a long time, then strode from the shrine.

I was afraid to go to him. I ached; my breasts felt bruised and my abdomen had swelled a little. I thought at first that tension and fear had brought about the aches, and then realized that I would soon begin to menstruate. I had not bled at all since leaving the city and had worried that the rigors of my new life had affected my cycle, but I did not welcome this bleeding now. I remembered my happiness when I first experienced this sign of my womanhood; out here, it was only another sign of my weakness.

At last I rose and went outside. Arvil had rendered the deer's fat and stored it in entrails; he was now picking over what remained of the carcass for useful bones. He did not look up at me. I went to the edge of the clearing, collected more wood, and carried it back, setting the wood down near him. The day had grown warm; I took off my heavy coat and sat down on it.

'Arvil.'

He glanced at me. 'You must cover yourself. Someone may come and see what you are.'

'Arvil, listen to me. You ask me questions, and I answer them. You say you want to know the truth, but hearing it only angers you. I know how hard it is for you to bear, but you frighten me. If I anger you enough, you might injure me in your rage.'

He looked up sharply. 'I would not hurt you. I couldn't, even now.'

'I fear that you may without meaning to do so.'

'Never.' He sat back on his heels. 'Those garments you wear – you must change them. Only a small boy who has come from an enclave wears such things, and they reveal too much of your form.' He got up and went to Wild Spirit, then opened a sack.

He returned with a shirt and pants he had taken from the men in the shrine by the plateau. He worked at them with a piece of bone and cut at the edges of the pants with a knife. 'You should wear these.' I hesitated. 'If you must hide your form from me, then put them on inside the shrine.'

I stood up. 'I must wash first, in the stream. It's warm enough. Will I be safe?'

'I shall stand guard,' he said. 'You must be ready to cover yourself quickly.'

I picked up my coat and my clothes and hurried into the shrine, relieved that his anger had passed. Taking off my cloth garments, I tore my shirt into strips, knowing I could use them while I bled and wash them out to be used again. I pulled on my coat and held it tightly around me as I went outside.

Arvil picked up his bow and quiver, then followed me down to the stream. He turned his back to me as I dropped my clothes, took off my boots, then crouched by a tree to remove my coat.

I tested the stream with one foot before plunging into the water. The stream was shallow, warmed a little by the sun. I sank down, letting the water flow over me, loosening my hair as I bent my head back. When I felt clean, I climbed out. Arvil was watching me; he turned away slowly. I hid behind the tree while making a loincloth with my belt and three thick strips of cloth; I looped the cloth through the belt and pulled it up between my legs.

As I reached for the leather shirt, I realized that Arvil was looking at me again. I held the shirt to my chest, feeling shamed and vulnerable. 'Please. You mustn't look at me yet.' He did not look away. I pulled on the shirt and picked up the pants.

'Why do you wear that loincloth under pants?' he asked.

I blushed. 'I must explain something else to you. Every twenty-eight days or so, a woman bleeds from her female parts.' He started and stepped toward me. I was burning with embarrassment but knew that I could not hide this from him for long. 'It isn't an illness, and the blood does not come from a wound. It's something that happens to all women. Inside a woman's belly there is a womb in which she carries her child, and from time to time the womb sheds its wall. I wear this cloth so that . . .' I could say no more.

'Does it pain you?' he asked.

I shook my head. 'I ache sometimes. There was never much pain for me.'

'I must wash,' he said suddenly as he handed me his weapons. He stripped off his clothes quickly, not troubling to conceal himself, and then walked into the stream. His arms thrashed at the water; he ducked under it and rose, his hair streaming.

He climbed out on to the bank. His clothing had hidden how muscular he was, had made him seem leaner. His member seemed to swell a bit as he gazed at me; he walked out from under the trees and stood in the sun. I clutched at my coat and retreated to the fire. Still naked, he carried his clothes to the horses, took out the other shirt and pants, and went into the shrine.

I stood near the fire, waiting for my hair to dry. My mother had once taken me to the wall, after I had become a woman, to show me the images of men who were inside after being called. Most women would have shrunk from showing such sights to a daughter that young, but Yvara had defied custom in this as she had in so many other matters. I had glimpsed Arvil's body in the shrine where I first saw him, when he danced, before revulsion made me look away. I knew what a man looked like and had been prepared for what Arvil's nakedness would reveal.

I had not been prepared for my reaction to this sight of his body. The men I had seen on the screen had seemed ugly and misshapen, with their body hair, flat chests, and stiff members covered by tubes; they had been no more than providers of sperm for new generations. But Arvil's body did not seem ugly to me. The water on his pale smooth skin had glistened in the sunlight, and, for a moment, I had seen beauty in his form, in the body hardened by his life.

He came outside and sat down near me. I looked away as I tied my hair back with a leather thong. 'Those clothes are looser on you,' he said. 'They will hide much of your form, although I wish it did not have to be hidden.' He pulled the deer hide to him and began to scrape at the skin with stone. 'You will need another garment to conceal what you are, and the weather will grow too warm for your coat. I'll make you a garment from this hide.'

I seated myself and watched as he worked at the hide, making it supple. He would make me a garment; I was strangely moved by the gesture. Occasionally, he glanced at me and opened his mouth, as though about to speak, and then he set down his tools and held his hands against his abdomen.

'In here,' he said, 'in this part of yourself – it is where you say a woman keeps her child before it is born, as an animal carries her young.'

I nodded.

'But you must put a man's seed there with your own. How do you take this seed and put it inside you?'

I kept my eyes down. 'When you join with the spirit-woman, it is taken from your male member. A woman who wants a child . . .' I swallowed. 'The seed enters her body through her female parts. It's taken from the man and brought to her. It is inserted with a syringe – a device we have – and then a child begins to form inside her.' I could hardly force these words out. 'What the spirit-women do allows us to collect your seed.'

'It is from the joining. I had wondered – there was a mystery in this joining, and now . . .' He was leaning closer to me; I could feel his breath on my face. 'But why must it be that way? If seed comes during such a joining, why don't you come to us yourselves instead of sending spirits? The spirit-women have pleasure with men, as we have with them . . . why could you not . . ?'

I jumped to my feet, disturbed and frightened by this turn in our talk. 'There would be no pleasure in it for us,' I cried. 'We can find that only with our own kind. We can no longer feel that with a man.'

'Are you saying that once you . . .'

'I don't want to speak of this!' I paced by the fire, then spun around. He gazed at me as he picked up the hide.

'You asked me not to grow angry at the truth,' he said. 'Now it is you who grow angry at it.'

I moved closer to him. 'In ancient times,' I said as calmly as I could, 'some women could bring themselves to enjoy a man, but it is no longer so. Men could use that pleasure to enslave women, and often they sought their own enjoyment whether or not the woman was willing. We're free from that now.'

'Perhaps men were also enslaved by it. You enslave us now with spirit-women in the shrines and enclaves. Even men with strong lusts and willing boys and men to satisfy them can find the Lady's blessings greater. If we didn't have the knowledge of the Lady's pleasures, perhaps we would find more enjoyment with each other and more love. With your magic, you might find a way to take our seed and give us boys without such blessings, but you would rather bend us to your will with that reward.'

He reached up suddenly and seized my wrist. I tried to pull away; he got to his feet. 'I cannot wear the circlet now,' he continued, 'without the risk of betraying you again. There will be no more spirit-women and their pleasures for me. I have no friends to love. You are all I have left. What am I to do, Birana? I can hold myself back, but I don't know if I am strong enough to do it for ever.'

'You will find friends in time. It may be . . .'

He pulled me to him. His hand gripped my hair, and my face was against his chest. 'It is you I want now,' he said. 'You tell me that women can love each other, and I have seen how the spirit-women perform with a man. Would it be so hard for you to show me what you do with another of your kind, and for me to give blessings to you, so that we could share some pleasure?'

'What you ask is impossible!'

He held my head so that I was forced to look up at him. 'I saw how you looked at me when I came out of the water. For a moment, in your eyes, I thought I saw your spirit warm toward me a little.'

I tore myself from his grasp and stumbled toward the shrine, huddling against the wall. I could hide nothing from him, not even my fleeting thoughts. Could he have seen something in me I could not acknowledge to myself? I was nearly sick at the thought.

I knew then what I would have to say to protect myself. As he came toward me, I lifted a hand. 'Listen to me,' I said. 'If you shared any pleasures with me, you would want to join with me all the more. If that happened, if your urge was too strong to control and your seed entered me, a child would be created inside me. I'd be ill at first, and then my belly would begin to swell. I would be much more of a burden to you then, because my body would grow large and clumsy. There would be no physician to guide me through the birth; my pain would be greater than any you have ever felt, and it's likely that both the child and I would die. Even if we lived, you couldn't care for us, so we would die anyway. I would give birth in agony, and then I would die, for I would have none of the help a mother has in a city. That's what joining would be for me. The pleasure you long for would mean my death.'

His face was drawn, his grey eyes wide. 'Birana . . .'

'Think of that, and perhaps restraint will be easier for you – that is, if you want me to live.'

'You know that I do. I'll try to put these thoughts from my mind.' His voice was strained, his eyes unhappy. He turned away and went back to the fire.

I waited for Arvil to tell us when we might ride on, but he seemed content to linger by the shrine, the most peaceful place we had yet found. From the deerskin, using a bone needle and strands of gut, he fashioned a coat for me. With the cat's fur, he made a short cloak for himself. He led me through the forest bordering the shrine as he gathered plants, showing me how to recognize them and where they might be found; he fished in the stream with his spear, and found a berry bush with ripening fruit.

He asked no more questions, and I grew easier with him during the days; but at night, I felt his eyes watching me and wondered what he might be thinking. We had taken to sleeping inside the shrine, one of us resting while the other kept watch by the door. Sometimes I would awaken and sense him standing near me and hear him sigh.

My bleeding stopped at last. I washed out the last bit of cloth I had worn and put it in my pack with the others, then led each of the horses to the stream to drink.

Arvil was walking Star around the shrine when I motioned to him. 'This place has been a kind of refuge for me,' I said, 'but we must look for another soon. The horses are growing restless.'

'I wonder if we'll find a place as peaceful.'

'We must try.'

'We shall leave soon. Now I'll hunt for the last time in this place. I have seen ducks not far from here.' He took up his bow and arrows and vanished into the wood.

I tethered the horses, practised with my sling, and then went back into the shrine. Ever since our talk of blessings and what they meant, Arvil had been careful not to come too close to me. He no longer smiled or took my hand for a moment, and I realized that I missed those signs of friendship. Why couldn't he be my friend without longing for more? I knew the answer to that. It was my kind that had awakened such desires in him.

I heard the door whisper open; Arvil could not be back so soon. Perhaps he had decided not to hunt. I turned, intending to smile and say something kind to him, and met a stranger's eyes.

I caught my breath and drew my deerskin coat around me. The man's brown hair was plaited in two long braids; his blue eyes narrowed as he watched me. He wore a loincloth with leather leggings that reached above the knees, and a furry hide covered his shoulders. He did not look pleased at finding me there.

I wanted to run from him, useless as that would have been. I waited as he walked toward the altar.

The stranger set down his small pack and weapons, knelt in front of the image, and bowed his head. I might have run outside, but he could follow, and nothing would prevent him from harming me there.

He finished his prayers and sat back on his heels. I sat down next to the altar, hoping the coat Arvil had made hid my breasts. 'A truce while we speak,' I said in my own language.

'There is always peace in Her presence.' He peered at me; I forced myself to gaze at him steadily. 'You did not travel here alone.'

'That is so.'

'What are you called, lad?'

I thought of the name Arvil had given me. 'Spellweaver,' I replied.

He nudged the spear in front of him with his foot. 'I am Narid, and perhaps that is all I should tell you, for I have heard of the horsemen beyond the Ridge in the west who would rid the world of those on foot.'

He did not look like a man who wanted a truce; I could not fight him. If he went outside, he could strike at Arvil when he returned, and if I tried to stop him, I would die as well. He had seen what we possessed and might take it all. I would have to reach a more lasting truce with this man and did not know how I could persuade him to one.

'What you have heard of the horse folk is not true of my band,' I said at last.

'Do you speak truth?'

'Can I lie in the Lady's presence?'

He frowned as he considered that. 'You might shape your words so that you do not utter a lie and yet conceal the truth.'

'I swear this before the Lady,' I pitched my voice as low as it would go. 'We do not seek your land. We want only peace with any who live here. I would pledge a truce if you pledge one for yourself and your band, one that would protect us both when we leave this holy place.'

He scowled. 'You are only a boy. How can a band be bound by the truce of a boy?'

I had no answer to that.

'Perhaps your horsemen seek new lands, and you are here as scouts. Perhaps I should leave your bodies outside for your band to find, so that they will know this is not their place. You may be willing to pledge peace for now and wait for a battle to come later.'

'If you kill us, others will not rest until your band is dead, until any band in this region is dead. Would you bring that upon yourself from horsemen who do not seek your land and do not wish to act against you?'

He stroked his brown beard as he considered this.

'We have horses,' I continued, 'and men on foot are no match for those on horseback.' My terror had made my words harsher than I had intended. 'You will only bring death to your band.'

Narid lowered his eyes to my hands; I suddenly wanted to hide them from him. 'I see your weakness, lad. Your wrists are thin; your hands are not strong. You cannot fight me.' He reached for his belongings and stood up. 'I go outside to await your companions. There cannot be more than two, perhaps only one judging by the signs I see. He will not be expecting attack. Do not think you can warn anyone, for if you set one foot outside, you will surely die. I offer you this, since we are in a holy place. Stay here, under Her protection, and you will live until hunger and thirst force you to leave. I can wait. Perhaps when your friends lie dead, and I have eaten of your food, my spirit will grow more merciful. I might take what you have but leave you your life.'

He backed away, keeping his eyes on me until he reached the door; it opened and then closed behind him.

I put my feet under me and rose. I could reveal myself to him; he would spare us both then. But then there would be another man who could betray me in shrines, or who would tell his band of what he had seen here. Unless I dwelled with them, I could not protect myself, but if I did, I might never reach a refuge.

I walked toward the door, knowing what I would have to do, wondering if I could find the courage for it. Arvil might die if I did not act. It was not only fear of my helplessness without him that drove me, but also the thought of his body lying in the dirt, of the loss of my only friend.

The door slid open. Narid was moving toward the trees to the south, preparing to conceal himself. He spun around and lifted his spear, aiming it, ready to hurl the weapon. 'You heard me, lad. You will die when you step from holy ground.'

'Your spear might miss me,' I said, unable to keep my voice from quavering. 'Then I will have a chance to strike. But I know you are more able than I, and maybe you'll take my life. I will be certain that, before I die, I stain this wall with my blood to warn my companion of danger. I will cry out with my last breath, and he will hear, for he has not gone far. You won't surprise him, and he will hunt you for killing me.'

This man, in order to surprise Arvil, would have to drag my body away and hide the corpse. He would strip off what he could steal from me, and then he would know what I was. The shock of that would make him believe he was cursed. His fears would chase all thoughts of lying in wait for Arvil out of his mind. I thought of my mother then, of how she had died outside a shrine, of how one of her murderers had screamed in despair.

'Don't be a fool,' Narid said.

I took a breath and stepped from the door, ready to dodge his spear however I could. I knew there would be no chance to reach for my sling before he threw.

He stared at me for a long time, then lowered his spear as he strode toward me. I shrank back as he slapped me on the back with such force that I staggered and almost fell. 'You show some bravery, lad. I see what your band must be if it has such boys. I have no wish for a battle with such men.'

My legs were weak with relief, but somehow they carried me inside. Perhaps he had only been testing me; maybe his words had been as empty as mine. We walked toward the altar. 'Will your companion grant me a truce?' he asked.

'I swear to you that he will, and that you have nothing to fear from him,' I answered.

'Then I shall swear one to you, and, when I return to my band, I will tell them they are not to harm you as you pass through our land.' We swore our oaths in front of Hecate's image, and then Narid began to move toward a couch; I realized he was about to put on a circlet. He looked back at me, apparently noticing my apprehension.

'What is it, lad?'

'It is nothing.' He knew me only as a boy called Spellweaver; he could not betray me. I moved away from him and sat down by the door to wait.

Narid said little to me, and I kept my distance from him as I watered the horses and gathered wood. He sat down outside the door, cleaning and sharpening his weapons as he watched. Arvil would, I knew, take care in approaching the shrine, but if he saw me outside, unharmed, he would know I had a truce with the stranger.

He returned in the afternoon with two ducks; he and Narid went inside to pledge their truce. The two were soon talking freely as they plucked the ducks; I carried wood to the fire and breathed on it to set it blaze.

The evening air was cooler; Narid rubbed his hands as he warmed them by the fire. 'I came here from an enclave,' he said.

'This is the second time I was called, and yet I have no boy. I pray that there will be one for me before long.'

Narid's talk, filled with digressions and stories of his band's exploits, finally revealed that he had travelled for nearly two months to reach an enclave. 'So far?' Arvil asked.

'It is not so hard as it may seem. A band with whom we have a truce lies some twenty days to the south, and I hunted with them before going on. It is hardest during the cold season, when food is not so easily found, but I made my journey then.'

'It would be hard to return on such a long journey with a boy,' Arvil said.

'A boy must show what he is made of early. One with a boy can stay with that band for a time and allow him to learn a few things before travelling on. In this season, my band begins to move south, through these lands, so it is good you have a truce with us. The other band will move north to join us. We hunt together in summer until it is time to return to our camps and prepare for the cold time. There is enough for us, for few men dwell here. It is why we choose to live here, even so far from the enclave. But I have spoken enough of myself. Let me hear of why you have travelled to this place, for few come here from beyond the Ridge.'

'We have heard,' Arvil said slowly, 'that there are bands east of here, near a great lake, who have seen a holy vision. Because our Headman seeks holiness, he has asked us to learn the truth of this tale.'

Narid turned his head toward Arvil; rage flickered in his eyes. 'You will find no holiness in the east,' he muttered.

'I was told that those by the lake knew of such a vision, and that they cannot be far from here. Did the man who told me this speak falsely?'

Narid stood up. 'I wish now I had not sworn a truce with you, Arvil and Spellweaver. It would have been better for you to die here than go to a land where you'll only stray from the Goddess's path.'

He stomped around the fire, scowling and moving his arms; I was afraid to look at him. Arvil motioned to the man. 'Please tell us what you know, Narid. What you tell us might help us shield ourselves from unholiness. I was told that the men who dwell by the lake won't harm a stranger who comes to them in peace, and that a holy vision of the Lady was seen there. That is all I know. I would hear what you know now.'

Narid sat down and gazed at the roasting fowl, as though his hunger was battling with his desire to be away from us. 'You will not turn back?' he asked.

'I cannot turn back,' Arvil said. 'Whatever is there, I must see it with my own eyes before I return.'

'You may never return. Should you wish to go on this foolish journey, you must travel south for one rising and setting of the sun, and you will come to land where the trees are not so thick. From there, go east to where the oaks jostle the pines. I cannot tell you how much farther you must go from there, for that is as far as I've travelled.'

Arvil nodded. 'I am grateful for this knowledge, Narid. I'll happily share our meal with you in return and will give you some of our dried meat so that you can return to your camp more quickly, without the need to hunt.' Narid glanced at him suspiciously. 'I swear to you that I'll think on your words and will not be deceived by unholiness. I would know why talk of this lake stirs your anger.'

'It is this way,' Narid said as he began his story. Long ago, before Narid had been taken from an enclave, his band had travelled east. They had come to a land of felled trees and stumps, a land scarred by unholiness, where his band was set upon by a great horde. Many had died; the rest had fled back to their own lands, and their anger against those in the east had grown, for they had no way to take revenge against the horde for the lives that had been lost. Much of his tale was mingled with curses, but I understood that his band had been attacked by those Ilf had said would meet strangers in peace.

'My band heard from a traveller of this vision you seek,' Narid went on, 'and yet he could say little of it, only that by the lake there is a camp that few men see and none who enter leave again. It is said that the vision appeared there, but he could not tell us anything about it. I think it's a lie used by the lake bands to make others fear them.'

What could this tale mean? I did not know whether I could hope or should feel fear. 'Did your band go to this lake in peace?' Arvil asked.

'It is said unholiness marked their land, that they did not live as men should. We could have no peace with such men, and without peace, a band should take what it can from those who are weaker. There were few of them, and then suddenly there were many, more than my band could count, and my guardian's guardian was among those who fell.' Narid spat on the ground. 'You see now why my anger is kindled against you. I made a truce with you, and you travel toward those who took lives of my band.' He smiled grimly. 'But I'll cool my anger with this thought – they may take your lives as well.'

'They may not harm two travellers who seek only word of their vision.' Arvil sounded uncertain.

'I have pledged you a truce, much as I curse myself for it, for I could have slain you both, but we are bound by our oath. It is said some go east. It is said that almost no one returns. It is said that even the Goddess turns Her eyes from what lies beyond the lake.' He gestured with one hand and made a sign. 'You should pray hard before you leave this shrine, for you will need the shield of the Lady.'

Narid sulked in silence until Arvil handed him some food; he stared at it sullenly before taking it. 'It may be,' Arvil said, 'that we will not go to the lake. I shall ponder your warning, for I am thinking of turning back.' I looked away, wondering if Arvil was only trying to soothe Narid or if the story had made him more fearful.

Narid relaxed a bit, and soon he was telling us tales of the spirits in the woods who sang when the wind moved the pines, of the joy the Goddess took in their song, of how the first tree had appeared at the beginning of time. I barely listened, hardly noticing what he was saying, as I worried about what Arvil might be planning.

We slept in the shrine that night; Narid had said there was no need to keep watch. He was gone when we awoke, and we found he had taken nothing from us, not even the dried meat Arvil had promised him.

ARVIL

Narid did not frighten me with his talk about how few men returned from the east. Birana and I could not return, whatever happened. But I was worried about his story of what had befallen his band. Ilf had said that the men of the lake would not harm strangers, but Narid knew more about them than Ilf had, and he feared them. I told myself that Narid's band had not gone to the lake in peace, that they had brought their deaths upon themselves. I thought of the vision and what it might mean, of Birana's hope for a refuge.

'What shall we do?' Birana asked as we left the shrine.

'You must say what we are to do. Will you risk travelling to this lake? Perhaps one of your kind appeared there, and perhaps those men know where you might find safety, or it may be only a tale with little truth.'

'I know one thing,' she said, as she carried her belongings to Flame. 'Any refuge I can reach would lie somewhere to the east. We'll have to go on.'

I touched her arm lightly. I had not come so close to her for the past days. I kept my hand on her. She did not pull away, and then I remembered what she had said, that my desire for her would bring her suffering and death. My hand dropped. 'I haven't heard how you reached a truce with Narid, though he said you spoke bravely.'

I tried not to smile when she spoke of how she had stood up to his threats, of how she had dared him to kill her outside the shrine. 'He was all bluff and arrogance,' she finished.

I grew solemn then. 'He was not, Birana. He could have followed his threats with deeds, while you couldn't. It may be all that saved you from him was his weariness and not your brave words. Brave as you were, you risked too much.'

'Even if he had killed me, you would have been safe. He would have seen what I was, and then he would have been no match for you. He would have thought himself cursed; he might have welcomed his death then.'

I stepped close to her. 'You think so much of me, to save me in that way?'

'I couldn't . . . without your help, I wouldn't have lived long anyway.' She looked away before she mounted Flame, and I knew that she had left other words unsaid. My heart leaped.

We came that evening to rolling land where high grass grew and where the trees to the east stood with much grassland around them. Birana fetched kindling from the edge of the wood while I found stones to set around the fire. What Narid had revealed of this land in his rambling way had told me that we did not need to fear men, and the fire would keep other creatures away.

The air was cold again, and we put on our sheepskin coats. With wood and my old coat, I set up a shelter above us, then stretched out on the ground. Birana crawled out and began to lie down a few paces away.

'I didn't make this shelter only for myself,' I said.

'I can sleep here.'

'The night grows colder. We would be warmer if we lay together.'

She sat up. 'No.'

'Do you think I forgot what you have told me? I want only warmth, no more.'

She came back and lay down next to me. I moved toward her until my chest was against her back. She tensed, but did not push me away. I put one arm across her, around her waist, over her coat.

She did not protest but accepted this. My soul sang with that triumph, and then it came to me that there might be caresses we could share while I kept my seed from entering her. My member hardened as I thought of the touch of the spirit-women, of how their hands had stroked me, of how mine had roamed over their bodies. It was my joining with her that would bring her harm, not my touch.

It was hard for me to put such thoughts from my mind. It might be even harder for me to resist joining with her if I shared more with her. I steadied myself, and at last my weariness brought me sleep.

As we rode, I pointed out plants to Birana and told her which ones could be eaten. I discovered that pokeweeds and dandelions were plants Birana had once scorned.

'When we find such things in the city,' she said, 'and we still do sometimes, those who garden pull them out and throw them away.' I was struck by that, the notion of her kind throwing away plants that could feed them. Their magic seemed to grow greater, the more I knew of them, while they themselves grew less fearsome. Only their magic gave them strength – that, and the power they held over life.

Birana's eyes grew sadder as she spoke of the enclave. Whatever I had awakened toward me in her soul, she would have forgotten if she could have returned to her home. She sought a refuge. I wondered if there would be a refuge for me without her. Perhaps if she found one, I would not be welcome in it.

We could have remained in the land where we rode. I could reach an understanding with Narid's band, one that would allow us to dwell apart from them so that they did not discover Birana's true nature. I could convince him that my band, who lived only in my false words, would not follow us east, and he would be pleased that we had turned from seeking that which was unholy. With our horses, we could aid his band and the other they sometimes joined, and I could teach Birana how to hunt and track. This land was nearly empty of men. We would be as safe here as anywhere. This might be as much of a refuge as we would find.

I dreamed of this but did not speak of it to Birana. I feared that, if she believed there were no other refuge but this, she might lose the will to live. We would have to go to the lake, whatever that quest brought us.

I counted the days as we rode, and by the seventh, we had still seen no sign of the lake. But we had come to a land of more trees and, as Narid had told us, giant oaks stood among the towering pines. The days had grown colder, as they will in the spring before the warmth of summer drives the spell of the north away, and from time to time, the clouds released their rain.

A wind would blow, and the trees would release their seeds, undulating as the wind stirred their limbs. Their seeds dropped around us, to lie on the ground and take root. Since hearing of the truth from Birana, I saw these trees with new eyes. A story Narid had told came to me.

The first tree, at the beginning of Earth, had sprouted and grown tall. At the sight of the land under his roots, the tree grew hard with desire. The spirit of Earth and the Lady caressed him, and Her land welcomed his roots and made him long for Her so greatly that bark grew around him and kept him stiff. A passion filled the tree, and his first seeds fell, to be borne away by the wind, but as boys are given to men by the Lady, so other trees rose around the first and became his band.

Earth accepted the seed of the trees, as the females of other creatures accepted the seed of their males. But men, by doing evil, had cast their seed carelessly and had lost it in ancient times. No new life came from us, for that was part of our punishment, but in a forest far away, Narid said, the first tree waits, still spilling its seed, and when men have moved closer to redemption, the seeds of the first tree will fall upon them and restore their own seed.

Narid had seen nothing more in this story than that trees, like the creatures around us, were yet another sign of what we had lost. But now, as the oaks stirred above Birana and me, I saw them as a sign of what I still was. Men had their seed still, and Birana's kind took it from us. The limbs fluttering overhead brought images of men dancing before other men whom they loved, of ghostly aspects beckoning to a man. Women had not robbed us of our seed but had hidden theirs from us.

All these thoughts only aroused me more, and I would have nothing from Birana but the warmth of her body while I slept. I kept my eyes on the ground, away from the limbs above.

At last we began to see the signs of men.

By a stream running through the wood, I saw that men had dug for roots and gathered plants there. Birana peered at her compass, and we rode on. Soon we were on a trail winding among the trees, a place where men had walked. We did not ride along the trail but kept it in sight as we continued east, concealing ourselves among the trees.

As we rode, I seemed to feel eyes upon me; yet, when I looked around, I saw no one. I was sure we were being watched but heard no sound except the birds.

'I come in peace,' I called out in the holy speech. Birana looked at me, startled, for she, it seemed, had sensed nothing. 'We mean no harm. I swear it to you in the Lady's name.' We moved back to the trail and rode along it. If men were watching, it would be useless to hide from them now.

Then we came to a place along the trail where stumps of trees stood among others that still lived, and where bark had been stripped from other trees. I sniffed the air and knew we were near water.

'I come in peace,' I cried again.

An arrow flew past and struck a tree in front of us. Flame reared as Birana clung to her reins.

'Hold!' a voice shouted in the holy speech before I could act. This man was hidden by the trees but seemed to be above us.

'You two are alone?' another voice called out from behind me.

'We are alone,' I answered, 'and we come in peace. I swear it to you.'

'If that is so,' the first voice said, 'then cast down all the weapons you carry and drop to the ground from the beasts that carry you. If you do not, you will die here.' The holy speech sounded strange in this man's mouth. I recalled what Birana had told me, that the holy speech was different in other places. This man drew out his words and then bit them off at the end.

We had to obey. Birana and I threw down our spears and the knives we carried, then dismounted. I tensed as I waited for the other arrows to fly. A small pouch dropped past my face. I picked it up, opened it, and saw a small piece of dried fish. They would not be offering us food if they intended to kill us.

'Lead your beasts on along this trail,' the first voice said.

239

'Remember that you will feel the wrath of all our band if you harbour evil intentions toward us.'

We led the horses forward. As we walked, I heard the men drop to the ground behind us but dared not turn. Ahead of us, more trees had been stripped of bark and more stumps stood on the land. I had never seen land so marked by men, and wondered how many could be in this band. I was feeling our helplessness. The men had made the gesture of offering us food but had not promised a truce.

Soon we came to a place where many trees had been felled, and I saw a long, low wall of dirt and stone. Beyond lay the lake, so wide it seemed to cover all the horizon; I could see no shore to the east, where the lake met the sky. Ten men stood on the wall. Four held spears while the others, all with the beardless faces of boys, carried bows. Two of them stood on either side of a passage that led through the wall.

I turned. Two other men were behind us, carrying the weapons we had dropped. They were dark-haired, without the beards of men, and nearly as tall as I. One of them pointed at the passage. 'Enter our camp,' he ordered.

We led our horses through the wall, and I nearly gasped aloud when I saw what lay inside. The land had been cleared, and men were toiling among straight rows of plants, green shoots just beginning to sprout. A path led past these plants to dwellings, round structures built of the trunks of trees that stood upright on the ground. I looked at the men on the wall, at those working, at those who stood near the dwellings, and knew that this band was as large as Truthspeaker's had been before the Lady destroyed it.

The two men carrying our weapons moved ahead of us, leading us to a wide clearing around which the dwellings stood. No fire burned at the centre of the camp, but from openings in the roofs of the dwellings smoke was rising. One dwelling, smaller than the others, stood apart from them and nearer to the wall. I wondered who lived there, then looked toward the lake, where other men rode the water in two floating vessels made of wood and bark. Other vessels lay on the shore below.

This was the richest camp I had ever seen. The sight of the men and their strong bodies told me that they did not feel hunger even after the deprivations of the recent winter. This, I thought, might be why so few returned from the east; a man would not want to leave such wealth. But perhaps other travellers had also died here. These men might not want to share what they had.

We were led past the clearing to a place by the shore, below the dwellings. 'You may rest here,' one of the men said. I now saw that even though he wore no beard, he was older than he had first seemed. 'Make your camp here. You may take water from the lake and tie your beasts to the trees there. I'll send my charge to tend to you.'

'We thank you for your kindness,' I said.

He held up my metal knife, studying the blade, then tossed it in front of us with our weapons. 'We leave you these. I don't think you will be so foolish as to use them against anyone here.'

He and his companion left us and walked back up the gentle slope toward the dwellings. As I glanced around, I noticed that the wall surrounded this camp, stretching nearly to the shore at either end. We could not escape without being seen by the men there.

We watered the horses, then tethered them by the trees. By the time I had set up a shelter of sticks and draped Tal's old coat and my own over them, a boy was making his way toward us, carrying a sack. He set the burden down, then bowed a little from the waist.

'Greetings,' he said. 'I am called Tulan.' He squinted at me with his black eyes as he pulled out a basket woven of reeds from the sack. 'Do you carry meat in your packs?'

I nodded.

'Then I shall leave you only these foods.' He took the top from the basket, then glanced at the horses. 'I have heard of horses. Perhaps they will eat of this.' He pulled out a large clay pot and offered it to me. I lifted off its top and saw a watery mixture of grain.

'We thank you,' I said.

'It is nothing.'

Nothing, to give away food to strangers and to feed our horses as well? His generosity was making me uneasy. The boy sat down and, after a moment, we seated ourselves in front of him.

'You are very kind to strangers, Tulan,' I said.

'Those who are mighty and blessed can be kind.' He grinned, and there was assurance in his smile. 'What are you called?'

'I am Arvil. The one with me is called Spellweaver, for he knows something of the powers of the mind. I would ask you a few questions.'

'That is why I am here, to answer them.'

'I would have you speak more slowly,' I said, 'for even the holy speech sounds strange to me in your mouth. How many men and boys are in your band?'

Tulan put out his hands once, then twice, then yet again until he had thrust his fingers at me eleven times. 'It is a great band,' I murmured.

'It is, and we have a truce with other lake bands with as many men.'

'You have much, but I see that you can guard it against others who would seek it.'

'That is so,' he responded, 'and each of the lake bands is bound to protect the others and to fight with them if one band is attacked.'

So this part of Ilf's story was true. I longed to ask the boy about the holy vision and what it might mean, but held myself back.

'I am to tell you,' Tulan continued, 'to stay here until it's time for others to speak with you. If you must relieve yourselves, go to that place.' He pointed at a ditch shielded by several shrubs. 'I'll bring you food. Others will not speak with you until we have learned more about you.' He leaned forward. 'Had you come on foot, we might have welcomed you more readily, but we have heard tales of those who have tamed the horse.'

'Some of those tales are not truthful.'

'Do others follow you?'

'No one will follow,' I admitted.

He seemed relieved to hear that. 'I'll tell you some of our lore.' I supposed that he was happy to have new ears for his talk.

He went on to tell us a story of long ago, when members of this band had first come to the lake. The Lady, in the form of a doe, had led them there, and because they had been a band that had not hunted does with young, but only bucks and other deer that had grown old, they had been rewarded with the bounty of the lake. In the form of a bear, the Lady had shown them the abundance of fish that lived in the waters and had taught them to make nets and boats. As a goose, She had led them to flocks of birds that came to the lake during their migrations. As a wren, She had shown them the plants that grew on the land, and a holy vision had revealed that certain plants could be cultivated and not simply gathered.

Other visions had shown them new arts, and they had prospered. They had also learned that truces with other bands around the lake would strengthen rather than weaken them. Although they lived very far from the Lady's enclave and had to travel for days even to reach a shrine, they honoured the Lady in all that they did. They often journeyed to a distant shrine in groups, and men of their number were called often enough to bring new boys to the band, while others had joined them after travelling to the lake from other regions. This last statement eased my mind a little.

I looked past him, seeing that a few men had entered the clearing; they carried a large deer hanging from a pole over their shoulders. Tulan turned his head toward them. 'The hunters are back,' he said.

'Are you not all hunters?' I asked.

He shook his head. 'When we are boys, the men see who is best at hunting or tending plants or fishing or toolmaking.' He struck his chest. 'I am one who will hunt. Those who are weaker must tend plants. Those whose hands are skilful craft tools, but it is from the hunters that our Headman is chosen.'

'You are all one band,' I said. 'Can one be more or less than another in a band?'

Tulan lifted his head. 'Do you not have a Headman, and isn't he higher than all?'

'Even a Headman must listen to his men and heed their words before he acts.'

The boy smiled. 'Our Headman heeds his own voice and listens only to those around him who have proven their strength, and others must follow. He does not hunt or fish or tend plants or make tools or baskets or pots unless he wishes to do so, for it is his task to watch others and to guide us all. When he grows older, he must choose another Headman.'

I thought of Geab. 'What if he doesn't want to give it up?'

Tulan gaped at me. 'But he must. He knows when it is time. When our Prayergiver dies, the Headman must become the Prayergiver and choose a new Headman. He then lives in the small hut apart from our other dwellings, and there he prays to the Lady throughout the days until his soul leaves us. He leaves our camp no more, and we honour his holiness, for his prayers protect us.'

I considered all he had told me. The men on the plateau had trained some of their number to fight with spears, others with bows, but all had laboured together at other tasks, according to Bint. The customs of this lake band were much stranger and seemed contrary to all I knew of what a man's life should be. Wanderer had heard of places where men tilled the soil, yet even he had not come upon so strange a band.

The men in the clearing were butchering the deer. Another man left one of the dwellings, and my mouth dropped open as I watched him gesture to the others. He was the largest man I had ever seen. His belly was swollen under his leather garments while his arms seemed thicker than my thighs. I waved an arm at him. 'Is that giant your Headman?' I asked.

Tulan turned. 'He is. You see our greatness in how well we have kept him fed.' He stood up. 'You'll hear more in time, and we will learn of you when the time for truthsaying comes.' He picked up his sack and left us.

I looked inside the basket he had given us and found pokeweed, ripe strawberries and asparagus. We ate this with the dried fish and then fed our horses, who ate readily of the grain. After we had drunk and filled our waterskins at the lake, we sat down under the shelter. From the camp, I could hear the voices of the men speaking in their own tongue as they entered their dwellings.

I stripped the red skin from the pokeweed that remained, chewed on the leaves, then divided the berries we had left. Birana shook her head as I offered one to her. 'I'm full.'

'I cannot eat them all.'

She accepted a few. I looked down at her belly, hidden by her coat. 'You grow rounder with more food, Birana. Your chest grows fuller and your hips more curved.'

She narrowed her eyes and drew back a little. 'I know,' she whispered, although there was no one near enough to hear us. 'If we stay here, they'll see what I am.'

I rested my head against my knees. 'We cannot escape.'

'We should never have come here.'

I felt the burden of her then. 'We are here because you seek a refuge, because you thought others of your kind might have found this land. I see none of them here, but this place can be a refuge for you. If you show these men your true nature, they would honour you and serve you, and your life would be an easy one, as would mine.'

'I would be betrayed the next time one of them went to a shrine. I can't teach them all . . .'

'You told my old band that they didn't have to travel to shrines while you were among them. Can't you tell these men the same?' I was warm with anger at her. Here was a camp where she could be safe, where I might find new friends, yet she still dreamed of a refuge that might not be. I wanted to break her hold on me then, to tell her I would travel no more.

'The boy said nothing of seeing one of us,' she said.

'Perhaps his band does not speak of such things in front of strangers.' I could still hope.

I stretched out under the shelter. Birana lay at my side, her arm by mine, seeking nearness to me instead of only enduring it. I clasped her hand tightly and felt her hair against my lips.

We stayed by the lake, and Tulan brought us another small basket of food. Although men passed by us on the way to their boats, they did not answer any of my greetings. We tended the horses but did not ride, and my idleness soon grew wearisome.

On the next day, when Tulan came, I motioned to him to sit, then went to the horses and fetched what remained of our meat. I carried it to the boy and put it into his sack, keeping only enough to eat later. 'You have given to me and to Spellweaver,' I said as I sat down. 'So I shall give to you. This is most of the meat we have, and you are welcome to it. Share it with others. I am sorry there is no more.'

Tulan grinned. 'I told them you were a good man,' he burst out. 'My band will be happy you did this now.' I saw then that I had passed some sort of testing.

'I must ask you to do something for us, Tulan. I want to speak to one of your men, your Headman or another who is respected among you.'

He rose. 'I will fetch Jerlan, my guardian. He's one of our best hunters and a man to whom even the Headman sometimes listens.'

He scurried off as Birana shot me a glance. 'What are you going to do now?'

'You will see,' I answered.

Tulan returned quickly with a tall, black-haired man, the one who had guided us to the camp and given us back our weapons. We greeted each other, and then I said, 'It is not right for us to take from you while giving nothing. I must take up the tasks of a man if I am to stay with you.'

'And do you wish to stay?'

'If your band will allow it. Our band is dead. We have no band. We travelled far to reach this place.'

Jerlan's dark eyes seemed kind, but I saw that he was also a man who would not listen to foolish or false words. I told him a little of our travels and how far we had come, and he grew more attentive to my words as I talked. I said that I had heard that the men of the lake lived in holiness and treated strangers kindly.

He nodded at this. 'We are kind to those who, when the time for truthsaying comes, show that they are worthy men. To others we are not so kind.' He was silent for a moment while I wondered what he meant by the time for truthsaying. 'What do you offer us besides the meat you have already given?'

I glanced at Birana. 'Spellweaver is not strong,' I said carefully, 'but my band kept him for his skill with horses and because he has a brave heart. He can teach some of you how to ride if you don't fear our beasts too much, and perhaps he can learn the art of plant tending from you.' She looked away as I spoke. 'I can hunt and gather wild plants. I can make tools and weapons.' I spread the ones I had before him.

'You didn't make this one,' he said as he picked up my knife. 'This is not a blade of stone.'

'I did not make it. The man who owned it is dead. I can also fight and can tell you stories of the land to the west.'

His lip curled at that. 'We know something of the west.'

'Do you know of the land beyond the Ridge, that wall of rock? Do you know of the plain beyond that? Do you know of the plateau where some men fell so far into evil ways that they would prey upon strangers inside shrines, on holy ground?'

Jerlan stared steadily at me. 'Of such things we have not heard.'

'You will hear of them in time, and of more as well.' I let a silence pass to feed his curiosity, then said, 'We can also find a way of making our horses useful to you. As you can see, they're able to bear burdens too heavy for a man. I am told you live far from shrines and the Lady's enclaves, but, with these horses, you can reach them more easily.'

'Travelling as we do tests our strength. Horses are only something else to feed, and they are wild and impart their wildness to men.'

'These horses are not wild.'

He shrugged. 'There may be something in what you say, Arvil. We can talk of the horses later when the time for truthsaying is past.' He drew his brows together. 'We'll see how you hunt. As for the boy there, he may spend the days showing my charge Tulan what he knows of these horses. We'll see what sort of men you are.'

I was to hunt with Jerlan and five other men the next day. The air had grown warm again, and Birana had put off her sheepskin coat to wear the one I had made for her.

'Your form is hidden well enough,' I said.

She held out one hand. 'Arvil, I'm afraid to stay here alone.'

'Tulan won't harm you. Do as his guardian asked, and show

him how to care for our horses and what their habits are. Say little to him – let him believe you are one of few words.'

I followed Jerlan and the others from the camp, but when we were outside the wall, they allowed me to lead. They told me nothing about the land or where game might be found, for it was my skill they wanted to see. Deer would avoid the ravaged land around the camp, and it came to me that, with so many men there, we might have to venture far to find game.

As we moved through the wood, I marked my position by the position of the sun overhead and also noted signs on the land – the faint marks of a trail, a glade to the south, the clumps of berry bushes near a thorny shrub. We had gone deep into the forest before I saw a place where deer had passed and where they had found forage among the plants. Still my companions said nothing as I followed these tracks.

We came to a pool fed by a creek, and there I waited, certain that deer would soon come to drink. The men were silent as they watched. When a buck at last appeared, I raised my bow and took aim, but only wounded the creature. My companions made no move to help me, and I marvelled at the wealth of those who could give up this chance at more food only to test me.

I leaped up and ran after the bleeding deer, tracking it until I was close enough to hurl my spear. This weapon brought the buck down, and I was able to take its life. Jerlan and his men followed and sat down to watch as I cleared a place for a fire.

When the fire was ablaze, I began the work of butchering. It was night by the time my labour was done and a haunch was roasting over the fire. I sat down and waited for someone to speak to me.

'You might make a hunter,' Jerlan said. 'You will share our meal now. We'll sleep here and return to our camp in the morning.'

The roasted meat restored some of my strength. I was with a band once more and felt how much I had missed the company of other men. 'It is not only hunting we want from you, but tales of your land,' Jerlan went on. 'Tell us a story of it now, while we eat. Tell us your tale of the evil ones who would violate a shrine.'

The other men muttered at this. 'Such men could not live,' one whispered as he made a sign against evil.

'Arvil told me that he knew of such men.'

'It is so,' I said. As I prepared to begin my story, I remembered what Shadow had told me about men preferring tales with some invention. In my words, the plateau became a place where an evil spirit dwelled and caused men to turn from the Lady, and I spoke of how the men there had seen that those who entered a shrine and expected peace within its walls could be easily robbed and slain. The Lady could not suffer such evil and sent Her weapons against these men, but the evil spirit among them was strong enough to protect a few from Her wrath. I spoke of two lone strangers who had come to a shrine, how the evil men had attacked them, and how the Lady, enraged by this desecration, had given Her strength to the travellers.

'The spears of the travellers became Her rays,' I said, 'and the evil ones fell before them, and then their bodies vanished, as if they had never walked the earth. I swear by the Lady that my words are true.'

'That is quite a story,' Jerlan said, 'yet I wonder if it was only a boastful fool who told it to you.'

I gazed into his face. 'No one told it to me, for I was one of those two travellers, and it was to me that the Lady imparted Her strength. I saw Her weapons destroy those men on their plateau and was spared because I followed Her way and not theirs.'

'Arvil makes his deeds greater than they are,' one man said.

'I have sworn it is true,' I replied.

'Deeds can grow in the telling,' Jerlan said, 'and men become mightier in the past when they view it from the present, but we'll know the truth of this tale when the time for Arvil's truthsaying comes.'

I wanted to ask him what he meant by that but held my tongue. Perhaps they would take me to a shrine, since men had to speak truth there, but I knew the truth of the Lady and could say what I wished. 'I have told a story,' I said, 'and now I would ask one of you. I have heard that there is holiness here and that a vision of the Lady appeared to a lake band not long ago.'

One of Jerlan's companions leaned toward him. 'I don't know if we should speak of that to him now. It would be better if he passed through his truthsaying first.'

Jerlan waved a hand. I had already seen that the other men deferred to him and waited to hear what he would say. 'He has hunted with us. I believe he may become one of us before long, and, if he doesn't, telling him the tale will make no difference.' He drank from his waterskin and then began his story.

Some years before, not long after the band's present Prayer-giver had assumed those duties, a lake band to the east had begun to bar its camp to all others, even those by the lake with whom that band had a truce. Although they would leave their closed camp to travel to others along the lake, they would allow no man to enter theirs.

The other lake bands, Jerlan's among them, grew suspicious of this and wondered if this band might be harbouring evil intentions. Always the men of the lake had welcomed those from other such camps to their own, and even traded among themselves if one camp's gardens flourished while another's did not. The other lake bands whispered among themselves as they worried about what evil might be taking root, and the mystery grew. Whenever a man from the closed camp was seen, he would say only that there was holiness that had to be hidden from the eyes of other men, but that the vision had promised blessedness to all the men of the lake.

Anger and doubts grew in the hearts of the other bands, and yet they feared to act; they had sworn a truce to the other band for all time and could not attack their camp. They also knew that, if the vision was a true one, they would be cursed for attacking men who had been blessed.

At last the Headmen of all the bands decided to travel to that camp, and there they were met by its Headman and Prayergiver outside the camp's wall. The Prayergiver swore mighty oaths and then told the others to bring their own Prayergivers back to that place. The Prayergivers would be allowed to see the truth of the vision and would attest to it, but the Lady willed that no others should behold this apparition.

All the Headmen swore more oaths and then returned to fetch their Prayergivers. This promise had not been an easy one to keep, for a Prayergiver was one who never left his camp to travel, and many of these old men were weak. Some were borne to the eastern camp on litters and others could walk only a short distance at one time; but at last they came to the camp, and there all those with them waited while the Prayergivers entered.

A day passed, and then the Prayergivers came outside, and all who saw them knew before they spoke that they had seen holiness, for a new light shone from the eyes of the old men. They swore that they had seen a holy vision, and all believed them, but the Prayergivers never again spoke of what they had seen.

'The Prayergivers swore not to speak of their vision,' Jerlan said, 'and that camp is still closed to all who will not join their band, but some word of the vision they saw has found its way to our ears. Some say that an aspect of the Lady appeared to them, while others say only that She speaks through the mouth of their Prayergiver and lends him Her form, but all know that the camp is blessed and has given its blessing to all of us. The proof of that is that we have all prospered and that life here is good.'

Jerlan's friends were looking about uneasily. His shoulders twitched as fear crept into his eyes. 'It is not wise to dwell on this holy mystery overmuch,' he continued. 'It is something to hold deep in the mind. We do not speak of it often, for it is best to veil such a vision, lest its power burn our souls.'

I said, 'I would go to that camp and see this for myself.'

'You cannot,' Jerlan replied. 'Only a Prayergiver or one of the boys who has won the right to join their band would be allowed to enter.'

'Boys join them?' I asked.

'From time to time a man from that camp comes to ours or to another, and the boys compete in contests before him. The boy who wins then goes to that camp to dwell there and is happy to live near holiness.'

'But . . .' I started to say.

'We have spoken enough of this,' one man said angrily.

'Is this another tale that has grown in the telling?' I said.

'Silence,' Jerlan muttered. 'I told you that we don't often speak of this. Even in a holy shrine, we will bury our thoughts of this vision. The Lady has blessed us, but She may also turn from us if we grow too proud. This tale is as I told it to you, for I was a boy when the Prayergivers journeyed to that camp, and the Prayergiver who dwells with us now was one who saw the holy vision.'

I considered this. 'And will he travel there again?'

'He will not, for the men in that camp guard their vision.'

'I must speak to your Prayergiver.'

Jerlan shook his head. 'You must not unless he summons you. A man doesn't enter his hut unless he is called there, lest his prayers be disturbed.'

We stretched out to sleep while one of the men kept watch. My thoughts tumbled inside me, keeping sleep at bay. I would have to learn more, but the beginning of a plan was already forming in my mind.

We returned to the camp the next day with our game. The Headman was standing among the plants, watching as those tending them poked at the ground with antlers and sticks. He beckoned to Jerlan, then led him to one of the dwellings.

I hastened to Birana, who was standing with the horses while they drank from the lake. Tulan held the reins of Wild Spirit, and I saw that the horse seemed gentler with him. He grinned at me.

'Spellweaver must teach me to ride this creature,' he said.

'We'll see. Your guardian is with the Headman. You should go to him now.' As the boy hurried away, I murmured to Birana, 'I have much to tell you.'

We tethered the horses and sat down under our shelter while I told her Jerlan's tale. Her face was ashen when I finished.

'It might be,' she whispered. 'If women were among them, or that band has seen them, they would still have to hide from others. And you say that the Prayergivers never leave their camps, so they wouldn't be able to betray what they know in a shrine. She clutched at my sleeve. 'We must go there.'

'We cannot simply ride out of here and seek them out.' I frowned. 'Jerlan keeps speaking of a truthsaying. Has the boy told you anything of that?'

She shook her head.

'We must speak to the Prayergiver somehow, and yet we cannot unless he summons us. I fear these men will strike at us if we approach that man.'

Jerlan was walking toward us. I stood up as he came near. 'Our Headman Irlan has spoken to me,' he said. 'He has said it is time for you and Spellweaver to have a truthsaying. Tomorrow, our band will prepare a feast, and you will both be led to the Prayergiver's house. There, outside his hut, we will learn what lies inside you.'

This did not sound too fearful. 'Must I swear a holy oath,' I said, 'so that you will know the truth of my words?'

'You may swear one, but it isn't an oath that will draw the truth from you both. You will drink a potion we'll prepare, and that which shapes your words and thoughts will be stripped from you, and you will speak freely of all that is in you. Should evil abide in your thoughts, you must die; but, if it does not, you may remain with our band.'

I was afraid to speak.

'Are you not pleased?' he said. 'We do not force a man to stay, but it is my hope that you'll join us.'

'I am pleased,' I managed to say. As he left us, I took Birana's hand and felt the iciness of her fingers.

The camp was silent as the men slept. I moved closer to Birana and felt the trembling of her body as she lay next to me. My fear had driven away any longing for her.

'Can you teach me to hold my mind still when I swallow that potion?' I whispered. 'Can you control your own thoughts?'

'I don't know. We don't know what we'll be drinking, or what it does.'

Everything in me, all of the thoughts they would see as unholy and blasphemous, might escape from me. All the truth Birana had told me might be revealed to them. They would know what Birana was, and if they learned that the Lady had ordered her death and that I had disobeyed this command, they might slay us both.

On the wall of dirt and stone, a few men were guarding the camp. I could not go to the Prayergiver's hut without being seen.

I put my lips to Birana's ear. 'Listen to me,' I said softly as I began to tell her what we would have to do.

The dawn promised fine weather for the ceremonies the men had planned. Some set out to gather wood and to relieve those who had watched during the night. The plant tenders carried baskets to their gardens and began to gather food.

I crawled out of the shelter and stood up as Birana got to her feet. 'Are you prepared?'

She nodded.

'Do not look at the men as we pass and keep your hands at your sides.' I had taken my knives from my belt. She dropped her knife next to mine.

We walked up into the clearing. A few men were standing in the doorways of their dwellings, and I could feel their eyes on us. We crossed the clearing. The Prayergiver's hut was ahead; a reed mat hung in its entrance. I knew the man was inside, for I had not seen him leave his hut, had not seen him at all during our time in the camp. We continued toward the small dwelling until we were only a few paces from the entrance.

'Stop there!' a man shouted from the wall in the holy speech. His spear was raised, while a man near him was already aiming an arrow at Birana. I was as close as I dared to go.

We sat down. 'I would speak to the Prayergiver,' I called out, hoping he would hear me.

Two of the men who had hunted with me strode toward us. 'He has not asked to speak to you. Get away from here before you're punished for your boldness.'

I held out my hands. 'We carry no weapons.' I opened my coat to show that I had no knife. 'We mean no harm, but there are matters I would speak of to your Prayergiver.'

Jerlan left his dwelling and hastened toward us, Tulan at his heels. He halted in front of me and shook his fist. 'I led you here,' he said. 'I hunted with you, I told the Headman you were worthy. You abuse my trust. Our Prayergiver is not to be disturbed in his holy tasks.'

'I would speak to him of holiness,' I replied, making my words clear and sharp. Jerlan was about to strike me when Tulan grabbed at his arm, holding him back. 'There is a holy truth I must reveal to him and to no one else.' Jerlan stepped back. 'So that you will know I speak truly, Spellweaver will show you the magic he carries.'

I gestured at Birana. She pulled out the chain around her neck, drew it over her head, and held out her compass. Jerlan leaned over to peer at it. 'Do you see the device upon it? A powerful spell holds that tiny spear, which always points to the north. With this magic, a man can always know where he is travelling, even in unknown lands where the sun may be hidden by trees or the stars by clouds. It is this magic that helped to guide us here, and it is a gift of the Lady, for Spellweaver brought it out of an enclave.'

Jerlan thrust up one hand while the other men made signs. Tulan's dark eyes widened. 'There are many spells,' Jerlan said, 'and not all are good.' He gazed at the compass, as Birana turned it in her hand, then backed away.

'Let your Prayergiver decide our fate,' I said, nearly shouting the words. 'I think he will want to know of this spell.'

'I do not hear him call,' one of the hunters said. 'He won't summon you.'

I stared at the reed mat. Perhaps the Prayergiver was so deep in prayer he had not heard our talk. He might be sleeping still. I did not know the customs of this band well; I had risked too much.

'I believed you were a good man,' Jerlan said solemnly. 'Yet after you hunted, you told me of such unholiness that I could hardly believe such things could be, and now you show us this unholy magic. It is our duty to shield our Prayergiver from evil intentions. I am sorry for this, but I know what I must do.'

He dragged me to my feet swiftly. Another man seized Birana by the hair as he drew out his knife.

'Hold!' a voice shouted.

A hand lifted the reed mat. A grey-haired man stepped outside. Jerlan let go as this man motioned to me.

'I shall call these two travellers to speak to me,' the Prayergiver said. 'I'll decide if they are holy or unholy. The Lady will protect me from any unholiness, and I am not so feeble that others must protect me as well. Let them enter, then leave this place so that we may talk freely.'

Birana hung her chain around her neck. We entered the Prayergiver's hut.

The man let the mat fall. Now that I was closer to him, I saw that, despite his grey hair, he was younger than I had expected. 'You may sit,' he said. 'The others are gone. Don't think you can strike at me, or you will die when you leave this house.'

I showed him my empty hands, keeping them before me as I sat down. Light shone through an opening between the roof and the upper part of the wall. From a hole in the centre of the roof, a wide beam of sunlight fell on ashes surrounded by rocks. On the ground, set against the wall of upright trunks, lay a mat and two hides, but another object had caught my eyes. A small figure of wood, crudely carved, stood next to the mat. The head of this image had no features and its arms were only stumps, but two mounds had been carved on its chest while the space between its legs was smooth.

The Prayergiver seated himself. 'I heard you speak of spells and holiness,' he continued. 'Know that I am one who has seen true holiness and lives with it daily. You cannot deceive me.'

'I am called Arvil,' I responded, 'and I too have seen holiness. Gaze upon the one with me, the one called Spellweaver, and tell me what you see.'

He leaned forward. Birana stood up, knowing what she would have to do, but her eyes were lowered and her face aflame. She took off her shirt and then lowered her pants. I wanted to leap up and conceal her body from this man, from all men.

'Tell me what She is,' I said.

He held up a hand. 'She is a holy aspect, and you are Her messenger.' He stared at her for a long moment, then covered his eyes. Birana's hands trembled as she put on her garments.

As she sat down, she began to speak the words I had given her the night before. 'I come among you to test you. It was My wish to reveal Myself to you, a holy man, but to keep the guise of a boy before others because they must not know what I am. Arvil is My true servant, for I chose him from among all men to travel with Me to this place.' She said these words calmly, but strain and fear marked her face.

The Prayergiver's hand fell, but he kept his eyes down. I had thought he would grovel. Perhaps he was too awed to move, or perhaps he was certain of his place in the Lady's thoughts. 'You are to have a truthsaying. Shall my band know of You then, Holy Lady?'

'There must be no truthsaying for Arvil and Me, Prayergiver,' she replied. 'If the magic in us were released, it would overcome your band. They must not know what I am, though I will bless them in My thoughts.'

'I know Your nature, Holy One. No longer will Your garb conceal Your form from me, for I know what is hidden. Others with sharp eyes will know a vision has been imparted to me when I step from this house. If You dwell among us for long, others will see what You are.'

'I cannot stay here,' she said. 'I must travel to another place.' He looked up at her then. 'I think I know what You seek. You are not the first holy vision I have beheld.'

Birana's eyes widened. 'You will take us to the place where you saw this vision.'

The Prayergiver shielded his face. 'Forgive me, but I do not know if I can. I was told I must never enter that place again.'

Birana said, 'You will be going there with Me.'

'Lady, forgive me, but they may not see what You are when we approach. I see that You wear a body of flesh and bone, and although You must have the power to shield Yourself, You may bring a curse on that other band should they raise their weapons against You before they know the truth. You may bring a curse upon me for leading You into such danger.'

This man was wise, and his eyes saw much. He believed Birana had hidden powers she could use, for his awe of the Lady would not allow him to think anything else. Yet his eyes had seen her weakness, had shown him her vulnerability.

'I cannot stay here.' Her voice was fainter, more desperate.

'Forgive me, Holy Lady, but it might be best if You did for a time. A man of that other band may come here to fetch a boy to take back with him, and I could tell him of the vision You have shown me. You could then travel safely with him to the place where all the Prayergivers saw holiness.'

Birana was silent. I knew that she wanted to ask exactly what he had seen there, but could not without revealing that she was not as all-knowing as the Prayergiver thought.

'Will such a man come here soon?' I asked.

'I cannot say. He will come, but he may not travel here this season or the next. He might come during another summer. I cannot know, unless it is in Your power to summon one here.'

Birana's hands tightened into fists. I wondered what she would say. The Prayergiver was studying her, perhaps curious about how many powers she seemed to lack.

'I shall do my best,' he said at last, 'to see that Your secret is kept here if that is Your will.'

'I cannot wait,' she said. 'You must find a way for Me and My servant Arvil to travel to the place where you saw your vision. Whatever befalls this form I wear, I promise you that you will be free from blame and that your band will not suffer. You must guide Me. My powers grow weaker in your world and must be restored to Me in that other place. I am testing you. You must not fail My test.'

He sighed; his beardless face had the look of a man contending with himself. 'I fear this test,' he said, 'but if You will it, then I must go with You. I shall bring the best men with me to lead You there.'

She shook her head. 'No others. We must go alone. It is only you who must know what I am, and on you rests the fate of your band. You must never tell your men what I am.'

'I swear to You I will not. I've kept holy secrets for a long time.' His dark eyes narrowed. 'But my men will be wondering what has been said in here. How can I utter false words before an aspect when I speak to them?'

'You need not say false words,' I said, 'only words that do not reveal all of the truth.'

He rubbed at his face, then got up, bowed to Birana, and went to the spot where his belongings lay. From under the hides, he took a small round object with a piece of hide across it.

We followed him outside. The clearing was empty, but eyes peered at us from the doors of dwellings. As we sat down, the Prayergiver struck the hide with his hands and made the sound of a heart beating. 'Come out!' he cried. 'Your Prayergiver has words for you.'

Men and boys emerged from the dwellings and quickly seated themselves in the open space. On the wall, the men guarding the camp looked toward us. 'You, there,' the Prayergiver said to the nearest boy. 'Mark my words, and then go to those on the wall and to those hidden by the trail and tell them all that I have said.'

The men waited. Their Headman sat among them, his wide bulk dwarfing those next to him, his face set in a frown. 'You will prepare the feast,' the Prayergiver said, 'and we shall eat it tonight, but I tell you that these two travellers will not join our band.'

The men muttered at this. The Headman suddenly stood up

and strode toward us, then sat down before the Prayergiver. 'I'll say what will happen.' The Headman struck his chest. 'You have honour as our Prayergiver, but I am Headman. We have not yet had our truthsaying. These two cannot leave until they have passed through it.'

'There has been another kind of truthsaying inside my house. These two have been touched by holiness and have revealed a vision to me, one of such power that I cannot speak of it. Their place is with the band to the east where I saw a holy vision so long ago. We shall have our feast and honour them for revealing more holiness to me, and then I'll take them to that other band.'

'It must be so,' Jerlan called out. 'I see by the Prayergiver's face that he speaks truly.'

The Headman hit the ground with his fist. 'I am Headman! I say that they must drink so we know the truth about them.'

'Do you question me, Irlan?' The Prayergiver tensed. 'I know more of holy matters than anyone here. Do you question one who must live closer to holiness than all of you, and who will know a true vision?'

Irlan's lip curled. 'Even a holy man might be deceived. How do you know that some evil hasn't cloaked itself in the guise of good? You say these two were touched by holiness. I see only a strange boy, who tends beasts and has not shown skill at other crafts, and a strange man, who is hardly more than a boy himself. Jerlan says they have no band, but perhaps they have lied and will lead their band here later.'

'They wish nothing from us, only to be led to that other camp.'

'If you take them there, you may only bring evil upon us all.'

The men in the clearing were now whispering among themselves in their own tongue. Some were looking at Irlan, while others gazed at the Prayergiver, as if not knowing which man to believe.

The Prayergiver leaned forward until his face was close to the Headman's. Still using the holy speech, he said. 'The vision I saw was a true one, and I won't have you bring a curse upon us by denying it.' He spoke so softly that none of the others could hear, and even I, sitting beside him, could barely catch his words. 'Perhaps we must settle this as we settle other disagreements. I can cast off my holy duties for a time, and we can contend as two men only. The victor can decide what comes to pass.'

Irlan grinned. 'You are an old man, Prayergiver.'

'And you are a fat one who has not hunted for many seasons. When I contend with you as Girlan, the man I once was, we will be matched.'

'I am ready to fight you,' Irlan whispered.

'Never before has a Prayergiver had to contend with a Headman, and I wonder what will come of it. There is no way to settle this with only a test of skill. This must be a battle to the death.'

Irlan pressed his lips together,

'If I die, you must become Prayergiver. You will then know what these two travellers are when their vision is imparted to you, and you will suffer for knowing I spoke truthfully. You will spend the rest of your life in prayer, inside my house, atoning for your deed and saying the prayers we require, and I don't know if you are ready for such a life.'

The Headman's eyes shifted a little.

'But I may win, for the spirit of the Lady guides me. I may choose to be merciful and spare your life, but the others will see that you cannot remain Headman and cannot be Prayergiver, either. I wonder if you could stay among us then. Very well, Irlan. Say now if we must put aside our bond as band members to settle this. I have spoken softly, and no one has heard. You won't lose your pride if you rise up now and tell the men we will do as I wish.'

Irlan was silent, then lifted his head and gazed at me with such hatred that I almost looked away. I had witnessed his loss of face. It came to me that the Headman would seek to regain it somehow.

Irlan stood up, grunting as he lifted his heavy body, then turned to face the others. 'It is my duty to protect this band,' he bellowed, 'but I see now that we are in no danger from these two travellers. I shall heed the Prayergiver, and we'll have our feast, but there will be no truthsaying tonight.' He puffed out his chest as he walked toward his men.

The Prayergiver rose and motioned to us. 'I shall walk with the travellers to their shelter.'

The men parted as we walked past. Jerlan nodded at me while Tulan smiled. Jerlan, I saw, had forgotten his angry words. Irlan stood with a small group of men, but their eyes were hard as they gazed at us. The Headman had spoken, but he had not settled this matter in his mind.

'I would have you abide in my house,' the Prayergiver said to me as we came to my shelter, 'but a Prayergiver must dwell alone. Since you are not to join us, you should remain here, outside our dwellings.'

'You spoke bravely to the Headman,' I said.

'I drew courage from the Holy One.' He made a gesture of respect to Birana. 'She would have lent me Her strength in a fight.'

I frowned. 'But he is still angry.'

'Irlan is full of bluster. When I chose him as Headman, he was strong and brave, and yet I sensed then that he might be one who should follow rather than lead. But the others wanted him as Headman and would not easily have accepted another, so I chose him.'

'We didn't seek to divide your band, Prayergiver.'

'You will soon be gone, and Irlan will bluster and then forget. Rest easy, Arvil.' But I saw the doubt in his eyes before he turned away.

For the feast that night, we were taken to one of the dwellings. The men had placed mats around their hearth, and there they sang songs and spoke among themselves as they passed soup and fish to us. One of the men began to ask me what I had revealed to the Prayergiver, but the older man, who had come to sit with us, shook his head.

'Know that the magic I saw,' he said in the holy speech, 'was for my eyes alone, and that it would dazzle one who has not lived in prayer and contemplation for as long as I have.'

From that dwelling we passed to another, where we ate meat and leaves from their gardens, and then to the house where Irlan lived with the hunters closest to him. As the others feasted, Irlan's face darkened, and his eyes were often on me.

When the feast was over, some of the men left their dwellings to dance in the open space. The hunters gestured with their spears while those who gardened made motions at the ground with tools made of antlers and wood.

Jerlan came to me as Birana and I watched this dance. 'I'm sorry you won't stay with us,' he said. 'I am sorry that you didn't tell me your true purpose when we hunted together. I would have sat outside the Prayergiver's hut myself, waiting until he summoned me, and would then have asked him to summon you.'

'It wasn't time to speak of it, Jerlan. My vision bid me to stay among you for a time until your virtue was revealed.' The false words fell easily from my lips. I looked down at Birana and felt a sadness then. I might have found a place with this band. I might have hunted with Jerlan and become his true friend.

I saw life then not as one life, but as many forking paths, and a phantom Arvil seemed to stand with me, one who had walked another path and had come to another place. I saw that other Arvil join these men, and he seemed as real to me as my own body.

I shook off these thoughts. Had Birana not been with me, I would never have seen this camp at all, or have known of its ways. I would have been with Wise Soul and Wanderer, living as they did, with my questions for ever unanswered.

Birana had led me here, and each turn in our path had led to something new and perhaps better than what I had left behind, however much I mourned for what I had lost. Our destination might be better still. She could have left me here, now that she had the Prayergiver to guide her. She might, in front of the Prayergiver, have ordered that I stay here, and I would have followed that command or risked the Prayergiver's wrath. She still wanted me at her side; I would follow the path she walked.

'We must sleep soon,' I said.

Jerlan walked with us to our shelter. A fire burned near it. Tulan was with the horses over by the trees, and I guessed that he had made the fire. As we settled ourselves around the flames, the boy hurried toward us.

'I fed the horses,' Tulan said. 'Even Wild Spirit will take food from me. I wanted them to share the feast.' His smile faded as he sat down next to his guardian. 'Will you take the horses away, too?'

'I think we must,' I said. 'We'll no longer be here to teach you more about them.' I was also thinking that, if we could not enter the other camp, we would have to travel on.

Tulan's mouth drooped. 'I'll miss them, Arvil.'

'You will not miss them,' Jerlan said. 'We had no need of such beasts before.'

'I will miss you, Arvil,' the boy murmured. 'I will miss Spellweaver, who was to teach me how to ride. I wish . . .'

'What is it you wish?' his guardian asked. Tulan did not reply. 'I believe I know.' Jerlan scratched his head. 'I have a question, Arvil and Spellweaver. Might Tulan travel to that other camp with you and the Prayergiver? It may be that he won't be allowed to enter, but if they admit him, he could live close by their holy vision and be touched by it. I would be happy knowing that Tulan was so blessed, and that would ease the pain of giving him up.'

Tulan gazed at me expectantly. 'May I?'

I glanced at Birana. A look of sadness and longing was in her eyes. Could she have grown closer to the boy? I burned with jealousy, then chided myself silently. Tulan was only a boy who could not have left an enclave more than six summers ago. Perhaps Birana only wanted a friend who was not yet old enough to share my longing for her.

'We would gladly travel with him,' I said. Tulan clapped his hands together. 'But it is your Prayergiver who must agree to this as well.'

Jerlan put a hand on the boy's shoulder. 'If that camp accepts you,' he said, 'you cannot return here.'

The boy leaned against his guardian. 'I'd miss you, Jerlan, but I want to go. I want to be with them both, and hear their tales, and learn more of their beasts. I'll become a man in that other camp if they take me. Someday I may come here to fetch another boy for them.'

Jerlan ruffled his hair. 'We'll see what the Prayergiver says. He risks much going to that camp, even if he is to bring them news of holiness.' He got up and pulled Tulan to his feet. 'We must rest now.'

The heaviness of the food inside me soon brought me sleep. A dream came to me, one in which aspects of the Lady gathered along the shore of the lake and held out their arms to me. Birana was among them, beckoning to me, and the part of my soul apart from the dream saw this as a sign that I would find a true refuge. Their hands gestured to me, and then another hand clutched at me. I was suddenly awake.

I was dragged from under the shelter. Our fire was low, revealing only the shadows of several men. 'Seize them,' Irlan's voice said, 'and bear them to the place of testing.'

Two men held my arms against my sides. Two others gripped Birana; she did not struggled against them. We were led swiftly through the empty clearing and along the path by the gardens until we were outside the wall. Guards ran along the top of the wall but made no move to help us when they saw Irlan. One man gestured at a guard, and soon three torches had been set in the ground around us.

'No blood will be shed inside our camp,' the Headman said, 'but we will settle this while the others sleep. You won't have a truthsaying and so I cannot know if you have deceived our Prayergiver. Even one so holy can be led astray. You must there-fore contend with me. If there is true holiness inside you, let it shield you now.'

261

'You had better believe your Prayergiver,' I said. 'You accepted his word about the holy vision he saw before. Why do you doubt him now?'

'He travelled there with all the Prayergivers, and all saw the vision. Here, there is no other witness to the vision he claims you showed him. He may see holiness in you, but I see only two who have come here on the backs of beasts and have already begun to alter the ways we follow. I will fight you, who claim to be a man, and if your death proves you aren't holy after all, the boy will soon lie at your side.'

'You don't know what you will bring down upon yourself!' I shouted with all my power. One man stepped back while others glanced at one another. Two guards climbed down from the wall and raced back toward the dwellings.

'I am willing to test what I know with my own body, and prove its truth.' Irlan's chest swelled. He took off his garments until he was bare to the waist.

He was, I saw then, a man uneasy with his power. Perhaps others besides the Prayergiver thought he was full of bluster. I had seen him back down in front of his Prayergiver; now he would prove that he was a man after all.

His men made a wide circle around us. I flexed my arms and took deep breaths as I pulled off my shirt. Irlan reached toward his belt and took out his knife, and I saw how we were to fight. My hand grasped the hilt of my metal blade, but I took little comfort from my knife. Irlan's stone knife was sharp, and there were cords of muscle under his fat.

More men had now gathered on the wall and others were running toward us from the camp. 'He has shared a feast with us,' Jerlan cried from the wall. 'You heard what the Prayergiver said. He is to take them from this place tomorrow.'

'If holiness were truly theirs, I would allow it!' Irlan bellowed. 'It is that I will test now. You will see that I'm right. Haven't we thrived since I became Headman? Do you wish to see evil come upon us if these two travel east? Do you want that other band to discover that no holiness is in them and that we have harboured evil in our midst?'

'Headman,' Jerlan responded, 'if you contend with this man, you must set aside the bond that binds you to us for that time.'

'And I'll take up that bond again when he lies dead at my feet. You will see I was right, and there will be no more talk of how I've grown weaker in my leadership.'

He faced me, legs apart. The Prayergiver was now on the wall above me, but this matter had gone too far even for him to stop the fight. I glanced at Birana. The men standing with her had released her. Her hands were on her coat, as though she was ready to tear the garment from herself. By revealing what she was, she could save me.

Anger burned in me. 'I shall fight, Spellweaver,' I shouted, 'and you will watch.' She dropped her hands. This was a matter between Irlan and me, and I would be diminished if she revealed herself to save me. Then I forgot everything except the man who wanted me dead.

I danced toward Irlan, muttering curses in my old tongue. His powerful arm slashed at me. I leaped back, unharmed. His body swayed on his heavy legs. I could dodge his sweeps, but would only tire myself with the effort. He moved and swung his arm, staying close to the circle of men so that I could not get behind him. His knife darted at my face and I ducked. If he got too close to me, he could knock me to the ground with one blow. He slashed at me again and I feinted.

Thus we went on, lunging forward, darting to one side and slashing the air, probing each other for weakness. His body gleamed with sweat from his exertions as he slashed at me. I thought of what I would have to do against him. His sweat became rivers flowing down his chest and shone on his unbearded face. Strong as he was, he had grown too fat to fight easily. I began to see that he might tire first.

We went on in this way until it seemed half the night had passed. I panted for breath. Irlan's fist grazed my face and nearly sent me to the ground, but I regained my footing.

'Come, Irlan,' I said in the holy speech as I swept my knife before me. 'You are Headman of a great band, you are large with the wealth of your camp, and yet you cannot defeat me.' I paused for breath and heard his louder gaspings for air. 'I am shielded from you, Irlan. Your knife cannot touch me. When you lie before me, I will set my foot on your neck and grind your face in the dust.'

His face grew red. I went on tormenting him with the foulest words I knew until his face flamed and his breath came from him in great gusts.

He stepped away from the circle and lumbered toward me. I jumped quickly to one side. His back was open to me. Before he could turn, I passed my knife to my left hand and struck him in the lower back with my strongest blow. He staggered. I hit him again and felt him give way.

He fell, and the ground seemed to shake with his falling. I leaped to his head and dropped down to his arms on my knees, pinning him to the ground. He kicked helplessly, his face in the dirt, his body heaving under me. My blood sang in my ears, throbbing with a sound like the Prayergiver's drum. Very slowly, I made a long scratch along Irlan's neck with my knife and then another along his back.

I got up. 'I have won,' I shouted with the little breath I had left. 'You see I had the power of death over him.' My chest heaved as I gulped air. 'But he is your Headman, and so I won't take his life. You must decide his fate.'

All of the men were looking toward the Prayergiver. Irlan sat up, raised one trembling arm, then let it fall. 'I am one of you,' he said feebly.

The Prayergiver put out one hand, palm open. 'You put off your bond when you fought. You said to Jerlan that you would take it up again when Arvil lay at your feet. He doesn't lie at your feet. You are no longer one of us. You did evil, Irlan. Now the Lady has shielded him from you and shown what he is. You can no longer be Headman, for you failed the contest you yourself sought. Your contest was to be to the death, and it is death you have won.'

I went to Birana as the circle closed around Irlan. We walked together toward the opening in the wall. None of the men followed us. Irlan's screams were already sounding through the night as we walked past the gardens. I did not look back. Birana halted, and I heard the sound of retching.

I put my hands on her head, trying to steady her. 'You are safe,' I said, 'and I'll sleep soundly now.'

I had thought that only preparations for the journey remained, but now the camp was without a Headman and a new one had to be chosen. The Prayergiver left his hut, took up Irlan's knife and spear, and went from one dwelling to another as both Prayergiver and Headman to learn what was in the men's hearts. At the end of the day, he surrendered the weapons to Jerlan, and it was Jerlan who became the new Headman.

This change required more prayers from everyone in front of the Prayergiver's house, where each man had to pass before the Prayergiver and Jerlan and kneel as he spoke holy words to the pair. Birana and I were the last to honour Jerlan, but because we were not members of the band, we bowed and did not kneel. Jerlan smiled at us then, for if we had not come here, perhaps he would not have been Headman.

Even after this, the band was not ready for us to leave. Jerlan had said Tulan might travel with us. Now he was Headman, and worried that showing his charge such favour might bring about hard feelings. He decreed a contest among the boys, saying that the winner would go with us.

My mind was not on these contests, although I hoped that Tulan would win them. We sat with the Prayergiver as the boys wrestled, shot arrows, ran footraces to the wall and back, threw spears, aimed stones in slings at targets, and threw knives at a bare spot on a distant tree. Jerlan made signs in the dirt at the end of each contest while I watched and longed to be away.

When the contests were over, Tulan had won the footraces and the stone-slinging, while his arrows had found their targets more often than those of others. No other boy had won as many contests, and perhaps the way Birana had smiled at the boy had cheered him. I praised him when he came before his guardian and saw the pride in his face. His journey was no longer a gift, but a prize he had won.

Jerlan stood up, beaming at his charge, and then spoke. 'We rest tonight. Tomorrow we shall gather food for the travellers, and on the next day say farewell to them. May the Lady bless us all.'

Before we left, Jerlan wished us well and hugged his charge, and although Tulan's eyes shone at this leave-taking, he held himself in and did not let his tears fall.

The Prayergiver walked ahead of us as we led the horses through the wall. We walked south and then east, following a faint trail through the wood. When the camp was completely hidden, Birana mounted Flame.

'It would ride,' Tulan said as he gazed up at her.

'You must learn how to sit on a horse first,' she replied. 'When we stop to rest later, I'll show you.' Tulan grinned as she spoke. We had decided to keep Birana's secret from the boy until we reached the other camp and learned whether those men would accept him, but Tulan was already seeing her as a friend.

The Prayergiver shook his head. 'I am too old to learn such a thing.' Old as he was, he walked with the sure step of a younger man. Through the trees, the lake below glistened as the sun shone upon it. I was leading Star and told the Prayergiver a little of how the horse had carried me to this land from the west.

'I'll tell you this,' the Prayergiver murmured when we were farther ahead of Birana and Tulan. 'You have brought me some joy, whatever awaits us, for if I did not have to lead, I would have remained in my camp until I died. I'm grateful for the privilege of praying to the Lady for my band, but such a life has been hard for me.'

I thought of the Wolf and how he had died as an Elder. 'It is not a bad life for an old one to be cared for by those who are younger,' I said.

'But I was a young Headman when the Prayergiver before me died, and the thought of spending my days in my house has sometimes weighed heavily on me.' He glanced back at Birana and made a sign. 'May the Lady forgive me.'

'The Lady would understand.'

'The Lady is good, and, had I not been a Prayergiver, I would not have beheld Her form two times.'

These were welcome words, and again I wanted to know the secret of the camp to the east.

'Often,' he continued, 'I went to the wall at night and tested myself with one of the guards at the skills of men. Sometimes the men would question me for doing this, but I would say that I had given the days to my prayers and that the nights were my own. I often told the Headman who came after me that he would do well to hone his arts from time to time.'

'Irlan should have listened to you,' I said politely, although I was grateful he had not.

'Do not speak his name. He was an unholy fool, and it's good that he's no longer able to bring a curse upon us. I am older now and have made a wiser choice. Jerlan will be a better Headman and even those closest to that other man will see that as time passes.'

We did not speak again until we stopped to water the horses and eat a meal. The Prayergiver asked for a story to carry back to his band, and I told him Wanderer's tale of the man who had dwelled in a shrine and taken on the Lady's form. I hoped this would lead him to talk more of his first vision, but he did not speak of that.

As we talked, Birana showed Tulan how to mount, how to sit on a horse, and led Flame in a circle around us while the boy sat on her back. When we set off again, Birana allowed Tulan to ride Flame with her, and without his shorter steps slowing us we were able to increase our pace. The lake wrinkled as the sun gleamed in its folds, and the trees sang their songs to us as their limbs sought to embrace the sky.

*

We made our camp by the lake. By morning, a mist hung over the water, and as we went back to the trail, rain began to fall.

'We have needed more rain,' the Prayergiver said, 'but even more rain will not restore our soil.' He went on to tell me of how growing plants tired the soil even when some was left fallow for a season, and of how his band might have to move its camp in seasons to come.

'It would be hard to move such a camp,' I said.

'Yet it has been moved before. Once it lay farther from the shore, and before that to the north of where it is now.'

The old man led us off the trail later that day. 'Another camp lies ahead,' he told me in a low voice. 'Although they have truce with us, it is better if we don't stop with them, for they might wonder about our purpose.'

We made camp that night far above the lake, and below to the west, I saw the distant smoke of a camp's fires. The rain was only a drizzle by now, moist droplets that seemed to hang in the air. Even from this place, the northern shore of the lake was hidden, and I could not see where to the east it ended.

The rain stopped during the night but did not cool the land. By morning the sun gave off much heat, and the air hung still and heavy. Tulan had taken off his shirt, and the Prayergiver and I wore only our pants to protect our legs, but Birana dared not pull off her deerskin coat. By the time we came to the trail again, I could see her discomfort.

When evening came, the heat still clung to the land. As we made camp, Birana came to me and whispered, 'I must bathe.'

'We shall see,' I replied, then took the Prayergiver aside while Tulan rubbed down the horses. 'My companion wishes to bathe,' I said. 'In this form, Her body is as ours, but She does not wish that men set eyes upon Her lest the sight rob them of their souls.'

He assured me that another camp's boats would not pass this way on the water and that travellers were unlikely to move along the trail in the evening, but promised to keep watch with Tulan by the trail.

'I'll go with my companion to the lake,' I said, 'and bathe there when She is done.'

His brows lifted above his wise eyes. 'Best that you also do not look too long upon Her, Arvil, however favoured you are. Her spell lies heavily upon you.'

Birana and I made our way down to the lake and found a sheltered spot where we could not be seen from above. I told her what I had said to the Prayergiver, and she covered her mouth as she laughed.

'Lest the sight of me rob them of their souls!' She shook her head, and I did not say that she had stolen mine. She turned her back to me as she took off her garments; this time, she did not ask me to look away, and I did not turn aside. Did this mean she had grown easier with me? Perhaps it meant only that she knew I would not dare to seek blessings now that I was aware of what they might lead to for her.

She crept down to the water and my heart raced as I beheld her. Her face, neck and hands had grown browner, but her skin was pale as moonlight, and I longed to put my hands upon her. Soft cries escaped her as the coldness of the lake raised tiny bumps on her skin. She put out her arms and moved upon the water. Her arms curved as they carried her forward and her buttocks rose above the surface as she kicked.

Suddenly she disappeared below the lake. Her feet poked above the water, and then she was gone. I jumped down to the edge of the bank, helpless, fearing for her, and then her head bobbed up. I let out my breath.

'You go too far!' I cried.

She laughed and sank below the water again, then reappeared closer to the shore. 'You were to bathe,' I said, 'not to make me fear for your safety.'

'I'm only swimming. Don't you know how to swim?'

I shook my head.

'I'll show you how.' She moved her arms and came closer. I looked around. Tulan and the Prayergiver would call out if anyone approached. I shed my garments quickly and entered the lake.

Birana did not look at me until the water was up to my waist, and then she moved her arms and showed me how to move mine. I struggled and splashed about, unable to bring my arms and legs to work together, for the water kept pulling me below. Birana swam out, but I followed her only to a place where I could stand with my head above the lake.

'Didn't your band ever swim?' she asked when she had drifted nearer.

'We had no need, but if I am to live by a lake, I see I may have to learn.'

Her feet rose up as she floated. The nipples of her breasts were hard. I lifted my own feet and again gulped water as my arms flailed. She laughed as she watched me. I looked foolish before her and yet felt joy at hearing her laugh, at feeling the cool caresses of the lake's currents. I had made her laugh and echoed her laughter.

As we left the water, I reached for her, only meaning to take her hand, although I wanted to press her body to mine. Her brown hair hung in wet curls around her face and shoulders. Her belly was taut between the rounded curves of her hips and her breasts glistened with droplets. As my hand touched hers, she started, pulled away, and hunched over, covering her breasts with one hand and the hairy place between her legs with the other.

We did not look at each other as we dressed. When I had finished putting on my garments, she was sitting on a rock by the water, brushing grass and pine needles from her feet. The foot-coverings she used inside her boots were worn. I sat on the ground beside her as I glanced at her callused, scabbed feet.

'I should make new foot-coverings for you,' I said, 'and softer boots to wear over them.'

'Tulan asked me about my boots,' she said. 'He said others in his band had noticed them. I told him that they were taken from a scavenger.' Her voice was high, and she kept her eyes from me.

I said, 'I meant only to touch your hand, Birana.'

'I saw what was in your eyes.'

'You were easy with me. No barrier stood between us. I wanted only to touch you as I would a friend.' Then more words I had not meant to say flowed from me. 'No, that isn't so. I wanted to touch your hand, and then other parts of you, and I wanted to feel your hands on me.'

She stood up quickly. 'You mustn't say this.'

I got to my feet and pulled her toward me. Memories of aspects came to me, recollections of how the spirit-women had put their mouths on mine. I held her against me as my hand lifted her face to mine, then pressed my lips to hers.

Her mouth was hard. Then her lips softened a little under mine, parting. My mouth opened. She quickly turned her head from me and twisted in my arms until I released her. She sat down and covered her face.

'Birana . . .'

'I was only thinking – you are like someone I knew.' She huddled on the rock, her body stooped. 'I forgot myself. I won't let it happen again. I won't uncover myself in front of you. I should have asked you to turn away.'

'Don't say such words to me. You grant little else. At least let my eyes know you.'

She pulled on her boots. We climbed up toward our camp. When we were close to it, and she could not protest without drawing the Prayergiver's attention, I leaned toward her and took her arm for a moment. 'I shall treasure that time,' I whispered, 'when I brought laughter to you and our souls communed for a time in that laughter.'

She turned her head from me, but not before I had seen her eyes grow gentle and knew that I had moved her.

The Prayergiver and Tulan bathed at dawn before we left our camp. Later that day, we again left the trail and skirted a cove where, the Prayergiver said, men often went in boats to fish.

The next day, we circled around another camp of men. By this time, Tulan had grown more used to the horses and was even able to ride Wild Spirit for a little while, something I still feared to do. 'You would make a good horseman,' I said to him.

He smiled with pride. 'The band will have to take me,' he said. 'I can do anything they can do, and I can ride as well.'

'Hold your tongue, young one,' the Prayergiver muttered. 'It is the band who will decide matters, not your pride.'

Tulan tossed his head as Birana rode up to his side. He seemed happy to be with her. Although he still thought of her as an older boy, she was unlike others he had known; she did not order him around and listened patiently to his tales of his life. I almost wished myself in the boy's place, for Tulan was able to be her friend without aching for her.

As we moved closer to the lake again, I saw what seemed to be the northern shore, then understood that the land was an island. The lake still stretched on, without end. The Prayergiver had grown more solemn, and the prayers he murmured from time to time as we walked became more frequent. I guessed that we were finally coming closer to our destination.

That evening, after we had made our camp and collected wood for the fire, the old man motioned to us.

'I must say this now,' he said. 'We draw closer to the camp where I saw my vision, and we must be more careful. I believe their truce with me will keep them from harming us, and yet I am returning when I promised I would not. It may be that they won't accept us in their camp.'

The Prayergiver made a gesture at Tulan, then told him to fetch water from the lake. When the boy was gone, the old man continued, 'If they learn what She is, they will accept Her. They may turn you away, Arvil, even if you are a holy messenger. Tulan and I can go back to our camp, but your presence among us might create hard feeling in those who were close to the former Headman. I would have Jerlan able to take up his duties without that problem.'

'I understand.' I said.

'You might find a place among another lake band, but you'll have to pass through a truthsaying with them. You would reveal the visions you have had.'

'Then I'll go east.' The words pained me. I did not care where I went without Birana.

The Prayergiver shook his head and made a sign.

'Do you know what lies to the east?' I asked.

'There are two camps on the easternmost shore, and a gorge through which a river feeds the lake. It is said that evil ones once preyed upon the lake bands in ancient times, and that they lived in the east. I don't know what lies there now and don't want to know. Even the Lady turns Her eyes from that land.' He made another sign.

'I will want Arvil with Me,' Birana said. Despite my worries, her words eased me. She had said nothing about what had passed between us by the lake, and I had feared she might want me away from her side.

The Prayergiver was silent for a moment. 'May the Lady forgive me for saying this, but I cannot hide my thoughts from Her and will speak them aloud to You, Holy One. You showed me a holy vision. The Headman who came after me challenged the truth of this vision, and now he is dead, and perhaps that shows the truth of it. But it comes to me that an evil one can also have power over men and seek to deceive them. Your presence in our camp caused us to lose our Headman, and foolish as he was, that's not a good sign. Such things, when they happened in the past, were evil omens. I believe You holy, but let me tell You now that the band You go to will see the truth of You.'

'They will not harm Her,' I said, wanting to believe it.

When the boy returned, the Prayergiver beckoned to him. 'Tulan, your guardian asked me to say this to you when we were close to that camp. If they allow you to enter, you will not leave.'

'I know that.'

'But you have not thought much about what I will say now. It is said that those men, because a vision has come to them, are not required to travel to shrines to be called. It is why they come among the lake bands to seek boys. You're too young to know much of the special blessings the Lady sends to men and older boys in shrines and in Her enclave. Such blessings are the greatest joys and pleasures a man can know, and I don't know what blessings this other band can give you in place of them.'

Tulan lifted his head. 'Living near a holy place will be enough for me.'

'You think that now, but when you are older, your body will burn for such blessings.'

'There will be men,' Tulan said, 'and other boys.'

'Pleasant as those joys are, they are less than the Lady can give, for She touches the soul as well as the body.' The Prayergiver sighed. 'Jerlan asked me to say this so that you would know what it is you're choosing. If you wish, we can say nothing to that band about your desire to join them, and you can return to your camp. There will be no disgrace in that for you.'

'No,' the boy answered. 'I want to go.'

The old man rubbed his chin. 'I wonder if it is holiness you want or simply the chance to stay with those beasts.'

'I want to stay with Spellweaver and Arvil, too.'

I smiled at the boy's words. Perhaps, knowing that I could never again go to an enclave and be given a boy, and that young Hasin would have to live his life without me, I was growing to care for Tulan. Yet the day might come when he would feel his soul stir, and I wondered how he would look at Birana then. I might have to protect her from him. Any affection for Tulan would end.

'Ah.' The Prayergiver shrugged. 'The young often seem to want what is new and different until they learn some wisdom.'

'You also seek some newness,' I said. 'Here you are with us, not quite sure of what lies ahead.'

'You speak truly. Some youth is in my soul still.'

We slept and, in the morning, the Prayergiver said many prayers as we prepared to go to what I hoped would be our refuge.

Toward midday, I felt eyes upon us and knew we were being watched. I caught no sight of anyone. These men had the stealth of Jerlan and his band and betrayed themselves with no sound. As we walked on, the cries of birds echoed among the trees, but something in their song made me wonder if it was birds that sang it.

As we reached a clearing that looked out over the lake, a voice behind us said, 'Cast down your weapons.'

We obeyed. Four men dropped to the ground from the trees around the clearing, lifted their bows, and aimed their arrows at us. 'We come in peace,' the Prayergiver said.

One man lowered his bow. 'You wear the garments of the lake bands,' he continued in the holy speech, 'as does that boy, and yet you bring two strangers here, and beasts as well. You know that you cannot enter our camp.'

'I am Prayergiver for my band. I have travelled here before and have seen your holy vision.'

The man gestured angrily. 'Then you know you were not to return.'

The Prayergiver held out his hands. 'If I cannot enter, then bring your Prayergiver outside your camp, and I shall speak to him of another vision I have seen.'

'Another vision?' The stranger scowled.

'I shall tell your Prayergiver of holiness.'

'He's too old and weak to leave the camp,' another man said.

'Then bring out your Headman, so that I may speak to him. I tell you that, blessed as you are now, your blessings will be multiplied if you heed me and welcome these travellers. If you do not, a curse will fall upon you.'

The first man who had spoken laughed. 'Do you think we, so loved of the Lady, can be cursed by you?'

'It will be so if you don't welcome these two travellers.'

'We take strangers into our camp no more and speak to them only away from it. I shall tell these two now that, if we do not like what we hear, they must die. We have a truce with you, Prayergiver, but not with them.'

'I must speak to your Headman,' the Prayergiver said firmly. 'You know that I wouldn't have travelled here and left my band without my prayers for something of little consequence.'

The men spoke among themselves, and then another stepped forward. 'You may turn back now, and we shall let you leave safely.'

The Prayergiver shook his head. 'I'll stay until your Headman speaks to me.'

'You risk breaking your truce with us, old man.'

'Then I'll risk it.'

The men said more to the Prayergiver in the lake tongue, and he replied in the same speech. At last one man turned and ran into the wood while the others remained.

'He will fetch their Headman,' the Prayergiver said. 'It is he who will have to decide about us. It seems that while we wait, we must make our camp here.'

By nightfall, no one had come for us. We would have to sleep under the eyes of the men who guarded us.

The horses had been tethered, but our guards kept well away from them. I raised a shelter for Birana and then lay down beside her. 'If the Headman doesn't come,' I said, 'you will have to show them what you are.'

She shivered. 'But the Prayergiver seems to think it's important to speak to this Headman.'

'It doesn't matter. Would you rather feel an arrow in your chest?'

She said no more that night, but once she called out in her sleep. I put my hand on her shoulder to calm her, wondering if it had been wise to come here.

In the morning, the Prayergiver took out some food, but I had no appetite for it. I gazed at the piece of dried fish in my hand for a moment, then rose and walked toward our guards. 'For you,' I said, 'so that you will know we mean no harm.'

One man stretched out a hand, but his companion slapped his arm down. 'Don't take it. We will not take food from one who may have to die at our hands.' His brown eyes were hard as he looked at me.

I walked back to Birana and sat down. 'Can this camp be so far?' I asked the Prayergiver.

'It isn't far, but perhaps the Headman must decide if he should come here.'

'And if he does not?'

The old man glanced at Tulan, then spoke softly. 'If he doesn't, hope those others see the truth before you die. I have a truce with them. I can defend you only with words.'

I waited impatiently, thinking of trying to escape with Birana on our horses before they could stop us. But it would be useless to flee. We did not know this wood, and the horses, slowed by underbrush, might not be able to outrun the men.

Three men suddenly emerged from the trees. A fourth man followed them into the clearing, and I knew before I was told that he was Headman here. He was tall, even taller than I, and his spear was decorated with feathers as Irlan's had been. His unbearded face, with its strong chin and even features unmarked by blows, was one of beauty. His light brown hair fell to his shoulders and though his bare, broad chest was nearly as wide as Irlan's, he carried no fat on his body. I did not want to risk a contest with this man.

The Prayergiver rose quickly and bowed; Birana and I followed his example. The Headman spoke a few words in the lake tongue.

'Greetings, Headman,' the Prayergiver answered in holy speech. 'I would speak to you in this tongue, for it is holiness I bring to you.'

'Do not stain your soul with false words, Prayergiver,' the Headman replied in the same speech. 'You were not to travel here again, but now I'm told you have seen a vision. What holiness can you bring us that we don't already have?'

'I bring holiness, and you will see it and be sorry for your words. I swear by the Lady that I'll offer my life freely to you if you do not find holiness, for I don't want to live if my vision was a false one.'

These words had clearly moved the Headman. He handed his spear to one of his men, then said, 'And how will I know the truth of this vision?'

'You will see it.' The Prayergiver waved a hand at me. 'Our Headman challenged the truth this man told me, and contested with him, and died for his foolishness. This boy proved himself in contests before we came here and wants a place with you. I would have you accept both of them among your men.'

The Headman looked at Birana. 'And this other boy?'

'That one will show you that my holy vision was true.'

The Headman's lip curled. 'We will take the smaller boy if I find you have been truthful. If not, he will carry the news of your death, the death you chose, and word of the deaths of these strangers back to your camp.'

'They are my friends!' Tulan cried out. 'You mustn't hurt them.'

'Be silent,' the Headman said. I put a hand on Tulan's shoulder, moved by his words but afraid of what the Headman might do. He looked down at Tulan from his great height and the shadow of a smile touched his lips. 'Brave words are empty unless followed by deeds, and you are too small to give your words force.' He looked around at his men, then turned back to the Prayergiver. 'You say that your Headman challenged the truth of your vision. Didn't a truthsaying reveal the truth?'

The old man said. 'There was no need for a truthsaying, as you will see.' He moved closer to Birana. 'This one will show you.'

As the Headman gazed steadily at Birana with his dark eyes, a look of wonder and then understanding passed over his face. I was suddenly sure, without knowing why, that he had guessed what she was. 'Prayergiver,' he said, 'you will come with this one and with me, and we shall see what truth is revealed. If an evil one has deceived you, I will not have my men stained by the evil.'

He walked toward the trees. Birana, head bowed, followed him, the Prayergiver at her side. I wanted to follow her, to shield her however I could.

I sat down with Tulan to wait. I would never forgive myself if harm came to her; I would contend with this Headman even if it meant my death. A long time seemed to pass, and then there was a shout from the trees. My throat was dry with fear.

The Headman came into the clearing, holding out an arm as Birana and the Prayergiver emerged from the trees. 'Holy messenger!' he cried to me. 'Forgive me for my words.' I knew then that we were safe and yet saw no awe or fear in this man's face, only triumph and pride. 'Kneel!' he shouted to the others. 'Know that we who are blessed are blessed again. The Lady has come among us in this guise, and a holy aspect is among us.'

Birana had taken off her coat and held it at her side. Her belt was over her shirt, around her waist, making the swell of her breasts and hips apparent. This was enough to convince the men, who knelt and struck their heads on the ground. Tulan gaped at me for a moment, then threw himself on to the grass.

'She and Her messenger seek to live among us,' the Headman continued. 'Give thanks that we have been found worthy once more.' Hope rose in me. His words could mean only that he had seen at least of Birana's kind before. Yet still he did not bow but stood easily at her side, as though this vision were no more than his due.

Birana was pale. Fear marked her face, and her hands trembled at her sides. She did not look like one who had found a refuge. She staggered, then righted herself, and I wondered what she feared now.

I helped Birana mount Flame. Her hands were cold to my touch. 'She is truly holy,' one man said, 'for Her power has tamed even these beasts.'

'Tulan shall guide Her horse,' I said as I handed the reins to the boy. He smiled at me, his eyes wide with awe.

A dark look passed over the Headman's face as he came to my side, and then vanished as he nodded at me. I thought I had seen anger, but how could I have angered him? 'I'll lead you to my camp,' he said.

The Headman walked with Tulan while I followed with the other horses. The Prayergiver and the other men walked behind me. Soon we came to land where tree stumps stood, and then to a patch of cleared land where only some grass and a few shrubs grew. Ahead was a wall of dirt and stone much like the one around the Prayergiver's camp.

'An aspect of the Lady comes among us,' the Headman shouted to the men on the wall. They cast down their weapons and bowed before us as the Headman turned toward the Prayergiver. 'You swore that you would not enter our camp again, so you must make camp here, but I'll send out men to guard you. You will be brought some of our feast and will be given food and water and men to travel with you when you return to your own camp.'

The Prayergiver bowed his head.

'Blessed are you, who brought Her to us.' The Headman held out a hand, palm down. 'May your band thrive, but you must not speak of these holy matters to them.'

'I swear that I'll tell them only that you have accepted the travellers and the boy.' The old man embraced Tulan, then gripped my arm for a moment.

'I thank you for guiding us here,' I said.

'It is you I must thank, Arvil, and the Lady.' I felt sadness at this parting, but curiosity about what I would find here dispelled my sadder thoughts.

We went through the opening in the wall and passed gardens where other men bowed and knelt. This band seemed even larger than Jerlan's. We were led to a clearing surrounded by dwellings made of tree trunks, and there Birana dismounted.

'Our Prayergiver must see the vision now,' the Headman murmured as he took her arm and led her toward a small hut a few paces from the wall. I wondered that he could bring himself to touch her. They entered the hut and remained inside for a short time. When they came out again, Birana was even paler than before.

I tied our horses to a sapling near the Prayergiver's house. Mats were set outside his door, and the Headman motioned to us to sit. 'I must leave You for a while, but You may wait here while the men prepare our feast.' He bowed to Birana and then strode away.

The Prayergiver came out of his house, leaning on a stick. He was thin, older and more feeble than the Prayergiver who had guided us. He knelt before us, chanting many prayers as he made motions in the air with his clawed hands, then beckoned to Tulan. 'Sit by me, young one, and tell me of your band and what happens now among them, and leave the Lady and Her messenger to await our bounty.' Another mat was brought, and the Prayergiver and Tulan sat down several paces from our side.

The men of the camp hurried into their dwellings to prepare their feast. Boys and gardeners passed us with baskets but did not speak to us. Most of the men in this camp, as in Jerlan's, wore no beards or kept them short around their faces; Tulan had told me this was so the men would more closely resemble the Lady.

We were facing the lake and I saw that the camp overlooked a bay. Just below the clearing, on the shore, several boats were overturned. The Headman and two others were setting one of the boats in the water. The Headman climbed in and settled himself in the centre while the two men paddled out on to the lake. An island lay out on the bay and seemed to be their destination. I narrowed my eyes but could not see what might lie there.

I glanced at Birana; her hands trembled. I lifted my eyes to her unhappy face. 'You are safe now,' I murmured. 'This band has more than did that other band, and you cannot be betrayed by these men if they don't go to shrines. Why do you seem so sad?'

She looked toward the Prayergiver, but he was deep in talk with Tulan and too far from us to hear. Her jaw tightened. 'The Headman,' she said between clenched teeth. 'He didn't just look at me, he put his hands on me, and so did the old man there, and they kept saying their holy words, but their hands were on me as if they saw nothing wrong in touching me. I wanted to scream. The Headman kept saying how holy I was, but I saw what was in his eyes.'

My face flamed. To have others look at her was bad enough; to think of their hands on her was more than I could stand. I struggled with my rage. 'I am with you. No harm will come to you.' These were empty words, I knew.

'I thought this might be a refuge,' she said, 'but there are only men.'

'You heard his words. He has seen your kind before.'

'Perhaps he dreamed it.'

'The Prayergiver didn't,' I said. 'A whole band would not have the same dream.'

The sun was lower in the sky. Men carried torches from their dwellings and set them around the clearing. Others followed, carrying baskets and food in clay pots to us. After they had set them down, they began to dance and chanted songs in their own speech. I ate of the food, but Birana took only water.

The men continued to dance, strutting before us, lifting their legs and jumping as they displayed themselves. The sun soon dropped behind the trees in the west, and still they danced and sang. Tulan swayed from side to side as he watched. Birana was still and silent, refusing to eat.

A young, dark-haired man with a bold face wove his way among the dancers and knelt before us, holding out meat. 'Take my food, Holy One,' he said. 'Take mine, if that of others displeases You.' Two others appeared at his side, also carrying food. 'May we have Your blessing, if that is Your will.' Birana said nothing.

'You must eat,' I whispered. She made no sign that she had heard me.

The crowd of men in the clearing hid my view of the shore, but I thought I saw the light of a torch out on the lake. The dancers were growing more subdued and began to sing a more solemn song. Suddenly they drew apart and stood in lines on either side of the clearing.

Two boats had landed on the shore. A man carrying a torch climbed up from the bank. The Headman was walking behind him. Six men followed, bearing a litter on their shoulders. As the light of the torches around us illuminated this litter and the one who sat upon it, I nearly cried out.

A woman rode on the litter. Her black hair fell past her shoulders but could not hide her full breasts, only partly covered by her leather shirt. This was one who could not have come among them disguised, as Birana had. She gazed in my direction as the men bore her litter toward us, and even I, who knew the truth about Birana's kind, trembled at the fierceness of this woman's gaze.

The litter was set down in front of us. The woman pushed aside the fur that covered her feet and slowly stood up. She and Birana gazed at each other for a long moment. When I saw the joy on Birana's face, part of me rejoiced, yet another part was saddened that her eyes had never held such joy when she looked at me.

'I welcome you, Sister and Holy One,' the black-haired woman said in a husky voice.

Birana leaped to her feet and embraced this woman. Her shoulders shook as the woman held her. 'Please, some decorum,' the strange woman murmured in a voice I could barely hear. 'Our worshippers expect it.'

Birana stepped back and wiped at her face with one sleeve. 'I rejoice to see you, Holy One,' she said in her higher, lighter voice.

In this way, our life with this band began.

BIRANA

A woman lived among this band. I wanted to speak with her, question her, but could not until we were alone. My legs were weak. I sat down again quickly; she seated herself next to me.

'We'll be here only a short time,' she said in an undertone. 'You must eat.' She pushed a pot toward me, but I was too excited to eat.

We were silent as the men danced some more. A few of their gestures disturbed me. The young ones held out their arms as if seeking an embrace, while others came as close to me as they dared and motioned at their groins. I swallowed hard and looked down.

At last the dancing stopped, and the men settled themselves on the ground as boys carried food to them. The woman said nothing to me as they ate, then held up her hand.

The Headman rose and walked toward us. 'I'll tell him we must leave now,' the woman whispered. 'You must ride on the litter with me.'

'What about my companions?' I whispered back.

'Companions?'

'The man with me and the boy with the Prayergiver.'

'They cannot come with us.'

The Headman stood before me. I repressed a shudder as I gazed at his face. 'I would share in your celebration,' the woman said in her husky voice, 'but I wish to be with My sister aspect, and want to return to My home now.'

The Headman bowed. 'It will be as You wish, Holy One.'

I glanced at Arvil. He was staring back at me. I had to do what I could for him now. I did not know this band's customs and wondered if Arvil or Tulan would be forced to pass through what these men called a truthsaying.

I stood up. The woman tugged at my shirt, obviously wanting me to remain silent; I ignored her. 'I say this to all of you.' I put as much resonance into my voice as I could muster. 'This man, Arvil, who sits at My side, is the holy messenger to whom I first revealed Myself. The boy, Tulan, is My true friend. I have seen into their souls, and so there is no need for them to pass through a truthsaying with you. I ask you to let them dwell among you in peace.'

The Headman's dark eyes glittered as he looked at me. I remembered how he had put his hands on me in the forest, how he had touched my breasts and let his hands fall to my waist; I had nearly been sick. My throat locked for a moment.

He bowed again. 'Because they came with You, Holy One, we will obey and treat them as members of our band.'

I found my voice once more. 'Arvil and Tulan will tend My horses.'

The Headman nodded. 'It will be so, Holy One.'

I turned toward Arvil for a moment. He smiled a little. I had done all for him that I could but was suddenly afraid to leave his side, anxious as I was to find out how this woman had survived.

We were carried down to the lake on the litter, which swayed a little as we moved. I gripped one of the poles, hoping that the men would not stumble. When the litter had been set on the ground, the Headman helped us into a boat, bid us farewell, and then walked back up toward his camp.

One man climbed into the bow; the other pushed the boat out and then sat in the stern. Three more men went ahead of us in a second boat; one held a torch while the others paddled.

My companion was silent in the presence of the men. The air was warm and still; someone in the camp behind us was singing a song. His voice faded until the only sound I heard was the soft lapping of the water against the boat and paddles.

Our destination, it seemed, was an island I had seen earlier from the camp. I wondered what was there, and if other women dwelled on that island. Somehow, I doubted it; surely they would have been brought to the camp as well. I tried not to feel too disappointed. I would have one friend at least and from her could learn more about this land and what lay beyond it.

The boat whispered through a few reeds as we neared the island. Above the muddy shore, a few flat rocks jutted out from the land. The men in the other boat got out of their craft, dragged it ashore, and lifted baskets from it.

When our boat had landed. I followed the woman and the men along a trail leading up to higher ground. Near the top of this slope, land had been cleared, and a square structure of wood stood under the trees, a hide hanging in its entrance. The men set their baskets down by the doorway, put a long torch in the ground next to them, then stepped back.

'What do You wish from us?' one man asked.

'Go to your boats now,' the woman replied. 'I would be alone with My companion.'

'We are blessed, Holy One,' the man replied.

When the men were gone, I embraced this woman again, unable to hold back my tears. 'I never thought . . .'

'I know, girl, I know. I believed I'd never see another woman again.' She released me. 'I had better show you my home.'

She led me to a sheltered ditch in back of the hut where I could relieve myself, and then we carried the baskets inside. As I sat down in the darkness, she went outside and brought in the torch. Wood had been set inside a fireplace circled by rocks in the centre of the floor; she held the torch to the wood until a fire started to burn.

The inside of the hut was now visible. Mud and clay filled the spaces between the logs of the hut; in one corner, a wide mat was heaped with hides and furs. A wooded platform held several pots, baskets and neatly folded garments of leather and fur.

My companion set the torch outside the door, then sat down at my side, reaching for my hand. My mind was filled with questions, but I could not speak.

'We can talk freely now.' Her low voice shook a little, as if she were as overcome as I was. 'Two of the men will stay below by the boat to guard us while the others return to their camp.'

I let go of her hand. 'You've been alone here?'

She nodded. 'I must ask you – did you tell them your name?'

I realized I hadn't and shook my head.

'Good. They don't know mine, either. It's best that they don't. We're simply the Holy Ones to them. My name is Nallei, but use it only when we're by ourselves.'

'I am Birana.'

She leaned toward me. 'You don't know how much I've wanted to hear another woman's voice. When Yerlan, the Head-man, came here to tell me you were in the camp, I couldn't believe it until I saw it for myself.' Her hazel eyes narrowed as she spoke of the Headman. 'But you've already caused me some worry. These men were supposed to keep my secret. How did you find your way here?'

'My companion and I found our way to another camp by the lake. We were told a holy vision had been seen here, but not what it was.' I went on to tell her of how the Prayergiver had guided us after I had revealed myself to him, but said little of my first meeting with Yerlan. This woman might despise me for allowing him to touch me, for not commanding his respect.

'How long have you been here?' I asked when I had finished.

'Nearly sixteen years.'

I gasped, horrified.

'I've kept track of the years there.' She pointed to a place on the wall where long marks had been scratched on one of the trunks. 'I was in my twenties when I came.'

I peered at her face. Sixteen years, and yet somehow she had kept her beauty. 'What did you do to be expelled?'

She scowled, and I knew I shouldn't have asked. 'That's of no importance now. Did I ask how one so young got herself expelled? You'd better forget your former life.'

I gazed at the fire. I would be staying here with Nallei; that might be easier if I did not know her crime. She might have been one like my mother, angry and quick-tempered, or her crime might have been planned and deliberate. I would be at her mercy, yet she was still another woman; I tried to take some consolation from the fact.

'I was sent out for my mother's deed,' I said, 'not my own.'

'You must have had some part in it, then, but enough of that.' Her voice was hard; I supposed that living out here had hardened her. 'Wasn't she expelled as well?'

'My mother is dead. Men killed her before seeing what she was.' I bowed my head.

'I'm sorry, Birana.' She touched my shoulder lightly. 'But you'll be safe here, as safe as you can be anywhere. These men worship me, and they'll worship you, too. They'll tend to all your needs. Just be cautious around Yerlan. He worships me, but . . .' She paused. 'He is used to being in a woman's presence now. He can sometimes forget himself.' Nallei fell silent once more, then said, 'Why were you so anxious about those two who came with you? Their fate isn't anything that should concern you.'

I was suddenly wary. I had told much to Arvil and had grown closer to him than I had intended. I remembered how he had held me, how I had let him press his mouth on mine. I had been thinking of Laissa then, but also of him, and my confusion had kept me from resisting him at first. I didn't know what Nallei would think of Arvil; although I longed to pour out my story to her, I held back.

'They have been friends,' I said carefully, 'as much my friends as a man and a boy could be. Arvil saved me from harm. I wanted to show some gratitude, that's all.'

'I see.'

'But I want to know about you, how you came here.'

Nallei rose, went to one of the baskets, and took out a jar and two earthen cups. As she sat down, she handed me a cup and then poured. I lifted my cup and tasted the sweetness of berries. The drink warmed me; I realized it was a kind of wine.

As I drank, Nallei told me of her life.

She had been expelled in the summer. She did not tell me where her city lay. She had not been forced to brave the storms of winter, and after walking through an empty land for three days, she had reached a shrine. By then, she was out of food and water. She had been prepared to die there alone, and then two men entered the shrine.

They saw what she was immediately. She was wearing light garments, and her body even then was too rounded to be concealed by her clothes. The two men hunted for her, and when she was strong enough to travel, took her with them to their band.

'Their camp,' she continued, 'was even more primitive than this one. They lived by following herds, and I worried that other tribes might find out about me, even though this band had sworn to protect me. But I listened to their stories, and learned that other bands lived in different ways. I told them I could stay among them only for a short time, and they sent out scouts to learn of other bands or places where I might live as a Holy One should.'

By the end of summer, one of the scouts had heard a story of the lake bands from a traveller, of how the men of the lake lived far from shrines and built walls around their camps. Nallei, thinking of the hardships winter would bring, decided to chance her journey and to see what the lake bands might offer. She spoke to the band that had cared for her, extracted a promise that they would, now that she had lived among them, no longer travel to shrines, and then she and three of the strongest men had set off for the lake.

Nallei paused for a moment. I supped my wine, then said, 'That band will die out. If they can't go to a shrine or be called, they'll have no more boys, and then . . .'

'I know that. It's not my concern. They think they'll be honoured in the next world. If they die out and can't betray me, so much the better.' She looked sharply at me. 'You show more concern for them than you should.'

I denied this as forcefully as possible. I saw then how much she still despised men, even after being among them for so long.

She poured more berry wine and went on with her tale. After a long journey and after many hardships, which she did not detail, she and her companions finally reached the land by the lake. One of the men had met his death at the hands of one of the others some days earlier; Nallei did not tell me why, but I guessed that by that time they might have come to some disagreement over her. Perhaps one had longed for her as Arvil had longed for me.

The two surviving men had been weakened by the trip; weak as they were, they still gave Nallei the greatest share of the little food they were able to find. As they pressed on, one of these men at last lay down on the frosty ground to die and asked for Nallei's prayers. Not long after, when Nallei's own despair made her almost ready to give up, she and the surviving man reached Yerlan's camp. The journey had robbed that man of the last of his strength, and he died three days later.

'You see, it worked out well for me,' Nallei said. 'No one was left alive who could reveal that I had come here.' Her voice held contempt, and her coldness disturbed me. I had seen the vileness and ugliness of men but had observed other qualities as well. Even my short time with Arvil's old band had given me a bit of sympathy for them, much as some of their ways repelled me. Nallei had lived with a band for a season and three of its members had died bringing her to a safer place. She had lived among men for years and yet seemed to have no compassion for any of them. I repressed these thoughts. I had not lived outside for as long as she had; I could not judge her. Whatever she felt, she was still one of my kind.

A feast had been held, and she had dwelled in the Prayer-giver's house until a hut was built for her on the island. At Nallei's command, the band also began to bar their camp to others and were told that they no longer had to visit the Lady's shrines.

Nallei soon learned enough about the band to realize that the other men of the lake would have to be dealt with, and so this band was prepared when the Headmen of those other tribes came to their wall. Knowing that Prayergivers would never leave their camps again and so could not betray her, she ordered the band to summon those old men. The Prayergivers were taken to the island, and there Nallei revealed herself while the Prayergivers swore that they would not speak of what they had seen and would say only that they beheld a holy vision.

Even then, Nallei feared that she might not be safe, that some word of her existence would find its way back to the cities. But as the years passed, her worries faded. Her band, which now sought its boys from neighbouring bands, would continue to serve her.

'One thing keeps me alive,' she said, 'knowing that I live in spite of what my city condemned me to.' She sounded like my mother then.

She had told me her story, but some of my questions were still unanswered. How had she lived among men for so long without provoking their lust, as Arvil told me I had with his former band? I thought of how Yerlan had handled me. I could not have misread his expression, and Nallei's full breasts and lovely face should have attracted him even more. How did she control him? What was her life like here from day to day, and how did she pass the time? How much had she revealed to the men, and how much had she kept hidden? There was no point in asking this; I would find out soon enough.

I finished another cup of wine; the beverage was making me giddy. 'I had to take off my clothes in front of the Prayergiver who brought me here,' I said. 'I had to take them off here, too.' A mirthless giggle escaped me. 'Who would have thought taking your clothes off could produce such reactions?'

She chuckled. 'You should have seen the Prayergivers when they beheld me in this hut.' She threw back her head and laughed. 'Oh, holiness! Oh, Sacred One! Oh, how blessed are we!'

She slapped the ground. I laughed, and then tears came, and then I was huddling next to her, sobbing against her chest.

'Birana,' she murmured. 'It's over, I'll make sure that you never go through that again.' She dried my face gently with her sleeve. 'I'd like to hear your story, but we both need to rest now.'

She led me to the mat. I lay down on her furs and she stretched out beside me. For a moment, I though she might want some love from me, since she had been without it for so long, but instead she held me as a mother might hold a small child.

In the morning, while Nallei still slept, I gathered up the cups and jar we had drunk from the night before, intending to wash them by the lake. I lifted the hide hanging in the doorway and stepped outside.

A man was climbing the trail toward me. 'Holy One!' he called out as he bowed. 'Is there anything You wish of me?'

I shook my head. 'I require nothing. I am only going to wash these.'

He bowed again, shook his dark hair, and held out his hands. 'I shall do that for You, Holy One.' I let him have the cups and jar, then began to explore my new home alone.

The island was in a bay; north of the bay, the lake still stretched on, with no shore visible. I came to a cove at the island's northern end; I might be able to swim here because the cove was hidden from the camp. I continued to walk, climbing over the rocks and moving through the reeds near the water's edge, until I had nearly circled the island.

A boat lay on the shore facing the camp. In the distance, men were already gathering in the clearing. Below, near the boat, a man sat on a flat rock, dangling his legs over the water. A twig cracked under my feet; he jumped up.

'Holy One,' he said as he bowed. 'Is there anything You wish?'

'No.'

He stared at me. He had a boy's face and a mass of short but curly red hair. 'I would be happy to lead You around this island.'

'I've seen most of it already. It isn't that large.'

'I shall fetch You food and prepare it if You wish. I shall light Your fire for You. I shall . . .'

'Stay where you are,' I said, suddenly irritated.

He turned away, crestfallen. I walked back up to the hut and went inside.

Nallei was awake but seemed groggy from the wine. She sat up slowly and pushed a fur aside. 'The fire's out,' she said. 'Call one of the men to light it and ask him to make us some tea.'

'I'll light it myself.' I went outside, gathered some wood, then went back inside. As I knelt, I took out my flints.

'Where did you get those?' Nallei asked.

'From a dead man.'

'Sounds as though you have a story to tell, girl.'

'I do.' I held tinder in my hands and blew gently on the spark until it became a flame, then lit the wood. While the fire burned, Nallei fetched a waterskin, a pouch of herbs, and two more cups. Tulan's band had made tea for me during their feast, and I had watched them. I waited until the stones around the fire were hot, covered my fingers with part of my leather sleeve, plucked out two small stones, and put them in the cups to warm the water. I sprinkled herbs into the cups, waited for them to steep, then handed one cup to Nallei.

She sipped. In the light of the fire, with more light entering the hut through the opening in the roof, Nallei seemed older than she had looked the night before. Two tiny creases were on either side of her wide, full mouth, and her thick black lashes did not hide the lines around her large hazel eyes. Strands of silver were in her long, black hair, and the skin of neck and chin sagged just a little. She was beautiful still but beginning to age. I gripped my cup. She should not have been ageing so soon; she should have had years of youth still. But her youth would pass quickly here with nothing to renew it. I would begin to age.

'You needn't do this sort of work yourself,' she said. 'The men will serve you.'

'I don't want them to serve me. I must have something to do.'

'You shouldn't be too reckless, Birana. Serving us is an honour for them, and it underlines our place. You wouldn't want them to lose respect for you.'

'I don't see how they can lose their respect if they see that we know some of their arts.' I sat back on my heels. 'You must have mastered some of them after all this time.'

She shook her head. 'I haven't had to do much. Oh, I know about their ways, but I hardly have to hunt or fish or gather plants. They're happy to do all of that.'

I gazed at her, annoyed; I had been hoping to pick up a few skills from her. 'You'll have to tell me everything you know of them,' I said at last.

'I shall, but I thought I would hear your story this morning.'

Of course she would want to hear it; she had probably heard no new tales for some time. I finished my tea. As I spoke, I sensed that it might not be wise to let her know how much I had told Arvil. From the way the men treated Nallei, I guessed that she had told them little about us. She might see Arvil as a danger if she knew what I had told him; she might turn others in the band against him or find a way to be rid of him. I told her of what had hapened to us, but nothing of what had passed between Arvil and me, and he became in my story only a young man who worshipped me, and who had sworn to bring me to a safe place. I said little about Arvil's old band and nothing at all about how he had been commanded to kill me.

I had wanted to be completely open with Nallei. It hurt me to feel that I should conceal a few events from her, that it was necessary to shade the truth. It hurt more to relive my mother's death.

'That's quite a story,' Nallei said when I had finished. 'It's remarkable that you survived at all.'

'Without Arvil, I couldn't have,' I replied. 'You can see why I tried to learn as much from him as I could. If he hadn't shown me how to use a sling . . .' I waved one hand.

'I'm sorry about your mother. I wish she could have been here with both of us.' She lowered her eyelids. 'But at least she didn't have to endure certain kinds of suffering.'

I wiped at my eyes. 'She was so sure there was a refuge for us. It was only that hope that kept her alive even for a few days.'

'You have a refuge here, but never forget that our lives hang by a thread. I still worry that we might be betrayed somehow.'

I shivered. 'There was another sort of refuge my mother sought. She imagined a place of several women, perhaps a community, not just one or two survivors.'

'All I've heard tells me there is no such place.'

'There are abandoned lands east of the lake. Maybe there . . .'

She shook her head. 'There's no refuge there.'

'How can you be sure?'

'I heard it from the men. A long time ago, apparently when men first came to this lake and settled here, a band that had gone to those eastern lands attacked one of the camps. They killed most of the men and carried off the youngest of the boys. They didn't go to shrines, you see, so the only way they could add to their numbers was by capturing young boys and raising them. The lake bands made a truce after that, and then went east and killed every man of that band they could find. No one has ever attacked from the east again, but it's said the easternmost band along the lake still keeps watch over the east.'

I was silent.

'No one can live there, Birana. There are no shrines, so the men can't be called. Any woman who found her way there wouldn't know how to live alone. You would find no one there.' She patted my hand. 'Don't look so solemn, child. Life here won't be so bad for you. We'll be as safe as we can be anywhere.'

I spent the following days in the simple tasks of preparing the food the men brought to us, keeping the hut clean, and listening to Nallei tell me about the customs of this band, which except for her presence among them and the changes she had brought, seemed much like those of Tulan's old band.

Yerlan, the Headman, led the men. He consulted with Nallei from time to time, but she had learned to leave most of the decisions to him except for those matters that concerned her directly. She had seen that the band would need to bring in new members occasionally and had ordered that boys be fetched from the other lake bands. She could not prevent the deaths of older or weaker band members; the men had noted that, but believed that their souls, having seen her in this world, would be blessed in the next.

Every month if weather permitted, during the first night of the full moon, Nallei was taken across to the camp to preside over a ceremony and to hear the Prayergiver's prayers in his hut. Only twice, before my arrival, had strangers come to this camp from other regions. The first group of three men had passed through a truthsaying and joined Yerlan's men, and only then had Nallei been brought to the camp for them to see. Two other men had appeared there a few years later, but she had never seen them. She later found out that they had raised doubts about their virtue and courage during their truthsaying and had been killed. She had told the band to bring no strangers into the camp after that, but to speak to them only beyond the wall.

She told me much about the band, and yet most of her talk was of what the men had told her or had revealed during their various feasts and festivals. Except for her ceremonial function, Nallei was not really part of the band's life but lived apart. In her early years, to stave off boredom, she had often asked the men to take her to the camp, where she would watch as the gardeners went about their tasks, the boys tested themselves in contests, and the hunters returned with their game. Sometimes the men took her out on the water in their boats, though they never ventured far from the bay. The novelty of these pursuits wore off, and after a while Nallei kept to her island. She now eased her boredom with jars and skins of the wines the men made from berries and other fruits and plants, making sure that the men gave her an ample supply.

I learned to do each task I set myself with deliberation, making the work last as long as possible so that empty hours did not stretch ahead of me. I drew out Nallei in conversation; our talks could continue for some time with little being said. I explored every part of the island on foot until I seemed to know the place of every rock and shrub, but the island was small, and soon I was arranging large stones along the sides of the trail simply to have something to do.

At first, the men tried to help me with the stones until I made it clear I did not want their aid. Two men, and sometimes three, were always on the island. They would remain for two or three days, and then another boat arrived to replace them with two or three others. Each time a boat came, I went down to the water's edge, hoping that Arvil might be among the men, and was surprised at the depth of my disappointment when he was not. I supposed that guarding us was an honour, and that such a privilege might not be given to a newcomer, even if he was considered my messenger. I was afraid to ask for Arvil, not knowing if others might resent that; I also wondered how Nallei might react to him. I had watched one evening as the men assembled in their clearing, had caught a glimpse of Arvil's blond hair as he was led before Yerlan; the two guarding me had told me that Arvil was making his pledge. He was one of the band now; he would be safe.

In all Nallei's talk about the infrequent highlights of her restricted life, I began to feel that she might be concealing as much from me as I was from her. Occasionally, when she spoke of some ceremony, she would break off and discuss something else, instead of elaborating as she usually did. Once in a while, I wondered what she might be hiding.

A morning came, after I had been on the island for nearly two weeks, when I thought of the endless days ahead and could hardly bring myself to stir from the mat. Summer weather had come; we had put away the furs. I had to do something different that day, something more than marking time.

I roused Nallei, made us breakfast, and then announced that we were going to take a walk together. She grumbled as I led her outside. 'It's too hot to walk.'

'You need the exercise. You get none at all. We'll walk down to the water, and then we'll swim. I'm tired of washing in the hut.'

She muttered complaining words under her breath. 'Don't you know how to swim?' I asked.

'I can swim. I haven't for years. We could catch a chill, you know. One has to be careful here.'

'All the more reason to build up your strength.'

We walked down the slope until we came to the northern cove. One of the men was walking along the shore; he hurried over to us, 'Holy Ones,' he called out, 'is there anything You wish?'

I shook my head. 'We wish to be alone here. Go back to your boat until I call you.'

When he had hastened away, I took off my clothes quickly. 'Come on, Nallei. You'll feel better after a swim.'

'You're my only friend, and you insist on tormenting me.'

'Don't be silly.'

She sighed as she took off her garments. Her waist was still small, but her large breasts had begun to sag, and her long, slender legs were growing flabby. We entered the water together. The lake seemed cold at first, but the sun was already warming the shallower water in the cove. She splashed about awkwardly but soon her strokes grew more graceful as she paddled around me. I swam back and forth, then out to deeper water and back until I was panting.

Our two guards suddenly appeared on the hill above us. 'Lady, Lady!' one cried as they descended. 'You must be careful!'

'Do you think that We cannot move safely on water?' I shouted. 'Go back to your boat and don't disobey Me again.' I waited, treading water, until I was certain they were gone, then left the water to stretch out on one of the flat rocks.

Nallei lay on a rock below me. 'Those men had better keep away,' she murmured. 'When I used to come here, the bolder ones would sometimes try to sneak up to watch.'

I lifted my head, but heard nothing, and hoped the two would be too intimidated to try anything like that. 'We'll come here every day we can,' I said as the sun warmed me. This time, Nallei did not protest.

My monthly time came and passed. Nallei showed me how to use pieces of soft hide she kept for this purpose and how to clean them. The full moon arrived. I expected to be taken with Nallei to the Prayergiver's hut and was longing for that change in our routine, but a wild storm raged over the lake that night. We remained in our hut while the men celebrated their rites without us.

Now it was Nallei who urged me down to the cove to swim. Her body was growing browner and firmer. I wanted her to grow healthier and stronger, not just for her sake, but for mine; I feared being left alone.

At last I summoned one of the guards. Out of Nallei's hearing, I asked him a few questions about Arvil and Tulan. Tulan had proven himself in a few contests with other boys and was making friends; he had already accompanied some of the men on a hunt. Arvil was learning various new skills, such as fishing from a boat and making the clay pots the band fired in a pit, but it was clear that hunting was his most useful skill. Both had continued to care for the three horses, which most of the men avoided, although Tulan was teaching two of the boys to ride. Arvil, it was said, was also trying to learn about healing from one of the older men.

The young guard told me little else, and that night, I woke from a dream. I could not recall much of the dream, which was fading in my mind even as I struggled into consciousness, but Arvil had been part of it. I suddenly felt a longing for his presence that was so sharp I started, nearly awakening Nallei.

I kept still until her breathing returned. Now that she was drinking less wine, she no longer tossed restlessly or cried out in her sleep. Somehow, in the dream, I had felt that Arvil was lying at my side, his hand on my arm protectively. I realized how much I missed him then, even with Nallei's company, and decided to find an excuse to go to the camp.

I woke up later than usual, then found I was alone. I went outside, but Nallei was nowhere in sight. She did not return to our hut until I had finished preparing our tea.

'Where were you?' I asked as she entered. 'Are you swimming so early now?'

Her face seemed troubled as she sat down; she shook her head as I held out a cup. 'I had to speak to the men. I want them to give a message to one of those who will replace them.' She paused. 'I think you should go to the camp today. We need more clothing. You can ask the men to show you some hides.'

She must have sensed my wish. 'You'll come with me, won't you? I don't know if I could speak to them alone.'

'You ought to learn, then. I can't go with you, Birana. Stay there for the day and come back in the evening. Remember, Yerlan is the leader, and he's proud, so be sure to speak with him if he's there.' Her voice was flat; she refused to look at me.

'Nallei, what's wrong?'

Her smile seemed forced. 'There are matters I must attend to here.' She did not explain what they were, and felt I should not ask.

I dressed in one of her shirts; it was too loose on me and I put my belt over it, pulling it in at the waist. After combing out my hair with my fingers, I put on a necklace of coloured stones one of the men had made for her.

As I was about to step outside, I turned. 'I could wait until you're finished with what ever you have to do, and we could go together.'

She shook her head violently. 'Go!'

I hurried outside and descended the trail. Another boat was approaching the island. The two men on shore greeted the arrivals in their own tongue, then helped me into their boat. Three men had come to the island; as my boat left the shore, one of the three began to climb toward Nallei's hut.

'Honour is his,' the man behind me said in the holy speech.

'May we be so honoured again,' the second man replied.

I paid little attention to them. I might see Arvil soon, and that thought made me happier than I had expected to be. I hoped that he was not out with a hunting party, and that he would want to speak to me. The thought that he might not, that he was with men now and could form new friendships, suddenly lowered my spirits.

When the boat had landed below the camp, other men carried the litter to me. I seated myself, and they bore me to the clearing. Several men were seated in front of dwellings, working at spear points and shaping arrows; Arvil was not among then.

'Holy One!' the Headman called out as he left his house. He bowed as he came near; even from the height of my litter, he was an imposing figure. 'I pray that You will smile upon us,' he continued. 'If there is anything You wish, You need only ask it of us.'

I smiled at him as kindly as I could, and he beamed, as though I had given him a great gift. I realized he was younger than he had seemed at first; he could not have been much past childhood when he had become the leader. Nallei had warned me about his pride, and for one so young to be made a Headman had to mean that he was one I should treat carefully; he had been chosen over older, more experienced men.

'I would speak to you, Yerlan,' I said, sensing that if I asked for Arvil immediately, he might be offended. My litter was set down in front of the Prayergiver's house; the old man hobbled out to greet me, bowed, murmured a few words, and then left us.

Yerlan seated himself in front of me. 'He will continue to pray,' he said. 'You see that we are greedy for Your blessings, Lady, and continue to pray for more.' He raised a hand to his forehead in a gesture of respect. Necklaces of bead and stone hung around his neck, but his chest was bare; the light brown hair on his head was thick, yet his chest was smooth and the fair hair on his arms had been bleached by the sun. I was ill at ease with him; fortunately he kept his eyes lowered. 'What is it You wish, Holy One?'

'My companion and I need more clothing. I would see what hides you have for Us.'

He shouted to others in the lake language, and several men were soon carrying hides to me. An older man came with them; he peered at me intently and summoned a boy who was close to my own height and size.

'I would be honoured to make garments for You,' the older man said as he measured my form with his eyes.

'Do so,' I replied, pointing to two of the hides. The man quickly took the boy aside and began to measure the hides against him.

'Tell Me of your band's activities during the past days, Headman,' I said. Yerlan spoke of their food stores and of their preparations for the harder seasons of fall and winter; unlike Irlan, he still hunted with his men. I waited in vain for him to speak of Arvil and was soon searching the clearing for a sign of him as Yerlan droned on, emphasizing his own prowess as a hunter and leader.

As he paused for breath, I said quickly, 'You have done well. I am pleased.'

He gazed into my face, then lowered his eyes to my chest, and I had a sudden impulse to cover myself with one of the hides on which I was sitting. I could not let him see my fear. 'It is said that My messenger Arvil is now one of you,' I continued.

He scowled for a moment before composing himself. 'It is so. He is Arvil no more, but Vilan, one of the men of the lake.'

I wanted to speak to Arvil then but was afraid to ask for him immediately; instead, I asked Yerlan to summon Tulan.

The boy was soon running toward me, trailed by a few other lads. He knelt at my feet, his face aglow while his friends watched him enviously. I asked him about the horses, and he assured me they were well, that he exercised them every day, and that he and Arvil had found ways to use them as beasts of burden. 'But some,' he finished, 'have complained about the stink of their wastes.'

'They should not. Take those wastes when they are dry and mix them with the soil of the fallow garden. They'll help to restore the soil.' I nodded at Tulan. 'You have done well. Now I would see My messenger.'

Yerlan's mouth tightened. Tulan scurried to one of the dwellings and beckoned to those inside by the entrance. Arvil emerged and walked toward me, head lowered; I couldn't tell if he was happy to see me or not. He bowed to Yerlan and then to me.

'I would ride with My messenger for a time,' I announced.

Yerlan was still smiling, but his face darkened a little. 'And after that, I will share a meal with you, Yerlan, in your dwelling, with you and the men closest to you.'

The Headman got to his feet as I stood. 'I will have You carried to the horses, Lady.'

I shook my head. 'I shall walk.'

I felt Yerlan's eyes upon us as I followed Arvil. The horses had been tethered to a tree just beyond the circle of dwellings. Flame nuzzled me as I stroked her head. As I mounted, Arvil murmured, 'I thought you had put me from your mind.'

'I didn't forget. I wanted to see you before.' I patted Flame and murmured to her soothingly as he mounted Star. 'I was afraid that if I asked for you to be one of my guards, I might offend Yerlan somehow. My companion tells me he's a proud man.'

'That is so, and it's Yerlan who chooses those who are sent to the island, but your companion is free to ask for others as well.'

'Then I'll ask for you,' I said.

He glanced at me from the corners of his eyes. 'It would be better to let Yerlan choose me. He's a man who seeks to be higher than others in the Lady's thoughts.'

The horses trotted along the pathway between the gardens. 'We must stay near the wall, where the men can see you,' he said. I sighed. Honoured I might be, but I was a prisoner as well; I wondered if these men would ever allow me to leave them.

We rode through the opening in the wall; the guards watched as the horses slowed their pace. We were far enough from them to talk without being overheard. 'Birana,' Arvil said, 'have you been happy here?'

'I have a new friend. The men bring us everything we need.' I shook back my hair. 'But the days are long with so little for me to do.'

'Is the other one kind to you?'

'She's been kind, but she doesn't know how much I've told you. I don't want you harmed, and I'm afraid she might think you're a danger if she realizes how much you know. It seems she's told these men little of the truth.'

'You may be wise,' he replied. 'There's a mystery about her, and no one speaks of it to me. Sometimes men are called to her, and all long for this more than anything. During their rite of the full moon, it is said that Yerlan is taken to the island. I saw his anger when she could not come to the camp this time, although he tried to hide it. No one will tell me of the rite – I am told only that I will learn of it in time.' I thought of how evasive Nallei had seemed with me.

We had come to this end of the wall and turned back to retrace our tracks. 'Perhaps,' he went on, 'it is her beauty that makes her spell on them so strong. She's like the spirit-woman I remember.'

I felt a twinge. Maybe I no longer seemed as beautiful to him; there was another to compare me to now. I was surprised at how much this disturbed me; I didn't want to talk of Nallei any more. 'Tell me how you've passed your time,' I said.

He had hunted with the men; he was now learning some of the healing arts from a man named Wirlan, arts most of the band had not mastered. 'There is one plant,' he said, 'that brings an ecstasy to the soul, but Wirlan told me I must not drink of the potion the men brew with it. Once this band used it for certain rites of prayer, but now it is drunk only by those summoned into the Lady's presence.'

'I suppose that accounts for some of her spell,' I muttered, as I reined in Flame. 'Arvil, I must find something to do. It's wearying to have every need met with little effort on my part.'

'I understand. Every man needs his tasks.'

'And so do women. I should learn the language of these men.'

'I could teach it to you. I'm learning it quickly now.'

'And I should know other things,' I said, 'more about hunting, how to gather plants, how to use a spear and bow. I'm helpless now.'

'These men can protect you, Birana. You wouldn't need to know such lore unless you were planning to leave this camp. It seems this isn't enough for you, that the new friend you have found is not enough, that you still dream of another refuge.' He spoke softly, but a vein near his temple stood out. 'I have new friends here, and learn new arts, and know that you are safe, and yet you would leave that behind. And I would be bound to follow you.'

'I wouldn't ask . . .'

'How could I not follow? My soul still burns.'

I lowered my head. 'My companion says that she knows of no refuge except this one, and I must learn much before I can chance leaving this camp.' I paused. 'Is there anyone here you can love?' I asked. Is there one, I thought, who can give you what you can never have from me?

'Wirlan is kind, but he treats me as his charge. There are a few men of some beauty who have sought pleasures with me. Would that I could grant them, but instead I think of you.' His voice was hard. 'And have you sought love with your new friend?'

I shook my head. 'She doesn't seem to want love. She also treats me as a charge.' He gazed at me intently. 'I'll have to find a way for you to teach me certain skills,' I said quickly. 'I may never need them, but I must have some way of passing the time.'

'I'll hope for that, so that I can be with you.'

We rode back to the open space. Yerlan was sitting outside his dwelling, clearly anxious for me to join him and his men. He leaped to his feet as Arvil and I dismounted. 'Our food is prepared,' the Headman said. 'I would have Vilan join us, for I see that his company is pleasing to You.' His mouth twitched a little.

Before I could reply, Arvil spoke. 'If you order this,' he replied, 'I shall honour your wish. But the Lady has already graced me with Her words as we rode, and it isn't fitting that I join such worthy men while they dine with Her.'

'My servant speaks truly,' I said.

Yerlan smiled. Arvil seemed relieved and led the horses away, while the Headman guided me inside the house.

Yerlan's men had prepared deer, eggs, fish and vegetables. Because I did not want to demean his hospitality, I ate as much as I could. We sat on mats around the hearth while the men entertained me with legends of their band – stories of a hunter whose skill was so great that the Lady came to hunt with him; of a gardener who learned a spell that could make a seed grow into a plant that reached the sky in one day and upon which he climbed to the moon; and of a small boy who healed an injured eagle and was carried by that bird to the Lady's realm. Throughout these narratives, I felt Yerlan studying me and could not meet his eyes.

Later, I was carried to the gardens to see what grew there, and then some of the boys held a contest with spears, which Tulan won.

Yerlan and the Prayergiver sat with me during this contest. When it was over, the Headman leaned toward me. 'The full moon will come again,' he murmured; I wondered why he was stating this obvious fact. 'I shall come to the island on the day after the full moon appears, as I always do. Since You have come among us, Holy One, I have prayed that You will honour me.'

His dark eyes were fierce. My voice caught in my throat. He

continued to stare at me until I said, 'I thank you for all you have shown Me today, but I would return to My companion now.' His lip curled a little. For a moment, I was sure he had seen how frightened I was of him.

Near the island, a small flock of ducks was feeding among the reeds. The men, Nallei had told me, did not hunt the ducks when they came there, since they were considered under her protection. The three men who had come that morning were sitting by the rocks near their boat. One lifted his head and stared at me as I stepped ashore.

I hurried up to the hut, certain that Nallei would want to hear about my time in the camp. The inside of the hut was dark; the fire had gone out. I lifted the hide across the doorway and looped it over the pole that held it so that the setting sun could provide a little light.

Nallei stirred. She was sprawled on the mat; a leather shirt covered her body. Two empty jugs lay on their sides near her. She had been drinking again, probably for much of the day.

I leaned over her. 'Nallei.'

She started up and threw a hand over her eyes, then clutched at the shirt. 'No!'

I knelt. 'Nallei, what's the matter?'

She shook her head, then buried her face in her arms. Her shoulders shook; I thought I heard a sob. I reached for her shoulder, but she shied away. 'You were drinking,' I said. 'It's no wonder you feel this way. The men brought us some wild strawberries. I'll have them carry them up here. We can . . .'

'Get away from me.'

I got our fire burning again and sat near it while she slept, then laid a hide next to the fire. I slept uneasily that night, getting up occasionally to be sure Nallei was covered and to feel her brow. I worried that she might be ill but felt no fever.

She was better in the morning. She accepted a cup of tea and listened as I told her of my time in the camp, but said nothing until I had finished.

'I should apologize to you,' she said at last. 'It was the wine that made me so irrational. I just want you to know . . .' She held out a hand. 'You'll be safe, Birana. I'll see to it.'

'But what . . .'

'Enough! I've said what I have to say.' Her tone cowed me into silence. 'It's time for us to go to the cove.'

*

The time of the full moon came once more, and Nallei grew solemn as she prepared for her journey to the camp. She sat passively as I combed out her dark hair with my fingers and trimmed the curls around her face with a sharp stone. The sun had given her face a golden glow and the skin over her cheekbones was tighter, while her body was firmer from her swimming.

'You are beautiful, Nallei,' I told her.

She grimaced. 'Beauty's useless here.' She picked up a deerskin shirt and pulled it over her head, then hung a necklace of feathers around her neck.

'I'll wear this one.' I picked up a shirt that had been made for me.

Nallei pulled on a pair of leather pants, then straightened. 'You're not going with me, Birana.'

'But I thought . . .'

'You're not going. This is something I must do alone. The men will be told that your duty is to commune with invisible aspects of the Lady during this time. They'll believe me.'

'But why . . .'

She grabbed my arm, twisting its flesh so hard that it hurt. 'You'll do as I say. I'll decide things here.'

'Very well,' I muttered resentfully. I had hoped I might see Arvil in the camp, but knew there would be little time to speak to him during a ceremony, and tried not to feel too disappointed.

Nallei had drunk half a jar of wine by the time the men came for her; I wondered how she would stay awake while the Prayergiver prayed before her in his hut. Her voice was fuzzy and slightly slurred as she told the men why I would be remaining on the island. I watched as she walked with our guards toward the boat; the distant camp was already ablaze with torches.

I was now completely alone on the island for the first time, for the guards would remain in the camp until these ceremonies were over. I hurried to the cove, delighted at the chance to swim and lie on the rocks without worrying that a man might try to glimpse me there. Perhaps Nallei had sensed that I might want this time alone; I was grateful to her then, sorry that I had tried to argue with her.

It was dark when I returned to the hut. From across the bay, I heard the songs as the men chanted. I set wood on the fire, ate my supper, and sipped some of the wine Nallei had left. As the wine warmed me, I found myself wishing that I had asked for Arvil to be sent here now; we might have spoken freely with no one to overhear us. I could have shown him the cove.

I shook myself. It would have been mad to take him away from a ceremony of such importance to these men. The wine was going to my head. I closed my eyes and imagined that Arvil was with me, sitting with me by the fire. I seemed to feel his hand on my arm. I remembered how he had looked at me, how he had pressed his lips on mine, how I had felt for a moment.

My eyes shot open. I clutched at my belly, afraid I might be sick. I had felt some longing for him in that instant. I heard his voice as he spoke of the images in shrines, of the pleasures I might show him, and nearly cried out. I hated myself as I struggled with my thoughts; my time among men was making me unnatural, perhaps even insane. I had to root out this sickness, destroy it before Arvil saw me again.

I crawled toward the mat and stretched out until sleep came to me.

I tried to keep busy during the next day, but by afternoon, my solitude was growing oppressive. I cleaned out the hut, re-arranged our belongings, aired out the hides we used on the mat. I could not keep still, afraid that if I did, more disturbing thoughts would come to me. I cleared the hearth of ashes; as I carried more wood inside, I heard voices out on the lake.

It was nearly evening. I lit a fire, cleaned my hands, then stood by the door, ready to greet Nallei and hear of the ceremony.

Yerlan soon appeared on the trail below; he was carrying a torch. A short, dark-haired man was at his side; he had dined with me in Yerlan's dwelling, and now he carried a basket. Nallei walked behind them; as she looked up at me, I saw the strain on her face.

The shorter man set down his basket, then bowed. 'I greet you,' I said, feeling that they expected some words from me. 'I rejoice to see My companion again.'

Yerlan's mouth tightened. I could not look at him and turned quickly toward Nallei. She swallowed; her eyes stared past me.

'Fellow aspect,' she said. 'Go from here to Our cove, and commune there with the unseen spirits. You shall be summoned later. It is Yerlan I must summon now.'

I stepped back, apprehensive at the look in her eyes. She and Yerlan clearly had important matters to discuss.

'Go!' she shouted. I stepped back as she went inside. Yerlan set his torch in the ground, then followed her.

I began to walk down toward the cove. The other man was following me. I spun around. 'Leave Me.'

'Holy One.' He bowed, pressing his fingers to his forehead. 'I am here to serve You.'

'Go back to your boat.'

I came to the cove and sat down on a rock. The night spread slowly across the bay; the disk of the moon sailed on the black, calm waters. I sat there for a long time, waiting for someone to call me, wondering what business Nallei had with Yerlan. At last I got up. Their talk might concern me, and what happened in this camp was now my business. I had been learning how to tread over the ground silently and had surprised Nallei a couple of times; I would test myself and see if I could overhear part of their discussion. Nallei was keeping secrets from me; I did not think of those I had kept from her.

I crept cautiously up the slope toward our hut, circling around until I was among the trees overlooking it. I moved silently past the ditch, then hunkered down in the dark place under the trees where I could see the door. Yerlan's torch had nearly burned out; there was no sound from the hut.

The hide hanging in front of the door was suddenly lifted. I held my breath as Yerlan came out. He was bare to the waist; he reached down to adjust his belt. He threw his shirt over his shoulder and stumbled down along the trail as if intoxicated.

When he was gone, I hurried to the door and peered inside. The fire was burning low. Nallei lay on the mat, one arm flung over her eyes. Two empty jugs lay by the hearthstones. Nallei was naked. I stared at the disordered hides around her, at her bare, golden skin, at the tiny bruises fingers had made on her thighs.

I nearly screamed. I ran from the hut, heedless of the tree limbs that slashed at my face as I stumbled down the hill. When I was above the cove, my chest began to heave; I retched until my stomach was empty.

My feet carried me towards the rocks. I knelt to wash my face. I would leave this place, ride out on Flame and never return. I would not let the men stop me; I did not care where I went. I would swim out into the bay until I was too far from the island to swim back, then let the waters of the lake close over my head.

'Holy One,' a voice said.

I turned, startled. Yerlan's companion was walking down the slope toward me. 'Holy One,' he repeated as he came to the rocks. 'The Headman has passed through the holy state and now sleeps soundly in the joy of that blessing. He sent me to guide You back to Your house.'

I got to my feet and stumbled towards him. My arms flew out as I struck him hard with my fists. He did not hit back but cowered as I punched at him. I wanted to hurt him, to hurt all of his kind; my nails bit into his arms.

'Lady!' he cried.

I stepped back, struggling for control. 'That's so you will understand your place,' I gasped. 'My kind could sweep you from the face of the Earth.' Tears stung my eyes; I wiped them away.

'I have angered You with my evil thoughts. I cannot hide them from You. I dreamed of the holy state with You while Yerlan was with the other Holy One, saw You before me, thought of joining . . .'

I hit him again. 'Forgive me, Holy One!'

I panted for breath. 'Never think such thoughts again.'

'Yerlan will find out I've angered You. He will punish me.'

My anger was gone. I gazed down at this frightened man, despising him. 'Yerlan won't learn of this from Me,' I said at last. 'Get away from Me now. Go back to your Headman.'

He scrambled up the hill as I sank to the ground.

I remained by the cove until the eastern sky was grey with light, then stood up and walked along the shore.

The men were sleeping by their boat. I prodded the dark-haired one with my foot; he sat up quickly. Yerlan slept on.

'Holy One,' the man whispered as he passed his hand protectively over his face.

'My companion and I have matters to attend to,' I said. 'I do not want either you or the Headman to come anywhere near Our dwelling until We summon you. Do you understand?'

He nodded. 'I shall offend You no more.'

I walked up the trail, took a deep breath, and entered the hut. Nallei was waking; she raised herself on one elbow and stared at me. I sat and stirred the embers of the fire with a stick, then put on more wood from our pile.

She said, 'You know.'

I said nothing as I went through the motions of preparing tea. 'Listen to me,' she went on. 'I wanted to tell you before. I knew you would have to find out, but I couldn't say it to you.'

'What you do is disgusting.'

'Keep your voice down. The men might hear.'

303

'I told them to stay where they are until we called them.' I picked up stones and put them into the cups. 'So this is how you've lived, degrading yourself.'

'This is how I have survived.'

'And this is what I've come to.'

She sat up and pulled on her shirt. As she crawled toward me, I saw that her eyes were red and smelled the sour odour of wine on her breath. 'When I came here,' she said, 'I had to tell them they could no longer seek blessings in shrines, but they still wanted them. Some of the bolder ones were soon saying that I must have come here to give them such blessings. The mindspeakers have taught them that the Lady seeks their embrace and rejoices in it. They've been conditioned to long for and respond to a woman's form and to want that even more than they want each other. Our cities have done their work all too well.'

My tea was nearly ready, but I could not swallow any.

'One day, a man came to my hut and tried to take me against my will. I called out, and his companion beat him so senseless for the deed that he died soon afterward, but I knew someone else might try the same thing and discover I couldn't stop it. I couldn't change their impulses, I could only try to control them. Yerlan was one of those who was saying I had come to grant the band blessings. He became Headman two years after I came here. I knew I had to act then.'

'It was you who started the full moon ceremony,' I said.

'It was that, or finding a way for the healer Wirlan to bring me poison. I considered that – I could have told Wirlan that such poisons would have no power over me. But I couldn't give up my life even then.'

She had been carried into the camp for the first ceremony, and there she had entered the Prayergiver's hut and had joined with him. She had fortified herself with wine and even then the Prayergiver was too old to do much more than lie upon her. But Yerlan, as Headman, also expected to be summoned, and she had brought him back to the island. He had been quite different from the Prayergiver, strong and young and fueled by the potion he had drunk. Even the wine had not blurred the torment of meeting his demands.

Nallei soon realized that she would have to call others of the band from time to time. What had begun as an evil and sordid necessity soon gave her a stronger hold on the men. Those who had been called worshipped her all the more; those who had not could hope to win her favour.

'The wine dulls my senses,' she said. 'The man drinks of the potion the healer prepares, and I become all women to him. The wine makes my mind rise from me until he is only touching a body while I watch from afar. It makes it easier to endure, and sometimes I can drink enough to forget.'

'It's horrible,' I whispered.

'I'll tell you what I hate most about them. I can no longer seek love with anyone and take pleasure from it. I couldn't lie with you without thinking of them.'

I set down my cup. 'I have to get away.' I glanced wildly around the hut. 'They'll expect the same thing from me.'

Her hand clutched my arm. 'I told you that you'd be safe. I said at the ceremony that you would summon no man, that it's your task to commune with spirits and not with them. I said this before all of them, so even Yerlan must be bound by it. He was angry, though he tried not to show it. His thoughts were turning to you, but there's nothing he can do about it now. If he hurt you, his men would see that he suffered for it, and he knows that.'

I had despised her; now, I was moved by her. She had thought of protecting me from what she had endured, and I had not thought of her at all.

'It may be that fewer of the men will seek our blessing,' she said. 'The younger ones, those who were boys when I came here or who were brought here from other camps, have never known these things. They want to be with me only because it's an honour, but it's other men they desire. They haven't had the cities and shrines to instruct them. I've summoned few of them. They drink their potion, but only lie at my side and have no memory of what happened later.'

My gorge rose. 'How could you do this?'

'I'm alive. One lives how one must, you foolish girl. You would have been forced to do the same thing if you had been alone.'

I thought of Arvil's old band and how they might have dealt with me, then remembered how I had imagined Arvil sitting with me in the dark of the hut. I had no right to condemn Nallei. She only endured the touch of a man, while I had, however fleetingly, responded to Arvil.

I drew up my legs and pressed my forehead against my knees, tormented by these thoughts, then raised my head. 'But what do you allow ... how do they ...' I could hardly say the words. 'You must have found some way to keep from having a child.'

Nallei picked up her cup of tea, swallowed a little, and set the cup down. 'Surely you know how to chart your cycle, Birana.

Women have to know when they're most fertile and ready for the insemination of sperm. You must have learned how to use a scanner to detect the time when you're ovulating. Here, I must use similar methods to avoid a pregnancy. I keep a bit of hide with me always, and chart the days of my cycle on it. I don't have a scanner now, of course, but I can know when my fertile time comes and allow for it.' Her mouth twisted. 'It doesn't often happen that I have to endure a man during that time, but when it's necessary, I find other ways to satisfy him.'

I pressed a hand against my mouth, not wanting to think about what those ways might be.

Nallei straightened. 'You might as well hear the rest. You won't despise me any more than you do already. I was careful as I could be, but in spite of my precautions, I became pregnant ten years ago.'

'But the child . . .'

'There was no child. I aborted it. Do you understand? I couldn't have a child here, couldn't let them see . . . As soon as I was sure, I aborted it. I had to use a stick. I began to haemorrhage; I thought I would die. Somehow I found the strength to bury it and sent one of the guards for Wirlan. He came and gave me some of his potions for three days. I told him that an evil spirit had struggled with me but that I had won over it, and then swore him to secrecy. He has never spoken of it since.'

This was more horrible than anything else she had said. I knew that in ancient times, when our biological sciences were not as advanced, abortions had occasionally been necessary, but none had been performed for centuries. Women chose a time to give birth; defects in newborns or fetuses had been eliminated long ago.

I thought of Nallei, alone here, of how helpless she must have felt when she realized her condition. No one could have helped her, not even the healer. She could not have given birth without showing the men the truth about their existence; she could not have raised the child here. She could not even know what sort of child it might have been, whether it would have been strong enough to live. I could not condemn her for this.

'I was even more careful after that,' she said, 'and it never happened again. Now I think I must have destroyed my ability to have children. I couldn't have borne them here, but I hate the men for that, too. I suppose I should be grateful that, in a few years' time, my monthly bleeding will be past.'

I lifted my head. She had reminded me of how quickly we would age.

'Now you know about me,' she said. 'Despise me if you must, but I've done what I can to keep you safe. And think of this as well. You found your way here – perhaps some other woman will. You spoke of finding another refuge, but it may be that you'll have to create one here instead.' She paused. 'If you can no longer bear to live with me, I'm sure that men will build you another hut.'

I moved closer to her. 'I won't do that. If you hadn't done as you did, there might not have been a safe place for me.' I put my arm around her. 'You are my mother now.'

I knew I would have to go to the camp again, but the thought of doing so repelled me. I knew what the men had done to Nallei; I would understand their thoughts only too well when they looked at me. Yet I had to go to the camp to learn the skills I might need.

I did not speak of this to Nallei, but I had not given up hope of an escape. A stranger might come to the area outside the camp with some tale of a possible refuge. I could leave on horseback, and the band would be at a disadvantage if they followed me on foot. I did not plan to leave Nallei behind; I would find a way to take her with me. I could not believe that, with all she had suffered, she would not willingly leave this camp.

I rose one morning and announced to Nallei that I was going into the camp. I did not want to go, but it was becoming too easy to while away the days in swimming and talk, accompanied by jugs of wine. If I did not go to the camp soon, it would be difficult to bring myself to go at all.

I boarded a boat with one of the guards, commanding the other one to remain. The man with me protested when I sat in the prow and took up a paddle, but I silenced him. I had watched the men in their boats and was able to use the paddle, however awkwardly. My shoulders ached when we landed below the camp, but I refused to sit in the litter and walked up to the clearing. A boy fetched a mat for me; I sat down a few paces from the Prayergiver's house.

'Where is your Headman?' I said to the boy.

'He rests, Holy One, for he returned with hunters only a short time ago.'

'I would speak to him.'

Yerlan was soon hastening toward me from his dwelling; he bowed and sat down. I tried not to think of what he had done to

Nallei. Some of my guards on the island had often commented enviously on Yerlan's handsome face and well-formed body, but I could see no beauty in him, only a man whose strength had made him brutal.

'It is My wish,' I said, 'to spend some time with My messenger and to visit the land that lies around this camp. We shall ride out today.'

'It will be as You wish, Lady, but You would be safer here.'

'I shall be safe enough with My messenger.'

He scowled. 'If any harm comes to You, he will pay for it.'

'And because you have shown Me such hospitality before,' I said, 'I would dine with you and your hunters when I return.' I struggled to keep my bitterness and hatred for him out of my voice. 'But I ask only that you give Me what you would eat by yourselves, and not a feast more suitable for a special occasion. The Lady is not well served if the band She honours takes food from other mouths to feed Her, for it is Her wish that your fine band has enough for all.'

He brightened at that, then sent one of his men to fetch Arvil, who, it seemed, was at the edge of the camp gathering herbs and plants with Wirlan. Another man was sent to speak to the sentries beyond the camp so that Yerlan could be certain no travellers were near.

We rode out from the camp on Flame and Star, keeping to the trail before leaving it to stop in a glade. 'There are no sentries here,' Arvil said as we dismounted. 'We can speak freely. There is something I must tell you.'

'What is it?'

His hands moved nervously over his bow. 'The one who dwells with you . . . I know what the ceremony of the full moon is. She . . .'

'I know what happened, Arvil.'

'She joins with Yerlan, and sometimes with others. She calls them to her, yet she said there is to be no joining for you. What does this mean?'

'She's protecting me. That's why she said that.'

'But you told me what would happen if I joined with you. Isn't the same thing true for her?'

'There are ways . . .' I burst out before falling silent. I would be admitting that what I had told him about these matters was not entirely true. 'She's older,' I said at last. 'She can have no children now. A man's seed can no longer grow inside her.'

'But . . .'

'Why must you speak of this? Are you hoping she'll call you? There's no pleasure in it for her. She endures it because she must, but she hates the men for it as much as I would.'

He gazed at me steadily. 'She is fair, but I don't hope for that. You know who it is I long for, but if it cannot be, I can take comfort from knowing you are safe from others. I think of you lying with Yerlan or with other men, and I feel such rage that I would kill anyone in this band, even those who are becoming friends.'

'Arvil . . .' I touched his arm. He reached for my hand and held it for a moment. 'You mustn't think about this. I need your help now. There's much I have to learn. You must teach me the language of these men and show me how to use this spear and bow.'

He smiled at last. 'I shall try.'

It became my practice to go into the forest with Arvil as often as possible. He had seen that his spear and bow would not do for me, and so I practised with weapons he had made for Tulan. It was good that we practised in secret, for the band would have thought little of my powers and my dignity if they had seen me struggling with the bow or had watched my arrows drop only a pace or two away. My efforts with the spear often reduced Arvil to laughter.

I did, however, grow more skilled with the sling, since that weapon required skill and accuracy rather than strength. A day came when I aimed at a rabbit and struck it, but my joy at finding the target faded when I picked up the creature's tiny body. I would never match Arvil's skill with the bow and could not hurl the spear as far, but gradually I grew a bit more practised with those weapons.

Occasionally Tulan rode out with us, and Arvil swore him to secrecy about these sessions. The boy was happy to keep the secret, and being asked to come with us had raised him even higher in the estimation of the other boys. With Tulan, I learned how to block blows and how to use my arms and legs in a fight, although it took several days to convince him that he was not being disrespectful if he used his full strength against me. Tulan, like all boys, had learned to fight at an early age, and I soon bore the bruises of his efforts.

It was, I knew, also better to learn these skills with Tulan instead of Arvil. Arvil was strong enough to injure me severely without meaning to do so, but I also feared provoking him with so much bodily contact. Whenever he moved my fingers along the bow or spear into a proper grip, I saw that he prolonged the touch and welcomed it. Tulan was still too young to feel such impulses and could lock his arms around me with no other thought than trying to keep me from breaking his hold.

Because I did not want others to resent any favour I showed Arvil and Tulan, I also spent time listening to Yerlan and others tell me of their deeds. I presided over contests among the boys and went with them when they gathered berries or hunted for stones to make into points. I walked among the gardens and listened as the plant tenders told me of their crops.

All of this brought me to the camp nearly every day, and after almost a month, Nallei agreed to come with me. She smiled when I told her what I was learning, scolded me when she noticed my bruises or strained muscles, but finally grew curious enough, or lonely enough, to accompany me.

She had not been on a horse since before her exile but was able to ride on Flame with me when I went into the wood with Arvil and Tulan. She refused to learn the use of weapons, but watched while I practised. At first, she laughed at my mistakes, but as the days passed, she grew more solemn. Often she glanced from Arvil to me, and a thoughtful look would pass over her face.

Several days after she had first begun to come to the camp with me, I was chiding her as we prepared supper in our hut. 'Surely you could try the sling,' I said as I set wild onion around our cooked fish. 'Arvil can make one for you. You might need the skill someday.'

'I won't need it here.'

'Life is uncertain out here, even on this lake. We might have to leave someday.'

'There would be nowhere to go.' She gazed at me over the fire. 'And I wonder if you would want to leave Arvil.'

I stiffened. 'He's been a friend. I think he would follow me.'

'I'm sure he would.'

'Just what do you mean, Nallei?' I said, annoyed.

'Do you think I'm blind? I've seen how he looks at you, and there's no deference in his eyes. He's not looking at a Holy One, but at a young woman. I think he sees what you really are. Perhaps he learned that during your travels. Maybe you told him more than you should have.'

I sensed a threat in her words. 'He's no danger to you, Nallei. He's happy with this band, and he'd do anything to protect me. He proved that during our journey many times.'

'You're saying that he loves you.'

I pushed the stone platter of fish toward her. 'He's a friend,' I said at last.

'His feelings will grow. A time may come when he can't control them. Remember that there was one who tried to force himself on me. You may not mean to do so, but you lure him on by spending so much time with him. You're often alone with him in that wood. You smile at him and let him put his hands on yours.' She sighed. 'I'll do nothing against him, girl, but you'd better decide if it might be wiser to avoid him as much as possible and let those feelings in him die.'

The thoughts of having no moments with Arvil was more painful than I expected. 'He's only a friend,' I insisted. 'It would hurt him if I began to avoid him. He's done too much for me – he's been kinder than anyone I've known except for you.'

'What shall we do, Birana? He'll need to ease what's inside him somehow. By the standards of men, he is handsome. More important, he seems to have a touch of intelligence and sensitivity. He might not be as brutal as others. I've been through so much that one more man won't matter. I could summon him here. It might make matters easier for you.'

'No!' I cried out without thinking. 'I wouldn't have you endure that for me,' I said more calmly, but I was also thinking that, when he saw her beauty, he would lose his feelings for me. Jealousy tore at me; I squeezed my eyes shut to keep from weeping. I was being a fool. I could give him nothing but would keep him from finding pleasures with her.

I swallowed hard, then opened my eyes. Nallei studied me for a long time, then said, 'Very well. I won't summon him.' She picked up a piece of fish and began to eat.

Throughout the summer, the camp was alive with activity as the men made preparations for the harder seasons that lay ahead. Plants had to be gathered and stored, the gardens had to be weeded and harvested, meat had to be butchered and smoked. Arvil and Tulan showed me how to recognize certain roots and plants, and we brought as many back to the camp as we could.

I was unable to put Nallei's warning from my mind, but all she had done was to make me more awkward when I was with Arvil. I started when he tried to guide my hand and lost some skill with the weapons. Sometimes I smiled at him inadvertently and looked away quickly when he responded with a grin. I tried to be distant but could not maintain that pose for long.

He seemed troubled by my changing moods, but the work of the band left him little time to dwell on them. The men often went far from the camp to hunt for game, and Arvil would sometimes be gone with the hunters for three or four days at a time. This should have eased me, but my moods were no different when he was gone.

Being idle for short periods of time offered too many chances for disturbing thoughts to plague me. I began to look for ways to aid the band. By midsummer, the men were going out in boats to gather wild rice along the shore and in small inlets. I went with them and watched as they paddled their boats into clumps of rice, pulled out clusters with their hands, and struck the plants with their paddles so that the seeds fell on to hides that covered the bottoms of the boats.

When we returned to the camp, we carried the rice into the clearing and laid it out inside one dwelling to dry. I insisted on helping with this task and the men, after a few protests, allowed me to do so.

One of the men was called Kirlan; he was a short, dark-skinned young man who had been sent to the island several times before. I motioned to him.

'You will tell Me,' I said haltingly in the lake tongue, 'what is now done with this rice.'

His eyes widened in surprise. 'Lady, does our speech now fall from Your lips? It is not worthy of You, for it is a poor speech compared to Your holy tongue.'

'It is not a poor speech. I shall honour you by uttering it from time to time, but now we shall speak in My tongue.' I had learned some of their language by then, but was far from fluent. 'What do you do with the rice now?'

'It must dry for two or three days, and then it must be husked between the hands, so.' Kirlan rubbed his palms together. 'Then it must be parched over a fire and stored until we need it.' He scratched at his dark, curly hair. 'But the Holy One knows this already. Did not the Lady teach us all arts in ancient times?'

'She did,' I replied, a bit taken aback, 'but She wishes to see how well you have learned them and how the boys are instructed. I shall come here when it is time to husk the rice and will work with you.'

He gaped at me. 'But it is we who serve You. Your fellow aspect has never shared our toil.'

'The Lady will share some of your work with you from now on,' I said firmly, 'for She wishes to honour the band that has honoured Her.' I searched my mind for another pompous phrase, since this was the sort of talk they expected. 'My fellow aspect has watched over you and has not found you wanting, and the time has come for Us to aid you in whatever way these incarnations allow.' Nallei, I knew, was not going to be pleased by this new policy. 'Let it not be said that the Lady does not return honour when honour is paid to Her.'

Kirlan bowed, then hastened off to spread this news.

Nallei complained, as I had expected, but I bullied her into coming with me to work; almost against her will, she soon took some satisfaction in the extra tasks. She learned how to scale fish and grew skilled at husking the rice. She cared little about easing the band's burden in our small way but took some pleasure in knowing that a little of our food was the product of our own efforts. We walked together along the edge of the wood picking berries and helped the men store their dried meat.

Nallei's days were no longer as tedious, but she had worried that the band might lose their respect for us if we worked at their side. Instead, we seemed to inspire them. They redoubled their efforts to prepare the camp for colder weather, labouring from dawn until nightfall. The gardeners swore that their plots had never yielded so many plants; the hunters exclaimed that deer willingly accepted their arrows and that wildfowl landed at their feet, while those who fished claimed that fish leaped into their boats. Even the trapping of a large and dangerous wild boar that had begun to forage nearby was attributed to our presence among the men.

Nallei grew slimmer and stronger and glowed as though her body were, even without the techniques of our cities, rejuvenating itself. We still swam nearly every morning before crossing to the camp, and often we returned to our hut too tired to do more than fall on to our mat to sleep. Whenever I saw Arvil now, others were usually with us, and we did not often go into the wood alone to practise with spears and bows. It was easier for me not to think of him at other times.

Only the full moon ceremonies marred this season. Nallei drank heavily on those days; I looked on sadly as her boat drifted away from the island. I had solitude then, too much time to dwell on thoughts of Arvil. My illness of the mind had the most power over me then. I saw his grey eyes, heard his voice, felt his hand on mine, and cursed the world for not having made him a woman I might love.

*

In early autumn, spots of colour began to appear amid the trees on the hills around the lake. The oaks were beginning to change. Nallei and I kept to the island, wanting to enjoy as much time in the cove as possible before it grew too cold for swimming.

Guards came to the island and left it. Used to seeing me among them, they spoke more easily with me now, but they still used terms of respect. Wirlan came once, although Yerlan rarely sent him in case his healing arts might be needed in the camp. He told me of what Arvil was learning from him but did not speak of the time he had tended Nallei. A red-haired man named Resilan gathered mushrooms for me under the island trees; a hunter named Aklan told me of his hunts. Nallei avoided these guards much of the time except when she needed a task done. I listened to their stories and tried to feel some kindness for them, although it was hard not to think of how they had used Nallei. I would have to live among them, whatever they were.

I was following Resilan along the island shore when he pointed at a boat crossing the bay. 'Your next guards come,' he said. 'Holy Lady, it is Your messenger, Vilan.'

I lifted a hand to my throat; I had already seen Arvil's blond hair. He would be here for two days, possibly three; we would have all of that time together. I told myself that I was only happy to see a friend, and yet warmth was already rising to my cheeks.

'I see that You are pleased, Holy One,' Resilan said. I lowered my eyes, trying to compose myself. 'I'll tell the Headman of Your happiness, and perhaps he will send Vilan to Your island more often.'

'You must not tell him that,' I replied warily. 'I am as happy to see any of you. I'm as happy to see the Headman himself.' I wondered if Yerlan's feelings toward Arvil had eased, if he was learning to trust him more.

Tulan was in the boat with Arvil. I stood on a rock and watched as they dragged the boat ashore, then bid farewell to Resilan and his companion.

'The Headman chose us,' Tulan said as he came to my side. 'He said that because You have sought our company before, it was right for him to send us to guard You.' He struck his chest with one fist. 'And I'm the youngest one he has ever sent here.'

Arvil was lifting a basket from the boat. He set it down and looked up as Tulan started to strut. 'Be proud,' he said to the boy, 'but do not brag.' He stood up and gazed at me. 'Since You have let him tend Your horses, perhaps he grows too proud.' He spoke the words gently.

'I am pleased to see you,' I said, as stiffly as I could, but was unable to keep all my joy out of my voice. My mind was darting from one thought to another; I wished I had put on another shirt, trimmed the curls around my face, or worn Nallei's necklace of feathers.

'I am pleased to see You,' he said softly.

'The horses are well,' Tulan said. 'More of the boys ride them now, and Wild Spirit is not so wild.'

'Greetings, Holy One,' Arvil said suddenly.

I turned. Nallei had come down the trail and now stood on the slope above us. 'So you are to be Our guards now,' she said. 'Greetings, Tulan and Vilan – or perhaps I should continue to call you Arvil as My companion does.'

Tulan bowed; Arvil stared at her a moment before lowering his head. 'You may call me whatever You wish.'

She glanced from Arvil to me. I gestured awkwardly at the basket. 'Arvil and Tulan will carry up this food,' I said.

Nallei did not reply right away. She's going to summon him, I thought; she'll do it to protect me. At last she said, 'The boy and I can carry that, and he can tell Me what he has been learning. Perhaps You might show Arvil Our island, since he has not been here before.'

I was bewildered. She had talked of protecting me before; now, she was leaving me alone with Arvil. She walked toward the basket and lifted one end as Tulan picked up the other.

As they walked up the trail, I motioned to Arvil. 'We'll walk along the shore,' I said. 'I'll show you the cove where we swim.' I had learned more of the band's language and continued to speak in that tongue as we circled the island. I spoke of our hut, of a patch where blueberries grew, of the ducks that would soon fly away from the bay, and kept my eyes averted from him. I had nearly run out of words by the time we reached the cove.

'This is where we swim ,' I said, waving a hand at the water.

'So you have said.'

'The water is shallower here, and the sun warms it.'

He moved a little closer to me. 'I am a better swimmer now.'

I groped for more words. 'Tell me what you've been doing during the past days.'

He sat down on one of the rocks; after a moment, I seated myself next to him, careful not to get too close. 'I should tell you this,' he said in my language. 'You must remain cautious in how you treat Yerlan. He still harbours a longing for you. He doesn't admit it openly, but when he speaks of you, I hear what is in his voice. He wonders how favoured a place I have in your thoughts.'

'Yet he sent you here,' I said.

'He has a liking for Tulan, perhaps because he has no charge of his own. The boy is bold, and when the Headman said he would send Tulan here, Tulan asked if I could go with him. Yerlan agreed, but he didn't seem happy to do so.' He paused for a bit. 'You haven't spoken alone with him for some time. Perhaps you should when I leave here.'

'I'd rather be near him as little as possible.'

'You can sit in the clearing. He can do nothing there. It would make him happy to speak more to you of his doings, and it may make matters easier for me. I want him to send me here again, and perhaps he will if you show him some favour now.' He reached toward me. 'I've missed you, Birana.'

I let him hold my hand as all the feelings I wanted to deny flooded into me. I wanted his hand on mine; I wanted him close to me – further than that my thoughts did not go.

I said, 'I have missed you, Arvil.'

He released my hand and slipped his arm around my waist. I sat very still, hardly able to breathe. 'My longing is still great,' he said. 'Even your absence does not weaken it.'

'You mustn't speak of that.'

'I know what you have told me, and now I am learning Wirlan's lore. He has taught me much, and he's also told me a little of what has passed here since your companion came. What his private thoughts of the Lady are, I cannot say, but he knows the lore of ill or weak bodies, and he sees that your companion has a body not unlike our own.'

'What has he told you?' I asked, remembering what Nallei had told me.

'Only that the Lady's spirit is trapped in such a body. He has joined with her, as have others. Do you think a man who knows his lore can so easily put it aside and believe that you or your companion are something other than what he sees or feels? Others may be blinded by the worship they have been taught, but Wirlan is not such a man.'

I thought of the healer. I had felt uneasy with him, when he was on the island, but had attributed that nervousness to what I knew about him from Nallei; he had said nothing to provoke it.

'You shouldn't be telling me this,' I said. 'If Nallei . . .' I paused, but I had said her name and could not call it back. 'If my companion knew of this . . .'

'She will do nothing against him, and I do not think you will. He's silent about such thoughts except with me, and even you and your friend may need his healing in time.' His arm tightened around my waist. 'But it is this I wanted to say. You told me of what would happen when a man joined with a woman, and yet your companion has joined with many, and with Yerlan often, and nothing has come of it. You say a woman would grow large, and a child would come from her body. Your companion could not have hidden this, especially from Wirlan.'

'You don't understand. She . . .'

'You say she is older and a man's seed doesn't grow in her. She could not have been old when she came here. You have not been honest with me.'

I thrust his arm from me.

'You said that to join with you would mean your death, and yet she lives and thrives. You didn't tell me the truth. You wanted only to keep me from you, to frighten me with your story because you knew I cared too much for you to harm you. Am I so hateful to you? Is my body so hateful? Then why do you call me friend and smile at me? Why do you sit with me now and then draw away?'

'Nallei hates what they do,' I whispered. 'I would hate it as much.'

'But you would not. Look at me and tell me that your soul doesn't long for me.'

I forced myself to raise my head. He embraced me and his lips found mine. He drew me down next to him on the rock. His mouth was gentle against mine as he stroked my hair with his hands.

My lips parted. I had been without love too long, I told myself; I could not have responded to him otherwise. I tried to push my mind outside my body, as Nallei did, but was trapped inside myself. His hands gripped my waist and slipped under my shirt to cup my breasts.

I pushed his arms away violently and sat up. 'Are you going to tell me now you don't long for me?' he said softly. 'Can you not find a way to share yourself with me? I cannot force myself upon you – there would be no joy in that for me. Tell me if there's a way I can be with you without causing you harm.'

I bowed my head, shamed, unable to answer.

'Birana, I cannot bear this much longer. I could hold myself from you when I believed I might harm you, but now I know that doesn't have to happen. I am tormented. Tell me that you can never be with me, and I'll accept it and leave this camp. I can find another band, and you will be safe here. Perhaps then I can forget.'

I could not bear the thought of losing him altogether. 'I can't let you go,' I said. 'If you left . . .' I gazed at him, unable to say more.

He raised himself on one elbow. 'You will have to guide me, Birana. If a time comes when we can be together, you will have to show me what to do. I can wait if I know such a time will come.'

What could I tell him – that it was only my fear of losing him altogether that might make me surrender? That I was only showing gratitude for all he had done? That I still saw Laissa when I looked into his eyes? This would be part of the truth, but not all of it.

I heard a sound above us and looked up. Nallei was descending the hill. She could not have seen us or heard our words, and yet I felt that somehow she had.

'Tulan is by your boat,' she announced. 'Go there and stay with him until We have need of you.'

Arvil got to his feet, nodded, and walked back along the way he had come. When he was gone, Nallei undressed and plunged into the water without speaking. I followed, but the water had grown too cold for us to remain in it for long. We climbed out and stood on the rocks shivering as we waited for the sun to dry us, then pulled on our clothes.

Nallei sat down and began to comb her wet hair with her fingers. 'You were pleased to see Arvil here,' she said.

'Of course. He's my friend.'

'Birana, he's more than that to you.'

My hands fell from my hair. 'Just what do you think I am? Do you think I'm deranged? Do you think I could . . .'

'Haven't I been honest with you? Do you think I could despise you after what I've had to do? I think it's time you were honest with me. We have only each other. I might be able to help you.'

I choked, and then my head was against her shoulder as I wept. 'I don't know what I feel,' I whispered between sobs. 'When I'm with him, something in me . . . Nallei, what's happened to me? At first, I saw something in him, a resemblance to one I loved, but now . . .'

'Calm yourself, girl.' She patted my shoulder and dried my tears with her sleeve. 'I think it's time to tell me what you haven't said. What has passed between you both?'

'There's something I didn't tell you before, about my journey.' I began to tell her of my first meeting with Arvil, how he had gone to the enclave and returned with a command to kill me. She listened without interrupting. I told her everything I had revealed to Arvil about the cities and how I had made sure that my city would believe me dead.

When I was finished, she stood up and paced along the shore, deep in thought, and then climbed back up to me. 'He cared for you enough to overcome his fear of your city,' she said as she sat down. 'He cared for you enough to throw aside all of his beliefs, because to hold on to them would mean you would have to die. Even when he knew that you had no way to resist him, he didn't force himself upon you. I wouldn't have thought a man was capable of such feeling. Is it any wonder that he seems to have awakened some feeling in you?'

'What I feel is sick and contemptible.'

'So those in the cities would think. We're not in a city now. The cities wanted us dead . . . does it matter what they think? You're young, at an age when the urge for love is strong. Had you been in your city, with young women who might have been your partners, that urge would have been satisfied, but you're here now. I think that maybe there were few such partners for you and that your capacity for love had no outlet, but your feelings are there, and Arvil has somehow awakened them. Long ago, women felt such feelings for men, and perhaps that capacity still lies inside some women. Perhaps those dormant feelings, in the absence of a woman to satisfy you, have been roused.'

'It can't be true. I couldn't . . .'

She leaned toward me. 'Birana, I'll tell you what the men here have been to me. They feel awe, and grovel, and do my bidding. They worship the spirit that they believe lives in me. They also long for a body they've been conditioned to want. When one enters my hut, it's only his lust he wishes to satisfy, and then it is I who must humble myself. That's all there is for me. They worship me and then take what they want from me. There isn't one who ever felt even a bit of compassion or caring for *me*. It had to be that way for me. Perhaps if even one of them had seen past that, had seen me as I am, it might have been different, but too many years have passed and too many men have used me to make that possible. It doesn't have to be that way for you.'

'What are you telling me to do?'

'I can't tell you to do anything. You must decide that. I can't feel scorn for you whatever you do, and I think you've feared that.'

'Arvil may leave this camp,' I said. 'He may leave because of me.'

'You might be losing much.' She helped me to my feet. 'You had courage when you found your way here. Try to show some of that courage now.'

Nallei and I shared a meal inside the hut, and when we were done, she left the hut and walked down the trail leading to the boat. I laid more wood on the fire, then went outside to wash out our cups.

Arvil was climbing toward me as I poured a little water into the cups; I poured it out quickly and stood up, clutching at the cups and the waterskin.

'Your companion said you might have need of me,' he said. 'She has gone with Tulan in the boat – she said she wished to spend the day on the water.'

We were alone then. I stepped back, nearly dropping the cups. He took my belongings from me and set them on the ground.

'You can swim in the cove if you like,' I heard myself say. 'The water will be warmer now.'

'Tulan and I swam before, when you were with your companion.' He touched my hair lightly and rested his cheek against the top of my head. 'I have wanted a time alone with you, and the one you call Nallei has given it to us.'

I shivered.

'Even she has seen my longing.'

I stumbled away from him. He caught me around the waist. I tore myself away from him and hurried into the hut.

On the platform lay a piece of leather. Nallei had been marking the days of my cycle there with a stone so that I would be prepared for the days when I bled. I picked up the leather and counted, noting the days.

The hide over the door was lifted; Arvil's silhouette darkened the entrance. He stepped into the light of the fire. 'Do you wish me to stay?' he asked. 'You must tell me now. There will be few such moments for us.'

I set down the hide. 'There would be no danger for me now,' I said, surprised at how steady my voice was. 'A woman's body has its cycle, as does the moon. There are days when a man's seed won't grow inside her. This is such a day for me, I am sure. My cycle has been regular since I came here.' Nallei had seen this, I thought. She had sent him here; she had forced this decision upon me, but she had also known I would be safe. I wanted to be angry with her, yet she was only giving me a chance to settle what was between Arvil and me. I could still send him from the hut, uttering words cruel enough to make certain I never saw him again.

'Birana,' he murmured.

'I'll need some wine,' I said. 'It will deaden my thoughts, and then you can do as you like. If I must do this to keep you as my friend, then I'll do it.'

He came closer to me. 'Do you think that's how I want you, having you suffer my touch instead of welcoming it?'

'Give me the wine.'

He picked up a jug and poured some wine into a cup. My hands shook as I took it from him; I gulped it down, then drank another cup.

He moved toward the mat, picked up a hide, and lay it on the dirt floor. He reached for me then and drew me down to him.

The wine, instead of dulling me, had sharpened my awareness. If I closed my eyes and felt only his hands without looking at him, I could pretend he was a woman, forget what he was. I could imagine that the hands lifting my shirt, the hands touching my breasts, were not Arvil's. I lay at his side, and his gentleness made it easier to pretend he was not a man.

He took my hand and pressed it against his chest; I could no longer pretend. He had taken off his shirt; with his other hand, he loosened the belt around his leather trousers. He drew my hand to his abdomen.

'Birana, Birana.' He repeated my name, as if it were a chant. He lay across me, pressing my back against the hide while I tried to push him away, but he was too inflamed with longing by then to release me. He drew my hand to his groin, still covered by his garment, and held it there; he was hard against my palm.

He gasped; his breath was hot against my ear. He let go of me suddenly and sat back on his heels. 'I long for you too much,' he said as he untied my belt and slipped my pants over my hips. I closed my eyes again, listening to his movements as he took off the rest of his clothing.

He lay down at my side. His hand cupped my cheek for a moment as he kissed me, then dropped to my breast. I had thought he would be impatient, yet his hands lingered on me, circled my waist, slipped under me to caress my buttocks and stroke my thighs.

Perhaps the wine had robbed me of any power to resist. I

321

thought to myself: It is a woman with me, but my mind summoned no images except that of Arvil.

I opened my eyes and gazed into his face. How could I ever have thought of him as ugly? A friend looked out from those eyes, a friend who loved me. 'You must help me,' he said. 'Show me how I can give pleasure to you.'

I could not speak. His hand moved across my belly and between my legs. I had expected roughness, but his fingers were gentle as they probed.

'I have learned something from the spirit-women,' he whispered, 'but you must guide me now.'

I was now watching myself from afar and yet still feeling what my body felt. My hand dropped to his as I guided him, feeling my wetness on his fingers, leading him along my folds and to the tiny nub that nestled there. My back arched as he touched me; I heard myself moan as I opened my legs.

I released his hand. He would want to enter me now; I would have to endure it. The tip of his finger slid inside me, and then he was exploring my folds again, moving his hand tenderly over my nub. I could no longer hold back, crying out as the tiny spot of pleasure grew and then blossomed. I moved against his hand as my body shuddered with my response.

His organ was in my hand. He drew my fingers along his shaft, then clasped his hand tightly around mine as he moved against me. He groaned as his seed suddenly spurted from him; he had spent himself without entering me.

He stretched out next to me. 'You felt some pleasure with me, Birana. You cannot deny it now.'

'You didn't . . .' I said.

'You must be ready for me. I felt that you weren't, but I have had pleasure from you. This is enough for now, to take this smaller joy and have the greater one of knowing that you can accept my touch.'

My head was clearing. A man had touched me; he had brought me to completion, and I had welcomed it. He had seen me respond; he knew that I would remember this and long for him again. He had restrained himself, not entered me even when he must have ached for that; but I could not think kindly of his restraint, only that I had given him even more power over me.

I sat up. The sight of his nakedness should have repelled me. His chest rose and fell as he sighed. His eyes were closed; one muscular arm was curled under his golden hair. His penis, so large in my hand, seemed smaller as it rested against his thigh. I thought of how he had touched me and felt my belly tighten.

I jumped up and grabbed at my clothes. 'Birana!' he called out. I darted from the hut and ran down toward the cove, heedless of the twigs and brambles lashing at my legs and the pebbles under my bare feet. I dropped my clothes on a rock and threw myself into the water, wanting to cleanse myself.

I dived down under the surface and moved through the dark and silent depths. I thought of what Yvara would have said, what every woman I knew would have said. I was ill, besotted, sick and twisted; I had done a shameful deed, had shown that they were right to expel me, that they had somehow sensed the evil that was inside me.

My head broke through the water; I gulped for air. Arvil was standing by the shore. He set down his clothing and waded in as I swam toward him.

'Birana . . .' he said.

'Don't speak to me now.' I climbed out on to the rocks, feeling his eyes on me. I wrung the water from my hair, then pulled on my clothes.

Arvil ducked down under the water, rose, and then swam away from the shore. His stroke was smoother, although still awkward. As he swam out of the cove and into deeper water, I called out to him. 'Arvil! Don't go so far!'

He turned and swam back, then climbed out of the water. 'You do not have to shout,' he said.

'I was worried. You haven't known how to swim for very long.'

'A voice carries over the lake. Would you have the camp know that we've come here together to swim?' He shook the moisture from his hair and began to dress.

We sat next to each other, not speaking. At last he said, 'Like a spirit-woman, you vanished from my side. I had thought it would be different with you.'

I turned my head from him as I combed my hair with my fingers. 'I don't want to speak of this.'

'You feared me when you thought I could bring you no pleasure, and now you fear me because I do. If this is how it will be, I won't come to you again. There's not so much enjoyment in it that I cannot satisfy myself in other ways.'

I was stung. 'So I've lowered and demeaned myself for nothing.'

'That is how you think of it – lowering yourself?'

I got to my feet. 'Find someone else, then,' I snapped. 'There are enough men in the camp. I can ask Nallei to call you. She would do it for me.'

'You say your friend hates what they do. Would you have her do what she hates, and grow to hate me? Do you think I could take any joy in that?' His hands shook; his face was taut with anger. 'Do you think so little of us?'

I turned as he leaped to his feet. He grabbed my arms and pulled me toward him. I expected him to utter more angry words; instead, he pressed his lips against mine.

I wanted to feel his touch then. I pushed him away and climbed quickly toward the hut; he did not follow. I was crying with shame and hurt as I entered the dwelling. He had lain with me, and I wanted him to come to me again but could not say the words aloud to him.

I threw myself on to the mat and wept, hoping he would come to me but knowing he would not.

Nallei said nothing to me when she returned toward evening. As I set out our meal, she began to speak of Tulan. 'The boy was honoured to be asked to take me out on the lake,' she said. 'He would be happy to do so again.'

She was clearly waiting for me to tell her what to do, but I said nothing.

'He told me of his friends,' she continued. 'Since you gave him the horses to care for, he's been quite proud of himself. Of course, he seeks Yerlan's approval as well. It's a pity he can't remain as he is, but sooner or later I suppose he'll become like the others, bullying those who are weaker. Already he allows only certain boys to ride the horses with him. Maybe you should speak to him about that, encourage him to be a little more generous. You brought those horses here – he might listen to you.'

'He would listen to you, too.' I did not want to speak of Tulan.

I had been drinking during the meal and had finished nearly a jug of wine by myself; Nallei was noting that but still asked me nothing about what had happened. She stood up, yawned, and walked toward the mat. 'I must sleep.' She looked back to me. 'Birana, is there anything you want to say? I might not be able to help, but I can listen.'

I shook my head, then got up to clear our platter and cups from the hearthside.

I sat at her side, drinking wine until she was breathing deeply and evenly. I could not sleep yet, and the wine had made my head ache. The fire was burning low. I remembered the first time

I had been alone in the hut, how I had imagined Arvil near me.

The hut seemed to be closing in around me. I went outside to breathe the cool night air until my head was clearer, then walked along the trail, not caring where my feet carried me.

I was soon standing above the place where the boat had been beached and swayed unsteadily on my legs. A banked fire glowed on the ground; Tulan lay next to it, asleep. Arvil was gazing toward the camp; he turned his head and saw me.

I backed away and stumbled into the trees. Branches snapped and rustled behind me. I hastened on, then tripped; I thrust out a hand as arms caught me.

The wine had made me weak and dizzy. I was sinking, falling against a soft, mossy spot as arms lowered me gently to the ground. The darkness hid him from me. I thought: He has come to me once; it doesn't matter what he does now; I can tell myself I was too weak to stop him.

He drew my trousers down and covered my mouth with his. My lips parted as he probed my mouth with his tongue. His hand moved over my belly and then lower as my legs opened. Warmth flowed through me; again I was taking his hand and guiding his fingers. I told myself that it was not Arvil touching me, but a hand that might have belonged to a woman, but it was impossible to pretend even in the darkness. I felt the muscles of his back; his organ was hard against my thigh.

I gasped. He withdrew his hand and took mine; I gripped him tightly as he had shown me how to do. He guided my thumb to his moistened tip; I wanted to pull away from him then, but he kept his hand over mine. He moved against my hand and groaned softly as his semen spurted from him.

An odd elation filled me for a moment. I could do this for him; in return for the power I had given him over me, I had been given this power over him. He was no longer a man trained to ache for a woman without knowing why; he was Arvil, my companion, who sought only my touch.

His penis was soft in my hand. I continued to hold it, then ran my fingers lightly over the testes beneath. He shuddered and sighed. 'Birana, this is more than I felt with you before. This is closer to the holy state of the spirit-women, and yet more than that because it comes from you.'

He kissed me again, moving his tongue inside my mouth. His hand was probing my cleft; I spread my legs wider, opening myself to his touch. 'Is there another way?' he whispered. 'Is it only my hand that can do this? A man will sometimes use his mouth with his partner. Should I put my mouth on you?'

A moan escaped me; I did not have to speak my answer. He lowered his head and kissed my belly as his hands pressed against the inside of my thighs.

His mouth was suddenly on the place between my legs, kissing me as he had kissed my lips. His tongue moved into me, flicking against my inner lips as he nuzzled me awkwardly. I heard myself whispering to him, telling him what to do. His fingers spread my folds open as his tongue licked and probed.

I drew up my knees as a wave of pleasure flowed over me. My hand was against my mouth to stifle my moans as his tongue slid over me. My hips moved under him; I felt my pleasure would never stop, that it would ebb and flow and then wash over me once more.

At last it flowed from me and did not return. He lay at my side, stroking my breasts tenderly as if he now sought no more than the feel of my skin. I touched his body and felt the harder muscles of his chest and then the downy patch just below his abdomen. His body, so different from mine, no longer seemed so repulsive, so alien.

No one had given me such joy before. Perhaps if I had known a woman or girl who had truly loved me, it would have been impossible for me to accept any love from Arvil. I had longed for love even more than I realized.

'Your kind has a power men do not,' he murmured. 'A man burns, and then his pleasure rushes from him, while yours seems to move over you as though it would never cease.'

The images in shrines conditioned men to want what they provided; it had not occurred to me before that they might also show men how to give us pleasure. Those ancient images, created in a time before women had completely separated themselves from men, had shown Arvil some ways to love me; people long dead still worked through him and through me.

Arvil drew his shirt and mine over us to protect us from the cold. We lay there for a while, and soon his hands were caressing me more insistently. This time he did not have to guide my hand to him. His body moved more slowly as he spent himself and sighed softly. I felt no wave of pleasure as he touched me, but only a small spasm of joy that might have come to me in a dream.

He kissed my face and neck, stroked my hair, then sat up. 'I would stay here with you,' he said, 'but I must go. Tulan may wake and wonder where I've gone.'

I rose reluctantly. He helped me dress, then put on his own

clothes. His hands slipped around my waist. 'I want too much, I know,' he said. 'Tell me that I can come to you again.'

I could not speak.

'Tell me that I can hope, that you will welcome me again.'

'I will.' I had said it at last. 'I don't think I could turn you away now, Arvil.'

He released me and vanished among the trees.

Nallei said little in the morning as I prepared our herb tea, but I had sensed she was feigning sleep the night before when I crept back into the hut. She must have known that something had changed, must have guessed that Arvil and I had been together.

I was awkward making the tea and nearly burned my hand on one of the small stones. I could hardly bring myself to eat any of our fruit. As we finished our meal, I heard a voice outside.

Nallei rose and left the hut; I followed Arvil and Tulan were walking up toward us. 'Is there anything You need, Holy Ones?' Tulan asked.

My cheeks burned. I glanced at Arvil from the sides of my eyes. His face was flushed; he looked away and poked at the ground with one foot.

Nallei cleared her throat. 'Tulan told me yesterday of the contests the boys will hold soon to mark this season. Since My companion and I will be presiding over them, I would like Tulan to tell Me more about what is planned this time. I shall go out on the lake with him again today and return for Our noontime meal.'

Tulan shook back his straight black hair and clapped his hands together, obviously pleased. 'You honour me again, Holy One.'

My face grew hotter as Nallei glanced from Arvil to me; I had confirmed her suspicions by not objecting while she spoke to the boy. 'Perhaps Tulan and I can go out in the boat this afternoon,' I said quickly.

Tulan beamed still more. 'I would be honoured.'

'I must tend to my tasks,' I muttered, and ducked back into the hut. Nallei was speaking to Arvil, telling him that she would welcome him and Tulan at our hut for our meal. I felt feverish as I knelt by the fire and wondered if I was becoming ill. I reached toward a jar of berry wine, then let my hand drop.

'They have gone,' Arvil said as he entered the hut and sat

down near me. Perhaps he only wanted to talk now; there had been little enough talk between us since he arrived. I kept my head lowered as I stirred the fire.

'You would rather be with Tulan this afternoon than with me,' he said. 'I had thought . . .'

'I'm being cautious. Would you want him to tell others that we were often alone while you were here? Yerlan might find it odd.'

'They cannot know what has passed, and Tulan would say nothing. I am almost a guardian to him.'

'So is Yerlan. We must be careful.'

He nodded. 'It is so. I'm too greedy. I think I must have every moment with you I can.' He paused. 'I think Tulan is coming to care for you more.'

'He is only a boy.'

'He won't be a boy for too much longer.' He ran a hand through his wavy, blond hair. 'I shouldn't say this, I know, but now that you have shared some pleasures with me, you may wish others to share them as well.'

'Never!' I cried. 'I've shamed myself enough.'

'Is it still shameful to you, Birana?'

I sat back on my heels. 'I didn't mean to say that. It seems that way afterward, not when I'm with you. Try to understand. No woman longs for a man. My city would call what I feel a sickness. I can tell myself it isn't so, but I can't forget that. They would think that what Nallei has done is bad enough, even though she takes no joy in it.'

He took my hand and helped me to my feet. 'We have little time.' He bent his head and put his mouth on mine. His hair and body smelled of the lake, as though he had bathed earlier; his tongue slipped inside my mouth and I remembered the feel of his tongue in me.

His hands pulled at my clothes. When we were both naked, he led me to the mat. No darkness shielded us now; the morning light shone under the hide over the door and the fire glowed. I saw his body clearly in the shadows. Below his tanned chest and paler belly, his organ had already begun to swell.

I lay next to him as he touched my breasts and guided his hands to my nipples. He rubbed his thumb over them until they were erect, then felt my thighs as he parted my legs.

'Birana,' he whispered as his fingers caressed me. 'I want . . .' He was suddenly upon me, his penis between my legs. I pushed against his chest, resisting, until he rolled to one side.

'Arvil, don't.'

'You said there would be no danger before. Is there danger now?'

I sat up, pulling part of a hide over me. I could tell him that there was danger but wondered if I could lie to him now about anything. 'No, there's no danger. I know my own body, I've counted the days carefully.' I did not want what had happened to Nallei to happen to me.

'Then why do you push me away?'

'I don't know if I can explain. What I've done with you . . . I might have done that with a woman. I can tell myself that, and then it doesn't seem so . . .' I bit my lip. 'But this other thing . . . it can only be done with a man, and that makes it seem worse.' I swallowed. 'It may hurt me, too. I'm afraid of the pain. I'm afraid my body can't take all of you inside me.'

'I know I can please you now. I can make you ready for me. I must try. If you cannot, I'll take my pleasure in the other way.'

I wanted to trust him; he had been gentle before. Perhaps I would only have to endure this once; if he hurt me or saw I took no joy in this practice, he might not want it again.

I lay back. He fondled me with one hand, but his touch was different this time. When I moaned, he hesitated before exploring me further. He lowered his head between my thighs and probed first with his hand and then with his tongue, arousing me and yet not satisfying me. His finger slipped inside me, then out, then in again more deeply.

I lifted myself a little, thinking I might have to guide him. I was completely open to him, aching as he rubbed each fold lightly and his tongue flicked against my nub. I fell back, unable to bear much more.

He lifted my knees and knelt between my legs. I felt the tip of his penis on my cleft. 'If you feel pain, I will stop,' he whispered, although I wondered if he could, if his own desire might already be too great. He rubbed against me some more; his tip pushed against me. 'Do you feel pain now?'

I shook my head. I could not have deceived him; everything in me was aching for release by then. He cupped my buttocks and continued to thrust gently, moving a little deeper inside me each time, and then entered me fully with one final thrust.

I cried out as he fell across me; this time, I felt pain. I twisted against him as his thrusts came more rapidly, but as he moved inside me, my pain was transforming itself, becoming a burning ache. At last he cried out, and my own cry answered his as my pleasure mingled with the pain.

He slipped from me. Our bodies were drenched with sweat. He sighed as he held me. He had done this thing, had given me some pleasure with it, something I had not expected, something I had thought impossible. This was not the same pleasure his hands and tongue had given, but I had responded even to this.

He leaned over me for a moment and then drew back. 'I've hurt you,' he said. 'There is a little blood on the hide. Have I done something wrong?'

'No, Arvil.'

'Has your time come to bleed?'

'No, it isn't that, only a small obstruction inside me that's now been broken. You won't make me bleed again.'

He rested his head on my chest as I stroked his hair. 'You are not a spirit-woman,' he murmured. 'With them, a man can thrust without fear. With you, I must be gentler, as a kind man would be with a younger one who has not yet known love. But this is different from what I felt with the spirit-women. They were more like creatures in a dream, but this was real, with you, and that makes it better. I'll make it better still.' He slipped one arm under my waist. 'And for you, Birana – what was it for you?'

'I can't say. There was some pain, but pleasure too.' I did not know what else to tell him; this was still too new to me. I had taken pleasure with a man in a way that had not existed for centuries, in a way that had died out long ago. I saw now why women had separated themselves from this act, how the need for it could enslave a woman and rob her of her reason. The act itself was foolish and dangerous. To love a woman exposed one to no dangers except the chance that one's heart might be broken; to love a man meant embarking on a journey with an uncertain end. There was the chance of a child if I were not cautious, and Yerlan and his men might learn somehow of what we had done. But even the thought of those dangers was not enough to make me want to give it up.

Arvil's hand moved over my abdomen, and then lower, and I forgot everything except the sensations he was reawakening in me.

Thoughts of Arvil distracted me for the rest of the day. I made an effort to listen to Tulan as we paddled the boat around the bay, but my mind was elsewhere, and I scarcely heard what he said. When I swam with Nallei that evening, I remembered how Arvil's body had looked when he emerged from the water.

That night, while Nallei slept, I went out to the place under the trees where I knew I would find Arvil. This time, he showed me something else he had experienced with the mindspeaker images. I learned that I could kneel, my legs on either side of him, that I could guide him into me and feel more pleasure in that way.

As we lay under the trees, my hands searched his body, coming to know him better. There was a small scar near his left shoulder, the legacy of a boyhood fight; another scar marked his right thigh. I found that he delighted in feeling my thumbs against his nipples and welcomed my touch along the soft downy region between his thigh and groin.

'I thought of this all afternoon,' he said. 'I thought of it while you were with Tulan.'

'I thought of it, too.'

'I wonder if I can ever stop thinking of it.'

I raised myself on one elbow. 'We must be even more careful now. We may not be able to . . .'

He touched one finger to my lips. 'We must find a way. I'll be sent here again. There may be other places away from the camp where we can go.'

I climbed back to my hut reluctantly, wondering how I would bear it when he left the island. As I pulled the hide over the door aside, I saw that Nallei was awake, sitting by the fire.

'You know what has happened,' I said as I sat down next to her.

'I know. Is this the end of what's between you, or the beginning?'

'I can't imagine it ending now.' I rested my head on my knees. 'When I'm with him, he's all there is for me, and when I leave him, I feel it's a madness, a disease of the mind. I never felt this way about anyone except one other.' I paused; it was still hard to speak of Laissa, who had drawn away from me, who had wanted me dead. 'Arvil looks like her. I think they had the same mother and father. The resemblance was why I felt more sympathy for him at first, but now . . .' I shook my head. 'His sister never loved me. I never told her how I felt.'

'We are more malleable than we realize,' Nallei said. 'Why wouldn't we come to love women in the cities? There is no one else to love. In ancient times, there were women who loved only other women, and men who loved men, but it was they who thought they had a disease of the mind. I know something of the past; I have read about it.' This was the closest Nallei had come to speaking of her former life. 'Sometimes it seems as if we insist on creating worlds in which some kinds of love are accepted and honoured, while others are despised. We chose our way long ago, partly because we believed the kinds of love sanctioned in the past, those that bound us to men, helped to bring about the Destruction and made us powerless to protest what men had done. I have had some doubt about that. Perhaps there simply wasn't enough love among those people for others. Perhaps if they had been free to love whomever they chose, to open their hearts willingly to anyone who might love them, and to let this love grow to encompass everyone in some way, they might have found a way to avoid the destruction of others they loved. Perhaps by denying certain kinds of love, they warped their ability to love anyone truly or to love the Earth that they nearly destroyed. At the very least, I can't see how accepting all the ways one might love and any partner one might choose could have added to the horror of what they did.'

I wondered if Nallei had spoken such thoughts to others in her city, if this, as much as any crime, had been responsible for her expulsion.

'If you and that young man had denied the capacity that was in you,' she continued, 'perhaps you would only have poisoned yourselves, twisted your love into something else. I'm sorry I couldn't be the one to love you, but that capacity has died in me – it would have been easier for us both if it hadn't. But you have another kind of love now, and you mustn't torment yourself about the rightness of it. I fear you may suffer enough without that guilt.'

She covered my hand with hers. 'Be careful, Birana. There are risks with this love, as you know. You can't grow reckless now. I wouldn't want to lose you and be alone here again, but I almost think it might be better if you and Arvil left this camp.'

'I couldn't leave you here alone. I won't leave you, Nallei.' If we left, I would have to find a way to take her with us. But the thought of escape was already far from my mind; I would think of that later. For now, I was safe enough here. I would be careful, would take no chances. It was easier to think this away from Arvil, easier to forget that when I was with him only those moments at his side mattered.

ARVIL

I had longed for Birana, yet even with what the spirit-women had shown me, I had not known what to expect. The aspects in the shrine and the enclave had felt like women of flesh and bone, but they had been ghosts without names, only bodies to arouse and then satisfy me.

I had seen Birana in that way at first, as one who might grant me blessings but who in every other way was apart from me. Instead, her soul had reached out to mine.

She was like the spirit-women and yet unlike them. With her, there was the smoothness of her skin and the curves of her body, but also an uncertain groping, the awkwardness of a fearful soul, the sweat and smell and salty taste of her. The spirit-women were beings who vanished when I was sated, while Birana remained to rest with me and to rouse me again. I remembered the look of her dark hair spread out on the mat, the rosy glow of her face after I loved her. Even my uncertainty with her and the need to give her a more prolonged pleasure that spirit-women did not seek added to my longing.

After our first time on the island, Birana went to the camp to sit alone with Yerlan in the clearing and listen to his tales. Although I had told her it would be wise to show him such favour, I felt anger when they sat together but swallowed my rage. Yerlan was pleased by her growing friendliness toward him. He soon learned that each time he sent Tulan and me to the island, Birana would come to him and listen to his talk.

That autumn was marked by the harvest of what remained in the gardens and by a great hunt. All in the camp were busy with butchering deer, drying fish, smoking our meat, curing hides, storing the food we would need for the winter, and patching spaces between the logs of our dwellings with mud and clay.

Birana and Nallei did what they could to aid the camp. With some of the boys, they gathered nuts and acorns and learned how to dig up roots. Birana was not skilled enough with her weapons to hunt, but she followed the hunters on horseback and showed them how a conveyance of wood and hide might be made for each horse to pull; on these litters, she was able to bring game back to the camp. I had worried about how we might feed the horses during the winter, but the band had seen their usefulness. Along with our own food, we stored much dry grass and some wild grains for the beasts. We would feed them what we could; if they grew weak, they could provide us with meat.

Birana had grown more beautiful. Her skin was as rosy as a wild rose's petals, her dark brown hair was streaked with red and gold from the sun, and she strode proudly among the men of the camp, as if the pleasures she had taken with me had filled a need in her soul. She smiled more often and spoke more kindly to some, and the men took this as a sign of her favour.

I rejoiced in this new beauty, but feared for her. I knew the thoughts of some men, for I had heard the bolder ones whisper them to one another. A time might come when the younger Holy One would no longer commune with spirits on the night of the full moon, when she too would summon men to her side. They whispered that Birana's smile showed her anticipation of the day she would enter the holy state with those she would call. More men found reasons to be near her, to help her in the work of gathering food or wood for the fires.

I did not seek her out often when others were near and lowered my eyes when she passed, afraid that others might see what was in my thoughts and mark by the way I gazed at her that we had grown closer. A hunter, I knew, could read many things in the stance and gaze of another.

I had won her, won her body and the love of her soul. I had overcome the obstacles the world had set in my path and had conquered my fear and hers. At times, I wanted to shout this to the others, to let them know she had chosen me; but I held my peace, knowing that I would only destroy what I had won.

I sat with Birana by the island cove; Yerlan had sent me to guard her for the sixth time. The oaks had lost nearly all of their leaves by then, and the camp often woke to the sight of frost on the ground.

Our pleasures that day had been given with hands and lips because it was a time when my seed might have grown within her. I had shown her how to take me into her mouth, as a man might do, but this had not been easy for her. I hoped that a time would come when she would welcome the taste of me, as I delighted in hers.

She cut at my hair with my metal knife, working gently at each strand until my hair curled against the top of my neck, then drew my curls through her fingers as I pressed my mouth to hers. 'Now for your face,' she murmured. I had little hair on my face but allowed her to draw the knife carefully across my cheeks.

I said, 'I may want a man's beard in time.'

'Your face is too pleasing to hide with a beard.'

'I think that's why Yerlan has no beard – not because it's the custom among many of these men, but because he cannot bear to hide his beauty.'

'Yerlan!' She sniffed. 'How tedious it is to listen to him sometimes, with all his talk about how strong he is, and how no one has ever beaten him in a contest. When I smile and tell him how fine he is, I feel like a fool.'

I took the knife from her. 'Birana, it isn't wise to think of Yerlan that way. He is a Headman, he became one when he wasn't much older than I am now. He may not have the cleverness or wit of some others, but he watches and sees more than you know.'

She lowered her eyes. 'Now you're frightening me.'

'I mean to frighten you. You must be on your guard with him, as I am. If you're careless in your dealings with him or show contempt, he will be shamed, and a shamed man can do reckless deeds.'

'All that posturing!' she burst out. 'All the bragging, the preening and strutting, all those competitions to see who's better with a spear or who can wrestle someone else to the ground.'

'We must be strong and skilled at such things if we're to live. We must know where another might be weaker, or how he might fail us.'

'The men don't have contests only for that. They want the enjoyment of beating someone else, of being better.'

'It would be good if you shared some of those feelings,' I said. 'You might grow better at such arts if you did.'

'I might improve if, every time we try to practise them here, you didn't start wanting to do other things.'

I pulled her to her feet. 'I do not see you resist those other things.'

I wanted to be alone with her for the rest of that day but knew that Tulan, who was with Nallei, would begin to look for me soon. I worried a little about Nallei as well. Although she did not complain, she moved more stiffly in this colder weather, as though her bones had started to ache. My time with Wirlan had made me able to see such signs and mark what they meant. I was concerned about Nallei for her own sake, but also for Birana's as well. Birana's companion protected her, and I feared what might happen if Nallei could no longer do so.

That autumn, I was allowed to lead a band of hunters from the camp. We had hunted deer before, bringing some of those creatures down with our spears and stealing other carcasses from the cats and wolves that had killed them. This time, we hunted bear, tracking a creature that might injure or kill us. Yerlan, I was sure, was testing me by allowing me to lead this hunt. I did not want to fail.

We tracked a bear for a day, rested that night, and found him the next morning. As our spears flew toward him, he rose up on his legs, maddened by this assault. My spear found his throat as he staggered toward us, bringing him down only a few paces from my feet.

We lashed the bear to a sturdy tree limb. He was fat with the food he had eaten to sustain him during his winter's sleep, and it took much of our strength to carry him back toward the trail.

'You did well, Vilan,' Aklan said, using the name that meant I was one of the men of the lake. 'We'll have fat to render and good eating for many days, and you will have a fine hide.'

'I'll have to speak to the Headman before I can take it,' I said.

'It was your spear that brought death to this bear. The Headman will let you have the hide. You may have need of it, for winters grow cold by the lake.'

I had my sheepskin coat and would not need this hide as well. It came to me that Yerlan might not be pleased by my success. Even after nearly two seasons, Yerlan had not warmed toward me, and I pondered what I would say to him.

It took us the rest of the day to reach the camp with our burden. The hunters rested as other men laboured over the carcass. Tired as I was, I roused myself and went to Yerlan.

He sat outside his dwelling; a furry hide protected him against the cold night air. Behind him, the fire of his hearth glowed. His head was bowed as though he were deep in thought.

'Greetings, Headman,' I said as I sat down. 'We have brought back a bear, and it was my spear that carried his death to him.'

'Then you'll have a hide, Vilan.'

'I have this coat I wear and the skin of a cat as well. They'll serve me during the coming season. I have seen your skill as a hunter and, had you been with us, your spear would have brought him down, not mine. I would give this hide to you.'

He scowled. 'I've proven myself as a hunter. I have hides enough. I do not need the gifts one would give to an old man.'

I had only insulted him with my offer. 'I have not spoken well,' I said quickly. 'It is my wish that you have this hide to take to the Holy Ones.' I was thinking of Nallei, of how she shivered in the cold. 'It is you who should make this gift to Them, not I, for it is you who are the leader and the greatest hunter here. The Holy Ones will thank you for it.'

He was silent. His eyes were hidden by the darkness, and I did not know what he was thinking. One mistake, I knew, could turn him against me.

'I am pleased,' he said at last. 'The Holy Ones do me honour, but it is you the younger One smiles upon most often.' I steadied myself. 'Now, She will smile upon me, and thank me.'

The other hunters were drawing near. Yerlan waved them away. 'My words are for Vilan,' he said. 'Leave us.' The others backed away. 'What favour do you seek, Vilan? Another time with the Holy Ones on Their island? I have sent you there often enough.'

'It is always an honour to serve the Holy Ones,' I said carefully, 'but it's also an honour to be part of your band.'

'I have sent you there, and the Holy Ones don't find you displeasing, and yet the black-haired Lady has not yet called you to Her side. She calls fewer now, and almost none of the younger men. Do you think that displaying yourself before Her more often will cause Her to call you?'

'A man always prays for the Lady's blessing.'

'You may pray for it. I receive it at the time of the full moon, always.' His hand passed over his groin. 'I say this to you now. A part of me knows that it's right that She grants Her blessing to others, and yet my soul rages when She lies with another man.'

'She would not prefer me to you, Headman. I don't think She will call me.'

'Perhaps is isn't the black-haired Lady you long for most, beautiful as She is. Perhaps it is the younger One you want. A time may come when She will welcome the holy state, when the invisible spirits guide Her to us. If that is so, it is I who will lie with Her, who will feel Her body under mine.'

I swallowed hard. My face burned. I wanted to mar his handsome face, to bury my knife in his chest.

'It's the brown-haired One you long for,' he continued. 'I see it when She walks by and you lower your eyes to hide your thoughts. Do you think you can hide them from Her? Do you think you can hide them from me?'

'I have only the longing the others in the band share,' I replied.

'There is more in your eyes than their longing, more than their awe.'

I was frightened then. 'It was to me that the Lady first revealed Herself,' I said. 'During our journey here, I came to hope that I would have a special place in Her thoughts, but that was not to be, although She honours me as Her messenger. She will not call me, Yerlan, and will call no one else. To me, She shows only the kindness She would show any man who had protected Her and brought Her to this fine band. It's true that I long for more than Her kindness, but I am content with that.'

Yerlan began to murmur to me then of the pleasures he had shared with Nallei. Although he used holy words to speak of them, his talk made my gorge rise. No respect was in his voice, and he spoke of Nallei as if she were no more than a vessel for his lusts.

It came to me then that Yerlan, who had been with Nallei so often, might have grown aware of her true nature. In all of his talk, there was also a message for me. I am the Headman, Yerlan was saying. This pleasure will be mine; it will not be yours unless the Lady chooses you, and it may be that I can see She does not choose you. I wondered what he would think if he knew that Nallei hated what he did.

Somehow, throughout his coarse talk, I kept my senses. Birana had come to me. Yerlan would never know those pleasures; he would never have Birana welcome him.

'I am honoured that you speak of these holy matters to me,' I said when he was finished, 'but it isn't my place to hear them.'

'It may be time you had a higher place,' he said. 'You haven't done badly for one who came to us as a stranger, for one who is still so young. You are a worthy enough hunter, and Wirlan tells me you begin to master some of his healing lore.' He paused. 'It is my wish that you move your belongings to my hearth, to my dwelling, and that you become one of those closest to me.'

I had not wanted this honour, nor had I expected it. He was not doing this in the hope I would lie with him, for the others had told me he sought no love from men since lying with Nallei. He was not just showing respect; he wanted me close, where he could watch me. I would be in more danger now.

'I am honoured,' I replied, putting as much conviction into the words as I could.

*

338

My place at Yerlan's hearth and the knowledge that he would be watching me was enough to make me cautious. My worries tainted even those few moments I had alone with Birana. I was afraid to take too much pleasure with her for fear that the Headman might glimpse my joy and wonder at its cause when I returned to the camp.

We brought baskets of food, enough for days, to the hut, for, during the winter months there were times when the band could not reach the island. The bay, shallower than the rest of the lake, froze during the coldest times. Sometimes men could walk over the ice to the island, but on other days, the ice was too thin, and we often had to pound at the ice and break it to make a path for the boats. Twice the full moon came and went without a ceremony while snowstorms hid the island from view.

I had thought the winter might take the Prayergiver from us, but the old man, frail as he looked, grew no weaker. Others were not so fortunate. One of Tulan's friends burned with a fever, lost the power to breathe, and died. A man nearly as old as the Prayergiver died quietly in the night. Another man, while fishing by a hole in the ice, fell through it and was claimed by the lake. It was Nallei's task, and Birana's, to stand over the bodies and recite holy words, telling the band that the souls of the dead ones were at peace with the Lady. The band accepted this, believing that the two had not used their powers to save the men because their souls would be happier in the next world.

These deaths, along with the fevers and aches that came over many in this season, led me to spend even more time with Wirlan. He shared his lore of herbs and potions that could cool a fevered one or calm the belly of a man who could not hold his food. I learned how to clean wounds, how to bind a broken limb, how to keep an injury from festering. I also learned more of his thoughts.

We had tended Dagelan, one of the hunters, for four days, fearing for his life until his fever broke and we knew he would live. As I left his dwelling with the healer, I said, 'The Headman will send me to the island tomorrow. I would have more datura to take to the black-haired Holy One.'

He glanced at me. 'Does She drink so much of it now?'

'It eases the aches of the body that holds Her spirit.'

His brown eyes narrowed, and a thoughtful look passed over his thin face. He pulled his hood over his greying hair, then drew me aside. 'The Holy Ones share many of our weaknesses,' he murmured.

'It is Their bodies that share them, but Their spirits . . .'

'I know of bodies. I do not know of spirits. Lirilan and Paslan learn from me of the body but think their chants and spells hasten the healing. I don't object, for if an ill man believes in such things also, he may be eased; but you, Vilan, are wiser than that.'

We walked toward the lake. Wirlan halted at the edge of the ice and stared out at the island. 'Dagelan will grow stronger, not because of spells and prayers, but because he's young and able to fight his illness. Metlan will die this winter or next, not because the Lady wants him in the next world, but because the few teeth he has left don't allow him to chew the food he needs. I can share such thoughts with you, and you may become a better healer for seeing this. Paslan and Lirilan would only shake their heads and make signs against evil.'

I had not protested when Wirlan first spoke to me in this way. Although I had hidden my own thoughts from him, my silence as I listened and his knowledge that I kept his words to myself had convinced him that he could be open with me.

'I have been called to the Lady's side,' he continued, 'and not just to share Her holy state but for another reason, years ago. I swore that I would not speak of it, but I shall tell you this. Her spirit has little power over Her body, and I fear that She may grow weaker still.'

'You have told me of this,' I said.

'I have not told you what I will say now. Since She came among us, the faith of others has grown, but I have become more troubled. I see a being not unlike us, and when I think of the enclave now, I imagine other beings with such bodies hiding behind their wall so that we can't see what they are. I don't know where a man's soul goes when he dies, but I do not think it goes there, to the Lady's realm. Perhaps it is only carried away by the wind and is no more. I have seen many men die and know what has brought their death to them. I have seen no sign of spirits. I have seen no sign of the Lady's power even though two of Her kind dwell among us.'

'It is said that the Lady tests our faith when we're tempted to doubt,' I said.

'Why would the Goddess test us in that way, by having us see weakness and by wanting us to believe She is other than what we see? It is what we can see and touch and learn about that makes us wiser and better servants of the Lady. Only a malign spirit would seek to show us one thing and have us deny the evidence of our eyes. But I know of no evil spirits, either – only of the illnesses and pains life brings, and my eyes tell me that the two Holy Ones are subject to the same ills.'

I wanted to tell him of what I had learned from Birana but held back. Even Wirlan might betray me if he knew what was between us, and now I feared that, if he could see some truth, other men would as well.

'I do believe this,' I said at last, 'that Their bodies are much like ours. But there may also be power in Them that we cannot see. Because we cannot see a spirit or power, it does not mean that it isn't present. I'll never see most of the men of Earth and yet know that they exist.'

Wirlan pressed his thin lips together, clearly disappointed in me.

Whether Yerlan still doubted me, I could not tell. He had wondered at my refusal when others of his men wanted to lie with me, but I was often with Tulan, and it was easy to allow the Headman to believe that I lay with the boy. I asked Yerlan's advice and listened to his tales while telling him some of those Wanderer had told me. I hunted with him on warmer days for fresh meat. A bond of a sort began to form between us, and our actions were those of two friends, whatever lay hidden in his heart and in mine.

Perhaps I would have been more wary of Yerlan if I had been enjoying Birana's body during that season, but the winter had made that impossible. Birana could not urge Nallei to leave the warmth of the hut without risking her companion's health, and the two of us could not lie on the snow or the frozen ground. When we walked around the island, practised with our bows, or rode on the horses along the trail, I came to know a calmer joy with her. I had thought my desires would grow. Instead, they grew duller and more distant, as if it were the satisfying of them that fed them. I could be easier with Yerlan then, for I had nothing to conceal.

So the winter passed, that time when men keep close to their camps, live off what they have provided for themselves, and tell stories around the fire. This winter was easier than others I had known, for we had enough food and our dwellings were warm. Wirlan's potions eased Nallei's aches, and although there were more strands of silver in her dark hair, her face kept its beauty. I knew some peace, both at Yerlan's hearth and in my soul.

During the winter, Birana told me more of life in her enclave. She spoke of mothers and daughters and clans of women who were related, and I saw that the enclave had bands of women, although they lived peacefully together. She spoke of how men were called and why the seed of many men was sought, speaking of men and women as the band's gardeners sometimes talked of their plants. I knew that my seed had been taken and wondered if it now grew inside one of her kind.

There was sadness in her as she spoke of the enclave. At first, I believed this was because she longed for her old comforts and the enclave's easier ways. But she was saddened also because of the things she would now never know and that the enclave's magic might have revealed to her.

The enclaves had many strange arts, and one of these was the use of signs by which the women could set down the words they spoke and thought. Not only could they speak to one another through their magic windows and hear the words of one far away, but they could also look at markings and know the thoughts of those long dead. Their legends were tales Birana called history, and it was through their symbols, not just through stories passed by an older woman to a younger one, that they learned of ancient times. As she told me of these symbols, she traced markings in the snow with a stick and said that these signified my name. Then she traced other markings and said that they were her name. I gazed at them in wonder, afraid to sweep them away, as if I might erase us from the world.

Other markings were used to set down numbers, and these were even more mysterious. The women did not use these symbols only to count, but to understand magic that could not be put into words. It was this magic, which Birana called mathematics, that she had been learning before she was sent into my world.

This was what I learned when we spoke – that there was a world in Birana's mind that grew ever more mysterious as she told me more about it, a world that men had known and mastered and had lost, a world I could never share with her. I had not felt this when my body met hers, but I felt it now, and the pain of knowing it grieved me. She spoke of a time before there was time, and of days when the stars were young. She spoke of dark stars where even the light was held by a mighty power and could not escape to shine upon the Earth. She told me of the end of time, when the stars would die as they were drawn together. I listened in wonder, afraid to speak, unwilling to let her see how little I understood.

A day came when tiny green shoots appeared on the land and I smelled the scent of approaching spring. My body was roused again, and Birana came to me in the night while Tulan slept. Her body was new and fresh to me, and yet I knew how to pleasure it now.

Birana grew more skilled with her weapons. During that spring and summer, we often left the camp on our horses to hunt small game or to scavenge what predators had left. On a hillside to the south of the camp, near the top where I could see what lay below, I found a small glade where we could lie together without fear, where our voices could cry out our joy aloud. We sought each other out as much as we dared, knowing that winter would come again.

At other times, I rode out with Tulan. He spoke so often to me of his doings that I did not see that he might be hiding other thoughts. I was at ease with the boy. He had told no one that Birana and I were often by ourselves on the island. I believed myself safe until a day when he revealed that he had seen more than I knew.

We had ridden out to a strawberry patch where fruit was plentiful. Tulan had found the patch before, but it was far from the camp and I decided we would rest there and pick the berries in the morning before our return.

'The Holy Ones will be happy to have fruit,' I said as I lit our fire, 'and there is enough here for many of the men as well.'

Tulan drew up his legs. 'You do not need to bring the Holy Ones many gifts. The brown-haired Holy Lady would favour you greatly even if you brought Her nothing.'

I glanced at him. 'She favours me no more than others.'

'The others may believe that, but I am the one with you when you guard Her. She often seeks solitude with you.'

I told myself that he could have seen nothing, that I would have heard his movements if he had been near. 'The black-haired Lady also seeks solitude with you, Tulan. She knows that Yerlan has some liking for you and that you can speak of him together, but She also enjoys hearing of what you and the boys are learning. She does not often have the chance to speak with a boy.'

'You leave my side in the night,' he said then. 'You think I sleep, but sometimes I am awake.' He looked away and covered his face with his dark hair, as though suddenly sorry he had said those words.

I sat very still. 'Sometimes I cannot sleep,' I said carefully. 'Sometimes the brown-haired Lady is also awake, and we talk where we won't wake you or Her companion.'

'Then why do you talk only when you think I'm asleep? Does She say words to you that She cannot say to me? Why do I feel you waiting as I lie next to you? Couldn't you talk to me? Could She not come and speak to you there when I'm awake?'

I wanted to force him to tell me what he suspected but kept calm. 'It is only . . .' I searched for words. 'What is it, Tulan? Do you think that She doesn't welcome your presence? She has a liking for you – you are the one who cares for Her horses. You came here with us, you'll always have a special place in Her thoughts.'

His mouth twisted. 'It is not Her thoughts I care about,' he said softly. His brown cheeks reddened. 'I am closer to you than to anyone. Some of the men say you lie with me. You don't deny it, you let them believe it. Yerlan believes it, too.'

'Do you want me to deny it?' I asked.

'I want you to make it true,' he answered.

I had been blind, so full of thoughts of Birana that I had not seen what was in the boy's heart. 'Tulan,' I said gently, 'I do not deny such talk, because men might force themselves on you otherwise. This way, they believe I would protect you. Isn't that why you allow the band to believe it?'

He shook his head. 'I want them to believe it, that you want me, that you will come to me.'

'It is this way,' I said, as I stirred the fire. 'I cannot lie with one so young. You must know of such men – Wirlan is another like me – who can only be satisfied with a man close to their own age, instead of with a boy who is weaker and unable to resist.'

'I am not weak and I'm not a small boy any more.' It was so. He was broader in the chest; he had grown taller during the winter, and his voice had deepened a little. 'I wait,' he continued, 'and you do not lie with me. You lie with no other. You would rather talk to Her than lie with me. Her spell is strong on you.'

'Be careful what you say.'

'I will say it!' he shouted. 'I long for the day when She may be taken from us so that you'll come to me. I look at Her and dream that She will vanish, that She'll break the spell She has on you.'

I grabbed his wrist. 'Those are evil words.'

'They're true words! Let Her strike me down for it! If I cannot be with you, I don't care what happens!' He pulled me to him then, pressing his face against my chest as I tried to think of how to reply.

'She would not harm you,' I murmured, 'but She will see into your soul. If you harbour such thoughts about the Lady, She will no longer welcome us on Her island, and then we would both be dishonoured before Yerlan and the band. Do you want that?'

He clung to me as I held him. He knew nothing of the spirit-women's pleasures, for he had been too young to learn of them before coming here. I had hoped he might find another boy to love. Birana had made it impossible for me to love him as he wanted, and I felt a pang at that.

None of that mattered. What mattered now, I told myself coldly, was that Tulan had become a danger to us.

'Listen to me,' I said. 'I care for you more than for anyone here. I think of you as my true friend, almost as a charge. Can't you be happy with that?' I swallowed. 'A day may come when I will lie with you.' I had expected those words to sound false, and yet there was some truth in them, as if I already saw a time when my longing for Birana would fade and I would seek the fiercer, sharper pleasures of knowing a man.

I spoke to him gently for some time, holding him and soothing him with my words while silently cursing him for his love.

I no longer sought out Birana so often when we went to her island. I saw questions and doubts in her eyes but did not speak of what Tulan had told me, knowing that this would only make her fearful. Instead, I found more reasons to leave the camp with her or to wait for her in our glade. We were careful to hide our tracks, tethering our horses below.

The others marked the season by which plants were ready for gathering or harvesting, by the movements of the fish in the lake or the animals on the land, by hunts and contests and journeys to another of the lake camps. I marked the season by my times with Birana. On a day in midsummer, I tasted of her as the light shining through the trees above dappled her skin, making new patterns upon it as she moved. On a day after the band had gathered wild rice, I knelt before her and gazed at the sight of my member thrusting into her. On a day when the leaves had begun to turn, I moved inside her as she lay on her belly and felt her hips and cleft with my hand.

In this way, I measured time; I measured it also by the changes that came to our bodies. Her arms were stronger when they held me, her breasts fuller and heavier in my hands. More hair grew on my face and I had to hone my metal blade into fineness to cut it away.

Another winter came, and another spring followed. Tulan

seemed lulled by my words of a love that might be his later, and my love for Birana flowered again. But this summer was not to be like others.

The winter now past had weakened Nallei, although the season had been milder than others and little snow had come. Streaks of silver marked her hair while her body grew more stooped. She ate little, and the potions I brought to her did not increase her hunger. She became thinner until her pale skin hung loosely around her face and the blue veins of her arms were visible. Only her golden eyes reminded me of her former beauty.

The men whispered of this and of the weather as well. Little rain came that spring and by early summer, the air was thick and still. Often it grew so close inside our dwellings that men took up their mats and lay in the open space.

At first our hunting was good. The deer could no longer drink at streams now dry, and came nearer to the lake. Predators followed, leaving carcasses we could steal. A pack of wolves roamed near the camp; we killed several and drove the rest away. After that, we found less game. We had enough water to drink but spent long days digging a trench from the lake to carry it to the gardens. Even then the plants did not thrive.

The sun beat down on the land until the leaves of the trees grew browner and more brittle. Banks once covered by the lake became a sea of mud, then dried and cracked. We had to range farther for game until we risked moving on to the territory of other lake bands. We feared building fires when making camp away from the lake lest a stray spark set the forest ablaze. Even in early summer, we counted our supplies and thought of the winter ahead.

The times of the full moon, when Nallei was carried into the camp, were no longer times of joy. The men gazed at Nallei's ageing face and greying hair and saw the thinness and weakness of her body. They whispered that she was losing her powers, that her body would soon shed her spirit, that she was too weak even to call down the rain.

Something had caused the Lady to curse the band and the land around the lake. The men murmured this, and Tulan was one of those who said it most often. He did not say it before me, but I heard his friends speak of this curse and of what Tulan had told them. The boy was watching me even more closely now; I did not dare go to Birana when we were on the island. We shared our love only during our meetings away from the camp, and there were few such times because we had to labour harder to find food. We lay together on dry ground covered with brown needles and dead leaves, knowing that at least we were safe for a little time, and yet I sometimes sensed the eyes of one watching. Such fears were often with me, and I no longer trusted my own instincts. I could no longer love Birana without thinking that each time together might be our last.

A day came when Wirlan and I were sent to the island together. The healer went up to the hut alone while Birana and I waited by the boat.

'It will be well,' I said to her. 'I don't know enough of healing to be of much use, but Wirlan will find ways to help her.'

She sat down on one of the flat rocks, her legs dangling over the edge. Once the tops of her feet would have nearly met the water, but the lake was lower now. 'She may be dying,' she said. She had not said this before in my presence and perhaps had not admitted it to herself. 'Arvil, she's in pain, she can hardly walk. She can't eat, and often she can't even keep down the potions you bring her. She tries not to complain, but I see her suffering. I can do so little for her now.'

I knew all this. I had sat outside the hut as Birana tended Nallei and had heard Nallei's moans as Birana tried to soothe her. 'Wirlan will make her better,' I said, trying to believe it.

'I don't think she wants to get better. I think she wants to die.'

'There is something I must say,' I murmured as I sat beside her. 'This land is dying now. We can leave this camp. We can ride away, as we have done before, and never return. We could ride far before they know we are gone for good.'

'I can't.'

'You dreamed of escaping before.'

She gazed at me. She had pulled her hair up and tied it back from her face. Hollows were in her cheeks, as if she had eaten little for the past days. 'I can't leave Nallei now. If there's a chance she can live, she'll need me. If there isn't, I can't let her die alone.'

'If you wait too long,' I said, 'you'll have no chance to escape. We'll need food and there are three horses in the camp. They will provide meat if it's needed, and that will be the end of our hope of escaping on them.'

'They are my horses. I'll forbid it.'

She seemed more concerned for the animals than for herself. 'How long do you think the men will obey you now? They say they are cursed, that the Lady cannot lift this curse from them. They will begin to rage at you. Nallei would want you to find what escape you can.'

'That isn't so, Arvil. She clings to me now, I'm all she has left. Do you think I could go from here knowing I'd abandoned her?' She paused. 'The men here won't harm me. Yerlan would never allow it. I could call on him for help if there were any danger, but there won't be. I can tell the men the curse will be lifted. This weather can't go on for ever. We'll have a chance to escape later. I can't leave Nallei now.'

I saw the torment in her face, her fear for us and her concern for Nallei; yet an evil in my soul emerged then, as though the sun and the heat had burned away the bonds that held my wicked thoughts. 'I know what lies inside you now,' I heard myself say. 'I have shown you pleasures. Now you tire of me and see that you can share them with others. Perhaps you want Yerlan at your side and would welcome his strong body. You don't even have to risk the danger of his seed growing inside you, for you can show him other ways to reach the holy state.' My anger grew as I spoke, but somehow I was roused as well. I wanted to fling her upon the rocks and take her at that moment, and the thought of Yerlan lying with her fed both my fury and my desire. 'Perhaps you want two men to lie together with you. Perhaps your need has grown too great for me to satisfy it alone.'

Her hand darted toward me. She struck such a blow that my cheek burned. As she got to her feet, I rose and lifted my arm. My open hand found her face. She fell, nearly striking her head on the rock.

I dropped to her side. Her cheek was red where I had hit her, but somehow I had held back the full force of my blow. I cupped her head in my hands. 'Forgive me,' I said. 'Birana, what's happening to us?'

She pushed me away. 'Don't come near me.'

'Birana . . .'

'If that's what you've been thinking, then leave the camp by yourself. I don't care if I never see you again. I should have known how little love there was inside you.'

She sat with her back to me. At last I said, 'There's little love in you if a few evil, careless words and one blow I already regret can divide us.'

She turned her head. As I was about to say more, I heard a sound behind us.

Wirlan was walking down the trail. I stood up, afraid that he might have heard our angry voices, but his long face was solemn, his mind elsewhere. 'I must speak to you, Vilan,' he said.

'You must say what you have to say to Me as well,' Birana said as she rose.

'Lady, my words are not of the Holy One's spirit, but about the body that holds Her. The body is dying. I have seen such an ailment only a few times before, in older men, but Hers is like theirs. Something grows in Her belly and feeds on Her – it is a claw that is tearing Her life from Her. She has been marked by death, Holy One. There is nothing I can do for Her now except ease Her pain.'

'No,' Birana whispered.

'The other Holy One knows it is so. I told Her of Her approaching death. My words did not surprise Her. I shall go to the camp now and bring what I can for Her. She rests, but She will need you soon.'

Birana said, 'There must be something you can do.'

Wirlan's mouth twisted. 'Unless You have some magic You can use against death, there is nothing that can be done.'

Birana let out a cry, then stumbled up the path. I stared at the healer, unable to speak. 'This illness is a great evil,' he said. 'It isn't a pestilence carried out by the wind, or a fever that leaps from one man to another. It is as if the very body turns upon itself and creates its own death from inside.'

'And you can do nothing?'

'This is also part of being a healer, Vilan – knowing that one can only make a death that must come a little easier. I must go and fetch what I can for Her. Yerlan will have to be told.'

'How can you tell him this?'

'He will have to know and prepare the men for Her passing. He can no longer deny it or hide from it. I have sensed for some time that there was a weakness in Her body.' His hand rested on my shoulder. 'I must go. The Young Holy One may need your help now until I return.'

He pushed the boat into the water. I could not bring myself to go to the hut to witness Nallei's pain, to see the anger in Birana's eyes. I thought: The love that brought me here is dying with everything else.

Other men came to the island the next morning, while Wirlan and I returned to the camp. I had expected the Headman to rage against us for being unable to heal Nallei. Instead, he listened to us in silence, then went to sit in front of his dwelling, refusing to speak, gazing about the clearing with unseeing eyes.

Tulan, once so attentive to the horses, had been neglecting them, and it was left to me to find what I could for them. Flame's coat no longer shone, and I could feel her ribs under my hand. Wild Spirit's legs seemed almost too thin to carry her, and Star was often weary.

I was feeding them the few roots I had gathered when Aklan ran through the gardens toward the clearing. He stopped before Yerlan and began to speak, waving his arms wildly. The Headman did not move. Wirlan left his dwelling to speak to Aklan, and then the two men came up to me.

'Vilan, you must come with us.' Aklan pulled at my arm. 'The hunters of another band wait beyond the wall. They cannot enter the camp and see what is here now, but we must speak to them.'

'This is business for the Headman,' I said, wondering how much longer Yerlan would refuse to act.

'He will not come,' Aklan replied. 'He didn't even seem to hear my words, and the Prayergiver is too weak from the heat to be carried outside. I have fetched the healer instead and would have you come with us as well.'

'I can be of little use,' I said.

'Among them is the man who led you and the blue-eyed Holy One here,' Aklan said. 'I think they will speak to you.'

They led me from the camp as I wondered what the other band wanted from us. We walked along the trail until we came to a glade where four hunters stood with the Prayergiver who had guided me here.

I went to him and gripped his arms. He was thinner now, his hair a bit greyer. He embraced me, then stepped back. 'Where is your Headman?' he asked.

'He is unable to leave the camp now,' Wirlan answered. 'I am healer in this camp. I'll speak for him.'

The Prayergiver glanced from him to me. 'I came here hoping that you, who are so blessed, would know of a way to break the evil spell that lies on us. Now I see that the spell holds you as well.' He motioned his men away, then leaned toward us. 'Are the Holy Ones who dwell with you also powerless?' he said in a soft voice.

'I do not know,' Wirlan said. 'We wait, as you do, for the spell to be broken.'

'This is what I feared.' The lines around the Prayergiver's mouth deepened. 'Another band not far from us has left their camp to travel west. We have known for some time that we might have to seek other lands. Jerlan, the Headman of my band, asked me to travel here, but I'll have no good tidings to carry to him. We will have to leave the lake and live elsewhere. Perhaps we can return in another season.' He paused. 'And will you leave also?'

'We cannot leave,' Aklan said. 'The Lady . . .' Wirlan gestured to him to be silent. 'We cannot leave,' Aklan repeated.

'Return to your camp then,' the Prayergiver said. 'Send my greetings to your Headman and Prayergiver. I see that I'll have to pray for your band as well. I would speak alone to this man now.'

The Prayergiver drew me to one side as Wirlan and Aklan left us. 'When I travelled with you and the Holy One,' he murmured, 'I thought that She might not be what She seemed, and yet this band accepted Her. My doubts were quieted, but now they come upon me again. I wonder if it was holiness I brought here.'

'It was holiness,' I said. 'The Lady struggles against the evil. She'll find a way to bring life to this band and the lake once more.' I tried to sound convincing.

'We cannot wait. We grow weaker. We must travel to other lands while we still have the strength to do so.'

'They will be strange lands, and you know this one,' I said. 'The lake will still give you water and some fish. Other creatures seeking the water may come here and give us game, and there are still the plants that grow on the banks. You know what dangers you face here – you'll face new ones in another place.'

The Prayergiver shook his head. 'It is not only the drought that drives us away, but what it signifies. Holy Ones dwell with you, and yet the Lady has turned Her face from this land. I now wonder what I brought here. But we have a truce with these men and are not strong enough to force the truth from them, even if we did not. I have prayed. The Lady is telling us that it is time to leave this lake until She smiles upon it once more, until the evil is gone.'

I said nothing.

'Jerlan wants to lead us south,' he continued, 'for a traveller not long ago told us that the south still thrives. It may be that the time has come for me to say my prayers in a shrine again, to appeal to the Lady in that way.'

I gripped his arm. 'You cannot do that. The Lady . . .'

'Can saying my prayers in a shrine bring any more evil upon us?'

What could I say to him? I could not tell him that those in an enclave might probe his mind and learn of Birana and Nallei. 'I am a member of this band,' I said at last, 'and our customs are yours. It's the duty of a Prayergiver to pray in his camp, wherever that camp might be. Your men will need to see you praying for them even more now and keeping to your customs in another land. Others can pray for your band in the shrines.'

He nodded gravely. 'There is something in your words,' he said, but I could not tell if he would heed them. 'I shall pray for you, Arvil. I must leave you now with whatever lies inside your camp. Tell Tulan that his guardian . . .' He was silent for a moment. 'Jerlan would want the boy with him, but Tulan's bond is with this band now. Farewell.'

Even word of Jerlan's band and their decision did nothing to rouse Yerlan. He continued to sit before his dwelling, brooding in silence, sleeping on the ground in front of the entrance. He ate little of the food left for him, and others took what remained, spoiled and fly-marked as it was. Stubble grew on his face, and his light brown hair grew darker with dirt. It was left to Wirlan and Aklan to guide the band, and others did not follow them easily. Often, the men would sit on the shore, as silent as their leader, looking up at the sky for signs of rain or gazing out at the island hopelessly.

I knew what I had to do, yet days passed before I could force myself to approach Wirlan. I still feared that Birana would not speak to me, that I had wounded her too deeply. At last I went to the healer and asked him if I could go to the island. He agreed easily, for some of the men had grown fearful of the island, and there were few willing to go.

Tulan came with me. I had grown used to his sullen silences and to the dark look in his eyes when he gazed at me. But he seemed happier this time and spoke to me with his old friendliness. I felt easier with him by the time we reached the island, happier that he was with me.

I left him by the boat and climbed toward the hut. Nallei was lying outside on her mat, away from the closeness of the air inside. Her body seemed no more than bones under her loose shirt, while her hands were claws folded over her chest. Her bare legs were so thin that I might have circled one thigh with the fingers of one hand. Birana looked up at me, then covered Nallei with a hide.

A fire burned outside the hut. I knelt there, brewed a potion, and handed it to Birana. I had used one of Wirlan's most powerful roots, one he had dried on his rack for years, one he gave only when a pain was too great for even a brave man to endure. Birana lifted Nallei's head and held the cup to her lips. Nallei drank, gave out a cry, and fell back. Her clawlike hands clutched at Birana's sleeve as she moaned piteously.

The sight of Nallei's suffering tormented me; I saw now why Wirlan viewed the world as he did. There was no meaning in such pain, no purpose; no evil deserved such agony. Nallei cried out, bit her lip until it bled, then began to grow quieter.

'I am not very brave,' Nallei rasped.

'You are braver than many men would be,' I said. She smiled a little; I marvelled that she could smile in such a state. 'Birana,' I continued, 'I must speak to you.' Her blue eyes gazed at me coldly. I had said nothing to her since the day I struck her. 'I have much to say to you.'

'I can't leave Nallei now.'

'Then later, when she rests. Come to me tonight at the place where we have met before.'

She said nothing.

I stood up. 'I'll wait for you, and if you do not come, then there's nothing more I can do for you. I cannot force you to save yourself.'

Nallei lifted a hand. 'She will come, Arvil,' she murmured in her weak voice. 'I'll see to it.'

Tulan, who had tried to cheer me during the day, grew more solemn as we ate our evening meal. As he stretched out to sleep, he reached for my hand. 'Vilan . . .'

'What is it?'

'I still wait. Can you lie with me?'

'Tulan, I cannot think of such things now while the Holy One grows weaker.'

'You will never come to me, then.'

'This isn't the time to speak of it,' I said harshly.

He let go of my hand and turned his back to me. I touched his head gently. He pushed me away.

I listened impatiently to the sound of his breathing until I was sure he was asleep, then went to the place under the trees where I was to meet Birana. I sat there for a long time, lost in my thoughts. Perhaps she would not come, perhaps her anger with me was still too great.

I did not hear her approach. She was suddenly before me, a shadowy form in the darkness. I got to my feet.

'Nallei's asleep,' she said. 'She sleeps so little now. I couldn't leave her before. She kept insisting that I go to you, but . . .' She came toward me and rested her head on my chest. 'I don't want to be angry at you any more, Arvil. I know you didn't mean it. I thought you might never . . .'

'Listen to me. We must escape – now, as soon as we can. Tomorrow you will come with me to the camp and we'll ride away together.' She did not speak. 'Are you going to tell me you must stay with Nallei still? I cannot believe she would ask it if you would be safer somewhere else.'

She lifted her head. 'She wants me to leave with you. She told me so before. Even in her pain, she was able to tell me that.' Her shoulders shook as a sob escaped her. 'She keeps trying to protect me even now, and I can do so little for her.'

'I'll have Wirlan come to tend her. I don't think she will suffer much longer.' I stroked her hair. 'Will you come with me?'

'Yes.'

I drew her down beside me, feeling how much I had missed her. My hands moved over her until her breath came in short, sharp gasps as I loved her in all the ways she loved best. We would escape and find a place, where we could love without fear. I felt her warmth around me as I entered, and my soul sang.

I was awake. I searched the ground next to me and knew that Birana was gone. I opened my eyes as I sat up. The sky was growing grey. Tulan might be awake, searching for me. I could tell him that I awoke early and had gone to tend Nallei.

I stood up and stretched. The midsummer heat was fierce even this early in the day. The air was still. Only a distant, whining sound reached my ears.

I suddenly understood what I was hearing. As the whine grew louder, I threw myself to the ground and crawled under a log. A ship was overhead. I caught a glimpse of its gleam as the orb flew over the island and on toward the camp.

I waited but heard no cries of terror, no sound of men falling under the Lady's deadly rays. At last I strugged to my feet and hastened to the hut.

The fire still burned near Nallei. Birana stood in the doorway of the hut. 'I was inside,' she said. 'The ship didn't see me, but Nallei . . .' She waved a hand at the mat.

I bent over Nallei. Her eyes were closed, her face peaceful in sleep. I wondered if she had seen the ship. 'What can it mean?' I asked.

Birana shook her head. 'I don't know. It may have been a passenger ship on an unusual course, or a city might have sent it here. Someone may suspect . . .'

'We have to leave now,' I said.

She came to Nallei's mat. 'Farewell,' she whispered. Only the slight movement of Nallei's chest showed that she still lived. She might welcome a ship now, I thought. At least such a death would be a quick one.

'Farewell,' I said.

We hurried down the trail. Voices were already reaching us from the distant camp. The men would be wondering what the ship's appearance meant. I picked up my pace, then slowed so that Birana could catch up to me. We came to the end of the trail and stopped by the rocks.

The boat was gone. Birana sank down on to a rock. I gazed over the lake, bewildered. 'It is nothing,' I forced myself to say. 'Perhaps Tulan is fetching more food. He'll return soon.' I sat down next to her, trying not to show my fear.

A boat came, but Tulan was not aboard. As the two men paddled toward us, I stood up to greet them.

'Greetings, Balan,' I said to one of the men, expecting to see his quick smile. He continued to frown and said nothing to me as he stepped from the boat. 'I'll help you pull the boat ashore.'

Balan shook his head. 'You are to return to the camp with Dagelan. I'll wait here to guard the Holy Ones. The Headman is himself again and wishes to speak to you. The portent we saw at dawn has returned his spirit to him.'

'I shall also return to the camp,' Birana said.

Balan's dark hair swayed as he shook his head. 'Forgive me, Holy Lady, but it is the Headman's wish that You remain here.'

'I want to go to the camp. Will you disobey Me?'

Balan drew himself up. 'Forgive me, Holy One, but Yerlan would have You rest here where You will be free to commune with the invisible spirits that might lift our curse from us. We have seen one holy sign today, a sight the men have seen only during the times we once travelled to Your holy enclave. We believe the Lady may break the spell and reward us for keeping You safe even during this troubled time.'

'The Holy One will stay,' I muttered, knowing we had no choice.

I climbed into the boat. I felt Dagelan watching me as we moved over the water, but he did not speak.

Yerlan had left his dwelling. Dagelan led me to the garden. Yerlan was pacing over the dry, dusty ground, Tulan at his side. He faced me as I approached; he had cut the stubble from his face. He smiled, showing his teeth.

'I have seen a portent,' he said. 'Smell the air, Vilan.' He came closer to me. 'Do you not smell the scent of rain to come?'

I could smell nothing but dust and the sweat of his body. A few of the hunters gathered behind me, and I was suddenly wary of keeping my back to them. The gardeners near us set down their tools and stood by their wilted plants.

'It was Tulan's duty to aid me in guarding the Holy Ones,' I said. 'He should have told me he was coming here.'

Yerlan put an arm around the boy's shoulders; Tulan's lip curled as he watched me. 'He awoke. You were not at his side. He was sure that you were tending the golden-eyed Holy Lady and thought you might have need of more herbs from the healer. He would have returned to you, but then the Lady's holy sign appeared. In his wonderment, the boy forgot to fetch the herbs.'

'I will take them to Her now,' I said.

'I'll take them. It is time I went to the island. Wirlan will come with me, and Tulan also, since he has served both me and the Lady so well. You will remain here, Vilan.'

He turned, his arm still around Tulan, and walked toward the tree where the horses were tied. Star lifted her head and neighed softly as Wild Spirit tossed her mane. 'These beasts are too weak to do much labour for us, and yet we must feed them some of what little we have.'

'They can become food,' one of the men behind me said.

'It is so,' Yerlan replied, 'but see how thin they grow. Such meat would be hard to chew.'

'Even such meat would be welcome now,' Dagelan muttered.

'Indeed,' the Headman said, 'but perhaps it's not only lack of food that makes them weak. Perhaps some illness is in them that might be passed to us. And there is this to consider. A Holy One brought these beasts to us. We promised Her they would not be harmed. Can we break such a promise now that the Lady has sent us a portent?'

'We cannot,' another man said.

Yerlan stroked his chin thoughtfully. 'We cannot harm them but must feed them while they are here. There is only one answer to this. They must be set free.'

'No,' I shouted.

'Do you question me?' Yerlan cried.

'They are the Lady's. She will say what should be done.'

'I will say what should be done! The Lady has sent me a sign; Her power is in me now. She will speak through me to you. She would have us save what food we can until the rains come again.

We cannot feed the horses, so they must be set free.'

I lunged toward him. He knocked me to the ground with one blow. Two men grabbed my arms and pulled me to my feet. 'Be careful, Vilan,' the Headman muttered, 'or there will have to be a contest between us.' He waved an arm. I watched helplessly as Tulan ran toward the horses, untied them, and slipped the reins from their heads.

'Go!' Tulan cried, lashing their backs with the reins. The horses trotted away, then slowed; Flame lifted her head and looked back toward us. 'Go!' Tulan ran after them, lashing at them unmercifully until they passed through the wall. The guards on the wall whistled and threw clods of dirt at the animals until they had disappeared.

My hope for an escape was gone. I gazed into Yerlan's dark, angry eyes, certain now that he knew everything, that he had even learned of our plan to escape. Only one could have told him, could have overheard me tell my plans to Birana. Terror filled me as I wondered what else Tulan might have seen. I had spurned him. He had paid me back by betraying me.

'You have questioned me,' Yerlan said as Tulan returned to his side. 'You have raised your hand to me, a Headman who honoured you with a place at my hearth. There is an evil inside you, Vilan.'

I believed he would kill me at that moment. His hand reached for my neck, but his touch was light as he drew his fingers down my chest and then touched my member. 'But you are also a man who brought a Holy One to us.' He stepped back. 'Aklan, you will watch over the camp while I go to the Holy Ones. Let Vilan labour to dig us a new trench for our wastes and to cover the old one. It is time he learned to be more humble. Be certain that he doesn't leave this camp.'

He strode toward the boats with the boy as I was led away.

BIRANA

Nallei was sleeping. I sat with her, wanting desperately to speak to her, but knew that awakening her would only make her conscious of her pain.

I had expected her to unburden herself before dying, but she suffered silently. During the past days, she had even stifled her moans at night, as though she feared waking me. I wanted her to open her eyes one last time, to listen as I told her how much she had meant to me, and yet I also hoped that she might slip away peacefully. I did not want her to learn of the ship; I wanted her to die easily, believing I would still live.

Balan was squatting by the hut; he stood up and pointed down the slope. Two men were climbing toward us along the trail. My hopes for escape had already faded; when I saw Yerlan walking toward me, the little hope I had left died.

Wirlan was with him. The healer knelt by the fire and set out his pouches of roots and herbs. Yerlan watched me for a long moment, then beckoned to Balan. 'Go to the boat,' he commanded. 'The boy Tulan waits below. Stay there while I speak to the Holy Ones.'

As Balan left, Yerlan sat down at Nallei's side. His hand trembled as he smoothed back her silvery hair. His face contorted; he cried out and gathered her up in his arms. 'You cannot leave me. You cannot die.'

Nallei stirred and moaned softly as I moved toward them. 'You mustn't,' I said. 'She's in terrible pain. You must let her rest.'

He set her down gently and lay at her side, his hand covering hers. Wirlan gave me a cup; Yerlan took it from me and guided it to her lips. The healer stood up and motioned to me. 'Let us leave them for a little,' he said.

We went into the trees; he stopped and leaned against a trunk. 'Lady,' he said, 'I must tell You something I think You would want to know. Yerlan has returned to himself, but he is now angry with Your messenger, Vilan. The Headman has raised his hand to Vilan and shamed him before the band, but at least he allows him to live.'

I clasped my hands together. 'Is he all right?'

'He won't be harmed for now, but I urge You to be cautious with the Headman.' Wirlan folded his arms. 'The sight of the Lady's ship has changed him. He speaks of our curse being lifted, of rains that will come. This morning, after we sighted the Lady's orb, he went to the horses and freed them.' I let out a gasp. 'He said he would not harm them, but that we could no longer feed them. I know they were Your creatures, but they might have given us meat. The Headman did a foolish thing for You, Holy One.' He paused. 'Vilan spoke against this act and raised his hand to Yerlan. It is a wonder the Headman didn't kill him then.'

I tried to calm myself. 'Wirlan, I'll tell you what that ship might mean. This camp may be in danger now. Don't ask Me how I know this, just believe Me. The men would be safer if they left, if they went far away. Someone has to tell them this. There may be little time.'

He shook his head. 'They will not listen to me.'

'I can tell them. Take Me to the camp – they'll listen to Me.'

'You cannot lift this curse. This is what they will say. They see hope in the omen. They won't abandon the land where they have lived for so long. Your power wanes, Lady. Don't give them a reason to believe that an evil spirit might be speaking through You and that it was evil You brought with You here.'

'Is that what you believe?'

His lip curled. 'I do not deal with spirits, only with what I can see. What I see is that You may have reason to lie in order to keep Your messenger safe from Yerlan.'

'I'm not lying!'

'I cannot know that, Lady.'

I held out my hands. 'Please listen to Me.'

'I have served the Headman and the one before him for all my life. I won't turn against him now, when our band may need him most. You would be wiser to give the Headman no reason to vent his rage upon Vilan. He is still the best of those who have learned healing from me, and I would not want to lose his skill.'

I went back to the hut. Yerlan sprawled at Nallei's side, stroking her hands. He lifted himself on an elbow and looked across at me. 'I hear Her moans,' he said, 'I feel Her pain.' Nallei's lips moved; he bent to hear her.

As Wirlan came near, Yerlan sat up. 'Healer, I must ask you this now. What would you do for a man who suffers in this way?'

'I can only ease the pain until death comes.'

'And if you knew he would suffer for many days before death could claim him, what would you do then?'

Wirlan's face hardened. 'I shouldn't say this to you, for it is a secret of my craft. There is a potion I can give that will bring an easy death.'

Yerlan cradled Nallei's head in his arms. 'If you could restore Her to what She was, I could bear the sight of Her pain. If you could take Her disease and pain from Her, while leaving Her as She is now, I would rejoice that She lived, and the memory of Her beauty would make Her seem beautiful to me again. But I cannot bear to see Her pain prolonged when there's no hope.'

'There is no hope, Headman.'

'Then you know what you must do,' Yerlan said. Wirlan

nodded. 'Brew your potion and then go to Balan and the boy. I would have them go to the camp and bring those who are closest to me here. We will not speak of your potion. I won't have them know that it is we who will free Her spirit at last.'

Yerlan sat with her for the rest of the day. It was he who cleaned her, gave her what little she could drink, covered her with a hide when she shivered, and soothed her with whispered words. A covered jug with Wirlan's potion stood next to him, yet he held back from giving it to her.

He would not let me tend Nallei. Tears glistened in his dark eyes, but he did not let them fall. I thought of all the times he had entered the hut with her and of the cruel smile on his face when Nallei had ordered me away from the hut so that he could lie with her. I had not known there was any tenderness in him.

By late afternoon, we heard the sound of voices below. Wirlan stood up, 'Headman, your men approach,' the healer said. 'It is time.'

Yerlan closed his eyes for a moment, then reached for the jug, pouring the liquid into a cup. He held Nallei as she drank. I watched as he gave her another cup; he warded me off as I tried to move closer.

The men gathered below us; Arvil was not among them, although I knew Nallei would have wanted him there. Wirlan raised his arms. 'The Lady's body weakens,' he said. 'I believe Her spirit will leave us soon.'

The men had known she might die, but a few cried out at this; Aklan covered his face as he leaned against Balan. Only Tulan, head bowed, was still. I saw Nallei whisper to Yerlan as he folded her arms over her chest.

I could no longer restrain myself. I crawled to her side and leaned over her, ignoring Yerlan. 'I'm here,' I whispered.

'You will live, child,' she said faintly.

'Because of you, because you helped me.'

She closed her eyes. The men were whispering prayers. I knew she was gone when Yerlan threw himself across her body and wept.

The men fell to the ground, hitting their heads against the earth as they covered their hair with dirt. Wirlan pulled at the Headman's shoulders and helped him to his feet.

'We must not weep,' Yerlan said at last. 'The suffering of Her body is past, and Her spirit will live. It is the time to bury Her body and remember Her spirit. The Lady gave us a sign today.

Her ship came to call this Holy One's spirit to the Goddess. Now Her soul is free, and the evil that lies over the lake will be lifted.'

The men began to dig a grave in the clearing. I knew that they expected some words from me, but I could not speak, knowing I would weep if I did. It was evening when Yerlan placed her body in the grave. I stood with Wirlan, keeping back my tears as Nallei was covered with earth.

Yerlan looked from the grave to me, then held up a hand. His tears were gone; the harder look with which I was so familiar had returned to his face. 'The Holy One whispered Her last words to me,' he said, 'and I must now reveal them to you. She is gone, but a Holy One still lives among us. Part of Her spirit remains inside this Lady.' He moved his hand in my direction. 'She told me that it is now the task of this Holy One to take up Her duties. A full moon comes again in three days. The Lady will be carried into our camp and will commune with the Prayergiver, and will grant Her blessing to me when we return here.'

I gazed at him in horror, too shocked to protest. My legs shook; I stepped back and leaned against the wall of the hut. Yerlan was still speaking to the men. 'Return to the camp, all of you. Tell the others that our sorrow is past and that the Lady will smile upon us again. Tulan will wait by my boat for me while I pray here.'

The men filed away from the grave. Weak with sorrow and fear, I sank to the ground. Yerlan stood by the grave, head bowed.

'You lied,' I said at last. 'I know what My companion would have said. She never told you such things.'

He lifted his head. 'I waited. I wanted her to tell me that she regretted leaving this life, that she understood my longing, that she wanted me with her.' He was no longer speaking of Nallei with the formal words the men used in talking of us; I tensed. 'I wanted to ease her, and all she told me was that she would be rid of me, that she wanted to die, that she was happy she was dying at last. She cared nothing for me even then.' He shook a fist. 'All those times I went to her, and yet whatever pleasure I took, I could give none to her. She didn't fight against me – even that could have roused my passion a little. She endured me and drank her wine so that she could forget.'

'It wasn't in Her power to care for you that way,' I said.

'I longed for her, and she only suffered me. There were times when my power failed me and I couldn't grow hard with her. She said the potion might have robbed me of my strength, but I rarely drank of it. I didn't need it to long for her, to worship her. It was she who took my power from me.'

'She hated the touch of men,' I said. 'You might have been kinder, reached out to Her, been a companion who didn't force himself on Her, but you couldn't do that. You'd rather take what you want even from one who couldn't bear the sight of you.' It no longer mattered what I said; he could do little more to me.

'I wanted her to welcome me, and she shrank from my touch. You will never be what she was to me, but perhaps I can forget my grief with you. I know now that you don't despise the touch of a man.'

I felt the blood draining from my face. 'What are you saying?' I whispered.

He walked toward me; I could not look up at his face. 'I have other eyes,' he said. 'Tulan has been my eyes. He has seen what has passed between you and Vilan. Vilan was foolish. He allowed the boy to long for him but did not return his love. He didn't see that a boy's fierce love might become hatred and a longing for revenge. Vilan let me believe that he lay with the boy. He would have been wise to do so, but the Lady's spell was over him by then, that spell that can keep a man from seeking out other men.'

My chest was so tight that I could hardly breathe.

'The boy saw Vilan longed for you,' he continued. 'He saw that you were often alone here and that you rode into the wood together. He followed you at a distance and discovered where you went. He began to go out there and wait for you this spring, concealing himself so that you would not discover him. He saw what you and Vilan did under the trees.'

'He lied,' I managed to say. 'He's trying to turn you against Arvil.'

'He did not lie. He could not lie about such a matter. He waited, and you came there. He saw you move your body upon his and described to me what you did. He was frightened when he first saw this – he believed you might punish him for seeing it, and so he kept what he knew to himself, thinking this might be some holy matter he did not understand. Then the land grew parched, and no rain came, and he began to believe that you and Vilan had brought the curse upon us. He knew that you were not to lie with us, yet you lay with him. Perhaps if Vilan had shown him love, he would have kept his secret, but Vilan did not. Tulan heard you both when you were together, planning to escape from us. It was then he knew that he would have to come to me. He told me of your secret this morning, before the omen appeared. He told me much of how you sought pleasures with Vilan.'

I clutched at my stomach, afraid I might be sick. 'It is not for you to question My ways,' I said. 'You know what I am. Would you bring a greater curse upon yourself?'

'You'll bring no curse,' he muttered. 'You have no powers. I learned this with your companion long ago, that she was a being like us, for I knew her body well. I learned that she had no power over us, that I could do as I liked. But it served me to keep this knowledge to myself to strengthen my position as Headman. It served me to let her believe I still worshipped her so that she would not betray me to others. It will be different with us. You will see me as I am, and I shall know the truth about you.'

'I'll never lie with you,' I said. 'If you carry me into the camp, I'll denounce you – tell them all you lied.'

'Then Vilan will be the first to die.' He dragged me up and pushed me against the wall of the hut. 'Consider his fate before you speak. Tulan will keep your secret for now, but if I don't have what I want from you, he will speak of what he knows. I will not even have to order Vilan's death – the men will take his life for bringing a curse upon us.'

He pulled at my shirt as I struggled against him. 'Get away from me,' I whispered. He dragged me away from the wall and pushed me through the hut's entrance; I fell to the dirt floor.

He came toward me; I tried to kick him with my legs. He grabbed my ankles and forced my legs apart, then fell across me, pinning me to the ground. My hand darted toward his face, ready to scratch at his eyes; he held me down with one arm as he fumbled at my belt.

The holds Arvil had taught me were useless. His bare chest was a heavy weight squeezing the breath from me; I was afraid I would faint. He twisted against me as he loosened his belt. I tensed, clenching my teeth.

'I see why she hated you,' I said with what breath I had left. 'She hated you, and she mocked you, and sometimes she even pitied you.' He felt at me roughly, hurting me. I stiffened and turned my head from him, unable to struggle any more.

He pushed his member against me, then sat back on his heels. His hand struck me hard across the face; I took the blow and tasted blood. 'My power is gone from me,' he muttered. 'Do you have an evil power after all?' He raised his arm, as if to strike me again, then struggled to his feet. 'It had better be different when

I'm with you again. If I am not roused, you'll find ways to rouse me, or you will see Vilan die.'

As he was about to walk through the door, I said, 'You will bring Arvil with you when you come to take me to the camp. Otherwise, I have only your word that he lives.'

'I'll bring whom I please.'

'You will bring Arvil. When I know he is safe, I'll do whatever you want.' I forced myself to say those hateful bitter words. 'You won't regret it, Yerlan. I want him restored to his former place and honoured by you, I want to know that he won't be harmed, and then you'll see what pleasures I can show you, but if you hurt him your powers will never return.'

He strode from the hut without answering. I crawled into a corner and lay there, bruised and aching with sorrow. I had no hope that Arvil would live for long. Yerlan's jealousy would grow; or Tulan would eventually tell others what he knew; and sooner or later, I was sure, a ship would return to strike at this camp. I had only the hope of seeing Arvil once more before he was lost to me for ever. I wanted him to know that it was he whom I loved, whatever Yerlan might tell him now.

I sat in my hut the next morning, staring at my knife, knowing that a slash at my throat could free me. Nallei would have wanted me to live somehow. Arvil would suffer if Yerlan discovered I had taken my life; the Headman would not make his death an easy one.

At last I went outside. The sky was still clear, but the air had grown stickier. I took my sling and aimed my stones at the trees, imagining that each trunk I hit was Yerlan. The Headman would come for me and return with me to the hut. Arvil had shown me that I could love a man; Yerlan would teach me to hate all men. I searched the sky, hoping that a ship would come, wanting to die before Yerlan killed what was left in my soul and heart.

I tucked my sling under my belt and descended the trail. Aklan and Resilan were below, guarding the island; Resilan got to his feet. 'What is it You wish, Holy One?'

I was silent.

'Rain will come,' Aklan said as he turned his head. 'I feel it in my bones. We will be blessed by You in many ways now.' A new look of anticipation was in their eyes: the hope for rain, the wish that I might summon them to my side soon.

I left them and walked along the shore. I would not go to the camp; I would find a way to prevent it, whatever the cost.

*

The evening came when Yerlan was to fetch me. I had prepared myself, tested the bow Arvil had made for me. I tied back my hair, shouldered my quiver, and walked toward the trail.

I moved along the path until I was close to the shore, then left it to creep through the trees. Resilan and Aklan sat on the rocks, waiting as another boat moved toward the island. I squinted and saw Arvil's blond head in the dusky light. He sat in the prow of the boat, hands at his sides as Yerlan paddled behind him.

The men below had not heard my movements. I had practised creeping silently through the wood during the day, moving close to them without giving myself away. I stood against a tree as the boat came nearer.

Resilan got up and pulled Yerlan's boat ashore. As Arvil stumbled from the boat, I noticed that his legs were bound, hobbling his movements. Yerlan put down his oar, picked up a spear, and handed Aklan a leather cord as he stepped on to the island.

'Bind Vilan's hands,' Yerlan said.

'Why is he bound?' Resilan asked.

'Vilan has not yet learned his place,' Yerlan replied. 'I think that, if he were freed, he would try to fight me even now.' He put a hand on Arvil's neck as Aklan tied Arvil's arms behind his back. 'I would have to kill him then, and I would not want to lose so fine a man. I must protect him from himself. He brought a Holy One to us, and the Lady would be unhappy if he could not share our joy tonight. His anger will cool when he sees us blessed, and perhaps then I can free him from his bonds. I'll allow him to share in our celebration, even bound as he is.'

Yerlan fingered the feathers around his neck as he gazed at the sky. 'Rain is coming,' he said. 'I saw the feathery clouds today. Even now the sky darkens.'

'The Lady will not be pleased to see Her messenger bound,' Resilan said.

'She will be pleased that I guarded him from himself, kept him alive.' Yerlan prodded Arvil with the point of his spear. 'We will see what She ordains for him later. Wait here.'

Resilan was frowning. I retreated up the hill, moving as quickly as I dared until I was near the top of the trail. I took out one arrow, notched it to my bow, and waited under the trees. My heart was pounding so wildly that I scarcely heard anything else, but my hands were steady.

Yerlan's voice drifted toward me. 'This will be a new joy for me,' he was saying. 'Pray that the Lady gives me everything I wish, because for every pleasure She does not grant me, I will bring pain to you.'

'She will never allow you to treat me this way.'

'She will allow it. She has no power to do otherwise.'

'You'll have my life anyway. She'll understand that. Tulan won't keep silent for ever – he will speak about what he knows and then your men will demand my life. You will never have what you want from Her.'

I heard the sound of a hand striking flesh. 'Tulan will be silent for as long as I wish. Seeing you live and suffer for scorning him will give him more joy than a death that might bring you peace. The Lady will do as I wish for a time to keep you alive, and then I'll teach Her to long for me. That is when you will die, Vilan – when She no longer longs for you.'

They were near me at last. Arvil walked stiffly, inhibited by the cord between his ankles. Yerlan was behind him, his spear at Arvil's back. I held my breath as they passed. They moved into the clearing; their backs were to me. Arvil stumbled forward and fell to his knees.

'Holy One,' the Headman called out.

I stepped from the trees and took aim. The arrow flew, embedding itself in Yerlan's back. He swayed and turned to face me. His eyes were wide with surprise. I saw no anger in his face, only hurt and an odd look of appeal.

My courage nearly left me then. He still held his spear and might have hurled it at me as I aimed another arrow, yet he did not lift the weapon. The second arrow landed in the base of his throat. He dropped the spear, clutched at his neck, and toppled forward.

I ran to Arvil and cut away his bonds with my knife. He crawled to Yerlan, searched the body with his hands, then pulled a knife from the dead man's belt. 'My weapon,' he muttered. 'He took that from me as well.' He sat back on his heels. 'You've killed our tormentor, Birana, but you've left us no escape.'

I was nearly sick. Arvil stood up and caught me before I fell. 'It doesn't matter. We're dead already.' I could not look at Yerlan. 'He could have killed me easily. Something held him back.' I shuddered as I leaned against him.

'Aklan and Resilan are waiting. If he does not come, they'll climb up here. Are you prepared to take their lives as well?'

'I don't know,' I said weakly. 'I've killed already. Maybe it becomes easier the more one does it.' I pushed his arms away. 'I wanted him dead. I didn't think of what would happen later. At least we can die together now.'

'No, Birana. I won't have him dead only so that we can lie at his side.' He lifted his head. 'Yerlan spoke truly when he said that the rains will come. I sense a storm approaching.'

The wind was rising; trees swayed above us. I had been so intent on my deed that I had not noticed the sky. 'The clouds will thicken,' he continued, 'and hide the moon. There may be a small chance for us. One of the boats below can carry us from here. If it grows dark enough, we may not be seen.'

'There are also two men below,' I said.

'Send them away. Tell them you will lie with Yerlan here and come to the camp when the storm is past. They'll listen. Tell them that you'll lift the curse in this way.'

I dropped my quiver and bow, then walked toward the path. Arvil picked up my weapons and followed. We would never escape, whatever Arvil thought. The sky might darken enough for us to paddle away from the island, but even if we were not seen, a storm would force us toward land. We would have to flee through the wood on foot if rain came. Someone was likely to come for Yerlan in the morning; Tulan would tell his story when he knew the Headman was dead. The band would not rest until they hunted us down. We would, at best, have only a few more days.

Arvil left the trail and concealed himself among the trees as I stepped toward the rocks. Across the bay, in the camp, torches flickered in the open space as the men there waited for me. The wind wailed a little and then died down.

Aklan stood up. 'A storm is coming,' I said quickly. 'It is My wish, and that of the Headman, that you return to the camp before the rains arrive. I shall celebrate My rites with him here, and with the messenger he has kept from harm. In this way, I will end this evil time.'

The two men were still. 'Go,' I commanded.

'Why has the Headman not come to tell us of Your wishes?' Aklan asked.

I searched for words. 'He prepares himself for My blessing,' I replied. 'Go.' Aklan and Resilan were hesitating. I pressed my lips together for a moment. 'Obey Me, and it may be that I shall summon both of you before long.'

They bowed, then pushed their boat into the water. I watched as they drifted out on to the lake. The surface of the water was growing choppier; their arms rose and fell swiftly as they paddled. The distant sound of a song reached me from the camp, a song about the mercy the Lady showed to worthy men. The sun was gone as clouds swept toward us from the west.

Arvil came out and sat beside me on a rock. 'My life here was a good one,' he said, 'until this season. I learned much and there were friends for me. I had your love.' He was speaking as though he knew he would die soon.

I reached for his hand. This might be the last peaceful moment we would know. The men in the camp sang as they danced. Thunder rumbled softly and faded away; I heard a faint hum.

Arvil tensed as the hum grew louder. 'A ship,' I whispered.

He grabbed me; we rolled together into the water, then hid under the rocks jutting out from the island's edge. The gleam of three ships appeared in the south, over the hill above the camp. We sank down under the rocks until the water reached our necks; Arvil held me tightly. The men still waited in the open space, watching as the ships approached. Cries of joy escaped them.

Beams lighted the night as rays found targets. Flames blazed from the thatched roofs of the dwellings. Men fell from the wall as others ran helplessly toward the lake. Resilan stood up in his boat as a beam found him.

I pressed my face against Arvil, unable to look, but the screams of the dying men reached us. We huddled under the rock, hidden from the ships' eyes. Beams struck behind us; I smelled smoke and burning wood. The humming faded and then grew louder as the ships made another pass at the island and flew on toward the camp. Rays shot from the ships; the camp blazed with light. The dwellings burned as men lay scattered on the ground. The wind caught the flames, tearing patches of burning thatch over the low dirt wall. Men were running from the open space; they shrieked as the beams struck them.

I hid my eyes again. Arvil buried his face in my hair; his body was shaking. Even then, the ships continued to strike at the camp, their sound becoming fainter as they retreated and louder as they returned; I knew they would not stop until every man was dead.

The island burned behind us. I was choking; I covered my mouth and nose with one hand. Smoke burned my eyes. Sparks glittered among the trees beyond the camp. The parched forest was suddenly ablaze.

The ships hummed above us, flew over the camp, and disappeared in the south. The land around the bay was an inferno; I glimpsed a deer trying to outrace the flames along the shore. The only sound now was the roaring and crackling of the fire. I was afraid to leave the shelter of the rock, even when I was certain the ships were gone. The smoke was soon so thick that I gasped for air, keeping my face close to the water. My legs were numb; I slipped below the water. Arvil held me up.

The sky rumbled; lightning flashed above the smoke. Arvil quickly pulled me out on to the shore. Thunder slapped against my ears as sheets of rain began to fall. The flames continued to burn for a while. The rain washed over us and beat down on the lake until the fire died.

The storm broke before dawn. We climbed toward the hut in silence. The path was lined with blackened, burned trees; I saw no sign of life. The hut was a mound of ash and burned logs; Yerlan's body lay under a black tree trunk.

I knelt and sifted through the rubble, too stunned and empty to care if I found anything. Almost everything was gone – the clothes, the hides, the baskets of food. I dug through the ash and found one jug of wine, then sat down and pressed the heels of my hands against my eyes. I hated my kind, hated myself.

Arvil was standing by Yerlan's corpse. 'You may have shown him some mercy,' he said. 'At least he didn't live to see this.'

Nallei had, without knowing it, saved my life. Her city, or another, had saved me by wanting to be sure that she was dead, and that all the men who knew of her were dead. The gift of my life seemed meaningless now. The struggle to live had been the reason for all of our actions, including the cruelest ones. So that Arvil could live, Yerlan had to die. So that the Earth could live, men had to die, before they could threaten Earth again.

I looked up. Now that the tops of the trees and their leaves had burned away, I could see the camp from the hill. I saw no movement, no sign that anyone had survived. The men must have thought of the ships as a good omen in that brief moment before the rays struck; they had been easy targets.

Arvil sat down next to me. I drank from the jug and handed it to him; he did not drink. I took the jug from him and swallowed more wine.

'Enough,' he said as he pulled it from my hands. 'We must find what we can and leave this place.'

'I didn't want my life at this price.'

'It doesn't matter how you have it. It is yours, and mine as well. We must go to the camp and salvage what we can.'

He pulled me up. Too weak to protest, I followed him down to the boat. The hull was charred, but it was still sturdy enough to carry us across the bay. We climbed in and paddled toward the camp.

The lifeless bodies of men littered the banks, the open space, the top of the dirt wall. The dwellings had burned to the ground. Mud sucked at our feet as we left the boat. Arvil stopped near one body, then covered his face; he was weeping. I looked down and recognized the charred body of Tulan.

Arvil wiped the tears from his face. 'We must search now. There may be some food, some spear points – other things we can use. I may find some of Wirlan's roots and herbs.'

I shook my head. 'I can't . . .'

He gripped my arm. 'Don't be useless to me now. We must search. Try not to touch the bodies.' He turned away and walked toward what was left of Wirlan's old dwelling.

He was right, of course. We had to search, and quickly. A ship could return to make certain the entire camp had been destroyed. Wings fluttered nearby; I looked up. Already, black birds were settling amid the rubble, pecking at the dead. Dagelan's body lay in front of the burned logs that had been Yerlan's dwelling. Wirlan lay across a boy, as though he had tried to shield the young one from the ships. Other men lay along the path leading through the gardens, caught by the rays before they could escape.

I searched listlessly, able to find little. The birds flew from me, then alighted behind me as I passed. In that place of death, we salvaged what we could for our own lives.

Only one undamaged boat remained on the bank. We dropped our packs into the boat and paddled away from the camp. I knew that we would have to go east; we paddled on, keeping near the shore, not speaking.

At last Arvil said, 'We must stop now to rest. Others may see us from shore. We can go on at night.'

We were near a small inlet. On the shore, green trees and some foliage remained, a small untouched spot surrounded by burned trees. We pulled the boat up and concealed it among the ferns, then stretched out on the ground.

I had been dreaming for seasons, for years. The dream had suddenly become a nightmare during the past days, and now I was finally waking from my reverie. All of the past months and seasons had been dominated by my need for Arvil; I had thought of little else, it seemed. The men in the camp had been figments of my dream, unable to affect me; I had believed myself safe and had grown careless.

The dream was over. I looked at Arvil, wondering how my need for him had grown so great. He stared back at me with lifeless, grey eyes. I did not want him now; I might never want him again. I thought of all the times we could have left Yerlan's camp, of how we might have persuaded Nallei to come with us, while she was still strong, and thus saved the camp from its fate. Our bodies and our dream had kept us from acting.

During our time with the lake band, we had learned of what lay on the eastern side of the lake. Three days later, we came to the gorge where a river fed the lake. The water cascaded over the rocks, spilling into the lake with such force that we had to paddle around the falls before landing on the eastern shore. To the north, invisible to us, lay the easternmost camp of the lake bands, and beyond that, unknown territory.

The fire had not spread here; the land was renewing itself after the recent rain. Flowers poked above the ground; tiny green leaves opened to the rising sun.

I studied the gorge and saw immediately that we could not paddle against the river's strong currents. Arvil handed me a little dried fish. 'We must decide what to do,' he said.

'We can carry the boat farther up the river,' I said, 'and find out what's along the banks. We'd have water and may come to a place where we can use the boat again.'

'We are also likely to come to a place where there are men.'

'There's a camp not far from here.'

Arvil shook his head. 'There may be no place for us there. They will learn of what happened to Yerlan's men and perhaps blame us for it.'

They would be right to blame us, I thought. 'You see what I've brought you,' I said then. 'You can leave me and go west. Another band would take you in; you could forget all of this.'

His mouth twitched. The stubble of his beard was beginning to grow; his face was haggard, the face of a man who had endured too much. I expected him to pick up one of the packs, to walk away from me.

He lifted a hand to my shoulder. 'We'll leave the boat. Our way lies to the east now. We may find that refuge you once sought.'

'There is no refuge.'

'Then we will make our own. I won't leave you now. I have

suffered too much for you, as you have for me. It seems I am bound to you.'

'You don't want to be bound any more, do you?'

His smile was bitter. 'I am, none the less.'

We tied our packs to our backs, picked up the weapons we had salvaged, and began to walk east. I believed that we would find only the refuge of death, that this summer or the coming autumn could be our last season.

We found water and fish; I gathered plants and roots while Arvil found us a hare or a bird. We came to a wide river we could not cross and went north until it grew narrow enough for us to reach the other side. We found berries one day and gorged ourselves until we were nearly sick. We left the forests behind and came to grassland, and saw no signs of men. Always, we continued east.

I grew more skilled at catching small game, and Arvil found herbs and roots like the ones Wirlan had gathered, but our walking tired us both. We did not speak of the past, or of what might come to us, but only of the route we would travel and of what food we might find. From time to time, we stopped for two or three days to make camp and to rest.

A night came when I felt Arvil's hand on my arm. We were lying at the top of a hill under a shelter of hide and wood he had set up for us. By then, I was used to lying at his side and feeling him turn away from me, keeping to himself as he had when we first wandered together.

He held me for a moment and then embraced me, pressing his lips against my neck. He did not love me in the passionate way he had before, but as if he were seeking solace; his moans were filled with sadness and pain. He withdrew from me before his seed came from him and rested his head on my chest.

Our love had not died after all. We could not let it die. We had paid for it too dearly.

The days were growing shorter; the nights colder. The tracks of a herd led us south, and we found a fawn being devoured by two wolves; we killed one wolf with our arrows and frightened the other away. We would have to find a place to spend the winter, begin to think of shelter and provisions; yet, after we had dried what was left of the carcass, we were travelling east again. As long as we kept moving, there was still some hope of finding a safe place.

We came to hills where few trees grew, and here I saw the

marks of the Destruction. Boulders and bits of rubble were the only signs of what had once been roadway; a bit of glass, lumps of fused metal, and piles of stone were all that was left of what might have been a dwelling or a town. We forded a stream and stumbled up a bank to another hill.

Arvil gestured at the slope. 'We could stop here,' he said. 'We would have water. We could make a shelter here – begin to set food by. We must think of these things now.'

I sighed. 'We'll find no one on this land.'

'Then at least we'll be safe. Perhaps later, in the spring . . .' His voice trailed off.

I searched through the brush on the hillside. A piece of shapeless metal, another sign of ancient times, lay under a bush; I picked it up, wondering what it might have been, as I circled the hill. At the bottom of the slope, nearly covered by trailing vines and branches, was an opening. I approached and swept back a few vines, then gazed into the black space of a small cave.

'Arvil,' I called out. As he hastened toward me, I entered the cave and thrust out my hand. My fingers touched a metal wall. I pulled back more branches to allow light to enter.

I was looking into a small room. Overhead, a light panel had been set into the ceiling, but no light shone from it now. I walked inside and crossed to the far wall, where stones and dirt lay against a door, then pressed my hand to the wall. The door did not open; I had not expected it to move. I suddenly knew where I was.

'What is this place?' Arvil asked behind me.

'It's the entrance to a shelter.' My voice sounded hollow. 'These shelters were where our world began. Men and women lived below, raised their children, tried to stay alive. Men were sent out first when the Earth had started to heal. After a while, women saw that life might be better if they lived apart from men.'

'And there are no men and women here now?'

I shook my head. 'They left long ago.' I waved a hand at the door. 'There's probably a lift on the other side of that door, but there's no power to feed it now or to open the door so that we could go below. We would find very little anyway.'

He sat down next to me. I thought of the corridors underneath, the rooms where men and women had once lived, clinging to life together until the next struggle came, the one that had separated my kind from men for ever. Ghosts seemed to haunt the room, and I thought of the bones that lay under the ground, the dust of men and women mingled in death.

I said, 'We might be able to make a shelter here.'

373

'Something has led us here, Birana.' He stood up. 'Perhaps it's a sign, this place where life had to begin again, where men and women were once together.'

We searched the hills during the next few days but found no other entrances that might lead us to the corridors underneath. We returned to the room, dug a space for a fire just outside the entrance, and set rocks around it. We had seen no signs of men in that deserted land; there was no need to hide our dwelling from other eyes. A ship was unlikely to pass overhead; the cities had abandoned this land centuries before.

We went out hunting and had luck once more. A herd of wild cattle had begun to move south through the hills. We tracked them, searching for a weak one or a slow beast who would not keep up with the rest. We found a straggler, hurled our spears, and tracked it until we were able to bring it down.

We dragged it back to our shelter, knowing that now we would have enough to eat for some time. We swept out the room with branches, then laid out our smoked meat, herbs, plant foods, roots, some apples Arvil had found in a grove near the stream, and dried fish. Our weapons were laid neatly against the walls, along with two coats of fur, two cups we had carried from the camp, and Arvil's healing herbs and roots. Our bed was made with the hides of the fawn and the wild cow, while our packs were our pillows.

In that dark room, safe from the autumn winds that often raged outside and from the cold rain lashing the land, I could forget what lay outside, could almost imagine that I had gone back into the past to a time when another man and another woman might have clung together.

We continued to forage and to hunt small game until winter dominated the land and a blanket of snow covered the hills. During that season, we kept near our shelter, leaving it only to gather wood or collect snow to melt for water. Arvil found a large rock shaped like a bowl and insisted on dragging it back to our room; into the bowl we could pour water, wait for it to warm, and then bathe.

'You are my true friend,' Arvil often said to me. 'You are more to me than anyone else has been.' For the first time, we could share our love without desperation, without the fear of being discovered. I had thought we knew all the ways we could give each other pleasure; now we found ways to prolong and heighten it.

We were at peace, and yet as the winter wore on, some of our contentment started to fade. Arvil was often silent; at other times, he would speak of those he had known, as if wishing for new companions. He grew more insistent during the time he lay with me, as though this pleasure had to make up for all he had lost. Sometimes I could not respond, and Arvil would withdraw from me for a few days, refusing to touch me until I came to him. I was all he had and worried that I might not be enough for him. When the weather allowed, I found excuses to leave the shelter – to look for mint, to search out small game – refusing to admit the true reason to myself, that I needed time away from him.

Spring came late that year. I knew it was upon us not just because of the warmer days, or the tiny green leaves that showed where carrots and other roots were growing, or the sound of birds, but also because of Arvil's restlessness. We roamed farther from the shelter to look for food; we strengthened our bodies and prac- tised with our spears, arrows, and slings. Arvil's eyes were often on the horizon, searching; I knew he longed for companions, for men to hunt with and boys to teach. Often, I felt in the evening that our room was closing around us, imprisoning us.

Nallei occupied my thoughts as well. I missed her even more than I had earlier and wondered if I would ever hear a woman's voice again.

I had expected to welcome the spring, to feel myself awaken as if from a long sleep, to grow more alert. Instead, as the weather warmed, my head ached when I awoke and there were days I had to force myself to rise. Foods I had eaten easily before grew distasteful; my efforts at cheerfulness grew increasingly false. Arvil noticed this but said nothing; he too seemed to be fighting a darker mood in himself.

I awoke. The air seemed oppressively warm; I had thrown off the hide covering me in the night. I sat up and pulled on the soft boots Arvil had made for me that winter.

He was awake, sitting by our rock, splashing water on his face as he cut at the beard he had grown during the winter with the sharp edge of his knife. 'You've cut yourself,' I said.

He glanced at me. He had shaved nearly all of his beard away, but tiny cuts marked his face. 'They will heal,' he muttered.

'You didn't have to . . .'

'I did it for you. I know that you would have me without a beard, that my face is more pleasing to you this way.' He scowl- ed. 'I do little enough to please you now.'

I was about to reply when a wave of nausea flowed through me. I stumbled out of the shelter toward the trench he had dug for our wastes and felt my stomach heave.

He came to me and held my head as I vomited. 'You're ill!' he cried.

I gasped and wiped my mouth on my sleeve. 'I'm all right now. This will pass.'

'You must rest.' He guided me into the room and made me lie down. 'I will make a potion for you.'

My stomach had settled by the time he handed me a cup, but I drank the herbs anyway. 'I wanted to explore the land to the east during the coming days,' he said, 'but I cannot leave you if you're ill.'

'I'm not ill.' I sat up. 'Something I ate disagreed with me, that's all. I can take care of myself while you're gone. I'm sure my company's grown quite tedious by now. You want some time alone, that's why you want to explore.'

'It isn't so.' He looked away as he spoke.

'It is so. I feel the same way. I'd welcome some time to myself.'

'I see.'

'There's enough food here for me,' I said, 'and all I'll have to do is gather wood. I'll be safe enough while you're gone. I wish you would go. You obviously want to go.'

His face darkened. I picked up my spear and went outside, then hurled the weapon, pulled it from the ground, hurled it again and ran after it. Arvil watched for a while and then began to put some food and a waterskin into one of the packs.

He shouldered his quiver, picked up his bow and spear, and came outside. 'You seem well enough now,' he said. 'Perhaps you will miss me while I'm gone and welcome me when I return. You'll have your time by yourself. I cannot seem to make you happy when I am here.'

'Farewell,' I said as I hurled the spear again. He walked away and soon disappeared among the hills.

I was suddenly dizzy. Swallowing hard, I grabbed my spear and leaned against it as I went back to the shelter. I rummaged through my belongings until I found a small piece of hide. I had marked the days of my cycle on this hide with a piece of rock. I counted, then counted again; I had not bled when I should have. I had refused to see this before. The hide fell from my hand.

A child was growing inside me; I was sure of that now. Perhaps it had started during a night when Arvil had taken me without seeming to care about my response; I had lain there passively, too tired to resist and provoke another argument. Maybe it had happened during another night when I had sat astride him as he entered and had felt warmth and pleasure as I had not for some time. I could not know. We had lain together so many times; I had felt myself safe.

I thought of what Nallei had done, what I might have to do. Arvil's pouches of herbs were in front of me. A poisonous potion might rid me of the child; the risk to me would be no greater than the one I faced if I did nothing. A stick could be sharpened; some datura might dull the pain. Arvil would never have to know. I could lie, invent an illness I had endured while he was away. Nallei had done this thing and had survived.

I would have to summon all of my courage now. My hand reached for one of the sticks in our pile of wood; I took out a stone and began to sharpen a point.

ARVIL

Anger burned inside me. She did not want me near her. During the spring, when I had sought pleasures with her, I had never known if she would welcome me, endure me, or shy away. Bitterness filled me as I remembered all the times I had longed for days alone with her. Now there were too many days when I wanted to strike her or to throw myself upon her and force her to love me again.

I walked on, scarcely seeing where I went, and at last my anger cooled. I too had sought time away from her, had been happy for moments away from her sullen gaze. Perhaps love only thrived when barriers had to be overcome before having it. Perhaps danger had fired our passion and made our times together more precious.

Birana had told me that she was well, yet I wondered. During the winter and spring, I had grown used to the pattern of her cycle, of the times she would bleed and wear the soft skins we had taken from small game. It came to me that she had not bled for some time. I had not spoken of this to her, knowing that she grew shyer when that time came and blushed if I spoke of it. She had not bled, and that could be a sign of illness.

I halted and cursed myself silently. My anger had been so

strong that I had not thought of her at all. I had learned healing from Wirlan and had forgotten to be a healer. I should have stayed, tried to find out what might be wrong. She had wanted me to leave. She was trying to hide her illness from me, perhaps hoping it would pass while I was gone. She would have turned to me for help before, would have trusted me.

I had to go back, yet hesitated, surprised at how much I feared what she might say. I could walk on, could still return before evening after seeing more of this land. I climbed to the top of a hill and looked east, then to the south.

Southeast of the hill, at the limits of my vision, a black form fluttered near the ground. I descended the hill and began to run toward this sight. As I neared it, I saw that black birds were feeding on a carcass.

The birds spread their wings and flew away as I approached. Panting for breath, I gazed down at the carcass. A small calf had died. The birds had pecked away much of its meat while flies and tiny worms were now feeding on the rest. I would get no meat from this calf, but my mind was not on food.

An arrow was lodged in what was left of the animal's shoulder. I blinked, hardly able to believe what I saw, then leaned over and pulled the shaft out. Another arrow lay among the calf's ribs.

I turned the arrow over in my hands, put it into my quiver, and began to search the ground. The trail, barely visible amid the grass, led south. Someone had shot this creature but had failed to track it here – for what reason I did not know.

Someone lived on this land, perhaps not far from me. I wanted to follow this trail while it was still fresh, find out where it might lead me, and then remembered Birana. This trail might be a long one that would carry me far from her. Better to return to our shelter, to see if she was well enough to travel, to follow this trail together.

I ran as fast as I could, slowing only when the hill covering our shelter was in sight. Birana sat by the fire, head bowed, hands around a sharpened stick. As I came nearer, I saw that her shoulders were shaking.

She looked up. Tears streaked her face. 'Birana,' I said, 'I decided I could not leave you alone if you might be ill, and now – I have found something.'

Her eyes gazed at me in despair. I sank down beside her. 'Birana, are you still ill? You must tell me so that I can help you.'

'You can't help me now. I'm pregnant.'

I gaped at her, not sure I understood.

'I'm pregnant!' she shouted. 'There's a child growing inside me now. How can I have a child out here?'

I could not speak for a moment. 'But you told me . . .' I said at last. 'You said there were times this could not happen. I've been careful. Much of the time I held my seed back so that it wouldn't enter you. How can this be?'

'It seems we weren't careful enough.' She dropped the stick. 'I was going to abort it while you were gone, stab inside myself with this stick to kill it. I couldn't do it.'

I reached for her; she pushed me away. 'This is what you've done to me, and I let you do it.'

'I didn't mean for this to come to you,' I said. 'If I could change it . . . Birana, what can we do?'

'I might die if I have this child. I might also die if I abort it.'

I cursed myself for my helplessness, for my love for her. My eyes fell to her belly, and then another feeling came to me, that awe I had felt when I had worshipped her kind. 'This child inside you,' I murmured, 'it has my seed. It's inside you and is part of you, but something of me is in it as well.'

Her arm lashed out at me; I took the blow without flinching. 'Is that all you can think, that it's yours? See what you think of it when I'm dead, when you won't be able to care for the child and it dies as well.'

I seized her by the arms and shook her. 'I would see it die to have you live. But if its death would bring death to you . . .' My hands dropped. 'Those in the enclaves bring such children out of themselves and yet do not die.'

'They have physicians – healers.'

'I've learned some of the healing arts. Can't I use them to help you somehow?' I pondered all she had told me. 'You said that men and women lived together in ancient times before your kind mastered its magic. They must have known ways to pass through such a time. You must tell me what you know, what will happen inside your body, so that I can help you.'

'I've told you what will happen,' she said. 'My belly will grow very large. Eventually, it'll be hard to walk. I won't be able to hunt after a while, and you'll be caring for me alone. The birth will cause great pain, and there's a chance I won't be able to deliver the child. Even if I do and manage to survive that, the child may die. It'll be a helpless, tiny creature for a long time, completely dependent on me, and I'll be completely dependent on you. You can't care for us both alone.'

I set down my quiver and took out the arrow I had found. 'Perhaps I won't have to care for you alone. I discovered a dead animal not far from here. This arrow was in the body, and another lay beside it. Do you see what this means? Others live on this land.'

Her face grew paler. 'That can't be true. A band couldn't live here for long. There are no shrines, no places where men can be called.'

'Here is the arrow,' I replied, 'and it is not one of ours. Someone aimed it at that calf but did not track it here. Perhaps those men fear the north or found other meat closer to their camp. Perhaps they have come to this land for a time, to hunt and then return to their own regions. We can follow that beast's tracks. If we were with a band again, all the men could care for you and that child.'

She shook her head. 'How could we possibly explain that to them?' She stood up and paced by the fire. 'You know what it was like when we lived with a band. These men may want what I've given to you when they learn what I am. I couldn't bear it.'

'There is something else. You hoped for a refuge once. You said it would have to be here, far from the enclaves, on land where men do not wander. Perhaps this arrow came from such a place.' I wanted to believe this, wanted to give her some hope, however small.

'There's no such place, Arvil. I'm sure of that now. It's a story a condemned woman tells herself when there is no other hope.'

'We've lived, have we not?' I said softly. 'Couldn't there be others like us?' She clasped her hands together as her eyes widened; I had awakened some hope in her. 'We have a summer to seek for those who made this arrow. Wouldn't it be better to look than to stay here? If we find no one, we cannot be worse off than we are. If they're men with whom we cannot live safely, we can return here and prepare for the winter. They'll be too awed by you to stand against you if you wish to leave.'

She folded her arms and stared at the fire.

'We'll have to go soon, while I can still find the trail,' I said. 'This is all I can do for you now. This arrow is a sign we must heed.' I could not let her die and refused to believe that she might.

'Very well,' she whispered. 'Anything's better than staying in this accursed place. We'll go. We'll leave now.'

We scattered the rocks and ashes of our fire. Vines and leaves would hide the entrance to our shelter. We strapped our packs and quivers to our backs, picked up our spears and bows, and began another journey.

I led her to the calf's body. Drops of blood marked the creature's path; we followed the trail through the grasslands until it grew too dark to see. I made a shelter with our spears and coats; Birana stretched out on the ground. As I lay next to her, I put my hand on her arm.

'You can do what you like with me,' she said. 'You can't possibly do anything more to me than you already have.'

Shame and guilt filled me. 'Do you think I want that now? Do you think I can lie with you and have you hate me for what I've done?'

'It might have been better if you had forced yourself on me in the beginning. I would have learned to hate you then, I would have given you as little as possible, and maybe this wouldn't have happened.'

'Do not say that. You'll live and this will pass.' I ached to hold her, to comfort her somehow. 'If you wish it, I'll never lie with you again.'

She drew my hand to her belly. 'I brought this on myself. I can't blame you for everything. Even if I had known this would happen, I might still have lain with you.' She sighed. 'All my life, before I was expelled, I looked forward to the time when I would have a child. I wanted to be a better mother to it than my mother was to me. I wanted a daughter I could love, who would know her mother loved her. Even now, while I hope this child is never born, I think of when I longed for one.'

'I will help you, Birana. I'll do everything I can for this child.'

'Even if it lives, what kind of life can it have?'

'It will have what we can give it.' I held her, stroking her hair until she slept.

The trail led us south and then east. We moved slowly as I searched the ground for signs. The calf had grazed at a clump of grass, had fallen by a pool. We followed the trail for three days; Birana rarely spoke, and when she did, her voice had the flat tone of one without hope.

On the fourth day, I lost the trail but found another sign of men. A place on the rocky ground was marked by charred wood. Someone had camped here, had come this far before turning back. I looked toward the rockier, more forbidding land to the east. 'There,' I said, pointing at a bush. 'Those branches were broken by someone who passed that way. We may have another trail to follow now.'

We walked on. Although there were many rocks to tread upon,

these men had walked over the marshier ground around them, not troubling to hide their tracks. We came to another pool of water, but a brackish smell hung over the pool, and we did not drink.

Birana clutched at her stomach; I wondered if her sickness was upon her again, as it had been during the past days. She had explained that it would pass, that it was only an early sign of the child inside her, but I worried that her body could not feed the child if she did not hold her own food. 'We'll have to find water before long,' she said.

'Those who made these tracks would have needed water as well. They will lead us to it.' I heard a cry above me and looked up. Great white birds flew overhead, birds I had never seen before. This was a new land, unlike any I had seen, and I wondered what it might hold.

We continued east while I noted other signs – a tiny, torn bit of leather, a hole in the ground where a man might have leaned against his spear, wastes where another had relieved himself. They had moved over this land as though they felt no danger from enemies who might follow.

By afternoon, I grew aware of a sound I had heard before. A distant roar drummed at my ears, a roar that swelled and faded and swelled again, a sound like a mighty wind and yet unlike it.

'What is that?' I asked.

'I don't know what you mean.'

'That sound.'

Birana stiffened. 'I think . . . I'm not sure . . .'

I bounded over the grassland amid the rocks, drawn by the roar, which grew louder as I ran. Birana hastened after me. We scrambled up other rocks and then before me, rolling toward a shore of sand and rock, was a body of water that seemed to stretch to the ends of the earth.

I let out a cry. The roar drowned out my voice. The blue-green water rose and fell as white waves crashed against the shore.

I ran toward the water, drawn by the sound and the salty smell, and danced as the waves lapped at my feet. I had thought of the lake as vast, yet this body of water dwarfed the lake. There was no end to it.

Bright objects lay scattered on the sand. I picked one up and touched its spirals, marvelling at its stripes. 'What magic made this?' I shouted above the roar as I turned to Birana.

'No magic,' she cried back. 'The sea made it. This is the ocean,

Arvil. This is as far east as we can go.' She sank down on to the sand.

I filled my lungs with the air of the sea. Birana's kind had retreated from this shore. It came to me that only the strongest spirits could live here, ones who could look upon the sea and meet its power with their own courage, for this sea retreated from the shore and then covered it again, pounding against the sand and crushing the treasures that lay there while depositing new ones.

I dropped my belongings, took off my shirt, and lay on the warm sand. The ocean's sounds surrounded me. I had never seen the ocean before, and yet its rhythmic sound seemed familiar.

'A man could build a great boat,' I said at last, 'and move upon this sea.'

'Men did so once.'

'Perhaps they will again. I would do so if I could.' I sat up and gazed to the south. I had lost the trail in the sand, but a black spot marred a white patch of shore. Birana stood up as I got to my feet. 'There,' I said. 'Another fire. These strangers have gone south.'

Her hand slipped into mine. 'We can turn back,' she said. 'We have water for only three more days, maybe four, and we can't drink the sea. If we go on and find no water, we may be unable to turn back by then. We know this route now – we could return another time with more supplies.'

'Is that why you talk of turning back?' I asked. 'Or is it that you fear what we may find?' She did not reply. 'Birana, they may move their camp in this season. If we leave and return later on, any trail will be harder to find. We might have to roam far to discover where they've gone.' I released her hand. 'But I must do as you wish. I have brought enough harm to you. I won't force you on a journey you do not want to make.'

She pressed her lips together, then said, 'I suppose we must go on.' She stared down at her belly. 'Maybe the effort will cause me to lose this child.'

'Do not say it.' Somehow I felt that her life was now tied to the life within her, that if the child were lost, I would lose her as well.

The sea was ever-changing. Storm clouds appeared in the east, and I was unable to tell if the storm would reach shore and lash us with its wind or drift away. The ocean's greenish waters became grey as the sky clouded, then darkened as the waves rose to white peaks. I huddled with Birana by a rock as a storm raged.

383

Near another place, where a fire had been built, lay the bones of fish. The waves washed other fish ashore, but we ate none of them. We had a little food left, and I did not know these fish well enough to be sure they were safe to eat. I gathered a few of the most beautiful objects the sea gave up to us. The ocean had robbed me of my will. I imagined wandering along the shore endlessly with each day bringing me another treasure, revealing another of the sea's many aspects.

Birana had shed her shirt. Her skin grew browner, and although she was thinner, her breasts had swelled. I thought of when I had first seen her and how she had tried to cover herself. I knew her body well, and yet now her form would become something new to me.

We drank as little of our water as we could, but on the fourth day of our journey along the shore, I knew we would have to find more. I retreated from the ocean's edge to the steeper slopes bordering the beach, then waited for Birana to catch up to me.

'We must leave this shore and search for water,' I said to her. 'This sea will steal my soul if we remain.'

She nodded. We climbed up the slope with difficulty, feeling the sand shift under our feet until we came to the top.

I now saw more of the land to the south and knew we had come to water we might drink. Farther ahead, the ocean had formed a bay. Through the rocks on the shore, a wide river fed the sea, flowing under willows with drooping limbs and on through marshland around the shore.

'We'll have water,' Birana said.

'Those men might have made their camp along the river.' I turned toward her. 'Perhaps you should cover yourself.'

She shook her head. 'Better that they see what I am.'

We picked up our pace and were soon among the trees. I ran to the riverbank, tasted of the water, and drank from my hands. As I rose, a small object on the ground caught my eyes. I bent and picked it up.

'Look at this stone,' I said. 'It was part of a tool. A hand shaped this and made the edge sharp. Look here.' I touched a fern. 'Someone has cut at this plant, has foraged here not long ago.'

She filled a waterskin, drank, then faced me. 'They may be upriver,' she said. Fear flickered in her eyes. 'We had better find out what kind of men they are.'

'Wait here. I can go alone, see if it is safe first.'

'No, Arvil. I can't go back now no matter what lies ahead. I'll come with you.'

I gripped my spear as we walked up the river. The banks narrowed until the other side was clearly visible. As we crept through underbrush, a voice reached me, a high, light voice like a boy's.

Near the bank, two foragers clothed only in loincloths stooped over the ground. A hand pulled at a root and tossed it into a leather sack. The foragers stood up, turned toward us, dropped their sacks, and let out wild cries.

Birana gasped. I nearly cried out myself, but my voice caught in my throat. I stared at the pair's beardless faces and then at their breasts, hardly able to believe what I saw.

Before I could speak, a man lunged from the trees behind them, spear raised. He gaped at Birana. His arm fell.

'We come in peace,' I said slowly. The man looked from Birana to me. One of the women raised her hands to her face. 'We mean no harm.' I took a breath and dropped my spear and bow. After a moment, the man cast his spear on the ground.

'We have found your refuge,' I murmured as we walked toward them.

The three were older than they had seemed from afar. The man's brown beard was streaked with grey, while lines and wrinkles marked the faces of the women. Their bare breasts were pendulous and their bellies sagged.

The man began to speak as we approached. The two women stood behind him and covered their mouths as they peered at us. I had picked up my weapons but set them down once more as the man spoke. I could not make out his words, and although he kept glancing at Birana, his words seemed meant for me.

'We come in peace,' I said again when he fell silent.

He stroked his beard and spoke more slowly. His distorted and slurred words now sounded much like the holy speech, and I was able to make out a few. He was greeting us, offering to guide us to his camp.

'I know your words now,' I said, 'but you must say them to us slowly.' He nodded, showing that he understood me.

'We would like to come to your camp,' Birana said. 'We have little food left, but if you guide us there, we will share what we have with you.'

The man's eyes narrowed. He did not move. One of the women was shaking her head.

'My companion and I will come with you,' I said. He nodded again; I wondered why he was able to understand my words and not Birana's. 'Are there others with you?'

'There are others,' he replied.

'Then I'll put on my shirt,' Birana muttered to me as she reached into her sack. The woman giggled as she donned her garment, perhaps wondering why Birana wanted to cover herself.

The man led us along the bank. The women trailed behind, stopping from time to time to gather other plants. 'This is a joyous day.' The man spoke carefully, making each word clear. 'We have always hoped to see others, and now it has come to pass.' Birana and I slowed to allow the women to catch up to us. He gestured impatiently. 'Come. They know the way. Let them do their work.'

The ground was thick with shrubs and flowers. We pushed past the hanging limbs of willows and came to a path through the growth. We walked over a small rise and below, on the riverbank, I saw their camp.

Two dwellings of wood with grassy roofs stood on either side of a clearing where meat was roasting over a fire. A smaller dwelling had been built at the edge of this clearing. I looked at these huts for only a moment. Two men sat by the fire and two other women were feeding the flames with sticks.

'Rejoice!' the man at my side called out. 'A man and a woman have travelled to our land.' I could not make out the rest of his words. The men below jumped up as the women dropped their kindling. Two naked young boys ran out from one dwelling. As we walked down to the camp, a third young one emerged from the other dwelling. I saw this child's limp and then the hairless slit between her legs.

'A little girl,' Birana whispered to me. I caught my breath. Children were here, and these women must have borne them. They had lived. There would be help for Birana.

The men and women gestured, bowed, then surrounded us, laughing and babbling in their slurred speech as they poked at us gently with their hands. We set down our belongings and seated ourselves by the fire. One woman ran into a dwelling and came out with a basket of food.

They grouped themselves around the fire, the two women and the girl at our right, the three men and the two boys at our left. The other two women had reached the camp by then. They set down their sacks and sat next to the girl.

The man who had guided us to the camp struck his chest. 'My band welcomes you,' he announced. 'I am Tern, leader here.

Next to me is Gull, and next to him is the man called Skua.' He did not say the names of the boys, or the women.

'I am called Arvil,' I responded, 'and my companion is Birana.'

Tern muttered other words I could not catch, then said, 'We will feast while we talk.' The women cut off pieces of roasting meat with stone knives and handed food to the men and to me before taking any for themselves or for Birana. I took out what was left of my dried meat and gave it to Tern.

I glanced at the women, who bowed their heads, refusing to meet my gaze. These women lived among men, yet seemed shy before me. I had already learned something of this camp and its people. The site of the dwellings on lower land and the path that led so clearly to the camp showed that these men and women did not fear attack and seemed to have no enemies.

'Are you alone?' the leader asked. 'Or will others follow?'

I wondered how much to admit, but these men and women had welcomed us in peace, had shown no sign of fear or suspicion. 'We are alone,' I said.

Tern frowned. 'I had hoped there might be others, but we are grateful even for two.'

I reached into my quiver and took out the arrow I had found. 'I think this is yours. This arrow guided me here.'

Tern took the arrow from me. 'It is mine. We had gone too far from our own land and had to turn back. I hope our prey gave you some meat.'

'It gave its meat only to birds and worms, but that arrow was worth more to me than the meat.'

The man laughed. 'You are welcome to dwell here for a time, to remain among us if you wish.'

'You are kind,' I said, surprised by his offer.

'You are needed.' He did not explain what he meant.

Birana was watching the women. One of them had a belly so big that I wondered how she could rise, and then it came to me that she, like Birana, carried a child inside her. Birana had said that her belly would swell; the sight of this woman's belly terrified me. How large would the child be when it emerged, as large as Hasin had been when I first saw him? That could not be. Was it possible that a woman could live through such an ordeal? Guilt swept through me; I touched Birana's hand for a moment, fearing for her.

I peered at the women again, then noted that all had the same light brown hair, although that of the older two was growing silver. They held their hands over their mouths in the same way, and their thin, pinched faces and narrow noses were alike. One glanced toward me with her yellowish-brown eyes and drew her hair across her face. I turned back toward the men. They also resembled one another and had the same thin faces.

Birana said, 'We would hear of how you came to this place.'

Tern gestured at her. 'We did not ask you to speak.'

Birana flushed. 'I'll speak without being asked.'

Tern scowled. 'You are not to speak. He will ask the question.'

I frowned, then motioned to Birana as she was about to reply. We did not know this band's customs. Perhaps they still feared her kind even after living among them. 'How did you come here?' I asked.

Tern finished his meat, then set his hands on his knees. 'It happened in this way. In the west, there lived a band of men, and out of the west, death came upon them. Many died at the hands of another, larger band, and only two lived. They cursed the spirits that had brought such evil to them, and then they journeyed to one of the citadels where the minions of the one called the Lady rule. There, within sight of the wall, they cursed the Lady and all of the men she holds in thrall, for they believed she had sent the band against them.'

Tern seemed to share their anger as he spoke of the Lady, and I wondered at the words he used in speaking of Her. 'Then from that wall,' he continued, 'a vision appeared to them, and an aspect of the Lady came out to them.'

This woman, Tern said, had revealed many truths to the two men, who learned from her that the Lady had little power in the lands to the east. From this woman they had also learned of the pleasures they could share with her and of how life could spring from them. From her body, two males and two females had come, and from the bodies of those two females, two males and three females, and from theirs, six had come to the river where Tern's band now lived, although the six had died many seasons ago. Tern sang out the names of all these men and women in a chant until he ended with his own name and those of his men.

'We live here now,' Tern said, 'and although we were blessed in the past, we have known sorrow these past seasons. These three, and the one Hyacinth carries inside herself, are our only children. Another was born not long ago, but it did not live. One was born two summers ago, but so monstrously shaped that it could not be allowed to live.' He waved a hand at the little girl. 'The child called Lily has a limp and also an affliction that makes her shake like a leaf in the wind – it was always so with her from the time she entered the world.' The child lowered her eyes. 'I thought that the Lady had somehow reached out to curse us, but now that you are here, perhaps it is a sign that new ones will be born among us.'

His words filled me with horror. I had never known of a boy who did not leave an enclave fit and strong – his only defects of body would be those brought by illness, injury, or age. Birana had told me her kind made certain that their children were born strong and healthy. What would happen to her child here, away from her enclave's magic? Would it also be afflicted? I tried to steady myself. The two boys seemed fit enough, and the girl had lived.

Birana's face was white. 'I thank you for telling me this story,' I said. 'I too have tales to tell, but I would speak to my companion for a moment.'

Tern nodded. 'Perhaps you do not wish to share our burdens. I cannot force you to stay but will tell you this – in all my life, I have seen no others except those here and the ones who brought us into the world. You will find no one else in this land.'

I took Birana's arm and led her down to the riverbank. We were still within sight of the group but could speak softly in the lake tongue. 'These afflictions Tern spoke of,' I murmured. 'Could such things befall the child inside you?'

She drew her brows together. 'I don't know. I keep telling myself that your strain and mine are healthy ones, but I can't be certain of what traits my child might carry. I can't use gene-scanning techniques out here, can't repair defective genes.' She went on in this way, using other words in her own tongue I did not know. 'I don't even know if I'll have a boy or a girl, and there's a chance the birth itself might cause some injury.'

'Is that what has happened here? Did afflictions come upon their young ones because of that?'

She shook her head. 'I'm not sure, but they're all descendants of the same mother, and they've been inbreeding ever since. It means more of a chance for defects to show up in their children, and there's no way to prevent that out here. They're all related. That's why they look alike. Their gene pool is too small.' She used other words then, both in the lake language and her own speech, and at last I understood that there was an illness of some sort in the seed of these men and women that had weakened their children.

'Is there a way to heal them?' I asked.

'Not here. No wonder they're so happy to see us, although

they don't know why. We mean new genes.' She signed. 'What kind of refuge is this? It might be better to force my child from me now.'

'No, Birana. These women have had their children and have lived. They must know how to help you, and this band has welcomed us peacefully. We would be safe.' I looked up at Tern's band. The men stroked their beards as they watched us. The women smiled.

'And what kind of life will we have? What kind of life would the child have if it lives?'

'You wanted a refuge. You have found it – a place where men live with women. There is nowhere left for us to go. We must stay for a time at least, until . . .' I took her hand. 'I curse myself for what I have brought upon you. A time may come when we can seek out other lands, but we must stay in this camp for now.'

'You're right. I suppose I should be grateful even to have found this much.'

I wanted to hold her, comfort her somehow. We walked back to the fire; Tern gazed up at me hopefully. 'Birana and I have decided,' I said, 'but there is a question I would ask. Children have come to you. Can these women aid another when a child comes from her?'

The women giggled. 'We aid one another,' one of the older women replied. 'We know of birthing.'

Tern glared at her; she lowered her head. 'That is women's business,' he said. 'Why do you ask this, Arvil?'

'I ask it because Birana carries a child inside her now.' I paused. 'If she can be helped, we will stay with you.'

Tern jumped to his feet. Joy glowed in the faces of the others. 'We are truly blessed,' he shouted as he grasped my shoulders. 'Welcome, friend.'

We feasted with the band that afternoon. Although Tern asked me about my travels, I told him only that Birana had appeared to me in a shrine, that we had travelled and found shelter with bands of men before finding our way to the sea. Tern and his men seemed satisfied with that and showed little curiosity about what lay west. Their land was here, and other regions were only places of danger, lands where men raised their hands against other men and where the minions of the Lady ruled. No awe of the Lady lived in the souls of these men, who gestured angrily whenever I spoke Her name.

In the evening, the women carried off what was left of the

feast. I rose to help them, but Tern motioned to me to sit. One of the women came to Birana and then said, 'You will come with me to our house.'

Birana walked toward the dwelling. I was about to follow when Tern touched my arm. 'She will live with the women. You will dwell in our house.'

'We have spent our nights together at the same hearth.'

'When you wish a night with her, you may join her there.' The leader pointed at the small hut near the trees. 'And if you wish one of the others . . .'

The other men grinned. I was wary, unsure of their customs. Birana disappeared inside the women's dwelling. 'I am content with Birana,' I said.

Skua chuckled while the two boys dug their elbows into each other's sides. 'Your seed grows in her now,' Skua said. 'Should it also take root in another, it can only mean new life for our band.'

I wondered what the women would say to that but held my tongue. 'There is a story I didn't tell you before,' Tern said in a low voice. By now, I was more used to his speech even when he spoke more rapidly. He glanced at the women's dwelling, then leaned closer. 'You are not the first stranger who has come here. Some time ago, when I was a boy no older than young Pelican here, a man was found not far from this camp. He was injured, but those who found him carried him back here in the hope that he might live and provide his seed. He died not long after of his wound, and although the band grieved, perhaps it was just as well. You see, he was still under the Lady's power. When he saw the women in this camp, he spoke strange words to them, addressed them as beings who were set here to rule over him. Such things are not good for women to hear.'

My neck prickled. 'So men are taught in other places,' I said. 'The Lady has great power.'

'But we know the truth. We learned it long ago. The minions of the Lady cloak their weakness with guile and magic; but, stripped of it, they are not more than we. You must also have learned this truth from your companion.'

'Birana has told me some truths,' I admitted.

'And you have lain with her and know that a child is in her, so you know her true nature. You must have come from a place where the Lady rules over men or she could not have shown herself to you, but you've seen the truth now. You know that what you once believed is a lie, but though you do not bow before the woman you led here, there is awe in you still. You hover over her. You allow her to speak when she should be silent.'

My anger nearly burst from me. 'I am her friend,' I said steadily, 'as she is mine. She doesn't rule me and I do not rule her. It is not my place to command her.'

'It is your place,' Gull muttered. 'That is the rest of the truth we have learned, the truth the Lady's minions hide – that it was men who once ruled over her.'

I could no longer control myself. 'That is so,' I answered, 'and you must also know what came of it – a time of trouble and devastation. I care nothing for who ruled then or who rules now. Birana is my friend, and I will treat her as my friend.'

Tern scowled. 'You say you will live among us. You will follow our ways. What will our women think if they see that your companion has power over you? You would make trouble for us.'

I took a breath. I wanted to rise and take Birana from that camp, but even if they let us go, I would only be taking her from those who could help her.

'I shall do my best to abide by your customs,' I said, 'and Birana will do the same, but what passes between us when we are alone is our concern. I will treat her kindly. She carries a child. You say your band needs new young ones. You must let us live how we will.'

Tern glanced at the others, but there was little he could say to that. At last he stood up and led me to his dwelling.

I wanted to speak to Birana alone the next day, but the three men had decided to go on a hunt, and I was to hunt with them. I asked if any of the women would come with us.

Gull shook his head. 'Women do not hunt.'

'Birana has hunted with me.'

'Women do not hunt,' he insisted. 'She carries a child – she should not hunt. When the young ones are small, the women must carry them or keep them close, so it is their work to gather plants and tend the camp. They will smoke or cook what game we bring back.'

It appeared that the women had spoken to Birana about their ways, for as we gathered around the fire for our morning meal, Birana kept her eyes lowered as she helped the women fetch food. I took the food she brought to me, then saw her tightened mouth and the anger in her eyes. 'When we are alone,' I murmured quickly in the lake speech, 'things will be as they were. I don't want you to bow to me then.' Her mouth softened a little.

The men, I learned during the days that followed, were companionable enough among themselves, but in the camp with the women, they wore stern faces as they ordered the women about or waited to be served. Hyacinth was carrying Gull's child, yet he often forced her to stand beside him while he ate, weary as she was from her work and the weight of her belly. Willow, the other young woman, was expected to comb Skua's hair and beard with the spine of a fish, although he could have groomed himself. Cress and Violet, the older women, dragged heavy loads of wood into the camp, sometimes helped by the boys, Egret and Pelican, but never by the men.

The women gathered plants, fished in the river, went down to the seashore to look for fish and shells, laid away food for the winter, and kept the camp clean. The men hunted, made tools, garments and weapons, and patched the huts. There was work enough for all, but the men accepted the labour of the women as their due while expecting the women to be grateful for what the men provided.

Whenever one of the men wanted to lie with a woman at night, he made a quick gesture toward his groin with his hand and the woman followed him to the small hut. The women gave no sign that they sought this joining or welcomed it, and I never saw one beckon to a man. I soon saw that Gull always lay with Hyacinth, in spite of her large belly, while Skua went to Willow and Tern summoned either Cress or Violet.

It was Tern who explained that each woman could lie with only one man, but that if enough time had passed without his seed taking root inside her, another man could summon her for a while. This was, he told me, so that each man would know where his seed had grown. Thus Tern knew that Pelican, born of Cress, carried Tern's own seed, while Egret, born of Violet, was Skua's child.

'Skua has lain with Willow for some time,' Tern told me, 'but nothing has come of it.' He shook his head. 'Another man will have to try her soon. Egret will be old enough before long.'

'You could try your luck.' I found the words distasteful but was trying to banter with him as the other men did.

Tern was shocked. 'That cannot be. My seed gave her life in Cress's body.' A man, it seemed, could not lie with a woman born of his seed or with a woman who had carried him inside herself. A man could lie with a woman born of the same mother or with one who shared the same father, but only after both had lain with others.

'You see why you are needed,' he said. 'Let us hope that others are born to you and Birana.'

I did not reply. To have her endure this ordeal once was painful enough. I could not let her suffer it again. I had wanted to bring her to safety; now I worried about what this band might do to her spirit.

Several days after I had come to the camp, I went to the women's house and called out to them. Cress came to the entrance and peered out at me.

'I want to see the child Lily,' I said.

'Forgive me for asking this, but what can you want with her?'

'I have learned some healing lore from another man. Perhaps I can help her somehow.'

Cress shook back her greying hair. 'There is nothing you can do,' she said, but led me into the hut. Lily sat by the hearthstones weaving a basket of reeds. A tremor passed over her; she dropped the basket as her hands fluttered.

'The man Arvil wishes to see you.' Cress glanced at me suspiciously. 'I humbly ask you to be quick about whatever you wish to do. I must gather more wood before dark comes but will not leave her alone with you.'

I sighed. 'I mean her no harm.'

'Forgive me for saying this, but I have known men to become roused by young ones not much older, even when they know they cannot be summoned and are too young to bear children. I would ask you if I can wait here.'

'You may wait,' I answered.

She beckoned to the girl, then sat down next to me. Her gold-brown eyes gazed at me directly as I passed my hands over Lily's small body. Except for the cleft between her legs, her body was like a boy's.

'It is hard for her to be the only girl-child here,' Cress said. 'Already Egret and Pelican try to fondle her.'

'If you made her garments so that she could cover herself, perhaps she would not rouse them.'

The woman shrugged. 'When the weather is warm, it is easier for them to run naked. We shall put on garments soon enough. The men don't like it when the weather grows cold.' She tugged at her loincloth. 'They would rather see our bodies and display their own. You should tell Birana that she need not wear so many garments in this season.'

'You should think of your own wants sometime, and not only those of the men.'

Cress pursed her lips. 'Birana said that you were not a man like others. You are more different than I thought.'

Lily shuddered again. The tremor passed. 'How long has she trembled?' I asked.

'I saw it not long after she was born. She has always been thus. Hyacinth has borne much sorrow – first Lily and then a child who had to die.' She made a sign. 'I pray that her next child will be unmarked.'

I felt Lily's hip. 'This hip is not set like the other,' I said. 'That's why she limps. It is as if her leg bone was pulled from its socket.'

'It was hard for her to walk at first. She would fall.'

'Someone injured her. How did it happen?'

Cress was silent.

'Do you know? Can you tell me?'

Cress lowered her eyes. 'You must tell me,' I said in the commanding tone the men used.

'When she was born, her foot came through the passage first.I had to pull her out, there was no other way.'

'Tell me more of this, Cress.'

She threw up her hands. 'I cannot! You're a man. I cannot speak of these things to you.'

I patted Lily on the arm and then released her. She crept back to the hearth and sat down, bowing her head. 'Then think of me as a healer and not as a man,' I said. 'Birana will have a child. I must know that she will be helped and not harmed.'

Cress pulled her hair across her face. 'It's the head of a child that should come through the passage first, but that did not happen with Hyacinth. I did what I could. I did not want to injure the child, but this was all I could do. I swear to you that I'll do my best to keep Birana's child from harm.'

'Do what you can for Birana,' I whispered. 'If she is harmed, I won't care about the child.'

Cress cleared her throat. 'There is a strong feeling in you for her. It cannot be only your man's need.' She got to her feet. 'You're an odd man, Arvil. There is a man's strength in you, and yet you are unlike the others. You listen to my words even when I do not ask permission to speak them. You scrape the hairs from your face even though it is only women and children who have hairless faces.' She shook her head. 'And Lily? Can you bring any healing to her?'

'I can do nothing,' I said bitterly. 'I cannot force her leg into its proper place without risking more injury to her. I don't know what causes her to tremble. The man who taught me healing was wise, but even he could have done nothing. I am sorry.'

'May I leave you now? I must gather wood.'

I nodded. She picked up a long leather sling and left the hut.

'I am sorry,' I said to Lily. 'I would give you herbs or a root to see if that might stop your trembling, but such potions might make it worse. Often it is best for a healer not to act when he doesn't know an ailment's cause. Perhaps it is an illness that will heal itself in time. You are brave to face it without complaint.'

She glanced at me from the sides of her eyes, then picked up her reeds. I went outside. Birana was walking into the clearing with a small sack of plants she had gathered. All my fears for her suddenly welled up inside me.

I motioned to her. 'I must be alone with you,' I said in the lake tongue. 'Will you come with me to the small hut tonight? I'll make the sign in front of the other men, but we do not have to share pleasures – your company will be enough.'

She set down her sack. 'You don't have to ask.' Her mouth twisted. 'The other men need only make the sign, it seems.'

'I shall always ask. I won't make that sign unless you wish to come with me.'

She smiled, but her eyes were still sad. 'I'll go to the hut with you, then.'

By evening, my desire for her had grown, but the sight of the men grinning and winking as I made the sign nearly robbed me of my longing. We walked together to the hut. Tern whispered to Skua, who laughed.

We entered; I picked up a hide and laid it over the mat on the ground. 'Do you want a fire?' I asked.

Birana shook her head. 'It's warm enough without one. Anyway, the men would expect me to fetch the wood here for it.'

'Birana, you will do as you wish when you're with me.'

She stretched out on the hide. I meant only to hold her, but my hands reached under her shirt as my lips met hers. I wanted her, then remembered what my past pleasures would force her to endure.

I released her. 'I cannot,' I whispered. 'I fear what may happen to you. I looked at Lily today. Cress told me how she entered the world, and now I fear even more for you.' I paused. 'I can do nothing for the girl.'

'She has a palsy of some kind. I had thought such things were gone from the world, but here . . .' She turned her head toward me. 'The women will help me, Arvil, and I've always been strong. You mustn't worry. It may be easier for me than it was for any of them.' I felt she was saying this only to soothe me.

'It isn't right for the men to treat them as they do.'

She sighed. 'They don't know anything else.' She went on to speak of stories the women told among themselves, although not to the men.

The women lived in the hope that others of their kind would some day come to the camp and restore their magic to them. They took Birana's presence as a sign that this might happen soon. They accepted the labour that they did, met the demands of the men, and told themselves that their ability to bear children showed their greater power. They knew nothing of the cities except that others of their kind lived there and that their Goddess was to be feared. The men might say bitter words about the regions the Lady ruled, but the women, in secret, occasionally prayed to Her.

'What have you told them about yourself?' I asked.

'Only that I was sent out of a city. They don't know why. They want so desperately to believe I was sent here to help them, that others will come too. I don't know how to tell them it isn't so. They have so little to hope for.' She reached for my hand. 'You mustn't tell that to the men, though.'

'I understand.' I wondered what other secrets the women kept from the men. 'Wouldn't an enclave help these women if . . .'

'Women who live with men as they do? I don't know. Such women aren't supposed to exist. Now they're harbouring me. They'd probably die simply for that.'

Her voice was so despairing that I searched for a way to cheer her. 'Tomorrow,' I said, 'I shall leave this camp with my spear and your arrows and bow. Meet me and we'll hunt together again. We don't have to say anything about it to the band.'

'The women wouldn't say anything about it anyway, although they'd probably scold me for it. I can't go. They'll expect me to do my own work.'

'You will hunt with me, and I'll forage with you.' I held her close to me until we slept.

We hunted together only a few times that summer. Birana seemed strong, but as her belly began to swell, she grew more listless. At first, she risked the anger of the men by glaring at them when one ordered her about or by speaking without asking permission. Soon, she was doing her work without protest. I remembered how proud and brave she had been and despaired.

We had to work to lay aside enough provisions for the winter to come. The men had described the winter of this land to me. It would not be as harsh as some I had endured, but as the summer drew to an end, a sharp wind often blew through the camp from the sea.

At night, when the camp was quiet, I sometimes sensed the distant roar of the sea. I welcomed the sound, which called to my soul. Sometimes, I would leave the camp and sit alone on the shore with my thoughts, marking the movement of the water as it crept up the sand.

A day came at the end of the summer when the women went to the sea to dig for clams in the wet sand. I had watched them at this work before, but they would not let me help and seemed to want this time away from men. I followed but sat on the hill above the beach to watch. The band had come to the shore often, had built a fire, and dug a pit in which to steam the clams along with salty wet seaweed, but the weather would soon be too cold for this work. All of the women wore shirts and leggings now. Hyacinth's shirt was tight over her belly and Birana's would soon be too small for her.

They laughed and chattered as they dug for the food. I had brought a hide with me and worked at the leather with my stone, happy to see the women in this easier mood; I recalled a dream of women beckoning to me from another shore. They picked up their burdens of shells and began to climb toward me, all except Willow, who was putting her clams into her sack. They smiled as they passed me; Birana was about to speak, and then her eyes grew distant and cold.

I turned. Skua was behind me, approaching the shore. The women passed him silently. He came to my side, stared at Willow for a moment, then scrambled down the sandy slope toward her.

He strode up to her. I expected him to help her with her sack, unlikely as that was. He was speaking, although I could not hear his words. She backed away, shaking her head. Skua seized her arm. She tore herself away from him. He leaped after her and threw her face down on the sand, then pulled at her leggings and loincloth. She scrambled to her knees as he tugged at his own loincloth. He pulled her toward him by her hips and entered her, thrusting against her as she clawed at the sand.

I jumped to my feet. The woman had given no sign that she wanted this and many signs that she did not. I hastened toward them, but even as I pitied Willow, I could not take my eyes from this coupling. Something in me was roused by this sight, however I fought against it.

Skua finished, stood up to adjust his loincloth, and caught sight of me. I thought he would be angry, but instead he beckoned to me. Willow curled up on the sand, weeping; the marks of his fingers were on her hips.

'You have hurt her,' I said. I held out my hand, but Willow shook her head and covered her face with her hair. I wanted to comfort her but had only shamed her by witnessing this act.

Skua shrugged. 'She is often thus. Perhaps a child will come of it this time.' He narrowed his eyes. 'If she doesn't grow a child soon and yours is born without flaw, perhaps you should try her.'

I recoiled at his words, which he said as though Willow were not with us. 'I shall see what Willow wishes,' I replied.

'She has nothing to say about it.'

'I seek no pleasures with one who is unwilling.'

'You had better learn what you are and what a woman is.' Skua lowered his eyes. 'You do not say it, but I see that she has roused you.'

He had seen what I could not admit, for my member had grown stiff. The sound of his laughter followed me as I stumbled away.

An evil entered me. I could not put what I had seen from my mind; I had been without pleasures for too long. I walked on toward the camp, struggling with my thoughts, aching to feel a woman around me.

In the camp that night, I made the signal the men used to Birana. I had never done this before without knowing earlier that she wanted to be with me. Her lips tightened as I gestured. The men had seen me make the sign, and she could not refuse me.

She spun around and walked toward the small hut. Skua's lip curled as I stood up. I thought of his hands on Willow's buttocks, of how his member had plunged into her, of how her helplessness and protesting movements might themselves have aroused him. My desire was sharper than it had ever been before.

The inside to the hut was nearly dark. Only a little moonlight shone through the openings under the roof. As Birana sat down, I knelt behind her and pulled at her skirt.

'What's wrong with you?' she whispered in the lake tongue.

'I must … I need …' I forced her down on her belly.

'You're hurting me.'

'I must . . .'

She twisted away and struck me. 'Oh, I understand. How quickly you adapt. Well, you're still stronger than I am, especially now. Go ahead, do what you like. If I resist too much, you can call out to the others. They'd probably come here and hold me down for you, and then tell you what a fine man you are for taking what you want.'

She stretched out on the mat. The thought of her lying there enduring me, hating me, suddenly repelled me. 'My need is too great,' I whispered. 'Today, I saw Skua with Willow, on the shore. I knew she didn't want him, and yet . . .'

'I can imagine what you saw. I've heard the women talk of what the men do.'

'Yet they stay here,' I said. 'There must be some pleasure in it for them.'

'Where can they go, Arvil? How would they live? They come here with the men because they'd be beaten if they didn't. Sometimes they have some pleasure, and often they don't, but it's worse if they fight it. The men only deceive themselves by thinking that the women want it. Is that what you want from me?'

'This place has poisoned me,' I said. 'I've seen men have their way with weaker ones before, but the sight never roused me – I remembered what it was like to be a boy at the mercy of men. But a boy can grow strong enough to have his revenge on one who torments him too much. Willow will never grow stronger than Skua. He'll always have his way with her.' I sighed. 'These men see the women only as ground for their seed. I hate myself when I think of what they do, and yet their evil is in my soul.'

'You mustn't . . .'

'Perhaps your kind was right to draw away from us and teach us to worship you.'

'No, Arvil. What's true for these men and women isn't true for us.'

I lay down next to her. She was silent for a long time, and then her hand touched my hair, brushing it back from my face. 'Whatever you felt, you didn't act on it. I couldn't have fought you, but you held back. There's evil enough in all of us – what matters is whether or not we act on it.' She paused. 'You're still my friend, aren't you?'

'You shame me by asking. You're more than my friend.'

'I need your friendship here. My child will need you. I fear what will happen even if I live through this birth. I'll have to have another child, and then another – the others will expect it.'

'No,' I said. 'I can't let you suffer this again.'

'If we don't have another child, the men will wonder why. They'll begin to think that one of them might produce a healthy child with me. I might be forced to lie with one of them.'

'Never,' I muttered. 'We'll have to leave this place.'

'How? With a baby? Do you think they'd let us leave now?' She nestled at my side. 'Arvil, I'm afraid to stay here, and yet the women have been kind to me. They have some hope even if it is an illusion. It would be hard just to abandon them although I can do little for them.'

Her lips touched my cheek. Her hands caressed me; she was seeking my touch. My longing swelled inside me.

'Isn't it better this way,' she whispered, 'having me want you?'

Her body was new, her breasts full, her belly large against me. I lay on my side as I drew her toward me.

Hyacinth's time came a few days later.

As she stood next to Gull, holding the food she was to serve him, she suddenly doubled over. The meat and the stone platter fell from her hands. Gull lifted his hand as if to strike her, then let his arm fall.

'It is her time,' Cress said without asking if she could speak. The other women got up and led Hyacinth to their hut. Cress turned toward Birana. 'You had better come too. We may have need of you.'

Birana's hands trembled as she stood. I was about to follow when Tern motioned to me. 'This is not our business,' he muttered.

'I have learned of healing. I should learn of this as well.'

He shook his head. 'This is not something for a man to see.'

We finished our food and cleared the space around the fire ourselves. From time to time, Hyacinth moaned or let out a cry. The men made no sign that they heard this, but each of her cries made me tense with fear.

As I lay in the men's hut that night, her cries grew louder until they resounded through the camp, and I shuddered at the pain she must be enduring. Tern and Pelican, on their own mats, breathed evenly as they slept on. Even Gull, who had brought this upon Hyacinth, slept soundly. I could not sleep, could not understand how the men could sleep.

Birana would suffer in the same way.

I slipped silently from the hut. Firelight flickered in the entrance to the women's dwelling. Hyacinth was screaming almost without pause. I crept toward the light and peered inside.

The screams suddenly died. Hyacinth panted rhythmically, reminding me of the moans Birana sometimes made when I joined with her. The women crouched around Hyacinth, and then Cress and Violet took hold of her arms as she squatted. Her body shone with sweat. A tiny head bright with blood was emerging between her legs.

I gasped with fright. Willow turned. 'Get away.' She jumped up and pushed me from the entrance. 'This isn't a sight for you.'

I backed into the clearing and sat down by the banked fire. I felt terror, but mingled with the terror was awe of what I had seen.

I had viewed women as those who ruled Earth and men as beings who were separated from the ways of other creatures by our ancient punishment. But in the enclaves, women still bore their young as Hyacinth did, whatever magic they used to ease it, and men still gave their seed without knowing that they did. Now I saw how linked to Earth we all were, how Earth's ways still ruled us.

I had found something new to worship in place of the faith I had lost – life itself, the ability of women to bear their young, the power of men to make young ones with their seed. I thought of how the seed of another man and woman lived in me and of how part of me might live on in the child Birana carried. Tal lived inside me still. This was the destination of our souls – to live on in those that followed us on Earth, not in the Lady's realm in the next world.

Someone was near me. I looked up at Birana's shadowed face. 'It's over,' she said. 'Hyacinth is well.'

'And her child?'

She lowered her eyes. 'The child is a girl. She lives, but she's weak. Cress said that she was born too soon.'

I took her hand. 'And when your time comes?'

'Don't fear too much. The women have more knowledge of these matters than I thought – they know how to help with the breathing, that their hands and the knife they use to cut the cord must be clean, other things. Perhaps the ancestor who was expelled long ago was able to pass on some knowledge to them.'

'She cried out so much . . .'

'Her labour was hard, but it was over quickly. It may not be so hard for me.'

I stood up. 'I must tell the men. Gull will want to know.'

'Let them sleep. It'll be morning before long. They'll celebrate, and for once Gull will wait upon Hyacinth for a day. You'd better rest now.'

I held her for a moment before returning to the hut.

*

We feasted the next day. The men passed by the women's dwelling and peered in at Hyacinth and her child as they sang. I could not keep from gazing often at the mother and child and watching as the young one sucked at Hyacinth's breast. That was how, I learned, such a child had to be fed, and I wondered at how a woman could give not only life but nourishment as well.

I had not expected the child to be so small. Once a woman had held me in that way, had fed me. All those memories had been taken from me, and even the dreams I had once had of such a time had faded. Now they returned to me when I slept, and I heard the voice of the one who had borne me sing to me again.

The men were joyous, the women more sombre. By the looks that passed between the women, I knew that they feared for the child. The camp's celebration was short-lived. Three days after her birth, the child breathed her last.

Hyacinth stumbled from her dwelling and wailed; Gull answered her wail with his own. They stood together, the woman weeping while Gull tore at his hair and beard. 'My seed is cursed,' he cried. 'First Lily, and now this. What have I done?' He threw himself on the ground and pounded with his fists until Tern and Pelican led him away.

Cress, surrounded by the other women, carried the small body out of the camp. I followed with the men. We walked until we came to the hill overlooking the sea, then made our way down to the shore. There, the weeping women lay the child on the sand. Gulls shrieked as they circled overhead, adding their cries to ours.

We waited until the waves reached the body. As the child disappeared into the sea, Hyacinth screamed while Violet held her. Birana's hand was over her belly as she glanced at me.

The men averted their eyes, but not before I had seen the fear of death in them – not fear of the death of one, but the fear that their entire band might die out soon.

Tern moved closer to me as the women left the beach. 'It seems,' he murmured, 'that our hopes now lie with your child.'

BIRANA

Often I thought of my mother and how she had hoped for a refuge. She had, I supposed, imagined a place where women lived in a settlement not unlike a primitive city, where they practised what arts they could and ruled over the male servants they might need to survive. My time with Arvil had given me another image of a possible refuge, a place where men and women might have learned to love, to live as comrades.

I now saw how foolish such hopes had been. A settlement large enough to be viable, to avoid inbreeding, to be able to move from a life of hunting and gathering to farming, would grow too large to escape the notice of roaming bands of men and, eventually, the attention of the cities. Only small bands were possible, groups that might cling precariously to life for a few generations, until they grew too weak and too few in numbers to survive.

I had hoped to find companions, women who had retained some knowledge of the cities and their accomplishments, with whom I could talk of what I had read and learned; I had imagined men who might open their minds to this knowledge. But such ideas were useless in this world, where the only knowledge that mattered was of which plants to gather and which animals to hunt and how to make tools and shelters.

These women had lost the knowledge of their ancestors, and the cities were only fabled places of magic to them. The demands of their children, the fact that the women had to bear them and nurse them and look out for them when they were small, forced them to depend on the men. The men in turn exacted their price for this dependence.

Violet, the oldest of the women, did not see things this way. She took pride in the women's endurance, in those children they had been able to bear, in their ability to do their work and tend to the men's needs. Although the men might glory in their greater strength, the women, among themselves, mocked this pose while dreaming of the day the cities would reach out to them and raise them up. They lived among men, and yet in some ways their lives were as separate from the men's as they might have been in a city, for they hid many of their thoughts and allowed the men to believe what they wished.

When I first arrived in the camp, they waited until the men were asleep and then came to me with questions. If I had been sent out of a city, did that mean that others would follow me? Was this a sign? I had answered them vaguely, saying that the Lady had hidden Her purpose from me, for although I did not want to encourage false hopes, I could not bear to dash them either. They believed that the Lady would send others to them – if not this season, then the next; if not during their own lives, then during the lives of those who followed them. They believed that their souls would be reunited with the Lady at death, but that the men might be punished for scorning the Goddess.

Other questions, asked of me in secret when we dug for roots together or sat around the hearth at night, were usually about life in the cities. The women did not seek knowledge, but tales of a place where food appeared whenever it was wanted, or where women rode through the air in ships, or where it was always warm and snow never fell. They marvelled at my compass, a sign of the city's magic, but grew distracted when I tried to explain magnetism to them. The technology that had made the cities possible – the energy that powered them, the discoveries in physics that had produced our shields, the chips and circuits that allowed the cyberminds to mimic human thought – was of no interest to them. The fact that the cities had once dreamed of building upon their scientific knowledge, or of exploring the cosmos, but now clung only to what they had, was not something these women could understand. Only Lily seemed interested in my talk of the stars above and what lay beyond the Earth, but the demands of her life, I knew, would dull her curiosity in time.

The women listened patiently when I encouraged them to change their conduct toward the men but scorned such an idea. 'Let them believe in their strength,' Violet said. 'It keeps them content and holds back their anger, and we know the truth of it anyway.'

'You should not be so easy in Arvil's presence,' Hyacinth advised me. 'It will only enrage him, and then he may hunt for you no longer, or give you no more children. He may stop summoning you and find one who is more yielding.'

'Better to act as they believe us to be,' Willow would murmur. 'A time will come when we're raised above them and will have magic that can bend them to our will.'

Only Cress did not offer such advice to me. 'Arvil is not like other men,' she would mutter, 'and Birana has some of the Lady's magic in her still. Let them act as they wish as long as they do not offend the men. Perhaps if their child is a healthy one, our men will note that and treat us as Birana is treated.'

The air was often damp and heavy, making the days seem colder than they were. The wind from the sea, so fresh and soothing in the summer, was now cold and often fierce. The band abandoned the central fireplace for fires inside the huts, as they had before whenever it rained. Instead of serving the men and then eating with them, we carried food to their hut before eating by ourselves in our dwelling. We had stored food but could not rest; wood was collected, mint, nuts, and other plants were gathered, fish were taken from the river. The men hunted whenever the weather broke.

I soon thought of little except my child. I moved through the camp as though my surroundings were only part of a dream, doing my work automatically until I could rest. I told few tales of the city and passively followed the commands of the men instead of bridling at their words. Only the child was real; even my body and brain were no more than a host to serve it. I did not want to think of what might happen after it was born, how it would live, how we might escape this place.

Cress fed me green plants, fish, and potions made with finely ground shells and bone, assuring me that these would aid my child and keep me strong as well. Arvil practised his healing with the men, bandaging a wound on Skua's leg so that it did not fester, draining an abscess in Tern's mouth and removing a rotting tooth. It seemed that we might pass through the winter without illness or misfortune.

The first light snowfall came and a colder wind with it. Violet began to cough, then to rasp when she breathed. Two mornings after the snow fell, she was unable to rise from her mat. I touched her fevered face, then ran to fetch Arvil. He covered her with hides, brewed potions, wiped her brow. Violet babbled wildly as her fever raged, twisting and turning as she tried to throw the hides from her body. Arvil sat with her during the day and Cress tended her at night.

Violet struggled against her illness for three days, and then her body grew quiet as her breathing became more laboured. Lily sat in one corner, trembling as Hyacinth held her. Arvil turned his head toward me.

'Will she live?' I asked in the lake language.

'No,' he replied. 'Her chest fills. She cannot breathe. The fever has burned away her strength.'

Violet opened her yellowish eyes. 'Do not fear,' I said. 'You will be with the Lady. Your soul will struggle no more.' It did not matter what I said as long as she was comforted.

'My son,' she whispered.

'I will get him.' I hurried from the hut. Skua, who had given Violet her son, was standing by the men's dwelling. He had not come to see her, had refused to believe she might die.

'Skua!' I cried out, forgetting the phrases the women used when addressing the men. 'Fetch Egret. Violet would see her son now, before . . .'

The boy came out of the hut as Skua drew himself up. 'Do not order me about, Birana.'

'I beg you and the boy to come now.'

He strode toward me, the boy at his heels. 'Be gentle with her,' I said more softly.

'Do not tell me what to do.'

'Forgive me, brave spirit,' I said harshly. 'These may be Violet's last moments and if you and Egret won't make them easier for her, then leave us so that I can.'

'She cannot die. Arvil will heal her.'

'Arvil has done all he can.'

Skua groaned, pushed me aside, and entered the hut. I waited outside until Egret's wail told me that his mother was gone.

We carried Violet's body to the shore and shivered on the snowy beach as her body drifted into the sea. The band sorrowed, but Violet had been old by their standards. She had given birth to no children for some time, had been weaker that year; if she had lived, she might have become just a burden. The band, grieved as they were, could accept her death.

Only a few days later, another illness came to the camp, one which struck all three of the children. They burned with fever and vomited while their bowels ran. The women refused to let me near them, fearing for me and my child.

Arvil carried the children to the small hut. There, he and Cress tended them, doing what they could. Egret and Pelican survived. Lily, unable to recover, died.

The men had paid little attention to the girl. Even Willow and Violet had sometimes mocked her tremors and her lisping speech. Yet Lily's death affected the band more deeply and drew more sobs from them than Violet's had. Lily, whatever her afflictions, had been one who would have grown into a woman and given new life to the band.

Once again we bore a body to the beach and laid it at the edge of the grey, wintry sea. The women tore at their hair and wept while the men mourned silently. As the waves carried Lily off, I felt the eyes of the band on me. Violet was gone, Willow was still without a child, Cress would probably bear no more children, and Hyacinth seemed doomed to have children who could not live. I sensed them all clinging to life through me.

I left the camp to gather wood. A snowstorm had blown through the camp two days before, forcing us to retreat to our dwellings; from the women's hut, I was barely able to see the men's house through the swirling flakes.

The snow now lay in drifts along the riverbank, in mounds under the trees and along the path leading up from the camp, covering what wood was on the ground. I searched for twigs that had been blown into shrubs and dead branches that rested in the lower limbs of trees; my belly made it impossible for me to stoop very low. I could no longer recall what it was like to move freely, to bend, sit and stand without the burden of my child.

In the city, I would have been anticipating the child's birth. I would have spent time with other pregnant women, would have prepared a room for the child, heard reassuring comments from women about their own pregnancies and deliveries. A physician would have tended me; I would have known what my child was to be. I wondered what I would bear, whether the baby would die, whether I would live. I wanted the birth to be over and yet dreaded it.

As I reached for a piece of dead wood, a sharp pain stabbed at me; I groaned as my belly cramped. My time was coming. Somehow I remembered to pick up my wood before stumbling down toward the camp.

I set down the wood and called out; Cress ran toward me from the riverbank. 'It is time,' I said, and nearly doubled over with the next pain.

'Are the pains coming often?'

I straightened. 'This one is passing.'

'You must go inside before the next one comes.'

I clutched at her cloak. She led me to our hut and fed the fire while I knelt on my mat. 'I'll stay with you now,' she said. 'The others will come soon.'

Cress helped me prop my back against the wall. All my fears were suddenly amplified. The child might be born with a defect; I might be unable to deliver it at all. I might have it and be unable to nurse. Then the pain took me again, and I could think of nothing else.

Between the pains, Cress forced me to my feet, supporting me with her warm arm as we walked around the hearth. The pains were soon sharper, the contractions closer together. I moaned as Cress settled me on the mat. 'I can't . . .' I started to say.

'You are strong enough, Birana. You mustn't fear.'

Dimly, I could hear the voices of the men as they returned to the camp. 'Cress,' I gasped, 'fetch Arvil.'

'I cannot. This is not for him to see.'

I clenched my teeth. 'Please! I want him with me.'

She shook her head but got up and left the hut. Another pain shot through me; I forced myself not to scream. When it had passed, Arvil was at my side.

'Birana, is it painful for you?'

'I'll be all right. Stay with me.'

'I shall. I must make something for you.' He went to the fire and crouched as he took out a pouch of herbs. Cress and Hyacinth entered; I closed my eyes.

'Birana.' Cress was handing me Arvil's cup. 'You should drink this. It will dull your pain and won't harm the child.' She glanced at Arvil. 'We also know of this herb.' She held the cup to my lips as I drank.

Hyacinth said, 'The man must leave us.'

Arvil rose. 'I will not have Birana face this without me.'

'You cannot . . .'

'It was I who brought her to this,' he said firmly. 'I'll stay.'

'If the child is cursed,' Hyacinth muttered, 'it will be on your head.'

'Stop it!' I cried, frightened. 'I won't hear of curses now! I want him to stay.'

Cress murmured to me, reminding me of how to breathe. I took in air and exhaled, panting. Cress handed me a soft piece of leather as more pain seized me; I put it into my mouth and bit down. Hands pulled off my clothes, then laid a hide over me. Willow was near, massaging my thighs as the other two women washed their hands in hot water. My fingers dug into Arvil's arm. His face was pale; each time I moaned, he winced. I expected him to flee, to hide from this with the other men.

Throughout that night, I was in labour. The pain forced

everything else from my mind; my body was fighting itself, trying to force what I carried from me, and yet it seemed the child would never be born. I promised myself I would not scream in Arvil's presence and broke that promise many times. I didn't care about the child; I only wanted the pain to end.

I screamed and gasped for air, throwing the hide from myself. My body's struggle and the heat of the fire were making me feverish. Hands kneaded my belly and thighs and then forced my legs apart.

'I see the head,' Willow said. Cress leaned over me. 'It is coming now.'

'Birana, you must bear down, you must push the child out. You are open enough, but you must help.' Cress gripped me as a hand reached inside me. 'Push!'

I panted and bore down. Arvil was still with me; I caught a glimpse of his terror-filled face before he lifted a hand to his mouth. 'Arvil!' Cress said sharply. 'If your courage is going to fail you now, then leave us. I cannot tend to you now!'

'I will stay.' His voice sounded faint. He took my hand. I cried out, feeling the child leave me, then pushed again as fluid flowed from me.

'So much blood!' Arvil cried. He dropped my hand. Hyacinth was speaking, chiding him. I fell back on the mat.

The pain was gone. I opened my eyes. Cress dipped a soft piece of hide in warm water and began to wash me. Something lay on my chest; it squirmed in my arms. I heard another cry, a baby's cry.

'Is it . . .' I whispered.

'See for yourself,' Cress answered; she was smiling.

Hyacinth thrust her stone knife into hot water, then cut the cord. I drew my child to my chest, touched the small body, counted the fingers.

'A girl,' Cress said. 'You have been blessed. Our band is blessed.'

'Arvil.' I turned my head. He was at my side; he had not run from the hut. Too exhausted to say more, I drifted into sleep.

When I awoke, Cress was holding my daughter, now clothed in a tiny fur robe. Someone had covered me with a hide.

'Birana.' Arvil was speaking. 'The women say you'll be well, that the child will live.'

'She is hungry,' Cress said as she handed the child to me.

Arvil eased me up. I pulled at my nipple until milk flowed; the baby nursed at my breast.

'She is so small,' he said. 'I didn't know how she could come from you, how she could pass through your opening, but now she seems so small.'

'She'll grow.' Her eyes were blue; the fine hair on her nearly bald head was as pale as Arvil's.

'She will grow strong, I will teach her how to hunt.'

Hyacinth shook her head. 'You should not have been here to witness this, and now you speak of teaching a man's tasks to her.'

'Be silent,' Cress murmured. 'He has brought no harm to the girl. Perhaps the other men will think on this when another child is born and won't huddle in their hut away from us.'

My mind cleared; I was suddenly aware of my dilemma. This band would want more children from me now, would expect me to bear as many as I could. My child was a girl. I thought of her growing up among these people. The women, kind as they were, would dull her mind with their tales and teach her to submit to the men. Arvil might protect her for a time, but when she was old enough to bear children, the men would summon her with no thought of her wishes. Whatever children she and I might have would only prolong this group's tenuous hold on life, without altering its eventual fate.

I had cursed my daughter by giving her life. I looked down at her round face, at the pursed lips sucking at my nipple, and thought of putting a hide over her mouth and nose when we were alone. No one was likely to guess what I had done; children had died here before. I gazed at my daughter, held her to me, and knew that I could not commit such an act.

'That child will live.' Cress sounded as proud as if she had borne the baby herself. 'She should have a name.'

'Nallei,' I responded almost without thinking.

Willow drew her brows together. 'Nallei?'

'She was a woman who was like a mother to me. She might have wanted a daughter of her own, but . . .' I swallowed. 'In a way, she made my child's life possible. Nallei is dead. I want my child to have her name.'

'Nallei,' Arvil whispered as he gazed down at our daughter.

The winter soon passed; in spite of the cold, Nallei thrived. I had enough milk to feed her. Arvil went far from camp in search of meat for me but helped me care for Nallei whenever he could.

The other men muttered at this, clearly wondering why a man would bathe a child or hold her while she slept, but said little. When they mocked Arvil, they did so gently; our child, after all, was whole and healthy. Arvil's behaviour could be excused.

With Nallei tied to my back or resting in a sling against my chest, I was able to forage. Days came when the wind from the sea was warmer and green shoots began to poke their way through the light covering of snow. I was stronger; Arvil delighted in his child, still wondered at the apparent miracle of her birth. The guilt that had haunted him was gone; the band was content; Nallei and I were safe.

I wondered if I could bring myself to leave. I could free Nallei from this life, yet when I thought of the journey that might lie ahead, my mind faltered. I knew where I could take her but also pondered the obstacles that I would face along the way. It was easier not to think of leaving, to tell myself I could make my plans later.

I was searching for greens along the bank when Arvil finally spoke to me of his own thoughts. He untied the straps holding Nallei to my back and held her as I dug at ferns and watercress.

I smiled at him as he made a face at the child. 'The men will mock you again,' I said.

'Pelican will, but he is only a boy. Even Tern now says that a man with such good seed may act as he wishes, although he would not treat a child this way.' Nallei whimpered and let out a wail; he rocked her until she quieted. 'Before she came into the world,' he went on, 'you and I spoke of leaving this place.'

'Yes.' I would have to tell him my thoughts now. I looked up, making certain no one was near. 'I've been afraid to think of that, but we can't wait much longer.'

'This is not what I think, Birana. She is so small still. If anything happened to one of us, the other could not tend her alone. If we were both . . .'

I stood up and adjusted the sling holding my plants. 'What are you trying to tell me?'

'There are others here who can help care for her. We can wait until she grows, until she's able to walk and travel with us, and then . . .'

'You know what will happen if we stay. We've had one child, and the others will want us to have more. And we have to think of Nallei, too. You know what her life would be like here, and when she's older, she may not be able to leave, may be afraid to go.'

He handed the baby to me. 'I have thought of leaving. I've thought of everything you say. You think that, if my seed doesn't flower in you again, the others will summon you, but I won't let it happen, I'll find a way to stop it. You say we must think of Nallei. I am thinking of her. Even if we left this camp now, where can we take her? Will you leave her alone in this world with no friends when we're gone?' He took a breath. 'Even this life would be better.'

I gazed into his grey eyes, steeling myself. 'There's a place we can take her where she can have a life.'

'Where?'

'My city.'

His mouth dropped open. 'But they cast you out. You said . . .'

'They cast *me* out. Nallei's a baby, she did nothing. They can't punish her for what I did – even the cruelest ones there wouldn't harm a baby girl. They'll have to take her in.'

He gazed at Nallei, then lifted his head. 'Your enclave wanted you dead. When they see that you are alive . . .'

'Let them see it!' I moved closer to him. 'You don't have to come to the wall with me. They needn't know about you at all. I can protect you if you wish.'

His face hardened. 'You are saying I'm a coward.'

'I'm saying you can do what you like.' I sighed. 'I don't want to make this journey. I could go on here, become like the others. But how could I forgive myself if I saw Nallei growing up with nothing to hope for except keeping this pitiful group alive for a few more generations? Do you want to see us both become like the women here?'

Arvil did not reply.

'She could have a life in the city. It's worth the chance. I can accept whatever happens to me if I know she's safe there.'

'When she is older . . .' Arvil started to say.

'When she's older, it'll be too late. The city might take a baby, a small one who wouldn't remember this world. They wouldn't take an older child, one they'd have more trouble training, who might not be able to adapt.'

'In the city,' he said, 'she'll learn to hate us, if she learns of us. She will despise me for being a man and scorn you for what you have done.'

'She may learn to understand us in time.' I spoke with more confidence than I felt. I could not believe that the city would willingly condemn my daughter, an innocent and one of their own kind, but they would know how she had come into the world and many would scorn her for it. Nallei might grow up as an outcast, yet her life there would surely be better than what she would endure here; she might be grateful for that. 'Perhaps, when she is grown, she may try to change the way things are.'

'You would enter the enclave yourself if you could. You would leave me and forget what I've been to you.'

'It's useless to say such things. I can't enter the city again.'

He turned toward me. 'This journey . . . it would be harder than the one that brought us here. We might not live through it. We would be on foot, with Nallei. Who will help us?'

'We must try, for Nallei's sake.'

He glowered at our child; I held her closer to me. 'It is all for Nallei now – everything you do.'

'That may be true.' I touched his face. 'A mother's bond with her child is a strong one. I thought a father's might be as strong if he knew that the child was his.' He shied away from me. 'Arvil, if you won't come with me, I'll have to go alone.'

'You cannot make the journey by yourself.'

'I will make it one way or another. Let the city take my life if I reach the wall. Part of me will live on in her.'

He paced along the riverbank as I waited for his response. Whatever I had said, he knew I could not make the journey alone, that I would never reach the wall. He could go to Tern now, see that I never left the camp; he could comfort himself by believing he was protecting me.

He stopped pacing and folded his arms. 'You know how to use the Lady's circlet.'

'Of course,' I murmured, wondering why he had mentioned that.

'Perhaps there is no need for you to go to the wall. It might be better to take Nallei to a shrine, to summon a few of your kind there and leave the child for them, escape before they can reach us. We will have to think about this.'

My heart leaped; he was agreeing to travel with me. 'Arvil, I . . .'

'Do not thank me. You may find cause to regret this. I may curse myself for leading you back into danger.' He took my arm as we walked back toward the camp.

During the following days, I collected the things I would need for the journey. Each day, I carried a piece of dried fish or meat or a tool to the hole I had dug by a tree's roots, then covered it with a stone, making certain no one had followed me there. I supposed that I could hide my preparations from the women by stealing only a little every day.

I was not prepared to find Cress standing by the tree as I crept there early one morning. I wanted to run but forced myself to approach her. 'I thought you had gone out to forage,' I said. 'You will find little here.'

Her eyes narrowed. 'What did you carry here this time?'

I swallowed and shook my head.

'I know what you're doing, Birana. I have seen what lies under the rock. Did you think you could take things from our hut unseen?'

'Who else has seen me?' I asked.

'No one else yet, but they will soon know. Why do you steal and hide what you take?'

I reached into Nallei's sling and took out the dried fruit hidden under her covering; she stirred and clutched at my hair with her small hand. 'I'm not stealing. I've taken only what I use or haven't eaten. I won't take anything that belongs to you.'

'Why?' The wrinkles around her mouth deepened. 'But I do not have to ask, do I? You need food for a journey. You're planning to leave us.'

I could not deny it. 'It's true,' I whispered. 'Arvil and I are going to leave with our child.' I waited, expecting her to rail against me, to run back to the camp and summon Tern.

'Why, Birana? Have we been so evil to you?'

Her question pained me. 'No, Cress. You've been kind; you've been my friends. If I were alone, I might stay with you, but I have to think of my daughter. Please try to understand. In the citadels of the Lady, she can be given a home and a better life than she has here. That's where I'm going to take her.'

'That was the Lady's purpose for you? To send you out so that you could bring this child back to Her?'

I shook my head. 'But She'll take the child.'

'We cannot go to the Lady's realm, Birana. Always we were told this – my mother told this to me, and hers to her. We must wait for the Lady to come to us. I thought that you might bring Her . . .'

'I came out of a citadel. Now I must take my child there.'

'And will the Lady take you back?'

'No,' I replied. 'My child may find a home there. They won't take me back.'

She bowed her head; tears ran down her wrinkled face. 'You'll be taking our last hope with you. Hyacinth's children die, and

Willow lies with Skua and brings forth no young. My sins keep me from bearing more young. There will be no mates for our boys. We might as well cast ourselves into the sea.'

I put my arm around her. 'You mustn't say that. You could still . . .'

'Don't speak falsely to me now. There will be nothing for us.'

'There would be nothing if I stayed.'

'There would be children!'

'Yes,' I said, 'and children for them in time, but after a while there would only be what you have now – children born weak or ill. If I thought there was a chance for something else, I would stay, but there isn't. You'd need many more men and women here for your children to thrive – the seed of one man and one woman isn't enough.'

Cress wiped her face with one sleeve. 'Now I see that the Lady has forgotten us. I helped you bring your daughter into the world, and now you'll take her from us.'

'I've told you what life is like in a city. Nallei will learn the Lady's magic, ride in Her ships, dwell in Her towers. If you could give that to a daughter, would you keep her here? Cress, listen to me. There may be one chance, a small one, for you and the other women. I can tell you how to reach a city – you could even follow me. A city might take you in, might find some place for you, might . . .' I paused.

'You're not saying this because it's true, but only to comfort me. The Lady is punishing me. I brought no more children into the world when I might have, and now She's taking yours from us.'

'No, Cress,' I said as firmly as I could. 'The Lady would never punish you for that. Those in Her cities choose when to have children and don't bear them against their will. When they can have no more, they guide those who are younger. The Lady wouldn't want you to . . .' I stepped back as I drew Nallei's head to my shoulder. 'You can go to Tern, tell him what I'm doing. It would be hard for me to escape then. I can't stand against all of you.'

She leaned against the tree. 'That will not help our band, to bind you against your will. Break your bond with us if you must, but I won't break mine with you.' Her words moved me. 'Perhaps I deserve to see your child taken from us.'

'Why do you keep speaking as if you've done something wrong?'

Her pale brown eyes gazed steadily at me. 'I can tell you this now. There's a plant I gather, one that yields tiny berries. I learned of it from my mother. I can brew a potion with it, and it keeps a man's seed from taking root in me. I could never let the men know of it and worried that I was doing an evil thing, but then I would think that such a potion couldn't be evil. I used it only so that my body could heal itself before I bore more children. My last time was a hard one – the child died, and I nearly died myself. I told myself that I was only strengthening myself until it was time to bring new life into the world, that the Lady would understand. Then you came to us, and I believed it was better to stay alive and help you care for your young ones rather than risk death for one of my own. Now you'll leave, and my body may be too old for more children.'

I wanted to ask her about this plant, but she needed my comfort then. 'You didn't do wrong,' I said. 'You must believe that. You were here to help me. I won't forget you. Nallei will know of you some day, and maybe the Lady . . .'

Hope gleamed in her eyes for a moment. I wondered if this undoubtedly false hope, my last gift to her, would be enough to sustain her. 'The Lady wouldn't want you to bring children into this world when there's so little hope for them,' I continued. 'She'll understand when you're with Her again. There's some hope for your boys. There are men to the west they can join, and perhaps the Lady will call them to Her side someday.'

'And if you're not to enter a citadel yourself . . .'

'I'll be with Arvil. We'll find another place together. Perhaps we'll even find our way back here in time, if there's a way . . .'

Her lips curved into a brief smile. 'Arvil is more than I believed a man could be. Even Tern's been touched by his spirit a little. His soul is gentler than it was. He'll need my comfort when he knows you are gone.' She reached into her coat and took out a pouch. 'You will need a gift from me, Birana. Take this. The berries of which I spoke are in this pouch, those that will keep another child from growing inside you. I'll tell you of how to make a potion. Show these berries to Arvil. He knows the lore of plants and healing – he'll know where to find this plant.'

I put out my hand. 'You'll do this for me?'

'For you and for Arvil. I see the strength of his need whenever he looks at you, even when he doesn't summon you, and I sense that your need for him is as great. You cannot bear a child while you wander the Earth, but must wait until you find a place to rest.'

I could not speak for a moment. 'Cress, I . . .'

'Don't weep before me now.' She patted my hand, then let hers rest on Nallei's blond head. 'You'll have to leave soon, before the others learn of your plan. Leave in the morning. The men will think you're foraging. By the time you are missed, it will be too dark for them to search, but they may try to follow. Where will you go?'

'To the north, from where we first came. There's a place we can stop before going west.'

'Then I'll tell them I saw you go toward the river's bend to the southwest. They'll search there first. They will not go far from this land, as you know. They fear the lands beyond.'

I blinked back my tears. 'I'll never forget what you've done.' I pressed my shoulder to hers and wept.

Cress was awake when I rose; Willow and Hyacinth still slept. I fed Nallei, bound her to her tiny litter, then calmed her until she fell asleep again. Cress tied the leather straps of the litter across my chest as I adjusted those over my shoulders. She did not speak as I picked up my empty pack and thrust it under my coat. She handed me my sling; I was about to say farewell, but she glanced at the other women and put a finger to her lips.

I crept from the hut; Cress followed. Arvil had told the men he was going to hunt today; he would be gone already, waiting for me. The other dwelling was silent, the men still asleep. Cress watched as I walked through the clearing and began to climb the hill. When I looked back, she raised a hand before turning away.

The sun was rising by the time I had removed my things from where they were hidden and had put them into my pack. Arvil had said he would meet me here and lead me to his secret cache. I was closer to the ocean, could hear the waves rushing toward the shore.

A twig cracked; Arvil emerged from the trees. He carried only his weapons and a smaller pack. 'I left a false trail,' he said as he took my pack from me. 'Tern will think I went to the shore to gather shells instead of hunting. He'll look for me there when I don't return.'

We began to walk north, careful to leave no signs of passing. Nallei stirred and whimpered; a smile flashed across Arvil's face before he grew solemn again.

'I don't know if we will survive this journey,' he murmured. 'We may never see your enclave again. I go only because I cannot stay without you.'

'We will live,' I replied.

The
SHRINE

LAISSA

I waited for Eilaan. She had sent no message, but I knew she would come; her curiosity, if nothing else, would bring her to my rooms. She might think that I had finally put our shared deed behind me, that I had even forgiven her for her part in it.

I could understand her better now. Her years on the Council had made her what she was. I had thought she was using me to shield herself but had done nothing Eilaan could not have handled alone. Her life – her actions, everything she had done – rested on her view of the world, a view I had questioned. The cities had to be preserved at any cost; to question or seek change would put the world at risk once more. The death of a few and the torment of others were justified for the sake of the many. By becoming her accomplice, I had implicitly accepted her beliefs and confirmed her in them.

Our shared deed would be Eilaan's legacy to me and to our city. The deed would bind me to her, would harden and temper me, would lead me to take on her attitudes, if only to avoid the guilt I would otherwise feel. So Eilaan must have believed.

I saw her only once after our meeting on the wall. I told her that Birana was dead and that my twin Arvil might be for ever tormented by having had to kill the young woman he had once worshipped. Eilaan was not concerned by that; perhaps she was even amused at the notion of a man suffering such guilt. Arvil was a tool to be tempered by terror, used, and cast aside. I was another tool, but one not so easy to dismiss.

She waited as I delivered my message, apparently expecting me to demand some favour as payment for my cooperation. She listened to my words and Arvil's recorded ones and then dismissed me. I asked her for nothing then. I wanted nothing from the Council, nothing from anyone else.

I told myself I was protecting my mother, but she was not the same afterward. She came to her senses, not long after Button's departure, but went about her work passively, saw few of her friends, endured my visits with a sad smile and an abstracted, distant mien. Her patients were soon requesting other physicians, and my mother was finally assigned some simpler tasks in the wall's genetic laboratories. She never asked about Birana, although she must have guessed what had happened; she seemed to have forgotten Button.

Eilaan believed that my mother had healed, had come to some peace. I knew better; my mother was broken.

I had my studies still, under the guidance of my mentor Fari; I withdrew from almost everything else, and soon had the reputation of a solitary; except for Zoreen, my old friends soon fell away. My self-imposed solitude, at first a punishment I inflicted upon myself, became a kind of solace. I was apart from the city, my only reality the thoughts inside myself. Slowly, without the distractions of other companions and the need to mould and modify my ideas in their company, I came to know my own mind and the kind of purpose I might find in my work.

I had suspected that Birana was dead even before Arvil confirmed it, for his old band had travelled to a shrine with a strange tale. Birana's coat had been found, but no trace of her or Arvil. From these facts, a man called Wanderer had fashioned a story: Arvil had discovered Birana, and she had shown him more favour than she had to the other men. She had come among the men to bless them, and Wanderer had guessed that Arvil would be the first to be honoured. Arvil had gone to a place alone with her to receive her blessing; Birana had taken such joy in him that she had carried him to the Lady's realm, to dwell always at her side. The band honoured Arvil's memory, believing that he and Birana still watched over them all; the following years seemed to prove the truth of the story. They found other horses and believed Birana's spirit helped in taming them. They made truces with a few other bands and often sensed the ghostly presence of Arvil during these parleys. In Wanderer's story, Arvil and Birana embodied the band's hopes and spirits; the young man, who undoubtedly feared the men too much to return to them, had become a kind of deity.

I had no reason to contradict this tale; it didn't matter what the men believed as long as they honoured the Goddess. I did not think much about the story when I first heard it, but Wanderer and his men journeyed to shrines often, and I was soon hearing other tales.

Wanderer, I learned, made stories from many events. When my progenitor, Tal, disappeared – perhaps a victim of a predator or another group of men – Wanderer recalled his prowess as a hunter and spoke of how Tal now hunted at the Lady's side. A rainstorm became the tears of the Lady, wept for the sins of men; the damp, greener ground was a sign of the Goddess's forgiveness. Wanderer knew other stories as well, narratives of men in far places and the legends they told.

Occasionally, I probed Wanderer's thoughts through the mindspeaker. Partly out of guilt and partly out of curiosity about Button's welfare, I had taken to tending this band and answering their prayers. I was soon more interested in the stories themselves. Bren had told me I would become a chronicler; the cities knew little of the stories men told to one another, tales that revealed much about their hopes, fears, feelings and beliefs. I imagined myself fashioning a new chronicle from them, one that might illuminate the outside world. I wanted to hear more of such tales. I supposed the Council in time might find them useful and informative as well, which meant that they might aid me in what I would propose to do.

Even when I understood my purpose, a year passed before I could bring myself to make my proposal to the Council. I did not fear their reaction; I felt I could no longer be touched by anything they did to me. I did not worry that I would be refused; Eilaan would become my tool now. But I wondered if I had the courage to carry out my wishes.

My guilt finally moved me to act; whatever grief came to me would be deserved. I made my proposal and waited for Eilaan to come to me.

Eilaan was outside my door. I rose and went to greet her. She was alone as I had requested. I led her to a chair and seated myself across from her.

She glanced around the room, frowning in disapproval as her gaze fell on the piles of books and documents on the floor and the couch. 'How untidy,' she said. 'I wonder how you can keep your materials sorted.'

'We do well enough. Most of this is Zoreen's. The documents and transcripts I've been using are in the corner there, and I keep the rest in my bedroom.'

'Your guests must find it quite disorderly.'

'You know perfectly well we don't have many guests.' I folded my arms.

'Laissa, this proposal of yours – it's out of the question. Surely you see that.'

'I've discussed it with Fari,' I said. 'She thinks it may yield something of value. If I have the courage to pursue it, she won't stand in my way.'

'Fari.' She scowled, clearly disapproving of my mentor. 'It doesn't matter what she thinks.'

'It may matter what my old advisor, Bren, thinks, now that she's on the Council. She's encouraged me in the past. She'll stand with me this time.'

'The Council will never allow this.'

'You had better persuade them that they should.' I leaned forward. 'I did your bidding a few years back. I kept silent. Your reputation is safe enough for now. But if you don't speak up for my proposal, I may decide to spread a few rumours.'

'You can't frighten me with that. Anyone would agree that I did only what I had to do.'

'Some will,' I replied, 'and some won't. Such a tale would certainly create doubts about your abilities, since you weren't even willing to take the responsibility on to yourself. I had to see to things for you when I was hardly more than a girl. Many would wonder about the propriety of that. Even if they agreed about the rightness of your actions, they would wonder why you couldn't carry them out yourself.'

'The Council is aware of what happened.'

'But perhaps not of my role.' Eilaan averted her eyes; I had guessed correctly. 'And I needn't worry about my own reputation being sullied. I have little enough as it is.'

Her mouth twitched. 'You'd drag out what's past after all this time?'

'I'm a chronicler. The tale of how Birana met her end might be interesting both as a story and as a historical footnote.'

'Dorlei played her part in those events for reasons some might question. You know the state she was in. Don't you have any concern for her, of how she might react if you . . .'

'Don't you dare speak of my mother to me.' I stared steadily at Eilaan until she looked away again. 'I think very little could touch her now.'

'One might almost think,' the old woman said, 'that you feel you must unburden yourself of your guilt, make it public.'

'I have much to feel guilty about. It isn't just Birana's death that weighs on me – I could have done little about that once she was sent out. But I might have been her friend earlier. I might have spoken up for her before her sentence was passed. Maybe the Council wouldn't have punished her so harshly if someone had pleaded for mercy. She didn't deserve expulsion.'

'She was Yvara's daughter and her mother's accomplice. You saw what kind of creature Yvara was.' Eilaan shook her head. 'We're well rid of that strain. It's past, and it's useless to speak of it now. It's this proposal of yours that concerns me at the moment. You must give it up.'

'I am going to do my chronicle of the men's tales. If I am to hear these tales, I must go outside. There will be little danger. I'll be in a shrine; the men who come there won't harm me; and my presence will only confirm them in their faith. I'll do nothing to rob them of their illusions.'

She gripped the arms of her chair. 'It's mad to go outside. You'll learn no more from those men than you would if you listened to them with the mindspeaker.'

'That isn't so. We learn a little, but they're often preoccupied with prayer, with wanting to appease the Lady, with the desire for erotic encounters.' She grimaced at those words. 'I can learn more by questioning them directly, by letting them tell their tales to me. The stories would make a new and interesting chronicle, and some scholars might find them illuminating. We know too little now about the outside.'

'We know enough.'

I tapped my fingers impatiently. 'Eilaan, if we had known more, maybe Devva wouldn't have had to destroy that settlement years ago. Maybe the city of Lasan wouldn't have had to destroy another settlement later because they believed an exiled woman was living among those men. That kind of action only makes more sensitive souls wonder at the necessity for such cruelty. It causes a few to question matters they might ignore if we showed more mercy.'

'Those men were a danger to us,' she said firmly. 'That's how it begins, with larger groups and the need to organize them, and it leads to the breeding of plants and animals, and then to questions about why things are as they are and what the true role of men is. You think there's no threat. Would you wait until they discover metalworking, until they begin to master some of the knowledge they lost, until they pose a direct threat to the cities?'

'Then argue my case, Eilaan. Get approval for my proposal. The more we learn about the outside, the more able we'll be to distinguish a true danger from something we can leave alone. We've been hiding in our cities too long. If I find something of interest, others might go out from other cities and learn more. We might even find new means to control men, ways that are more subtle and less drastic. Their stories can tell us much about them.'

She was silent.

'You see,' I continued, 'I can suffer my guilt but I can also put it aside. Whatever I did, it was to preserve our city and our lives as they are. Now I would like to do more. I asked nothing of you before, but I'm wiser now and need your help. We both have the same end in mind, and I'll be sure to acknowledge your contribution if anything worthy comes of my work.'

She smiled a little at that, as if responding to a kindred soul.

'We should leave our daughters more knowledge about the outside,' I said. 'We should not leave them with the necessity to remedy our negligence and our mistakes.'

'You should be thinking of a daughter of your own soon,' she murmured.

'Time enough to consider that when I return.'

'You talk of preserving our cities, Laissa. I know your actual thoughts, and Fari's as well. You're wondering if it's time for change.' She gestured wearily with one hand. 'I'll speak up for you, but I promise nothing.'

'Think of what I might mention to others if you fail, and I'm sure you'll be persuasive.' I stood up and led her to the door.

'I fear for you,' Zoreen said.

'You needn't. I'll be safe enough.'

'Women haven't gone outside this city in ages.'

'It's time someone did.'

'This isn't a little jaunt to Devva in a ship. You'll be alone. You may not be able to summon help if there's danger.'

'I'll be careful.' I turned toward her. She was lying beside me on my bed.

Zoreen had come to love me during the past years, and I cared for her in a placid, abiding way that would have been impossible with Shayl. My former love, according to gossip, kept her lovers ensnared in uncertainties, never letting them know if she would continue to accept them. With Zoreen, I had some peace. I had become so accustomed to her body that our lovemaking, once filled with the excitement of discovering her needs and teaching her mine, was now a respite; touching her body was little different from touching my own. My desires were reflected in hers, while hers mirrored mine.

'You once dreamed of the outside yourself,' I said.

'I know now that I couldn't go out.' She drew my head to her chest. 'You'll be alone. That's fearful enough.'

'I'm used to being alone.'

'You mustn't say that to me. Maybe they won't give you permission to go. That would disappoint you, but I'd be relieved.'

'They'll let me go.' I caressed her with one hand, wanting her to forget her worries for a little while. Her belly moved against my palm. I suddenly thought of Birana; she would not have been a lover expecting only the familiar; her wilder spirit would have been a constant surprise. Why was I thinking of her now?

'What is it?' Zoreen asked; she had sensed the change in my mood. I shook my head, unable to answer. 'You're afraid. Don't think of it now.' She eased me back on the bed; I seemed to feel my own hands touching me.

I was granted the permission I sought. Eilaan herself came to me with the news, although she was clearly not pleased.

I had prepared myself, learning from a pilot how to operate my small ship if it was necessary to take control. My immune system was bolstered, and I was given a small medical kit, although I would return to the city at the slightest sign of an illness. I had equipment to record my encounters.

After saying farewell to Zoreen in our rooms, I went to board my ship. No one, not even my mentor, Fari, had come to see me leave. I had expected at least a small crowd of the curious, perhaps a few who might try to dissuade me. I entered my ship; it rose from the wall as I set my course and began to move southwest.

My destination was a shrine to the Wise One that stood near a small lake. From Wanderer's band, I had learned that other bands came to that lake to hunt during the spring and summer; I wanted to hear the tales of various bands but did not want to go to a shrine where too many more would gather.

I peered through my window at the green of summer. Two men cowered in a clearing as the ship passed overhead. I soon sighted the lake but saw no signs of men near the shrine. As the ship sent out its signal, the shrine's dome slowly opened to receive me. The ship dropped and alighted on the altar as the dome closed.

Women had tended the shrines once, returning from time to time to make what repairs were necessary; the cyberminds had freed us of that task. I sat inside the ship, suddenly afraid to leave it. Birana had been discovered in this shrine; I had learned that much from Wanderer's men. In the safety of my room, it had seemed fitting to come here, to face the last refuge Birana had known, to remember her while I did my work. Now I regretted my choice.

At last I went out and set up my recorder near the ship's door. The Council had placed some restrictions on my project; I was to tell the men as little as possible, offer no aid or advice, affect them as little as I could while listening to their talk. Yet I could not observe them and speak to them without affecting them in some way.

I sat down to wait, keeping the wand that was my weapon near me, clinging to what courage I had left.

I did not leave the shrine, afraid even to step from its door. I waited for two days and spent two nights inside the ship before my first visitors arrived.

Two men and a boy entered the shrine, then threw themselves on the floor when they saw me seated on the altar. I wore a clinging shirt that outlined my breasts, my hair was loose around my shoulders, and I had set the instruments of the Wise One in front of me. I wanted to be sure that the men saw what I was immediately – a woman, carried by a ship from the Lady's realm.

'Holy One,' one of the men cried as he looked up.

'I have come to dwell among you for a time,' I said. The three covered their heads with their arms. 'The Lady wishes to honour you by speaking to you in this form. She wishes to hear your stories.'

'Oh,' one man groaned, 'have mercy, Lady.'

'I shall not harm you.'

I could get nothing out of them; they were too terrified to speak of themselves. One muttered incantations while the others beat their fists against their foreheads. At last I dismissed them. They ran from the shrine, not even pausing to make the customary observances.

I was trembling by then, drained by this brief encounter; I was disappointed but not discouraged. These men were sure to tell others about what they had seen; more men would come.

The next day a group of ten males appeared; I thought I recognized the three I had seen. The three boys with the group were sturdy, broad-shouldered lads with brown or dark blond hair; the men all had brown beards, although two were beginning to go grey. They dropped to the floor and covered their heads.

'You may rise.' My voice shook, and I swallowed. 'You will not be harmed.' They sat back on their heels; none raised his eyes to me. 'I have come among you for a time, to dwell here and to hear your words. The Lady would hear you speak of your lives.'

One man got awkwardly to his feet. 'You honour us, Lady.'

'I would hear your tales now. Sit down and tell Me of yourselves.'

The men settled on the floor, folding their legs and keeping their heads bowed. 'We serve You,' the man who had spoken before said. 'We pray. Several of us have been called.' He went on in that vein for a while, stressing the honour he had always paid to the Goddess. When he was finished, another man spoke, saying nearly the same thing.

I was learning little. After a third man had told me of his frequent prayers, I said, 'It is your lives I wish to hear about – how you hunt, your customs, the stories you tell yourselves.'

'Surely You know all of that Lady,' one bold boy said. 'Do You not see all?' The man next to the boy struck him with the back of his hand; I tried not to wince.

'The Lady sees all,' I replied, 'but I wish to hear of your lives from you and to see if you speak the truth.'

'Could we do otherwise than speak truth before You?' a man asked.

I repressed a sigh. 'Speak of yourselves.'

More vague talk about the band followed. They lived not far from this lake; they fished and hunted birds there; they had made a truce with another band – I wasn't told why.

At last I said, 'I shall dwell here and hope to see you again.' That did not seem impressive enough, so I added, 'Do not neglect Me.'

'Our band is truly honoured.'

'I do not honour only your band but will welcome anyone who visits this shrine.'

'Yes, Lady.'

I dismissed them, wondering if I would ever learn anything.

Others soon began to come to the shrine. At first, each arrived alone, or with a friend, but by the middle of summer, larger bands were arriving, many from some distance. Often as many as four or five bands were vying to tell me their stories.

As they became accustomed to my presence, they grew more relaxed, sprawling on couches or sitting nearer to the altar. They maintained a respectful distance, and a sharp glance or a harsher tone from me still cowed them. I kept my weapon with me, prepared to stun anyone who seemed threatening with a beam from my wand; I sat just outside the ship's door, ready to retreat.

Some of the men were better tale-tellers than others, able to describe their doings in detail or to hold everyone in suspense while they related stories of battles or the hunting of large and fierce creatures. I rewarded those who told the best stories with pieces of fruit or sweets, and found that this encouraged others to emulate them. Although fear of me undoubtedly kept them from lying outright, I suspected that a few were not above embellishing their tales by making enemies more fearsome and numerous or animals more dangerous and bloodthirsty. This did not matter; how they regarded themselves was of interest, and their lives, even unadorned by invention, were brutal enough.

I had hoped for understanding, had even imagined acquiring a little sympathy for these men. Instead, my repugnance and loathing grew, and I often had to retreat inside my ship to collect myself. They were filthy; I smelled their sweat and body odours even though they stayed below the altar. Among themselves, their behaviour was crude at best; younger boys were struck or beaten for the slightest reason. Violence and murder were commonplace in their lives, most of their stories were of hunting and fighting, and they showed more respect for the game than they did for one another.

They were little better than beasts, and I marvelled that I could ever have believed that they might be more. Yet once in a while, I saw men gaze with affection at boys who might have been their sons or heard a story of the friendship and loyalty among members of a band, or a tale of bravery and self-sacrifice, or of a strong love between two men, and these rudimentary signs of humanity would lift my spirits for a time.

Always, there were stories passed down through the years of how the Lady had appeared in various guises to teach a band or to guide it to a new region. I heard nothing in these tales that indicated that they doubted their faith or that they longed for change. Men had been punished long ago, but the Goddess let them live, rewarding them in the enclaves and in the next world for lives well spent.

I let them speak and asked few questions. Whenever one turned to me for guidance or posed a problem for me to solve, I answered ambiguously or cryptically, so that my answer would seem correct whatever befell the man later. I revealed none of my own thoughts. None the less, my presence was affecting them.

A few of the tribes that came to the shrine were horsemen; although they could not fight inside the shrine, there was obviously bad feeling between the horsemen and those on foot. But as the men began to spend more time in or near the shrine, often staying away only long enough to hunt for food, they started to speak among themselves. Soon several bands made truces with those they had once hated.

I noted this and thought of discouraging it but did not act. When men were divided, only the strongest survived; I knew that keeping them divided served our ends. Yet some seemed willing to accept more peaceful ways. I suppose I had a vague hope that the men might some day show that they were worthy of better treatment.

I recorded their stories and noted my own observations and reactions, wondering what I would glean from this mass of material when I had the chance to reflect upon it. At times, I feared that the project would be useless. What was there to be gained? Only the knowledge, it seemed, that men were largely as we believed them to be. Perhaps my work, instead of adding to our understanding, would only increase our fears.

I could do nothing about that in any case. I would record the tales, provide transcripts for those who were interested, and put together a chronicle. It was likely that only a few would read the stories; most would find them too disturbing. As a chronicler, I might shape the stories and my commentary on them in any way I wished; how the chronicle was used in the end was not my business.

Later in the summer, I began to hint that I would soon be leaving the shrine. I expected the men to drift away to their camps. Instead, the shrine grew more crowded as distant tribes, hearing of the wonder, travelled to see me, while some of those already present seemed reluctant to leave.

I was flooded with tales, each man speaking rapidly and with passion as though afraid I would never hear of his life otherwise. Those who had told me their tales related them to men who had not heard them before.

I had triggered a flood of words and an orgy of self-examination among the men. They told their stories, listened to others, and reflected on their lives; this was something new for most of them. They began to sit closer to the altar, appearing to forget my presence as they spoke. Many of the tales were variations on what I had heard before, but I recorded them all.

I had gone inside the ship, welcoming the silence. After resting for a bit, I checked my supplies. I had eaten little during my stay. The supplies would last me for some time longer, and the ship could recycle water indefinitely, but I had been outside the city too long. Eilaan would soon send a message, asking why I had not returned; Zoreen would be worrying about me.

I could not bring myself to leave. Wanderer's band sometimes travelled to this shrine; I realized that I was hoping they might find their way here. Surely some man had told them about my appearance; those who had seen one aspect of the Lady and who believed themselves blessed would be curious about this new aspect. I could see Button, now called Hasin by the band; he would not remember me, but I might give my mother word of him. I might hear more from the band of the brief time Birana had spent with them.

Birana had come to this shrine. She haunted me most when I was alone in the ship; I wondered if she had welcomed the death that had freed her. At last I stood up, dropped a new spool into my recorder, and left the ship.

As I stepped out on to the altar, I noticed that some of the men had left but that another band had arrived. After setting down the recorder, I seated myself, still clinging to the wand I had never needed to use.

The men remaining in the shrine knelt, and then a member of the new band stepped forward. He was a beardless young man clothed in a leather vest and leggings; a neckpiece of feathers hung over his chest.

'I would hear your tales,' I said as I pressed the recorder.

'We are honoured, Holy One,' he replied. 'A traveller told us an aspect dwelled here and spoke to men. Although we have not come to this land before, we travelled far to see this holy vision.' He waved an arm at a small group of men dressed as he was. 'I am not our Headman, but those in my band have asked me to tell You our tale. I pray that You will find my words pleasing.'

'You may seat yourself and tell your story to Me.' I waited, expecting to hear another version of stories already recorded.

He sat down near the altar, shaking back his long black hair as he gazed up at me. 'We are blessed by Your holy presence,' he said. 'Our blessings are great, for I did not think we would behold an aspect again in this life.'

I restrained a cry of surprise but could not speak for a moment. 'You have seen an aspect before?'

'I must speak truth in a shrine, and You, Holy Lady, will know the truth of any words I speak. Many seasons ago, I beheld one of Your aspects, yet Her true nature was not apparent to me for She

432

wore the guise of one of our kind. Only Her messenger spoke to me, and then they left our land. Later, She returned to us, and we learned what She was.'

'Go on,' I managed to say.

'The Lady was with Her messenger and a child. This child was not like the young boys who leave Your walls, but one even smaller and more helpless. The child did not eat, but took nourishment from the Lady herself. This child . . . I do not know how to say it, Holy One. The child had no male member but shared the Goddess's nature. We knew then that we had seen one of the holiest of visions. The Lady dwelled in our camp for a time, but although we begged Her and Her messenger to remain with us, She told us that She must return to Her realm.'

'That cannot be so,' a man called out.

'It is so,' the young man answered. 'Let the Holy One strike at me if I lie.' He turned back to me. 'The aspect told us this, that the Lady's magic is great, but that it does not reach to all of Earth. She said that She had dwelled with Her messenger and had come to know his soul, and that the child She carried in Her arms partook of both his spirit and Hers. Then She bid us live in peace with other men and said farewell.'

A man from another band jumped to his feet. 'Blasphemy!' he cried. 'You should die for saying this here!'

'We came here to honour the Lady,' the young man said. 'We saw this vision, and when a traveller told us an aspect had appeared in this shrine, even though it is far from our lands, we hastened here, for we knew that something new had entered the world.' He held out a hand. 'Is it so, Holy One? Can it be that the Lady will forgive us at last?'

'Hold back your words,' a tall bearded man shouted, 'or I shall . . .'

'Silence!' I cried. The angry muttering among the men died down. 'I am here to listen, and it is I who shall decide what is offensive to Me.' I leaned toward the dark-haired young man. 'When did you see this vision?'

'Not long ago, at the beginning of this season.'

The closeness of the air and the shock of hearing this story had made me feel faint. I clutched my wand tightly.

'What does this vision mean, Holy One?' the young man asked. 'Why do You appear? Is the world . . .'

'It is not time for you to know what it means.' I struggled for breath. 'The Lady works in ways unknown to you.' I got to my feet. 'I thank you for your story. I must now seek solitude in My sanctuary.' I went into the ship; the door slid shut behind me.

I collapsed on a seat, knowing the true meaning of this astonishing tale. An exile had managed to survive out here; she had given birth to a child. A man must have taken her against her will, forced himself upon her; somehow, she had lived through the birth. The thought of that made me so ill that I doubled over, afraid I might be sick.

Why then had she spoken to the young man and his band as if she bore them no ill will, when such an experience could only have scarred her and made her hate men all the more? Why had she kept the child alive when no life could be possible for her?

The man who had forced himself upon her must have learned her weakness and used her as he wished. Perhaps he had beaten her into submission, into a poor, frightened creature who had to do his bidding. He would know the truth now, would no longer worship what he had been taught to venerate; he would know that his world had been built on a great deception. The birth of the child would have taught him what his kind had forgotten. I could imagine the hatred and rage he would feel and how he would express it against the woman he had used.

My work had come to this – a story that showed how necessary our ways were. Men could not live with us, knowing what we actually were, without making us their victims. Occasionally, in fanciful conversations with Fari, I had imagined a careful, gradual guiding of men to a more civilized state, perhaps even to the point where, someday, they would have their own cities. Fari thought it possible. The men might be given ways of reproducing themselves, or we could continue to send our boys to them. We could guide their development, even become their friends in time.

It would never happen. We controlled them with our greater knowledge as they had once ruled us with their brute strength. They could never be allowed to become a threat. Eilaan would have her views confirmed.

I thought of something else Fari had said. Perhaps it was time to rid the outside world of those beings still bound to us. We could refuse to call them to our walls, give them no more boys, let them disappear. All of the world would be ours at last.

I stood up and left the ship. The young dark-haired man was gone, along with the rest of his men; I had forgotten to command them to stay, had missed the chance to question them, although perhaps I would not have wanted to hear their answers. Three bands remained.

A stocky, bare-chested man rose. 'Forgive us, Holy One. We swore peace in Your presence, but the tale of that young man has angered us. His band saw this and went from this place. I do not know how a man could speak falsely before You, and yet . . .'

'He did not speak falsely,' I said wearily. 'He saw something and took it to be other than what it was. It is not a lie if he believed it to be true. An evil spirit deceived him with an illusion, but the Lady has power over such spirits, who are sent only to test your faith.' I suddenly wanted to be rid of them. 'The summer will soon draw to an end. You must leave this shrine and return to your lands. I shall not forget you, and the Lady will watch over you.'

Several filed past me, uttering farewells, while others picked up their weapons and packs. As they made their way to the door, one boy turned. 'Will You return to us, Lady?'

'I cannot tell you now. The Lady appears when She chooses to appear and what She will choose must be hidden from you.'

'Farewell. Blessed be the Goddess!'

Others took up the cry: 'Blessed be the Goddess!'

The shrine was empty. I sat on the altar, pondering what I had heard, then stood up, and walked toward the door. I took a breath as the door slid open, then stepped outside. I had not dared to leave the shrine before. A few ducks sat on the shore, resting, their bills tucked against their chests. The sun was beginning to set. I smelled the clean air of the lake.

Just beyond the door, several rocks had been set over a small mound. Yvara had died here; I had nearly forgotten that. Two men with Arvil had buried her; I had learned this from a member of Wanderer's band. I shivered; only death lay outside. I stepped back and let the door close, breathed deeply until my heartbeat slowed, and then walked back to the altar.

I gathered up most of my equipment. I listened to several recordings, looked at images on my small screen; I sorted the recordings and filed them away. The men's images would live on; their voices would continue to repeat their tales.

Few messages had come from the city during much of my stay; I sent brief messages to Fari, Eilaan and Zoreen each week to let them know I was well. Lately, their messages to me had become more frequent and insistent: Why do you wait? Why don't you return? Haven't you heard enough?

There was nothing to hold me to this shrine, and yet I waited. Perhaps I sensed that the tales were not yet at an end.

*

A few days after the bands had left, the ship's sensors told me that someone had entered the shrine. I rose and went out to the altar. My recorder lay at my feet; I knelt and turned it on. Two men, heads down, stood by the door. The shorter one was clothed in a loose shirt and pants and wore a hood over his head, in spite of the heat.

'I have come to dwell among you for a time,' I said automatically as I stood up again. 'I would hear what tales you have to tell.'

'There is one tale you may wish to hear.' The tall man raised his head. 'I know You, Lady. I have seen You when I don the Lady's crown.'

Startled, I gazed at his dark face. 'Wanderer,' I whispered.

He strode to the altar; his companion, still concealed by the hood, followed. 'We have heard of the wonder here,' Wanderer said. 'At first, I thought it was only a wild tale. When it came to me that it was true, I feared to come here for another reason. But I did not think it was You who had come among men.' He gazed steadily up at me, showing no fear.

Before I could speak, his companion suddenly leaped on to the altar. I raised my wand; a hand chopped against my wrist. The wand fell and rolled across the floor. I tried to dart toward the ship and was seized, my arms pinned against my sides.

The hood of Wanderer's companion fell back. I looked into a ghost's blue eyes.

'It can't be,' I gasped.

'Laissa,' Birana hissed. 'It was you who listened to Arvil's story about my death, wasn't it?' Her fingers dug into my arms. 'Is that why you came outside, Laissa? Did you want to be sure I was dead?'

I tried to pull away, but her grip was too strong. 'Let me go!' I glanced at Wanderer, but he made no move to help me.

'Why did it have to be you?' she cried. 'Of all the women in the city, why did it have to be you?'

Wanderer stepped toward her. 'Birana, this One has spoken to our band often. She is not . . .'

'She wanted me dead.' Birana twisted one of my arms. 'Don't think Wanderer will help you. He knows more about what we really are now.' She pulled me down from the altar and pushed me toward a couch. 'You'd better admit what you've done, Laissa. When Arvil sees you, he'll know.'

'Is he . . .'

She shoved me, forcing me to sit. Her face was browner than it had been, her body leaner; her hand gripped the knife at her belt. 'Why are you out here? Why were you sent?'

'To gather stories,' I answered. 'I swear it's true. It's a project of mine, assembling tales and legends of the men. It has nothing to do with you.'

She turned toward the altar and saw the recorder, then pointed. 'Destroy that thing.' Wanderer stepped on to the altar and raised his spear.

'No!' I clutched at Birana's sleeve. 'I'll turn it off if you want, but you mustn't . . .' She shook off my hand. 'Please.'

Wanderer hesitated. Birana frowned, then went to the recorder, leaned over it, and slapped it with her palm. 'Very well. It's off now.' She sat down at the edge of the altar as Wanderer settled next to her.

The way to the ship was blocked; there was no safety outside for me even if I made it to the door. Birana tapped her fingers against her knee. 'You say you came out here to gather stories? What kind of a project is that?'

'It was time to learn more about the outside. I'm a chronicler now. I've questioned Wanderer and his men through the mind-speaker, and Wanderer's stories interested me. I thought I might hear even more if I came outside, I wanted to find stories we hadn't heard before. I sent my proposal to the Council. They weren't very pleased but knew my work might be useful to them, and one of them had other reasons for pleading my case. They gave me permission to come here.'

'You, a chronicler?' Her mouth twisted. 'And what do your old friends think of that?'

'They're not my friends any more. I no longer care what they think.'

'You wanted their approval so badly once.' She leaned forward. 'Why did you do it, Laissa? How did the Council ever come to you to be certain of my death?'

'I had no choice. They used my mother against me.' I went on to tell her of my mother's collapse, the reasons for it, Eilaan's appeal to me. 'It was that,' I finished, 'or having all of that man's band destroyed to be sure you were dead as well. I could change nothing, but I could prevent that. It would have been the final blow to my mother, to know that Button – Hasin – was dead, given her state at the time – she cared for him too much. As it is, she's never been the same.'

'I suppose,' Birana murmured, 'that you also thought it didn't matter what happened to me anyway.'

'I've been tormented by it ever since. All these years, I've thought of the times I might have been of some help to you, when I could have tried to be your friend, when I could have spoken up for you. The opinions of my friends, the approval of others seemed so important then. In the back of my mind, I think I believed that eventually I'd make it up to you, that we'd both change when we were older, that there'd be time – and then you were expelled. I had to put it all behind me, but I couldn't.'

'How moving,' she said bitterly. 'The fact that your life is now in my hands has no doubt provoked this little speech. You are desperate, aren't you?'

'I meant every word.' I forced myself to look directly at her. 'We live so long we think we have time to remedy any hurt. Then you were gone and that chance was lost.' I bowed my head. 'You have the upper hand now, Birana. You can have your revenge against the city through me. I can't fight you out here, and things can't be worse for you no matter what you do to me.'

I waited, wondering what she would do. Despite my words, I was frightened. If she had lived this long outside, she had surely seen other deaths, hardened herself to them.

'Is that true?' she asked. 'You regretted it all and thought of making things up to me?'

'Question me in any way you want. It's true.'

'And if you could do something for me now, would you?'

I lifted my head. 'Yes. But what can I do? I can't take you back to the city. I'd do it if that's what you want, but there would be nothing for you there. They'd expel you again, or find another punishment – perhaps a worse one. Now that you've shown a woman can live outside, the city may have to find other punishments.' I took a deep breath. 'I can do this much. Leave this place. I can destroy that spool before you go – there'll be no record that you were here. I'll say nothing. The city will never know about you.'

Her eyes narrowed. 'And as soon as I step out that door, you'll be inside your ship summoning others.'

'Tie me to this couch, then. By the time I'm able to get free, you can be far away, and I won't want the city to know of my carelessness. I'll have to keep silent after that.' Even as I spoke, I was struggling with myself; I was contemplating a crime against the city, one that would condemn me in the minds of the Council if they ever learned of it.

Birana stared at me for a moment. 'I won't ask that. There's something else you can do, though, and the city, whatever it thinks, won't punish you for it. You can ease your guilt while risking little.' She motioned to Wanderer. 'You may fetch Arvil now.'

He rose and walked towards the door. 'You'd better prepare yourself,' she continued. The door whispered open behind me; I heard the sound of feet and then a small wail.

I turned. Arvil had entered; with him was a young man who had to be Wanderer's son Shadow, but I did not look at him long. A bundle was in Arvil's arms; I saw a small face and tiny fists. He was carrying a child.

'My daughter,' Birana said then. 'Mine, and Arvil's.'

The shock was nearly too much for me. I swayed dizzily on the couch, unable to stand, afraid my legs might give way if I did. Arvil walked toward the altar and handed the child to Birana. She did not recoil from my twin; she smiled briefly at him as she took the child.

The horror of what I was seeing roused me at last. 'What have you done?' I cried. 'What has he done to you?'

'He's done nothing against my will. He's been my protector and friend. He's loved me and I've come to love him as well.'

I could not bear to listen. I stumbled up. Wanderer and Shadow were sitting by the door; Wanderer lifted his spear as I took a step toward him. I turned back toward the altar, helpless. 'What are you saying?'

'He was sent to kill me. He couldn't do it. I showed him how to induce a trance, how to respond over the mindspeaker so that you'd think he had killed me. We were bound together after that, exiles from both his band and the city. We had only each other. He was only my friend at first. Later, he became something more.'

'We shall wait outside,' Wanderer said. I glanced back as he and Shadow rose. 'Do not be too hard with this One, Birana. I hear truth in Her voice, and She has watched over us for many seasons. I think She will help you now.' The two stepped through the door. Wanderer's story, the one he had invented to explain the disappearance of Birana and Arvil, had contained more truth than he knew at the time.

'I love Arvil,' Birana said. 'At first, it was because I saw you in him and thought of what might have been. You should have loved me, Laissa. I would have loved you, I longed for you.' Arvil's mouth tightened as she spoke. 'Even now, I can still long for you, but it's because I see Arvil in you.'

I sank down on to the couch, stricken with guilt once more.

'Why do you sit there?' she asked. 'Come and look at my daughter, Nallei.'

I got up and approached her; she thrust the child into my arms. The girl had soft blond hair and Birana's blue eyes. I guessed that she was seven months old, perhaps more; her face seemed a bit pinched, as if she lacked for food. 'How can she live out here?' I murmured.

'She can't.'

'What will you do?'

'I came here to ask you to take her into the city.'

'But how . . .'

'What can they do? Refuse to take an innocent little girl? She's committed no crime. Even the Council wouldn't condemn a baby to exile and death.'

The child stirred in my arms and began to cry. Birana took her from me, adjusted the baby's soft leather diaper and coat, then lifted her shirt as she held Nallei to her breast. 'I travelled far to bring her here,' Birana said. 'I knew there was a chance for her in the city. I was going to go to a shrine, then summon someone outside through the mindspeaker. We found our way to Arvil's old camp. I knew he wouldn't be harmed by the men if I was with him. By then, the band had learned an aspect was here in this shrine. I wanted to come here right away, but too many bands had been seen here. We had to make camp near this shrine and wait, hoping we could speak to the woman here alone. I didn't want the men to come with me, but Arvil wouldn't leave me, and Shadow and Wanderer were willing to face any danger there might be. The others agreed to wait.'

'You knew that the weapons of the city could have been brought against you,' I said.

'I knew it. The men knew it. It's why I wanted to come alone. I didn't care what happened to me as long as Nallei was safe. You can understand that, can't you?' She lifted the baby to her shoulder and rubbed her back. 'Even my life out here hasn't robbed me of everything. I know my obligations to my child. I wonder how many in the city would have done as much for a daughter. Laissa, will you take her back with you?'

I looked from her to Arvil. The child could not be blamed for what they had done. I would have to take her back, could not have Nallei on my conscience; I bore too much of a burden already. Even Eilaan could not stand against me.

'If I take her back,' I said, 'I'll have to tell them how I found her. They'll have to know about you.'

'I can wait here while you send a message. Just give Arvil and the others enough time to get safely away. You can say I came alone. I know I have to die here. You'll have done your duty, and I won't ask for more from you.'

No!' Arvil cried out; he put his arm around Birana's shoulders protectively. 'If you wait, I must wait with you. I won't leave you now.'

'You know what that would mean,' I said. He nodded. 'And you'd do it? You care that much for her? You'd die here with her?'

'How can you doubt it?'

I sat down beside him; my own eyes gazed out at me from his face. 'Do you know what I am?'

He frowned, apparently puzzled.

'There is a bond between us of a kind,' I continued. 'You are my brother, Arvil, and my twin. We were together inside our mother's womb before she bore us, the same blood flowed through our veins. We both came from the same woman's body and the same man's sperm. It means that there is a kind of bond between me and this child as well. Can you understand that?'

'I see it.'

'I'll take the girl with me, do what I can for her. She'll have a home.' I stood up and held out my arms. 'Let me take her into the ship. I have food I can give her – milk, soft fruit.' Birana drew back. 'I won't call to anyone now, I just want to see if she's well.'

'I'll come with you.'

She followed me into the ship while Arvil waited on the altar. As the door closed, she sat down in the front of the ship. I took out my small medical kit, removed the scanner, and passed the cylinder over Nallei's body. 'When was she born?' I asked.

'In winter.'

I peered at the scanner's small gauge. 'She's underweight, but she seems strong enough. I'm not a physician, though. She'll have to be thoroughly scanned when I take her back, but the physician can tend to any problem.'

I fed her soft cereal and a little fruit; Nallei squirmed, swallowed a little, then began to cry. I rocked her, soothing her before handing her back to her mother. 'Do the men who came here with you understand how she . . . how you . . .'

'Wanderer and Shadow understand,' she said. 'Wise Soul comprehends a little less. The others seem to see Nallei as a kind of mystery or miracle.'

'You've endangered them with your actions.'

'They're not the only ones who've seen her. There are others, bands who sheltered us during our journey here. What is the city going to do – destroy them all? You won't ever know which bands they are. Leave them alone, and what they know will only become another legend other men won't believe.'

'Some stories can be powerful in time,' I said.

'Is that why you came out here, Laissa? Do you think the stories you carry back will change anything?'

'I don't know. I'm not sure I want change.'

'Maybe you've learned enough to strengthen the power of the cities over men.'

'Perhaps. Maybe I'm preserving a record of beings who will soon be allowed to die out. I can't tell what will come of this work. Some will conclude that those outside are hopeless, that there is no way they could ever be guided to peaceful and civilized ways.'

'Would you say that about Arvil?' she asked. 'Would you believe that of Wanderer and Shadow? They knew they were taking a risk by coming here, but they were willing to share it with us. Wanderer told me that he thinks my child may soften the hearts of women toward men eventually. He wants you to know that some of his kind can hope for more.'

'We're alone now,' I said. 'You can be honest with me. Did Arvil force himself upon you? Has he so abused you by now that you're afraid . . .'

'You still don't see. Can't you see the love in him, can't you hear it in my words? He gave me back my life, what's left of it, and I'm his life now.'

'You say that, but if the city would take you back, would you go?'

She closed her eyes for a moment. 'Yes. It would pain Arvil, but he'd want me there if I could live. Do you think that means I don't care for him? I'd never forget him. I'd want the city to know what he's been to me.'

I leaned toward her. 'I came out here to gather stories. I should listen to yours and his.'

'And what would that accomplish?'

'Perhaps little, but at least your daughter could hear it when she's older, know the truth about you. There will be many who will try to tell her other stories.' I rose. 'I'm willing to listen, record your words.'

'You'll do well for yourself, Laissa. You'll have a story no chronicler has ever told and can make sure I'm finally dead. Some day, they may put you on the Council for it.'

'I care nothing about that.'

She stood up. 'You may find portions of this story hard to bear .. you'd better steel yourself. You'll have my last words. I supopose it must be told before you . . .'

She turned and left the ship; I followed her out. Arvil was by the door, speaking to Wanderer and Shadow; he looked back. 'Will you call to your enclave now?' he asked. 'Shall I tell my friends to leave this place?'

I shook my head. 'They can wait outside. I want to hear your story first, yours and Birana's, as much of it as you're willing to tell. Please let me hear it. I must have something to tell the child later.'

Wanderer put a hand on Arvil's shoulder, murmured to him, then backed away as the door closed. 'They will wait and watch the horses,' Arvil said. 'It is a long story, Lady – it may take some time to tell.'

'I'll listen.' I sat down by the recorder.

Arvil spoke first, and when his voice grew strained, Birana continued their tale. Their story was not easy to hear, and several times I asked them to be silent so that I could regain my composure. Much of the story – the brutality they had endured, the violence they had seen – made me ill; I wanted to retreat inside the wall, think no more of the outside, imagine that such a world did not exist. Their shameless talk of their longings and how they had fulfilled each other's needs repelled me, but I forced myself to listen.

I pitied Birana and sorrowed with her; I had expected that. Yet she had won some joy for herself throughout her suffering; she had reached out to Arvil in a way I thought impossible, while Arvil had sacrificed much to love her.

They spoke almost without pause, and as they neared the end of their tale, I began to question them, curious about gaps in the narrative. They answered willingly about their journey east and their years by the great lake but said less about how they returned to Arvil's old camp, as if wanting to protect those who had helped them. I did not press for more answers.

I shut off the recorder and rubbed at my eyes. Nallei had fallen asleep in Arvil's arms hours before; I wondered if it was already morning outside.

. 'I can imagine what you think,' Birana said, 'how you feel about what I've done.'

'I don't know what I think.'

'I want my daughter to know what Arvil was to me. She mustn't think that an act of force brought her into the world, or feel hatred and contempt for her father. I want her to know love gave her life.'

'I'll tell her,' I said, 'although it might be easier for her if she believed otherwise. The city would understand an act of force and have more pity for her.'

'She must know of Birana,' Arvil said. 'If she learns of her mother's courage, perhaps her own will grow.'

Nallei stirred and began to cry. I went into the ship, picked up a shirt, and tore it into strips. 'This is for you,' I said as I came back out and handed the cloth to Birana. 'She needs to be changed, I think. If you like, you can clean her inside the ship.'

She took the child from Arvil and left us alone. 'Are you going to summon your kind now?' he asked.

'I must rest before I do anything. I'm sure you're tired also.'

'There will be rest for me soon enough, for ever.'

'You needn't stay. Leave with your friends. I can say that you threatened me, that you left and I couldn't stop you.'

'Do you think I could leave her now?'

I stood up, clutching the recorder. 'I don't suppose you could.' I shook my head. 'You're just one man, Arvil, a man who was somehow able to become something better, and you won't change a thing. The rest of your kind will always be as they are now.'

'Your kind has helped to make us this way. You don't want us to be anything else.' He gazed at me solemnly. 'If you saw into our souls, you would have to look into your own.'

I retreated into the ship; Birana picked up the child as I entered. 'I must sleep,' I said.

'Are you going to . . .'

'I have to sleep.' I threw myself into a seat and closed my eyes.

I was alone when I awoke. I stumbled from the ship. Arvil lay on a couch as Birana nursed Nallei; I had expected them to flee, to leave Nallei on the altar for me, to take this decision out of my hands.

Wanderer and Shadow entered the shrine. 'It will be dark before long,' Shadow said, 'and the men will be wondering what has happened here.'

Arvil sat up. 'Go!' Birana cried.

'Wait.' I held up a hand, then swayed, feeling an abyss open up beneath me, afraid I would fall. 'I'll take this child to the city, but I will not see the city act against you. You can all leave this shrine together. I'll wait until you're safely away before I send any message. You've hidden this long – you can find another hiding place.'

Birana set Nallei next to Arvil. 'Laissa, you risk too much.'

'I'll take the risk. I can atone for having failed you before, when it would have cost me little. I can say that you overcame me, that by the time I could act, you were gone. I'll be believed.'

'You may be punished.'

'I won't be punished.' I could say that to her, but did not believe it myself. The Council had ways of getting the truth from me.

I was throwing aside everything I had been taught for the sake of a man, a woman, and a child. I was setting myself against the city, and for what? So that Birana and Arvil could have a few more years of a very hard life, years of pain and struggle during which they would have to live in fear of both the cities and men? Death might be more merciful.

'Why are you doing this?' Birana said.

'So that I don't have to tell your daughter some day that I was responsible for your death. So that I don't have to live with your ghosts.'

Arvil got to his feet. 'Is this so? Or do you only want us to die farther from this place?'

'You have to trust me now. Go as far from this region as you can – I don't want to know where. If your band scatters, that will make it more difficult for the cities to find you.' I sighed. 'But you know more of this world than I.'

Arvil took Birana's hand; she rested her head against his arm. 'You would do this for us? she said.

'Yes, but you may not thank me for it later. You may wish you had taken the chance for a quick death.'

Birana picked up her daughter; I looked away as she wept.

I went outside with them. Birana stood over the grave of her mother in silence as the men fetched their horses. She clung to the child in her arms as if suddenly afraid to give her up.

I had collected supplies from my ship, wrapping them in one of my shirts; I handed them to her. 'There's food for you here,' I said. 'You won't have to search for more.' I took the child from her as she accepted the supplies. 'There are some medical supplies, too – antiseptics and other things. The small scanner's in there as well – I won't need it now.'

Her eyes widened. 'But how will you explain . . .'

'I'll find a way.' I swallowed. 'I'm sure you understand how useful the scanner will be,' I said in a lower voice. 'You'll be able to chart your cycle accurately with it; you'll have something more reliable than those berries you were given. You won't have to fear Arvil's attentions at least.'

'Laissa . . .'

'I've aided an exile. Giving you help to pursue your perverted practices safely is a small thing next to that.'

Tears welled in her eyes. She touched Nallei's blond head briefly, then embraced me.

'Farewell,' I whispered. 'I can give you a few days, no more. My friends will be expecting a message by then.'

Birana touched my cheek. 'I wish . . .'

'I know. I should have . . . think of me sometimes.' I could say no more. 'Go.'

Shadow led a white horse to her; she mounted and Arvil climbed up behind her. 'Farewell,' Arvil said.

The sun was setting as they rode away from the lake. I stood near the ashes of their fire, wondering where they would go.

'I have committed a crime for your mother,' I murmured to Nallei. 'Your father put aside all that he believed for her, and now I've done the same. I wonder what you will become.'

I waited inside the ship for five days, knowing that my crime grew more serious with every hour that passed. I listened to Birana's story again before filing it with my other spools. Eilaan might want to destroy the recording; I could not let that happen.

I wrote out my message to Fari before I sat down in front of the ship's small screen, wanting to be sure she grasped its importance. My mentor was not in her room; I read the message and then called Zoreen.

'Listen to me,' I said before she could speak. 'I've finished my work, I'm coming back. Fari has a message from me, and I've asked her to speak to Bren. I'm hoping that Bren will take my recordings to the Council – I don't want Eilaan to hear them first.'

'Laissa, what . . .'

I motioned at the small face on the screen. 'I'm bringing back something else.' I held Nallei to the screen; Zoreen gasped. 'This little girl was born outside months ago. I'm bringing her into the city.'

'But how . . .'

'Birana bore her.'

She gasped.

'Zoreen, you must tell as many women as you can, anyone you can find, about this child and the fact that I'm returning with important records. The Council is not going to destroy them and then pretend they never existed. The historians will want them preserved and will fight for that.' I paused. 'This may mean some trouble for you, but I'll bear most of the blame.'

'I can do that much for you,' Zoreen replied. 'But that child . . .'

'My twin Arvil is her father. The city can't turn away an innocent child, especially if it's widely known that I'm bringing her back. The Mothers of the City will pity her, and those we serve are sentimental. I'll return tomorrow.' I shut off the screen before she could say more.

My ship landed on the wall. The wind whipped my hair as I climbed out of the ship with Nallei in my arms. As I had expected, several women had come there to greet me. Bren stood with Fari and two other historians; Zoreen was next to two patrolwomen. Eilaan was not with them, although she must have known I would be returning.

All of the women wore masks over their mouths and noses. As Zoreen started toward me, I saw that my mother was behind her; she reached for Zoreen's arm, holding her back.

'They'll have to be scanned,' Mother said then. 'I don't expect there's much wrong, but we must be careful.' Her voice was firm, as though some of her old spirit had returned to her.

I glanced at Fari. 'My recordings are in the ship,' I said. 'I imagine the Council will want to hear and view them right away. You'll understand how important they are after you've heard them all. It may take some time – I made many. The most important ones are on top of the case – you should listen to them first.'

Fari nodded, then went to the ship. 'I didn't expect to see you here,' I said to Mother.

'Zoreen gave me your message. She said the child was . . . that your twin is the father. How did he . . .'

'It isn't what you think. He didn't force himself on her.'

A patrolwoman nudged her. 'They must be scanned.'

Mother lifted her head. 'Come with me.'

Zoreen remained with the historians and Bren as Mother and I were led inside the wall. The patrolwoman guided us to a room in the area where men were kept, then left us alone with Nallei.

I sat down on one of the beds and laid the child beside me. 'How long will this take?' I asked.

'You'll have to sleep here tonight. I don't expect we'll find anything wrong with you, so you may be able to leave in a day or two. The girl may be here longer.' Her voice was muffled by her mask. 'She not only has to be scanned, but we'll have to map her genes as well.' She shuddered. 'I can hardly bear to think of how she must have been born. The poor child.'

'Birana risked a lot to see that she was brought here,' I said. 'She and Arvil both wanted me to take her.'

'Laissa, how . . .'

I looked up at the screen on the wall, wondering if anyone was listening to us. 'I'll tell you the story another time. All you have to know is that Nallei was born of love, strange as that may seem. I think Arvil cares almost as much for her as Birana does.'

'You saw them both in that shrine?'

I nodded.

'And they still live?'

'Yes. I have much to tell you, Mother, but not here.'

'Perhaps it's better if I don't know.' She went to the screen to summon another physician.

Nallei was taken to another room; Mother had promised to watch out for her. No messages came for me; after a day, I went to the screen and tried to send one to Zoreen. Letters flashed on the screen; no messages would go out. I tried the door; it remained closed.

I was a prisoner. From time to time, a physician I did not know came to the room, examined me, and left without speaking. I noticed that she wore no mask and worried about why I was still being detained.

The Council was keeping me in that room, perhaps debating over what to do with me. Outside, in my ship, I had supposed that the value of the recordings I had brought back might mitigate any punishment. Now I knew I was lost. I spent days staring at the door, waiting for it to open. I would be led to the Council, would plead my case, would be isolated again and perhaps expelled.

I lost track of time. I slept when I was tired, paced the room when I was awake. Patrolwomen brought me food; I ate little. I was lying on my bed, wondering when the torment of waiting would be over, when the door opened. I looked up, expecting to see the physician or a patrolwoman.

Eilaan entered and sat down on the bed next to mine. 'We've gone through your recordings,' she said. 'I found them repulsive. I'd destroy them, but of course the historians won't have that, and several Council members are on their side. They're not about to listen to what I think now – I won't be on the Council much longer.'

'That's some consolation,' I said as I sat up. 'What's happened to Nallei?'

'She's still inside the wall. Dorlei's looking after her. That wretched child is safe enough.' Her eyes narrowed. 'You spoke to an exiled woman. You didn't send a message to us. Certain supplies are missing from your ship.'

'Birana took what she wanted. She had men with her. I could do nothing.'

'Do you expect the Council to believe that? Do you think I believe it? You might have called for help as soon as they were gone, but instead all you did was send messages to your mentor and friend to make certain your disgusting recordings would be saved.'

'There was nothing I could do.'

'Don't add lies to your crimes.'

'I suppose that you're angry that I brought the child back,' I said. 'You would probably have preferred to see her die with her mother and father.'

'Don't speak of those wretches to me. The child will suffer enough when she learns of how she was born. You may have shown her a little mercy.'

'She's alive, at least. Isn't that our reason for everything, Eilaan – life?' I was silent for a moment. 'Are you going to send out ships to search for Birana?'

'We've already done so. They've found nothing. What are we to do – have all the cities search the continent for one woman? Wipe out every band that might have seen her? Bren is now saying that it's better to let Birana go, that it's likely she'll flee to abandoned land far from men, that in time she'll become only part of another story the men tell, and that this can't affect us. She wants mercy, and the Council is heeding her words. How clever you were to make those recordings, Laissa. Some on the Council were so moved by those images of Birana with her child, by her tale of woe. You made it possible for that wretched woman to plead for herself directly.'

'We might learn much from her story,' I said.

'We've learned quite enough. Do you think what has passed

between her and that man means anything? You heard the rest of her story; you know what happened to other women who lived among men. No life is possible with men for long – even Birana will learn that. The man with her will revert to what he is eventually and take advantage of her weakness.'

'You're wrong,' I said. 'I saw what he was.'

'Always we've exiled those who had committed grave crimes. Now some wonder if we can resort to that punishment again, for if Birana could survive, so could others. But others are saying that such a life outside may be punishment enough, that many would fear expulsion all the more if they heard Birana's story.' Eilaan closed her eyes. 'I've loved this city; I've worked for it all my life. You think of me as heartless – you can't look into my mind and see my struggle. I've had my moments of doubt but put them aside for the city's sake. Now I see the beginning of the end of all we have tried to do.'

'Do you think we're so weak?'

'This is how it begins,' she answered, 'with one misplaced act of mercy, with setting one life above one's duty. It will lead to other such acts. More wrongdoers may be expelled and may survive, and some will want to show them mercy as well. Our lives – very slowly, perhaps – will change. We won't have to worry about the men discovering our limitations. We'll weaken ourselves.'

'Do you think mercy shows weakness? Maybe if we'd trusted in our own strength more, we could have shown more mercy in the past. We think we restored peace to Earth. We only built places to hide.'

Eilaan gazed at me steadily, then slumped forward. 'I can do nothing now. The Council has questioned my competence. I'll have no voice.'

'What will happen to my recordings?' I asked.

'The historians will have them. They're used to such sordid material. No one else will be interested. Historians have so many documents others scorn – that story may be forgotten in time, even by them.'

I took a breath. 'And what will happen to me? Am I to be expelled?'

Eilaan brushed back a lock of grey hair. 'Oh, no. You won't be expelled, Laissa. You'll be allowed to plead for yourself before the Council and offer what explanation you can for your actions, but I already know what your sentence will be. I'll have the satisfaction of telling it to you now.'

I waited.

'You'll never be a Mother of the City. You'll leave the towers and live among those we serve, and even they will probably have little to do with you. You'll do whatever work is found for you.'

'I can accept that. I'll have a daughter some day. My daughter or hers will join the Mothers of the City again.'

She shook her head. 'There will be no children for you. That's the rest of your punishment. You'll never go to the wall; you'll never have a child. You'll vanish and leave no direct descendants.'

'No,' I whispered. My throat constricted; I clung to the side of the bed, afraid I might slip to the floor.

Eilaan rose. 'You'll be allowed to raise the child Nallei. You brought her here, after all. You can think of the daughters you'll never have when you raise her. She can think of the life she might have had in the towers if you had done your duty.' She walked toward the door. 'The Council will summon you soon. Don't expect anything from them. You might have been exiled. Bren argued against that, but even she knows that an example must be made.'

I endured my day before the Council in a trance, almost unable to focus on their words. I answered their questions passively, offering no arguments, refusing to fight for myself. The sentence was passed, as Eilaan had predicted.

A house was found for me at the northern end of the city, a structure of stone and glass at the end of a path. To the north lay the wall; to the south, the distant spires of the towers reminded me of what I had lost. A patrolwoman brought Nallei to me, put her in my arms, and took me to my new home. My personal belongings had already been moved, but my books and papers were not among them.

As I cared for Nallei or walked along the path near my house, I thought of the times I had sought solitude. My neighbours spoke to me only when necessary and did not urge me to trade with them for their handmade items. Those with small daughters did not bring them to the house. My work, what little there was of it, consisted of monitoring the cyberminds managing that part of the city and noting where a malfunction might occur; it was work I could do inside the house by my screen.

The women living near me did not seem aware of exactly what I had done. I had gone outside, I had spoken to men, but they barely understood what a man was, shielded as they were from the deliberations of those who lived in the towers. I had aided an exiled woman, had brought her child into the city; to them, Nallei might as well have been the offspring of a woman and a fabled beast. They whispered among themselves, fell silent when I passed, then murmured again, not seeming to care if I heard. All they had to know was that I was disgraced, deprived of the right and duty to bear children – that I was as removed from the life of the city as if I had been expelled.

I might have given in to despair, but Nallei depended on me. At first, I tended her automatically, making sure that she was fed, cleaned, sung to, and given toys; but as I grew accustomed to her presence, I warmed to her. I saw Birana in her eyes, Arvil in her face. She was a child of my twin and the only child I would ever have. Perhaps giving her to me had not been part of my punishment, but a consolation for what I had lost.

I was sitting in front of my door, watching Nallei crawl in the grass, when I saw Zoreen walking along the path toward me. She stopped in front of me and folded her arms. 'You've been here almost two months,' she said. 'I haven't heard a word from you. Is that any way to treat me?'

'I didn't want to cause you any more trouble.' I moved closer to Nallei as Zoreen sat down. 'You probably shouldn't have come here. You can always leave a message on my screen.'

'I don't want to leave you messages.' She glanced behind me at the house. 'Seems you have room enough for a friend or two to live here.'

'I have no friends.'

'I came to ask if I could live here.'

I gaped at her, surprised. 'But that's impossible.'

'You have to live here,' she said, 'but the Council never said that others couldn't live here with you.'

'They didn't have to say it. Zoreen, your place is in the city's centre. You don't have to make some gesture to me out of pity.'

She took my hand. 'It isn't pity. Can't you see that?'

'But you . . .'

'I'm not highly thought of as it is. I'd rather live here than alone in my rooms. I can do my work here as easily as anywhere else. I'll be planning to have a child before long, and I have a feeling Nallei may need a friend. I don't want to live without you, Laissa.'

I looked away.

'I listened to your recordings,' she said, 'with Fari and Bren, before Bren took them to the Council. I think I know why you acted as you did. I think you came to love Birana, in a way. I was jealous at first, but she's gone and I'm here, and I won't do less for you than you did for her. Tell me I can stay.'

'I might have loved her. It's past now.' I leaned against her, feeling a loose lock of her brown hair under my cheek. 'I want you to stay.'

'Then I'll move my things. I suppose I'll have to be neater. I wouldn't want Nallei getting into my books and papers.' Nallei crawled toward us and settled next to Zoreen. 'I don't suppose you know this, but the ships haven't found a trace of Birana. The Council will keep looking, but I don't think they're trying too hard. Maybe she's found a hiding place by now.'

'She may be dead,' I whispered.

'That settlement she spoke of, the one where those poor women live with men – they haven't done anything about that, either. Those women couldn't adapt to our life, most likely, and the settlement won't survive anyway. Fari's put your recordings into the system. Most of the historians have looked at them and listened to them by now, and we've had messages from cities that hardly ever speak to us asking for them. You did some important work, you see. The historians now know more about the outside than we've known for some time.'

'They're the only ones who will care, I said. 'In time, that tale will be no more than a curious sidelight even to them. The cities will go on as they have. You've spent some time among those we serve – walk down this road and listen to their talk. They don't want to think about what makes their peaceful lives possible. If you offered them a chance to have a voice in any change, most of them would refuse it and tell us to leave things as they are. How can I blame them? They live without having to struggle. To tell them that a life without any struggle and pain leads only to weakness and decline would seem an abstraction to them – they'd look at the cheerful, calm faces of their daughters and wonder what I was talking about.' I sighed. 'Anyway, that isn't my concern. I have other tasks.'

'You sound much like one of those we serve,' she said softly.

'I am one of them now.'

Within a few weeks, Zoreen's room was filled with the disorder of her books and documents. She discussed her work with others over the screen or went to see them in their rooms. I never asked her about what she was doing; after a few tentative overtures, she refrained from discussing her work with me. I expected her to tire of me, to find an excuse to leave me before long; I saw worry and disappointment in her green eyes whenever she looked at me. Yet she stayed on, as if hoping I might become what I once had been – a companion to whom she could speak freely, a lover who knew her thoughts.

My mother began to leave messages, but I did not seek her out. I had disgraced her, had made her own position more precarious; she would only want to weep over me or utter angry accusations. She might expect me to wallow with her in her own guilt as she talked of how she had failed me. I refused to answer her; speaking to her now would accomplish nothing.

I was unprepared for her visit to my house. Her gaze was steady; she did not look like a tormented woman. She embraced me without speaking, holding me as she had when I was a child.

I ushered her into my front room. Zoreen looked up from her book. 'Where is Nallei?' Mother asked.

'She's asleep.'

'Don't disturb her, then. I'll see her another time.'

'You shouldn't have come,' I said. 'It'd be better for you to forget me.'

'A woman doesn't forget her daughter.' She sat down on the couch next to Zoreen. 'I came here because your mentor – your former mentor, Fari – asked me to bring you this.' She reached inside the pocket of her blue tunic, took out two spools, and handed them to me. 'She would have brought them herself, but – I suppose she knew I'd want to see you.'

'What are they?' I asked as I sat in the chair nearest to her.

'Copies of recordings you made outside. The story Birana and Arvil told to you.'

'You shouldn't have brought them,' I said harshly. 'That work is over now. My papers were taken from me.'

'Perhaps Zoreen can keep the recordings. Nallei might want them some day.'

'What good can they do here? They'll only remind her that it would have been better if she'd never been born.' I looked down at the spools. 'Why did Fari want me to have them?'

'I'm not sure,' Mother said.

'Maybe she thinks I need a reminder of my crime.'

'Oh, no. I'm sure she didn't think that.' She put her hand on the arm of my chair. 'I listened to them. I hadn't known the whole story before. It was a hard thing to hear, and I'm sure most wouldn't want to listen to it, but – Arvil is my son, after all. That meant little to me once. Now I find myself remembering what he was as a child, and I wish I had loved him more.'

'You loved Button too much.' I sat back in my chair. 'In a way, that's what brought me here, I suppose. That's how it all started.'

'I know that,' Mother said softly.

'Thank you for bringing the recordings, but they're useless to me.'

Zoreen set down the pages of her book. 'You're a chronicler, Laissa,' she said. 'There's a story on those spools the cities have never heard.'

'I'm not a chronicler any more.'

'Do you need to have the Council call you one to be one?' she asked. 'Must an adviser tell you that's what you are?'

'No one wants to hear that story.'

'You mean that they don't want to view those recordings. What would they see and hear? An exiled woman talking about a world we can barely understand and a man who would probably terrify most of them. I suppose only historians and a few others would have the stomach for it. But you could write a chronicle. You could make that world live for others, Laissa. You can help them understand it. You can find a way to make others want to read that story, and maybe a few can find some compassion for those people in it.'

I was silent.

'I think that may be why Fari wanted you to have those spools.' Zoreen continued, 'though she'd be too cautious to say so herself. You have your work if you want it.'

Mother rose. 'I'll visit my granddaughter another time.' She stroked my hair. 'Think about what your friend's said. I nearly lost the will to live once myself – I don't want to see that happen to you. Let Nallei believe some day that there's some purpose to her life and in the lives of those that gave her to us.'

I did not want to set down this chronicle. Perhaps I would not have begun to write it except for Nallei; in her, I seemed to see Birana and Arvil pleading for their story to be told.

Some will read these words and think that I have set myself against our cities. I do not want to destroy what we have built. We saved Earth and came to know our true power. Our daughters grow up unscarred by the wounds that marked the lives of women in ancient times; we must never go back to what once existed. Yet we have made this life for ourselves at the cost of the lives of those outside. To be free, we have enslaved them.

Those outside are our brothers. I do not mean that in the sense in which we usually use that term, which means only a male born of one's own mother and no more, but in the way it was once used. They are our fathers and our sons. There is something of us in them and something of them in us.

We were forced to choose this pattern once because our survival was at stake. I believe it may be at stake once more. We may stagnate, as life does when it holds to a pattern that is no longer needed, which can keep it from growing and becoming something more. It may be time for us and for those outside to begin to reshape ourselves and become another kind of being.

During the time it has taken me to write this chronicle, I have heard rumours circulating in the city of men who have gone to shrines and prayed for the Lady to dwell among them once more. I have heard of bands trying to preserve a fragile peace with others, who speak of the woman who listened to their tales in a shrine. There are more stories of the woman and the tiny girl-child who once revealed themselves to men. Near a shrine in the east, a crude carving in wood shows a man and a woman with a child in their arms; a ship's pilot has seen men worshipping there. And there is Nallei, who lives because a woman and a man somehow found love for each other.

We are being given a chance to reach out to our other selves. What we do will show what we are and determine what we shall become.

There is no word of Birana's fate or of Arvil's, no sign that they live, no rumour that they have been seen outside. Yet I cannot think of them as dead. They live on in my mind, freed by their love from her world and his. I imagine them on a distant shore near a refuge they have built for themselves dreaming of the oceans we might sail again and the stars we might seek. Perhaps we will join them on that shore at last.

Vernor Vinge
The Peace War £2.95

Paul Hoehler, mathematician of genius, had devised spherical force fields that allowed nothing – people, objects, light, air, radiation – in or out.

The ultimate defence initiative and supreme survival technology, it offered total power and the opportunity was not lost on Livermore Electronics Laboratories. Suddenly anyone in the vicinity of a government compound or a defence installation was 'bobbled', locked into a force field and lost to sight forever.

The new Peace Authority had global power in a world where war was obsolete. But outside the impregnable 'bobbles', mysterious plagues began their epic devastation.

And outside the 'bobbles', Hoehler, the man who had created the technology for total power, had become The Peace Authority's most feared enemy, the holder of the long-lost key of hope for a world dominated by soul-numbing repression . . .

Marooned in Real Time £2.95

The Extinction happened at some point in the 23rd century. Beyond that point, all that remained of humankind survived locked in timeless limbo inside spherical force fields known as 'bobbles'.

The rebuilding of civilization and the rescue of survivors fell to the 'high-techs', themselves survivors of the technologically advanced decades just before The Extinction.

When they reached the 'bobble' where the last members of The Peace Authority lived on in stasis, one of the 'high-techs' was murdered, cruelly abandoned in real time.

Wil Brierson, the last detective in the world, was called in to handle the case. Seeking the murderer through a complex web of mysteries, he stumbled on a plan for a new – and final – Extinction . . .

Susan Shwartz
Byzantium's Crown £2.95

After the death of his father it is Imperial Prince Marric who should rule in Byzantium with his sister Alexa. But in Marric's absence, his stepmother Irene has seized power.

Summoned secretly by Alexa, Marric returns to fight for their crown. Instead he ends up fighting for his life and soul. Captured by Irene, believing Alexa dead, Marric is tempted by the Consort's magic powers, then sold into slavery.

As the Empire is devoured from within by evil and attacked from without by its former allies, Marric learns to endure slavery and, through the love of the seeress Stephana, to come to terms with his destiny. He also learns that for the first time in centuries, the Empire needs a ruler who can control more than mortal powers . . .

The Woman of Flowers £2.95

The sorceress Irene has won the Empire through her powers of necromancy. The princess Alexa escapes her serpent clutches, travelling north under the protection of Audun, called Bearmaster, and his phalanx of white bear warriors.

Across wild waters, beset by the shape-changing battle hordes of Jomsburg's Reiver Jarl, they come to the northern fastness of the Aescir. There Alexa struggles to bring her fiery magic to Audun's aid, but as long as she remains with his people, the black bears of Jomsburg and the flame-tinged falcon of the sorceress will lay merciless siege to the Aescir.

So it is that Alexa journeys on to the Misty Isles of the Celtoi, where love seeks her out in the shadow of the standing stones. But Marric is coming. The prince who became a slave who became a warlord is destined to summon the woman of flowers back to far Byzantium . . .

Julian May
The Many-Coloured Land £2.99

Book One in the Saga of the Exiles

The year 2034 was when a French physicist discovered a one-way
fixed-focus timewarp into the Rhone valley of six million years ago. By
the start of the 22nd century, there are those who seek to escape a
world of technological perfection – the misfits and mavericks of the
future, who pass through the doors of time and enter a battleground of
two warring races from a distant planet.

'Grips the reader and doesn't let go' VONDA McINTYRE.

The Golden Torc £2.99

Book Two in the Saga of the Exiles

Exiled beyond the time-portal, six million years in the past the misfits of
the 22nd century become enmeshed in the age-old war between two
alien races. In this strange world, each year brings the ritual Grand
Combat between the tribal Firvulag and the decadent city-dwelling
Tanu, possessors of the mind-armouring necklet, the golden torc.

'Altogether enchanting and engrossing . . . I was captivated by its
glamorous, sinister movement through the misty forests of Earth's true
past' FRITZ LEIBER

Julian May
The Non-Born King £2.95

Book Three in the Saga of the Exiles

The dominion of the Tanu has been broken, and in the aftermath of
cataclysm Aiken Drum seizes his hour to grasp control of the Pliocene
world. Some, human and Tanu, rally to him – and others fear and hate
him. The Grand Master, Elizabeth, the mad Felice, the goblin hordes of
the Firvulag – all are thrust into a violent and stormy struggle for
irresistible power.

The Adversary £2.95

Aiken Drum is king of the Many-Coloured Land . . . the last chapter in
the saga of the Exiles has begun. The Firvulag are rising, and the
children of the metapsychic rebels are racing to reopen the time-gate to
the Galactic Milieu. Marc Remillard, defeated leader of the rebellion
takes up his destined role in the power play, determined to keep the
gate sealed and to create the new race of Mental Man. Which side will
he aid when Tanu meet Firvulag in the last great contest of the exile
world?

Vonda N. McIntyre
The Exile Waiting £2.95

The time is the distant future and Earth has been rendered uninhabitable by terrible storms during which its only city, Center, constructed around a natural cave system, is sealed from the outside.

Mischa, a young thief whose capabilities are enhanced by hereditary mutation, is trying to escape with her drug-addicted brother from the dominance of her uncle. So when a starship arrives, commanded by the twin alien pseudosibs, Subone and Subtwo, Mischa seizes her chance.

All goes well until Subone, in a moment of cruelty, lures Mischa's brother into a fight and kills him. Mischa exacts her revenge, but has to flee the wrath of the aliens and take refuge back in the deep caves underneath the city . . .

'A beautifully realized vision of the future Earth' IRISH TIMES

Dreamsnake £2.50

In a world devastated by nuclear holocaust, Snake is a healer. One of an elite band dedicated to caring for sick humanity, she goes wherever her skills are needed.

With her she takes the three deadly reptiles through which her cures are accomplished: a cobra, a rattlesnake, and the dreamsnake, a creature whose hallucinogenic venom brings not healing but an easeful death for the terminally ill.

Rare and valuable is this dreamsnake. When Grass is wantonly slain, Snake must journey across perilous landscapes to find another to take its place . . .

'A very beautiful work indeed . . . richly and beautifully imagined, very satisfying' THE SPECTATOR

Ira Levin
Rosemary's Baby £2.95

'This horror story will grip you and chill you' DAILY EXPRESS

'A terrifying book . . . I can think of no other in which fear of an unknown evil strikes with greater chill' DAILY TELEGRAPH

'A terrifying, wholly devilish book . . . gripping, starkly spine-chilling' SPECTATOR

'Diabolically good . . . the pay-off is so fiendish, it made me sweat' SUN

'A darkly brilliant tale of modern devilry that induces the reader to believe the unbelievable. I believed it and was altogether enthralled' TRUMAN CAPOTE

The Boys from Brazil £2.95

'Ninety four men have to die on or near certain dates in the next two and a half years . . . the hope and the destiny of the Aryan race lie in the balance'

Dr Joseph Mengele, September 1974

A phone call to Vienna in the dark hours of the morning. A message from thousands of miles away cut short by a killer put Yakov Liebermann on the trail of a nightmare.

For three decades he had hounded those who had escaped justice at Nuremberg. Now he must confront a conspiracy of fiendish imagining and a man whom history has branded The Angel of Death . . .

'Horribly credible, chilling, disturbing . . . a stunner' SUNDAY EXPRESS

'There's no way to stop once you've started' NEWSWEEK

'You won't stop reading . . . his best since *Rosemary's Baby*' PUBLISHERS WEEKLY

Gail Godwin
The Finishing School £2.95

'It is at once her most artful and accomplished novel and an old-
fashioned, irresistible page turner. The plot, like that of *A Mother and
Two Daughters*, is set in motion by the death of a father and the
adjustments demanded of the women he protected. But this time
Godwin has made it harder on the survivors, particularly the young
daughter who must endure a brief but harrowing rite of passage toward
maturity' TIME

'A finely nuanced, compassionate psychological novel'
THE NEW YORK TIMES BOOK REVIEW

A Mother and Two Daughters £2.95

'A novel about that richest of all subjects, families . . . funny, sad,
provocative, ironic, compassionate, knowing, *true* . . . everything that a
novel should be' WASHINGTON POST

'A major novel from a talented writer really hitting her stride'
KIRKUS REVIEWS

'A novel to live with and live in' NEWSDAY

All Pan books are available at your local bookshop or newsagent, or can be ordered direct from the publisher. Indicate the number of copies required and fill in the form below.

Send to: **CS Department, Pan Books Ltd., P.O. Box 40, Basingstoke, Hants.   RG21 2YT.**

or phone: 0256 469551 (Ansaphone), quoting title, author and Credit Card number.

Please enclose a remittance* to the value of the cover price plus: 60p for the first book plus 30p per copy for each additional book ordered to a maximum charge of £2.40 to cover postage and packing.

*Payment may be made in sterling by UK personal cheque, postal order, sterling draft or international money order, made payable to Pan Books Ltd.

Alternatively by Barclaycard/Access:

Card No.

Signature:

Applicable only in the UK and Republic of Ireland.

While every effort is made to keep prices low, it is sometimes necessary to increase prices at short notice. Pan Books reserve the right to show on covers and charge new retail prices which may differ from those advertised in the text or elsewhere.

NAME AND ADDRESS IN BLOCK LETTERS PLEASE:

....

Name ————————————————————————

Address ————————————————————————

————————————————————————————

————————————————————————————

————————————————————————————

3/87